evolution

STEPHEN BAXTER

a novel

evolution

BALLANTINE BOOKS · NEW YORK

A Del Rey Book
Published by The Ballantine Publishing Group

Copyright © 2002 by Stephen Baxter

All rights reserved under International and Pan-American Copyright Conventions. Published in the United States by The Ballantine Publishing Group, a division of Random House, Inc., New York, and simultaneously in Canada by Random House of Canada Limited, Toronto. Originally published in Great Britain by Gollancz, an imprint of the Orion Publishing Group in 2002.

Del Rey is a registered trademark and the Del Rey colophon is a trademark of Random House, Inc.

www.delreydigital.com

Library of Congress Cataloging-in-Publication Data

Baxter, Stephen.
    Evolution : a novel / Stephen Baxter.—1st ed.
        p.   cm.
    ISBN 0-345-45782-X
    1. Montana—Fiction.   2. Hominids—Fiction.   3. Evolution—Fiction.
I. Title.

PR6052.A849 E94 2003
823'.914—dc21

                                                                    2002031422

Manufactured in the United States of America

First American Edition: February 2003

10   9   8   7   6   5   4   3   2   1

To Sandra, again,

and to the rest of us, in hope of long perspectives

Judging from the past, we may safely infer that not one living species will transmit its unaltered likeness to a distant futurity. And of the species now living very few will transmit progeny of any kind to a far distant futurity.

—CHARLES DARWIN

On the Origin of Species by Means of Natural Selection,
or the Preservation of Favoured Races in the Struggle for Life (1859)

prologue

As the plane descended toward Darwin it ran into a cloud of billowing black smoke. The windows suddenly darkened, blocking out the Australasian summer light, and the engines whined.

Joan had been talking quietly to Alyce Sigurdardottir. But now she shifted in her seat, the belt uncomfortably tight across her bulge. This was a roomy, civilized airplane, with even the economy seats set in blocks of four or six around little tables, quite unlike the cattle truck conditions Joan remembered from a childhood spent traveling around the world with her paleontologist mother. In the year 2031, a time of troubles, not so many people traveled, and those who did were granted a little more comfort.

Suddenly, as danger brushed by, she was aware of where she was, the people around her.

Joan watched the girl sitting opposite Alyce and herself. The girl, aged around fourteen at a guess, with a silvery gadget stuck in her ear, had been viewing tabletop images of the toiling Mars lander. Even here, ten thousand meters above the Timor Sea, she was connected to the electronic web that united half the planet's population, immersed in noise and shining, dancing images. Her hair was pale blue—aquamarine, perhaps. And her eyes were bright orange red, the color of the Martian dust that filled up the smart tabletop. Doubtless she featured many other genetic "improvements" less visible, Joan thought sourly. Cocooned in her own expanded consciousness the girl had not even registered the presence of the two middle-aged women sitting opposite her—nothing save for a slight widening of the eyes at Joan's figure when she had sat down, a reaction which Joan could read like a book: *Somebody so old got pregnant? Yuck* . . .

But as the plane labored through the cluttered sky, the girl had turned to gaze out of the obscured window, distracted from her high-technology bubble, and the flawless skin of her brow was slightly furrowed. The girl looked scared—as well she might, Joan thought; all her genriched perfection wouldn't help her a bit if this plane fell out of the sky. Joan felt an odd touch of meanness, envy wholly inappropriate in a woman of thirty-four. Be an adult, Joan. Everybody needs human contact, genriched or not. Isn't that the whole point of your conference, that human contact is going to save us all?

Joan leaned forward and reached out her hand. "Are you all right, dear?"

The girl flashed a smile, showing teeth so white they all but glowed. "I'm fine. It's just, you know, the smoke." Her accent was nasal U.S. West Coast.

"Forest fires," Alyce Sigurdardottir said, her leathery face creased into a smile. The primatologist was a slender woman of about sixty, but she looked older than that, her face deeply lined. "That's all it is. The seasonal fires in Indonesia, and the Australian east coast; they last for months now, every year."

"Oh," the girl said, not really reassured. "I thought it might be Rabaul."

Joan said, "You know about that?"

"Everybody knows about it," the girl said, a hint of *dummy* in her intonation. "It's a huge volcanic caldera in Papua New Guinea. Just to the north of Australia, right? It's suffered minor earthquakes and eruptions every two years or so for the past century. And in the last couple of weeks there have been Richter one earthquakes like every *day*."

"You're well informed," Alyce said.

"I like to know what I'm flying into."

Joan nodded, suppressing a smile. "Very wise. But Rabaul hasn't suffered a major eruption in more than a thousand years. It would be a little unlucky if it were to come just when you happen to be within a few hundred kilometers, uh—"

"I'm Bex. Bex Scott."

Bex—for Rebecca?—*Scott*. Of course. Alison Scott was one of the conference's more high-profile attendees, a very media-friendly genetic programmer with a brace of beautifully engineered daughters. "Bex, the gunk outside the window really is from the forest fires. We aren't in any danger."

Bex nodded, but Joan could see that under her bluster she wasn't reassured.

"Well," Joan said brightly, "if we are all going to get crisped in a volcanic caldera, we ought to get to know each other first. My name's Joan Useb. I'm a paleontologist."

Bex said brightly, "A fossil hunter?"

"Near enough. And this lady—"

"My name's Alyce Sigurdardottir." Alyce extended a slim hand. "I'm pleased to meet you, Bex."

"Sorry, but your names are kind of strange," Bex said, staring.

Joan shrugged. "*Useb* is a San name—or an anglicized version; the real thing is pretty much unpronounceable. My family has deep roots in Africa, very deep roots."

"And I," said Alyce, "had an American father and an Icelandic mother. A military romance. Long story."

Joan said, "We live in a mixed-up world. Humans have always been a wandering species. Names and genes scattered all over the place."

Bex frowned at Alyce. "I know your name, I think. Chimpanzees?"

Alyce nodded. "I took over some of Jane Goodall's work."

Joan said, "Alyce is one of a long line of prominent female primatologists. I always wondered why women did so well in the field."

Alyce smiled. "Isn't that stereotyping, Joan? But, well, primate behavioral studies in the wild take—*took*—decades of observation, because that's how long the animals themselves take to live out their lives. So you need patience, and an ability to observe without interfering. Maybe those are female traits. Or maybe it was just nice to get away from all the usual male hierarchies in academia. The forest is a lot more civilized."

"Still," Joan said, "it's a powerful tradition. Goodall, Birute Galdikas, Dian Fossey."

"I'm the last of a dying breed."

"Like your chimps," said Bex, with surprising brutality. She smiled at their silence. "They're all gone from the forests now, aren't they? Wiped out by climate change."

Alyce shook her head. "No, actually. It was the bushmeat trade." Briefly she told Bex how, toward the end, she had worked in Cameroon, as the loggers had worked their way out into the virgin rain forest, and the hunters had followed.

"Wasn't it illegal?" Bex asked. "I thought all those old species were protected."

"Of course it was illegal. But bushmeat was money. Oh, the locals had always taken apes. A gorilla was prestige meat; if your father-in-law visited, you couldn't give him chicken. But when the European loggers arrived, it got much worse. Bushmeat actually became a faddish food."

The black hole theory of extinction, Joan thought: all life, everything, ultimately disappears into the black holes in the centers of human faces. But what next? Will we keep on eating our way out through the great tree of life until there's nothing left but us and the blue-green algae?

"But," said Bex reasonably, "there are still chimps and gorillas in the zoos, right?"

"Not all the species made it," Alyce said. "Even the populations we did save, like the common chimps, don't breed well in captivity. Too smart for that. Look: The chimps are our closest surviving relatives. In the wild they lived in families. They used tools. They mounted wars. Kanzi, the chimp who learned a little sign language, was a bonobo chimp. Did you ever hear of her? And now the bonobos are extinct. *Extinct.* That means gone forever. How can we understand ourselves if we never understood *them?*"

Bex was listening politely, but she looked distant. She has grown up with such earnest lectures, Joan thought. It must all mean little or nothing to her, echoes of a world vanished before she was even born.

Alyce subsided, the old frustration showing in her face. And meanwhile the plane continued to limp through the smoky sky.

To break the slight tension—she hadn't meant to lecture this girl, only to distract her—Joan changed the subject. "Alyce studies creatures that are alive today. But I study creatures from the past."

Bex seemed interested, and in response to her questions Joan told her how she had followed the example of her own mother, and about her work, mostly out in the desert heartlands of Kenya. "People don't leave many fossils, Bex. It took me years before I learned to pick them out, tiny specks against the soil. It's a tough place to work, dry as a bone, a place where all the bushes have thorns on them to keep you from stealing their water. After that you return to the lab and spend the next few years analyzing the fragments, trying to learn more of how this million-year-dead hom lived, how she died, who she was."

"Hom?"

"Sorry. Hominid. Fieldwork slang. A hominid is any creature closer to *Homo sap* than the chimps—the pithecines, *Homo erectus,* the Neandertals."

"All from bits of bone."

"All from the bone, yes. You know, even after a couple of centuries' work, we have dug up no more that two thousand individuals from our prehistory: *two thousand people,* that's all, from all the billions who went before us into the dark. And from that handful of bones we have had to try to infer the whole tangled history of mankind and all the precursor species, all the way back to what happened to our line after the dinosaur-killer comet." And yet, she thought wistfully, lacking a time machine, the patient labor of archaeology was all there was, the only window into the past.

Bex was starting to look distant again.

Joan remembered a trip she had taken to Hell Creek, Montana, when she was about this girl's age, thirteen or fourteen. Her mother had been working there because it was a famous dinosaur-extinction boundary site. You could see traces of the huge event that had ended the dinosaur era, there in the rocks, in a layer of gray clay no thicker than her hand; it was the Cretaceous-Tertiary boundary clay, laid down in the first years after the impact. It was full of ash, the fallout of a huge disaster.

And underneath the clay, one day, her mother had found a tooth.

"Joan, this isn't *just* a tooth. I think it's a *Purgatorius* tooth."

"Say what?"

Her mother was big, bluff, her face coated with sweat and dust. "*Purgatorius*. A dinosaur-era mammal. Found it right under the boundary clay."

"You can tell all that from a tooth?"

"Sure. I mean, look at this thing. It's a precise piece of dental engineering, already the result of a hundred and fifty million years of evolution. It's all connected, you see. If you're a mammal you need specialized teeth so you can shear your food more rapidly, because you have to fuel a faster metabolism. But if your mother produces milk, you don't need to be born with your final set of teeth; the specialist tools can grow in place later. Didn't you ever wonder why you had milk teeth? Joan, a lot of people are going to care a great deal about this. You know why? Because it's a *primate*. This little scrap could be all that's left of the most remote ancestor of you and me—and everybody alive—and the chimps and gorillas and lemurs and—"

And so on. The usual lecture, from the great Professor Useb. Joan, at age thirteen, had been a lot more interested in spectacular dinosaur skulls than ratty little teeth like this. But still, something about it had stuck in her mind. And, in the end, such moments had shaped her life.

"That's the point of the conference, you see, Bex," Alyce was saying. "It's a synthesis. We want to pull together the best understanding we have of how we got here, we humans. We want to tell the story of humankind. Because now we have to decide how we are going to deal with the future. Our theme is *the globalization of empathy*."

That was true. The real purpose of the conference, known only to Joan, Alyce, and a few close colleagues, was to found a new movement, establish a new way of thinking, a new approach that might actually stave off the human-induced extinction event.

Bex shrugged. "You think anybody's going to listen to a bunch of scientists? No offense. But nobody has so far."

Joan forced a smile. "No offense taken. We're going to try anyway. Somebody has to."

"And there's no point in all that stuff anymore, is there? Your archae-ology."

Joan frowned. "What do you mean?"

Bex clapped her hands over her mouth. "I shouldn't say anything. My mother will be furious." Her Martian eyes were bright.

Alyce had withdrawn into herself again; she gazed out of the window at the billowing debris of forest fires a thousand kilometers away.

Suppose I threw you down the strata, back into time, Joan's mother had said to her. *After just a hundred thousand years you'd lose that nice high forehead of yours. Your upright-walker legs would be gone after three or four million years. You'd grow your tail back after twenty-five million years. After thirty-five million, you'd lose the last of your ape features, like your teeth; after that you'd be a monkey, child. And then you'd keep on shrink-ing. Forty million years deep you'd look something like a lemur. And eventually—*

Eventually, she would be a little ratty thing, hiding from dinosaurs.

Sometimes she had been allowed to sleep in the open, in the cool air of the badlands. The Montana sky was huge and crammed with stars. The Milky Way, a side-on view of a giant spiral galaxy, was a highway across the night. She would lie on her back, gazing up, imagining the rocky Earth had vanished, its cargo of fossils and all, and that she was adrift in space. She wondered if that little *Purgatorius* critter would have seen the same sky. Had the stars swum about the sky, across sixty-five mil-lion years? Did the Galaxy itself turn, like some huge pinwheel in the night?

But tonight, she thought, the smoke from the volcano would hide any stars.

ONE

ancestors

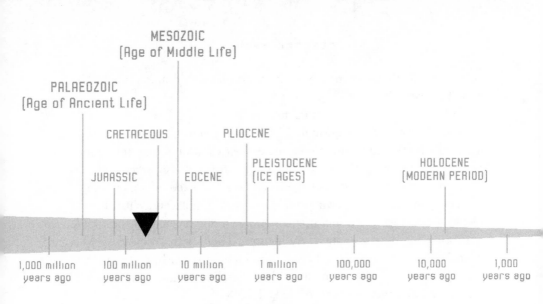

MESOZOIC
[Age of Middle Life]

PALAEOZOIC
[Age of Ancient Life]

CRETACEOUS   PLIOCENE

                                      PLEISTOCENE   HOLOCENE
JURASSIC   EOCENE   [ICE AGES]   [MODERN PERIOD]

1,000 million   100 million   10 million   1 million   100,000   10,000   1,000
years ago   years ago   years ago   years ago   years ago years ago years ago

CHAPTER 1

dinosaur dreams

▼ **Montana, North America. Circa 65 million years before present.**

I

At the edge of the clearing, Purga crept out of a dense patch of ferns. It was night, but there was plenty of light—not from the Moon, but from the comet whose spectacular tail spread across the cloudless sky, washing out all but the brightest stars.

This scrap of forest lay in a broad, shallow lowland between new volcanic mountains to the west—the mountains that would become the Rockies—and the Appalachian plains to the east. Tonight the damp air was clear; but often mists and fogs blew in from the south, born over the great inland sea that still pushed deep into the heart of North America. The forest was dominated by plants that could extract moisture from the air: Lichen coated the gnarled bark of the araucaria trees, and even the low magnolia shrubs dripped with moss. It was as if the forest had been coated with a layer of thick green paint.

But everywhere the leaves were soured, the moss and ground cover ferns browned. The rains, poisoned by gases from the great volcanic convulsion to the west, had been hard on plants and animals alike. It wasn't a healthy time.

Still, in the clearing, dinosaurs dreamed.

The thick night dew glistening from their yellow-black armor, ankylosaurs had gathered in a defensive circle, their young at the center. In the gentle Cretaceous air, these cold-blooded giants stood like parked tanks.

In the milky light Purga's large black eyes had fixed on a moth. The insect sat on a leaf, brown wings folded, fat and complacent. With an efficient lunge Purga caught her prey in her paws. She severed off the wings with a couple of nips of her tiny incisors. Then, with a noise like the crunch of a tiny apple, she began to munch with relish at the moth's abdomen. For this brief moment, with food in her mouth, Purga found a scrap of contentment in her crowded, difficult life.

The moth quickly died, its sparklike awareness incapable of recording much pain.

The moth consumed, Purga moved on. There was no grass cover here—the grasses had yet to dominate the land—but there was a green covering of low ferns, mosses, ground pine, horsetails, and conifer seedlings, even a few gaudy purple flowers. Through this tangle, scuttling between scraps of cover, she was able to progress almost silently. In the dark, solitary foraging was the best strategy. Predators worked by ambush, exploiting the shadows of the night; no group could have been as invisible as a lone prowler. And so Purga worked alone.

To Purga the world was a plain picked out in black, white, and blue, lit up by the uneasy light of the comet, which shone behind high scattered clouds. Her huge eyes were not as sensitive to color as the best dinosaur designs—some raptors could make out colors beyond anything that would be visible to humans, somber infrareds and sparkling ultraviolets—but Purga's vision worked well in the low light of night. And besides she had her whiskers, which fanned out before her like a tactile radar sweep.

Purga looked more rodentlike than primate, with whiskers, a pointed snout, and small folded-back ears. She was about the size of a small bush baby. On the ground she walked on all fours, and she carried her long bushy tail behind her, like a squirrel. To human eyes she would have seemed strange, almost reptilian in her stillness and watchfulness, perhaps incomplete.

But, as Joan Useb would one day learn, she was indeed a primate, a progenitor of that great class of animals. Through her brief life flowed a molecular river with its source in the deepest past, its destination the sea of the furthest future. And from that river of genes, widening and modifying as thousands of millennia passed, would one day emerge all of humanity: Every human ever born would be descended from the children of Purga.

She knew none of this. She didn't give herself a name. She was not conscious like a human—or even like a chimp or monkey; her mind was more like a rat's or a pigeon's. Her behavior was made up of fixed patterns, controlled by innate drives that constantly shifted in balance and priority, reaching a new sum each moment. She was like a tiny robot. She had no sense of self.

And yet she was aware. She knew pleasure—the pleasure of a full belly, the safety of her burrow, the snouts of her pups as they nuzzled her belly for milk—and, in this dangerous world, she knew fear very well.

She crept among the feet of dreaming ankylosaurs. As she moved beneath the immense bellies Purga could hear the huge rumble of the dinosaurs' endless digestion, and the air was thick with their noxious farts. With their crude teeth, all the work of processing and digesting their coarse food had to be done in the dinosaurs' vast guts, which labored even as the ankylosaurs slept.

The ankylosaurs were herbivorous dinosaurs. But this was a time of huge, ferocious predators. So these animals, larger than African elephants, were covered with armor, a fusion of bones, ribs, and vertebrae. Great yellow-black spines were embedded in their backs. Their skulls were so heavily reinforced there was little room left for brain. Their tails ended in heavy clubs that could smash legs or skulls.

The dinosaurs were too huge for Purga to comprehend. Hers was a small world, where a fallen log or a puddle was a major obstacle, where a scorpion could be a significant predator, where a fat millipede was a rare treat. To her, the dozing ankylosaur herd was a forest of immense stumpy legs and drooping tails that had no connection to each other.

But for Purga there was a rich prize here: dinosaur dung, immense heaps of it scattered in the muddy, trampled ground. Here, in fibrous mountains of roughly digested vegetation, she might find insects, even dung beetles, laboring to destroy the tremendous turds. She burrowed into the steaming stuff eagerly.

Thus had been the role of the ancestors of humanity, all through the long dinosaur summer: relegated to the fringe of the reptiles' great society, emerging from their burrows only at night, foraging for a living from dung, insects, and the small pickings of the forest.

But tonight the rewards were meager, the droppings watery and foul-smelling. The volcano-damaged vegetation had provided poor fodder for the ankylosaurs, and what came out the other end was of little value to Purga.

She moved across the clearing and into the forest. Here conifers towered grandly, rising to spreading mats of leaves far overhead. Among them were smaller trees a little like palms, and a few low bushes bearing pale yellow flowers.

Purga scrambled briskly into the angular branches of a ginkgo tree. As she climbed she used the scent glands in her crotch to mark the tree. In her world of night, scent and sound were more important than sight, and if others of her kind found this mark, any time within the next week, it would be a sign like a neon light, telling them she had been here, even how long ago she had passed.

It was pleasing to climb, to feel her muscles work smoothly as they hauled her high above the dangerous ground, to use the delicate balance afforded by her long tail—and, most of all, to jump, to fly briefly from one branch to another, using all her body's equipment, her balance, her agility, her grasping hands, her fine eyes. She was forced to shelter in burrows on the ground. But everything about her had been shaped by an existence in the complex three-dimensional environment of the trees, where almost all primate species, throughout the family's long history, would find refuge.

But the acid rain of recent months had withered the trees and undergrowth; the bark was sour, and there were few insects to be found.

Purga was perpetually hungry. She needed to consume her body weight every day: It was the price of her warm blood, and the milk she must produce for her two pups, safe in their burrow deeper in the forest. She clambered reluctantly back down the trunk of the ginkgo. Fear and hunger warring in her mind, she tried one or two more trees, but with no better luck.

But now she lifted her head, whiskers twitching, bright eyes wide, to peer into the green dark of the forest. *She could smell meat*: the alluring stench of broken flesh. And she heard a forlorn, helpless piping, like that of baby birds.

She scuttled away, following the scent.

In a small clearing at the base of a huge, gnarly araucaria there was a heap of roughly piled moss. At its edge, a small patch of debris-littered silt began to move. Soon the patch rose like a lid, and a small, scrawny neck poked out of the ground and through the layer of mud and debris. A beaklike mouth opened wide.

Its little head quivering, tiny scales and feathers still moist with yolk, the infant dinosaur took its first breath. It looked like an oversized baby bird.

It was the moment the didelphodon had been waiting for. This mammal, the size of a domestic cat, was one of the largest of its day. It was low slung, with a black-and-silver coat. Now it lunged forward and grabbed the chick by its thin neck, hauling it from its shell and flinging it into the air.

The chick's life was a handful of brief, vivid impressions: the cold air beyond its cracked shell, the blurred glow of the comet, a sense of *flying*. But now a hot cavern opened beneath it. Its skin still smeared with yolk, the chick died instantly.

Meanwhile more chicks were pushing out of the ground, hatching all at the same time. It was as if the ground were suddenly swarming with baby dinosaurs. The didelphodon, and more predatory mammals, closed in to feed.

An ancient survival strategy had been operating. Dinosaurs were reptiles who laid their eggs on the ground. Though some parents stayed with their brood, there was no way all the vulnerable eggs and chicks could be protected. So dinosaurs laid many eggs, and their hatchings were synchronized. There should have been dozens of broods hatching right now, scattered through this area of forest: hundreds of chicks. The idea was that suddenly the forest floor would be overwhelmed with baby dinosaurs, far too many for even the hungriest of predators. Most of the chicks would die, but that didn't matter. It was enough that some would survive.

But here, tonight, the strategy had gone wrong—horribly so for the dinosaur chicks. The mother of these chicks was a hunter isolated from her pack. Confused, hungry, scared of predation herself, she had laid her eggs in the old, familiar place—this rookery was millennia old—and covered them with rotting vegetation for warmth. She had done just what she should have done, save that it was the wrong time, and the eggs had been forced to hatch without the cover of hundreds of others.

The air was filled with the stink of blood, the low growls of the predators, and the sad peeping of the doomed chicks. There were many species of mammals represented here at this grisly banquet. The largest was the big didelphodon. There was a pair of deltatheridiums, ratlike omnivores, neither marsupial nor placental, a unique line that would not outlive the dinosaurs. Many of the creatures here had potential far beyond their present standing; one unprepossessing little creature was an ancestor of the line that would lead to the elephants.

But for now, all that concerned them was their empty bellies.

Dissatisfied with the slow emergence of the struggling hatchlings, the mammals had already started to dig into the loose silt, seeking unbroken eggs, scattering the cover of moss laid over the nest by the mother dinosaur.

By the time Purga arrived the rookery had become a killing pit, a squirming mass of feeding mammalian bodies. Purga, late to the fray, burrowed eagerly into the dirt. Soon tiny bones crunched in her mouth. And, so deeply did she immerse her head in search of the deep-buried goodies, she was the last to sense the return of the mother dinosaur.

She heard an angry bellow, felt the ground shudder.

Her snout sticky with yolk, Purga pulled her head out of the dirt. The other mammals were already vanishing into the forest's welcoming green black. For one instant Purga saw the whole creature, an unlikely feathered monster suspended in the air, limbs splayed, mouth gaping. Then a vast clawed hand flashed out of the sky.

Purga hissed and rolled. Too late she learned that this was the nest of a troodon: an agile, fast-moving killer—and a specialist hunter of mammals.

The troodon's name meant "Wounding Tooth."

Wounding Tooth, the size of a dog, was not the largest of dinosaurs, but she was intelligent and agile. Her brain compared in size to that of the flightless birds of later eras she somewhat resembled. Her eyes were as large and as well night-adapted as Purga's, and they could see forward, giving her binocular vision, the better to triangulate on her small, fast-moving targets. She had legs that enabled her to spring like a kangaroo, a long sicklelike claw on the second toe of each foot, and hands like spades evolved specifically to dig out and crush scuttling mammals.

She was coated in small sleek feathers, an elaborate development of scales. The feathers weren't meant for flying, but for warmth during the night's chill. In the equable climate that swathed the Earth in these times, you didn't need a hot-blooded metabolic engine to keep warm: If you were big enough, your cold-blooded body would retain its heat right through the night, even if you lived at Earth's extremes, at the poles. But smaller dinosaurs, like the troodon, needed a little extra insulation.

Small or not, she had one of the largest brains of all dinosaurs. All in all, she was a well-equipped hunter. But Wounding Tooth had problems of her own.

She could not know it, but they had been caused by the widening of the Atlantic, the huge geological event that had dominated the whole of this Cretaceous period. As the Americas were pushed west, North America's huge inland seaway had shallowed and drained, and close to the western coast—just a few hundred kilometers from the troodon's hatching site—that line of new volcanoes had erupted like an angry wound. The volcanism had disturbed the complex web of life in many ways. The young volcanoes were almost continually active, belching out smoke and ash ladened with sulfur that, mixing with the rain, turned to acid. Many species of plants had vanished, and trees on the higher ground had been reduced to bare trunks. Elsewhere the destruction had been more direct, with vast fingers of cold lava reaching deep into the forest.

The troodon's mammalian food, relatively close to the base of the food chain, had been less disturbed than most of the larger species of predatory dinosaurs. In fact, with their tiny bodies, deep burrows, and fast reproductive rate, the mammals were better equipped to live through such times of stress than the land's grander overlords.

But troodons were pack hunters. And this female had, some days ago, become isolated from her pack by a spectacular venting of hot steam from a fissure. Even though she was alone, Wounding Tooth was carrying eggs from her last fertilization. So she had come to the herd's ancient roosting site. A deep part of her had hoped to find others of her kind here. But there was no other here, only herself.

Wounding Tooth was growing older. At fifty, she found many of her much-stressed joints were racked with the pain of arthritis. And, because of her age and loss of strength and flexibility, she herself was under threat: This was, after all, a time of predators powerful enough to justify armor plating on creatures bigger than elephants. She had to reproduce; every instinct demanded it.

She had laid her eggs, as she had before. What else could she do?

The nest itself was a circular pit scraped out of the dirt, and she had arranged the eggs with an odd, almost surgical precision. She made sure the twenty eggs were not too close together, and that the top of each elongated egg pointed to the center so the emerging chicks would have a good chance of digging their way out. Then she had covered over the eggs with dirt and moss. She had returned several times to the nest, probing with her claws to tap the shells. The eggs had developed well; she could see it. But now the eggs had hatched—her young had emerged—but nothing was left of them except scattered bits of red flesh and gnawed bone. And here, in the center of the smashed nest, was a mammal, her face stained by blood and yolk and dirt.

Which was why Wounding Tooth leapt.

Purga helplessly squirted urine and musk, leaving a scent warning: *Beware! Mammal hunter about!* Then she ran out of the forest, back to the clearing of the ankylosaurs.

But on the edge of the clearing Purga hesitated. She had a choice to make, a choice of dangers. She had to get away from the pursuing troodon. She was heading back toward her burrow, where her pups waited. But by crossing the clearing again she was leaving the safety of the trees. The unconscious calculus rapidly produced a result. She took the gamble; she raced across the clearing.

A sleepy infant giant raised one bony eyelid.

The light seemed brighter than ever now, exposing Purga clearly. But there was no dawn; it was only the comet, its nucleus huge, blurred, and bright, the gas jets that erupted from it clearly visible, even through the haze of air. It was an eerie, extraordinary sight that sparked a dim curiosity in her agile mind, even as she ran.

A shadow fled at the corner of her vision.

Instinctively she darted sideways—just as a dinosaur hand slammed into the ground where she had stood. She ran back into the ankylosaur herd, darting this way and that, seeking cover in the shadow of the lethargic dinosaurs.

The troodon chased her around immense legs. But even the enraged mammal hunter was reluctant to disturb these huge armored beasts. Their clubbed tails could have crushed her in a second. Purga even slithered perilously *under* one ankylosaur's huge raised foot, which hovered like a falling moon above her, while Wounding Tooth, frustrated, hissed and scraped at the ground.

At last Purga reached the far side of the clearing. Her scent and instinct guiding her unerringly, she raced into the undergrowth.

Her burrow was pitch dark, too dark even for her huge eyes to make out anything. It was like entering a mouth set in the warm earth. But the burrow was full of the consanguineous smell of her family, and she could hear the snuffle of her two young as they squirmed blindly out of the dark. Soon their warm, tiny mouths were nipping at her belly, seeking her nipples. Her mate was not here; he was out foraging himself in this clear Cretaceous night.

But Wounding Tooth must be close; the scent of warm flesh, fur, and milk that had helped bring Purga home would draw the hunter here too.

The imperatives in her head shifted again. She tucked her infants behind her and pushed her way to the back of the burrow, away from its entrance. Purga, unlike the troodon, was young—just a few months old, in fact—and this was her first brood. And unlike the prolific dinosaurs, Purga's kind bore few young. She could not afford to lose her brood. And now she prepared to fight for them.

There was a crash behind her.

The roof of packed earth imploded, showering Purga and the pups with dirt. Comet light flooded in, startlingly bright after the few seconds of darkness. It was as if a bomb had fallen. A huge grasping hand reached out of the sky into the burrow. The pups squirmed and squealed, but one of them was impaled on a bloody claw. In an instant its life was over. It was lifted up and out of the burrow, a naked, lifeless scrap, and out of Purga's life.

Purga hissed her distress. She ran toward the burrow entrance, away from the claw. She could sense the remaining infant, naked and stumbling, hurrying after her. But the wily troodon had foreseen this. That claw now pushed into the entrance, breaking open its earthen walls. Reptile fingers closed, and the second pup's life was squeezed out, its skull and tiny bones crushed, its organs pulped.

Purga, her world broken apart in a few heartbeats, scrabbled away from the debris of the entrance, away from the broken roof, back to the deepest recesses of the burrow. But again and again that machinelike clawed paw slammed through the roof, breaking it down and admitting more milky comet light.

Purga's body urged her to flee, to find darkness, a new burrow, shelter—to be anywhere but *here*. She was even hungry; for such a fast-metabolizing creature as Purga, it had been a long time since she had supped the yolk of Wounding Tooth's eggs.

But suddenly the strength drained out of her.

She huddled at the rear of her ruined burrow, shivering, folding her paws over her face as if to clean her fur of mites. From the moment of her birth into this world of huge teeth and claws that could flash from the sky without warning, she had struggled to survive by instinct and agility. But now her young were gone. The innate imperatives dissolved, and something like despair settled on her.

And while Purga trembled in the remains of her burrow, a world trembled with her.

If she submitted now, she would leave no living descendants: The molecular river of inheritance would be blocked, here, forever. Others of her kind would breed, of course; other lines would go on into far distant futurity, to grow, to evolve, but not Purga's line, not *her* genes.

And not Joan Useb.

Life always had been chancy.

The great clawed hand slammed down one more time, centimeters from Purga. And now Wounding Tooth, impatient, rammed her great head into the burrow. Purga quailed before a wall of snapping teeth.

But as the dinosaur pressed closer, screeching, Purga smelled meat, and crushed bones, and a lingering sweetness of milk. The monster's hot breath smelled of Purga's babies.

With a spasm of rage Purga threw herself forward.

The great teeth snapped, scything through the air around Purga like some vast piece of machinery. But Purga squirmed to avoid their flashing arcs, and sank her own teeth into the corner of the dinosaur's lips. The scaly skin was tough, but she felt her lower incisors sink into the warm, softer flesh inside the creature's mouth.

Wounding Tooth bellowed and pulled back. Purga, hooked by her own teeth, was dragged out of her burrow and hauled up into the air, up through many times her own body height, up past the scaly belly of Wounding Tooth and into the cold night.

Her mist of rage faded. She twisted her head, ripping away a scrap of dinosaur flesh, and she tumbled backward through the misty air. Even as she fell a great clawed hand swept sideways at her, seeking to grab her. But Purga was a creature of the trees, and she twisted as she fell. Again luck favored her—though the grasping claw came close enough to make a breeze that ruffled the downy hairs of her belly.

She fell onto a patch of trampled dirt. She was momentarily winded. But already teeth and claws were descending again, painted silver by the eerie comet light. With a lithe wriggle Purga rolled over, got her feet under her, and ran into the roots of the nearest tree. Alone, eyes wide, mouth gaping, she huddled there, panting, twitching at every leaf that stirred.

There was a scrap of meat in Purga's mouth. She had forgotten that it had come from the dinosaur. She chewed it quickly and swallowed, for a moment assuaging the hunger that clamored at her even now. Then she peered around, seeking a safer refuge.

Wounding Tooth paced and bellowed out her frustration.

Purga had chosen life. But she had found an enemy.

II

The Devil's Tail was as old as the sun.

The solar system had been born out of a rich, spinning cloud of rock and volatiles. Battered by a supernova shock, the cloud quickly coalesced into planetesimals: loosely aggregated lumps of rock and ice that swam chaotically through the dark, like blind fish.

The planetesimals collided. Often they were destroyed, their substance returning to the cloud. But some of them merged. Out of this clattering violence, the planets grew.

Close to the center, the new planets were rocky balls like Earth, baked by the sun's fire. Farther out, huge misty worlds were born, globes stuffed with gases—even the lightest gases of all, hydrogen and helium, gases manufactured in the first few moments of the universe itself.

And around these growing gas giants, the comets—the last of the icy planetesimals—swarmed like flies.

For the comets it was a dangerous time. Many of them were dragged into the gravity wells of Jupiter and the other giants, their masses feeding those growing monsters. Others were hurled inward by the giants' gravitational slingshots to the warm, crowded center, there to batter the inner planets.

But a few lucky survivors were hurled the other way, away from the sun and into the huge, cold spaces of the outer dark. Soon a loose cloud of comets formed out here, all of them following vast, slow orbits that could reach halfway to the sun's nearest stellar neighbor.

One such was the Devil's Tail.

Out here the comet was safe. For most of its long lifetime its nearest neighbor was as remote as Jupiter was from Earth. And at the farthest point of its orbit, the Devil's Tail sailed all of a third of the way to the nearest star, reaching at last a place where the sun itself was lost against the star fields, its huddled planets invisible. Away from the heat, the comet quickly cooled and froze hard. Its surface was made black by silicaceous dust, and an epochal frost carved exotic, fragile ice sculptures on its low-gravity surface, a meaningless wonderland that no eye would ever see.

Here the comet swam for four and a half billion years, while on Earth continents danced and species rose and fell.

But the sun's gentle gravity tugged. Slowly, slower than the rise of empires, the comet responded.

And it began to fall back toward the light.

Red dawn light seeped into the eastern sky. The clouds had a bubbly texture, and the sky was tinged a peculiar bruise purple. In this remote time the very air was different—thick, moist, laden with oxygen. Even the sky would have looked alien to human eyes.

Purga was still traveling, exhausted, already dazzled by the gathering light. She had wandered far from any forest. There were only scattered trees here, spaced out over a ground made green by a dense mat of low-lying ferns. The trees were cycads, tall trees with rough bark that resembled palms, squat cycadeoids looking oddly like giant pineapples, and ginkgoes with their odd, fan-shaped leaves, an already ancient lineage that would survive into the human era and beyond.

In the stillness of the predawn, nothing moved. The dinosaur herds had yet to stir, and the hunters of the night had retired to their burrows and nests—all but Purga, who was stranded in the open, all her worn nerves sparking with an apprehension of danger.

Something moved across the sky. She flattened herself against the ground and peered up.

A winged form glided high over the roof of the sky, its profile picked out cleanly by the red-gray light of the dawn. It looked like a high-flying aircraft. It was not; it was alive.

Purga's instinctive computation relegated the pterosaur to a matter of no concern. To her the most ferocious flying creature was of much less immediate peril than the predators who might lurk under these cycads, the scorpions and spiders and ever-ravenous carnivorous reptiles, including the many, many small and savage dinosaur species.

She stumbled on, toward the gathering dawn. Soon the greenery started to thin out, and she scrambled over hard-packed dunes of reddish sand. She topped a short rise—and found herself facing a body of water, which lapped languidly to the horizon. The air smelled strange: full of salt, and oddly electric.

She had come to the northern shore of the great slice of ocean that pushed into the heart of North America. She could see vast, languid forms break the water's surface.

And to the southeast, where the dawn light was gathering, the comet was suspended in the sky. Its head was a milky mass from which immense fountains of pearl-white gas gushed, visibly evolving as she watched. Its twin tails, streaming away from the sun, flailed around the Earth, making a confusing, billowing mass. It was like looking down a shotgun blast. The whole immense, brilliant show was reflected in the shallow sea.

Listlessly she stumbled forward, descending to a shallow, sloping beach. The shore was littered with clam shells and half-dried seaweed. She prodded at this detritus, but the seaweed was stringy, salty stuff. And she could smell the salt in the water; there was nothing to drink here.

On her little rise, Purga was increasingly exposed, as if picked out by a spotlight.

She spotted a tree fern, no more than a meter tall. She stumbled to it and began to dig at its roots, hoping to make a rudimentary burrow. But the soft sand fell back into her trenches. At last, as the ruddy sun rose above the horizon, Purga managed to dig out a hole big enough to shelter her body. She tucked her tail in behind her, put her paws over her face, and closed her eyes.

The warmth and darkness of the burrow reminded her of the home she had lost. But the smell was wrong: nothing but salt and sand and ozone and decaying seaweed, the sharp stinks of this place where land met sea. Her home burrow had smelled of *herself*, of that other who was her mate, of the pups who had smelled like a mixture of herself and her mate—a wonderful mélange of selves. All gone now, all lost. She felt a deep pang of regret, though her mind was not rich enough to understand why.

As she slept out the long day her legs scraped and scratched at the gritty young sand.

Cretaceous Earth was a world of ocean, of shallow seas and shore.

A giant ocean called the Tethys—like an extension of the Mediterranean—cut off Asia from Africa. Europe was little more than a scattered collection of islands. In Africa, even the mid-Sahara was an ocean floor. The world was warm, so warm there were no polar ice caps. And for eighty million years the sea levels had been rising. The post-Pangaea spreading of the continents, and the formation of huge reefs and shelves of chalk around their coasts, had pushed huge volumes of solid matter into the oceans: It had been like putting bricks into an already full bucket of water, and the brimming oceans had flooded the continents. But the vast shallow oceans were almost tideless, and their waves were gentle.

Life in the sea was richer and more varied than at any other time in Earth's long history. Tremendous blooms of plankton filled the waters, drinking the sunlight. The plankton were the base of the ocean's vast pyramid of eaters. And in the plankton were microscopic algae called haptophytes. After a brief free-swimming phase, the haptophytes constructed for themselves tiny, intricate suits of armor from calcium carbonate. As they died, billions of tiny corpses sank to the warm seabeds, where they settled and hardened into a complex white rock, chalk.

Eventually tremendous chalk beds, kilometers thick, would smother Kansas and the gulf coast of North America, and stretch along the southern half of England and into northern Germany and Denmark. Human scientists would call this era the Cretaceous—after *creta*, meaning "chalk"—for its most enduring monuments, constructed by the toiling plankton.

When the light began to seep out of the sky, Purga emerged from her shelter.

She scampered with difficulty through dry sand that yielded with every step, sometimes billowing around her belly. She was rested. But she was hungry, and confused, and pulsed with loneliness.

She came to the top of the rise she had crossed yesterday. She found herself facing a broad, gently rolling plain extending to the rising smoke-wreathed mountains to the west. Once the great American inland sea had flooded this place. But now the sea had receded, leaving a plain littered with broad, placid lakes and marshes. Everywhere there was life. Giant crocodiles cruised like gnarled submarines through the shallow waters, some of them with birds riding on their backs. There were flocks of birds, and birdlike, furry pterosaurs, some of whom built huge rafts to support their nests at the center of the lakes, far from the land-based predators.

And everywhere she looked there were dinosaurs.

Herds of duckbills, ankylosaurs, and a few gatherings of slow, clumsy triceratops clustered around the open water, jostling and fighting. Around their feet ran and hopped frogs and salamanders, lizards like iguanas and geckos, and many small, snapping dinosaurs. In the air pterosaurs and birds flapped and called. On the fringe of the forest, raptors could be seen stalking, evaluating the jostling herds.

The hadrosaurs, the duck-billed dinosaurs, were this era's most common herbivores. Though they were larger than later mammalian equivalents like wildebeest or antelope, they walked on two legs like outsized ostriches, their strides long, their heads bobbing. Males led the way, elaborately ornamented by huge crests over their noses and foreheads. The crests acted as natural trumpets, capable of producing notes as low as a piano's bottom register. Thus the voices of the duckbills hooted mournfully across the misty plain.

In the foreground a herd of vast anatotitans was crossing the flood-plain. It was a convoy of flesh. These immense creatures looked oddly unbalanced, with powerful hind legs—each of them taller than an adult human—but comparatively spindly forelegs, and they trailed long, fat conical tails. The air was filled with their rumbles: the churning of the herbivores' huge stomachs and the deeper growl of their voices, reaching deep into the infrasonic, deeper than any human ear could have detected, as they called reassurance to each other.

The anatotitans converged on a grove of cycads. The cycads' mature leaves were thick and spiny, but their fresh growth, protected by a crown of older leaves, was green and luscious. So the anatotitans rose up on their heavy hind legs and cropped the new growth. As their great feet fell back on the undergrowth of ferns, clouds of insects rose up. The phalanx of titans would leave the cycads smashed and broken. Though the ana-totitans would scatter seeds for future growth far from here, the vegetation would take a long time to recover from the devastation they caused.

There was noise everywhere: the mighty foghorn honks of the duck-bills, the bellows of the armored dinosaurs, the screeching of birds, the leathery flapping of the huge flocks of pterosaurs. And, under it all, there was the ugly, unstructured roar of a female tyrannosaur, the area's top predator: All of these animals were within her domain, and she was letting them, and any competitor tyrannosaur, know about it.

The scene might have reminded a human of Africa. But though there were great herbivores to fill the roles of antelopes, elephants, hippos, and wildebeests, and predators who hunted like lions, cheetahs, and hyenas, these animals were more closely related to birds than to any mammal. They preened, displayed, fought, and nested with oddly rapid motions fueled by the rich oxygen of the thick air. The smaller, more lithe dinosaurs that ran or stalked through the undergrowth would have seemed surreal: There was nothing like these bipedal runners in human times. And there was no sight in twenty-first century Africa like the two ankylosaurs who now began to mate, backing their rear ends together with the most exquisite care.

It was a landscape of giants, in which Purga was a lost, helpless figure, utterly irrelevant. But to the west, Purga made out a storey of denser forest, layer on layer of it rising up toward the distant volcanoes.

Purga had run the wrong way, coming to this place of the sea. She was a creature of the forest and the dirt; *that* was where she must go. But to get there she had to cross the open plain—and evade all those mountainous feet. With trepidation she slid down the sand bank.

But now she glimpsed stealthy movement through low ferns. She hurried beneath an immature araucaria and flattened herself against the ground.

A *raptor*: Standing as still as a rock, it was studying the jostling anatotitans. It was a deinonychus, something like a featherless, flightless bird. But it was as still as a crocodile. The raptor had only a faint scent—its skin was not as glandular as mammals'—but there was a dry pungency in the air, a spiciness that filled Purga with a sense of peril.

It was very close to Purga. If it caught Purga the raptor would, of course, kill her in a second.

A bird was climbing into the tree above her. Its feathers were bright blue and it had claws on its wing bones and teeth in its beak. This creature was a relic of ancient times, of archaic linkages between birds, crocodiles, dinosaurs. The bird was climbing to feed its brood of fat, squawking chicks. Apparently it had not seen the raptor.

But for now the raptor was stalking larger prey.

The raptor watched the anatotitan herd with blank, hawklike eyes, its only calculation was which of the titanic herbivores might serve it as prey. If necessary, it would harass the herd, seeking to make one of them peel away and thereby become vulnerable.

But that proved unnecessary.

One of the adult titans fell behind the rest. This female, walking tiredly, was more than seventy years old. Her growth had continued all her life, and now she was the largest in the herd—one of the largest of her kind anywhere, in fact. Now she dipped a heavy head into the scummy water of a shallow pond.

The raptor began to stalk steadily, silently, toward the old titan. Purga cowered in the shelter of her araucaria.

The raptor was three meters tall—compact, agile, with slim legs capable of high-speed running and a long stiff tail for balance. It had a huge claw on each hind limb; while the raptor walked, its toes lifted the claws up and clear of the ground.

The raptor wasn't so smart. Its brain was small—no larger than a chicken's or a guinea fowl's. And it was a solitary hunter; it wasn't smart enough to hunt in a pack. But it didn't need to be.

The great anatotitan still had no idea of the danger it was in.

The raptor erupted from cover. It spun in the air, and its grime-crusted hind claws flashed cruelly. The strikes were made well.

Blood gushed. Bellowing, the anatotitan tried to back away from the water. But the titan's black entrails slid out of immense, deep belly wounds, steaming. At last she caught her forefeet in the slippery mess. With a sound like thunder she slid forward on her chest. And then, with a spasm, the great hind legs collapsed, rolling the great bulk of her body onto its side.

One of the other anatotitans looked back and lowed mournfully, a deep noise that made the ground under Purga tremble. But the herd was already moving on.

The raptor, panting rapidly, waited for the titan to weaken.

The dinosaurs had first emerged more than a hundred and fifty million years ago, in a time of hot dry climates more welcoming to reptiles than mammals. In those days the continents were fused into the single vast Pangaean landmass, and the dinosaurs had been able to spread across the planet. Since then, continents had fissioned, danced, and whirled, and bands of climate had shifted across the planet. And the dinosaurs had evolved in response.

Dinosaurs were *different.*

They did not hunt like the mammalian killers of later times. Their cold blood meant they were poor at sustaining speed for long distances; they could never be endurance hunters, running down their prey like wolves. But they had versatile, high-pressure hearts. And the design of their bodies had much in common with birds': This raptor's neck bones and torso contained a duct system that drew the air through its lungs, and oxygen could be supplied to its tissues at a tremendous rate. It was capable of short sprints, and could pour a great deal of energy into its attacks.

Dinosaur hunts were events of stillness, of ambush and silence and motionlessness, broken by brief bursts of savage violence.

Mammals were not poorly evolved compared to the dinosaurs. The product of her own track of tens of millions of years of evolution, Purga was exquisitely adapted for the niche in which she made her living. But the brutal facts of energy economics kept mammals caged in the neglected corners of a dinosaur world. Overall, a dinosaur killer made better use of energy than mammals: This raptor could run like a gazelle but it rested like a lizard. It was that combination of energy efficiency and lethal effectiveness that had kept the dinosaurs supreme for so long.

The raptor was something like a huge, ferocious bird, perhaps. Or something like a souped-up crocodile. But it was not *truly* like those animals. It was like nothing seen on Earth in human times, something no human eye would ever witness.

It was a dinosaur.

This raptor's preferred way of killing was to burst out of cover and slash at its prey, inflicting wounds that were savage but often nonlethal. The prey might flee, but it would be weakened by raking wounds to its legs and flanks—or hamstringing—blood loss and shock would result. The raptor had poor dental hygiene—its breath stank ferociously—and its bite passed on a mouthful of bacteria. The raptor would follow, perhaps attacking again, perhaps just following the scent of the stinking, infected wounds, until weakness disabled the prey.

Today this raptor had been lucky; it had disabled its victim with a single blow. All it had to do now was wait until the titan was too weak to do the raptor any harm. It could even take its food while its prey was still alive.

The raptor would not trouble with such small fry as Purga while such a giant meal awaited it. Moving cautiously, watchfully, Purga left the shelter of the fern, and scurried across the scrubby floodplain, through

the devastated track left by the anatotitan herd, until she reached the
security of the trees.

For the first time in four billion years, heat had touched the Devil's Tail.
Fragile ice sculptures older than Earth were quickly lost.

Gases boiled through fissures in the crust. Soon a shining cloud of
dust and gas the size of the Moon had gathered around the comet. The
wind from the sun, of light and sleeting particles, made the gas and dust
stream behind the falling comet nucleus in tails millions of kilometers
long. The twin tails were extremely tenuous, but they caught the light
and began to shine.

For the first time, uncomprehending eyes on Earth made out the
approaching comet.

Spitting, rotating, its dark nucleus founting gases with ever greater
vigor, the Devil's Tail swam on.

III

Another long, hot Cretaceous day wore away.

Purga slept through the day, her new family curled around her. She
slept even when her pups suckled. The snug burrow floor was littered
with the primates' soft fur—and it smelled, indubitably, of Purga, of her
new mate, and of the three pups who were half of herself.

Purga's mate gave himself no name, and nor did Purga name him, any
more than she named herself. But if she had—in recognition that he
could never be the first in her life—she might have called him Second.

As Purga slept, she dreamed. Primates already had brains large and
complex enough to require self-referential cleansing. So she dreamed of
warmth and darkness, of flashing claws and teeth, and of her own mother,
huge in her memory.

Purga, like all mammals, was hot-blooded.

All animal metabolisms were based on the slow cellular burning of
food in oxygen. The first animals to colonize the land—gasping fish,
driven from drying rivulets, using swim bladders as crude lungs—had had
to rely on metabolic engines designed for swimming. In those first land-
walkers the metabolic fires had glowed dimly. Still, their decisive move
onto the land had been successful; and now and into the future every
animal—mammals, dinosaurs, crocodiles, and birds, even snakes and
whales—would use a variant of the same ancient tetrapod body plan of
four legs, a backbone, ribs, fingers, and toes.

But some two hundred million years before Purga's birth, certain animals had begun to develop a new kind of metabolism. They had been predators, driven by selection to burn food more briskly in order to improve their luck in the chase.

It had meant a complete redesign. These ambitious predators needed more food, a higher rate of digestion, a more efficient system of waste elimination. All this had raised their metabolic rate, even when resting, and they had had to increase the size of heat-producing organs like the heart, kidneys, liver, and brain. Even the working of their cells had speeded up. In the end a new and stable high body temperature had been set.

The new hot-blooded bodies had had an unplanned advantage. Cold-bloods relied on drawing heat from the environment. But the hot-bloods did not. They could operate at peak efficiency in the cool of night, when the cold-bloods had to rest, or in extreme heat, when cold-bloods would have to hide. They could even prey on cold-bloods—frogs, small reptiles, insects—at times like dawn and dusk, when those slow movers were vulnerable.

But they could not topple the dinosaurs from their thrones; the dinosaurs' supreme energy efficiency saw to that.

Purga's dreams were disturbed by the immense stomping of the dinosaurs as they went about their incomprehensible activities in the world of day above. The ground would shake as if in an earthquake, and bits of the burrow walls crumbled and fell around the dozing family. It was as if the world was full of walking skyscrapers.

But there was nothing to be done about any of that. To Purga the dinosaurs were a force of nature, as beyond her control as the weather. In this huge, dangerous world, the burrow was home. The thick earth protected the primates from the heat of the day, and sheltered the still-naked pups from the night's chill: The earth itself was Purga's shelter against dinosaur weather.

And yet, at the back of her small mind, there was a tiny chapel of memory, a reminder that this was not her first home, not her first family—a lingering warning that she could lose all this, too, in another instant of light and flashing claws and teeth.

When the Earth turned and the air cooled and the dinosaurs settled into their nightly torpor, at their feet the dirt stirred. The creatures of the night emerged: insects, amphibians—and many, many burrowing mammals, rising like a tide of miniature life around the dinosaurs' pillarlike legs.

This night Purga and her new mate traveled together. Purga, a little older and more experienced, led the way. A few centimeters apart, proceeding in cautious fits and starts, they made their way down the shallow slope toward the lake.

They did not usually forage together. But the weather had been dry, and the priority for both of them was to get a drink.

This part of America had endured a long, epochal drying. Here the relic of the ancient inland sea was a great stretch of swampy land, drowned by new sediment from the Rockies to the west, young mountains eroding almost as quickly as they were born. And in this time of relative drought, any standing water was a focus for animals large and small.

And so the lakeshore was crowded with dinosaurs.

Here was a herd of triceratops, three-horned giants with huge bony frills that covered their shoulder regions. They were like heavily armed rhinos, dozing in their loose circles, the adults' ferocious horns pointing outward to deter any hungry, night-prowling aggressor.

There were many duck-billed hadrosaurs. Herds had gathered around this shallow lake, a bewildering, brightly colored array of them, and Purga and Second had to creep past forests of their great, immobile legs, like refugees in an immense sculpture park. Even now, as the duckbills slumbered, their unconscious snoring was a cacophony of deep and mournful hoots, honks, and cries; they sounded like fogbound ships.

At last Purga and Second reached the edge of the lake. The water had receded, and they had to cross a stretch of stony, half-dried pond-bottom mud, slick with mucus and sheets of green vegetation. In the eerie, still light, Purga drank quickly, her eyes wide and whiskers twitching.

Their thirst sated, the primates split up. Second began to track over the shallow beach, looking for the little piles of coiled sand that marked the presence of a worm.

Purga moved up the beach to the fringe of the scrub, following a more intriguing smell.

She soon found the source of the stink: a fish. It was lying in a heap of rusty fern fronds, its carcass shriveled within its silvery skin. Somehow stranded far from the water, it had been dead many hours. When Purga poked the fish's skin it burst, releasing a voluminous, noxious stench— and a squirming mass of ghost-pale maggots. Purga plunged her paws into the carcass. Soon she was pushing maggots into her mouth; the salty goodies burst between her teeth, releasing delicious body juices.

But now another fish came flying over her head, to land deeper into the scrub. Startled, she flattened herself, whiskers twitching.

A dinosaur was standing stock-still in the shallow water. She was tall and upright, some nine meters tall, with a jaw like a crocodile's and a great purple-red sail on her back. Her teeth were hooked, and her hands were equipped with claws like great blades all of thirty centimeters long. Suddenly she plunged her claws into the water, breaking the glimmering surface into shards. A handful of silvery fish flew up, wriggling and squirming, and the dinosaur skillfully snapped most of them out of the air with her long mouth.

This was a suchomimus, a specialist hunter of fish. Her kind was a relatively recent immigrant from Africa, having traveled the land bridges that sporadically connected the continents. She dragged for fish like a bear. She could take her prey with her claws or by scooping her crocodilian jaw through the water, relying on her hooked teeth. She was hunting in the night—when most creatures of her size had become dormant—because now was the time when the fish, lulled by the dimming of the daylight, came to the surface and the shore to feed.

Some meters behind her, a second suchomimus followed. This was a male; like many hunting dinosaurs, the suchomimus traveled in mating pairs.

The female suchomimus swiped again, and fish rained onto the dry shore, where they flopped briefly, suffocation quickly extinguishing their pinpoint sparks of consciousness. But the female suchomimus ignored such easy takings, apparently preferring the game of the hunt.

As did the watching deinosuchus.

The deinosuchus was a giant crocodile. She glided through the water of the lake, almost silent, hidden from view by a thin surface layer of aquatic fern. Her transparent eyelids slid over yellow eyes, keeping the tiny green leaves away.

This deinosuchus was a female: already sixty years old and twelve meters long, many of her offspring had grown to hunters themselves. A time like this—a time of drought, a time when animals came clustering to the water, in their thirst losing some of their native caution—was a bonus time for the crocodiles, a time of easy pickings. But the deinosuchus was a creature capable of taking on a tyrannosaur; she seldom went hungry, whatever the weather.

The crocodiles were already ancient, descended from bipedal hunters some hundred and fifty million years before. They were supremely successful, dominating the shallow waterways and lakes all over North America and beyond: They were among the few animals of the Cretaceous to die of old age. And they would survive to the time of humans and far beyond.

The exquisitely adapted nostrils of the deinosuchus could sense the motions of the suchomimus pair at the edge of the lake. It was time. Her mighty tail flexed once.

Purga saw a kind of eruption at the edge of the lake. Pterosaurs and birds rose from floating nests, cawing throatily in protest. The male suchomimus barely had time to turn his expressionless head before the crocodile's jaws locked around one of his great hind legs. The crocodile hauled backward, bringing the suchomimus crashing to the mud, crushing his beautiful crest. The suchomimus hooted and fought, trying to bring its long, bloody claws into play. But the crocodile slithered back toward the water, taking the suchomimus with her.

Barely a minute after the deinosuchus had emerged, the turbulence of its passing soothed away from the surface of the water. The female suchomimus seemed baffled by her sudden loss. She patroled the water's edge, hooting mournfully.

The crocodile had been a messy killer. The mud of the shore was left soaked in blood, and littered with scraps of the suchomimus—lengths of glistening entrails, chunks of ripped flesh, even its staring, dismembered head. The first scavengers on the scene were a pack of small, agile raptors; they burst from the undergrowth, hopping, jumping, and swiveling, lashing out at each other like kickboxers as they fought over the juicy scraps of flesh.

They were soon joined by pterosaurs, flapping in noisily. They landed on the mud and walked clumsily, with legs and elbows splayed like a bat's. Their heads were long, their beaks narrow and equipped with sharp teeth. The beaks dug deep into the remnants of the suchomimus. As more pterosaurs were attracted, the sky became darkened by their gaunt wings. One pterosaur in particular descended toward the two toiling primates.

Purga saw it coming. Second did not.

His only warning was a gush of leathery air, a glimpse of huge, hair-covered wings flapping across the sky above him. Then clawed feet fell out of the sky and enclosed him like a cage.

It was over before Second knew what had happened. From the comforting noises of the ground he was lifted into a silence broken only by the rustle of the pterosaur's huge flapping wings, the silky straining of its wirelike muscles, and by the rush of the wind. He glimpsed the land, dark green and pocked by blue-glimmering ponds, falling away beneath him. And then the view opened up spectacularly to the southeast, the direction where the comet lay. The comet's head was a vast unearthly lantern hanging over the tongue of sea that pushed into the land from the Gulf of Mexico.

Second longed only to get out of this cage of scaly flesh, back to the ground and his burrow. He thrashed at the talons that contained him, and tried to bite into the flesh; but the scales of the huge creature defied his small teeth.

And the pterosaur squeezed until small primate ribs cracked.

The pterosaur was an azhdarchid. She was the size of a hang glider. Her massive, toothless head, with a pointed triangular beak at the front and an elaborate crest at the rear, was sculpted to serve as an aerodynamic aid. Her hollow bones and porous skull made her remarkably light, and her body was tiny. She was nothing but wings and head. She looked like a sketch by Leonardo da Vinci.

The spar of each pterosaur wing was a single tremendous finger. Three remnant fingers created a small claw in the middle of the leading edge. The wing was held open by her hind legs. With all four limbs occupied in controlling the aerodynamic surfaces, the azhdarchid's relatives could never diversify, like the birds, into running or aquatic forms. But the pterosaurs had been astonishingly successful. Along with birds and bats, they had been one of only three groups of backboned animals to have mastered flight—and they had been the first. By now pterosaurs had darkened Earth's skies for more than a hundred and fifty million years.

The azhdarchid was capable of taking fish from shallow waters, but made most of her living as a scavenger. She rarely took live mammals. But Second—who had been engrossed in devouring a worm he was pulling from the sand—had not realized how visible the bright comet light had made him. He was not the only animal whose rhythms and instincts were disturbed by the new light in the sky. He had been an easy capture.

Second lay still, encased in pain, as cold air washed over him.

He could see the great outstretched wings above him, comet light shining blue through the translucent skin. Tiny creatures squirmed: a pterosaur's wing was an enormous expanse of almost hairless skin packed with blood vessels, a powerful lure for parasitic insects. Every square centimeter of the pterosaur's wing surface was controlled by an underlying mat of muscle fabric, enabling the azhdarchid to control her aerodynamics with exquisite precision; her body was a better engineered glider than any manufactured by human hands.

The azhdarchid banked to avoid a smudge of volcanic cloud that hung above the young mountains. It would be fatal for her delicate wings to be caught in such foul air. She was expert at spotting upwelling fountains of warm air—marked by cumulus clouds or over the sun-facing slopes of hills—that she could exploit for free lift. To her the world was a three-dimensional web of invisible conveyor belts, capable of carrying her anywhere she wanted to go.

The azhdarchid's nest was in a foothill of the Rockies, above the tree line. A steep wall of young rock soared above a guano-stained ledge littered with eggshells and bones and beaks. Chicks stalked noisily around this confined area, scattering the bits of shells from which they had emerged a few weeks earlier. There were three of them; they had already devoured a weakling fourth sibling.

The parent worked a spur of bone in her wrist that changed the shape of the wings' membrane: like air brakes, this enabled her to slow without stalling. She came to a halt a meter above the ledge, and dropped onto her hind legs. She stowed her delicate wing membranes, folded her flight fingers across her back, and walked forward, her knees bent outward and her elbows bent.

Second was dropped. He clattered against bare rock. He glimpsed the adult azhdarchid flap away. He scrabbled at the rock, but it was too hard to burrow into.

And little monsters closed in on him, blue-black in the comet light. Fed by their parents' proteinaceous offerings of fish and meat, the chicks were growing quickly. But their wings were still undeveloped, and their bodies and heads were relatively large. They looked like miniature dinosaurs.

The first beak nipped at Second's hind leg, almost playfully. The scent of his own blood evoked sudden memories of the burrow. He experienced a kind of regret. He bared his teeth. The ravenous chicks closed around him. It was over in a heartbeat, his warm body torn apart.

But now something moved, far above the mother azhdarchid. She twisted her sketch of a head to peer upwards. In these tall Cretaceous skies, fueled by the oxygen-rich air, a pyramid of predators had erected itself, with all the savagery of its landbound analogues. But when she saw the vast sprawled shadow, skimming over the comet-bright sky *above* the lowest of the clouds, she knew she was in no danger.

It was only an air whale.

The largest flying animal ever discovered by humans was a type of azhdarchid christened Quetzalcoatlus. Its wingspan of fifteen meters was four times that of the largest birds, condors; it had looked like a light airplane.

But the greatest pterosaur of all was an order of magnitude larger again.

The air whale's tremendous, delicate wings were one *hundred* meters across. His bones were little more than sketches, strut-filled and hollow, astonishingly light. His mouth was vast, a translucent cavern. His main danger was overheating in the unfiltered sunlight of the high air, but his body had a number of mechanisms to compensate, including the capacity to vary the flow of blood in his tremendous wings, and air sacs placed in his body that enabled his internal organs to lose heat.

He lived his life in that thin, high layer of air called the stratosphere, higher than the mountains, above most of the clouds. But even this far from the ground there was life: a thin ethereal plankton of insects and spiders, windblown. Sometimes mating swarms of midges, or even locusts, could be blown up into this lofty realm. This was the whale's thin bounty, which he scooped endlessly into his vast mouth.

Far below, if he had chosen to look, the air whale might have glimpsed the little drama of Second, the azhdarchid chicks, and the pterosaur. But from up here such remote events were of little interest. When he looked down over his airy domain, the whale could see the curve of the Earth: the fat blue band of thicker air that marked the horizon, and the glimmering of the sea in the light of the comet. The sky above faded to violet at the zenith. He was so high that there was too little air to scatter the light effectively; despite the brightness of the comet, he could see stars.

The air whale was capable of circumnavigating the globe, following the stratospheric winds and seeking updrafts, without once touching the ground. His kind made up a thin population—the aerial plankton could sustain no more—but they were scattered all over the planet. Three or four times in his life he had mated, summoned to the planet's highest mountain peaks by innate timing mechanisms triggered by the motion of the sun. Mating was perfunctory and uninteresting; such huge, delicate creatures couldn't afford the displays and courtship rituals of more terrestrial species. Nevertheless ancient instincts did sometimes come to the fore. There could be fights, often savage, almost always lethal, and when that happened, huge flimsy bodies would rain out of the skies, to baffle ground-based scavengers.

The whale was the end product of a brutal evolutionary competition, mostly aimed at removing weight; everything that had been surplus to requirements had, over the generations, been selected out or shriveled to insignificance. And, since nothing ever happened up here in the cool stratosphere, those diminished organs included the whale's brain. The whale was at once the most spectacular but among the most stupid of his great family; his brain, though a fine control center for his elaborate flight systems, was little more than an organic adding machine. So the magnificent astronaut's eye view before him meant nothing.

Only the warm oxygen-laden air of the late Cretaceous would allow such immense, delicate creatures to escape from gravity's clutches, and never again would there be a gene bank like the pterosaur's to supply raw material for similar evolutionary experiments. Never again would any creature fill this particular ecological niche, and in the future windblown insects would sail in peace.

And human paleontologists, piecing together this remote era from fragments of bone and fossilized plant, would learn little of the true giants. Most pterosaur bones found would be of marine and lakeland species, because that was where fossils were most easily preserved. By comparison the creatures that dominated the roof of the world, the upland areas and mountaintops, left few traces, for their habitats were subject to ferocious uplift and erosion. The highest mountains of the human era, the Himalayas, did not even exist in the Cretaceous.

The fossil record was patchy and selective. All through time there had been monsters and wonders that no human being would ever know had existed—like this immense flyer.

With the most delicate of touches from his immense extended forefingers the whale banked his wings and soared toward a particularly rich layer of aerial plankton.

The cruel night was not yet done with Purga.

Despite the loss of Second, she continued to forage. There was no choice. Death was common; life continued. There was no time to grieve.

But when she returned to her burrow a small, narrow face came pushing out of the dark toward her, a twitching, mobile snout, bright black eyes, quivering whiskers: one of her kind, another male.

She hissed and backed out of the burrow entrance. She could smell blood. The blood of her pups.

It had happened again. Without hesitation Purga launched herself at the male. But he was fat and strong—evidently a good forager—and he pushed her away easily.

In despair she ran out into the dangerous dawn, where mountainous dinosaurs were starting to stir, the air resonating to the first long-distance calls of the hadrosaurs. She made for an old fern she knew, around whose roots the ground was dry and crumbling. Quickly she dug herself in, ignoring the moist squirms of the worms and beetles. Once she was safe in her cocoon of soil she lay there trembling, trying to shut out of her head the dread stink of her pups' blood.

The strange male, on discovering Purga's scent marks—the scent of a fertile female—had followed them back to the burrow, carefully covering over her marks with his own in order to hide her from any other males.

When he had entered the burrow the pups had clustered around the stranger, his same-species smell overwhelming his warning aura of not-of-my-family. He could smell from the traces of fur and dung that a healthy, fertile female lived here. The female was of use to him, but not the pups. They did not smell of him; they were nothing to do with him. Without them, the female would have that much more incentive to raise the litter he would give her.

For the male, it was all utterly logical. The two larger pups had mouthed his belly, seeking milk, even as the male had consumed their younger sister.

The night after that the male found her again, having tracked her scent. He still stank of her dead babies, of the lost part of her. She fought him off savagely.

It took her two more nights before she accepted his courtship. Soon her body would begin to incubate his young.

It was hard.

It was life.

It would have been of no consolation to Purga to know that this brutal landscape, which had swallowed up two of her broods, would soon be overwhelmed by a wave of suffering and death to dwarf anything she had endured.

IV

Earth was now *inside* the comet's swelling coma, the loose cloud of gases that swathed the nucleus itself.

All over the night side of Earth the tail could be seen stretching away from the sun. It was as if the planet had drifted into a sparkling tunnel. The sky glittered with meteors, tiny bits of comet falling harmlessly into the high atmosphere, creating a light show glimpsed by uncaring dinosaurs.

But the comet's nucleus was bigger than any meteor. It moved at twenty kilometers per second, at interplanetary speeds. It had already crossed the orbit of the Moon.

From where it would take just five more hours to reach Earth.

All night long, the birds and pterosaurs sang their confusion; during the day, they slumped with exhaustion. There was no room in their neural programming for a new light in the sky, and they were disturbed at a deep cellular level. In the shallow seas, too, the unending light had disturbed the plankton and larger creatures like crab and shrimp; the cynical hunters of the reef fed well.

Only the great dinosaurs were unperturbed. The comet light made no difference to the air temperature, and when true night had fallen they slipped into their usual torpor. On the last night of a reign that had lasted nearly two hundred million years, the rulers of the Earth slept untroubled.

If not for the tyrannosaur eggs, the young giganotosaur would have spotted the disturbed troodon earlier. In the lee of the mountains, he stalked silently through the green shadows. His name meant Giant.

The forest here was sparse, spindly araucaria and tree ferns, scattered over a ground littered with sharp-edged volcanic rocks. Nothing moved. Anything that could hide had already hidden; anything else lay still, hoping for the shadow of death to pass by.

He came to a pile of moss and lichen. Superficially it looked like a heap of debris piled up at random by wind or the passage of animals. But Giant recognized the characteristic scrapings, the lingering smell of meat eater.

It was a nest.

With a rumble of anticipation, he fell on the nest and began to dismantle it with his stubby forearms. When he had exposed the eggs, Giant dug his clawed thumb, with a surgical precision, into the top of the largest. He pulled out the embryo head first. As the mucus and yolk drained from it, lurid colors bright, Giant saw the chick squirm feebly, even saw its tiny heart beat.

Just as the embryos of chimps, gorillas, humans would all be disturbingly similar, so dinosaur fetuses all looked alike. There was no way to know that this chick would have been a female tyrannosaur. Blind, deaf, immature, the embryo struggled to open her mouth, dimly imagining the hulking shape of a mother who would feed her. Giant flicked the embryo into his mouth and swallowed it without chewing. The chick's life ended in crushing, acidic darkness.

It didn't matter. Even if no predator had come this way, her egg would have been destroyed before she could have hatched by a monster even more terrible than a giganotosaur.

Giant was descended from South American stock that had crossed a temporary land bridge into this continent a thousand years earlier.

In a world of slowly separating island continents, the dinosaur fauna had become diverse. In Africa there were archaic-looking long-necked giant herbivores and creatures like hippos with fat, low-slung bodies and powerfully clawed thumbs. In Asia there were small, fast-running horned dinosaurs with noses like parrots' beaks. And in South America large sauropods were hunted by giant pack-hunting predators; there it was like a throwback to earlier times, to Pangaea. The giganotosaurs had cut their evolutionary teeth hunting the great South American titanosaurs.

Giant was an immature male, and yet he already outmassed all but the very largest carnivores of the era. Giant's head, in proportion to his body, was larger than a tyrannosaur's—and yet his brain was smaller. The giganotosaurs were less agile, less fast, less bright; they had more in common with the ancient allosaurs, equipped to kill with teeth and hands, whereas the tyrannosaurs, all their evolutionary energy funneled into their huge heads, specialized in immense, sharklike bites. Where the tyrannosaurs were solitary ambush hunters, the giganotosaurs were pack animals. To bring down a sauropod fifty meters long and weighing a hundred tons, you didn't need brains as much as raw strength, rudimentary teamwork—and a kind of reckless frenzy.

But, coming across that land bridge into a new country, the giganotosaurs had been forced to confront an established order of predators. The invaders had quickly learned that their takeover of a region could not succeed unless they first mounted a bloody coup against the ruling carnivore.

Which was why this young male giganotosaur was munching slippery tyrannosaur embryos. Resolutely Giant cracked one egg after another. The carefully constructed nest turned into a mess of shattered eggs, scattered moss, and chunks of dismembered chick. Giant was feeding well—and issuing a challenge.

It would be a transfer of power. The tyrannosaur had been the top predator, mistress of the land for a hundred kilometers around, as if the whole elaborate ecosystem was a vast farm run for her benefit. The prey species had come to terms with the formidable presence that lived amongst them: with their armor or weapons or evasive strategies, each of the hunted had reached a point where their losses to predators were not a threat to the endurance of the herd.

Given time, all that would have changed. The impact of the invaders' hunger would have rippled down the food chain, disturbing creatures large and small, before a new equilibrium could be established. It would have taken longer still for the prey species to learn new behaviors, or even evolve new coping systems or armor to deal with the giganotosaurs.

But none of that would happen. There would not be time for the giganotosaur clan to exploit their triumph. Not in the few hours left.

The nest destroyed, Giant wandered away. He was still hungry, as always.

He could smell putrefaction in the still, misty air. Something huge had died: easy meat, perhaps. He pushed through a bank of tree ferns and emerged into another small clearing. Beyond, through a screen of greenery, he could dimly see the black flank of a young volcanic mountain.

And there, in the middle of the clearing, was a dinosaur—a troodon—standing quite still above a scraping of earth.

Giant froze. The troodon had not seen him. And she was alone; there were none of the watchful companions he associated with the packs of this particular agile little dinosaur.

There was something wrong with the way she was behaving. And that, so the grim predatory calculus of his mind prompted him, gave him an opportunity.

Wounding Tooth should have been able to overcome the loss of a clutch of eggs.

This was a savage time, after all. Infant mortality rates were high; and at any time of life, sudden death was the way of things. This was the world the troodon had been evolved to cope with.

But she could not cope, not anymore.

She had always been the weakest of her brood. She would not even have survived the first days after her hatching if not for the chance decimation of her siblings by a roaming marsupial predator. She had grown to overcome her physical weakness, and had become an effective hunter. But in a dark part of her mind she had always remained the weakest, robbed of food by her siblings, even eyed as a cannibalistic snack.

Add to that a slow poisoning by the fumes and dust of the volcanoes in the west. Add to that an awareness of her own aging. Add to that the hammer blow of her lost brood. She hadn't been able to get Purga's scent out of her head.

It had not been hard to pursue that scent out of her home range, across the floodplain to the ocean shore, and now to this new place where the scent of Purga was strong.

Wounding Tooth stood still and silent. The burrow, her nose told her, was right under her feet. She bent and pressed one side of her head against the ground. But she heard nothing. The primates were very still.

So she waited, through the long hours, as the sun rose higher on this last day, as the comet light grew subtly brighter. She did not even flinch when meteors flared overhead.

If she had known about the giganotosaur that watched her she would not have cared. Even if she could have understood the meaning of the comet light, she would not have cared. Let her have Purga; that was all.

It was a peculiar irony that her high intelligence had brought Wounding Tooth to this. She was one of the few dinosaur types smart enough to have gone insane.

It was not yet dark. Purga could tell that from the glint of light at the rough portal to the burrow. But what was day, what was night in these strange times?

After several nights bathed in comet light, she was exhausted, fractious, hungry—and so was her mate, Third, and her two surviving pups. The pups were just about large enough to hunt for themselves now, and therefore dangerous. If there was not enough food, the family, pent up in this burrow, might turn on one another.

The imperatives slid through her mind, and a new decision was reached. She would have to go out, even if the time felt wrong, even if the land was flooded with light. Hesitantly she moved toward the burrow entrance.

Once outside, she stopped to listen. She could hear no earth-shaking footsteps. She stepped forward, muzzle twitching, whiskers exploring.

The light was strong, strange. In the sky cometary matter continued to fall, streaking across the dome of the sky like silent fireworks. It was extraordinary, somehow compelling—too remote to be frightening.

An immense cage plunged out of the sky. She scrabbled back toward the burrow. But those great hands were faster, thick ropy muscles pulling the fingers closed around her.

And now she faced a picket fence of teeth, hundreds of them, a tremendous face, reptilian eyes as big as her head. A giant mouth opened, and Purga smelled meat.

The dinosaur's face, with its great, thin-skinned snout, had none of the muscular mobility of Purga's. Wounding Tooth's head was rigid, expressionless, like a robot's. But though she could not show it, all of Wounding Tooth's being was focused on the tiny warm mammal in her grip.

Her limbs pinned against her belly, Purga stopped struggling.

Oddly, Purga, in this ultimate moment, knew a certain peace that Wounding Tooth would have envied. Purga was already in her middle age, already slowing in her movements and thought. And she had, after all, achieved as much as a creature like her could have hoped for. She had produced young. Even encased in the troodon's cold reptilian grip, she could smell her young on her own fur. In her way she was content. She would die—here and now, in heartbeats—but the species would go on.

But something moved beyond the troodon's bulky body, something even more massive, a gliding mountain, utterly silent.

The troodon was unbelievably careless. Giant didn't care why. And he didn't care about the warm scrap she held in her hands.

His attack was fast, silent, and utterly savage, a single bite to her neck. Wounding Tooth had time for a moment of shock, of unbelievable pain—and then, as whiteness enfolded her, a peculiar relief.

Her hands opened. A ball of fur tumbled through the air.

Before Wounding Tooth's body fell Giant had renewed his attack. Briskly he slit open the belly cavity and began pulling out entrails. He expelled their contents by shaking them from side to side; bloody, half-digested food showered the area.

Soon his two brothers came racing across the clearing. Giganotosaurs hunted together, but their society was fragile at the best of times. Giant knew he couldn't defend his kill, but he was determined not to lose it all. Even as he chewed on the liver of Wounding Tooth, he turned to kick and bite.

Purga found herself on the ground. Above her, mountains battled with ferocious savagery. A rain of blood and saliva fell all around her. She had no idea what had happened. She had been ready for death. Now here she was in the dirt, free again.

And the light in the sky grew stranger yet.

The comet nucleus could have passed through the volume of space occupied by Earth in just ten minutes.

In the great boiling it had endured the comet had lost a great deal of mass, but not a catastrophic amount. If it had been able to complete its skim around the sun, it would have soared back out to the cometary cloud, quickly cooling, the lovely coma and tail dispersing into the dark, to resume its aeonic dreaming.

If.

For days, weeks, the great comet had worked its way across the sky— but slowly, its hour-by-hour motion imperceptible to any creature who glanced up at it, uncomprehending. But now the bright-glowing head was *sliding*: sliding down the sky like a setting sun, sinking toward the southern horizon.

All across the daylit side of the planet, silence fell. Around the drying lakes the crowding duckbills looked up. Raptors ceased their stalking and pursuit, just for a moment, their clever brains struggling to interpret this unprecedented spectacle. Birds and pterosaurs flew from their nests and roosting places, already startled by a threat they could not understand, seeking the comfort of the air.

Even the warring giganotosaurs paused in their brutal feeding.

Purga bolted for the darkness of her burrow. The disembodied head of the troodon fell behind her, lodging in the burrow's entrance, following Purga with a grotesque, empty stare as the light continued to shift.

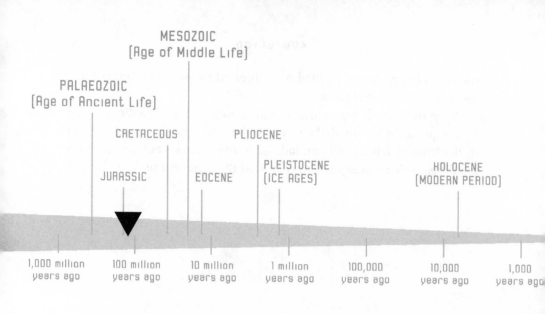

MESOZOIC
[Age of Middle Life]

PALAEOZOIC
[Age of Ancient Life]

CRETACEOUS   PLIOCENE

PLEISTOCENE   HOLOCENE
JURASSIC   EOCENE   [ICE AGES]   [MODERN PERIOD]

1,000 million   100 million   10 million   1 million   100,000   10,000   1,000
years ago   years ago   years ago   years ago   years ago   years ago   years ago

CHAPTER 2

the hunters of pangaea

▼ **Pangaea. Circa 145 million years before present.**

Eighty million years before Purga was born, an ornitholestes stalked through the dense Jurassic forest, hunting diplodocus.

This ornith was an active, carnivorous dinosaur. She was about the height of an adult human, but her lithe body was less than half the weight. She had powerful hind legs, a long, balancing tail, and sharp conical teeth. She was coated in brown, downy feathers, a useful camouflage in the forest fringes where her kind had evolved as hunters of carrion and eggs. She was like a large, sparsely feathered bird.

But her forehead might almost have been human, with a high skullcap that sat incongruously over a sharp, almost crocodilian face. Around her waist was a belt and a coiled whip. In her long, grasping hands she carried a tool, a kind of spear.

And she had a name. It would have translated as something like Listener—for, although she was yet young, it had already become clear that her hearing was exceptional.

Listener was a dinosaur: a big-brained dinosaur who made tools and who had a name.

For all their destructiveness, the great herds of duckbills and armored dinosaurs of Purga's day were but a memory of the giants of the past. In the Jurassic era had walked the greatest land animals that had ever lived. And they had been stalked by hunters with poison-tipped spears.

Listener and her mate slid silently through the green shade of the forest fringe, moving with an unspoken coordination that made them look like two halves of a single creature. For generations, reaching back to the red-tinged mindlessness of their ancestors, this species of carnivore had hunted in mating pairs, and so they did now.

The forest of this age was dominated by tall araucaria and ginkgoes. In the open spaces there was a ground cover of ground ferns, saplings, and pineapple-shrub cycadeoids. But there were no flowering plants. This was a rather drab, unfinished-looking world, a world of gray-green and brown, a world without color, through which the hunters stalked.

Listener was first to hear the approach of the diplo herd. She felt it as a gentle thrumming in her bones. She immediately dropped to the ground, scraping away ferns and conifer needles, and pressed her head against the compacted soil.

The noise was a deep rumble, like a remote earthquake. These were the deepest voices of the diplos—what Listener thought of as belly-voices, a low-frequency contact rumble that could carry for kilometers. The diplo herd must have abandoned the grove where it had spent the chill night, those long hours of truce when hunters and hunted alike slid into dreamless immobility. It was when the diplos moved that you had a chance to harass the herd, perhaps to pick off a vulnerable youngster or invalid.

Listener's mate was called Stego, for he was stubborn, as hard to deflect from his course as a mighty—but notoriously tiny-brained—stegosaur. He asked, *They are moving?*

Yes, she replied. *They are moving.*

Hunting carnivores were accustomed to working silently. So their language was a composite of soft clicks, hand signals, and a ducking body posture—no facial expressions, for the faces of these orniths were as rigid as any dinosaur's.

As they approached the herd, the noise of the great animals' belly-voices became obvious. It made the very ground shake: The languid fronds of ferns vibrated, and dust danced up, as if in anticipation. And soon the orniths could hear the footfalls of the mighty animals, tremendous, remote impacts that sounded like boulders tumbling down a hillside.

The orniths reached the very edge of the forest. And there, before them, was the herd.

When diplodocus walked, it was as if the landscape were shifting, as if the hills had been uprooted and were moving liquidly over the land. A human observer might have found it difficult to comprehend what she saw. The *scale* was wrong: Surely these great sliding masses must be something geological, not animal.

The largest of this forty-strong herd was an immense cow, a diplo matriarch who had been the center of this herd for over a century. She was fully thirty meters long, five meters tall at the hips, and she weighed twenty tons—but then even the youngsters of the herd, some as young as ten years old, were more massive than the largest African elephant. The matriarch walked with her immense neck and tail held almost horizontal, running parallel to the ground for tens of meters. The weight of her immense gut was supported by her mighty hips and broad, elephantine legs. Thick ropelike ligaments ran up her neck, over her back, and along her tail, all supported in canals along the top of her backbone. The weight of her neck and tail tensed the ligaments over her neck, thereby balancing the weight of her torso. Thus she was constructed like a biological suspension bridge.

The matriarch's head looked almost absurdly small, as if it belonged to another animal entirely. Nevertheless this was the conduit through which all her food had to pass. She fed constantly; her powerful jaws were capable of taking bites out of tree trunks, huge muscles flowing as the low-quality food was briskly processed. She even cropped in her sleep. In a world as lush as this late Jurassic, finding food wasn't a problem.

Such a large animal could move only with a chthonic slowness. But the matriarch had nothing to fear. She was protected by her immense size, and by a row of toothlike spines and crude armor plates on her back. She did not need to be smart, agile, to have fast reactions; her small brain was mostly devoted to the biomechanics of her immense body, to balance, posture, and movement. For all her bulk the matriarch was oddly graceful. She was a twenty-ton ballerina.

As the herd progressed the herbivores snorted and growled, lowing irritably where one mighty body impeded another. Under this was the grinding, mechanical noise of the diplos' stomachs. Rocks rumbled and ground continually within those mighty gizzards to help with the shredding of material, making a diplo's gut a highly efficient processor of variable, low-quality fodder that was barely chewed by the small head and muscleless cheeks. It sounded like heavy machinery at work.

Surrounding this immense parade were the great herbivores' camp followers. Insects hovered around the diplos themselves and their immense piles of waste. Through their swarms dove a variety of small, insectivorous pterosaurs. Some of the pterosaurs rode on the diplos' huge uncaring backs. There was even a pair of ungainly protobirds, flapping like chickens, running around the feet of the diplos, snapping enthusiastically at grubs, ticks, and beetles. And then there were the carnivorous dinosaurs, who hunted the hunters in turn. Listener spotted a gaggle of juvenile coelurosaurs, gamely stalking their prey among the tree-trunk legs of the herbivores, at every moment risking death from a carelessly placed footfall or tail twitch.

It was a vast, mobile community, a city that marched endlessly through the world forest. And it was a community of which Listener was part—where she had spent all her life, which she would follow until she died.

Now the diplo matriarch came to a grove of ginkgoes, quite tall, ripe with green growth. She raised her head on its cable neck for a closer inspection. Then she dipped her head into the leaves and began to browse, tearing at the leaves with her stubby teeth. The other adults joined her. The animals began simply to barge down the trees, snapping trunks and even ripping roots out of the ground. Soon the grove was flattened; it would take decades for the ginkgoes to recover from this brief visit. Thus the diplos shaped the landscape. They left behind a great scribble of openness, a corridor of green savannah in a world otherwise dominated by forest, for the herd so ravaged the vegetation of any area that it had to keep moving, like a rampaging army.

These were not the mightiest herbivores—that honor went to the giant, tree-cropping brachiosaurs, who could grow as massive as seventy tons—but the brachiosaurs were solitary, or moved in small groups. The diplo herds, sometimes a hundred strong, had shaped the land as no animal had before or since.

This loose herd had been together—traveling forever east, its members changing, its structure continual—for *ten thousand years*. But there was room for such titanic journeys.

Jurassic Earth was dominated by a single immense continent: *Pangaea*, which meant "the land of all Earth." It was a mighty land. South America and Africa had docked to form a part of the mighty rock platform, and a titanic river drained the heart of the supercontinent—a river of which the Amazon and Congo were both mere tributaries.

As the continents had coalesced there had been a great pulse of death. The removal of barriers of mountain and ocean had forced species of plants and animals to mix. Now a uniformity of flora and fauna sprawled across all of Pangaea, from ocean to ocean, pole to pole—a uniformity sustained even though vast tectonic forces were already laboring to shatter the immense landmass. Only a handful of animal species had survived the great joining: insects, amphibians, reptiles—and protomam-mals, reptilian creatures with mammalian features, a lumpen, ugly, unfin-ished lot. But that handful of species would ultimately give rise to all the mammals—including humans—and to the great lineages of birds, croco-diles, and dinosaurs.

As if in response to the vast landscape in which they found them-selves, the diplos had grown huge. Certainly their immensity was suitable for these times of unpredictable, mixed vegetation. With her long neck a diplo could work methodically across a wide area without even needing to move, taking whatever ground cover was available, even the lower branches of trees.

In the clever orniths, though, the diplos faced a new peril, a danger for which evolution had not prepared them. Nevertheless, after more than a century of life, the matriarch had absorbed a certain deep wisdom, and her eyes, deep red with age, betrayed an understanding of the nimble horrors that pursued her kind.

Now the patient orniths had their best opportunity.

The diplos still crowded around the wrecked ginkgo grove, their great bodies in a starburst formation. Their heads on their long necks dipped over the scattered foliage like cherry picker mechanical claws. Youngsters clustered close, but for now they were excluded by the giant adults.

Excluded, forgotten, exposed.

Stego ducked his head toward one of the diplo young. She was a little smaller than the rest—no larger than the largest African elephant, a gen-uine runt. She was having trouble forcing her way into the feeding pack, and she snapped and prowled at the edge of the formation with a massive birdlike twitchiness.

There was no real loyalty among the diplos. The herd was a thing of convenience, not a family grouping. Diplos laid their eggs at the edge of the forest, and then abandoned them. The surviving hatchlings would use the cover of the forest until they had grown sufficiently massive to take to the open land and seek a herd.

The herds made strategic sense: Diplos helped protect each other by their presence together. And any herd needed new blood for its own replenishment. But if a predator took one of the young, so be it. In the endless Pangaean forests, there was always another who would take her place. It was as if the herd accepted such losses as a toll to be paid for its continuing passage through the ancient groves.

Today it looked as if this runty female would pay that toll.

Listener and Stego took their whips of diplo leather from around their waists. Whips raised, spears ready, they crept through the rough scrub of saplings and ferns that crowded the edge of the forest. Even if the diplos spotted them they would probably not react; the diplos' evolutionary programming contained no alarm signals for the approach of two such diminutive predators.

A silent conversation passed in subtle movements, nods, eye contacts.

That one, said Stego.

Yes. Weak. Young.

I will run at the herd. I will use the whip. Try to spook them. Separate the runt.

Agreed. I will make the first run . . .

It should have been routine. But as the orniths approached, coelurosaurs scuttled away and pterosaurs flapped awkwardly into the air.

Stego hissed. Listener turned.

And looked into the eyes of another ornith.

There were three of them, Listener saw. They were a little larger than Listener and Stego. They were handsome animals, each with a distinctive crest of spiny decorative scales running down the back of its head and neck; Listener felt her own spines rise up in response, her body obeying an unbidden, ancient instinct.

But these orniths were naked. They had no belts of woven bark around their waists like Listener's; they carried no whips, no spears; their long hands were empty. They did not belong to Listener's hunting nation, but were her remote cousins—wild orniths—the small-brained stock from which her kind had arisen.

She hissed, her mouth gaping wide, and strode into the open. *Get away! Get out of here!*

The wild orniths stood their ground. They glared back at Listener, their own mouths gaping, heads bobbing.

A tinge of apprehension touched Listener. Not so long ago three like these would have fled at her approach; the wild ones had long learned to fear the sting of weapons wielded by their smarter cousins. But hunger outweighed their fear. It had probably been a long time since these brutes had come across a diplo nest, their primary food source. Now these clever opportunists probably hoped to steal whatever Listener and Stego managed to win for themselves.

The world forest was getting crowded.

Listener, confronted by this unwelcome reminder of her own brutish past, knew better than to show fear. She continued to stalk steadily toward the three wild orniths, head dipping, gesturing. *If you think you are going to steal my kill you have another think coming. Get out of here, you animals.* But the mindless ones replied with hisses and spits.

The commotion was beginning to distract the diplodocus. That runty female had already ducked back into the mass of the herd, out of reach of the hunters. Now the big matriarch herself looked around, her head carried on her neck like a camera platform on a boom crane.

It was the chance the allosaurs had been waiting for.

The allos stood like statues in the forest's green shade, standing upright on their immense hind legs, their slender forearms with their three-clawed hands held beneath. This was a pack of five females, not quite fully grown but nevertheless each of them was ten meters long and weighed more than two tons. Allosaurs were not interested in runtish juveniles. They had targeted a fat male diplo, like themselves just a little short of full maturity. As the herd milled, distracted by the commotion of the squabbling orniths, that fat male got himself separated from the protective bulk of the herd.

The five allos attacked immediately, on the ground, in the air. With hind claws like grappling hooks they immediately inflicted deep, ugly wounds. They used their strongly constructed heads like clubs, battering the diplo, and teeth like serrated daggers gouged at the diplo's flesh. Unlike tyrannosaurs they had big hands and long, strong arms they used to grab on to the diplo while dismembering him.

Allosaurs were the heaviest land carnivores of all time. They were like upright, meat-eating, fast-running elephants. It was a scene of immense and ferocious carnage.

Meanwhile the diplo herd was fighting back. The adults, bellowing in protest, swung their huge necks back and forth over the ground, hoping to sweep aside any predator foolish enough to come close. One of them even reared up on her hind legs, a vast, overpowering sight.

And they deployed their most terrible weapon. Diplo tails lashed, all around the herd, and the air was filled with the crackle of shock waves, stunningly loud. A hundred and forty-five million years before humans, the diplos had been the first animals on Earth to break the sound barrier.

The allosaurs retreated quickly. Nevertheless one of them was caught by the tip of a supersonic whip-tail that crashed into her ribs. Allosaurs were built for speed and their bones were light; the tail cracked three ribs, which would trouble the allosaur for months to come.

But the attack, in those few blistering moments, had been successful.

Already one great leg had collapsed under the male diplo, its ripped tendons leaving it unable to sustain its share of the animal's weight. Soon his loss of blood would weaken him further. He raised his head and honked mournfully. It would take hours yet for him to die—the allosaurs, like many carnivores, liked to play—but his life was already over.

Gradually the crackle of whiplash tails ceased, and the herd grew calmer.

But it was the big matriarch who delivered the last whiplash of all.

When the allosaurs had attacked, the orniths, suddenly united in terror, had fled the clearing. Now Listener and Stego skulked side by side in the forest-edge scrub, their unused weapons in their hands, their hunt thwarted. But it wasn't all bad news. When the allos were done feeding there might be meat to be scavenged from the fallen diplo.

Then came that last whiplash. The huge diplo's tail landed clean across Stego's back, laying his skin open to the bone. He screamed and fell, tumbling out into the open, his mouth agape. The slit pupils in his eyes pulsed as he gazed up at Listener.

And one of the allosaurs, not far away, turned with glassy interest. Listener stood stock still, shocked.

With a single bound the allo reached Stego. Stego screamed and scrabbled at the mud. The allo poked him curiously, almost gently, with her muzzle.

Then, with astonishing speed, the allo's head shot forward and delivered a single clean bite, all but severing Stego's neck. She grabbed him by the shoulder, lifting him high. His head dangled by a few threads of skin, but his body twitched still. She carried him to the edge of the forest, away from the herd, where she began to feed. The process was efficient. The allo had joints within her jaw and skull, so that like a python she could open her mouth wide and position her teeth, the better to consume her prey.

Listener found herself staring stupidly at an allosaur track, a three-toed crater firmly planted in the trampled mud. *A hunter without her mate is like a herd without its matriarch*: The ornith proverb sounded in her head, over and over.

The big matriarch diplo swung her head around to stare directly at Listener. Listener understood. The orniths' antics had given the allos their chance to attack. So, with her whiplash, the matriarch had exposed Stego. She had given him to the allos. It had been revenge.

The matriarch turned away, lowing, as if contented.

Something hardened, a dark core, in Listener's mind.

She knew she would spend the rest of her life with this herd. And she knew that the matriarch was its most important individual; providing protection to the rest with her sheer bulk, leading them with her wisdom acquired over long years. Without her the herd would be much less well coordinated, much more under threat. In a way, this matriarch was the most important individual creature in Listener's life.

In that moment, she swore vengeance of her own.

Each night the orniths retreated to their ancestral forest, where once they had hunted mammals, insects, and the nests of diplodocus. They scattered in little pockets, and surrounded the area with heavily armed sentries. That evening, the mourning was extensive. This ornith nation was only a few hundred strong, and could ill afford to lose a strong, intelligent young male like Stego.

Even as the cold of night drew in, Listener found it hard to rest.

She gazed up at a sky across which auroras flapped, steep three-dimensional sculptures of light, green and purple. In this age Earth's magnetic field was three times the strength it would be in the human era, and, as it trapped the wind streaming from the sun, the shining auroras would sometimes blanket the planet from pole to pole. But the lights in the sky meant nothing to Listener, and brought no comfort or distraction.

She sought refuge in memories of happier, simpler times when she and Stego, emulating their distant ancestors, had hunted for diplo eggs. The trick was to seek out a patch of forest floor, not too far from the edge, that looked apparently lifeless, strewn with leaves and dirt. If you put your sensitive ear to the ground you could hear, if you were lucky, the telltale scratching of diplo chicks in their eggs. Listener had always preferred to wait, to guard "her" nest from others, until the diplo chicks began to break out of their eggs and stick their tiny heads out of the scattered dirt.

For an inventive mind like Listener's, there was no end to the games you could play.

You could try to guess which chick would come up next. You could see how quickly you could kill a new emergent, snuffing it out within a heartbeat of its first glimpse of daylight. You could even let the chicks come out of their shells altogether. Already a meter long, with their flimsy tails and necks dangling, the chicks' only priority was to escape to the deeper forest. You could let a chick get all the way to a patch of scrub—almost—and then haul it back. You could nip off its legs one by one, or bits of its tail, and, crunching the little morsels, see how it still struggled, as long as its brief life lasted, to get away.

All smart carnivores played. It was a way of learning about the world, of how prey animals behaved, of honing reflexes. For their time, orniths had been very smart carnivores indeed.

Once, not more than twenty thousand years ago, a new game had occurred to one of them. She had picked up a handy stick in her grasping hand, and she used that to probe for unbroken eggs.

By the next generation the sticks had become hooks to drag out the embryos, and sharpened spears to stab them.

And by the next, the new weapons were being trialed on bigger game: juvenile diplos, younger than five or six years, not yet part of a herd but already a meat haul worth hundreds of embryonic chicks. Meanwhile a rudimentary language was born, of the subtle communications of pack hunters.

A kind of arms race followed. In this age of immense prey, the orniths' better tools, more sophisticated communication, and complex structures were quickly rewarded by bigger and better hauls of meat. Ornith brains rapidly expanded, the better to make the tools, and sustain societies, and process language—but there was a need for more meat to feed the big expensive brains, requiring better tools yet. It was a virtuous spiral that would operate again, much later in Earth's long history.

The orniths had spread all over Pangaea, following their prey herds as they crisscrossed the supercontinent along their vast ancestral corridors of parkway.

But now conditions were changing. Pangaea was breaking up, its backbone weakening. Rift valleys, immense troughs littered with ash and lava, were starting to open. New oceans would be born in a great cross shape: Eventually the Atlantic would separate the Americas from Africa and Eurasia, while the mighty equatorial Tethys would separate Europe and Asia from Africa, India, Australasia. Thus Pangaea would be quartered.

It was a time of rapid and dramatic climate change. The drift of continental fragments created new mountains which, in turn, cast rain shadows across the lands; the forests died back, and immense dune fields spread. Generation by generation—as their range disintegrated, and the vegetation no longer had time to recover from their devastating passage—the great sauropod herds were diminishing.

Still, if not for the orniths, the sauropods might have lingered much longer, even surviving into the great high summer of dinosaur evolution, the Cretaceous.

If not for the orniths.

Though Listener went on to take more mates and to raise proud clutches of healthy and savage young, she never forgot what had become of her first mate, Stego. Listener did not dare challenge the matriarch. Everyone knew that the best chance of the herd's survival was for the powerful old female to continue her long life; after all, no new matriarch had emerged to replace her.

But, slowly and surely, she drew up her plans.

It took her a decade. Over that time the numbers of diplos in the herd halved. The allosaurs too went into steep decline across the supercontinent as their prey animals became scarce.

At last, after a particularly harsh and dry season, the old one was observed to limp. Perhaps there was arthritis in her hips, as there evidently was in her long neck and tail.

The time was close.

Then Listener smelled something in the wind from the east, a taste she had not known for a long time. It was salt. And she realized that the fate of the matriarch was no longer important.

At last she achieved a consensus among the hunters.

The great diplo cow was now 120 years old. Her hide bore the scars of failed predator attacks, and many of the bony spines on her back had snapped off. Still she was growing, now massing a remarkable twenty-three tons. But the degeneration of her bones, after their heroic lifetime of load-bearing, had slowed her cruelly.

On the day her strength finally ran out, it took only a few minutes of the herd's steady, ground-covering trot for her to become separated from the pack.

The orniths were waiting. They had been waiting for days. They reacted immediately.

Three males moved in first, all of them sons of Listener. They stalked around the matriarch, cracking their whips, flimsy bits of treated leather that emulated the supersonic crackle of the diplos' tails.

Some of the diplo herd looked back dimly. They made out the matriarch, and her tiny predators. Even now the million-year programming of the diplos' small brains could not accept that these skinny carnivores presented any threat. The diplos turned away, and continued their relentless feeding.

The matriarch could see the capering, diminutive figures before her. She rumbled her irritation, the great boulders grinding in her stomach. She tried to lift her head, to bring her own tail to bear, but too many joints had fused to painful immobility.

Now the second wave of hunters moved in. Armed with poison-tipped spears, and using the claws of their hands and feet, they attacked the matriarch as allosaurs once had, striking and retreating.

But the matriarch had not survived more than a century by chance.

Summoning up the last of her energy, ignoring the hot aches that spread from the pinpricks in her side, she reared up on her hind feet. Like a falling building, she towered over the band of carnivores, and they fled before her. She crashed back to the earth with an impact like a sharp earthquake, her slamming forefeet sending waves of pain through every major joint in her body.

If she had fled then, if she had hurried after her herd, she might have survived, even thrown off the effects of the spears. But that last monumental effort had briefly exhausted her. And she was not given time to recover. Again the hunters closed in, striking at her with their spears and claws and teeth.

And here came Listener.

Listener had stripped naked, discarding even the whip around her waist. Now she flew at the diplo's flank, which quivered mountainously. The hide itself was like thick leather, resistant even to her powerful claws, and it was crisscrossed by gullies, the scars of ancient wounds, within which parasitic growths blossomed, lurid red and green. The stink of rotten flesh was almost overwhelming. But she clung there, digging in her claws. She climbed until she had reached the spines that lined the matriarch's back. Here, Listener bit into the diplo's flesh and began to rip away at the horny plates embedded beneath.

Perhaps in some dark corner of her antique mind the diplo remembered the day she had ruined this little ornith's life. Now, aware of new pains on her back, she tried to turn her neck, if not to swipe away the irritation, at least to see the perpetrator. But she could not turn.

Listener did not stop her frantic, gruesome excavation until she had dug down to the spinal cord itself, which she severed with a harsh bite.

For long days the mountain of meat served to sustain the nation of hunters, even as the young played in the cavernous hall of the matriarch's great ribs.

But Listener was criticized, in angry head bobs, dances, and gestures. *This is a mistake. She was the matriarch. We should have spared her until another emerged. See how the herd is becoming scattered, ill-disciplined, its numbers falling further. For now we eat. Soon we may starve. You were blinded by your rage. We were foolish to follow you.* And so on.

Listener kept her own counsel. For she knew the damage the loss of the matriarch had done to the herd, how badly it had been weakened, how much less were its chances of survival. And she knew it did not matter, not anymore. For she had smelled the salt.

When the matriarch was consumed, the hunting nation moved on, following the savannah corridor to the east as it had always done, walking in the herd's unmistakable wake of trampled ground and crashed trees.

Until they ran out of continent. Beyond a final belt of forest—beyond a shallow sandstone cliff—an ocean lay shining. The giant diplos milled, confused, in this unfamiliar place, with its peculiar electric stink of ozone and salt.

The herd had reached the eastern coast of what would become Spain. They were facing the mighty Tethys Sea, which had forced its way westward between the separating continental blocks. Soon the Tethyan waters would break through all the way to the west coast, sundering a supercontinent.

Listener stood on the edge of the cliff, her forest-adapted eyes dazzled by its light, and smelled the ozone and salt she had detected so many days ago. The matriarch was dead, destroyed, but it did not matter. For, after walking across a supercontinent, the diplodocus herd had nowhere to go.

The orniths might have fared better had they had a more flexible culture. Perhaps if they had learned to farm the great sauropods—or even simply not to pressure them so hard in this time of change—they might have survived longer. But everything about them was shaped by their origins as carnivorous hunters. Even their rudimentary mythos was dominated by the hunt, by legends of a kind of ornitholestes Valhalla. They were hunters who could make tools: that was all they would ever be, until there was nothing left to hunt.

The whole of the orniths' rise and fall was contained in a few thousand years, a thin slice of time compared to the eighty million years the dinosaur empire would yet persist. They made tools only of perishable materials—wood, vegetable fiber, leather. They never discovered metals, or learned how to shape stone. They didn't even build fires, which might have left hearths. Their stay had been too brief; the thin strata would not preserve their inflated skulls. When they were gone the orniths would leave no trace for human archaeologists to ponder, none but the puzzle of the great sauropods' abrupt extinction. Listener and her culture would vanish. Like the great air whale and innumerable other fabulous beasts, they would vanish forever.

With a sudden stab of loss, Listener hurled her spear into the ocean. It disappeared into the water's glimmering mass.

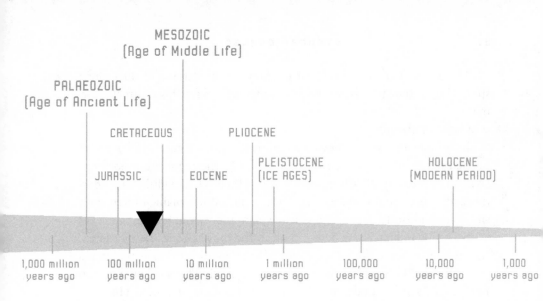

MESOZOIC
[Age of Middle Life]

PALAEOZOIC
[Age of Ancient Life]

CRETACEOUS

PLIOCENE

PLEISTOCENE
[ICE AGES]

HOLOCENE
[MODERN PERIOD]

JURASSIC   EOCENE

| 1,000 million | 100 million | 10 million | 1 million | 100,000 | 10,000 | 1,000 |
| years ago | years ago | years ago | years ago | years ago | years ago | years ago |

CHAPTER 3

the devil's tail

▼ **North America. Circa 65 million years before present.**

I

Once interplanetary impacts had been constructive, a force for good.

Earth had formed close to the brightening sun. Water and other volatiles had quickly boiled away, leaving the young world an empty theater of rock. But the comets, falling in from the outer system, delivered substances that had coalesced in that cooler region: especially the water that would fill Earth's oceans, and compounds of carbon, whose chain-based chemistry would lie at the heart of all life. Earth settled down to a long chemical age in which complex organic molecules were manufactured in the mindless churning of the new oceans. It was a long prelude to life. It would not have come about without the comets.

But now the time of the impacts was done, so it seemed. In the new solar system, the remaining planets and moons followed nearly circular orbits, like a vast piece of clockwork. Any objects following more disorderly paths had mostly been removed.

Mostly.

The thing that now came out of the dark, its surface of dirty slush sputtering in the sun's heat, was like a memory of Earth's traumatic formation.

Or a bad dream.

In human times, the Yucatan Peninsula was a tongue of land that pushed north out of Mexico into the gulf. On the peninsula's northern coast there was a small fishing harbor called Puerto Chicxulub (*Chic-shoe-lube*). It was an unprepossessing place, a limestone plain littered with sinkholes and freshwater springs, agave plantations, and brush.

Sixty-five million years before that, in the moist age of the dinosaurs, this place was ocean floor. The plains of the Gulf of Mexico were flooded up to the foothills of the Sierra Madre Oriental. The shallow Yucatan Peninsula itself lay under nearly a hundred meters of water. The sediments that would later form Cuba and Haiti were part of the deep seafloor, yet to be lifted by fault movements to the surface.

In an age dominated by warm shallow seas, drowned Chicxulub was an unremarkable place. But it was here that a world would end.

Chicxulub is a Mayan word, an ancient word coined by a lost people. Later, when the Mayans were gone, nobody would know for sure how it translated. Local legend said it meant the Devil's Tail.

In its last moments the comet flew in from the southeast, passing over the Atlantic and South America.

II

In bright, shallow waters the huge ammonite cruised.

This sea-bottom hunter, the size of a tractor tire, looked something like a giant snail, with an elaborately curved spiral shell from which arms and a head protruded cautiously. As it had grown, it had extended its shell's spiral structure, gradually moving from one chamber outwards to the next; now the linked, abandoned chambers were used for buoyancy and control.

The ammonite moved with surprising grace, its upright spiral cutting through the waters. And it scanned its surroundings with wide intelligent eyes.

The sunlit sea was crowded, translucent, full of rich plankton. Some of the creatures here—oysters, clams, many species of fish—would have been familiar to humans. But others would not: there were many ancient species of squid, the ammonite itself—and, dimly visible as shadows passing through the blue reaches of the deeper ocean—giant marine reptiles, mosasaurs and plesiosaurs, the dolphins and whales of the age.

As the daylight gathered, more of the ammonite's kind were rising, to hang like bells in the translucent water.

But the ammonite spotted movement on the seabed. It descended quickly, sensory tentacles pushing out of its shell. By sight and feel it quickly determined that the scuttling, burrowing thing in the gritty sand was a crab. More arms slid out of the shell and wrapped around the crustacean, tiny hooks on each arm helping to secure their grip. The crab was pulled easily away from the soft seabed. A heavy birdlike beak protruded, and the ammonite bit through the crab's shell, between its eyes. It injected digestive juices into the shell, and began to suck out the resulting soup.

As particles of meat diffused in the water, more ammonites came sliding in.

But the ammonite with the crab saw a shadow moving above, a shadow with a snout and fins, silently sliding, rapidly resolving. It was an elasmosaur; a marine reptile, a kind of plesiosaur with an immensely long neck. Abandoning its kill, the ammonite ducked into its shell. The opening in the shell was immediately sealed off with a heavy cap of hardened tissue.

The elasmosaur fell on the ammonite, pushed its shell over, and clamped its powerful jaws around the narrowest part of the spiral. But it could not break through. After breaking a cluster of teeth, the elasmosaur dropped the shell, letting it drift back to the ocean floor. Frustration and pain seethed in its one-dimensional awareness.

The ammonite had endured violent shaking, but it was safe in its armored home.

But one immature ammonite had not been so wary. It tried to flee, its jets pushing it this way and that.

The elasmosaur took its consolation kill well. Its teeth sliced expertly across the spiral shell at the place where the body was attached to the inner surface. Then it shook the shell hard until the ammonite, still alive, tumbled out into the water, naked for the first time in its life. The fish-lizard took its prize in a single gulp.

Now the elasmosaur spotted a cloud in the water. It plunged in without hesitating.

The cloud was a shoal of belemnites, thousands strong. The little squid had gathered for protection, and their defensive systems, of sentries and ink and shimmying, deceptive movements, were usually effective even against predators as fast as this elasmosaur. But they had been caught out by this creature's angry lunge. They darted away, venting ink furiously at the immense invader, or even leaping out of the ocean altogether and into the comet-bright air. Still, hundreds of them died: each a pinpoint of awareness, each of them in its way unrepeatable and unique.

Meanwhile, cautiously, the crab-killer ammonite had opened its shell once more. A tube of muscle protruded from the opening, and a high-pressure stream of water pulsed out, jetting the ammonite up and into the blue waters. It had lost the crab. But no matter. There was always another kill to make.

So it went. It was a time of savage predation, in the sea as on land. Mollusks hunted ammonites, boring through shells, poisoning prey animals, and firing deadly darts. In response, bivalves had learned to bury themselves deep in sediment, or had evolved spines and massive shells to deter attackers. Limpets and barnacles had forsaken the deep sea, colonizing shallow environments on the shore where only the most determined of hunters could reach them.

Meanwhile, the seas teemed with predatory reptiles. Carnivorous turtles and long-necked plesiosaurs fed on fishes and ammonites—as did pterosaurs, flying reptiles who had learned to dive for the riches of the ocean. And huge, heavy-jawed pliosaurs preyed on the predators. Measuring some twenty-five meters long, with jaws alone some three meters long, their sole stratagem to rip and shake their prey apart, the pliosaurs were the largest carnivores in the history of the planet.

The rich Cretaceous oceans teemed, enacting a three-dimensional ballet of hunter and hunted, of life and death. It had been so for tens of millions of years. But now a bright light was building above the glimmering surface of the ocean, as if the sun were falling from the sky.

The ammonite's eye was drawn upwards. The ammonite was smart enough to feel something like curiosity. This was new. What could it be? Caution prevailed: Novelty usually equated to danger. Once more the ammonite began to withdraw into its shell.

But this time even its mobile fortress could not protect it.

The comet punched through Earth's atmosphere in fractions of a second. It blasted away the air around it, blowing it into space, leaving a tunnel of vacuum where it had passed.

The ammonite was trapped right under the comet's fall. It was as if a great glowing lid closed across the sky. Its substance immediately vaporized, the ammonite died. So did the belemnites. So did the elasmosaur. So did the oysters and clams. So did the plankton.

The ammonites had stalked the oceans of the Earth, spawning thousands of species, for more than three hundred million years. Within a year, none of them would be left alive, none. Already, in these first fractions of a second, long biographies were being abruptly terminated.

The few dozen meters of water offered the comet nucleus no more resistance than the air. All the water flashed to steam in a hundredth of a second.

Then the comet nucleus hit the seabed. It massed a thousand billion tons, a flying mountain of ice and dust. It took two seconds to collapse into the seabed rocks, delivering in those seconds the heat energy released by all of the Earth's volcanoes and earthquakes in a thousand years.

The nucleus was utterly destroyed. The seabed itself was vaporized: rock flashed to mist. A great wave pulsed outward through the bedrock. And a narrow cone of incandescent rock mist fired back along the comet's incoming trajectory, back through the tunnel in the air dug out in the comet's last moments. It looked like a vast searchlight beam. Around this central glowing shaft, a much broader spray of pulverized and shattered rock, amounting to hundreds of times the comet's own mass, was blown out of the widening crater.

In the first few seconds thousands of billions of tons of solid, molten, and vaporized rock were hurled into the sky.

On the coastal plain of the North American inland sea, the duckbill herds gathered around the pools of standing water. They hooted mournfully as they clustered and nudged each other. Predators, from chicken-sized raptors upwards, watched stray duckbill young with cold calculation. In one place a crowd of ankylosaurs had gathered, their dusty armor glistening, like a Roman legion in formation.

An orange glow could be seen deep in the south, like a second dawn. Then a thin, brilliant bar of light arrowed into the sky, straight as a geometrical demonstration—straighter, in fact, than a laser beam, for the beam of incandescent rock suffered no refraction as it pushed out through the hole in the Earth's superheated air. All of this unfolded in silence, unnoticed.

The crocodile-faced suchomimus stalked the edge of the ocean, her long claws extended. Just as she did every day, she was looking for fish. The death of her mate days before was a dull ache, slowly fading. But life went on; her diffuse grief gave her no respite from hunger.

Elsewhere a group of stegoceras was foraging, scattered. These pachycephalosaurs were about as tall as humans. The males had huge caps of bone on their skulls, there to protect their small brains during their earth-shuddering mating competitions, when they would crash their heads together like mountain sheep. Even now two great males were battling, ramming their reinforced heads together, the bony clatter of their collisions echoing across the plains. This species had sacrificed much evolutionary potential to these contests. The need to maintain such a vast protective cap of bone had limited the development of the pachycephalosaur brain for millions of years. Locked in biochemical logic, these males cared nothing for shifting lights in the sky, or the double shadows that slid across the ground.

On this beach it was just another day in the Cretaceous. Business as usual.

But something was coming from the south.

By now the crater was a glowing bowl of shining, boiling impact melt, wide enough to have engulfed the Los Angeles area from Santa Barbara to Long Beach. And its depth was four times the height of Everest, its lip farther above its floor than the tracks of supersonic planes above Earth's surface. It was a crater ninety kilometers across and thirty deep formed in minutes. But this tremendous structure was transient. Already great arching faults had opened up, and immense landslides, tens of kilometers wide, began to collapse the steep walls.

And the seabed was flexing. The Earth's deeper rocks had been pushed down into the mantle by the comet's hammer blow. Now they rebounded, rising up through twenty kilometers, breaking through the melt pool to the surface. The basement rock itself, almost liquefied, quickly spread out into a vast circular structure, a mountain range forty kilometers across, erected in seconds. Meanwhile water strove to fill the pit that had been dug into the ocean floor. And already ejecta debris was falling back onto the crater's shifting floor, a rain of burning rock. Temperatures reached thousands of degrees—enough to make the air itself burn, nitrogen combining with oxygen to form poisons that would linger for years to come. It was a chaotic battle of fire, steam, and falling rock.

From the impact site, superheated air fled at interplanetary speeds. A great circular wind gushed out from the Yucatan, down into South America, and across the Gulf of Mexico. The shock wave was still moving at supersonic speeds ten minutes later, when it reached the coast of Texas.

To the south of the beach, the thin pillar of light had fanned outward. It became more diffuse, and changed color, becoming a deeper orange white. Tiny flecks of orange could be seen flying up around its base. And now a band of darkness spread over the southern horizon. Still, all this unfolded in silence. What was coming was still moving much more rapidly than sound. The dinosaur herds were oblivious; still the young pachy-cephalosaurs battled, locked into their Darwinian dance.

But the birds and the pterosaurs knew the sky. A group of pterosaurs had been working the ocean, skimming low over the surface seeking to scoop up fish in their hydrodynamically elegant beaks. Now they turned and headed inland, flapping to gain speed. A flock of small, gull-like birds followed, rising up on gray-white wings that seemed to pulse in the glowing rock light.

Of the thousands of dinosaurs, only the suchomimus reacted to the light show. She turned to the south, and her slit pupils narrowed at what she saw. Some instinct made her splash away from the water to run higher onto the shore. The warm sand was soft under her feet, slowing her down. But still the suchomimus ran.

Two young raptors, working playfully at the shell of a stranded sea turtle, lifted their heads with speculative interest as she passed. A corner of the suchomimus's clever mind rippled with alarm signals. She was breaking many of her innate rules; she was making herself vulnerable. But a deeper instinct told her that the stain of darkness spreading over the horizon was more of a threat than any raptor.

She reached a bank of low dunes. A ball of fur squirmed indignantly out from beneath her feet and fled with blurring speed.

Over the coastal plain, the light began to fade.

At last the dinosaurs were disturbed. The great herbivore herds, the duckbills and ankylosaurs, lifted their heads from their browsing and turned to face the south.

The fan of ascending rock was invisible now, hidden by a wall of darkness that spanned the horizon. But it was a moving wall whose front bubbled and writhed. Lightning flickered over the moving surface, making it shine purple white.

Even now, in these last seconds, there was little sense of strangeness. It was like an eerie twilight. Some of the dinosaurs even felt drowsy, as their nervous systems reacted to the reduced level of light.

Then, from out of the south, the shock front exploded. From silence to bedlam in a heartbeat. The front smashed the animal herds. Duckbills were hurled into the air, huge adults writhing, their lowing lost in the sudden fury. The competition among the hard-skulled stegoceras was concluded without resolution, never to be resumed. Some of the great ankylosaurs stood their ground, turning into the wind, hunkering down like armored bunkers. But the very ground was torn up around them, the vegetation ripped out and scattered; even the lakes explosively emptied of their water. The shallow dune exploded over the suchomimus, instantly burying her in gritty darkness.

But as quickly as it had come, the shock wave passed.

When she felt the ground's shuddering cease, the suchomimus began to scrabble at the earth. She sneezed the grit out of her nostrils, her great translucent eyelids working to clear her eyes, and clambered to her feet.

She stepped forward gingerly. The new ground was rubble strewn, uncertain, difficult to walk on.

The coastal plain was unrecognizable. The dune that had sheltered her was demolished, the wind's patient, centuries-long work erased in seconds. The plain was littered with debris: bits of pulverized rock, sea-bottom mud, even a few strands of seaweed and smaller sea creatures. Above her, clouds boiled, streaming north.

Still the noise continued, great crackling shocks that rained out of the sky as sound waves folded over on themselves. But the suchomimus heard none of this. She had been deafened in the first instant of the shock's passage, her delicate eardrums crushed.

Dinosaurs lay everywhere.

Even the largest duckbills had been smashed to the ground. They lay, broken and twisted, under scattered sand and mud. A group of raptors lay together, their lithe bodies tangled up. Everywhere the old lay with the young, parents alongside their children, predators with their prey, united in death. Most disasters, like floods and fires, selectively affected the weakest, the young and the old and the ill. Or else they targeted species— an epidemic, perhaps, carried by an unwitting host across a land bridge between the continents. But this time, none had been spared, none save the very fortunate, like the suchomimus.

The suchomimus saw a silver fish. It twitched, carried a dozen kilometers in seconds, still alive. The suchomimus's gut rumbled gently. Even now, as the world ended, she was hungry.

But the wind's work was not yet done. Already, over the ocean, the air was rushing back to fill the vacuum created at the impact site. It was like an immense inhalation.

The suchomimus, toying with her fish, saw the wall of darkness bear down once more. But this time it came from inland, and it was laden with debris, with dirt and rocks and uprooted trees and even a huge male tyrannosaur that writhed lifeless, high in the air.

Once more the suchomimus dived at the sand.

From the furies of the crater the shock front continued to spread out, like a ripple around a fallen stone. Further inland, where Giant had raided the tyrannosaur nest, the front had wrought devastation around a great circle big enough to have been wrapped around the Moon.

Tornadoes spun off the advancing front like willful, destructive children.

To Giant, the twister was a tube of darkness that connected sky to ground. At its feet, what looked like splinters rose up, whirled and fell back. The giganotosaurs' ancestors had invaded a continent. Now Giant reared up and hissed, bobbing his head, eyes triangulating on the approaching menace.

But this was no saurian competitor. As the twister approached it grew ever larger, towering high above him.

At last something in Giant's mind focused on those twigs scattered at the feet of this climatic monster. Those "twigs" were *trees*, redwoods and ginkgoes and tree ferns, scattered as easily as pine needles.

His brothers made the same calculation. The three of them turned and ran.

The base of the twister tore casually through the blanket forest, destroying trees, scattering rock. Animals weighing five tons or more were hurled into the air, great slow-moving herbivores suddenly flying. Many of them died of shock even before they hit the ground.

In her burrow, Purga was shaken awake by the rattling of the earth. She and her mate huddled closely around the two pups, and they listened to the howling of the wind, the clatter and crunch of trees being shattered, the scream of dying dinosaurs.

Purga closed her eyes, baffled, terrified, longing for the noise to stop.

And in the foothills of the Rockies, the mother azhdarchid sensed the approach of the mighty wind. Hastily she folded up her wings and waddled on wrists and knees toward her nest.

Her young clustered around, but she had no food to give them, and they pecked at her angrily. The chicks were still flightless, their wing membranes yet to develop. For now they had only loose, useless flaps of skin trailing between their flight fingers and hind legs. And yet they were already beautiful, in their way; the scales that clustered around their thin necks, a relic of their reptilian ancestry, caught the high sunlight, gleaming and glistening.

But now clouds raced across the sun. The twisters would not reach so high. But the shock front was still a broiling wall of turbulent air, still powerful even so far from the impact site.

A first gust buffeted the nest. The chicks screeched and stumbled.

Without thinking the mother flapped her wings, taking to the air. A primitive imperative had taken over. There would always be more broods, if she survived. The chicks, receding beneath her, squawked their anger and fear.

As the wall of wind approached, there was a moment of stillness.

The azhdarchid's airspeed dropped. She turned and spread her wings, instinctive responses coming to play. She held out her long flight finger and her hind limb, and subtle twitches of thigh and knee adjusted the tension in her wings. She was an exquisite flying device, an apparatus of tendons, ligaments, muscle, skin and fur, shaped by tens of millions of years of evolution.

But the comet wind didn't care about that, not at all.

The wind hit the nest first. The rock ledge was swept bare, the nest smashed to fragments. The bones of the pterosaurs' victims—including those of Second—were sent whirling into the air with the rest of the debris. The chicks flew: if only briefly, if only once, if only to their deaths.

And then, for the mother azhdarchid, it was as if she had flown into a wall of dust and spray, and even bits of vegetation and wood and rock. She felt her fragile bones snap. She was tumbled over and over, helpless as a dead leaf.

Once more the suchomimus struggled to her feet. She ached in her legs, arms, back, tail, and head, where she had been struck by bits of flying debris, the wreckage of a world.

Again the beach had become an utterly unfamiliar place. The ground was now littered by debris from inland, bits of smashed trees and crushed animals, dead or dying pterosaurs and birds, even lake-bottom ooze. Nothing moved—nothing but dying creatures, and the suchomimus.

She remembered the fish she had been about to eat. The fish was gone.

Above her, dark banks of cloud whipped across the sky, like a curtain being drawn. The sun disappeared; it would not be seen again for a long time.

And to the south, the lid of sky began to glow an eerie orange. A breeze wafted a sharp, distinctive smell to her nose. *Ozone.* The smell of the sea. She thought of lapping water, the glittering fish of the shallows. She must get to the sea. She had always made her living from the sea; there she would be safe. With a mournful lowing even she couldn't hear, she began to blunder in the direction of the scent, ignoring the grisly detritus under her feet.

The sea turtle had been fortunate. When the comet hit, she was cruising the sea bottom far from the impact zone.

Her kind was among the most primitive of the great reptile dynasties.

But, primitive or not, this turtle was an effective hunter. Her body was undemanding, requiring only a twentieth as much food as a dinosaur of the same weight. Heavily protected by her powerfully reinforced shell, cautious even as a hunter, the only risks she ran in her life were the annual assaults she had to make on the beaches to lay her eggs, before hurrying back to the safety of the water.

Her brain was small, her consciousness dim. She lived alone, in a world of colorless monotony. She had no bonds with her parents or siblings, no real understanding that the eggs she laid would produce a new generation. But she was ancient, wary, enduring.

Now, though, something disturbed her blue, lonely world. A monstrous current began to drag the sea toward the south.

Grimly the turtle paddled at the water, heading downward. Her instincts, honed by millions of years of tropical storms, primed her with a simple instruction: dive deep, get to the bottom, find shelter.

But this was like no current she had ever experienced. Through the increasingly muddy and turbulent water she glimpsed much larger creatures, even giant pliosaurs, being dragged backward by this mighty tide. And as she descended she was battered by debris, helpless ammonites, clams, squid, even rocks torn from the floor.

At last she found soft mud. All her four fins working, she began to work her way into the dirt, ignoring the hail of objects that clattered off her shell. Eventually she would have to surface, for air and warmth; but she could last for a long time, perhaps until this monstrous storm had passed away.

But now the sea's glimmering meniscus descended toward her—and the sea *drained away*—and she found herself in sunlight, with moist mud hissing all around her. Something like shock lit up her small mind. The world had turned upside down; this made no sense.

And now the sea bottom mud, exposed, began to shake.

By the shifting, strange light, at last the suchomimus saw the sea. With a hoarse cry of relief, she hurried forward.

But the sea ran away from her, exposing glistening mud. And as fast as she pursued it, the sea ran faster.

A fish flopped at her feet. She stopped and plucked it out of the dirty mud and popped it into her mouth. In the fish's tiny awareness was a kind of relief; this death was quick compared to the grisly suffocation it had endured on the new beach.

The sea bottom, uncovered for the first time in millions of years, was a glistening floor of life. It was littered with clams, crustaceans, squid, fish, ammonites of all sizes, all of them drowning in the air.

Further south there were giant shapes. The suchomimus saw a giant plesiosaur, stranded like the rest. Eight meters long, it lay gasping on the mud with its four huge flippers splayed and broken around it. It struggled, tons of marine carnivore flipping this way and that, huge fins waving, savage teeth snapping in rage at the fate that had stranded it.

On any other day it would have been a remarkable sight. The suchomimus turned away, bewildered.

When she looked north to the land, she could see creatures creeping out of the devastated forests, the wind-scoured marshland. Many of them were ankylosaurs and other armored creatures, protected thus far by the heavy armor that had evolved to fend off the teeth and claws of tyrannosaurs. They crawled toward the exposed seabed, seeking sanctuary, to drink, to feed.

But now the ankylosaurs opened their mouths and began to retreat once more. The suchomimus watched them, baffled. They were bellowing, but she couldn't hear them.

She turned back to face the sea. And then she saw what had frightened them.

As air, so water.

From the impact site, powered by the immense pulse of heat, a circular shock wave now marched outward through the body of the ocean. Its destructive power was limited because the impact had not occurred in deep ocean water. Still, as it neared the coastline of North America, the wave was already some thirty meters high. And as it reached the shallower water of the Texas coast, the tsunami gathered itself, rearing ten to twenty times its initial height.

Nothing in the suchomimus's evolutionary heritage had prepared her for this. The returning sea was like a moving mountain range, hurtling out of the retreated ocean. She could not hear it, but she could feel how it made the exposed seabed shudder, smell the sharp stink of salt and pulverized rock. She stood upright and bobbed her head, baring her teeth defiantly at the approaching tsunami.

The water towered above her. There was an instant of pressure, of blackness, a huge force that compressed her. She died within a second.

The tsunami rolled landward, dwarfing the lumbering ankylosaurs before crushing them, armor and all. On it went, ramming its way into the ancient, long-dried sea way. When it receded, the water left behind debris, great banks of it dredged from the sea bottom. It had been an immense slosh, from the stone thrown into this Cretaceous pond.

On the land, in Texas, nothing survived.

In the sea, only a handful of creatures lived through the oceanic catastrophe.

One of them was the sea turtle. She had burrowed deep enough into
the mud for the tsunami waters to spare her. When she could sense that
something like calm was restored, she struggled out of the mud, and
ascended up through water cloudy with debris and bits of dead animals
and plants.

The turtles, ancient, had already passed the zenith of their diversity.
But where more spectacular creatures had perished en masse, the turtle
had survived. In a dangerous world, humility made for longevity.

The impact had sent an energy pulse through the body of the Earth. In
North and South America, across thousands of kilometers, faults gaped
and landslides crashed, as the shocked ground shuddered. The rocky
waves weakened as they propagated, but the Earth's internal layers acted
like a giant lens to refocus the seismic energy at the impact's antipode,
the southwestern Pacific. Even there, the width of the planet away, the
ocean floor heaved in swells ten times higher than the 1906 San
Francisco earthquake.

The shock waves would continue to pass through the planet's body,
crossing, interfering, reinforcing. For days, the Earth would ring like a
bell.

Seen from space, a glowing wound was spreading out over the Earth
around the still-burning impact point. It was a great cloud of molten rock,
hurled into space.

In the vacuum the scattered droplets were beginning to cool and con-
dense into hard specks of dust. Some of this material would be lost to the
planet forever, joining the thin drizzle of material that swam between the
planets: In a few millennia fragments of Yucatan seafloor would fall as
meteors on Mars and Venus and the Moon. And some of the space-borne
material would, through chance configurations, enter orbit around the
planet, making a temporary ring around the Earth—dark, unspectacular—
that would soon disperse under the shifting gravitational tweaks of the sun
and Moon.

But most of the ejecta would fall back to Earth.

Already the great hailing had begun. The first to fall was the coarser
debris from the perimeter of the crater, much of it fragments of smashed-
up ocean-bottom limestone. These chunks had not been melted by the
heat pulse of the initial impact. But as they fell back into the Earth's

warm pond of air, they began to glow brightly. Streaks of light hundreds of kilometers long were drawn across the sky, like an insane geometrical exercise. Some of the debris chunks were large enough to crack open as they heated, and secondary tracks fanned out from sparking explosions.

Of all the creatures within a few thousand kilometers of the impact, the great aerial whale had been least affected so far.

He had watched the great light descend over the Yucatan Peninsula— had seen that stabbing laser beam of vaporized seabed and comet, had even glimpsed the formation of the crater, as great ripples of rock pulsed through the exposed seabed before congealing into place in a great chthonic clench. Had he been able to describe what he saw, the whale could have provided posterity with a compelling eyewitness account of the catastrophe, the most violent impact since the end of the formative bombardment four billion years earlier.

But the whale cared nothing for that. The whale had not even been troubled by the wind; he flew too high, and had been able to continue feeding as the great sheets of discolored air fled across the ground far beneath him. Distant lights in the sky, trouble on the ground—like the creamy-swirl weather systems that often crossed the land and oceans— meant nothing to a creature who flew at the fringe of space. So long as the wispy aerial plankton that fed him continued to drift up from the lands below, he prowled his thin niche untroubled.

But this storm was different.

The air whale was used to meteors. They were just streaks of light in the purple-blue sky above. Almost all of the billions of bits of cosmic debris that fell to Earth burned up far above the stratosphere, the whale's realm.

But some of these tracks were reaching *down* into Earth's thicker air, passing far below him. The whale had no hearing—he had no need of it in this thin, silent air, where no predators worked—but if he had he might have made out the thin howl of the meteors as they plunged back to the planet from which they had so recently been flung. He could even see where the first sea-bottom chunks fell: On the ground, far below, sparks of light bloomed like tiny flowers, one after the other. It was like the view from a high-altitude bomber.

For the first time since he was a chick the whale began to know fear. Suddenly this was no aerial light show but a *rain* of light and fire. It was a rain that was falling all around him—and it was getting thicker. Belatedly he turned. With a slow flap of his immense wings, he headed north.

Light pulsed.

The white-hot rock fragment was just a scrap. After the encounter with the whale it continued its descent toward the thick Cretaceous forests, only a fraction of its kinetic energy expended. But the whale's complex nervous system brought his small brain messages of agonizing pain. When he turned his great head to the right, he saw that the surface of his wing was torn and scorched.

If the meteor had hit near the center of the wing, it might have made no more than a puncture, and the whale might have lived a little longer. But the whale had been unlucky. The meteor had punched through the joint of an immense, fragile flight finger. The wing began to fold up in great sections around the broken segment of bone.

The blue-gray Earth tipped over. Though he thrashed inelegantly with his good wing, the whale was already falling away from the horizontal— falling out of control, out of the sky. Still he remained conscious, slowly twisting, crumpling like a broken toy kite. But the meteor hail thickened. Bulletlike meteors tore tunnels through the fine caverns of his body, ripping open air sacs, smashing his delicate, light-as-air filigree skeleton, further puncturing his magnificent wings.

The pain became overwhelming. His mind filled with comforting, creamy memories of gliding high over an undisturbed Earth. He died long before the remnants of his torso reached the ground, his lungs crushed by the thick air.

Giant was struggling to get back to his feet.

Before him a stegoceras lumbered, bewildered, the scarlet-coated cap of bone and flesh on his head absurd. Thanks to a chance sheltering in a dense crop of araucaria this young male had survived the tornado, suffering no worse injury than a snapped rib. But his clan was gone, scattered by the wind. He lifted his head and howled, a great mournful lowing. It was like a chick's call of distress, a lost call.

It wasn't his mother who responded, but two huge carnivores, giganotosaurs, who came stalking slowly toward him, their heads bobbing, their eyes fixed on him. Even now, the game of predator and prey continued.

But through the adrenaline-induced fear that flooded his system, the stegoceras noticed something strange. A third giganotosaur, as big and powerful as the rest, was showing no interest in him. The third monster was head-bobbing, threatening, reacting to something that approached from out of the sky. Confused, fearful, the stegoceras turned to the south, where a lowering cancerous orange continued to spread through the racing black clouds.

The first meteor screamed overhead like a glowing hornet. It flew low over the smashed forest and slammed against a foothill beyond. Young volcanic stone exploded, and a secondary shower of steaming fragments hailed out, pattering against the debris-strewn ground. All the dinosaurs turned that way, shocked and startled, their innate animosity briefly forgotten.

And the second meteor passed through the stegoceras's body, like a high-velocity bullet. A fraction of a second later, on meeting the impenetrable ground, the meteor dumped the last of its energy into the rock. The explosion burst apart the stegoceras's body before it had time to fall. In the brief rain of blood, Giant cringed, uncomprehending.

Now the meteors began to land in the remains of the smashed forest. Fire splashed.

Giant and his brothers panicked and ran. But still the meteor rain thickened. The meteors pounded the ground around the giganotosaurs, digging shallow craters and starting fires even in the scattered undergrowth. It was as if the brothers were running through an artillery barrage.

Purga, too, could smell the smoke.

The primates could ride out fires in their burrows, buried deep in the cool earth, to emerge into the debris of a charred and ruined forest. But, Purga's instincts warned her, this time was different. She pushed past her cowering mate and her pups, past the grisly severed head of the troodon. She emerged into daylight. She was immediately dazzled, her sensitive night-adapted eyes unable to cope with the unaccustomed flood of light. But she could nevertheless make out the main features of the terrible day: the spreading fires in the smashed blanket forest, the continual, incomprehensible rain of meteors.

She could not stay here. But where to go?

With much of the obstructing forest already demolished by the winds she could see the shoulders of the Rockies with their clouds of volcanic smoke lingering at their summits. And where the comet winds had pushed warm, moist air up the flanks of the rising ground, thick cumulus clouds clung to the mountain's upper slopes.

Shade. Darkness. Perhaps there would even be rain.

She took a step further into the open, whiskers twitching. She moved in rapid jerks, pausing every few paces, flattening herself against the ground.

She looked back. Beyond the fallen head of the troodon, she could see her mate and pups, three sets of wide eyes peering after her. Instincts honed across a hundred million years urged her to return to the cool earth, or to clamber into the trees where she would find safety, for otherwise the terrible claws and teeth and feet of this giant world would surely claim her. But the trees were smashed and broken, her burrow no longer a sanctuary.

She scurried away, toward the cloud-draped mountains.

Her mate followed, more cautiously. One of the pups followed him. The second, terrified, bewildered, bolted back into the recesses of the burrow. There was nothing Purga could do for the second pup. She would never see him again.

So the three tiny, shrewlike creatures—carrying all the potential of mankind within them—made their way slowly across the battered, smoldering plain while meteors rained around them.

The fire fed on itself. The scattered pockets of fire were beginning to link up. As the temperature of the air rose even the damp undergrowth was starting to burn. A wind began to gather, the smoke to spiral overhead. Here, and all over North and South America, the fires began to exert a logic of their own, becoming self-feeding, self-perpetuating systems.

Thus the firestorms began. Everything that could burn did so: every scrap of vegetation, even lake plants still soaked from their immersion. Animals simply burst into flame: Raptors burned like saplings and great armored herbivores cooked in their own monstrous shells.

The three giganotosaurs burst at last from the forest. They had come to a clearing centered on a large lake. They were overheated, their great mouths gaping, their heads filled with the stink of the smoke.

The open sky was extraordinary. A lid of blackness was rushing up from the southeast, as if a great curtain were closing. That eerie orange glow was spreading too, growing brighter and ascending to yellow. And still the meteors hammered into the muddy ground.

Near the lake itself a desolate scene greeted the giganotosaurs.

Dinosaurs stampeded. Great herds of rival duckbill species mingled, armored beasts like ceratops and ankylosaurs jostled for room, herbivores ran alongside giant predators. There were even mammals, blinking in the light, running amidst giant feet. All the animals charged in panic, their feet burned by the smoldering ground, clattering into each other blindly. This would have been unimaginable just a couple of hours ago. The intricate ecological relationships of herbivores and carnivores, of predators and prey, built up over a hundred and fifty million years, had utterly collapsed.

Giant pushed forward, barging his way through the panicking mob, driven to the water by a deep instinct. He plunged into the lake, ignoring the smoldering debris that floated on the surface. The deeper layers were still blessedly cool. But even with his head submerged he could see more meteors hitting the lake, creating bubble trails in the water like bullets.

And now a missile shape rose before him, a great mouth gaped white, and through the murky water he could see rows of conical teeth. He flailed back.

The crocodile had lain at the bottom of her lake, silent, patient.

A distant cousin of the seagoing deinonychus, so far the events of this tumultuous day had meant little to her. She had felt the shuddering of the Earth and the responding ripple of the water, noticed the peculiar lights in the sky. But she expected to ride out this storm, as she had ridden out many before. She could stay underwater for an hour at a time, as her metabolism was capable of shutting down almost completely when necessary. Her thinking was slow, patient. She knew that all she had to do was lie here in the mud, and the storm would pass, and once more her food would come to her.

But now a dinosaur came blundering clumsily into the water—not just skimming the fringe to drink and browse, like the stupid duckbills, but immersing itself, actually *swimming* in her domain. She felt anger at this intrusion, mixed with anticipation at any easy meal. She pushed herself away from the mud and rose toward the surface, which glimmered with meteor light. But more massive bodies plunged helplessly into the turbid water, struggling in the clinging mud of the lake bottom.

She attacked, of course.

Giant thrashed, evading the crocodile's reaching jaws, and in his blundering he managed to land a kick on the crocodile's snout. The crocodile backed away briefly. But soon she was returning to the attack. Giant might have withdrawn. But a crowd of animals was pushing into the water behind him. The crocodile fought and snapped at the invaders; and the animals warred amongst themselves.

But now there was a mighty surge, as an aftershock of the comet's seismic jolt shuddered through the basement rock. The ground was uplifted, cracked—and the water drained suddenly away, leaving Giant stranded amid drying vegetation and writhing animals.

The crocodile, suddenly exposed to hot, dry air, could not understand what had happened. She tried to burrow into the mud, instructed by instincts that had guided her as a baby from her shell to her first swim. But the mud was hardening, drying fast; she could not even dig into the ooze.

Still the meteors fell, lancing through the clouds of smoke like pillars of light.

The winds and the tsunami had already wiped out most of the living things, from insects to dinosaurs, in North and South America. Around the world, the gathering fires were now killing most of those who had survived.

But the worst was yet to come.

The coarser ejecta at the periphery of the comet impact had fallen back quickly, much of it pounding the disturbed ground within one or two diameters of the central crater, the rest falling as forest-igniting meteors. But the great central plume of rock vapor had continued to rise, propelled by its own heat energy. In the vacuum of space, solid particles condensed out of this glowing cloud, and, still white-hot, began to fall back to Earth. But where they had risen through a tunnel of vacuum, now they fell back into atmosphere, and they dumped their energy into the air. It was a lethal hail of fire, a planetwide blanket of uncounted billions of tiny, white-hot meteors.

All over the planet, the air began to glow.

Purga had reached a foothill. Her mate, Third, and her one surviving pup were at her side. They could go no further toward the true Rockies, for even here the land had been broken and jumbled by the ground waves, littered with boulders that were many times Purga's height.

This would have to do. She began to dig into the loose dirt, seeking to build a burrow.

She glanced back the way she had come. Under banks of billowing smoke the whole of the land glowed bright orange; it was an extraordinary sight. Even here, on this rocky rise, she could feel the heat; even here she could smell the stink of smoke and burning flesh.

She could see the clouds that had drawn her here. They were ragged, but still clustered around the upper slopes of the mountains. Against a sky as black as night the clouds glowed orange white, reflecting the glow of the burning land. But now, beyond the clouds, that orange light from the south crept overhead. The sky itself began to glow, like a dawn erupting all over the sky, all at the same time. The color quickly escalated to orange, then yellow, then a dazzling white, sun-bright.

The heat's first breath reached them.

The primates scrabbled desperately at the ground.

On the cracked pond floor Giant was somehow on his feet, surrounded by the dead. He couldn't breathe; his chest strained at air that was dense with smoke and bits of glowing, charred vegetation. It was like being in a gray fog. He saw nothing but smoke, dust, swirling ash.

Heat pulsed, hot as an oven. There was a stink of burning meat.

He felt a sharp pain in his hand. He lifted it in dim curiosity. His fingers were burning, like candles.

His last thought was of his brothers.

His death came in a moment of fulminant shock. He knew nothing about it: His vital organs were destroyed too quickly for his brain to process a conscious reaction. Then his muscles cooked and coagulated. They contracted his arms and legs, but his spine was extended, so that in this moment of death he adopted a posture oddly like a boxer's, head back, hands up, legs flexed. His flesh was seared away, and the enamel on his teeth began to shatter.

All this before Giant had time to fall to the ground.

And then the very rocks began to crack.

Jewel-like, its sudden brilliance reflecting from the ancient seas of its companion Moon, Earth was beautiful. But it was the beauty of a dying world.

Half of all the heat energy released by the burning air was injected into the deeper atmosphere and the ground. All over the planet, the sky was as hot and bright as the sun. Plants and animals burned where they stood. The trees of the mighty Cretaceous forests were consumed like pine needles. Any birds in the air disappeared in a puff of flame, and the pterosaurs vanished into the maw of extinction. The burrows of mammals and insects and amphibians turned into tiny coffins. Purga's second pup, whimpering and alone, was quickly baked.

Purga was spared. The last clouds, shadowed black, became ragged, dispersing quickly, soon vaporized into steam—but for the crucial minutes of the great heat pulse they served to shield the ground beneath them from a sky as bright as the sun.

It was just an hour after the impact.

III

After the first few days the Earth's shuddering died away, and the daily stamping of the great mountain-reptiles was gone.

Purga was used to darkness. But not to *silence*, this eerie stillness that went on and on.

For countless generations the dinosaurs had framed the lives of Purga's kind. Even after this cataclysmic shock, she had vague visions of arrays of dinosaurs waiting in silent rows to trap any mammal unwise enough to poke her snout out of her burrow.

But she could not stay here, in this hasty burrow. For one thing there was nothing to eat; the family had quickly excavated and consumed any burrowing worms or beetles they could reach. They didn't even know when it was day and when it was night. Their sleep cycles had been thrown off by their flight during the day of the impact, and they found themselves waking at different hours, their hunger conflicting with their fear of the strange, cold silence above. They bickered among themselves, snapping and biting.

And as time wore on the temperature plunged, from the intense heat of the hours of the burning sky to a bitter cold. The primates were sheltered by the thick layer of earth above them, but even that would not protect them forever.

Finally Third turned on the pup—*Last*, for she was Purga's last surviving child. Purga couldn't see Third. But with her whiskers and well-developed hearing she could sense her mate approaching the pup, step by step, mouth wide, as if stalking a centipede.

Third was angry, confused, frightened, and very, very hungry. But what he was doing made a certain sense. After all, there was nothing to eat here. If the flesh of the pup kept the adults alive a little longer, long enough for them to produce another litter, the genetic program would be fulfilled. The calculations were relentlessly logical.

Perhaps in other times Purga would have submitted to Third's aggression, even helped him finish off the pup. But Purga's life had already been long for her kind, and she had suffered a series of extraordinary events: the destruction of her first home, her dogged pursuit by Wounding Tooth—and now the nightmare of the comet impact and her stranding in this world of cold and silence.

The imperatives resolved themselves. She bit Third savagely on the thigh, and scrambled past him to stand alongside her daughter.

Last was just as confused as the others. But she figured out that her mother was defending her from some kind of attack by her father. And so she stood with Purga and bared her teeth at Third. For a full half-minute the burrow was filled with hissing and the sound of tiny paws scraping the ground aggressively; three sets of whiskers filled the space between the primates, each of them waiting for the other to strike.

In the end it was Third who backed off. He gave up quite suddenly, abandoning his aggressive posture and curling up alone in a corner of the burrow. Purga stood with her daughter until the anger and aggression had drained out of her system.

It was this final incident that changed the balance of the forces in Purga's mind.

They couldn't stay here, for they would starve, or freeze, if they didn't kill each other first. They had to go out, regardless of what mysterious dangers lurked in the newly silent world above. Enough was enough. When her body clock next woke her, Purga pushed away the dirt that clogged the entrance to the burrow.

And emerged into the dark.

After two days, the fire in the sky had died. But now, from pole to pole, dust and ash covered the wounded Earth, a black shroud laced with wispy, yellow-white clouds of sulfuric acid. The Earth had been transformed from a starlike shining to a dismal, gloomy darkness, darker than the core of the comet which had wrought such devastation. Dust and ash: The dust was comet fragments, and sea-bottom dirt, and even volcanic debris spewed out after the immense seismic shocks that had rippled through the planet. And the ash was burned life, trees and mammals and divergent species of dinosaurs from America and China and Australia and Antarctica, burned to cinders by the global firestorms and then burned again in the pulse of superheat, now mingled together in the choked stratosphere. Meanwhile, sulfur, baked out of seabed rock in the first moments of the impact, had lingered in the air, forming sulfuric acid crystals. The high, bright acid clouds reflected away sunlight and drove the cold deeper still.

Followed by Third and Last, Purga crept cautiously away from her burrow's mouth, whiskers twitching nervously. It was late afternoon, here in the chill heart of North America. If the sky had been clear, the sun would still have been well above the horizon. There was only the gloomiest of twilights, barely sufficient even for Purga's huge, sensitive eyes.

She stumbled forward over bare, scorched rock. Everything was wrong. There was no scent of green growing things, nor the pungent, spicy stink of the dinosaurs, not even of their dung. Instead, she smelled only ash. The whole of the great thick green-brown layer of Cretaceous life had been burned off: even the dead leaves, even the dung, all destroyed. All that was left were minerals, lifeless dirt, and rock. It was as if Purga had been transported to the surface of the Moon.

And it was *cold*, a deep intense cold that quickly penetrated through diminished layers of fat to her bones.

She came to the ruins of what had been a small stand of tree ferns. She scraped at the ground with her claws, but the ground was strangely hard—and it was cold, deep cold, so cold it hurt the pads of her hands.

But when she licked her hand, a slow trickle of water gathered in her mouth.

Just a few days earlier this had been a place of tropical forest and swamplands. No frost had formed here in millions of years. But now there was frost. Purga scrabbled at the ground, cramming the strange, chill stuff into her mouth. Slowly she got mouthfuls of water—and plenty of ash and dirt along with it.

She tried to dig deeper. She knew that even after the most ferocious fire there was food to be had: hardened nuts, deep-buried insects, worms. But the nuts and spores were trapped under a lid of frozen ground, too tough for Purga's small paws.

She moved on, feeling her way through the dark with her whiskers.

She came to a shallow puddle. In fact it was the footprint of a vanished ankylosaur. Her snout hit a hard surface: brutally cold and hard as rock. The cold that stabbed through her fur was intense. She backed up hastily.

Like frost, she had never encountered solid ice before either.

More cautiously she poked at the ice with her snout and hands. She scraped and scratched—she could smell the water that was somehow hidden here, and it maddened her to be able to get no closer to it. Frustrated, she began to circle the little puddle, pushing and probing. At last she came to a place where the ankylosaur's foot, pushing into what had been soft warm mud, had dug a somewhat deeper pit. The ice here was thin, and when she pushed at it, the surface cracked and lifted up. She jumped back, startled. The fragment of ice, upended, slid slowly into the black water. Cautiously she slid forward once more. And this time, when she tentatively dipped her snout, she found liquid water: chill, already frosting over with fresh ice, but liquid nonetheless. She sucked in great mouthfuls, ignoring the bitterness of the ash and dust that laced it.

Attracted by the sound of her drinking, Third and Last came hurrying to her side. They quickly extended the hole she had broken, jostling to slurp up the gritty water.

For the first time since the comet had struck, things had gotten better for Purga: not by much, but better.

But now something touched her shoulder: something light, cold. She yelped and turned. It was a wisp of white, already melting.

Now more flakes came drifting down out of the sky. They fell with a random, gentle movement. When a flake came close enough, she leapt up and took it in her mouth, like plucking a fly from the air. She got a mouthful of soft ice.

It was snowing.

Spooked at last beyond endurance, she turned and bolted for the security of the burrow.

The impact had hurled vaporized ocean water into the air. After weeks of suspension, it began to fall back.

There was a *lot* of vapor. An epochal rain fell, all over the planet.

But the rain itself brought further devastation. It was full of sulfuric acid from the ice clouds, and the impact had injected thin clouds of toxic metals into the atmosphere, metals that now rained out. Nickel alone reached twice the threshold of toxicity for plants. Runoff water washed substances like mercury, antimony, and arsenic out of the soils, concentrating them in lakes and rivers.

And so on. For years, every raindrop would be poisoned.

The great rain washed out the dust and ash. All over the world, a fine layer of blackened clay was laid down, a band of darkness that would forever show up as a punctuation in the sedimentary rocks of the future—a boundary clay, one day to be studied by Joan Useb and her mother, the last remnant of a biosphere.

After months of dark the sun showed, at last, through the planet-girdling layers of dust and ash. But it was only a pinprick, shedding barely any heat on the frozen land; there would be no more than a murky twilight for another year.

The returning sun illuminated a skeletal landscape.

Tropical plants, if not burned, had been killed by the sudden cold. Any surviving dinosaurs were succumbing to hunger and cold, their bones quickly stripped of flesh by the surviving predators. But here and there living things moved in the ash: insects like ants and cockroaches and beetles, snails, frogs, salamanders, turtles, lizards, snakes, crocodiles—creatures that had been able to hide in mud or in deep water—and many, many mammals. Their furry bodies and habits of burrowing into the shelter of the ground were protecting them from the worst of the cold. Their indiscriminate eating habits helped as well.

It was as if the world ran with rats.

And even now the survivors were breeding. Even now, despite the cold and the shortage of food, in the absence of their ancient predators, their numbers were increasing. Even now the blind scalpels of evolution took raw material adapted for a vanished world and cut and shaped it for the conditions of the new.

Alone, the female euoplocephalus stumbled through the endless cold, seeking the rough forage she needed.

She was of a species of ankylosaur. Her body was ten meters long and, before her slow starvation had begun, she had weighed as much as six tons. Her armor was bone: plates of it set in the skin of her back, neck, tail, flanks, and head. Even her eyelids were plates of bone. The plates were woven into a layer of tough ligaments, making the great carapace flexible, if heavy. Her long tail terminated in a fused mass of bone. Once she had used this club to lame a young male tyrannosaur, her greatest triumph—not that she was able to remember it; all that armor had left little room, and little need, for a large brain.

Though geologically sudden, the great death unfolding across the planet was not instant in the consciousness of those who endured it. For days, weeks, months, many of the doomed clung to life—even dinosaurs.

Relatively speaking, the euoplos had been well-equipped to survive the end of the world. Their massive bulk, great strength, and heavy armor—together with a fortunate placing beneath a thick layer of cloud close to the bank of a river—had enabled a few of her kind to endure the first few horrific hours. She had survived droughts before; she ought to withstand this unexpected calamity. All she had to do was keep moving and fend off the predators.

And so, wandering the freezing Earth, she sought food. And found hardly any.

One by one her companions had fallen away, until the euoplo was alone.

But, in a final irony, she had endured one last mating, from a male now dead; and she found herself heavy with eggs.

In this new world, a land of ice and blackness and a lid of gray-black sky, the euoplo had been unable to find the ancestral rookeries. So she had constructed a nest of her own as best she could, from the bare, cinder-strewn floor of what used to be a rich forest. She had laid her eggs, lowing, setting them carefully in a neat spiral on the ground. Euoplos were not attentive mothers; six-ton tanks were not well equipped to deliver tender loving care. But the euoplo had stayed close to her nest, defending it from the predators.

Perhaps, despite the cold, the eggs might have hatched. Perhaps some of the young could have survived the great chill; of all the dinosaurs, perhaps it was an ankylosaur who might have endured best in the new, harsher world to come.

But the stinging rain had leached away the nutrients the euoplo's body needed to manufacture successful eggs. Some of them had been laid with shells so thick no infant could ever break out, others were so thin they were broken as soon as she produced them. And then the rain began to damage the eggs directly, the grimy downpour etching away their protective surfaces.

None of the eggs had hatched. The euoplo, mournful, baffled on a deep cellular level, had moved away. Immediately after she was gone, a furry cloud of mammalian predators had descended on the eggs, in their squabbling reducing the nest to a muddy battlefield.

The last of her kind, the euoplo wandered the land, driven on by a final imperative: to survive. But the poison and the rain worked on her too. Creatures like Purga sheltered from the worst of the rain in her burrow, or under rocks—or even, once, under the scooped-out shell of a dead turtle. The euoplo was too big: There was nowhere for her to hide, and she could not burrow into the ground. So her back was ferociously scalded, and great bony plates of armor were stripped of flesh, the connecting ligaments etched and burned.

Unthinking, she staggered toward the sea.

Three months after the impact, Purga and Last stumbled across ground frozen as hard as rock.

They saw few animals: Sometimes a cautious frog would watch them go by, or a bird would flee at their approach, chirping with eerie loudness, abandoning some frozen bit of offal on the ground. The relics of the lush Cretaceous vegetation, the stumps of trees and patches of undergrowth, were now frozen as hard as blackened sculptures, and any attempt to gnaw them was rewarded only with a mouthful of ice, and more often than not a chipped tooth.

There were only two of them. Third had gone, lost to hypothermia.

Purga longed for security, to clamber into a tree or dig into the soft earth. But there were no trees—nothing but ash and stumps and bits of roots—and the ground was too hard to burrow into. When they needed to rest they could only grub in the looser debris, making loose nests of ash and burned leaves and bits of wood, where they would lie shivering, huddled to share body warmth.

After days of wandering, Purga and Last made their way slowly along the fringe of America's inland ocean.

Even here the gritty beach was frozen, and the sea itself, as charcoal gray as the sky above it, was littered with ice floes. But the gentle swell still breathed salty water over the sand. And here at the fringe of the ocean the primates found food—seaweed, small crustaceans, even stranded fish.

The oceans, too, had been devastated by the impact. The loss of sunlight and the acid rain had massacred the photosynthetic plankton that had populated the ocean's upper layers. With this key foundation of the ocean's food chain gone, extinctions were following like tumbling dominoes. On wounded Earth, death stalked every realm, and the ice-littered waters of the darkened ocean hid a holocaust as horrific as that which was unfolding on the land. It would take a million years for the seas to recover.

Purga came across a stranded starfish. Still new to ocean foraging, she had never seen such a beast before. She poked it with her snout, trying to determine which of her world categories it most closely fit: a threat, or good to eat.

Her movements were listless. In fact she could barely see the starfish.

Purga was weakening. She was constantly thirsty, with a nagging pain that clung to her mouth and throat and sank deep into her belly. Since the impact she had lost weight steadily, from a scrap of a body that had little excess to start with. And she was a tropical creature suddenly stranded in arctic conditions. Though her layer of fur helped trap heat, her body form was long and lanky, lacking the spherical, enclosing shape of creatures adapted to the cold. So she burned up even more energy and body mass in shivering.

She was bony, enfeebled, continually exhausted, her thinking increasingly fuddled, her instincts dulled.

And she was getting old. Living as vermin, the primates' principal survival tactic had been fast breeding: there had always been simply too many of them to be eliminated by the dinosaurs' ferocious hunting. For such creatures, there was no premium on longevity. Already Purga was coming to the end of her short, explosive life.

Last suffered, too, of course. But, younger, she had more strength to spend. Purga was aware of a growing distance between them. It was not a question of disloyalty. This was the logic of survival. Purga sensed, deep down, that the day would come when her daughter would see her not as a foraging companion, not even as a hindrance, but as a resource. After all she had survived, maybe Purga's final memories would be of her own daughter's teeth at her throat.

But now they smelled meat. And they saw more survivors, more rat-like mammals, scurrying across the beach. There was something to be had. Purga and Last struggled to follow.

At last, her awareness flickering like a failing lightbulb, the great euoplo stumbled to the shore of the ocean.

She looked down, uncomprehending. Water lapped at her feet, dappled by heavy raindrops. The sand was flecked with the black of soot and volcanic dust, and littered with the bones of tiny creatures. She made out the silvery bodies of fish, lifeless, their eyes pecked out by opportunistic birds. But the euoplo knew only her own weariness, hunger, thirst, loneliness, pain.

She raised her head. The sun, setting to the southwest, was a disk, bloodred, not far above a horizon that was charcoal against charcoal.

The euoplo stood motionless at the edge of the water. She was one of the last large dinosaurs left alive anywhere on Earth, and she stood now like a statue to her vanishing kind. Her head and tail felt very heavy, weighed down by all that armor. She let them droop. She was dying without ever having produced a single viable young. An abject misery clamored within the euoplo's small consciousness.

There was a sharp nip at the pad on the base of her foot.

It was a therian mammal. It was no more prepossessing than Purga, and yet equipped with teeth that scissored—just as, one day, a lion's would. It had run forward and *bit* her, with absurd boldness. The euoplo hooted her indignation. With a vast effort, she raised one immense foot. But when she slammed it down into the water she made only a splash; the scurrying mammal escaped.

But, all around her, more survivors gathered.

None of these animals were large. Purga and Last were here, and other mammals, little ratlike creatures that had kept themselves alive in their underground burrows, warmed through this long winter by their constant body heat. There were birds, protected by their hot blood and small size from an event which their more spectacular relatives could not endure. Here, too, were insects, snails, frogs, salamanders, snakes, creatures who had endured in burrows and riverbanks or deep holes. These small, scurrying creatures had been used to feeding off scraps and hiding in the corners anyhow; to them, the comet impact hardly made things worse.

Now they moved closer to this giant, the last of the monsters who had dominated their world for a hundred million years. In the long empty months since the impact, as they spread out through a world like a charnel house, many of them had learned to exploit a new food source: dinosaur flesh.

Times had changed.

Extinction was a terminus more drastic than death.

At least with death there was the consolation that your descendants would go on after you, that something of your kind would linger on. Extinction took away even that comfort. Extinction was the end of your life—and of your children, and all your potential grandchildren, or any of your kind, on to the end of time; life would go on, but it would not be *your* kind of life.

Dread though they were, extinctions had always been commonplace. Nature was packed thick with species, each connected to all the others through competition or cooperation, all endlessly struggling for survival. Though nobody could get permanently ahead, it was possible to fail— through bad luck, or disaster, or invasion by a better-equipped competitor— and the price of failure had always been extinction.

But the comet impact had now triggered a *mass* extinction, one of the worst in this battered planet's long history. Dying was occurring in every biological realm, on land, in the sea, and in the air. Whole families of species, whole kingdoms, were falling into the darkness. It was a huge biotic crisis.

At such a time it didn't matter how well adapted you were, how well you evaded the predators or competed with your neighbors, for the most basic ground rules were changing. During a mass extinction, it paid to be small, numerous, geographically widespread, to have somewhere to hide.

And, crucially, to be able to eat other survivors in the aftermath.

Even then survival depended as much on good fortune as good genes: not evolution, but luck. For all their smallness and ability to hide, more than half the mammals had gone extinct with the dinosaurs.

But the mammals owned the future.

The euoplo was not aware of her legs collapsing. But there was suddenly a damp cold under her belly, a gritty saltiness in her mouth where her head dangled into the water.

She closed her eyes. The heavy armor made the lids opaque. She rumbled deeply—a sound that another of her kind could have heard kilometers away, had there been any to hear—and tried to spit the brine out of her mouth. She retreated into her bony armor, like a turtle inside its shell. Soon it was as if she could no longer hear the hiss of rain on the sand and water, the scuffling of the ugly little creatures who surrounded her.

Even to the last she knew no peace, only a huge reptilian loss. But she felt little pain, when the small teeth went to work.

This last great dinosaur was a storehouse of meat and blood that fed the squabbling horde of animals for a week.

At the end of that time, as the acid rain began to leach the huge gnawed plates of the euoplo's back gleaming white, Purga and Last encountered another group of primates. There were several of them, mostly about Last's age or younger—so they had probably been born after the impact, and had known nothing, all their lives, but this strait-ened world. They looked lean, hungry. Determined. Two of them were male.

They smelled strange. They were not even distantly related to Purga's family. But they were undoubtedly *Purgatorius*. The males had no inter-est in Purga; her subtle scent told them she was too old to bear any more litters.

Last gave her mother a final glance. And then she scampered over to the others, where the males, whiskers quivering, began to sniff her and to nuzzle her with bloodied snouts.

After that day Purga never saw her daughter again.

IV

A month later Purga, wandering alone, came upon the carpet of ferns.

Entranced, Purga hobbled forward as fast as she could. These were only lowly groundcover growths, but their fronds made a dim green shade. On the underside she could see little spore sacs, brown dots.

Green, in a world of soot and ash gray.

Ferns were robust survivors. Their spores were tough enough to with-stand fire, small enough to be carried great distances on the wind. In some cases the new growths sprouted directly from surviving root sys-tems, black, creeping roots that were far more indestructible than the roots of trees. In times like this, as the light slowly recovered and photo-synthesis became possible, the ferns faced little competition. Amid the muddied ash and clay, the world was taking on a look it had not had since the Devonian age some four hundred million years before, when the first land plants of all—primitive ferns among them—had made their tenta-tive colonies.

She climbed. The tallest of these ground huggers gave her a platform just a few centimeters off the ground, but she clambered onto the fronds gratefully. It was enough to release in her a flood of inchoate memories of how she had scurried along the branches of the great, vanished Cretaceous forests.

Later, she dug. The rain still fell, and the ground was boggy, but by digging close to the tough roots of the ferns she was able to construct a satisfactory burrow. She began to relax, for the first time since the impact—perhaps for the first time since the crazed troodon had begun to pursue her.

Life had nothing more to ask of Purga. One of her pups had survived, and would breed, and through her the great river of genes would pass on, on into an unknowable future. And it was an irony that in former times she would surely already have succumbed to predation by now: It was the great emptying of the world that had preserved her life—a few extra months won at the expense of uncounted billions of creatures.

As content as it was possible to be, she settled to sleep in a cocoon of earth that still smelled of the great burning that had ended a world.

The planet was filling up with fast-breeding, short-lived creatures. Already almost all of Earth's population had been born into the new era, and had known nothing but ash, darkness, and carrion. But as Purga slept her hind legs convulsed and her front paws scrabbled at the ground around her. For Purga, one of the last creatures on the planet to remember the dinosaurs, the terrible lizards still stalked, at least in her dreams.

There came a morning when she did not wake, and the little burrow became her coffin.

Soon a blanket of sediment, deposited by the ocean, covered over the vast impact crater. The great geological deformation was eventually hidden under a layer of limestone a thousand meters thick.

Of the Devil's Tail itself, nothing remained but traces. The nucleus had been destroyed in the first seconds of the impact event. Long before Earth's skies cleared, the last remnants of the coma and the glorious tail—the tenuous body of the comet, now cut from its tiny head—blew away in the wind from the sun.

But still the comet had left a kind of memorial. In the boundary clay would be found tektites—bits of Earth that had been blasted into space and returned, melted into glassy dewdrop shapes like tiny space capsules by their re-entry into the air—as well as fragments of quartz and other minerals, shocked into strange glassy configurations by the impact energy. There were shards of crystalline carbon, normally formed only deep in Earth's interior, but baked on the surface in those few ferocious seconds: tiny diamonds, littering an ash of burned Cretaceous forests and dinosaur flesh. There were even traces of amino acids, the complex organic compounds once delivered by long-vanished comets to rocky Earth, the compounds that had enabled life to emerge here: a wistful present from a visitor who had come too late.

And as the dust clouds finally cleared and the chill dispersed, the comet's final gift to the Earth came into play. Vast amounts of carbon dioxide, baked out of the limestone of the shattered seabed, now lingered in the air. A savage greenhouse effect kicked in. The vegetation, striving to recover, struggled to cope. The first millennia were times of swamps, of marshes and rotting bogs, where dead vegetation choked lakes and rivers. All over the world coal was laid down in great seams.

At last, though, as spores and seeds blew around the world, new plant communities blossomed.

Slowly, Earth turned green.

Meanwhile, time worked on Purga's tiny remains.

Within hours of her death, blowflies had laid eggs in her eyes and mouth. Soon flesh flies were dropping larvae on her skin. As maggots burrowed into the little corpse, so the gut bacteria that had served her all her life burrowed out. Intestines burst. The contents began to rot other organs, and the cadaver liquefied, with a powerful stink, like cheese. This attracted carnivorous beetles and flies.

In the days after her death, five hundred types of insects feasted on Purga's corpse. Within a week, there was nothing left but her bones and teeth. Even the great DNA molecules could not survive long. Proteins broke down into their individual building blocks; amino acids in turn decayed into mirror-image forms.

Just a few days after that, a flood of acidic water swept away the little hollow. Purga's bones were dumped in a shallow depression half a kilometer away, jumbled with the bones of raptors, tyrannosaurs, duckbills, and even troodons: enemies made equal in the democracy of death.

With time, more layers of mud were laid down by floods and bankbursting rivers. Under pressure, the layers of silt turned to rock. And, in her rocky tomb, Purga's bones were further transformed, as mineral-rich water was forced into their every pore, filling them with calcite, so they became things of rock themselves.

Buried deep, Purga began a spectacular journey lasting millions of years. As continents collided, the land was uplifted, bearing all its entombed passengers like some vast ocean liner riding a swell. Heat and compressing forces fractured and twisted the rocks. But erosion continued, a relentless, destructive force balancing Earth's creative uplift. Eventually this land became an angular landscape of plateaus, mountains, and desert basins.

At last the erosion cut through the mass grave that had swallowed Purga's bones. As the rock crumbled away bits of fossil bone emerged into the light, corpses bobbing to the surface, waking from a sixty-five-million-year slumber.

Almost all of Purga's bones were lost, flashing to dust in geological instants, all that patient chthonic preservation wasted. But in 2010 a remote descendant of Purga's would pick out a blackened shard in a wall of gray rock, just beneath a strange layer of dark clay, and recognize it for what it was, a tiny tooth.

But that moment lay far in the future.

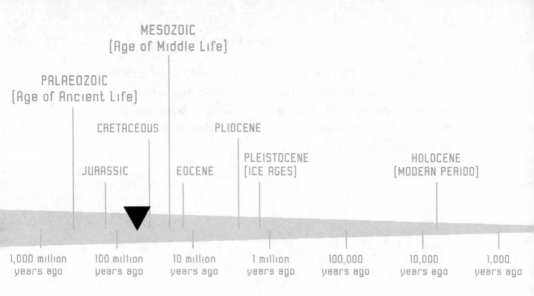

MESOZOIC
(Age of Middle Life)

PALAEOZOIC
(Age of Ancient Life)

CRETACEOUS   PLIOCENE

                                              PLEISTOCENE
JURASSIC   EOCENE   (ICE AGES)   HOLOCENE
                                                      (MODERN PERIOD)

1,000 million   100 million   10 million   1 million   100,000   10,000   1,000
years ago   years ago   years ago   years ago   years ago years ago years ago

CHAPTER 4

the empty forest

▼ Texas, North America. Circa 63 million years before present.

I

Through the endless forest, Plesi climbed.

Squirrel-like, she scampered up a scaly trunk and along a fat branch. Though it was close to noon, the light was dappled, uncertain. The canopy was high above her, the floor lost in green layers far below. The forest was silent save for the rustling of leaves in the warm breeze and the call of the canopy birds, those colorful cousins of the vanished dinosaurs.

It was a world forest. And it belonged to the mammals—including the primates, like Plesi.

She glanced back along her branch. There were her two pups—both daughters—who she thought of as Strong and Weak. About half Plesi's size, they clung to the angle of branch and tree. Even now, Strong was pushing Weak subtly aside. In some species the runtish Weak might have been allowed to die. But Plesi's kind bore few young, and in an uncertain and dangerous world, all of them had to be cared for.

But Plesi could not protect her pups forever. They were both weaned now. Though they had learned to seek out the fruit and insects that inhabited this, their birth tree, they must learn to be more adventurous—to move out into the forest, to seek out their own food.

And to do that, they had to learn to jump.

Hesitantly, scrambling at the scaly surface of the branch, Plesi tensed, and leapt.

Plesi was a plesiadapid: she belonged, in fact, to a species that would one day be called carpolestid. Plesi closely resembled her remote grandmother, Purga. Like Purga, she looked something like a small squirrel, with a low-slung body like a large rat's, and a bushy tail. Though a true primate, Plesi retained Purga's claws rather than nails, her eyes did not face forward, and her brain was little developed. She still even had the big night-vision eyes that had served Purga so well in the time of the dinosaurs.

The most significant development of primate bodies since Purga's time was in the teeth; Plesi's was a species adapted to husk fruit, as would be the possums of Australia, much later. It was a necessary response, if the primates were to find something to eat. Few animals of this time fed off leaves. In an equable world where tropical or paratropical forests spread far from the equator, there was little seasonal variation, and here in Texas the trees did not shed their leaves regularly. In fact, the trees loaded their leaves with toxins and chemicals to make them bitter or poisonous to curious mammalian tongues.

But still, since Purga, there had been little innovation in the primate line—even across two million years. It was the same for many other lineages. Long after the great impact, it was as if the emptied world had been shocked into stasis.

Plesi landed on her target branch without difficulty.

Her two pups were still huddled hesitantly against the tree trunk, and they made the mewling calls of babies. But, though the calls tugged at her, Plesi only raised her head and twitched her snout. She tried to encourage the pups to follow her by nibbling the fruit that clustered on this new tree.

At last the pups reacted. To Plesi's surprise it was the little one, Weak, who came forward first. She scampered to the end of the branch—nervous, hesitant, but showing good balance. She raised her tail and tensed her muscles—she backed off nervously, preened the fur of her face—and then, at last, she jumped.

She overjudged slightly. She came tumbling out of the air and collided with her mother, making Plesi hiss in protest. But her agile hands and feet soon gripped the lumpy bark, and she was safe. Trembling, Weak scampered to her mother and buried her face in her belly, seeking a nipple that was now dry. Plesi let her suckle, rewarding her with comfort.

But now there was a blur of movement from the other tree. Strong, left behind, suddenly lunged forward, her immature feet slipping on the bark. And—without looking carefully, without trying to use her innate skills to estimate the distance—she leapt into the air.

Fear prickled inside Plesi.

Strong made the branch, but she landed too hard. Immediately she slid backwards. For a heartbeat she hung there, her small hands scrabbling uselessly at the bark, her hind legs waving. And then she fell.

Plesi saw her tumble in the air, wriggling, her white underbelly exposed, her hands and feet clutching at nothing. Even now Strong made the peeping cry of a lost infant. Then she fell into the leaves, and in a moment she was gone, taken by the green below, which swallowed all the forest's dead.

Plesi clung to her branch, shuddering. It had happened so quickly. One young lost, one runtish weakling left. It was not to be borne. She hissed her defiance into the menacing green.

And, leaving Weak clinging piteously to the trunk of the tree, Plesi began to descend, down toward the green, down to the ground.

At last she reached the lower story of branches, and looked down into an oasis of light.

This was one of the endless forest's few clearings. Within the last few months, an ancient canopy tree had fallen, eaten from within, wrecked by a random lightning strike. When it had crashed down it had cut a swath through the dense foliage. This clearing would not last long. But for now the plants of the undergrowth, like those hardy survivors, the ground ferns, were taking the opportunity to germinate, and the forest floor here was unusually lush and green. And already saplings were sprouting, beginning a ruthless vegetable race to steal the light and plug that hole in the canopy.

The forest was an oddly static place. The great canopy trees competed with each other to trap as much sunlight as they could. In the gloom of the lower levels, the light was too weak to support growth, and the floor was customarily littered by dead vegetable matter and the bones of any animals or birds unlucky enough to fall. But under the silent ground, seeds and spores abided—waiting centuries, even millennia if necessary, until the day came when chance opened up a gap in the canopy, and the race to live could begin.

Plesi slithered down a buttressing root and reached the ground. Under the broad fronds of a ground fern she scuttled uneasily through a patch of direct sunlight. The solid ground, with no give or sway, felt very strange to her, as peculiar as the shuddering of an earthquake would have felt to a human.

There were other animals here in the clearing, drawn by the prospect of novel pickings. There were frogs, salamanders, and even a few birds, flapping across the air in bright bursts of color, seeking insects and seeds.

And there were mammals.

There were creatures like raccoons but more closely related to the hoofed animals of the future, and scurrying insectivores whose descendants would include the shrews and the hedgehogs. Here was a taeniodont, like a small, fat wombat. It grubbed in the soil, expert at digging out roots and tubers. None of the grubbing creatures in this clearing would have been familiar to a watching human. They were furtive, odd, ungainly, almost reptilian in their behavior, forever looking over their shoulders, like petty thieves expecting the return of the householder.

These mammals were holdovers from the Cretaceous. Then, it had been as if the whole Earth had been a vast city, shaped for the needs of its owners, the dinosaurs. But now the dominant inhabitants were gone, the great buildings erased, and the only creatures left alive were the urban species who had lived in the drains and sewers, subsisting on garbage.

But the recovering Earth had become a very different place from the dreamy Cretaceous. The Earth's new forests were much more dense now. There were no great herbivores: The sauropods had gone, and the elephants lay far in the future. There were no animals big enough to topple these trees, to smash clearings and corridors and make parklike savannah. In response the vegetation had gone crazy, filling the world with greenery of a density and profusion not seen since the first animals had walked onto the land.

But it was an oddly bare stage. In these thick jungles there were no more predatory dinosaurs—but neither were there yet jaguars, leopards, tigers. Practically all of the forest's inhabitants were small, tree-dwelling mammals like Plesi. For an extraordinary span of time—for millions of years—the animals would cling to their Cretaceous habits, and no mammal species would grow to even moderately large sizes. They still contented themselves with the darkness and the corners of the empty world, nibbling on insects, eschewing any evolutionary innovations more spectacular than a new set of teeth.

Like long-term prisoners, the survivors of the impact were institutionalized. The dinosaurs were long gone—but for the mammals, habits ingrained over a much longer span, a full hundred and fifty million years of incarceration, were not so easy to give up.

But things were changing.

At last Plesi heard the quiet mewling of her young.

At the edge of the clearing Strong was huddled, pathetically, in a kind of nest of browned fronds. After she had fallen out of the tree and tumbled into the clearing, at least she had had the sense to seek cover. But she was far from safe: a large, scarlet-bellied predatory frog was watching her, an absent curiosity in its blank eyes. When she saw Plesi, Strong dashed forward and fell on her mother. She tried to find Plesi's nipples, just as her sister had, but Plesi snapped at her, denying her comfort.

Plesi was deeply disturbed. A carpolestid who was strong in the nest but who had no instinct for the trees—who lacked even the sense to keep silent when exposed—had poor survival prospects. Suddenly Strong didn't look so strong after all. Plesi felt an odd impulse to find a mate, to breed again. For now, though, she merely nipped at Strong's flank with her sharp incisor teeth, and led the way back toward the tree from which she had descended.

But she had gone no more than a few body lengths when she froze.

The predator's blank eyes fixed Plesi with lethal calculation.

The predator was an oxyclaenus.

He was a sleek, four-footed, dark-furred animal: long-bodied, stout-legged, he looked like an outsized weasel, though his face and muzzle were more reminiscent of a bear's. But he was related to neither weasel nor bear. In fact he was an ungulate, an early member of that great family that would one day include the hoofed mammals like pigs, elephants, horses, camels, even the whales and dolphins.

This oxy might have seemed clumsy, slow, even unfinished to an eye used to cheetah or wolf. But his kind had learned to stalk prey through the sparse undergrowth of the endless forest. He could even climb, pursuing his quarry into the lower branches of the trees. In this archaic time, this oxy had little competition.

And, as he looked on Plesi's timorous, flattened form, two cold questions dominated the oxy's mind: *How will I trap you?* And, *How good will you be to eat?*

Plesi lay flat against the floor, quivering, her whiskers twitching, her small, sharp teeth bared. But she was equipped with instincts honed over a million centuries at the feet of the dinosaurs. And in the cold calculus of her mind, a reassessment of risk was beginning. In this open place she could not hide. She could not reach a tree to clamber out of the oxy's grasp. Surely if she tried to outrun him he would trap her easily with one of those cruel claws.

Only one option was left.

She arched her back, opened her mouth and hissed, so violently that she spattered the oxy with her spittle.

The oxy flinched at the unexpected aggression of this tiny creature. *But she is no threat.* The oxy, angered, quickly recovered his composure, and prepared to call Plesi's bluff.

But Plesi had vanished into the undergrowth. She had never meant to attack the oxy, only to gain a precious second of time. And she had left Strong behind.

The young carpolestid, transfixed by the carnivore's stare, flattened herself against the ground. The oxy crushed Strong with his paw, snapping the little primate's spine. Strong, flooded with pain, turned on her attacker, seeking to gouge his flesh with her teeth. In her final moments Strong discovered something like courage. But it did her no good.

The oxy played with the crippled animal for a while. Then he began to feed.

As the world recovered, so its changing conditions shaped its living inhabitants.

The mammals were beginning to experiment with new roles. The ancestors of the true carnivores, which would eventually include the dogs and cats, were still small, ferretlike animals, busy, opportunistic general feeders. But the oxyclaenus had begun to develop the specializations of mammalian predators to follow: vertical legs for sustained speed, strong permanent teeth anchored by double roots and with interlocking cusps designed to shred meat.

It was all part of an ancient pattern. All living things worked to stay alive. They took in nourishment, repaired themselves, grew, avoided predators.

No organism lived forever. The only way to counter the dreadful annihilation of death was reproduction. Through reproduction, genetic information about oneself was passed on to one's offspring.

But no offspring was identical to its parents. At any moment each species contained the potential for much variation. But all organisms had to exist within a frame of habitability set by their environment—an environment, of weather, land, and living things, which they shaped in turn. As survival was sought with ruthless ferocity, the frame of the environment was filled up; every viable variation of a species that could find room to survive was expressed.

But room was at a premium. And competition for that room was relentless and unending. Many more offspring were born than could possibly survive. The struggle to exist was relentless. The losers were culled by starvation, predation, disease. Those slightly better adapted to their corner of the environment inevitably had a slightly better chance of winning the battle for survival than others—and therefore of passing on genetic information about themselves to subsequent generations.

But the environment could change, as climates adjusted, or as continents collided and species, mixed by migrations over land bridges, found themselves with novel neighbors. As the environment, of climate and of living things, changed, so the requirements of adaptation changed. But the principle of selection continued to operate.

Thus, generation by generation, the populations of organisms tracked the changes in the world. All the variations of a species that worked in the new frame were selected for, and those that were no longer viable disappeared, sinking into the fossil record, or into oblivion altogether. Such turnovers were unending, a perpetual churn. As long as the "required" variation lay within the available genetic spectrum, the changes in the population could be rapid—as rapid as human breeders of domesticated animals and plants would find as they strove for their own ideas of perfection in the creatures in their power. But when the available variation ran out, the changes would stall, until a new mutation came along, a chance event caused, perhaps, by radiation effects, that opened up new possibilities for variation.

This was evolution. That was all there was to it: It was a simple principle, based on simple, obvious laws. But it would shape every species that ever inhabited the Earth, from the birth of life to the last extinction of all, which would take place under a glowering sun, far in the future.

And it was working now.

It was hard.

It was life.

Plesi had made an unspoken bargain with the oxy: *Take my child. Spare me.* Even as she clambered back through layers of green and into the safety of the trees, seeking her surviving daughter, that dreadful stratagem still echoed in her mind.

That, and a feeling that came from deep within her cells, a thought she might have expressed as: *I always knew it was too good to be true. The teeth and claws weren't gone. They were just hiding. I always knew they'd come back.*

Her instinct was right. Two million years after the uneasy truce imposed by the dinosaurs' death, the mammals had started to prey on each other.

That night Weak, bewildered, terrified herself, watched her mother twitch and growl in her sleep.

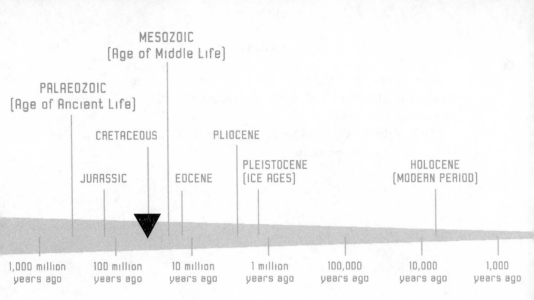

| PALAEOZOIC [Age of Ancient Life] | MESOZOIC [Age of Middle Life] | | PLIOCENE | | | |

MESOZOIC
[Age of Middle Life]

PALAEOZOIC
[Age of Ancient Life]

CRETACEOUS

PLIOCENE

PLEISTOCENE
[ICE AGES]

HOLOCENE
[MODERN PERIOD]

JURASSIC   EOCENE

| 1,000 million years ago | 100 million years ago | 10 million years ago | 1 million years ago | 100,000 years ago | 10,000 years ago | 1,000 years ago |

CHAPTER 5

the time of long shadows

▼ **Ellesmere Island, North America. Circa 51 million years before present.**

I

There was no true morning during these long days of Arctic summer, no authentic night. But as the clouds cleared from the face of the climbing sun, and light and warmth slanted through the trees' huge leaves, a mist rose from the swampy forest floor, and Noth's sensitive nostrils filled with the pleasing scent of ripe fruit, rotting vegetation, and the damp fur of his family.

It *felt* like a morning, like a beginning. A pleasing energy spread through Noth's young body.

His powerful hind legs folded under him, his fat tail upright, he squirmed along the branch to get closer to his family—his father, his mother, his new twin sisters. Together, the family groomed pleasurably. The nimble fingers of their small black hands combed through fur to pick out bits of bark and fragments of dried baby shit, even a few parasitic insects that made a tasty, blood-filled treat. There was some loose fur, but the adult adapids had already lost most of last year's winter coat.

Perhaps it was the gathering light that inspired the singing.

It began far away, a thin warbling of intertwined male and female voices, probably just a single mating pair. Soon more voices joined in the duo's song, a chorus of whooping cries that added counterpoint and harmony to the basic theme.

Noth moved to the end of the branch to hear better. He peered through banks of giant leaves that angled south toward the sun, like so many miniature parasols. You could see a long way. The circumpolar forest was open, and the trees, cypress and beech, were well spaced so their leaves could catch the low Arctic sunlight. There were plenty of broad clearings where clumsy ground-dwelling herbivores rummaged. Noth's eyes in their mask of black fur were huge—like his remote ancestor Purga's, well adapted to the dark, but prone to dazzling in the daylight.

The song's meaning was simple: *This is who we are! If you are not kin, stay away, for we are many and strong! If you are kin, come home, come home!* But the song's richness went beyond its utilitarian value. Much of it was random, bubbling, like scat singing. But at its best it was a spontaneous vocal symphony, running on for long minutes, with passages of extraordinary harmonic purity that entranced Noth.

He lifted his muzzle to the sky and called.

Noth was a kind of primate that would be called *notharctus,* of a class called adapid, descended from the plesiadapids of the early millennia after the comet. He looked much like a small lemur. He had a high conical chest, long and powerful legs, and comparatively short arms with black, grasping hands. His face was small with a pronounced muzzle, an inquisitive nose, and pricked-up ears. And he was equipped with a long, powerful tail, laden with fat, his winter hibernation store. He was a little more than one year old.

Noth's brain was considerably larger than Plesi's or Purga's, and his engagement with the world was correspondingly richer. There was more in Noth's life than the urgencies of sex and food and pain; there was room for something like joy. And it was a joy he expressed in his song. His mother and father quickly joined in. Even Noth's infant sisters contributed as best they could, adding their tiny mewling voices to the adults' cries.

It was noon, and the sun was the highest it would travel today, but it was still low in the sky. Shafts of low green-filtered light slanted through the trees, illuminating the dense, warm mist that rose from the steaming mulch on the floor, and the tree trunks sent shadows striping over the forest floor.

This was Ellesmere, the northernmost part of North America. The summer sun never set, but merely completed circles in the sky, suspended above the horizon, as the broad leaves of the conifer trees drank in the light. This was a place where the shadows were always long, even in high summer. The forest, circling the Earth's pole, had the air of a vast sylvan cathedral, as if the leaves were fragments of stained glass.

And everywhere the adapids' voices echoed.

Emboldened, the adapids began to clamber down the branches toward the ground.

Noth was primarily a fruit eater. But he came upon a fat jewel beetle. Its beautiful carapace, metallic blue green, crunched when he bit into it. As he moved he followed the scent marks of his own kind: *I came this way. This way is safe. . . . I saw danger here. Teeth! Teeth! . . . I am of this troop. Kin, come this way. Others, stay away. . . . I am female. Follow this to find me. . . .* That last message gave Noth an uncomfortable tightness in his groin. He had scent glands on his wrists and in his armpits. Now he wiped his wrists through his armpits and then drew his forearms across the trunk, using bony spurs on his wrists to embed the scent, and to cut a distinctive curving scar in the bark. The female patch was old; the brief mating season was long over. But instinct prompted him to cover the patch with his own multimedia signature so that no other male would be alerted by it.

Even now, even fourteen million years after the comet, Noth's body still bore marks of his kind's long nocturnal ancestry, like the glands for scent marking. His toes were tipped, but not with nails, like a monkey's, but with grooming claws, like a lemur's. His watchful eyes were huge, and like Purga he had whiskers to help him feel his way forward. He retained a powerful sense of hearing and smell; he had mobile radar-dish ears. But Noth's eyes, while wide and capable of good night vision, did not share the dark-loving creatures' ultimate adaptation, a tapetum, a yellow reflective layer in the eye. His nose, while sensitive, was dry. His upper lip was furry and mobile, making his face more expressive than those of earlier adapid species. His teeth were monkeylike, lacking the tooth comb—a special tooth used for grooming—of his ancestors.

Like every species in the long evolutionary line that led from Purga to the unimaginable future, Noth's was a species in transition, ladened with the relics of the past, glowing with the promise of the future.

But his body and mind were healthy and vigorous, perfectly adapted to his world. And today he was as happy as it was possible for him to be.

In the canopy above, Noth's mother was taking care of her infants.

She thought of her two remaining daughters as something like Left and Right, for one preferred the milk of the row of nipples on her left side, and the other—smaller, more easily bullied—had to make do with the right. The notharctus usually produced large litters—and mothers had multiple sets of nipples to support such broods. Noth's mother had in fact borne quadruplets. But one of the infants had been taken by a bird; another, runtish, had quickly caught an infection and died. Their mother had soon forgotten them.

Now she picked up Right and pushed her against the trunk of the tree, where the infant clung. Parked like this, her brownish fur blending into the background of the tree bark, Right would remain here until her mother returned to feed her. She was able to stay immobile for long hours.

It was a form of protection. The notharctus were deep enough in the forest to be safe from any diving bird of prey, but the pup was vulnerable to the local ground-based predators, especially the miacoids. Ugly animals the size of ferrets, sometime burrow-raiders who scavenged opportunistically from the kills of other predators, the miacoids were an unprepossessing bunch, but nonetheless were the ancestors of the mighty cats and wolves and bears of later times. And they could climb trees.

Now the attentive mother moved along the branch, seeking a comparable place of safety to leave Left. But the stronger child was happy where she was, clinging to her mother's belly fur. After gentle pushing, her mother gave up. Laden with her daughter's warm weight, she worked her way down a ladder of branches toward the ground.

On all fours, Noth walked across a thick mulch of leaves.

The trees here were deciduous, every autumn dropping their broad, veined leaves to cover the ground with a thick layer of decaying vegetation. Much of the mat on which Noth walked was made up of last autumn's leaves, frozen by the winter's hard cold before they could rot; now the leaves were mulching quickly, and small flies buzzed irritatingly through the misty air. But there were also butterflies, their gaudy wings making splashes of flitting color against the drab ground cover.

Noth moved slowly, seeking food, wary of danger. He wasn't alone here.

Two fat taeniodonts grubbed their way across the ground, their faces buried in the rotting leaves. They looked like heavy-jawed wombats, and they used their powerful forelimbs to dig into the dirt, seeking roots and tubers. They were followed by an infant, a clumsy bundle pushing at her parents' legs, struggling through the thick layer of leaves. A paleanodont scuffed for ants and beetles with its long anteater's snout. And here was a solitary barylambda, a clumsy creature like a ground sloth with powerfully muscled legs and a stubby pointed tail. This creature, scuffling gloomily in the dirt, was the size of a Great Dane—but some of its cousins, in more open country, grew to the size of bison, among the largest animals of their day.

In one corner of the clearing Noth made out the slow movement of a primate, in fact another kind of adapid. But it was quite unlike Noth himself. Like the loris of later times, this slow, ground-loving creature looked more like a lazy bear cub than any primate. It moved slowly across the mush of leaves, making barely a sound, its nose snuffling the ground. This adapid generally stuck to the deeper forest where its slowness was not as disadvantageous as it would be on more open ground. Here, its slow and silent movements made it almost invisible to predators—and to the insect prey it sniffed out acutely.

Noth wrinkled his nose. This adapid used urine as its scent marker; every time it toured its range it would carefully urinate on its hands and feet to leave its signature. As a result, to Noth's sensitive nose it stank badly.

Noth found a fallen beehive. He inspected it curiously, hesitantly. Hive bees were relatively new arrivals, part of an explosion of new forms of butterflies and beetles and other insects. The hive was abandoned, but there were whole handfuls of delicious honey to be had inside it.

But, before he attacked the honey, Noth listened carefully, sniffing the air. His sensitive nose told him that the others, high in the trees above, were still far away. He ought to be able to devour this food before they reached him. But he *shouldn't*. There was a calculation to be made.

Noth was low-ranking among the males in his group. What Noth was expected to do was to call out, letting the rest know he had found food. Then the other males and the females would come, take as much honey as they wanted, and—if Noth was lucky—leave him a little for himself. If he stayed silent and was caught with the honey, he would be severely beaten, and any food left would be taken away, leaving him nothing at all. But on the other hand if he got away with it he might get to eat *all* the honey, and be spared any punishment . . .

The choice was made. Soon he was working the honey with his small hands, licking it down as fast as he could, eyes flicking around to check on the others. He had finished the honey and wiped away any traces on his muzzle by the time his mother reached the ground.

She still had her pup, Left, clinging to her belly. She began to scrabble at the floor, her fat-ladened tail held out behind her, silhouetted against the bright shafts of light that pierced the forest's higher layers. She quickly uncovered more chunks of the fallen hive. Noth made a play of grabbing at the honey, but his mother pushed him away with a sharp shove and fell on it herself.

Noth's father now tried to join in the bounty, but his mate turned her back on him. Here came two of Noth's aunts, his mother's sisters. They immediately rushed to their sister's side and, with screeches, bared teeth, and handfuls of thrown leaves, drove Noth's father away. One of them even grabbed a chunk of honeycomb from his hand. Noth's father fought back, but, like most adult males, he was outsized by any one of the females, and his struggles were futile.

It was always the way. The females were the center of notharctus society. Powerful clans of sisters, mothers, aunts, and nieces, together for life, excluded the males. All this was a behavioral fossil: The dominance of females over males, and the tendency of male-female pairings to endure after mating, were more common in nocturnal species than those able to live in the light. This powerful matriarchy was making sure that the sisters had first call on the best of the food, before any male.

Noth took his own exclusion calmly. After all, the taste of illicit honey still lingered in his mouth. He loped away in search of more food.

Purga and Plesi had lived isolated lives, usually as females with pups, or as half of a mating pair. Solitary foraging was a better strategy for nocturnal creatures; not being part of a noisy group made it easier to hide from night hunters, who would wait in silent ambush for their prey.

But animals active by day did better to keep to groups, with more eyes and ears on the alert to spot attackers. The notharctus had even evolved alarm calls and scents to warn each other of different classes of predators—birds of prey, ground predators, snakes—each of which required a different defensive response. And if you were part of a group there was always the chance that the predator would take the next guy, not you. It was a cold-blooded lottery that paid off often enough to be worthwhile adapting for.

But there were disadvantages to group living: mainly, if there were large numbers of you, there was increased competition for food. As that competition resolved itself, the inevitable result was social complexity—and the size of the adapids' brains had increased so that they were capable of handling that complexity. Then, of course, they were forced to become even more efficient at searching for food to fuel those big brains.

It was the way of the future. As primate societies became ever more complex, a kind of cognitive arms race would continue, increasing smartness fueled by increasing social complications.

But Noth wasn't *that* smart. When he had found the honey, Noth had applied a simple behavioral rule: *Call out if the big ones are close by. Don't call if they aren't.* The rule gave Noth a good chance of getting away with maximum food and minimal beating. It didn't always work, but often enough to be worth trying.

It looked as if he had lied about the honey. But Noth was incapable of telling genuine lies—planting a false belief in the minds of others—for he had no real understanding that others had beliefs at all, let alone that their beliefs could be different from his, or that his actions could shape those beliefs. The peekaboo game played with human infants—if you want to hide, just cover your eyes; if you can't see them, they can't see you—would have fooled him every time.

Noth was one of the most intelligent creatures on the planet. But his intelligence was specialized. He was a great deal smarter concerning problems about the others of his kind—where they were, their potential for threat or support, the hierarchies they formed—than about anything else in his environment. He couldn't, for example, associate snake tracks with the possibility that he might stumble on a snake. And though his behavior looked complex and subtle, he obeyed rules as rigidly as if they had been programmed into a tribe of robots.

And still the notharctus spent much of their lives as solitary foragers, just as Purga had. It was visible in the way they moved: They were aware of each other, avoided each other, huddled for protection, but they did not move *together*. They were like natural loners forced to cooperate, uncomfortably imprisoned by necessity with others.

As Noth worked the forest floor, a troop of dark little creatures scurried by nervously. They had ratlike incisors, and a humble verminous look compared to Noth and his family, their black-and-white fur patchy and filthy. These little primates were plesiadapids: all but identical to Purga, even though she had died more than fourteen million years before. They were a relic of the past.

One plesi came too close, snuffling in its comparative blindness; Noth deigned to spit a seed at it; the seed hit the scuttling creature in the eye, and it flinched.

A lithe body, low-slung, slim, darted from the shade of the trees. Looking like a hyena, this was a mesonychid.

Noth and his family cleared off the ground quickly.

The plesi froze. But it was hopelessly exposed on this open forest floor.

The mesonychid hurled itself forward. The plesi squirmed and rolled, hissing. But the meso's teeth had already taken a chunk out of its hind leg. Now more of the meso's pack, scenting blood, came jostling toward the site of the attack.

The mesonychid was a kind of condylarth, a diverse group of animals related to the ancestors of hoofed animals. The meso was not an expert killer or a meat specialist but, like a bear or wolverine, it was an opportunistic feeder. All the condylarths were doomed to extinction ten million years before the age of mankind. But for now they were in their pomp, top predators of the world forest.

The other inhabitants of the forest floor reacted in their different ways. The lorislike adapid had a shield of thickened skin over bony bumps on its back, beneath which it now tucked its head. The big, dull barylambda concluded it was under no threat even from a pack of these small hunters; like the hyenas of later ages, the mesos were primarily scavengers and rarely attacked an animal much bigger than themselves. The taeniodont, however, decided that caution was called for; pompously it trotted away, its gaping mouth showing its high teeth.

Meanwhile the plesi fought on, inflicting scratches and bites on its assailants. One of the mesos was left whining, the tendons of its right hind leg badly ripped, blood leaking from torn flesh. But at last the plesi succumbed to their teeth and weight. The mesos formed a loose circle around their victim, their slim bodies and waving tails clustered around their meal like maggots around a wound. The rising stink of blood, and the fouler stench of panic shit and stomach contents, overwhelmed Noth's sensitive nose.

Though some of the ancient plesiadapids had specialized, learning how to husk fruit like opossums or to live off the gum of trees, they remained primarily insect eaters. But now they faced competition from other insectivores, the ancestors of hedgehogs and shrews—and from their own descendant forms like the notharctus. Already the early-form plesis had become extinct across much of North America, surviving only in fringe areas like this marginally habitable polar forest, where the endless days did not suit bodies and habits shaped during the nights of the Cretaceous. Soon the last of them would be gone.

Noth, high in the cathedral calm of the trees, could see the family as they climbed up toward him, their lithe limbs working smoothly. But something disturbed him: a shift in the light, a sudden coldness. As clouds crowded past the sun, the great forest-spanning buttresses of light were dissolving. Noth felt cold, and his fur bristled. Rain began to fall: heavy misshapen drops that clattered against the trees' broad leaves and pounded like artillery shells into the mud below.

It was because of the onset of the rain, and the overwhelming stink of the bloody deaths below, that Noth did not detect the approach of Solo.

Hidden in a patch of shadow, his scent blowing downwind, Solo saw the notharctus troop scurrying to safety.

And he saw Noth's mother with her infant.

She was a fertile, healthy female: that was what the presence of the infant told him about her. But there was a mate with her, and since she already had a pup, she was unlikely to come into heat again this season. Neither of those factors were an obstacle to Solo. He waited until Noth's family had settled on a branch, calming down, out of immediate danger.

Solo, at three years old, was a mature, powerful male notharctus. And he was something of a freak.

Most males roamed the forests in small bands, seeking out the larger, more sedentary troops of females where they might find a chance to mate. Not Solo. Solo preferred to travel alone. He was larger and more powerful than almost all the females he had encountered in his travels in this polar forest. Again, in this Solo was unusual; the average adult male was smaller than the average female.

And he had learned to use his strength to get what he wanted.

With a lithe swing Solo dropped down to the branch and stood upright before Noth's mother. He looked unbalanced, for his hind legs were comparatively massive, his forearms short and slender, and he held his long tail up in the air so that it hooked over his head. But he was tall, and very still, and very intimidating.

Noth's mother could smell this huge stranger: *not kin.* She immediately panicked. She hissed and pushed Left behind her.

Noth's father came forward. He raised himself up on his hind legs and faced the intruder. Moving with fast jerky gestures he rubbed his genital glands against the foliage around him, and swept his tail over his forearms so that the horny spurs above his wrist glands combed through his tail fur and impregnated it with his scent. Then he waved the lushly stinking tail above his head at the intruder. In the scent-dominated world of the notharctus, it was an awesome display. *Get away. This is my place. This is my troop, my young. Get away.*

There was nothing sentimental in the father's behavior. Producing healthy offspring that survived to breeding age was the only purpose of this father's life; he was preparing to take on the intruder solely through a selfish drive to see his own heritage preserved.

Usually this game of malodorous bluff would have continued until one or the other of the males backed down, without physical contact. But again Solo was unusual. He did not respond with any form of display, save for a cold stare at the other's feverish posturing.

Noth's father was unnerved by the newcomer's eerie stillness. He faltered, his scent glands drying, his tail drooping.

Then Solo struck.

With teeth bared he lunged at Noth's father, slamming into his chest. Noth's father fell back, squealing. Solo dropped to all fours and fell on him, biting into his chest through a layer of fur. Noth's father screamed and scurried out of sight. He was only slightly injured, but his spirit was broken.

Now Solo turned on the females. The aunts could easily have resisted Solo, if they had combined their efforts. But they scrambled out of Solo's way. Solo's assault had disturbed them as much as its victim. They had never seen anything like it. All of them were mothers; all thought immediately of the infants they had left parked in the high branches.

Solo ignored them too. With a carnivore's steely movements he advanced on Noth's mother, his principal target.

She hissed, she showed her teeth, she even kicked at him with her powerful hind legs. But he resisted her blows easily, walked through her kicking—and took the unresisting, baffled infant from her grasp. He bit quickly into the pup's throat, opening up the flesh, and rummaged there until he had ripped open the infant's trachea. It was over in heartbeats. He dropped the quivering scrap into the forest below, where mesonychids, alerted by the scent of fresh blood, ran forward with their eerie uncanine-like barking. His mouth and hands bloodied, Solo turned to Noth's mother. Of course she would not be fertile yet, perhaps not for some weeks, but he could mark her with his scent, make her his own, and repel the attentions of other males.

There was nothing truly cruel in Solo. If her pups were killed, it was possible Noth's mother would come into heat again before the end of the summer—and if Solo covered her then, he could generate more offspring through her. So, for Solo, infanticide was a good tactic.

Solo's brutal strategy wouldn't have been sustainable for everybody. Notharctus males were not equipped to fight. They lacked the canine teeth that later primate species would use to inflict damage on rivals. And this polar forest was a marginal environment where true fights were literally a waste of energy, a squandering of scarce resources, which was why the ritual stink fights had evolved. But for Solo, the exception, it was a strategy that worked, over and over, and which had won him many mates—and which had generated many offspring, scattered through the forest, whose veins ran with Solo's blood.

But it wasn't going to work this time.

Noth's mother, marked by the killer's scent, gazed down into the green void below. She had lost her baby—just as Purga, her remote grandmother, had once endured. But, considerably more intelligent than Purga had been, she was much more acutely aware of her pain.

Blackness filled her. She lunged at Solo, her small limbs flailing, mouth gaping. Startled, he darted back.

She lunged past him. And she fell.

Noth saw his mother fall into the pit where his infant sister had fallen before. Immediately her twisting form was lost under the slick, writhing bodies of the mesos.

Noth had been weaned a few weeks after he had been born. Soon would have come a time when he would have wandered from the troop. His link to his mother was tenuous. And yet he felt a loss as powerful as if his mother's breast had been ripped from his mouth.

And still the rain fell, harder all the time.

Noth, shivering, crawled through the branches. With the wind low, the rain fell in massive drops that pounded exposed flesh and hammered against the trees' broad leaves.

Following lingering traces of his mother's scent, he found his baby sister. She still clung motionless to the tree trunk where her mother had parked her—where she would have clung, probably, until she starved. Noth sniffed her damp fur. He huddled up close and wrapped his arms around her. She was a tiny shivering mass against his belly fur, but he was sheltering her from the rain.

He was drawn to stay with her. She smelled of family; she shared much of his genetic inheritance, and therefore he had a stake in any offspring she might one day have.

But the rain fell through a night and a day, as the sun continued its purposeless dance around the sky. The forest floor became sodden, and glimmering pools, laden with floating leaf debris, began to cover the ground, hiding gnawed and scattered bones.

And the continuing rain washed away the last traces of the scent markers of Noth's troop from the trees. Noth and his sister were lost.

II

As the endless day wore on, as the sun wheeled through its meaningless cycles, Noth and Right stumbled through the forest's branches.

They had already been lost for a week. They had found none of their own kind. But here in the forest canopy there were many adapids, cousins of the notharctus. Many of them were smaller than Noth. He would glimpse their glowing eyes, like eerie yellow pits, peering out of a shadowed nook. These miniature insect hunters looked more like mice. Some of them scuttled along branches, racing from shaded cover to cover. But one made a spectacular upright leap from tree to tree, its powerful hind legs dangling, its paws reaching. Its membranous ears swiveling like a bat's, it caught an insect, plucking it out of the air in its jaws in mid-jump.

One solitary little creature clung to the rotten bark of an ancient tree. It had a scruffy black coat, batlike ears, and prominent front teeth, and it tapped patiently at the wood with a claw-tipped finger, its large ears swiveling. When it heard a larva burrowing under the bark, it ripped off the bark with its teeth and plunged in a peculiarly long middle finger to hook the larva and deliver it to its gaping, greedy mouth. This was a primate that had learned to live like a bird, like a woodpecker.

Once Noth blundered into a giant, slothlike creature hanging upside down from a thick branch, its primate's hands locked around the wood. This monster's head swiveled to inspect Noth and Right, its eyes blank. Its mouth chewed slowly, crammed full of the fat deciduous leaves that were its principal diet. Its kind had been driven to larger sizes by the need to accommodate a gut big enough to break down the cellulose in the leaves' cell walls. The sloth-thing's face was oddly immobile, static, limited in its expressiveness. The social life of this gloomy hanging creature was unexciting; its slow metabolism, and lack of spare energy to devote to social activities, saw to that.

The world had warmed steadily since the terrible impact. Waves of vegetation had migrated away from the equator, until tropical rain forest eventually covered all of Africa and South America, North America to what would become the Canadian border, China, Europe as far north as France, and much of Australia. Even at the poles there were jungles.

North America was still joined by mighty land bridges to Europe and Asia, while the southern continents lay in a great band below the equator, like scattered islands. India and Africa were both migrating north, but for now the Tethys Sea still girdled the equator, a mighty current that spread warmth around the belly of the planet. The Tethys was like a river through Eden.

In response to the great warming, the children of Plesi and other mammals had at last thrown off their past. It was as if the Earth's inheritors had finally realized that the empty planet offered them a lot more than just another kind of grub to chew. While the reptilian survivors, the lizards, crocodiles, and turtles, clung on largely unchanged, soon the foundations of the successful mammalian lineages of the future would be laid down.

Plesi, like Purga, had been a low-slung crawler, with the typical mammalian four-footed head-down body stance. But her primate descendants grew larger, with more powerful hind limbs to support upright bodies and heads. Meanwhile the primates' eyes had moved forward to the front of their faces. This would give them three-dimensional vision, enabling them to judge their increasingly long leaps, and to triangulate on the prey insects and small reptiles that still formed part of their diet. And as they explored different ways to make a living, the primates would fan out into many different forms.

There was no design in this: no sense of improvement, of purpose. All that was happening was that each organism was struggling to preserve itself, its offspring, and its kin. But as the environment slowly changed, so through relentless selection did the species that inhabited it. It was not a process fueled by life, but by death: the elimination of the less well adapted, the endless culling of inappropriate possibilities. But the potential of an unseen future was no consolation to those who lived through the relentless culling.

Many of the adapids had become too specialized. This comfortable planet-swaddling warmth would not last forever. In cooler times in the future, as the forests became sparse and seasonal differences became more pronounced, it wouldn't seem so smart to be a fussy eater. Extinctions would follow, as they always had.

Meanwhile, amid this clutter of exotic primates, the siblings found no notharctus.

Exploring the forest floor, Noth found a plant with podded fruit, a kind of pea. He broke open a few pods and let his sister feed.

A kind of anteater, a meter long, approached a pillarlike ants' nest. It fell on the nest, wielding its powerful arm and shoulder muscles. As though it wielded a pickaxe, all its force was concentrated on a single point, the tip of its strongly flexed middle finger. The ants swarmed—they were huge, each some ten centimeters long—and the anteater quickly ingested them with its long, sticky tongue before the soldiers could unite in defense. The anteater was a descendant of South American stock, which had wandered here over temporary land bridges many generations before.

Noth and Right watched, wide-eyed. But as he kept an eye on the anteater, concern gnawed at Noth's unconscious.

He had tried to keep them both feeding, to fatten up their tails with the winter storage that would see them through the long months of hibernation to come. That was just as his innate programming instructed. But they weren't eating enough. Isolated from the support of the troop, he was having to spend much too much of his time watching for predators.

He could have gone back. Like all his species—the mobile males more than the sedentary females—he kept track of his position by dead reckoning, integrating time, space, and the angle of the slanting sunlight. It was an ability that helped him find scattered sources of food and water. If he needed to Noth could find his way back "home," to the stand of trees that had been the center of his troop's range. But he never heard the distinctive warbling song of his troop; his rudimentary decision-making machinery pressed him to keep searching for a troop that would accept him and his sister.

Meanwhile, though the sun still circled endlessly above the horizon, much of the daylight was tinged with the red of sunset, and here on the forest floor brown spores clung to the fern fronds. Autumn was coming. And then there would be winter. They were underfed, and time was running out.

Right became distressed, as she so often did. She dropped the pea pods and folded over on herself, rocking, keening softly, her hands over her small face. Noth took her in his arms and carried her to the crook of a branch, where he began to groom her. He worked carefully through the sparse fur on her back, neck, head, and belly, removing dirt, bits of leaf, and dried feces, untangling knots, picking out parasites that were attempting to feast on her young skin.

Right quickly calmed. The grooming's mixture of pleasure, attention, and mild pain flooded her system with endorphins, her body's natural opiates. Before she grew much older she would be addicted, literally, to this pleasurable scratching—as her brother already was. Noth badly missed the strong, nipping caress of adult fingers on his back.

But Noth was worried about her, on deep levels he could not understand.

Right's bewildering grief served a purpose. It was a signal to her that she had suffered a loss, that there was a hole in her world that she must fix. And though Noth was not capable of true empathy—if you didn't really understand that other people had minds and thoughts and feelings like yours, you couldn't possibly be empathetic—still the signs of grief in his sister triggered a kind of protectiveness in him. He wanted to put the world right for his sister: The instinct to help the orphaned went very deep.

But in the end obsessive grief was maladaptive. If Right was unable to recover, in the end there would be nothing he could do for her. He would have to abandon her, and then she would surely die.

As day followed day, the sun, at the lowest point of its arc in the sky, began to slip beneath the southern horizon. At first the brief nights were like twilight, and on clear nights purple-red curtains of light climbed into the tall sky. But quickly the sun's excursions into invisibility became longer, and there were increasing intervals when stars shone in a deepening blue. Soon true darkness would return to the polar forest.

The weather quickly became colder and drier. Rainfall was scarce now, and on some days the warmth of the sun barely seemed to penetrate the lingering mist. Already many of the birds of the forest canopy had departed, skein after skein of them flitting over the sky to the warmer lands to the south, watched by uncomprehending primate eyes.

Noth became exhausted, ragged, and his dreams were full of flashing teeth and biting claws, visions of his scrap of a sister taken by gigantic mouths.

Now their biggest problem was thirst. It had been so long since the last rain that the treetops were becoming parched. And already the trees were starting to shed; the last leaves were withered and brown. Soon Noth was reduced to licking the bark each morning for the cold dew.

At length, driven by their thirst, the siblings went in search of ground water. Near the closest large lake they scurried down a tree trunk, eyes wide.

Approaching the water, the primates crept past a pair of what looked like miniature deer. The size of small dogs with long, trailing tails, these fast, solitary runners, browsing on leaves and fallen fruit, were ancestors of the mighty artiodactyl family, which would one day include pigs, sheep, cattle, reindeer, antelope, giraffes, and camels. Right disturbed a frog, which hopped away, croaking in protest. She cowered back, eyes wide at its strangeness. Soon they saw more amphibians, frogs and toads and salamanders. Birds crowded the bushes, raising shrill cries that filled the dank air.

Noth was uneasy. The shore was too crowded: Noth and Right were not the only thirsty creatures in this shivering jungle.

A meter-long creature like a long-tailed kangaroo ran past; this was a leptictidium, a hunter of small animals and insects. Exploring the ground with its mobile nose, it disturbed a pholidocercus, a spiky-haired ancestor of the hedgehogs, that indignantly hopped away like a rabbit. Here was a close-packed herd of horses. They were tiny: no larger than terriers, with perfectly formed equine heads. Shyly these exquisite little creatures picked their way through the undergrowth. They walked on pads, like cats, and on each foot they had several hoofed toes. Their genus had emerged in Africa only a few million years earlier. A rough growl from an impatient carnivore startled the little horses, making them stir into sudden flight.

Through this exotic crowd the two primates proceeded cautiously, moving in scurries, in fits and starts.

The water itself was a languid sheet, dense with matted vegetation, dead reeds, and algal blooms. In places ice had already formed in thin gray slices. But on the open water birds waded, ancestors of flamingos and avocets, and huge water lilies rested languidly on the surface.

Over the open water a spider was suspended on a thread of silk, and huge ants flew, each as large as a human hand, on their way to found new nests. Through this crowd of insects flapped a family of delicate bats. Recently evolved, as huge and fragile as paper kites, the new flying mammals snapped at the insects. Primitive bony fish broke the surface and gulped at the aerial fodder, as did a twisting eel.

The primates found a place far enough from any of the predators to be able to drink unhindered. They bent and plunged their muzzles into the chill water, sucking it up gratefully.

The largest animals of all wallowed at the muddy fringes of the lake.

A pair of uintatheres stood side by side. These great animals looked like gargantuan rhinos, each with a set of six bony horns on its head and long upper canine teeth like a saber-toothed cat's. Their thick hides were coated with mud, which helped keep them cool and kept off insects. They cropped placidly on the soft vegetation of the lake bottom, sucking at water stained green by algae, while a fat youngster, more agile and lively, played around his parents' legs, barging their tree-trunk knees with a head ladened with stubby, unformed tusks. Noth watched their huge feet fearfully. Closer to the shore there walked a family of moeritherium. No more than a meter tall, the adults moved through the water with a stately calm, rumbling reassurance to each other, while their round-bodied infants splashed at their feet. They worked the lake bottom vegetation efficiently with their long noses. These were among the first proboscideans, the ancestors of elephants and mammoths. They were still more piglike than elephantine, but they were already clever and social animals.

Around the herbivorous herds circled carnivores. These were mostly creodonts; they looked like foxes and wolverines. And there was one pack of hoofed predators—like carnivorous horses—bizarre, terrifying creatures with no analogies in human times.

Many of these creatures looked slow and lumbering, oddly ill-formed, the results of nature's first experiments in producing large herbivores and predators from the mammalian stock that had survived the dinosaur extinction. Open grasslands still lay millions of years in the future, along with the fleet, long-legged, graceful herbivorous forms that would adapt to their open lush spaces, and the cleverer, faster carnivores that would arise to prey on them. When that happened most of the species around Noth would succumb to extinction. But the orders that would be familiar to humans—the true primates, the hoofed animals, the rodents and bats, the deer and the horses—had already made their entrance on the stage.

And there was no more complex and crowded an ecology anywhere on Earth right now than here on Ellesmere Island. This place was a pivot on the great migratory routes up through the Americas and over the roof of the world to Europe, Asia, and Africa. Here, pangolins from Asia, carnivores from North America, hoofed creatures from Africa, European insectivores like ancestral hedgehogs, and even anteaters from South America mingled and competed.

Suddenly Noth pulled back his head.

From inside the water two primates were looking out at him, a burly male and a small female. He could not smell the male, could not tell if he was kin or stranger. He screeched, baring his teeth. The male primate bared his teeth in response.

Enraged, Noth got to his feet and displayed his musk glands to the stranger in the water—who displayed back, angering him further—and then he stamped at the water until the reflected notharctus was gone.

Noth could recognize others of his species, could distinguish them as male or female, and as kin or not kin. But he could not recognize himself, for his mind did not contain the ability to look inward. All his life he would feel threatened by any such chance reflection.

A sleek form burst from the water itself and came lurching up on clumsy flippered limbs onto the rocky platform. Noth and Right stumbled back. Over a snout like a crocodile's the newcomer gazed at the two baffled primates.

This ambulocetus was a relation of the hyena-like mesonychids. Like an otter, it was covered in sleek black fur, and it had large, powerful back legs equipped with toes ten centimeters long. Ages ago this animal's ancestors had returned to the water, seeking a better living, and selection had begun its relentless molding. Already the ambulocetus looked more aquatic than terrestrial.

Soon its kind would take permanently to the oceans. Its skull and neck would become shorter, and the nose migrate backward, while its ears would close so that sound would have to pass through a layer of fat. Its legs would morph at last into fins, with more bones added, the fingers and toes becoming shrunken and useless, at last disappearing. When it reached the vast spaces of the Pacific and Atlantic, it would begin to grow—ultimately becoming as large compared to its present form as a human was to a mouse—but those mighty seagoing descendants would still retain within their bodies, like fossils of bone and molecular traces, vestiges of the creatures they had once been.

The walking whale stared uncomprehendingly at the two timid primates. Deciding this crowded shore wasn't such a good place to bask after all, it flexed its spine and swam gracefully away.

As the light faded, Noth and Right retreated to the shelter of the trees. But the branches were now all but bare, and cover was hard to find. They huddled in a branch's crook.

The herbivores splashed out of the water, family groups calling to each other. And the predators began to call, harsh doglike barks and leonine growls echoing through the sparse forest.

As the chill settled deeper Noth felt torpor steal over him. But he felt *cold*, stuck here like this with only his baby sister, cold away from the huddle of his troop.

And then, to his surprise, he was startled awake by a powerful musk scent.

Suddenly there were notharctus all around. They were on the branches above and below him, huddled shapes with their legs drawn up beneath them and their long, fat tails dangling. Their scent told him this was his kind, but not his kin. He had not detected their scent markings before; in fact the markings were sealed in by layers of frost. But the strange notharctus had noticed him.

Two powerful females gathered closely, drawn by the scent of an infant. One, who he thought of as Biggest, pushed aside the other—who was merely Big—to get a closer look at Right.

Noth's mind churned. He knew that it was vital that they be accepted by this new group. So he reached for the female closest to him, Big, and began, tentatively, to dig his fingers into the fur at the back of her legs. Big responded to his grooming, stretching out her legs with pleasure.

But when Biggest saw what was going on she hooted and slapped them both. Noth cowered, trembling.

Noth was bright enough to understand his own place on the social ladder—in this case, down on the bottom rung. But his social mentality had its limits. Just as he could not detect the beliefs and desires of others, so he was not smart enough to form judgments about the relative ranking of others in a group. He had got it wrong: Biggest outranked Big, and she expected this new male to pay her attention first.

So Noth waited as Biggest played with the drowsy Right. But at least she did not drive him away. And at length Biggest let Noth approach her and groom her own dense, rank-smelling fur.

III

Every day was shorter than the last, every night longer. Soon there were just a few hours of bright daylight, and the intervals between the darknesses were lit only by a pink-gray twilight.

The forest was all but silent now. Most of the birds and the large herbivore herds had long gone, migrated south to warmer, easier climes, taking their dinning cries with them. The buzzing insect swarms of high summer were a memory, leaving only larvae or deep-buried eggs, sleeping dreamlessly. The big deciduous trees had already dropped their broad leaves, which lay in a thick litter on the ground, welded together by the persistent frost. The bare trunks and leafless branches would show no signs of life until the sun returned in a few months' time. Beneath them, plants like the ground fern had died back to their roots and rhizomes, soon to be sealed into the earth under a lid of frost and snow.

The species here—derived from ancestral stock adapted to the balmy conditions of the tropics—had had to make ferocious adjustments to survive the extreme conditions at the pole. Every plant, wherever it lived, depended on sunlight for energy and growth, and during the endless days of summer the vegetation had lapped up the light with broad, angled leaves. But now there approached a season when for months there would be no light but that of the Moon and stars, useless for growth: If the plants had kept on growing and respiring they would have burned up their energy store. So the flora were heading for a vegetable hibernation, each according to its own strategy.

Even the plants were sleeping.

The notharctus troop was thirty strong, and they had huddled in the branches of a big conifer. They looked like big furry fruit, their hands and feet clinging to the branches as they slept, their faces buried in their chests, their backs exposed to the cold. Frost sparkled on their new winter coats, and where a muzzle showed breath steamed, glowing blue white.

Noth slept away the lengthening nights, his fur bristling, immersed in the body heat of the others of the troop. Sometimes he dreamed. He saw his mother fall into the jaws of the mesos. Or he was alone in an open space surrounded by hard-eyed predators. Or he was like a pup again, pushed out of a troop by adults bigger and stronger than he was, excluded by rules of which he had no innate understanding. But sometimes the dreams faded, and he fell into a kind of torpor, a blankness that prefigured the long months of hibernation to come.

Once he woke in the night shivering, his muscles involuntarily burning energy to keep him alive.

The sleeping world was full of light: the Moon was high and full and the forest glowed blue white and black. Long, sharp shadows striped the littered floor, and the vertical trunks of the leafless trees gave the scene an eerie geometrical precision. But the tangled branches higher up were a more complex and dismal sight, bone bare and glimmering with frost, a harsh contrast to the warm green glow of the leaves of high summer.

In its way it was a beautiful scene, and Noth's wide archaic eyes served him well, revealing to him detail and subtle colorations that would have been invisible to any human. But all Noth perceived was a *lack*: a lack of light, of warmth, of food—and a lack of kin in this group of strangers, save for his sister, whose still-growing body was buried somewhere in the huddling troop. And he knew on a deep cellular level that the true winter had yet to begin, long, drawn-out months of a kind of slow agony as his body consumed itself in order to keep him alive.

He squirmed across the branch, trying to force his way deeper into the group. Each of the adults knew that it was in everybody's long-term interests that she should take her turn at the edge of the group, briefly suffering the cold in order to shelter the rest; it wouldn't help to have outliers die of frostbite. But still Noth's lowly rank worked against him, and when the other males picked up his scent they sleepily combined to push him back out of the huddle, so he finished up almost as exposed as when he had started.

He lifted his muzzle and puffed out a breath, hooting mournfully.

These primates could draw no comfort from those around them. Noth found pleasure in grooming—but only in his own physical sensations, and in the effect it had on others' behavior toward him, not in how others felt. The other notharctus were simply a part of his environment, like the conifer trees and podocarps, the foragers and predators and prey: nothing to do with *him*.

These huddling notharctus, despite their physical closeness, were each lonelier than any human would ever be. Noth was forever locked inside the prison of his head, forced to endure his miseries and fears alone.

The morning dawned clear, but a freezing mist lay over the forest. Even though the sun grew bright there was little heat to be had from its rays.

The notharctus stretched limbs stiff with cold and long hours of immobility. Cautiously, watchfully, they headed down to the ground. On the forest floor they scattered slowly. The senior females moved around the edge of this loose clearing, using their wrists, armpits, and genitals to renew scent markers.

Noth picked through the frozen mulch. The dead leaves were of no use to him, but he had learned to burrow under places where the leaf litter was particularly thick. The mulching leaves could trap moisture and keep the frost away; here there was dew to lap up, and unfrozen ground to dig in search of tubers, roots, or even the rhizomes of hardy ferns.

A series of hooting cries broke out, startlingly loud, echoing through the forest. Noth looked up, whiskers twitching.

There was a commotion around a stand of podocarp. Noth saw that a group of notharctus, strange females with a scattering of pups, had come out of the forest. They were approaching the podocarp.

Biggest and some of the other females dashed forward. The troop's big dominant male—who Noth thought of as something like *the Emperor*—joined in the females' charge. Soon they were all displaying ferociously, hooting and scraping musk over their long tails. The strange females cowered back, but they responded in kind. The forest briefly filled up with the cacophony of the argument.

The female clans, the heart of the notharctus' society, were fiercely territorial. These strange females had ignored the scent markers left by Big and the others, bright warning signs in a notharctus' sensorium. At this time of year food was becoming short; in the final scramble to stoke up their bodies' stores for the rigors of winter, a rich stand of podocarp was worth fighting for.

The females, with babies clinging to their fur, went further in their wars than their males were prepared to. They quickly escalated the confrontation to lunges and feints and even slashes with canine teeth. The females fought like knife fighters.

But it wasn't going to work. Though not one notharctus laid a paw on another, the display by Biggest and the rest overwhelmed the newcomers. They backed off toward the long gray-brown shadows of the deeper forest—though not before one older pup had lunged forward, cheekily sunk his teeth into a cold-wizened fruit, and run off with his bounty before he could be stopped.

Suddenly aware of the vulnerability of their treasure, the females closed around the podocarp now, munching greedily at the fruit. Some of the older, more powerful males, including the Emperor, were soon feeding alongside Biggest and the rest. Noth, with the other young males, circled the feeding group, waiting his turn at whatever would be left.

He dared not challenge the Emperor.

Male notharctus had their own complex and different social structure, overlaying that of the females. And it was all about mating, which was the most important thing—the *only* thing. The Emperor had a large territory, including the ranges of many female groups. He would aim to mate with all the females in his territory, and so maximize his chances of propagating his genes. He would scent mark females to repel other suitors. And he would fight fiercely to keep other strong males away from his wide empire, just as Noth's father had fought to exclude Solo.

The Emperor had done well to hold on to his wide-ranging fiefdom for more than two years. But like all of his short-lived kind, he was aging quickly. Even Noth, the lowliest newcomer, made endless automatic computations of the Emperor's strength and fitness; the drive to mate, to produce offspring, to see his own line go on, was as strong in Noth as in any of the males here. Soon the Emperor would surely meet a challenge he could not withstand.

But for now, Noth was in no position to challenge the Emperor or any of the stronger males in the loose pecking order above him. And he could see that the supply of podocarp fruit was dwindling rapidly.

With a frustrated hoot he hurried over the forest floor and scampered briskly into a tree. The branches, slippery with residual frost, dew, and lichen, were all but bare of leaves and fruit. But it might still be possible to find caches of nuts or seeds, stashed away by providential forest creatures.

He came to a hollow in an aging tree trunk. In its dank, rotting interior, he saw the gleam of nutshells. He reached in with his small, agile hands and hauled out one of the nuts. The shell was round, seamless, complete. When he rattled it he could hear the kernel inside, and saliva spurted into his mouth. But when he bit into the shell his teeth slid over the smooth, hard surface. Irritated, he tried again.

There was an almighty hissing. He hooted, dropped the nut, and scuttled to a higher branch.

A creature the size of a large domestic cat came scrambling clumsily toward the nut cache. It raised its head to Noth and hissed again, showing a pink mouth with powerful upper and lower incisors. Satisfied that it had driven off the raider, it dug out one of its stored nuts and, with a clench of its powerful jaws, cracked the shell. Soon it was nibbling purposefully, widening the hole it had made. At last it reached the nut's kernel—Noth, tucked behind the tree trunk, was almost overwhelmed by the sudden sweet aroma—and fed noisily.

This ailuravus looked something like a rudimentary squirrel, with a mouselike face. It had a long bushy tail, the purpose of which was to slow its fall, parachute-like, every time it tumbled out of a tree, as it frequently did. Although it was clumsier than the notharctus as it moved about in the trees, lacking a primate's grasping hands and feet, it was more than big enough to have fought off Noth.

The ailuravus was one of the first rodents. That vast, enduring family had emerged a few million years earlier in Asia, and had since migrated around the world. This small encounter was a skirmish at the start of an epochal conflict for resources between the primates and the rodents.

And the rodents were already winning.

They were beating primates to the food, for one thing. Noth would have needed a nutcracker to eat hazelnuts or brazil nuts, and a millstone to process grains like wheat and barley. But the rodents, with their ferocious, ever-growing incisors, could break through the toughest nut and grain seed coats. Soon they would begin to consume the fruits of the best trees before they were even ripe.

Not only that, the rodents outbred the primates by a large factor. This ailu could produce several litters within a single year. Many of its young would fall to starvation, competition with their siblings, or predation by birds and carnivores. But it was enough that some should survive to continue the line, and for the ailu each of its young represented little investment—unlike the notharctus who bred just once a year and for whom the loss of a single pup was a significant disaster. And the rodents' vast litters incidentally offered up much raw material to the blind sculptors of natural selection; their evolutionary rate was ferocious.

Even though primates like Noth were much smarter than rodents like the ailu, his kind could not compete.

It wasn't just the plesiadapids that were becoming rare in North America. It was no coincidence that Noth's kind had been pushed up into this marginal polar forest. In the future Noth's line would migrate further, passing over the roof of the world to Europe and thence to Asia and Africa, adapting and reshaping as they went. But in North America the rodent victory would, within another few million years, be complete. A new ecology would arise, populated by gophers, squirrels, pack rats, marmots, field mice, and chipmunks. There would be *no* primates in North America: none at all, not for another fifty-one million years, not until human hunters, very distant descendants of the notharctus, came walking over the Bering Strait from Asia.

When the rodent was done feeding, Noth crept cautiously out of his hiding place. With his agile hands he sought out the scraps of kernel the ailu had dropped, and crammed them into his mouth without shame.

For a few hours a day the southern sky still grew bright. But the sun made its cycles beneath the horizon now. Almost all of the lakes were frozen over, and the trees were laden with frost, some of it gleaming in thick lacy shards where mist had frozen out on spiderwebs. The notharctus' movements through the trees and over the silent forest floor were sluggish and dull. But it didn't matter; the forest could offer them little more food this autumn.

There came a last clear day, when layers of red-tinged cloud stacked up against a violet southern sky, and the purple-green aurora rolled like a vast curtain over the stars.

The notharctus hurried to the ground and began to dig in places where the soil had been kept unfrozen by layers of leaves or under the roots of trees. Tonight would be the hardest frost of the winter so far, and they all knew it was time to get under cover. So the primates dug, building burrows in which Purga would have felt comfortable. It was as if the brief interval in the trees had been nothing but a dream of freedom.

In the deepest dark, Noth pushed his way through tunnels quickly worn smooth by the passage of primate bodies and over a floor littered with loose fur. At last his powerful nose guided him to Right.

Gently Noth sniffed his sister. She was already dormant, curled tightly up with her tail wrapped around her, close to the belly of Big. She had grown during their months with Biggest's troop, but Right would always be small, always retain traces of the runt who had been bullied by her now-dead twin. Still her winter fur seemed sleek, healthy, and free of knots and dirt, and her tail was fat with the store that should sustain her through the winter.

Noth felt a kind of satisfaction. Given their dreadful start to the summer, they had both beaten the survival odds better than expected. With no pups of his own, this was still the only kin Noth had—his entire genetic future depended on Right—but for now there was nothing more he could do for her.

In darkness, immersed in the scents and subtle noises of his kind, Noth snuggled as close as he could to his sister. He shut his eyes, and was soon asleep.

Briefly he dreamed, of fragments of summer light, of long shadows, of his mother's fall from the trees. And then, as his body shut down, his mind dissolved.

IV

The sun's rays, almost horizontal, shone like searchlights into the forest. Above the slowly melting ponds a chill mist hovered, shining in elaborate pink-gray swirls, pointlessly beautiful. From the gaunt tree trunks immense black shadows stretched north. But the first leaves were budding on the bare branches, tiny green plates hanging almost vertically to catch the sun's light. The leaves were already at work: The days of spring and summer were so short that these hardy vegetable servants had to gather every droplet of light they could.

It was just a glimpse, a dawn that would last no more than a few minutes. But it was the first time for several months that the disk of the sun had shown.

The forest was quiet. The great herbivorous migrants were still hundreds of kilometers to the south; it was weeks yet before they would come back, seeking their summer feeding grounds, and even the birds had yet to arrive. But Noth was already awake, already out, working.

Fresh from his burrow he was gaunt, his tail flaccid and drained of fat. His fur, ragged and stained yellow by urine, hung around him in a cloud, lit up by the sun, making him look twice his true size. There was still little fodder to be had in the trees, so he had to scurry over the littered, frosty ground. After the winter's chill, it was as if nobody had ever lived here, and everywhere he moved he marked rocks and tree trunks with his musk.

All around him, in grim competition, the males of the troop were foraging. They were all adults: Even those born less than a year ago were approaching their full size, while relative veterans like the Emperor himself, approaching his third birthday, moved more stiffly than last year. After their winter of starving sleep, all of them looked sick, and the lingering cold bit hard through their loose fur and into their fat-deprived bodies.

There were risks in moving around so early. In the burrows, the females still slept, consuming the last of their winter stores. The predators were already active—and as food was still scarce, early-bird primates made a tempting target. If one of the males did find an unexpected cache of food he was quickly surrounded by snapping, jealous rivals, making the empty forest echo to their hoots and yips.

But Noth had no choice but to risk the cold. The days of breeding were approaching, a time of ferocious competition for the males. Noth's body knew that the sooner it laid down a store of strength and energy for the battles to come, the better chance he would have of finding a mate. He had to accept the risks.

Navigating with a blurred recollection of the landscape map he had built up last season, Noth made his way to the largest of the nearby lakes.

The lake was still mostly frozen, covered by a lid of gray ice littered with loose, hard-grained snow. A pair of ducklike birds, early immigrants, padded over the ice, pecking hopefully at its surface. Beneath the gray Noth could see the chill blue of older ice, a lens of deep-frozen material that had failed to melt through last summer, and would likewise fail to melt this year.

Close to the water's edge he passed a gray-white bundle. It was a mesonychid. Like the Arctic fox of later times, it endured the winter above ground. But in a sudden cold spell during the winter this meso had become lost in a blizzard, and, succumbing to exposure, had died, here at the shore of the lake. Its body had quickly frozen, and for now appeared perfectly preserved. But as it thawed the bacteria and insects had begun feasting: Noth could detect the sweet stench of decay. Saliva spurted into his mouth. The half-frozen meat would be good, and maggots were a salty treat. But his thirst outweighed his hunger.

Near the lake's shallow, muddy shore the ice was thin and cracked, and Noth could smell dank open water. The water was greenish, already full of life, and littered by grayish chunks of old ice cover. Noth dipped his muzzle into the water and drank, straining out the worst of the mucous slime between his teeth.

He could see that the open water bulged with clusters of small clear gray spheres: the spawn of the lake's amphibian inhabitants, laid down as early as possible. And closer by, in the shallows at his feet, Noth made out tiny wriggling black forms: the first tadpoles. He ran his hands through the water, letting the slime cling to his palms, and crammed the slippery harvest into his mouth.

With a flexing strain his bowels moved, and watery shit pooled beneath him.

But now the surface of the water broke, the ice cracking with sharp reports. Something huge was coming out of the lake. Noth scurried back to the cover of the nearest trees, eyes wide.

Like Noth, the crocodile had woken early, disturbed from its slumber by the brightness of the day. As it rose from the lake, bits of ice tumbled from its back. With a single graceful motion it clamped its jaws on the frozen meso: frost crackled, bones crunched. Then the croc slid backward into the water, dragging the carcass effortlessly, making barely a sound.

The crocodile was hungry.

Before the comet the largest animals in each of the world's ecologies had been reptilian: the plesiosaurs and ichthyosaurs in the oceans, the dinosaurs on land, and the crocodilians in fresh water. The disaster had wiped away these great families, and in their empty realms they would soon be replaced by functionally equivalent mammals—all save the crocodiles.

The freshwater environment had always been a difficult place to live. While the supply of plant material on land and in the sea was pretty reliable in space and time, freshwater environments were very variable. Erosion, abrasion, silting, flood, drought, and extremes of water quality were all hazards.

But the crocodiles—and other enduring freshwater species like turtles—were resilient. Some learned to walk overland in search of water. Others could take to the sea. Or they would just bury themselves eight or ten meters deep in the mud, and wait for the next cloudburst. And as for food, even during the worst of the killings on land and in the sea, they would subsist off the nutrients that continued to leach off the corpse-littered land, a "brown" food chain that persisted long after the green, growing things and the creatures that browsed them had died.

In this way the crocodiles had survived across a hundred and fifty million years, through extraterrestrial impacts, glaciation pulses, sea level changes, tectonic upheavals, and competition from successive dynasties of animals.

After all this time they were still capable of evolutionary novelty. Briefly, after the comet impact, the top predators around the water courses had been crocodile cousins with long legs and hooflike claws. They had been a nightmare, running predatory crocodiles capable of chasing down animals as large as small horses. Crocodiles had even adapted to survive here at the pole, where the sun didn't shine for months on end; they would simply wait out the winter months in deep hibernation.

Unlike the dinosaurs, unlike the plesiosaurs, the crocodiles would not be forced out of their freshwater niches by upstart mammals: not now, not ever.

Noth had lost the meso carcass, but some scraps of flesh and crushed maggots were smeared over the ground where it had lain. Hungrily he licked at the frozen ground.

At last the days of breeding arrived.

The females of the troop gathered in the branches of one tall conifer. They were feeding on ripe young fruit, cramming their bodies with the resources they would need to survive the drain of motherhood to come. The females were loosely marshaled by the more senior among them, including Big and Biggest. Right was among them. She had survived her first winter. She was filling out quickly, and when her scrappy winter fur had blown away she had emerged as a small but elegantly built adult, ready to mate.

The Emperor himself was among his female subjects. He moved from one to the other, heroically humping. Already he had been accepted by Biggest twice, and had deflowered an unprotesting Right. Now he was taking Big. She was bent over, clinging to a low branch, her head tucked between her knees, her tail uplifted. The Emperor was behind her, arms wrapped around her waist, hips thrusting with a rapidity born of exhaustion and urgency.

This was the day toward which the Emperor had worked all year, and now was the time for him to spend all of his authority and energy by covering as many of the females as possible.

But the Emperor was already tiring. And this female troop was only one of several in the wider territory he commanded.

In this ferociously seasonal place, baby rearing had to be squeezed into a drastically short period, so that offspring were produced when food was abundant and their new mothers could eat enough to produce plenty of milk. Any female who mated outside the breeding season was unlikely to see her offspring survive to adulthood. And any male who missed the chance to mate with a fertile female would have to endure a whole year of hardship, danger, and privation before getting another chance.

For the notharctus, the breeding season was just *forty-eight hours* long. It was a frantic time.

Today, the start of the females' simultaneous estrus, the air was full of an invisible pheromone cloud, and there were males everywhere, helplessly drawn, erections poking out of their fur. Every male had prepared since the return of the sun, feeding to build up his strength, practicing spectacular tree swings and engaging in mock battles: They had been like athletes preparing for a contest. It was impossible for the Emperor to keep them all away, and there was intense competition. Today the hierarchy of males was stressed to the point of collapse.

The stress on the females would come later, during pregnancy and nursing, when the fast-growing fetus or newborn pup demanded the mother find a stream of high-energy food—and she must eat well at a time when almost every other adult female was nursing too. It was the heavy cost of reproduction that had led to the general dominance of females over males, and it was the reason why the females always got the best of the food.

It was the same all over the forest. Every notharctus troop was hitting its brief mating season simultaneously, the timing dictated by the invisible chemical scents that permeated the air for kilometers around. For today and tomorrow, the forest was filled with primate lust: a tremendous clamor of battling males, pheromone-laden females, and frantically thrusting hips.

Noth, pursuing another young male he thought of as Rival, hurled himself through a loose stand of conifers. He swung one-armed on spindly branches. On each dip the earth tipped up like a vast bowl, dead leaves and new green ferns and the dull forms of snuffling ground feeders fleeing under him.

He approached a gap between two tall trees. On the far side he saw Rival, standing upright, genitals pinkly visible, rubbing his scent markers on the bark. Rival barked a contemptuous challenge.

Without hesitating, Noth took a final huge swing. The branch flexed and hurled him on a smooth parabola high into the air. For a few heartbeats he flew, tail held high, hands and feet held out before him ready to grasp.

His head was filled with the stink of estrus. He had had an erection since he had woken this morning. Even now, as he sailed from tree to tree, his penis stuck out before him, pink and solid. He had yet to succeed in battling his way through the crowding males to get to a receptive female, and he felt as if his belly would burst if he didn't succeed soon. But even as he was consumed with inchoate lust, still he relished the power of his lithe body as he hurled it through the forest domain for which it was exquisitely adapted.

Noth had never felt so alive.

Noth landed in Rival's tree, just where he had aimed. He grasped the branches with faultless positioning of his hands and feet. But immediately Rival was on him.

Facing each other they stood upright, their spindly erections poking out. Noth, tail held erect, stalked toward Rival, vigorously rubbing his groin against the tree bark, chattering and barking. Rival responded in kind. It was a ritualized encounter, each of them responding to the other's movements in a kind of dance: tail waft followed by groin rub, wrist spread provoking a spitting glare.

Soon the air was filled with their angry stink. They came close enough for Noth to feel the tips of the other's bristling fur, and Rival's spittle sprayed his face.

Rival was about the same age as Noth, about the same size. He had joined the troop a little earlier than Noth and his sister. To him, Noth had invaded a troop that he had come to regard as "his." Noth and Rival were too similar, like brothers, too close to be anything but enemies.

Rival was marginally bigger and heavier than Noth, and if anything he had done better in the early-season feeding. But Noth's difficult year had forged an inner toughness, and he stood his ground.

Psychology won out. Rival subsided suddenly, his display collapsing. He turned his back on Noth and, briefly, symbolically, displayed his pink backside in a curt gesture of submission.

Noth hooted, relishing his moment. Briskly he rubbed his wrists over Rival's back, marking his victory with his scent, and released a stream of urine. Then he let Rival slink away along the branch toward a cluster of berries.

Rival would come to no harm. He would skulk alone in his tree for a time, perhaps feeding, withdrawing for a while from the fray. But his chances of mating were for a few hours reduced. Noth's urine would make him briefly sterile; it would even reduce his ability to make the special trilling calls used by the males to attract females.

For Noth it was a valid strategy. Today it was impossible for any male, however heroically he tried, to cover all the females. But he could reduce the number of competing males with such sensory intimidation.

With Rival defeated, Noth's penis throbbed anew; soon he would at last attain the satisfaction he craved. With fast, vigorous swings he hurled himself through the branches, across the forest toward the place the females clustered.

But he was not aware of the grim battle taking place there.

Still immersed in his females, the Emperor finished yet another mating. His penis raw and dangling, he stalked among the females, cuffing and snapping at any male he could reach.

And suddenly he found himself facing Solo.

The aging Emperor hauled himself upright, bared his teeth, and let his glands pump out still more of his potent musk. Hair bristling, muzzle working, he was a magnificent sight, enough to intimidate any other male.

Any but Solo.

Solo had spent a comfortable winter in a burrow with a female band not far from here. As soon as the light had returned he had joined in the early feeding, rapidly building his body to the peak of strength and power he had enjoyed last year.

And he had begun his roaming. Already today he had planted offspring in half a dozen females throughout the forest. Now he had come to take more—once he had eliminated the opposition.

Solo lunged at the Emperor, ramming his scarred muzzle into his belly.

The Emperor was knocked flat on his back on the branch, winded, and might have fallen from the tree if his quick-working primate hands had not scrabbled at the bark. He was as much shocked by the sudden physical assault as hurt. Save for cuffs and slaps by food-monopolizing females, and occasional inadvertent blows from other males, nobody had ever deliberately hurt him in his life.

But it was not over.

With a bound, almost graceful for a creature his size, Solo jumped on the Emperor. He sat on the older male's chest, compressing the Emperor's fragile ribs. The Emperor screamed. He chuffed and panted, and he beat at Solo's back. If he had used all his strength he might yet have driven the other off. But to injure another went against his instincts, and his punches were weak, his blows ineffective.

He had missed his chance.

Solo bent forward and pushed his muzzle into the Emperor's crotch. He teased aside fur that was stiff with semen and the vaginal fluids of several females. With a brisk, practiced lunge, he bit into the Emperor's scrotal sac, severing one testicle.

The Emperor howled, thrashing. Blood gushed, mingling with the mating fluids on his fur.

Solo climbed easily away. With a single firm motion of his foot, he pushed the Emperor off the branch. The older male's body went crashing through the foliage beneath, plummeting toward the ground. Then Solo spat out the bloody testicle, letting it fall into the green below.

Solo advanced on Right, Noth's sister, one of the youngest of the females. He fingered his rapidly swelling penis, preparing to take her.

But now here was Noth, young, eager, horny, plummeting out of the air to land at Solo's feet. Solo turned like a tank turret to face this new challenger.

Noth hadn't known Solo was here. But he remembered him.

Noth was a creature of the here and now. He had no real conception of yesterday or tomorrow, and his memory was not arranged in an orderly narrative; it was more like a corridor of vivid images, rendered in sight and scent. But the powerful stink of Solo brought images flooding back, shards and glimpses of that dreadful day in another part of the forest, his mother's despairing howl as she fell into the pit of teeth.

Conflicting impulses surged through him. He should display, stink-fight—or else he should show his submission to this powerful creature, just as Rival had submitted to him.

But *Solo didn't fit*. He didn't obey any of the unwritten rules that governed the notharctus' fragile society. He had just mutilated the troop's dominant male. Solo would surely not be satisfied with a symbolic victory. Solo, huge, still, meant to injure him, if not kill him.

And here was Right, Noth's only kin, cowering in the foliage at Solo's feet. Here were the females with whom he had lived for half a year, and whose swelling pudenda had filled him with anticipatory lust for days, weeks—and here was this monster, Solo, who had destroyed everything he had grown up with.

He stood upright and howled.

Solo, startled, hesitated.

Noth's wrists and crotch itched with musk. He performed a frantic, one-second display, an accelerated demonstration of his power and youth. Then, blindly, not understanding what he was doing, he lowered his head and barged at Solo's midriff. With a gasping hoot, Solo was knocked backward, finishing on his back in a clump of foliage.

If he had followed up, Noth could have capitalized on his surprise attack. But he had never fought a physical fight in his life. And Solo, with the instincts of an experienced fighter, twisted and slammed his knee against Noth's temple. Noth went down face first and instinctively scrabbled for a hold. An immense mass crashed into his back, crushing him against the bark. And now Noth felt Solo's incisors sink into the soft flesh of his neck. He screamed at the sharp pain. He twisted and thrashed. He could not shake off Solo—but the vigor of his movements tipped them both off the narrow branch.

Hooting, with Solo's teeth ripping at his flesh, Noth found himself plummeting through layers of foliage and twigs.

They crashed to the ground, their fall scarcely cushioned by the rotting leaf cover. But Solo was shaken free, his clenched jaw giving one last rip at Noth's shoulder. Solo made his own display of aggression. He roared, an ugly, unstructured noise. He stood upright and hammered his small fists into the detritus at his feet; bits of leaf flew everywhere, surrounding him in a loose, sunlit cloud.

It was a battle of two small creatures. But much larger animals, watching timidly, backed away from Solo's ferocity.

It was a one-sided contest. Solo advanced on Noth, stalking out of the settling leaf fragments. Noth watched, not even displaying, as if hypnotized. He looked down in horror at his shoulder, where a flap of skin hung loose and blood soaked into his fur.

But now a burly mass came flying at Solo. It was the Emperor. Even as the blood continued to gush from his ragged scrotum, the big notharctus slammed feetfirst into Solo's back, knocking him flat, facedown in the debris.

This time Noth did not hesitate. He threw himself at Solo and began to pummel his back and shoulders with feet, hands, and muzzle. The Emperor joined in—and so did more of the males, until Solo was immersed beneath a blanket of hooting, jostling, inexperienced assailants. Any one of them Solo would have defeated—but not all of them together. Under the rain of inexpertly aimed blows, it was impossible even for him to rise.

At last he burrowed like a taeniodont through the forest floor detritus, out from under the clamoring pack. By the time the ragged army had noticed he was gone, that their punches and kicks were either landing in the dirt or on each other, Solo was limping away.

Aching, battered, Noth clambered back into the tree. When he got there he found the females grooming each other calmly, picking bits of dried semen out of their crotch hair, as if the combat beneath had never taken place. The Emperor was sitting quietly with the female Biggest. His flow of blood had stilled—but his copulatory campaign was suspended forever.

And here was Rival, vigorously covering Right. Noth saw his sister's face buried in her own chest hair, low squeaks of pleasure emanating from her throat. Noth felt an oddly warm glow. He was not driven by jealousy of other males over his sister—even of this male whom he had bested, and who had apparently recovered very quickly. A deeper biochemical part of him recognized that with his sister pregnant, the line would go on: the shining unbroken molecular thread that stretched from Purga, through this moment lit by the low polar sun, on into unimaginable futures.

He heard a remote lowing. It was the call of a moeritherium, the matriarch of a migrant herd, walking slowly up from the south. With the return of the herds, summer had truly come again. And from all over the forest came a high keening: It was the song of the notharctus, a song of loneliness and wonder.

In just a few years Noth's life would be over. Soon his kind would be gone too, their descendants transmuted into new forms; and soon, as Earth cooled from this midsummer peak, even the polar forest would shrivel and die. But for now—bloodied, panting, his fur covered with leaf mold—this was Noth's moment, his day in the light.

The huge female Big approached him. He trilled gently. With a glance into his eyes, she turned her back and presented to him. Noth entered her quickly, and his world dissolved into unthinking pleasure.

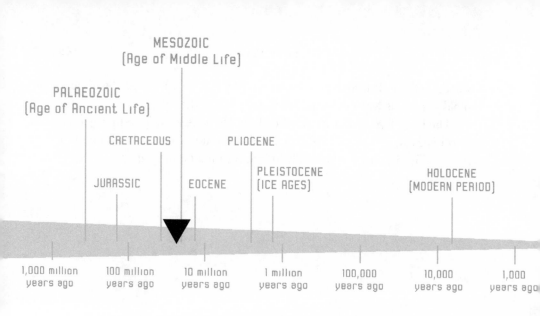

MESOZOIC
(Age of Middle Life)

PALAEOZOIC
(Age of Ancient Life)

CRETACEOUS

PLIOCENE

PLEISTOCENE
(ICE AGES)

HOLOCENE
(MODERN PERIOD)

JURASSIC

EOCENE

1,000 million
years ago

100 million
years ago

10 million
years ago

1 million
years ago

100,000
years ago

10,000
years ago

1,000
years ago

CHAPTER 6

the crossing

▼ Congo River, West Africa. Circa 32 million years before present.

I

Here, close to its final oceanic destination, the mighty river pushed sluggishly between walls of lush, moist forest. There were many meanders
and oxbow lakes, which, cut off from the flow, had turned into stagnant
marshes and ponds. It was as if the river were exhausted, its long journey
done—but this river was draining the heart of a continent.

And this late summer there had been much rain. The river was high,
and it spilled over onto land where the water table was already near the
surface. The dense, muddy water contained fragments of eroded rock,
mud, and living things. There were even rafts of tangled branches and
bits of vegetation drifting like unruly schooners down the river's tremendous length, relics that had already traveled thousands of kilometers from
their point of origin.

High above the water, in the forest's cacophonous upper story, the
anthros were making their daily destructive procession.

They were like monkeys. Running along branches, using their powerful arms to swing from tree to tree, they stripped off fruit, ripped open

palm fronds, and tore away great swaths of bark to get at insects. Crowds of females moved and worked together, occasionally stopping for a moment's grooming. There were mothers with infants clinging to their backs and bellies, supported by clusters of aunts. Males, larger, wider-ranging, made loose alliances that merged and fragmented constantly as they competed for food, status, and access to the females.

More than thirty anthros worked here. They were clever, efficient foragers, and where they passed, they laid waste. It was a joyful, clamoring racket of feeding, cooperating, and challenging.

Temporarily alone, Roamer was swinging from one thick branch to the next. Though she was high above the ground, she had no fear of falling; she was in her element here, her body and mind exquisitely adapted for the conditions of this tangled forest canopy.

Bordering the sea, to the west, there were dense mangrove swamps. But here, inland, the ancient forest was rich and diverse, full of tall trees with flaring buttresses: papaws, cashews, fan palms. Most of the trees were fruit bearing and rich in resin and oils. It was a comfortable, rich place to live. But it was a relic of a world that was vanishing, for a great cooling had gripped the Earth since Noth's time, and the once global and beneficent forests had shrunk back to scraps and fragments.

Roamer found a palm nut. She settled on a branch to inspect it. A caterpillar, fat and green, crawled over its surface. She licked off the caterpillar and chewed it slowly.

The troop moved noisily through the canopy around her. Alone or not, she knew exactly where everybody else was. In the long years since Noth's time the primates had become still more intensely social: To the anthros, other anthros had become more interesting than mere things—the most interesting objects in the world. Roamer was as aware of the rest of her troop as if they were a series of Chinese lanterns stuck in the foliage, diminishing the rest of the world to a dull, mute grayness.

Roamer belonged to no species that would ever be labeled by humans. She looked something like a capuchin, the organ-grinder monkey that would one day roam the forests of South America, and was about that size. She weighed a couple of kilograms, and she was covered in dense black fur topped by white shoulders, neck, and face; she looked like she was wearing a nun's wimple. Her arms and legs were lithe and symmetrical, much more so than Noth's: It was a body plan typical of the inhabitant of an open forest canopy. Her nose was flat, her nostrils small and protruding sideways, more like the monkeys of a later South America than those of Africa.

She looked like a monkey, but she was no monkey. Remote descendants of Noth's adapids, her kind was a type of primate called anthropoid—ancestral to both monkeys and apes, for that great schism in the family of primates had yet to occur.

Nearly twenty million years after the death of Noth, the grooming claws of notharctus feet had been replaced on Roamer's body by nails. Her eyes were smaller than Noth's, capable of a wide, three-dimensional field of view past her shorter muzzle, and each of her eyes was supported by a solid cup of bone; Noth's had been protected by a mere ring of bone, and his vision could even be disturbed by his own cheek muscles when chewing. And Roamer had lost many of Noth's ancestral relics of the times of night foraging. Her reliance on smell had diminished, to be replaced by a greater dependence on sight.

From Right's grandchildren had sprung a great diffusing army. They had migrated down through the Old World to inhabit the dense tropical forests of Asia, and here in Africa. And as they had migrated, so they had flourished, diversified, and changed. But the line of Old World anthropoids would not continue through Roamer. Roamer could not know that she would never see her mother again—and her fate was to be far more strange than anything that had befallen her immediate ancestors.

The whiteness of Roamer's fur made her face seem sketchy, unformed, and oddly wistful. But she had a youthful prettiness. In fact, she was three years old, still a year short of her menarche. A juvenile female independent of spirit, not yet fully absorbed into the troop's hierarchies and alliances, she retained something of the solitary instincts of more distant ancestors. She liked to keep herself to herself. Besides, the group wasn't a particularly happy bunch right now.

The last few years had been times of plenty, and the troop's numbers had expanded. There had been a baby boom, of which Roamer was a part. But growth brought problems. There was too much competition for food, for one thing. Every day there were squabbles.

And then there was the grooming. In a small group there was time to groom everybody. It all helped to maintain relationships and cement alliances. When a group got too big, there just wasn't the time to do that. So cliques were forming, subgroups fragmenting out whose members groomed each other exclusively, ignoring the rest. Already some of the cliques were traveling separately during the day, although they would still come together to sleep.

Eventually all of this would become too intense. The grooming cliques would fission off, and the group would split up. But the new, smaller groups each had to be large enough to offer protection against predators—the main purpose of these daytime bands in the first place—so it would be a long time yet, perhaps even years, before any fission was permanent. It happened all the time, an inevitable consequence of the growing sizes of primate communities. But it meant there was a lot of squabbling to be done.

So Roamer was happy to get away from all the bickering for a while.

The bug thoroughly masticated, Roamer inspected her palm nut. She knew that the kernel was delicious to eat, but her hands and teeth were not strong enough to break open the shell. So she began to pound the shell against the branch.

She became aware of two bright eyes watching her, and a slim, rust-colored body clinging to a branch. She was not alarmed. This was a crowder, a type of primate closely related to Roamer's kind but smaller, more slender—and a lot less smart. Beyond its slim form Roamer made out many more of its kind, clinging to the branches of this tree and the next, arrayed through the forest's green-lit world. The crowder was not competing for Roamer's nut, and was certainly not threatening her; all the little primate wanted was Roamer's leavings.

Roamer was mostly a fruit eater. But the crowders, like their common adapid ancestors, relied heavily on the caterpillars and grubs they snatched from the branches, and they had sharp, narrow teeth to process their insect prey. They lived in great crowded mobile colonies of fifty or more. This gave them a defense against predators and other primates. Even a troop of anthros would have had trouble driving off one of these agile, coordinated mobs.

But Roamer was a lot smarter than any crowder.

It would be tens of millions of years before any primate used anything that could be called a true tool. Much of Roamer's intelligence was of a specialized kind, designed to enable her to cope with the fast-shifting intricacies of her social life. But Roamer was clever at understanding the natural environment around her and manipulating it to get what she wanted. Smashing a nut against a tree trunk was hardly advanced engineering, but it required her to plan one or two steps ahead, a precursor of much greater inventiveness in ages to come. And such nut smashing was a cognitive leap beyond the grasp of any crowder, which was why the crowders were hanging around now.

Roamer heard a rustling far below. She clung to her branch, peering down into the green gloom.

She could see the litter of the forest floor, and a shadowy shape moving through the trees with a rustle of feathers, tentative pecks at the ground. It was a flightless bird, something like a cassowary. And when she tracked back the way the bird had come to the middle of the clearing, Roamer made out a rounded, polished gleam.

Eggs. There were ten of them, nestling in the bird's crude nest, each of them a reservoir of yolk as big as Roamer's head. In the stillness of noon, with her mate away, the bird had left her nest briefly unguarded, taking the chance that no harm would come to it while she briefly assuaged her hunger. She was unfortunate that Roamer's sharp eyes had detected the nest so quickly.

Roamer hesitated for a heartbeat. If she went after the eggs she would be taking a risk. Her nut cracking had already delayed her long enough for the troop to move away, and it would be bad to get lost. And the bird itself was a menace. A stalking monster, it was one of the last representatives of a twenty-million-year dynasty. After the comet, around the world, the land mammals had at first remained small, crammed into the dense forests—but some birds had grown large, and flightless monsters like this had briefly contested the role of top predator. Released from the weight limitations of flight they had become heavily built, muscular, and monstrously powerful, with beaks that could snap a backbone. But they had been out of time: When the mammalian herbivores grew large, so did mammal carnivores, and the birds could not compete.

The eggs were *there,* right below Roamer. She could take them easily.

If she had been older, more integrated into the group, her decision might have been different. But as it was she slid down the tree's rough bark toward the ground, her small mouth already moist with anticipation. It was this moment of decision that caused a great divergence in her own life—and the destiny of the greater family of primates in the future.

She had dropped the remains of her nut kernel. Behind her the little crowder, its patient wait over, fell on the sweet fragments. But in an instant more of its fellows came swarming over the branch to steal its prize.

As she climbed down the tree Roamer disturbed a troop of screechers. These primates were very small, with manes of fine silky hair and bizarre white moustaches. Startled by her passing they chattered and scurried away into the deeper recesses of the foliage, almost birdlike in the speed of their movements and the brightness of their furry "plumage."

Screechers made a living by digging into tree bark with their bottom teeth to make the gum flow. When they were done with a hole, they urinated into it to deter others from feeding there. There were many species of these little creatures, each specializing in the gum of one particular tree, and they were differentiated by their hairstyles. With their extravagant fur and trilling calls they made the forest canopy a place of color, life, and noise.

On the ground was still another form of primate. This was a potbelly, a solitary male. He was four times Roamer's size, his bulky body coated in thick black fur. He sat squat, steadily pulling leaves off a bush and cramming them between his powerful jaws. His muzzle was stained black: he had been chewing charcoal from a lightning-struck stump, a supplement which neutralized the toxins in his leafy diet.

As Roamer dropped lightly to the floor he glared at her, his mouth a ferocious downturn, and let out a roar. She glanced around nervously, fearing his call might have attracted the attention of the careless mother bird.

Roamer was under no threat from the potbelly. He had an enormous stomach with an enlarged lower intestine within which his low-nutrition food could be partially fermented. To let this mighty organic factory work effectively, he had to remain motionless for three-quarters of his time. This close she could hear the endless rumbling of his huge ungainly stomach. He was remarkably clean, though; given his lifestyle, he had to be sanitary, like a sewer rat. As she moved away from his precious patch of forest floor the potbelly subsided into a sulky silence.

The forest clearing was cluttered. Grasslands were still rare. In the absence of grass, the ground cover was rarely less than a meter tall, a clutter of low shrubs and bushes including aloe, cactus, and succulents. Most spectacular of all were giant thistlelike plants strewn, in their season, with psychedelically colored flowers. Such spectacles graced most of Earth's landmasses in this era, but it was an assemblage that would be unusual in human times; it was something like the fynbos flora of southern Africa.

To reach the bird's nest, Roamer would have to leave the cover of the trees. But the open sky today seemed very bright—bright and washed-out white—and there was a peculiar electric stink to the air. She would be exposed out there; she hesitated, uneasy.

Clinging to the edge of the forest, she tried to work her way closer to the eggs.

She skirted a marshy area, part of the mighty river's floodplain. She could see the water: Clogged with scummy vegetation, it glimmered, utterly flat, under a high sun. But there was a smell of salt in the air. Here, not far upstream of the river's delta, she was close to the ocean, and occasional floods and high tides had laden the soils with brine, making the vegetation sparse.

Animals moved through the clearing, seeking the open water. In low scrub a group of gazellelike stenomylus cropped, moving in a tight, nervous cluster and peering about anxiously as they chewed. They were trailed by a smaller herd of cainotheres, like small, long-eared antelope. Other deerlike browsers worked through the forest itself. But the stenomylus were not gazelles but a kind of camel—as were the cainotheres, with their oddly rabbitlike heads.

Close to the shore clustered a family of bulky herbivores reminiscent of rhinos. These were not true rhinos, and the sad curve of their upper lips gave a clue to their ancestry: They were actually arsinoetheres, creatures related to elephants. In the water itself wallowed a mating pair of metamynodons, very like hippos; wading birds stepped cautiously away from their clumsy passion. The metamynodons were actually more closely related to rhinos than were the arsinoetheres.

Where herbivores gathered, so predators and scavengers came to watch with their calculating eyes, as they had always done. The strange protorhinos and camel-gazelles were followed by cautious packs of beardogs—amphicyonids, predators and scavengers, walking like bears with their feet flat on the ground.

So it went. For a human observer it would have been like a fever dream—a bear like a dog, a camel like an antelope—shapes familiar if seen through half-closed eyes, and yet eerily different in detail. The great mammal families had still to find the roles they would occupy later.

But this age could boast its champions. At the forest's edge Roamer saw a shadow moving through the trees, immense, lumbering, menacing. This was a magistatherium. It walked four-footed, like a bear—but it was immense, twice the size of a Kodiak bear. Its canine teeth, five centimeters thick at the root, were twice the size of a tyrannosaur's. And, like the tyrannosaurs, it was an ambush hunter. For now it ruled these African forests—and it would prove to be the largest carnivorous mammal ever to live on land. But its shearing teeth, essential tools for a meat eater, came in pairs, unlike those of the true carnivores of the future, and more prone to damage. That slight design flaw would eventually doom the magistatherium to extinction.

Meanwhile, through the largest of the pools cruised the stippled back of a crocodile. *She* didn't care about any of this strangeness. As long as you were stupid enough to approach the crocodile's domain, as long as you had flesh that filled the belly and bones that crunched in the mouth, you could be any shape you pleased: Your fate would be the same.

At last Roamer came close enough to the nest. She dashed out of cover, attracting blank stares from the rooting herbivores, and reached her eggs.

The nest was partially covered by fallen fern fronds, and so she had some shelter to work in. With saliva flooding her mouth she picked up the first egg—and was baffled. Her hands slid over the egg's smooth surface, finding nothing to rip or tear. When she squeezed the egg against her chest, she did no better; the thick shell was too tough. There was no branch nearby against which she could smash the eggs. She tried cramming the whole egg into her mouth to bring her powerful back teeth into play, but her tiny lips could not reach around more than a fraction of its volume.

The trouble was, her mother had always cracked eggs open for her. Without her mother she had no idea what to do.

The light in the sky seemed to grow brighter, and a wind picked up suddenly, ruffling the surfaces of the ponds and scattering brown fronds across the ground. She felt a rising sense of panic; she was a long way from her troop. She dropped the egg back into the nest and reached for another.

But suddenly the sweet, sickly smell of yolk reached her nose. The egg she'd dropped, falling against the others in the nest, had broken. She jammed her hands into the jagged crack and pushed her face into the sweet yellow goo, and was crunching on half-formed bones. But when she took another egg, she couldn't remember how she had opened the first. She fingered the egg and tried to bite it, starting the whole trial-and-error process over.

Dropping eggs onto each other was how her mother had opened them before. But even if her mother had been here to demonstrate how to do it, Roamer would not have learned the technique, for Roamer was not capable of reading another's intentions, and so she couldn't imitate. Psychology was beyond the anthros, and every generation had to figure everything out from scratch from basic raw materials and situations. It made for slow learning. Still, Roamer soon got into another egg.

She was so intent on the food she wasn't aware of the lustful eyes that studied her.

Before she broke into a third egg the rain started. It seemed to come out of nowhere, huge droplets falling out of a blank, bright sky.

A great wind swept over the marshes. Wading birds took flight, heading west toward the ocean, away from the approaching storm. The big herbivores turned to face the rain, stoic misery in their posture. The crocodile slid beneath the surface of its pond, preparing to wait out the storm in the changeless depths of its murky empire.

And now clouds fled across the sun, and darkness closed in like a lid. To the east, at the center of the continent where the storm had brewed, thunder clattered. It was a storm of a ferocity that lashed the area only a few times in a decade.

Roamer cowered in the wreckage of the nest, her fur already plastered to her body. The droplets hammered into the ground around her, battering the dead vegetation and digging tiny pits into the clay. She had never known anything like it. She had always ridden out storms in the comparative shelter of the trees, whose foliage diffused and deadened the falling water. But now she was lost, stranded out in the open, suddenly aware how far she had come from her troop. If a predator had found her in those few heartbeats, then she might have lost her life.

But as it was, she had been found by one of her own kind: an anthro, a large male. He dropped to the sodden ground before her and sat still, studying her.

Startled, whimpering, she approached him cautiously. Perhaps he was one of the males who dominated her own troop—the loose, fissioning band she thought of as a kind of composite father—but he was not, she quickly saw. His face, the white fur beaten down with the rain, was strange, and a peculiar patterning of coloration gave him white drips down his black-furred belly, almost like blood.

This male—Whiteblood—was twice her size, and a stranger. And strangers were always bad news. She screeched and scrabbled backward.

But she was too late. He reached out his right hand and grabbed the scruff of her neck. She twisted and fought, but he lifted her easily, as if she were a piece of fruit.

Then he hauled her without ceremony back into the forest.

Whiteblood had spotted Roamer—a juvenile female wandering alone, an unusual opportunity. He had stalked her carefully, a fruit eater moving like an experienced hunter. And now the cover of the storm had given him the opportunity he needed to take her. Whiteblood had his own problems—and he thought Roamer might be part of the answer.

Like their notharctus ancestors, anthro females lived in tight supportive groups. But in this seasonless tropical forest, perpetually abundant, there was no need for their breeding cycles to be synchronized. Life was much more flexible, with different females coming into estrus at different times.

That made it easier for a small group of males—even a single male, sometimes—to monopolize a female group. Unlike the notharctus Emperor, it wasn't necessary for an anthro male to try to cover all his females in a single day, or to face the impossible task of keeping other males away. Instead it was enough that he kept rivals away from the small number of females who were fertile at any given time.

Though they were physically larger, anthro males did not "own" the females, or dominate them excessively. But the males, bound to the female group by a genetic loyalty—in a promiscuous group there was always a chance that any child born might be *yours*—would work to protect the group from outsiders and predators. For their part the females were generally content with the loose satellite male communities that accreted around them. Males were occasionally useful, obviously necessary, rarely troublesome.

But recently, for Whiteblood's troop, things had gone wrong.

Ten of the twenty-three females in the group had gone into estrus simultaneously. Soon other males had been attracted, drawn by the scent of blood and pheromones. Suddenly there weren't enough females to go around. It had been an unstable situation, intensely competitive. Already there had been bloody battles. There was a danger the group might fission altogether.

So Whiteblood had gone out hunting females. Juveniles were the preferred target: young and small enough to be handled easily, foolish enough to be easy to separate from their home groups. Of course it meant waiting a year or more before a child like Roamer could be mated. But Whiteblood was prepared to wait: His mind was complex enough for him to act now in the prospect of reward later.

For Whiteblood the situation was quite logical. But for Roamer it was a nightmare.

Suddenly they were swinging and running at a ferocious rate. Whiteblood kept hold of her scruff, seeming to find her no trouble to haul. Roamer had never moved in these great bounds, swoops, and leaps: Her mother and the other females, more sedentary than the males, moved much more cautiously than *this*. And she was being carried a long way; she could smell muddy water, for they were approaching the bank of the river itself.

And meanwhile the rain clattered down, pelting through the leaves and turning the air into a gray misty murk. Her fur was sodden and water ran into her eyes, making it impossible to see. Far below them, water ran across the sodden ground, rivulets gathering into streams that washed red-brown mud into the already swollen river. It was as if forest and river were merging, dissolving into each other under the storm's power.

Her panic intensified. She struggled to get free of Whiteblood's grasping hand. All she got for her troubles were cuffs on the back of her head, hard enough to make her squeal.

At last they reached Whiteblood's home range. Most of the troop, males, females, and infants, had clustered together in a single tree, a low, broad mango. They sat in rows on the branches, huddled together in sodden misery. But when the males saw what Whiteblood had brought back, they hooted and slapped the branches.

Whiteblood, without ceremony, thrust Roamer at a group of females. One female started poking hard at Roamer's face, belly, and genitals. Roamer slapped her hand away, hooting in protest. But the female came back for more, and now more of them crowded around her, striving to get close to the newcomer. Their curiosity was a mixture of the anthros' usual fascination with someone new, and a kind of rivalry over this potential competitor, a new recruit in the ever-shifting hierarchies.

For Roamer everything was bewildering: the sheets of lightning flashing over the purple sky, the hammering rain on her face, the roar of water below, the damp-fur, unfamiliar stink of the females and young around her. Surrounded by open pink mouths and questing fingers, she was overwhelmed. Struggling to escape, she lunged forward, and found herself briefly dangling over the branch.

And she looked down on strangeness.

Two indricotheres were lurking under the tree. These great creatures were a kind of hornless rhino. Looking like meaty giraffes, they had long legs, supple necks, and hides like those of elephants. They were oddly graceful in a slow-moving way, even if they did mass as much as three times as an African elephant—and so huge they were unused to being threatened by anything. Even now they reached up their thick necks and horselike faces to crop at the tree's soaking foliage.

But they were in danger. Muddy water flowed over the ground, washing around the indricotheres' legs, as if the tree and the indricotheres alike stood in the river itself.

At last a great sheet of muddy soil broke away from the riverbank, right next to the tree's shallow roots, and slid without ceremony into the river. One mighty indricothere lowed, its great flat elephantine feet scrabbling at a ground suddenly turned into a slippery, treacherous slope—and then it fell, fifteen tons of meat flying, its neck twisting and long tail working. It hit the water with a tremendous splash, and in an instant it was gone, swept away into the voracious river.

The second indricothere lowed its loss. But it too was in peril as the ground continued to dissolve under the water's relentless probing, and the bereft animal lumbered backward to safety.

But the tree itself was in trouble. Its roots had been exposed by the sudden erosion of the flash flood, and further undermined by the river's assault on its bank. The trunk creaked once, and shuddered.

And then, with a series of explosive cracks, the roots gave way. The tree began to topple toward the water. Like fruit from a shaken branch, primates of all sizes tumbled out of the tree and fell screaming into the turbulent water.

Roamer howled and clung to her branch as the tree tipped nightmarishly, all the way into the river.

The first few minutes were the worst.

Close to the riverbank the water was at its most turbulent, torn between the fast-flowing current and friction with the land. In this mighty torrent even the great mango tree was like a twig tossed in a brook. It bucked and creaked and twisted. First its foliage slammed into the water, then its roots, clogged with mud and rocks, would claw toward the sky. Roamer was rolled and dunked, plunged into cloudy brown water that forced its way into her mouth and nose, then carried into the air again.

At last the tree slid away from the turbulence near the bank and drifted into the center of the river, where its rocking and twisting quickly damped out.

Roamer found herself stuck underwater. She looked up through muddy murk at a glimmering surface littered with leaves and twigs. Already her mouth and throat were filling up, and panic overwhelmed her. With a bubbling scream she scrambled up through the tangled, broken foliage, clambering toward the light.

She broke through the surface. Light, noise, and the battering rain assaulted her senses. She hauled herself out of the water and lay flat on a branch.

The tree was floating branches first down the river. Its tangled, ripped roots reached up toward the lowering, lightning-strewn sky. Roamer raised her head, peering around for other anthros. It was not easy to recognize them through the thick rain-filled air, so battered and sodden were they, but she made out Whiteblood, the burly male who had abducted her, a couple of other males—and a female with an infant that had somehow hung onto her back, a little bundle of soaked, miserable fur.

Even though she was just as battered and half drowned as before,

Roamer felt suddenly better. If she had been left alone it would have been the most unbearable thing of all; the presence of others was comforting. But still, these others were not her family, not her troop.

More displaced vegetation coursed over the surface of the river, clustering along its spine where the water ran deepest. There were more trees and bushes, some of them washed by this precursor of the Congo thousands of kilometers downstream from the very different lands in the center of the continent. There were animals here too. Some of them clung to the floating foliage, like the anthros. She saw the flitting, nervous forms of a couple of crowders, and even a potbelly, sitting squat on the trunk of a walnut. The potbelly, a female, had found a stable place to sit, and the rain didn't bother her. She had already resumed her usual habit of feeding on leaves conveniently delivered to her clutching hands and feet.

But not all the animals in this gruesome assemblage had made it here alive. There was a whole family of fat, piglike anthracotheres, all of them drowned, stuck in the branches of a broken palm like meaty fruit. And the huge indricothere that had been washed into the river just before the fall of the mango was here too, a great carcass drifting in the water, long neck lolling back and powerful legs splayed, just another bit of floating detritus jammed in with the rest.

Gradually, as the river broadened, the subtle currents shoved these fragments together, foliage and roots tangling, and a makeshift raft assembled itself. The animals stared at one another, and at the churning river, as their crude vessel drifted on.

Roamer could see the forest, growing thick and green on shallow riverbank slopes of eroded sandstone. The trees were mangos, palms, a kind of primitive banana. Branches hung low over the water, and lianas and vines looped over the tangled terraces. Her arms ached for a branch to swing from, a way she could climb from here to there. But the forest was separated from her by churning water—and as the vegetable raft continued to sail downstream, those tempting banks receded further, and the familiar forest gave way to the mangroves that dominated the coastal areas.

The rain wasn't done yet. It actually fell harder. Fat droplets hurled themselves out of the leaden sky. The water was stippled with craters that disappeared as soon as they were formed. A white-noise harshness flooded her ears, so that it was as if she were lost in a kind of huge bubble of water, water below and around her, with only this broken mango to cling to. Moaning, chilled to the bone, Roamer burrowed into the branches of the mango and huddled, alone, waiting for everything to go away, and for her to be returned to the world she knew, of trees and fruit and anthros.

That, however, was never going to happen.

The storm, heavy as it was, blew itself out quickly. Roamer saw finger-thin shafts of light pushing into her shelter of foliage. The rain noise had gone, to be replaced by the eerily soft lapping of water.

She struggled out of the branches and clambered on top of the tree. The sun was strong, as if the air had been cleared, and she felt its warmth sink deep into her fur, drying it quickly. For a heartbeat she luxuriated in the warmth and dryness.

But there was no forest here: only this fallen tree and its cluster of broken companions, drifting over a gray-brown sheet of water. There weren't even any riverbanks. On three sides of the tree, all she could see was water, all the way to a knife-sharp horizon. But when she looked back the way the raft had drifted, she spotted land: a line of crowded green and brown, striped over the eastern horizon.

A line that was receding.

The raft of debris had been washed out to sea, out into the widening Atlantic, anthros, potbelly, crowders, and all.

II

After the days of Noth the geometry of the restless world had continued to evolve, and it continued to shape the destinies of the hapless creatures who rode the continental rafts.

The two great cracks that had doomed ancient Pangaea—the east-west Tethys Sea, and the north-south Atlantic Ocean—closed and opened respectively. Africa was undergoing a slow collision with Europe. Meanwhile India was drifting north to crash into Asia, and the Himalayan Mountains were being thrust into the air. But immediately after the young mountains were born, the rain and the glaciers had begun their work, gouging and eroding, washing the mountains back to the sea: On this turbulent planet, rock flowed like water, and mountain ranges rose and fell like dreams. But as the continents closed, the Edenic flow of the Tethys was doomed, though fragments of the shrinking ocean would survive as the Black, Caspian, and Aral Seas, and in the west as the Mediterranean.

As the Tethys died there was a great drying, right across the belly of the world. Once there had been mangrove forests in the Sahara. Now a great belt of semiarid scrub spread around the old track of the Tethys, across North America, southern Eurasia, and northern Africa.

Meanwhile, the huge land bridge that had closed off the northern Atlantic, spanning from North America to northern Europe via Greenland and Britain, was being severed, and the Atlantic reached up to the Arctic Ocean. As the ancient east-west ocean passage was being closed, so a new channel from south to north was opening.

Thus ocean currents were reshaped.

The oceans were great reservoirs of energy, restless, unstable, mobile. And all the oceans were laced with currents, great invisible Niles that dwarfed any river on land. The currents were driven by the sun's heat and the Earth's rotation; the top few meters of the oceans stored as much energy as the whole of the atmosphere.

Now the huge equatorial currents that had once rolled around the Tethys belt were disrupted. But already the great flows that would dominate the widening Atlantic were in place: A precursor of the Gulf Stream flowed, a mighty river sixty kilometers across, running south to north with the force of three hundred Amazons.

But this change in circulation patterns would reconstruct the planet's climate. For while equatorial currents promoted warming, north-south interpolar currents provoked a vast refrigeration.

To make matters worse, Antarctica had settled over the Earth's southern pole. Now its great ice cap had begun to gather, for the first time in two hundred million years. Vast, cold circumpolar ocean currents gathered in the southern seas, feeding the great northward currents of the Atlantic.

It was a crucial change: the start of a mighty planetary cooling, a downturn of the graph, that would persist to human times and well beyond.

All over the planet, the old climate belts shrank toward the equator. Tropical vegetation types survived only in the equatorial latitudes. In the north, a new kind of ecology appeared, a temperate woodland of mixed conifers and deciduous trees. Vast swaths of it covered the northern lands, stretching across North America, Europe, and Asia from the tropic to the Arctic.

This climatic collapse triggered a new dying—what paleobiologists would later call the Great Cut. It was a drawn-out, multiple event. In the ocean the plankton population crashed repeatedly. Many species of gastropods and bivalves disappeared.

And on the land, after thirty million years of comfortable success, the mammals suffered their first mass extinction ever. Mammalian history was cut in half. The exotic assemblages of Noth's times finally succumbed. But new, larger herbivores began to evolve, with heavy-duty ridged teeth able to cope with the new, coarser vegetation typical of seasonal woodland. By Roamer's time the first proboscideans, properly equipped with trunks and tusks, were already walking the African plains. The trunk, unparalleled for muscular flexibility save for an octopus's arm, was used for stuffing the animal's mouth with the vast quantity of food it needed. These deinotheres had stubby trunks, and odd, downward-curving tusks that they used for stripping the bark from trees. But, unlike their moeritherium ancestors, they *looked* like elephants, and some already grew as tall as the African elephants of later times.

And this was a time of success for the horses. The descendants of the timid creatures of Noth's forest world had diversified into many woodland browser types—some of them as large as gazelles, but with tougher teeth than their ancestors had had to take leaves rather than soft fruit—along with longer-legged plains animals slowly adapting to a diet of grass. Most of the horses now had three toes on both their front and back feet, but some plains-living runners were starting to lose their side toes, and were putting all their weight on their central toes. But as the forests shrank this diversity was already falling; soon many of the forest species would disappear. The rodents, too, were diversifying, with the appearance of the first gophers, beavers, dormice and hamsters, a great diversity of squirrels—and the first rats.

But the new conditions were not kind to the primates. Their natural habitat, the tropical forests, had shriveled back to the southern tropics. Many of the primate families had gone extinct. Fruit eaters like Roamer lingered only in the tropical woodlands of Africa and southern Asia, clinging to the year-long food supply these forests still provided. By the time Roamer was born there were no primates left north of the tropics, and—since the rise of the rodents—none in the Americas at all: not a single species.

But that was soon to change.

The sea around Roamer was a sheet of gunmetal gray across which waves rippled, languid as mercury. Roamer was in an utterly baffling place: a sketchy, elemental two-dimensional environment, static yet full of mysterious churning motion, that could not have been more different from the forest.

She felt nervous climbing around on top of the vegetation. She expected some ferocious aerial predator to bite into her skull at any moment. And as she moved she could feel the uneasy raft shift under her, its loosely tangled components rustling with the slow breathing of the sea. It felt as if the whole thing might disintegrate at any moment.

There were just six anthros: three males, two females—including Roamer—and the infant who still clung sleepily to the fur of its mother. These were the only survivors of Whiteblood's troop.

The anthros sat on a tangle of branches, eyeing one another. It was time to form provisional hierarchies.

For the two females the priorities were clear enough.

The other female, the mother, was a burly individual more than a decade old. This child was her fourth and—though she could not know it—now her only surviving offspring. Her most noticeable characteristic was a fur-free patch of scar tissue on one shoulder where she had once been burned in a forest fire. The infant, clinging to Patch's chest, was tiny, small even for its age, just a scrap of fur. Patch, the mother, studied Roamer dismissively. Roamer was small, young, and a stranger, not even remote kin. And, as a nursing mother, Patch would always have priority. So she turned her broad back on Roamer and began to stroke her infant, Scrap.

Roamer knew what she had to do. She scuttled over the branches to Patch, and dug her fingers into fur that was still moist and began to comb out tangles and bits of debris. When she probed at Patch's skin, she found knots of muscle, and places which made Patch wince to be touched.

As Roamer's strong fingers worked, Patch relaxed slowly. Patch, like all of them, had been battered by her precipitate removal from the forest, and was stressed by her sudden dumping into this extraordinary emptiness and the loss of her family. It was as if she could, for a moment, under the magic of the other's touch, forget where she was. Even the infant, Scrap, seemed soothed by the contact between the two females.

Roamer herself was calmed by the simple, repetitive actions of the grooming, and by the subtle social bond she was building up with Patch.

The males' negotiations were more dramatic.

Whiteblood found himself facing two younger males, brothers, in fact. One had a peculiar crest of snow-white hair that stuck up around his eyes, making him look permanently surprised, and the other had a habit of using his left arm predominantly over his right, so much so that the muscles on his left side were much more heavily developed than those on the right, like those of a left-handed tennis player.

Both Crest and Left were smaller and weaker than Whiteblood, and, younger, they had not outranked him back in the forest. But now Whiteblood had lost all of his allies, and together these two might defeat him.

So, without hesitation, he launched into a display. He stood upright, shakily, hooted and shrieked, and threw handfuls of leaves. Then he turned around, spread his backside and blew shit through moist fur.

Left was immediately intimidated. He shrank back, arms folded around himself.

Crest was more defiant, and answered Whiteblood's display with a shrieking tantrum of his own. But he was outsized by Whiteblood and, without the support of his brother, could not hope to best the older male. When Whiteblood began to cuff him about the head and neck, Crest quickly backed down, tumbling onto his back and spreading his arms and legs like an infant, showing his submission. All of this was halted only when an incautious stamp plunged Whiteblood's leg through the foliage and into the cold water. He yelped, pulled back his leg, and sat with legs folded beneath him, subdued.

But he had done enough. The brothers approached him now, their heads bent and postures humble. A brief interval of frantic mutual grooming ensured the new hierarchy was reinforced, and the three males started to pick bits of shit out of each other's fur.

The rough-and-ready communities of Noth had been like street gangs, held together by not much more than brute force and dominance, with each individual aware of little more than her own place in the pecking order. But by now the advantages of social living had driven primate societies to baroque intricacy, and had spurred the development of new types of mind.

Group living required a lot of social knowledge: knowing who was doing what to whom, how your own actions fit in with this, who you had to groom and when, to make your life easier. The larger the group, the greater the number of relationships you had to keep track of, and as those relationships changed constantly, you needed still more computational capacity to handle it all. By allowing their group living to develop to such extremes of complexity, primates continued to get relentlessly smarter.

Not all primates, though.

Through all this the big potbelly had sat on the comfortable branch she had found, methodically stripping it of leaves. She had no interest in the peculiar displays and hairy fiddling of the anthros.

Even among her own kind the potbelly knew little of the society of others. She ignored other females and let herself be bothered by males only when she felt the urge to mate—which, in fact, was on her now. When they were in season anthros like Patch and Roamer showed sexual swellings on their rumps. That would have been of little use to a creature who spent most of her time sitting on her backside, so on the potbelly's chest pinkish blisters had swollen brightly in an unmistakable hourglass shape. But as there was no male potbelly around, nobody was doing anything about it.

Not that the potbelly cared much. She didn't understand where she was and what had become of her any more than the anthros did, but it didn't trouble her. She could see there were plenty of leaves on this fallen tree to last her through the day. She had no real idea that there could be such a thing as a tomorrow different from today, that it might not find her in an endless forest full of nutritious leaves.

Already the anthros were starting to feel hungry; their low-nutrition diet worked through their systems quickly. They broke up their grooming circles and spread out over the branches of the fallen mango. The tree had lost much of its fruit, along with most of its inhabitants, when it fell from the bank. But Crest, one of the brothers, quickly turned up a cluster of fruit that had gotten lodged in an angle of branch and trunk. He hooted to summon the others.

The new miniature society worked efficiently. Though Crest managed to grab one piece of fruit for himself, he was quickly pushed away by Whiteblood. But Whiteblood was in turn usurped by Patch. Though she was not much more than two-thirds of Whiteblood's size, the infant clinging to her chest was like a badge of authority. Whiteblood took one fruit and, grumbling, moved back, giving way to Patch.

While this was going on Roamer, like the brothers, knew that she would get no nearer to the fruit until the dominant ones had taken what they wanted.

Alone, she walked carefully, all four limbs grasping, toward the edge of the raft, where the tangle of branches was a little looser. The two terrified crowders, huddled together, skittered away as she approached. Through the foliage she could see murky brown water, littered with bits of wood and leaf, rippling languidly. The sun glimmered in a hundred places, shining through gaps in the cover of the fallen tree, and the dancing light was entrancing, distracting.

Roamer was hungry, but she was also thirsty. She dipped her hand cautiously into the water—it was cool—and scooped up a mouthful. The water was mildly salty—not bitterly so, for even so far from land the river's powerful outflow diluted the ocean's brine. But as she drank the taste of salt began to build up in her mouth, and she spat out her last mouthful.

Hungry, bored, the brothers came to inspect her as she drank, head bent down into the foliage, arm outstretched, buttocks raised. They sniffed her curiously, but they could smell how young she was, too young to mate.

When the older ones were done, Roamer and the others fell on the fruit.

With their bellies full for now, the anthros were calming down. But already the haphazard raft had drifted out of sight of the land, already the anthros had eaten much of the fruit from the drowned mango tree. And already the potbelly, complacently munching, had stripped half the branches of their leaves.

And none of them had seen the pale gray triangle that slid silently through the water, not meters away.

The shark circled the crude, disintegrating raft. Alerted by the feeding frenzy as the drowned inhabitants of the riverbank forest were washed out to the waiting mouths of the ocean, the shark had been attracted by the scent of stale blood that leaked from the indricothere carcass. But now it sensed motion on the tangled foliage that floated overhead. It circled, calculating, patient.

The shark was not as intelligent as its parallels on land. But then it was not much like an animal at all. The bones of its back were not bone, but tough cartilage that gave the shark better flexibility than more advanced fish. Its jaw was cartilage too, in which were loosely attached teeth, serrated like steak knives, perfect for shearing flesh. Its projecting snout looked crude, but it cut through the water with the precision of a submarine's engineering, and it was equipped with nostrils that could detect minute traces of blood. Beneath the snout was a special organ with extraordinary sensitivity to vibration, enabling it to sense the struggles of a frightened animal across immense distances. Behind its small head, the shark's entire body was made of muscle, designed for power, for forward drive. It was like a battering ram.

Sharks had already been the ocean's top predators for three hundred million years. They had endured through the great extinctions, while families of land predators had come and gone. They had seen off competition from new classes of animals, some much younger, like the true fish. Over that vast period of time, the sharks' body design had barely modified, for there was no need.

The shark was relentless, unable to be deflected by guile, prepared to keep on attacking as long as its senses were appropriately stimulated. It was a machine designed for killing.

The shark could sense the great mass of dead meat drifting at the heart of this raft, but it could also hear the scurrying of live animals on its surface. The dead thing could wait.

Time to attack. It went in headfirst, its jaws open. The shark had no eyelids. But to protect its eyes, it rolled them back, so that they turned white, in the last instant before it struck.

Patch was the first to see the approaching fin, to glimpse the white torpedo body gliding through the water toward the raft, to look into the white eyes. She had never seen such a thing before, but her instincts yelled that this sleek form spelled trouble. She ran over the loose foliage to the raft's far side.

The other anthros were panicking. The two crowders were squalling like tiny birds, running and leaping this way and that. Only the potbelly sat placidly on its branch, munching another handful of leaves.

Scrap, separated from her mother, didn't react.

Patch was terrified. She had expected her infant to follow her to the far side of the raft. But the infant hadn't seen the approaching peril. A human mother would have been able to visualize her child's point of view, understand that the child might not be able to see everything she saw. That transference of understanding was beyond Patch; in that respect, just like Noth, she was like a very young human child herself, imagining that every creature in the world saw what she saw, had the same beliefs she did.

The shark rammed its blunt nose up through the loose foliage. To Roamer this eruption of a gaping mouth from under the world was a nightmarish vision. She hooted and ran helplessly, unable to escape the raft's confines.

The infant was lucky. As the raft shuddered under the shark's assault she lodged in an angle of branch and trunk. Her mother lurched across the spinning raft, leaping over the gaping hole the shark had ripped, and snatched up the child.

But the shark came again. This time it drove its wedge-shaped nose between two of the great trunks that formed the raft's crude structure. The trunks separated, a great lane of leaf-strewn water opening up between them. One of the crowders fell, squeaking, into the widening gap.

The shark's mouth was like a cavern opening up before it. The crowder's pinprick mind was snuffed out in a second. The shark was barely aware of taking the tiny warm morsel. Its work was barely begun.

The anthros screamed and ran to the edge of the raft, getting as far from the rift as they could—but they cowered back from the desolate ocean beyond.

Whiteblood saw that the fat, complacent potbelly sat where she had always sat, on her leafy branch, that ridiculous red swelling blazoned across her chest—even though the shark's vandalism had opened up the ocean right before her. In this instant of ultimate stress, new circuits closed in Whiteblood's inventive mind. It was a chain of logic beyond all but the brightest of his kind. But then, on average, every generation of anthros was just a little brighter than the last.

Whiteblood took a flying leap. Both his feet rammed into the potbelly's back. She was pitched precipitately into the sea.

This fat struggling creature was what the shark had been waiting for. It bit into its prey, in the middle of its torso. The shark's whole body flexed as it shook the potbelly, and its jagged-edged teeth tore a lump out of the hapless creature. Then, closing through a cloud of diffusing blood, it waited for its victim to bleed to death.

The potbelly was utterly bewildered, suddenly immersed in water, overwhelmed by stunning pain. But her brain flooded with chemicals, and the centers of her functional mind closed down, granting her a sort of peace in this bloody darkness.

Whiteblood sat panting over the scene of his assault, where nothing remained of the potbelly but a pile of thin, ill-smelling shit, and handfuls of crushed leaves. Gradually the gap in the raft closed, as if it were healing itself. The anthros cowered, too stressed even to groom.

And the sun climbed down into the western sky, in the direction they helplessly sailed.

III

Days and nights, nights and days. There was no noise save the creaking of the branches, the soft lapping of the wavelets.

The nights revealed a crushing sky from which Roamer wanted to cower.

But the light of day, under the glaring sun or gray lids of cloud, showed nothing but the elemental sea. There was no forest, no land, no hills. She could smell nothing but salt, and her ears brought her no calls of birds or primates, no herbivorous lowing. The river's outflow had dispersed now into the greater ocean, and even the other fragments of debris washed down by that torrential storm had dispersed, sailing over the horizon to their own mindless destinies.

The raft itself was diminished.

The anthracothere corpses stuck in the branches of the mango tree had long since slithered away. The last crowder had gone too. Perhaps it had fallen into the sea. The great indricothere had swollen as the bacteria of its huge gut ate their way out toward the light. But the invisible mouths of the sea had been at work on the indricothere, eating into it from beneath. As its meat was steadily stripped away, the huge corpse had imploded, at last sliding beneath the sea.

The anthros had long since eaten all the fruit.

They tried to eat the tree's leaves, and at first they would be rewarded at least by a mouthful of pleasing moisture that would, for a few heartbeats, ease their thirst. But the tree, uprooted, was dead, and its remaining leaves were shriveling. And, unlike the wretched potbelly, the anthros could not digest such coarse fare, and they lost still more fluid in the watery shit that erupted from their backsides.

Roamer was a small animal built for a life in the nourishing embrace of the forest, where food and water were always plentiful. Unlike a human, whose body was adapted to survive long periods in the open, her body carried very little fat, a human's main fuel reserve. Things got bad quickly. Soon Roamer's saliva became thick and tasted foul. Her tongue clung to the roof of her mouth. Her head and neck were very painful, for her skin was shrinking as it dried. Her voice was cracked, and she seemed to have a hard, painful lump in her throat that wouldn't dislodge no matter how many times she tried to swallow. She and the other anthros would have suffered even more, in fact, if not for the overcast skies that mostly spared them from the glare of the sun.

Sometimes Roamer dreamed. The dead mango would suddenly sprout, its roots reaching out like primate fingers to bury themselves in the unforgiving ocean-soil, the leaves would grow green and wave like grooming hands, and fruit would bloom, huge clusters of it. She would reach for the fruit, even crack it and bury her face in the clear water that mysteriously filled each husk. And here would come her mother and her sisters, fat and full of vigor, ready to groom her.

But then the water would evaporate, as if drying in the harsh sun, and she would find she was gnawing nothing more than a bit of bark or a handful of dead leaves.

Patch came into estrus.

Whiteblood, as the top male of this little lost community, was quick to claim his rights. With nothing else to do and nowhere to go, Whiteblood and Patch coupled frequently—sometimes too often, and the bout would be a perfunctory matter of a few dry thrusts.

In normal times subordinates like the brothers would probably have been able to mate Patch in these early days of her estrus. Whiteblood, with plenty of potential mates to choose from, would have excluded them only when Patch's peak of fertility approached and the best chance of impregnating her arrived.

This would have been in Patch's interests too. Her swelling was there to advertise Patch's fertility to as many males as possible. For one thing, the resulting competition kept the quality of her suitors high without requiring any effort from her. And if all the males in the group mated with her at some time, none of them could be sure who exactly was the father of an infant—so any male tempted to murder an infant to speed up a female's fertility cycle ran the risk of killing his own offspring. The swellings, her very public estrus, were thus a way for Patch to control the males around her at minimal cost to herself, and to reduce the risk of infanticide.

But on this tiny raft there was only one adult female, and Whiteblood wasn't about to share. Crest and Left looked on, sitting side by side, chewing on leaves, their comical erections sticking out of their fur. They could stare all they liked at Patch's refulgent swelling. But every time either of them approached Patch, let alone touched her for the most tentative grooming, Whiteblood would fly into a fury, displaying and attacking the perpetrator.

As for Roamer, she would always be subordinate to Patch, always a stranger. But in these stripped-down conditions she had quickly grown as close to Patch as to one of her own sisters.

While Whiteblood and Patch were coupling, Roamer would often take Scrap. After the first few days Scrap had accepted Roamer as an honorary aunt. The infant's tiny face was bald and her fur was olive-colored, quite different from her mother's; it was a color that triggered protective feelings in Roamer, and even in the males. Sometimes Scrap would play alone, clambering clumsily over the matted branches, but more often she wanted to cling to Roamer's chest or back, or to be held in Roamer's arms.

Sharing the load of child rearing was common among anthros— although it was usually only kin who would be allowed to serve as child minders.

Anthro infants grew much more slowly than had the pups of Noth's era because of the time it took their larger brains to develop. Though they were well developed at birth compared to human infants, with open eyes and the ability to cling to their mothers' fur, anthro pups were uncoordinated, weak, and utterly dependent on their mothers for food. It was as if Scrap had been born prematurely and was completing her growth outside her mother's womb.

This put a lot of pressure on Patch. For eighteen months an anthro mother had to juggle the daily demands of survival with the need to care for her infant—*and* she had to keep up grooming time with her sisters, peers, and potential mates. Even before her stranding on this raft, all these pressures had left Patch exhausted. But the society of females around her provided her with a ready supply of would-be aunts and nannies to take the infant away and give her a break. Roamer's amateur aunting was helpful to Patch, and besides it gave Roamer a lot of pleasure. It was a kind of training for her own future as a mother. But also it let her indulge in a lot of grooming.

They all missed grooming. It was the most difficult thing about this oceanic imprisonment. Even now Whiteblood was showing signs of over-grooming by his two acolytes; parts of his head and neck had been rubbed raw. So Roamer was happy to indulge the infant with long hours of gentle fur pulling, finger combing, and tickling.

But as the days went by the infant, perpetually hungry and thirsty, became increasingly unhappy. Scrap would wander around the raft, and even pester the males. Sometimes she would throw tantrums, tearing at the leaves or her mother's fur or racing precariously around the raft in her tiny fury.

All of which served to wear out Patch further, and irritate everybody else.

So it went, day after long day. The anthros, trapped together on this sliver of dryness in an immense ocean, were continually, intensely aware of one another. If there had been more space, they could have gotten away from the infant's annoying scampering. If there had been more of them, the younger males' jealousy of Whiteblood would not have mattered; they could have easily found more receptive females, and relieved their tension with furtive matings out of Whiteblood's sight.

But there was no larger group to soak up their tensions, no forest into which to escape—and no food but dry leaves, no water but the ocean's brine.

One featureless day it all came to a head.

Scrap threw yet another tantrum. She hurled herself around the raft, coming perilously close to the patiently waiting ocean, ripping at leaves and bark, making throaty cries. She had grown skinny, the flesh hanging off her tiny belly, her fur bedraggled.

This time, the males did not slap her away. Instead they watched her, all three of them, with a kind of calculation.

At last Patch retrieved Scrap. She clutched the infant to her chest and let her suckle, though there was no milk to be had.

Whiteblood moved toward Patch. Generally he approached her alone—but this time the bigger of the brothers, Crest, followed him, the spray of fur over his eyes gleaming in the harsh sun. With Whiteblood sitting alongside him, Crest began to groom Patch. Gradually his fingers worked their way toward her belly and genitals. It was a clear precursor to an attempt at mating.

Patch looked startled and pulled away, Scrap clinging to her belly. But Whiteblood stroked her back, soothing her, until she settled and let Crest approach her again. Though Crest continually cast nervous glances at him, Whiteblood did not intervene.

Slumped against the crook of a branch, Roamer stared at the males, baffled by their behavior in a way Noth could never have been. As the minds of the primates became steadily more elaborate, it was as if a sense of self was diffusing outward, from the solitary Purga to her increasingly social descendants. All this enabled the anthros to develop new, complex, subtle alliances and hierarchies—and to practice new deceptions. Noth had had a firm understanding of his own place in the hierarchies and alliances of his society. The anthros could go one step beyond this: Roamer understood her own rank as junior to Patch, but she also understood the relative ranking of others. She knew that a senior like Whiteblood should not be allowing Crest to behave like this, as if encouraging him to mate with "his" female.

At last Crest moved behind Patch and placed his hands on her hips. Patch gave in to the inevitable. Presenting her pink rump to Crest, she pulled the sleepy pup from her chest and held her out to Roamer.

But Whiteblood leapt forward. With the precision of the tree-dwelling primate he was, Whiteblood grabbed the infant from Patch's hands. Then he scampered over to Left, carrying the infant by her scruff, quickly followed by a nervous Crest.

Patch seemed baffled by what had happened. She stared at Whiteblood, her rump still raised to her vanished suitor.

The males had formed a tight huddle, their furry backs making a wall. Roamer saw how Whiteblood cradled Scrap, almost as if nursing her. The infant kicked her tiny legs and gurgled, gazing up at Whiteblood. Then Whiteblood put his hand over her scalp.

Suddenly Patch understood. She howled and hurled herself forward.

But the brothers turned to meet her. Both of these immature males outsized Patch. Though they were nervous about showing hostility to a senior female, they easily kept her at bay with slaps and hoots.

Whiteblood closed his hand. Roamer heard the crunch of bone—a sound like a potbelly biting into a crisp leaf. The infant kicked convulsively, and then was limp. Whiteblood looked down on the little body for a heartbeat, his expression complex as he stared at the olive-colored face, now twisted in final pain. And then the males fell on the tiny body. A bite at the neck and the head was soon severed; Whiteblood pulled the limbs this way and that until cartilage snapped and bones cracked. But it was not meat the males wanted most but blood, the blood that poured from the child's severed neck. They drank greedily of the warm liquid, until their mouths and teeth were stained bright red.

Patch howled, displayed, rampaged around the raft tearing at branches and dying leaves, and beat at the males' stolid backs. The raft shuddered and rocked, and Roamer clung to her branch nervously. But it made no difference.

Whiteblood had not lied, not really. Like Noth before him, he was unable to imagine what others were thinking, and therefore couldn't plant false beliefs in their heads—not quite. But anthros were very smart socially, and they had a good problem-solving faculty when facing new challenges. Whiteblood, a kind of genius, had managed to put these facets of his intelligence together to come up with the ploy that had succeeded in stealing Scrap from her mother.

With a final hoarse cry, Patch threw herself against the mango trunk and pulled broken foliage around her in a kind of nest. And still the males fed, to the sound of slurping tongues and bones crunching between teeth.

Her head full of the stink of blood, Roamer made her way to the edge of the raft, where dead branches trailed in the water like fingers.

The murky ocean water was like a thin soup, full of life. The upper sunlit layers were thick with a rich algal plankton, a crowded microscopic ecology. The plankton was like a forest in the ocean, but a forest stripped of the superstructure of leaves, twigs, branches, and trunks, leaving only the tiny green chlorophyll-bearing cells of the forest canopy floating in their nutrient-rich bath. Though the ecological structure of the plankton had remained unchanged for half a billion years, the species within it had come and gone, falling prey to variation and extinction like any other; just as on land this ocean-spanning domain was like a long-running play whose actors changed repeatedly.

A jellyfish wafted by. A plankton-grazer itself, it was a translucent sac, pulsing with a slow, languid dilation and contraction. It was strewn with silvery fronds, tentacles that contained the stinging cells with which it would paralyze its planktonic food.

Compared to most animals the jellyfish was a crude creature. It had a simple radial symmetry, and lacked substance and tissue organization. It didn't even have blood. But its form was very ancient. Once the ocean had been full of creatures more or less like the jellyfish. They had anchored themselves to the seafloor, turning the ocean into a forest of stinging tentacles. They did not need to be more active; they were untroubled by predators or grazers, as there had not been enough oxygen in the environment to fuel such dangerous monsters.

Roamer was baffled by the sea. To her water was something that came in ponds and rivers and cupped leaves, a fresh, salt-free stuff that you drank whenever you were safe enough to do so. Nothing in her experience or her innate neural programming had prepared her for suspension over a great inverted sky through which drifted such bizarre creatures as the jellyfish.

And she was thirsty, terribly thirsty. Her hand reached down, dipped into that murky soup, and lifted a palmful of water to her mouth. She had forgotten that she had done this not an hour ago, forgotten the bitterness of the brine.

The males had done feeding, she saw. They had fallen into a kind of stupor in the day's continuing heat. Of Patch, all that could be seen was a single foot, toes curled, that protruded from her lonely nest.

Cautiously, Roamer made her way to the place where the infant had been slaughtered. Blood stained the branches, smeared by the licking of anthro tongues. Roamer picked through the leaves carefully. She found nothing of the infant save a scattering of thin fur—and one perfect little hand, severed at the wrist. She grabbed the hand and retreated to a corner of the raft, as far from the others as she could get.

The hand was limp, relaxed, as if it belonged to a sleeping infant. Briefly Roamer ran it over her chest and remembered how Scrap would pull at her fur.

But Scrap was gone.

Roamer bit into the flesh of the forefinger, close to the knuckle. The meat was soft, irritating her dry palate. With a fast, jerking pull she stripped the flesh off the bone. She repeated that with the other fingers, then munched on the bare flesh of the palm. When the hand had been reduced to little more than skeletal, with a few scraps of cartilage and flesh still hanging off it, she bit through the tiny clattering bones, but there was only a dribble of marrow.

She dumped the bone fragments into the endless ocean. She glimpsed tiny silvery fish quickly clustering, before the bones sank out of sight into the greater deep.

Patch stayed in her nest of leaves for two days, barely moving. The males lay immobile in an untidy heap, occasionally picking at each other's increasingly sparse fur.

Roamer moved listlessly around the tree, seeking relief. Her mouth no longer generated saliva. Her tongue had hardened into a lump without sensation or mobility, like a stone in her mouth. She couldn't cry out or call; all she could make was a formless groaning. She even found herself picking at the dried shit left behind by the potbelly, seeking moisture, maybe a few nut kernels embedded in the waste. But the leaf eater's dung was thin and dry. She sank into misery, exhausted, drifting between sleep and wakefulness.

On the third day after Scrap's death, Patch stirred. Roamer watched listlessly.

Patch scrambled up to all fours. Dizzy, her fluid balance ruined by her long inactivity, she stumbled—and Roamer saw her grab at her belly. She was pregnant by Whiteblood, a pregnancy that was draining still more reserves from her depleted body. But she raised herself up and, doggedly, approached the males.

Crest sat upright as Patch approached, nervous, as if expecting an attack. Roamer could see his blackened tongue protruding from his mouth. His facial fur was still stained brown by Scrap's blood.

But Patch settled beside him and began running her fingers through his fur. The grooming was only a partial success. All their bodies had lost fur, and their skin was broken by ulcers and lesions that would not heal; as she worked she broke open scabs and probed at bruises. But he submitted, welcoming the attention despite the pain.

And then she moved away a little, turned her back, and presented her rump to him. She was hardly looking her best. Her fur was ragged, her skin broken, and her swelling had all but vanished, days earlier than it should have. But still, as she pressed her rump into his chest, Crest responded; a spindly erection soon poked out from his matted belly fur.

Now, at last, Whiteblood took notice of this violation of the hierarchy. This was not like his own deception; this was not acceptable. He lurched upright, uttering an incoherent roar around his ruined tongue. Crest backed away.

But Patch immediately attacked Whiteblood, ramming her head into his chest and beating him about the temples with her fists. He fell back, startled. Patch hurried back to the other males and made perfunctory presentations of her rump to them, uttering rasping hoots. And then she threw herself back on Whiteblood.

Subtly, alliances shifted, dominance dissolved. Without even looking at each other the brothers came to a quick decision. They joined in Patch's attack on Whiteblood. Whiteblood began to fight back, snapping and warding off the blows that rained down on him.

It was a grotesque battle, waged by four badly depleted creatures. The blows and kicks were soft and delivered in an eerie slow motion. And it was waged in a silence broken only by gasps of weariness or pain: There was none of the screeching and hooting that would normally have accompanied an attack by two juniors on a dominant male.

And yet it was deadly. For, under Patch's leadership, the brothers herded Whiteblood step by step toward the lip of the raft.

It was Patch who delivered the final blow: another ram to Whiteblood's belly, made with a hoarse, wrenching roar. Whiteblood toppled backward and fell through the raft's loose fringe of branches and into the water. He bobbed, splashed, and spluttered, his fur immediately becoming soaked and impeding his movements. He looked back at the raft, mewling like an infant around his blackened tongue.

Crest and Left were confused. They had not meant to kill Whiteblood; few dominance battles among the anthros ended lethally.

Roamer felt an odd pang of regret. There had been few enough of them already. Her instincts warned her that too small a pool of potential mates was a bad thing. But it was too late for that.

Whiteblood weakened rapidly. Soon the effort of keeping his mouth and nostrils above the water proved too much for him, and his struggling stopped. The shark, attracted by the blood that leaked from Whiteblood's stale wounds, took his body in a single bite.

After that, the suffering got worse. As the softly creaking raft drifted over the great unforgiving shield of the ocean, as these small creatures rapidly depleted their reserves, it could only get worse.

Roamer's limbs had swollen. The stretched skin ached continually and cracked easily. Her tongue squeezed past her jaws, as if her mouth were crammed with a great lump of dry dung. Her eyelids had cracked, and it felt as if she were weeping, but when she touched her fur she found blood leaking from her eyeballs.

She was undergoing a living mummification.

At last, one morning, she heard a cry, high and feeble, like a bird's.

She pushed away her covering of leaves and sat upright. The world turned yellow, and there was an odd ringing in her ears. It was hard to see anything; her vision was a blur, and when she tried to blink her eyes she got no relief, for her body could spare no moisture.

Still, she made out two anthros—Patch, Crest—sitting side by side over a dark, huddled form. Perhaps it was food. Painfully she pushed her way forward to join them.

It was Left, lying flat, his limbs splayed.

The sucking heat of the sun had done its work well. There was barely any of his white fur left on his head or neck. His flesh had shrunk on his bones. Roamer could see the shape of his skull, of the fine bones of his hands and feet and pelvis. His naked skin had turned purple and gray, and it was covered with huge blotches and streaks. His lips had shriveled to thin strips of blackened tissue, exposing teeth and cracked gums. The rest of his face was black and dry, as if burned. The flesh around his nose had withered, so his two small sideways-pointing nostrils were stretched, exposing the black lining of his nostrils. His eyelids had shriveled too, exposing his eyes in an unblinking, sightless stare at the sun. The conjunctiva that surrounded his eyes, exposed, had turned black as charcoal. He had been scrabbling at the bark, helplessly seeking food, and had cut his hands and feet. But there was no trace of blood; the cuts were like scratches in cured leather.

But he was still conscious, emitting dry, wistful cries. He moved his head gently and spread the fingers of his stronger left hand.

In the end, starved of input, striving to keep its vital systems running as long as possible, Left's body had consumed itself. Once its fat was gone, muscle had begun to be absorbed, a process that soon resulted in damage to the internal organs—which, badly deteriorated, were beginning to close down.

But in these last moments, Left was in no pain. Even the sensations of hunger and thirst had ceased.

Roamer watched, dizzy, bemused. It was like watching an animated skeleton.

Left's last eerie calls faded to silence. His fingers remained outstretched, frozen forever in his final gesture. His shrunken stomach growled, and a final noxious belch passed through his lifeless lips.

Roamer looked dully at the others. They were heaps of bone and damaged flesh, not much better off than Left, barely recognizable as anthros at all. They made no effort to groom, to make any kind of contact. It was as if the sun had baked away everything that made them anthros, had stripped them of the gains made painfully in thirty million years of evolution.

Roamer turned away and limped painfully back to her patch of soiled leaves, seeking cover.

She lay passively, shifting only to relieve the pain of suppurating sores. Her mind seemed empty, free of curiosity. She existed in a dull reptilian blankness. She would cram her mouth full of bark and dry leaves, but the dead stuff only scratched her broken flesh.

And she kept thinking about Left's corpse.

She got up slowly and crossed to Left's body. His chest had split open, a postmortem wound opened up by the drying of his skin. The stench, oddly, wasn't too bad. On this brine desert, the processes of decay that would, in the forests, have quickly absorbed Left's body were largely absent, and the slow mummification that had begun while he was still alive had continued.

Cautiously she pushed her hand into the wound. She touched ribs, already dried. She tugged at the flesh over his chest. It peeled back easily, exposing his rib cage.

There was barely any muscle tissue left on the body. There was no fat either, only traces of a translucent, sticky substance. Within Left's body cavity she could see his organs, his heart, liver, kidneys. They had been shrunken; they were like hard, blackened fruit.

Fruit, yes.

Roamer pushed her hand into the chest cavity. The rib cage split open with a crack, exposing the meaty fruit within. She closed her hand around his blackened heart. It came away easily, with a soft ripping noise.

She sat with the heart, and, as if it were no more exotic than a peculiar variety of mango, bit into it. The meat was lean, fibrous, and it resisted teeth that wobbled loose in her jaw. But soon she was tearing into the organ, and was rewarded with a little fluid, blood from its core that had not yet dried.

Instead of easing her hunger pangs, the meat only served to inflame Roamer's atavistic drive to eat. Saliva flowed in her mouth again, and digestive juices pumped painfully through her stomach. She vomited out her first mouthfuls, losing them to the sea, but she persisted until the hard, fibrous meat stayed down.

Left's eyes, milky white and opaque, still stared sightlessly at the sun that had killed him; and his left hand was curled in its final gesture.

Patch had stirred now. She came loping cautiously toward Roamer.

Her skin was a tight sack to which only a few clumps of her once-beautiful black fur still clung. Curious, she rummaged through Left's open chest. She came away with the liver, which she rapidly devoured.

Meanwhile Crest had not moved. Showing no signs of interest in the fate of his brother, he lay on his side, limbs splayed. He might have been dead, but Roamer made out a subtle movement, a slow rise and fall of his chest, slow as the ocean's swell, the last of his strength invested in keeping him breathing.

Instinct worked in Roamer now. Patch had been made pregnant by Whiteblood—but perhaps her body had destroyed the fetus by now, absorbing it like its own muscle and fat to keep itself functioning. Two females, alone, had nothing but their own deaths to look forward to. So Crest, the last male, must be preserved.

Roamer returned to the body and plucked out a kidney, another hard knot of blackened, shriveled meat. She carried it to Crest and pushed the meat into his shriveled mouth. At last he stirred. With a gesture as feeble as an infant's he reached up and took the lump of meat, and began to gnaw it slowly.

The food, such as it was, only made them more hungry, for it lacked the fat they needed to enable them to digest it properly. Still, all three of the survivors returned to the body over and over again, emptying the body cavity, gnawing flesh from limbs, ribs, pelvis, back. When they were done, only scattered bones remained—bones and a skull, from which eyeballs still stared at the sun.

After that the three anthros returned to their solitary corners. If they had been human, now that the taboo of devouring the flesh of their own kind had been broken, a kind of cruel mathematics would have begun to work in their minds. Another death, after all, would have provided the survivors with more food—and reduced the number who would share it.

It was, perhaps, a mercy that none of the anthros were able to plan that far ahead.

IV

The raft jolted under her. It was a sharper motion than the broad, slow swell of the sea. But she was beyond curiosity, and she lay passively in the raft's rough cradling, knotted branches poking into her thin flesh.

She was in pain constantly now. Her bones felt as if they were working their way out through her skin, which was like one giant ulcer. She could barely close her dried eyelids. Her memory was a disorganized hall of images: the feel of her sister's strong, grooming fingers, the warm, safe scent of her mother's milk, the brazen cries of the males who believed they owned them all. But then her soft dreams would be shattered by the irruption of great slavering jaws from the floor of the world . . .

Now came another jolt, a rustle of the dry timber around her. She heard the noise of waves breaking, quite different from the languorous lapping of the deep ocean.

Birds clattered overhead.

She peered up. They were the first birds she had seen since she had been washed from the land. They were brilliant white, and they wheeled high above her.

Something moved on her chest. It felt like fingers, tentatively scratching: perhaps someone was trying to groom her. With an immense effort she lifted her head. It lolled, her skin tight like a mask, her tongue a block of wood in her mouth. She had difficulty focusing her bleeding eyes.

Something was crawling over her: a flat orange shape with many segmented legs and big raised claws. She yelped, a thin, dry sound, and brushed her arm over her chest. The crab scuttled away, indignant.

With nostrils baked black as tar, she could smell something new. *Water.* And not the stinking brine of the sea, but fresh water.

She lifted an arm and grabbed at the foliage. Every scrap of her raw flesh, as scabs and blisters pulled and broke, was a source of lancing pain. With an immense heave she managed to get herself upright, her feet under her, her legs folded. Her head lolled, too heavy for her neck. It took her more energy yet to raise it, to squint through her broken eyes.

Green.

She saw green, a great horizontal slab of it, running from horizon to horizon. It was the first green she had seen since the last of the mango's leaves had curled and browned. After so many days of blue and gray, of nothing but sky and sea, the green seemed vibrantly bright, so bright it almost hurt her eyes, beautiful beyond imagining, and just looking at it seemed to strengthen her.

She levered herself forward, half crawling. The mango's dead foliage pricked and cut her, but there was no blood to flow, nothing but dozens of tiny sources of pain.

She reached the edge of the raft. No ocean, no water. She saw a shallow beach of coarse, young sand, stretching up a short rise to the foot of a sparse forest. Birds, bright blue and orange, flittered through the tops of the trees, piping brightly.

Her first impression could have been summarized as *I am home.* But she was wrong.

She pulled herself over the branches and half fell onto the sand. It was hot, very hot, and it burned her exposed skin. She mewled, pulled herself up, and limped forward, as if she had grown very old, up the beach toward the forest.

At the forest edge was an undergrowth of low ferns and blessed shade. Taller trees towered above her. On their branches were clusters of a red fruit she didn't recognize. Her mouth was too dry to salivate, but her tongue clicked against her teeth.

She glanced back the way she had come. The mango tree and its raft of vegetation was just a scrap of driftwood, broken, rotten, seaweed clinging to it, now washed up on this shore. She could see the unmoving form of an anthro—Patch or Crest—lying inert on the broken, salt-crusted foliage. And beyond the raft the sea rolled, huge, eternal, blue gray, reaching as far as she could see to a horizon of chilling geometric perfection.

Now there was a crashing tread, a great snapping of foliage. Roamer shrank back.

A giant form emerged from the forest, like a tank rolling through the undergrowth. Huge, squat, under a great bony dome of a shell, it looked like a giant tortoise—or perhaps an armored elephant—a great plated body supported by four stumpy legs. Behind it a tail swung carelessly, tipped by a spiky club. And as its small reinforced head pushed out into the light, armored eyelids blinked. This tremendous ankylosaur-like creature was a glyptodont. Roamer had never seen anything like it in Africa.

But then, this wasn't Africa.

The giant armored monster lumbered away. Cautiously Roamer followed the glyptodont deeper into the forest. She came to a clearing, surrounded by a wall of tall, imposing trees. The floor was carpeted by aloes. Experimentally Roamer nibbled at a leaf. It was succulent, but bitter.

She moved further forward, and found the glimmer of still water. It turned out to be a shallow, reed-choked freshwater pond. At its shore browsed a pair of huge animals. They grazed on the plants at the pond's edge with snouts like spatulas. They looked like hippos, but were actually immense rodents.

The pond was on the fringe of a broader plain. And there, dimly visible now, much stranger mysteries awaited Roamer. There were creatures that might have been horses, camel, deer, and smaller animals, like hoofed pigs. Alongside them moved a small family of dinomyids: bulky, bearlike grazers. They were giant rodents, the extravagant relations of dormice and rats. There were predators here too, creatures who ran in packs like dogs—but they were marsupials, only distantly related to placental counterparts elsewhere, shaped by convergent evolution, similarly adapted for a similar role.

From a green shadow near Roamer, a head turned, startling her. The head was upside down. Two black eyes peered at her dimly. Above the head was a huge brown-furred body, dangling from limbs that clutched a branch above. This was a sloth, a kind of megatherium.

Cautiously, Roamer crept forward, at last, to the pool. The water was muddy, greenish, warm. But when she plunged her face into it, it was the most delicious thing she had ever tasted. She sucked down great mouthfuls. Soon her shrunken belly was full, and agonizing pains shot through her, as if she were being torn apart from inside. She fell forward, crying out, and threw up almost all she had drunk. But she pushed her face back into the water and drank again.

This brackish pond was actually a sinkhole. Fifty meters deep, it had been caused by groundwater dissolving the underlying limestone. There were many such sinkholes in the area, aligned along great, deep-buried faults in the rocks.

Seen from the air, the sinkholes would have formed a huge semicircle some hundred and fifty kilometers across. The arc of sinkholes marked a boundary fault of the ancient, long-buried Chicxulub crater, the rest of which stretched under the Gulf of Mexico's shallow waters and sediments. This was the Yucatan Peninsula.

Expelled by an African river, riding westward currents, Roamer's raft had crossed the Atlantic.

Nowhere on Earth was truly isolated.

Everywhere was connected by the ocean currents, some of which covered as much as a hundred kilometers a day. The great currents were like conveyor belts that bore flotsam around the world. In later times, inhabitants of Easter Island would burn logs of American redwood, washed ashore after a journey of five thousand kilometers. People living on coral atolls in the deep Pacific would make tools from stones embedded in the roots of stranded trees.

With the flotsam traveled animals. Some insects rode the surface of the water itself. Other creatures swam: Westward currents could carry leatherback turtles across the Pacific from their feeding ranges near Ascension Island to breeding grounds in the Caribbean.

And some animals rode across the oceans on impromptu rafts— oceanic odysseys undertaken not by choice or design, but by the vicissitudes of chance, just as had befallen Roamer.

The Atlantic, which had been widening since the shattering of Pangaea, was still much narrower than in human times: no more than five hundred kilometers wide at its narrowest point. It was not an impossible distance, a traverse that could be survived even by fragile forest creatures like Roamer, with luck. Such crossings were improbable. But they were *possible*, given the outflows of mighty rivers, the narrow oceans, perhaps the help of hurricane winds.

On the longest of timescales, over millions of years, the workings of chance defied human intuition. Humans were equipped with a subjective consciousness of risk and improbability suitable for creatures with a lifespan of less than a century or so. Events that came much less frequently than that—such as asteroid impacts—were placed, in human minds, in the category not of *rare*, but of *never*. But the impacts happened even so, and to a creature with a lifespan of, say, ten million years, would not have seemed so improbable at all.

Given enough time even such unlikely events as ocean crossings from Africa to South America would inevitably occur, over and again, and would shape the destiny of life.

Thus it was now. In the trees that towered above Roamer there was not a single primate—not one, not in all the continent, for her remote cousins, other children of Purga, had succumbed to extinction here millions of years ago, beaten by the rodents' competitive pressure.

So, in this place where a world had ended, where differently evolved creatures foraged through different forests, a new life was starting, a new line of Purga's great family. From just three survivors—given enough time, and the slow plastic working of their genetic material—would radiate a whole spectrum of new species.

By any standards the New World monkeys would be successful. But on this crowded jungle continent, the fate of Roamer's grandchildren would be quite different from those of her sister's in Africa. There, the primates, molded cataclysmically by the shifting climate, would rapidly develop new forms. There, Purga's line would continue—through the apes—its slow shaping toward humanity. Even the later monkeys who Roamer so resembled would diversify away from the forest, finding ways to live in savannah, mountain plateaus, and even deserts.

Here it would be different. On a more equable continent, it would always be too tempting to stay in the vast rain forests.

Roamer's grandchildren would never leave the trees. They would never grow much smarter than they were now. And they would play no part in the future destiny of mankind—save as pets, or prey, or objects of scientific curiosity.

But all that lay in the unimaginable future.

Roamer already felt remarkably revived by her brief time in the green and the water she had drunk. She looked around. In the undergrowth she saw a splash of red, and she stumbled that way. She found a fruit, unfamiliar, but fat and soft-skinned. She bit into it. As she munched on the flesh, juice burst out and dribbled over her fur. It was the cleanest, sweetest thing she had ever tasted.

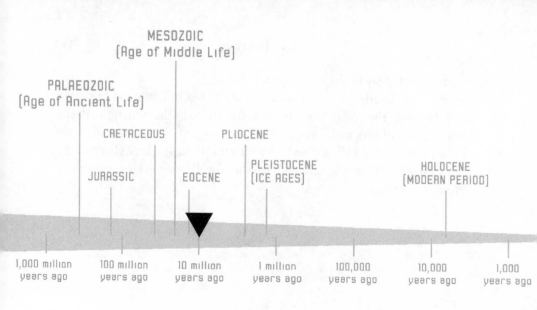

MESOZOIC
(Age of Middle Life)

PALAEOZOIC
(Age of Ancient Life)

CRETACEOUS   PLIOCENE

                              PLEISTOCENE   HOLOCENE
JURASSIC   EOCENE   (ICE AGES)   (MODERN PERIOD)

| 1,000 million | 100 million | 10 million | 1 million | 100,000 | 10,000 | 1,000 |
| years ago | years ago | years ago | years ago | years ago | years ago | years ago |

CHAPTER 7

the last burrow

▼ Ellsworth Land, Antarctica. Circa 10 million years before present.

I

The burrowers worked through the tough, scrubby grass that clung to the dunes. There were many, many of them. They were so crowded they looked like a ground-covering carpet of squirming brown-gray fur.

Dig spotted a dense patch of ferns on a little headland overlooking the ocean. The foraging crowd seemed a little less dense there, so she headed that way. In the shelter of the fern patch, she picked apart fronds with her agile, five-fingered hands, and she nibbled on brown spores.

At three years old Dig was already one of the oldest of the burrowers. She was just a few centimeters long. She was fat and round and coated with thick layers of brown fur, the better to retain her body's heat. She looked something like a lemming. But she was no lemming. She was a primate.

From here she could see the ocean. The sun hung low in the northern sky, over the endless, impassable water. As polar autumn drew on, the sun spent more than half of each day beneath the horizon. And already, far from the land, great sheets of pack ice had gathered. Closer to shore

Dig could see slushier gray ice forming in great sheets that rippled over the water's muscular swell. Her body knew what these things meant. The light-filled days of summer were a blurred memory; soon she would have to endure the winter months of continual darkness.

On one pack ice plate she saw a bloody stain, smeared over the gleaming surface, and an unidentifiable mound of inert flesh. Birds wheeled overhead, cawing, waiting their turn at the bloody pickings. And a shadow slid through the water, long, powerful. A huge snout pushed out of the chill water to take a share of the kill.

The seagoing carnivore was an amphibian, a descendant of a form called koolasuchus. Four meters long, it looked like a monstrous predatory frog. The frog was a relic of much more ancient times, when amphibians had dominated the world. In tropical climes, its ancestors had been outcompeted by the crocodiles, whom they closely resembled in size and form; the great amphibians had already been in decline when dinosaurs first appeared on the Earth, but they had clung on in the cooler waters of the poles.

Even from this distance, tucked under her ferns, Dig shuddered.

Suddenly a squat, feathered form came bursting from the tundra plain. The scrambling burrowers scattered in panic, and Dig cowered. The new arrival ran upright on long, powerful legs, and its hands, barely visible against thick white feathers, were grasping and equipped with cruel claws. This creature ran out into the water and splashed its way out to the ice floe. There it began to compete with the amphibian for scraps of the carcass, just as in later times Arctic foxes would try to steal the kills of polar bears.

This battling white-feathered predator looked like a flightless bird. It wasn't. It was a descendant of the velociraptors of the Cretaceous era.

On Antarctica, fifty-five million years after the comet impact, there were dinosaurs.

Dig made her way inland, away from the bloody scene at the shore. She moved cautiously, sticking to cover. Here and there she saw white feathers, discarded by the raptor in its haste to reach the kill on the ice.

As she clambered over the last dune, she could see the shape of the landscape.

It was a broad plain of green and brown, littered here and there by the blue of water. The grass was still thick, though it had begun to die back, and where it had not yet been cropped to the ground, it was turning golden brown. Most of the flowers had gone, for there were no insects to attract; but here and there bright, pretty blooms like saxifrage still lingered. Around the glimmering freshwater ponds, animals crowded, seeking drink. But the ponds were already gray with surface ice.

It was a classic tundra scene, part of a belt of such landscape that still encircled the continent.

And, over this tundra, dinosaurs walked.

A few kilometers to the southwest, Dig saw what looked like a dark cloud washing over the ground. It was a herd of muttas. Their breath created great clouds of steam that hung in the chill air. They were dinosaurs, huge herbivores. From a distance they looked like tuskless mammoths. But closer in it could be seen that they retained classic dinosaur features: Their hind legs were more powerful than their forelegs, they had powerful balancing tails, they behaved in an oddly skittish and nervous way, more like birds than any huge mammal—and sometimes they would rear up on their hind legs and bellow with the ferocity of a tyrannosaur.

The muttas were descended from muttaburrasaurs, beefy Jurassic herbivores that had once feasted on cycads, ferns, and conifers. As the cold had descended on Antarctica, the muttas had learned to subsist on coarse tundra produce. Their bodies had become squat and round, and they had developed a thick coat made up of multiple layers of dark-brown, scaly feathers. Gradually they became large, migrating tundra herbivores, a role later occupied elsewhere by animals like caribou and musk oxen—and mammoths. Their mournful hooting, made with inflatable skin sacs on their great horny snouts, echoed from the walls of ice to the south.

Once the muttas had migrated all over this continent, taking advantage of the short, rich summer. But as the ice had spread the muttas' numbers had been much diminished, and now, somewhat forlornly, the remaining herds wandered around the narrowing tundra fringe between ice and sea.

This mutta herd was being stalked by a solitary hunter.

Standing stock-still, the dwarf allosaur inspected the mutta herd. It looked like a golden, feathered statue. The allo was a dwarfed relic of a family of creatures long extinct elsewhere—a direct descendant, in fact, of the Jurassic lion who had killed Stego. But the herd was wary of the allo and stayed tightly bunched, their young at the center. This allo's movements were slow, as if it had been drugged. Its hunting had already been successful; with its store of fat laid in, its metabolism was already slowing as the air's chill gathered. Soon the allo would dig out its customary winter den in a snowbank, after the manner of polar bears.

Female allos laid their eggs toward the end of winter, and hatched them out inside their snowy dens, where they would be safe. For the mammals of Antarctica, spring was made more interesting by the possibility that from any snowbank there might suddenly erupt a clutch of ravenous allosaur chicks, snapping and squabbling in pursuit of their first meal.

Now there was a commotion among a throng of burrowers, not far from Dig, and the cold breeze off the ice cap brought her a sharp, meaty scent. *Eggs.*

She ran as hard as she could through the ferns and the long grass, for once reckless of her own safety.

The nest contained dinosaur eggs: the eggs of a mutta. This was an unusual find so late in the season, and far away from the muttas' usual nesting sites. Perhaps these eggs had been laid by a sick or injured mother. There were burrowers already at work here, and in amongst the squabbling crowd there were a few bulkier steropodons: clumsy, black-haired, oddly primitive-looking, these creatures were descended from mammals that had inhabited the southern continent since Jurassic times.

Dig was able to force her way into the nest before it was utterly destroyed. Soon her face and hands were coated with sticky yolk. But the competition for the eggs quickly degenerated into a ferocious battle. There were many, many burrowers here on the tundra this autumn, many more than last year. And Dig was smart enough to be worried by the burrowers' overcrowding on a deep, gnawing level.

There was no simple cause for rises in numbers like this. The burrowers were locked into intricate ecological cycles involving the abundance of the vegetation and insects they browsed, and the carnivores who preyed on them in turn. At times of excess bodies it was the burrowers' instinct to get away, to strike out blindly over the green land in search of empty places to establish new burrows. Many of them fell to predation, but that was the way of things: Enough of them would survive.

At least, that was how it had happened in the past. But now, as the ice advanced and the tundra shriveled back, there was nowhere left to go that wasn't already colonized. And so there were always great crowds like this, and you always had to fight.

Of course, it was bad for the mutta who had laid these eggs. The muttas hatched their eggs on the ground, as their ancestors had always done, which made them vulnerable to opportunistic predators like the burrowers. Indeed, the key cause of the decline in the muttas' numbers was the increasing competition for the protein locked up in their huge eggs. Giant mammalian herbivores, like mammoths or caribou, would have fared better here, as their young would have been safer at such a crucial moment in their lives. But the muttas, stranded like the rest when Antarctica had sailed away from the other continents, had had no choice in the matter.

Suddenly a claw came sweeping out of the sky. With an instinct more than two hundred million years old, Dig flattened herself against the ground, while burrowers squeaked and scrambled over each other.

The claw grabbed a small, immature burrower and popped her whole into a gaping mouth. Again the claw burned through the air, grasping as if frustrated. But the mammals had scattered. And after a time Dig heard the unmistakable sound of chewing, as a toothed beak crushed one mutta embryo after another.

This bandit was a leaellyn. Another dinosaur, it looked like an athletic chicken. Not equipped to be effective hunters of large prey, the leaellyns were mainly opportunistic scavengers. For this leaellyn, like the mammals, a mutta egg this late in the season was a rare treat.

As the leaellyn fed, Dig tried to lie still to avoid the killer's attention. But she was hungry. It had been a short, poor summer, and it had been impossible for her to fatten herself up as much as she needed to face the privations of winter. And the leaellyn was taking the eggs—taking all of *her* eggs.

Anger and desperation at last overrode caution. She raised herself up on her hind legs, hissing, her paws spread.

The leaellyn, blood and yolk smeared around its mouth, flinched back, startled by this sudden apparition. But, its small reptilian mind soon told it, this was not a threat to a leaellyn. In fact, this warm furry ball, for all its unusual posture, was good to eat, better than embryos and yolk.

The leaellyn opened its mouth and leaned forward.

Dig evaded and escaped. But she had to abandon the nest, and hunger burned inside her belly.

Dig could have traced her lineage back to Plesi, the little carpolestid who had inhabited the warming world a few million years after the fall of the Devil's Tail. Plesi's offspring had wandered the planet, using land bridges, islands, and rafts to cross from one island continent to another. One branch of the ancient family had crossed a land bridge between South America and Antarctica at a time when the southern continent had yet to settle over the pole.

And here it had encountered dinosaurs.

Even during the warm Cretaceous the dinosaurs of Antarctica had had to endure long months of polar darkness. So those chance survivors who had lived through the global catastrophe here had been well equipped to endure the comet winter that had followed while their contemporaries in the warmer latitudes had perished.

But the continents had drifted further apart, fragments of the wreckage of the ancient supercontinent still separating. Antarctica had spun away from the other pieces of southern Pangaea, soon traveling so far that no land bridge, no rafting was possible. And as the world recovered from the impact, the flora and fauna of Antarctica had begun to explore their own unique evolutionary destiny. Here the ancient game of dinosaur versus mammal had been granted a long, drawn-out coda—and here, still, thanks to the twin ferocity of the dinosaurs and the cold, the mammals had remained trapped in their humiliating Cretaceous niches.

But at last Antarctica had settled over the southern pole, and the great ice cap had slowly grown.

The days grew short, the crimson sun arcing only briefly over the horizon. The ground hardened with frost. Many plant species died back to ground level, their spores waiting out the return of the summer's brief warmth.

There was little fresh snow. In fact, much of the continent was technically a semidesert: What snow did fall came as hard crystalline flakes that rested on the ground like rock until the wind gathered it into banks and drifts.

But the snow, sparse as it was, was essential for the burrowers.

Those who had survived the summer and autumn began to dig into the snow drifts, constructing intricate tunnel systems beneath the hard-crusted upper layers. The tunnels were elaborate, humid, nivean cities, the walls hardened by the passage of many small, warm bodies, the air filled with a warm, damp-fur smell. The burrows were not exactly warm inside, but the temperature never dropped below freezing.

Outside, auroras flapped silently across the star-stained winter sky.

The leaellyn who had stolen the eggs from Dig was one of a pack, mostly siblings, who had hunted together in a small group centered on one dominant breeding pair. In the winter, as they felt their customary cold-weather torpor come on, the leaellyn pack huddled together.

The leaellyns were descended from small, agile herbivorous dinosaurs that had once swarmed in great nervous clans over the floor of the Antarctic forest. In those days the leaellyns could grow as large as an adult human, and they had big eyes well adapted to the darkness of the polar forests. But with the great chill the leaellyns had become dwarfed, fatter, and covered with scaly feathers for insulation.

And, as the megayears had worn away, they had learned to eat meat.

As the cold deepened, the pack members slid into unconsciousness. Their metabolisms slowed to a crawl, astonishingly slow, just enough to keep their flesh from freezing. It was an ancient strategy, shaped by millions of years of habitation in these polar regions, and it had always proven effective.

But not this time. For there had never been a winter as cold as this. In the worst of it the leaellyn group was overwhelmed by a storm. The savage wind took away too much of their body heat. Ice formed inside the leaellyns' flesh, shattering the structure of their cells; gradually the frostbite extended cold daggers deep into their small bodies.

But the leaellyns felt no pain. Their slumber was a silent, dreamless, reptilian sleep, deeper than any mammal would ever know, and it segued smoothly into death.

Every year the summers were shorter, the onset of winter harder. Each spring the great ice cap that lay over the center of the continent, a place where nothing could live, advanced a little further. Once there had been tall trees here: conifers, tree ferns, and the ancient podocarps, with clusters of heavy fruit at their bases. It had been a forest where Noth would have been at home. But now those trees existed only as seams of coal buried deep beneath Dig's feet, long since felled by the cold. It had been many millions of years since any of Dig's ancestors had climbed off the ground.

The primates of Antarctica had had to become adapted to the cold. They could not grow larger; competition with the dinosaurs saw to that. But they developed layers of insulation, fat and fur, designed to trap their body heat. Dig's feet were kept so cold there was little temperature difference between them and the ground, and little heat was lost. Cold blood coming up into her torso from her feet was pushed through blood vessels containing warm blood that ran the other way. So the descending blood was cooled before it ever got to her feet. The fat in her legs and feet was a special kind, made of shorter hydrocarbon chains, with a low melting point. Otherwise it would have hardened, like chilled butter. And so on.

For all her cold adaptations Dig was still a primate. She still retained the agile hands and strong forearms of her ancestry. And, though her brain was much diminished from her ancestors'—in this straitened environment a big brain was an expensive luxury, and animals were no smarter than they needed to be—she was smarter than any lemming.

But the climate was getting colder yet. And every year the remnant animals and plants were crowded into an increasingly narrow strip of tundra close to the coast.

The endgame was approaching.

Dig found herself laboring for breath.

In a sudden panic, she scrabbled at the snow above her, hands evolved for climbing trees now digging their way through a roof of snow.

She pushed her way out of the burrow and into a thin spring light, shockingly bright. A gush of fetid air followed her, steaming in the cold—fetid, and laden with the stink of death.

She was a bony bundle of urine-stained skin and fur on a vast, virgin snowscape. The sun was high enough above the horizon to hang like a yellow lantern in a purple-blue sky. Spring was advanced, then. But nothing moved: no birds, no raptors, no dwarf allo chicks erupting from their wintry caves. No other burrower emerged onto the snow; not one of her own kin followed her.

She began to work her way down the bank of snow. She moved stiffly, her joints painful, a ravening hunger in her belly, a thirst in her throat. The long hibernation had used up about a quarter of her body mass. And she was *shivering*.

Shivering was a great failure of her body's cold-resistant systems, a last-resort option to generate body heat with muscular movement that burned up huge amounts of energy. Shivering shouldn't be happening.

Something was wrong.

She reached the bare ground that fringed the sea. The soil was ice-bound, still as hard as a rock. And despite the lateness of the season nothing grew here, not yet; spores and seeds still lay dormant in the ground.

She came across a group of leaellynasaurs. In the cold, they had intertwined their limbs and necks until they had formed a kind of interlocked, feathery sculpture. Instinctively she flattened herself against the snow.

But the leaellyns were no threat. They were dead, locked in their final embrace. If Dig had pushed, the assemblage might have toppled over, frozen feathers breaking off like icicles.

She hurried on, leaving the leaellyns to their final sleep.

She reached a little headland that overlooked the ocean. She had stood in this place at the end of last summer, under a small stand of fern, watching raptor and frog battle. Now, even the fern's spores were locked inside the bare ground, and there was nothing to eat. Before her the sea was a plain of unbroken white, all the way to the horizon. She quailed before the lifeless geometry: a horizon sharp as a blade, flat white below, empty blue dome above.

Only at the shore was there a break from the monotony. Here the sea's relentless swell had broken the ice, and here, even now, life swarmed. Dig could see tiny crustaceans thrusting through the surface waters, gorging themselves on plankton. And jellyfish, small and large, pulsed through this havoc, all but translucent, lacy, delicate creatures that rode the swell of the water.

Even here, at the extremes of the Earth, the endless sea teemed with life, as it always had. But there was nothing for Dig.

As the great global cooling downturn continued, so the great clamp of the ice tightened with each passing year. The unique assemblage of animals and plants, trapped on this immense, isolated raft, had nowhere to go. And in the end, evolution could offer no defense against the ice's final victory.

It was a gruesome extinction event, hidden from the rest of the planet, drawn out over millions of years. An entire biota was being frozen to death. When the animals and plants were all gone, the monstrous ice sheet that sat squat over the continent's heart would extend further, sending glaciers to grind their way through the rock until the ice's lifeless abstraction met the sea itself. And though the deeper fossils and coal beds of ancient times would survive, there would be no trace left to say that Dig's world of tundra, and the unique life that had inhabited it, had ever existed.

Dispirited, she turned away and set off over the frozen ground, seeking food.

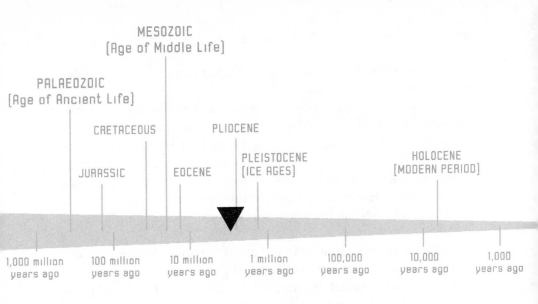

PALAEOZOIC
(Age of Ancient Life)

MESOZOIC
(Age of Middle Life)

CRETACEOUS

PLIOCENE

JURASSIC

EOCENE

PLEISTOCENE
(ICE AGES)

HOLOCENE
(MODERN PERIOD)

1,000 million
years ago

100 million
years ago

10 million
years ago

1 million
years ago

100,000
years ago

10,000
years ago

1,000
years ago

CHAPTER 8

fragments

▼ **North African coast. Circa 5 million years before present.**

I

As light leaked into the sky, Capo woke. Lying in his treetop nest he yawned, his lips spreading wide to expose his thick gums, and he stretched his long, furry limbs. Then he cupped his balls in one hand and scratched them comfortably.

Capo looked something like a chimpanzee, but there were not yet any chimps in the world. He was an ape, though. In the long years since the death of Roamer, the burgeoning families of primates had diverged, and Capo's line had split off from the monkeys some twenty million years ago. And yet—still some five million years before the rise of true humans—the great age of the apes had already come and gone.

Capo squinted into the sky. The sky was gray blue and free of clouds. It would be another long, hot, sunny day.

And a good day. He rubbed his penis thoughtfully. His morning erection felt tight, as it always did. Some of the most troublesome of the subordinate males had sloped off into the deeper forest a few days ago. It ought to be weeks before they were back, weeks of relative calm and order. Easy work for Capo.

In the stillness of morning, sound carried far. Lying here, his thoughts rambling, Capo could hear a distant roaring, like the endless grumble of some vast, wounded beast. It came roughly from the west. He listened for a few heartbeats, and his hairs prickled at the sullen majesty of the never-ending, baffling rumble; it was a sound of awesome power. But there was never anything there, nothing to see. It had been there in the background all his life, unchanging, incomprehensible—and remote enough not to matter.

He felt a nagging unease, but not about the noise. A vague concern crept up on him in such reflective moments.

Capo was more than forty years old. His body bore the scars of many battles and the patchy baldness of endless grooming. He was old enough and smart enough to remember many seasons—not as a linear narrative but in glimpses, shards, like vivid scenes cut out of a movie and jumbled up. And on a deep level he knew that the world was not as it had been in the past. Things were changing, and not necessarily for the better.

But there was nothing to be done about it.

Languorously he rolled over onto his belly. His nest was just a mass of thin branches folded over and kept in place by his weight. Through its loose structure he could make out the troop scattered through the tree's foliage, primates roosting like birds. With a soft grunt he let his bladder go. The piss sprayed messily from his penis, still half erect, and rained down into the tree.

It splashed Leaf, one of the senior females, who had been asleep on her back with her infant clutching her belly fur. She woke with a start, wiping thick urine from her eyes, and hooted her protest.

His time of reflection over, the last of his erection shriveling, Capo sat up and vaulted out of his nest.

Time to go to work. A great black-brown ball of fur, he proceeded to crash through the tree. He smashed nests, punched and kicked their occupants, and screeched and leapt. He kept this up until the whole tree was a leafy bedlam, and there was no possibility of anybody staying asleep, or not being aware of Capo's dominant presence.

He made one very satisfactory hard landing right in the middle of the nest of Finger, a stocky younger male with a very agile brain and hands. Finger curled up, chattering, and tried to lift his backside in a gesture of submission. But Capo targeted the backside with one well-aimed kick, and Finger, shrieking, went tumbling down through the foliage toward the ground. It was high time Finger was taught a lesson; he had been getting too cocky for Capo's liking.

At length Capo reached the ground, fur bristling, panting hard. He was on the edge of a small clearing centered on a clogged, marshy pond. He still wasn't done with his display. He threw himself back and forth around the line of trees, drumming with open palms on tree trunks, ripping off thin branches and shaking them so their leaves cascaded around him, screeching and hooting the while.

Finger had picked himself up from where he had plummeted. Limping slightly, he crawled into the shade of a low palm and cowered away from his master's display. Other males hopped and hooted in backside-kissing support. One or two females were already up. They kept out of Capo's way, but otherwise maintained their own morning routines.

As he finished his display, Capo spotted Howl, a female with a peculiarly high-pitched way of calling. She was crouching at the base of an acacia, picking lumps off a morel and popping them into her mouth. Howl was not yet pubescent, but she wasn't far off. Spying the tight pucker of her genitals, Capo immediately hardened.

Still bristling, panting a little, he swaggered over to Howl, lifted her hips, and smoothly entered her. Her passage was pleasingly tight, and Capo's supporters hooted and growled, drumming on the ground, urging on their hero. Howl did not resist, adjusting her posture to accommodate him. But as he thrust, she continued to pluck bits of morel, not much interested.

Capo withdrew from Howl before he ejaculated: too early in the day for that. But as a coup de grâce he turned his back on his cowering subordinates, bent over, and ejected a spray of shit that showered over them. Then he threw himself flat on the grass, arms akimbo, and allowed a few of his more favored subordinates to come close and begin the day's grooming.

Thus the great boss, the *capo di capo* of this troop—the progenitor of mankind, the ancestor of Socrates and Newton and Napoleon—had begun his day in suitable splendor.

The next priority was to fill his belly.

Capo selected one of his subordinates—Frond, a tall, sinewy, nervous creature—and, hooting loudly, delivered a series of slaps and blows to the cowering creature's head.

Frond quickly got the message. His assignment was to lead the troop's daily forage in search of food and water. He selected a direction—east, as it happened, into the light of the rising sun—and, his gait a mixture of clumsy knuckle-walking and upright sprinting, he ran back and forth along a trail that led that way, glancing back at Capo for approval.

Capo had no reason not to choose that direction. With a swagger, his big knuckles punching into the soft ground, he set out after Frond. The rest of the troop quickly formed up behind him, males and females alike, infants clinging to their mothers' bellies.

The troop worked its way through the trees at the forest fringe, foraging systematically, after their fashion. Mostly they sought fruit, though they were prepared to take insects and even meat if it was available. The males noisily postured and competed, but the females moved more calmly. The smallest infants stayed with their mothers, though older youngsters rolled and wrestled.

As they worked their endless way through the forest, the friendships of the females quietly endured. The truth of Capo's society was that the females were its foundation. The females stuck to their kinship groups and shared the food they found—a practice that made good genetic sense, as your aunt and nieces and sisters shared your own heritage. As for the males, they just went where the females went, their dominance battles a kind of showy superstructure, signifying very little of true importance for the troop.

With a moist dick and pleasantly aching fists, and the prospect of a belly soon to be filled, Capo ought to have been as happy as he could be. Life was good, here in the forest. For Capo, top of the heap, it could hardly get any better. But still that bit of unease lingered.

Unfortunately for Capo's mood, the pickings that morning were poor. They were forced to keep moving.

They came across other animals, here in the forest. There were okapi—short-necked giraffes—and pygmy hippos and dwarf forest proboscideans. It was an ancient fauna clinging to the conservatism of forest ways. And there were other primates too. They passed a pair of giants: huge, broad-shouldered, silver-haired creatures who sat massively on the ground, feeding on the leaves they plucked from the trees.

They were like the potbellies of Roamer's day. Capo's forebears had developed a new kind of teeth, the better to cope with their fruit diet: Capo had large incisors for biting, necessary for fruit, whereas his molars were small. These leaf eaters' teeth were the other way around; leaves didn't need much biting but took a lot of chewing. Closely related to the gigantopithecines of Asia, these great beasts, weighing a quarter of a ton each, were among the largest primates who would ever live. But the giants were rare in Africa now.

They were not in direct competition with Capo's troop, who, lacking the giants' immense multiple fermenting stomachs, could not feed on leaves. Still, it bothered Capo to have to divert his course to avoid these silent, patient, statuesque creatures. Not wishing to lose face, Capo knuckle-walked up to the larger of the giants—a male—and displayed, fur bristling, running in circles, drumming on the ground. The leaf eater watched, impassive and incurious. Even sitting down he towered over Capo.

Honor satisfied, Capo skirted the giants and moved on.

It wasn't long before the morning march came to an end, as the troop ran out of trees.

Here was the root of Capo's unease. This shrinking, half-flooded patch of forest was not as abundant a home as it used to be. It was just an island, in fact, in a greater, more open world.

Peering out of the trees, he glimpsed that world, still emerging from a misty dawn.

This scrap of forest lay in the palm of an extensive, glimmering plain. The land was like a park, a mix of open green plains and patches of forest. Much of the forest was palms and acacias, but there was some mixed woodland, both conifers and deciduous trees—walnut, oak, elm, birch, juniper.

What would most have surprised Roamer, Capo's distant great-aunt, was the nature of the ground cover that stretched over those open green areas. It was *grass*: hardy, resistant, now spreading with slow, unheralded triumph across the world.

And on the plain there were many, many lakes, ponds, marshes. Mist rose everywhere, the sun's early heat filling the air with moisture. A great river, having spilled from the southern highland, curled lazily over the plain. Around its banks stretched extensive floodplains, some of them marshy or sheets of open water. The land was like a full sponge, brimming with water. Some of the trees were dying, their roots in some cases actually standing in shallow water. The forest remnants, already shrunken by the world's continuing cooling and drying, were being drowned.

This soggy plain stretched to the north as far as Capo's eyes could see. But off to the south the land climbed to an immense wall notched by the outflow of that mighty river. Before that great ridge was a more barren area littered with wide, bone-white sheets of salt, on some of which stood small, stagnant-looking lakes.

There was a bellow from the north, and Capo turned back that way. The animals of the plain were going about their business. In the distance

Capo could see what looked like a herd of wild, overgrown pigs rooting in the long grasses. Their low-slung gray-brown bodies made them look like huge slugs. They were not pigs or hippos; they were anthracotheres, a holdover from much more ancient times.

Two huge chalicotheres worked their way slowly across the plain, plucking at shrubs with their huge paws. They picked only fresh shoots, and put them into their mouths, delicate as pandas. The taller, the male, was nearly three meters high at the shoulder. They had bulky bodies and stocky hind legs, but their forelegs were long and surprisingly graceful. But, because of their long claws, they could not put their front feet on the ground, and walked on their knuckles. In their bodies they looked a little like huge, short-haired gorillas, but they had long equine heads. These ancient animals were cousins of the horses. Once they had been widespread, but now the shrubs on which they depended were becoming scarce; this species was the last of the chalicothere kind.

Closer to hand, the apes could heard a steady, noisy rustling. Hesitant, they peered out. A family of a kind of elephant was working at the trees at the forest clump's edge, using their trunks to pull away branches and cram foliage into their mouths. These were gomphotheres, massive creatures. Each had four tusks, a pair protruding from both upper and lower jaws, giving its face the look of a forklift.

This was the heyday of the proboscideans. The very successful elephantine body plan had spun off a whole range of species across the world. In North America the mastodons would survive until humans arrived. Another family was the shovel-tuskers like these gomphotheres, with their hugely expanded and flattened lower tusks. And, walking through Africa and southern Asia, there were the stegodons, with long, straight tusks. They were the ancestors of the true elephants and the mammoths, who had yet to appear.

The sound of the gomphotheres' calls, carrying far in the cold morning air and echoing deep into the infrasonic, was eerie. These particular proboscideans were omnivorous. They were scarcely fleet-footed hunters. But on the whole a meat-eating elephant was best avoided.

That was when Frond, the spindly male, unexpectedly knuckle-walked out of the forest's shade and into grass tall enough to come up to his shoulders. The grass waved around him, stirred by a breeze, languid waves crossing the empty acres.

Hesitantly Frond got to his hind legs. For a heartbeat he stood upright, peering out into a world beyond the primates' reach, out into the green emptiness where animals walked, the antelopes, elephants, and chalicotheres grazing the abundant grass.

Then he dropped back to all fours and scuttled back into the forest's shadows, his nerve gone.

Capo gave him a sound beating about the head for taking such a risk. Then he led his troop back into the deeper forest.

Capo hauled himself up an acacia tree, seeking fruit and flowers. Capo climbed steadily. He used a kind of shimmying style, pulling himself up with his arms while gripping the tree trunk with his feet to provide a platform.

It was a feat Roamer could not have achieved—or indeed any monkey. Capo's apes had flat chests, short legs, and long arms. They had achieved greater flexibility by moving their shoulder blades to the backs of their bodies, which enabled Capo to reach up above his head. All this was equipment for hauling oneself up a tree trunk. Where Roamer had spent much of her life running along branches, Capo was a climber.

And this re-engineering for climbing had had another side effect, easily visible in Capo's long, narrow body. Working vertically, with a new bone structure and system of balance, Capo was already preadapted to walking on two feet. Sometimes he did this in the trees, holding on to branches for balance, trying to reach the highest fruit—and sometimes his kind would stand up out in the open, as Frond had demonstrated.

As their bodies had been redesigned, the apes had become smarter.

In these tropical climes fruit trees rarely fruited simultaneously. Even when you found a fruiting tree, you might have a long way to travel to the next. So the apes needed to spend much of each day searching for patchy resources, foraging alone or in small groups, collecting together again to sleep in the treetop refuges. This basic architecture of food gathering had shaped their social lives. For one thing they needed to understand their environment very well if they were to find the food they needed.

And, given the way they lived their lives, their bonding was loose. They could split and recombine, forming special relationships with other members of the community, even though they might not see them for weeks at a time. Keeping track of a multileveled, fissile social complexity required increasing smartness. As the apes juggled their relationships, it was as if they were living through a soap opera—but it was a social maelstrom that honed their developing minds.

In the first years after the great split of the archaic anthropoid stock into apes and monkeys, the apes had become the Old World's dominant primates. Though shrinking climate belts restricted them to the middle latitudes, there was plenty of room for them in a continuous band of forest that had spanned the whole of Africa and stretched across Eurasia from China to Spain. Following this green corridor the apes had walked out of Africa and spread through the Old World forests. In fact, they had migrated alongside the proboscideans.

At their peak there were more than sixty ape species. They had ranged from cat-sized to the size of a young elephant. The largest, like the giants, were leaf eaters, the midsized—those the size of Capo—took fruit, but the smallest, weighing under a kilogram or so, were insectivores, like their remote ancestors. The smaller the animal, the faster its metabolism and the higher the quality of the food it demanded. But there was room for everybody. It had been an age of apes, a mighty anthropoid empire.

Sadly for them it hadn't lasted.

As the world continued to cool and dry, the great forest belts had shriveled into isolated islands, like this one. The vanishing of forest connections between Africa and Eurasia had isolated the Asian ape populations, which would develop independently of events in Africa, into the orangutan and its relatives. With the reduced ranges had come a dwindling of numbers. Most ape species had, in fact, *already* long gone extinct.

And then had come the rise of a new competitor.

Capo reached a clump of foliage where, he knew, this particular acacia had an especially productive patch of flowers. But he found the spiny branches already stripped. When he pried them aside he was met by a small, startled black face, fringed by white fur and a gray topknot. It was a monkey—like a vervet—and juice dribbled from its small mouth. It peered into Capo's eyes, squealed, and shot out of sight before he could do anything about it.

Capo rested for a while, scratching his cheek thoughtfully.

Monkeys were a pest. Their great advantage was that they were able to eat unripe fruit. Their bodies manufactured an enzyme to neutralize the toxic chemicals used by the trees to protect their fruit until their seeds were ready to germinate. The apes could not match this. So the monkeys were able to strip the trees before the apes even arrived. They were even moving out into the grasslands, feeding off the nutlike seeds to be found there. To the apes, the monkeys were as tough a competition as the rodents had always been.

High over Capo's head, a slim form moved, swinging gracefully and purposefully. It was a gibbon. It raced through its forest canopy at extraordinary speed. It used its body as a pendulum to gain momentum, and, like a child on a fairground swing, it pumped its legs up and down to build up its speed.

The gibbon's body was a kind of extreme version of the apes' long-armed, flat-chested design. The ball-and-socket joints in its shoulders and wrists had been freed up so that the gibbon could hang from its arms and twist its body through a full circle. With its low weight and extreme flexibility, the gibbon could hang from the outermost branches of the highest trees, and it was able to reach the fruits that grew at the end of the thinnest branches, safe from even tree-climbing predators. And, able to hang upside down from branches, it could reach goodies out of the grasp of other apes, who were too heavy to climb so high, and even the monkeys, who ran along the tops of the branches.

Capo peered up at the gibbon with a kind of envy for a grace, speed, and skill he could not match. But, magnificent though it was, the gibbon was not a triumph for the apes but a relic, forced by the competition it had lost to the monkeys to eke out its living on the ecological margins.

Vaguely disappointed, still hungry, Capo moved on.

At length Capo found another of his favorite resources, a stand of oil palms. The nuts of this tree had rich, oily flesh—but they were enclosed in a particularly hard outer case that rendered them immune to most animals, even the clever fingers of monkeys. But not to apes.

Capo hurled handfuls of the nuts down to the ground, then clambered down after them. He collected the nuts together, carried them to the roots of an acacia he knew, and hid them under a heap of dried palm fronds.

Then he worked his way out toward the perimeter of the forest, to where he had stashed his hammer-stones. These were cobbles that fit neatly into the palm of his hand. He selected one and headed back to his nut stash.

On his way back he passed the adolescent Howl. Briefly he considered mating her again, but Capo's attention once a day was enough of an honor for any female.

Anyhow she was sitting with an infant, an odd-looking male with a peculiarly elongated upper lip: Elephant. He was actually one of Capo's sons. He was sitting on the ground clutching his stomach and moaning loudly. Perhaps he had a worm, or some other parasite. Howl was moaning along with him, as if some of the pain had transferred to her body. She was plucking bristly leaves and making the youngster swallow them; the leaves contained compounds that were toxic to many parasites.

And there were Finger and Frond, he saw, grubbing their way along the forest floor. The young males were aiming for a little light thievery, it seemed to Capo—in fact, he realized angrily, they had their eyes on Capo's own heap of fronds.

Capo contained his impatience. He sat under a tree, dropped his hammer-stone, picked up a stick and began to work methodically to clean out the spaces between his toes. He knew that if he made a dash for his palm nuts the others would get there first and pilfer the nuts. By loitering like this, he was making Frond and Finger believe that no nuts had been hidden at all.

Unlike Roamer, Capo was able to read the intentions of others. And Capo understood that others could have beliefs different from his own, that his actions could affect others' beliefs. It was a capability that even made a limited kind of empathy possible: Howl really had been sharing the suffering of Elephant. But it also made possible ever more elaborate modes of deceit and treachery. He was able, in a sense, to read minds.

This new ability had even made him self-aware, in a new way. The best way to model the contents of another's mind was to be able to study your own: *If I saw what she sees, if I believed what she does, what would I do?* It was an inward look, a reflection: the birth of consciousness. If Capo had been shown his face in a mirror he would have known it was *him*, not another ape in a window. His were the first animals since the hunters of Pangaea to have achieved such sophistication.

At last Frond and Finger moved away from the stash. Capo grabbed his hammer-stone and descended on his palm nuts. Capo would deliver beatings to the two of them later anyhow, on principle; they would never quite understand why.

He brushed aside the concealing fronds to expose his favorite anvil stone, a flat rock embedded in the ground. To protect his backside he spread some broad leaves over the moist ground. He sat down, legs tucked up to his chest. He set a palm nut on the anvil, holding it steady with finger and forefinger—and then brought down the hammer, snatching his fingers out of the way at the last moment. The nut rolled a little and squirted sideways unbroken; Capo retrieved it and tried again. It was a tricky procedure that took a lot of coordination. But it took Capo only three goes before he had cracked the first nut and was chewing out its flesh with his teeth.

Twenty-seven million years after Roamer and her habit of slamming nuts against branches, this was the height of technology on Earth.

Capo worked steadily on the nuts, losing himself in the tricky little procedure, pushing out of his mind the obscure worries that niggled him. It was high morning now, and for a time he felt content, satisfied in the knowledge that he had gotten enough food to stave off hunger pains for a few hours at least.

Elephant, drawn by the nuts' rich smell, came to see what was happening. This youngster's stomach problem had evidently been eased by

Howl's rough-and-ready bush medicine—or perhaps he had been faking it, to get some attention—and he was starting to feel hungry. He made out bits of nutshell scattered around the anvil stone, and even a few scraps of kernel. The youngster snatched these up and crammed them into his mouth.

Capo, grandly, let this pass.

Now Leaf came by with her infant clinging to her back.

Capo dropped his hammer-rock and reached for Leaf. Gently he began to groom her belly, an attention to which she submitted gracefully. Leaf, a big, gentle creature, was one of his favorite females. In fact she was favored by all of the troop's males, and they would compete for grooming time with her.

But that wasn't Capo's way. Very soon his lumpy penis had sprouted from his fur, and Leaf had had all the grooming she was going to get. Leaf carefully lifted the infant from her back and put her down on the ground. Then she lay back and let Capo enter her. She arched her back as he thrust, so that her head was upside down, her weight balanced on her skull. These apes often mated face to face like this. Empathy again: They could share each others' pleasure in grooming or mating.

Capo and Leaf were close. Though mating was promiscuous, sometimes Capo and Leaf would take themselves off into the forest for days on end—just the two of them—and during such safaris of tenderness, previsioning the sexual privacy of later kinds, most of Leaf's children by Capo had been conceived, including Elephant.

What Capo and Leaf felt for each other at such moments as this was nothing like human love. Each of the apes remained locked inside a wordless prison; their "language" still wasn't much more sophisticated than a cry of pain. But they were among the least lonely creatures on the planet, the least lonely who had ever lived.

Meanwhile young Elephant pored over Capo's tool kit. He started tapping nut against cobble, cobble against anvil.

Capo's apes, as they grew from infancy, had much to learn about their environment. They needed to learn where to find water and food, how to use occasional tools to get at the food, how to apply their simple bush medicine. They had been driven to live this way, in fact, because of competition from the monkeys: They had to figure out how to extract food the monkeys couldn't steal, and that took smarts.

But there was no schooling here. It wasn't that Elephant was trying to figure out what Capo had been doing. But by experimenting, using trial and error and the tools the adults left lying around—all the time driven by the lure of the delicious palm nuts—Elephant would eventually learn how to smash nuts for himself. It would take him three more years before he got it right. Elephant had to figure everything out from scratch himself, as if repeating in his own lifetime the whole intellectual progression of the species.

On and on he pounded at the shells, as if he were the first ape ever to try this trick.

Capo brought himself to a slow, shuddering orgasm, his first of the day. He withdrew from Leaf and rolled onto his back, rather unjustifiably proud of himself, and allowed her to groom him, picking knots from the fur of his belly.

But now his peace of mind was disturbed by a sudden cacophony from deeper into the forest: hooting cries, drumming, the rustle of large bodies clambering and swinging.

Capo sat up. In his world it wasn't good to have too much excitement in which he wasn't involved. He vaulted over a tree stump, drummed on a branch, routinely cuffed Elephant about the head, and loped off toward the source of the noise.

A group of young males were hunting a monkey.

To Capo's eye it looked like the little vervetlike creature he had disturbed munching on acacia flowers earlier. Now it sat cowering at the top of a young palm.

The hunters had spread out around the base of the tree, and were clambering stealthily up neighboring trees. Others, Frond and Finger among them, had gathered around to see the excitement. It was these spectators who were making all the noise; the hunters themselves moved with stealth and silence. But to the monkey the din was terrifying and disorienting.

Capo was unpleasantly surprised when he saw who the hunters were. They were the rowdy young males who had loped off not days before on a foraging trip to another part of the forest clump. Their informal leader, a burly creature called Boulder, had given Capo some trouble in the past with his rebellious ways, and Capo had been happy to see him go: Let him blow off steam, make a few mistakes, even get hurt, and he would soon defer to Capo's authority once more.

But Boulder had been away just days, where Capo had expected weeks to pass. And from the look of his bristling aggression, his jaunt hadn't made him any calmer.

Capo was worried by the hunt, too. Monkey hunting usually happened only when other food was scarce, such as during periods of drought. Why hunt *now*?

One of the clambering apes made a sudden leap. Chittering, the monkey jumped the other way—straight into the arms of a waiting hunter. The watching apes hooted and barked. The hunter swung the screaming monkey around and slammed its skull against a tree trunk. Its cries were cut off immediately. Then the hunter hurled the limp carcass to the ground, its smashed head making a bright red splash in the forest's green murk.

That was Capo's moment. He vaulted past Boulder to be first onto the body. He grabbed up the still-warm scrap, got hold of one ankle and twisted, hard, ripping the little limb loose at the knee.

But, to his astonishment, Boulder challenged him. The burly male leapt at him feetfirst, ramming him in the chest. Capo fell sprawling, an ache spreading along his rib cage, the breath knocked out of him. Boulder deliberately picked up the monkey limb and bit into it, blood spurting over his mouth. All the apes were madly excited now, and they hooted and drummed and scrambled over one another.

Ignoring the pain in his chest Capo leapt to his feet with a roar. He couldn't let Boulder get away with this. He scrambled up into the lower branches of a tree, drummed ferociously, hooted loudly enough to disturb birds that roosted high above him, and vaulted back to the ground. He let anger surge through him so that he bristled, and a proud pink-purple erection stuck out before him: a nice touch that, his trademark.

But Boulder kept his nerve. With the monkey limb wielded in his hand like a club, he began his own display, his stamping, leaping, and drumming just as impressive as Capo's.

Capo knew he couldn't afford to lose this one. If he did, given Boulder's circle of blood-stained hunters, he might lose not just his status but his very life.

With an agility that belied his years, he leapt forward, knocked Boulder flat, and sat on his chest. Then he began to batter Boulder about the head and chest as hard as he could. Boulder fought back. But, save for youth, Capo had all the advantages: surprise, experience, and authority. Boulder couldn't shift Capo's weight, and he couldn't bring his own powerful arms and legs fully into play.

Gradually, Capo saw, he was winning the battle in the minds of the rest of the troop, which was just as important as subduing Boulder. The young male's followers seemed to have melted away into the trees, and the whoops of excitement and approval Capo heard now seemed to be directed at him.

But even as he battled to subdue Boulder, a slow deduction worked through Capo's roomy mind.

He thought of the dying trees he had glimpsed beyond the fringe of the forest island, the speedy return of Boulder and his wanderers, their apparent hunger, their need to hunt.

Boulder had found nowhere to go. *The forest patch was shrinking.* That had been true all of Capo's life, and now it was becoming unavoidable. There was no longer enough room for them here. If he tried to keep the group here, the tension between them, as they competed for dwindling resources, would become too intense.

They would have to move.

At last Boulder gave in. He lay limp under Capo, cupped the older male's buttocks, and even briefly stroked his still-erect penis, all gestures of submission. To drive home his point Capo kept battering at Boulder's head for long minutes. Then he clambered off the prone younger male. Still bristling, he made his way into the forest, where he could afford to limp and massage the pain in his chest and nobody could see how he hurt.

Behind him the others fell on the vervet. Their stomachs could not digest flesh well, and later they would pick through their feces for lumps of meat to eat again. It was a digestive system that was going to have to improve, if the descendants of these rummaging creatures were to prosper on the savannah.

II

Since Roamer's time, grass had remade the world.

The great epochal cooling of the Earth continued. As water was locked up in the Antarctic ice cap, sea levels diminished, and inland seas shrank or became landlocked. But with more continental landmass exposed, there was less sea to buffer the climate from extremes of heat and cold, and the weathering rock drew carbon dioxide from the air, making it less able to retain the sun's heat. Cooler and drier: The planet had developed a vast feedback mechanism, driving its surface to still more arid, chilly conditions.

Meanwhile tectonic collisions created new mountain ranges: the Andes of South America, and the Himalayas of Asia. These new uplifts cast gigantic rain shadows across the continents; the Sahara Desert would soon be born in such a shadow. In the new desiccation, great belts of broad-leaved deciduous woodland spread from south and north toward the equator.

And the grasses spread.

Grass plants—huddling in their great crowds, able to rely on fertilization by windblown pollen—might have been designed for the new open, dry conditions. Grass was able to subsist on the sporadic rainfall that now fell, whereas most trees, with their roots delving ever deeper into the ground, found only dryness and could not compete. But the real secret of grass lay in its stems. The leaves of most plants grew from the tips of shoots, but not grass's. Grass blades grew from underground stems. So grass could be cropped by a hungry animal, right down to the ground, without losing its power to regenerate.

These unspectacular properties had enabled grass to take over a world, and to feed it.

The new grass-eating herbivores developed specialized ruminant guts able to digest the grassy fodder over long periods and hence extract the maximum nutrient from it, and teeth able to withstand the abrasive effect of silica grains in grass blades. Many herbivores learned to migrate, because of the seasonality of the rainfall. These new mammals were larger than their archaic ancestors, lean and long-legged with specialized feet and a reduced number of toes to help them walk and run long distances and at speed. And meanwhile there was a sharp rise in the types of rodents, like voles and field mice, able to eat grass seeds.

New carnivores rose, too, equipped to feast on the new herds of large herbivores. But the rules of the ancient game had changed. In the sparse cover of a grassland, predators could see prey from long distances—and vice versa. So predators and prey began a metabolic arms race, with the emphasis on speed and endurance; they developed long legs and quick reactions.

A new kind of landscape began to spread—especially on the eastern side of the continents that were sheltered from the predominantly westerly winds and the rain they carried: open, grass-covered plains marked by scattered scraps of bush and woodland. And in turn animals who adapted to the new vegetation were rewarded with a guaranteed food source that could spread across hundreds of kilometers.

But their specializations, and the stability of the grasslands, would lock in the grazers to the grasses, the predators to their prey, establishing a close codependency. In this period the deer, cows, pigs, dogs, and rabbits looked little different from their equivalents of human times five million years later—although many of them would have looked surprisingly large; they would later be outcompeted by their smaller, faster cousins.

Meanwhile the opening up of land bridges, caused by the falling sea levels, led to a great crisscross migration of animals. Three kinds of elephants—high-browsing deinotheres, omnivorous gomphotheres, and browsing mastodonts—crossed from Africa to Asia. Along with them traveled the apes, cousins of Capo. And in the other direction came rodents and insectivores, cats, rhinos, mouse deer, pigs, and primitive types of giraffe and antelope.

There were some exotica, especially on the islands and the separated continents. In South America the largest rodents that ever lived were flourishing; there was a kind of guinea pig as large as a hippo. In Australia, the first kangaroos appeared. And what would later be considered tropical animals could be found in North America, Europe, and Asia: In England, the Thames was broad and swampy, and hippos and elephants basked on its floodplain. The world had cooled greatly since Noth's time, but it still wasn't *cold*; the deepest chill would afflict later ages.

But still the drying continued. Soon the older mosaic of grassland and woodland able to support a wide variety of animals lingered only in the equator-straddling Africa; elsewhere the grasslands opened up into arid plains, the savannah, steppe, and pampas. In these coarser, simplified conditions, many species fell away.

This intense evolutionary drama was driven by the endless shifts in Earth's climate—and the animals and plants were as helpless as bits of flux on a great terrestrial forge.

The next morning there was no luxurious ball scratching. As soon as he woke, Capo sat up, hooted softly at the pain of yesterday's lesions and bruises, and voided his bladder and bowels in a fast, efficient movement, ignoring the chitters of protest from below.

He vaulted from his nest and began to shimmy down the tree. Just as yesterday he roused the troop by crashing into their nests, hooting, kicking, and slapping. But today Capo wasn't interested in displaying; this morning his purpose was not dominance but leadership.

His determination was still strong in his mind. The troop had to move. Where they should go wasn't part of his unsophisticated decision making yet. But what was very clear in his head was the pressure of yesterday, his competition with Boulder, what he had sensed of the overcrowding of this little patch of forest.

The troop gathered together on the ground, more than forty of them, including infants clinging to their mothers' bellies or backs. They were sleepy, wary, scratching themselves and stretching. No sooner had Capo gotten them gathered, of course, than they were drifting apart again, plucking at bits of grass and moss on the ground, reaching for low-growing figs and other fruit. Even among the males he saw reserve, rivalry, resentment; they might resist him just to make their own points in the endless plays for dominance. And as for the females, they were a law unto themselves, for all of Capo's noise and violence.

How was he going to be able to lead this lot anywhere?

He wasn't conscious all the time, as a human was. He was conscious intermittently. He was only truly aware of his own thoughts, of himself, when thinking about others in the troop, because that was the primary purpose of consciousness, to model the thinking of others. He wasn't conscious in the same way about other domains of his life, like food-gathering or even tool using: those were unconscious actions, as peripheral to his awareness as breathing or the working of his legs and arms when he climbed. His thinking was not like a human's; it was simplified, compartmentalized.

His mind was a sophisticated machine, basically evolved to handle complex social situations. And he had a good innate understanding of his environment. He had a kind of database in his head of the resources he needed to stay alive and where they could be found. He was even good at dead reckoning navigation, and could easily compute good shortcut courses from one site to another. It was his environmental awareness that had prompted his concern about the shrinking forest patch.

It was hard for him to put together the elements of this puzzle: the danger posed by the shrinking forest, what he needed to do with his troop. But the danger was very real to him, and every instinct screamed at him to get away from here. The troop had to follow him. It was as simple as that; he knew it deep in the fibers of his being. If they stayed here they would surely die.

So he roared to get his blood flowing, and threw himself into the most energetic display he could. He raced up and down among the troop, slapping, punching, and kicking. He tore branches from the trees and waved them over his head to make himself look even bigger. He swung and vaulted over branches and trunks, drummed ferociously on the ground, and—as a climactic gesture to reinforce his victory of yesterday—he threw Boulder to the ground and shoved his own puckered anus in the younger male's face. It was a magnificent spectacle, as good as any Capo had mounted even in his younger days. Males whooped, females flinched, infants cried, and Capo allowed himself a glimmer of pride in his work.

But then he tried to lead them away, toward the fringe of the forest. He walked backward, shaking branches and running back and forth.

They stared. Suddenly he was behaving like a submissive junior male. So he displayed again, drumming, vaulting, and hooting, and went back to the follow-me routine.

At last one of them moved. It was Frond, the spindly young male. He took a couple of tentative knuckle-walk steps. Capo responded with a chattering cry and threw himself at Frond, rewarding him with a burst of intense grooming. Now more came forward: Finger, a few more of the junior males, eager to be groomed in turn. But Capo noticed that Boulder aimed a sly kick at Frond's backside.

And then, to Capo's intense relief, here came Leaf, her infant riding on her back, knuckle-walking grandly if a bit stiffly. Where this most senior female came, others followed, including Howl, the near-pubescent youngster.

But not all the females followed—and not all the males. Boulder stayed behind, sitting squat under a tree with his legs ostentatiously crossed under him. Other males gathered around him. Capo displayed at them furiously. But they huddled and groomed each other as if Capo no longer existed. It was a deliberate snub. If he wanted to maintain his position, Capo was going to have to break up this knot of rebellion, perhaps even face down Boulder once more.

But, almost to his own surprise, he gave up his displaying and stood back, panting.

In his heart he knew he had lost them, that he had pushed them too hard, that his troop was fissioning. Those who chose to follow him would find their way, with him, to a new destiny—a destiny he himself couldn't yet imagine. Those who stayed behind would just have to take their chances.

He loped quickly away, out of the heart of the forest and toward the daylight, without looking back—although he was unable to resist a final valedictory liquid fart in the direction of the rebels.

In the end about half the males and rather more of the females stayed behind. It was a drastic diminishing of Capo's domain. And as he walked toward the bright light of the plain he could hear the whoops and howling of the males. The battles over the new hierarchy had already begun.

At the forest's fringe, on the edge of emptiness, Capo paused.

Just as yesterday, gomphotheres grazed on damaged, half-drowned trees. To the north the grassy plain stretched to its misty horizon, littered with glimmering lakes and marshes, herbivore herds passing like shadows. To the south, beyond a kilometer or so, the ground gleamed white as bone. The salt pan would be a difficult place to cross. But Capo could see how the land rose, up toward a green plateau, where—it seemed to his poor eyes, adapted for the short focuses of the forest—a thick blanket of trees lay draped over the rock.

South, then, across the dry land, to the new forest on the plateau.

Without glancing back to see if the others were following, he set off on knuckles and feet, pushing through grass that waved around him, shoulder-high.

The land rose, quickly becoming drier.

There were some trees here, but they were just thin-trunked pines clinging to arid ground, with none of the comforting density and moistness of the forest clump. So there was little shelter to be had from the high sun. Capo was soon panting hard, baking inside his thick fur, his knuckles and feet rubbed raw. He could not sweat, and his knuckle-walking gait, effective for clambering around the complex, crowded environment of the forest, was inefficient here.

And Capo, a creature of the forest, was intimidated by this great sweep of openness. He hooted softly and longed to cower, to hold his arms over his head, to hurl himself into the nearest tree.

There were animals to be seen, scattered over the dry plain: There were deer, some species of dog, and a family of grubbing animals like spiky-furred pigs. The larger animals were very few. But as Capo blundered on, many smaller creatures scampered away underfoot: lizards, rodents, even primitive rabbits.

The twenty or so of the troop who had followed him toiled painfully up the slope after him. They moved slowly, for they stopped frequently to feed, drink, groom, play, argue. This migration was more like a slow walk made by easily distracted children. But it was not in Capo's instincts to hurry them. They were what they were.

Capo crested a shallow, eroded hill. From here he looked back across the wet, glistening landscape with its islands of forest and crowding herbivores. But when he looked ahead, to the south, he could see the great dryness they approached. It was a broad, high, dry valley, scattered with thin trees and bits of vegetation. It was kept arid by an accident of geology which had left it cupped in a great subterranean bowl of rock, barren of springs, shadowed from rainfall.

It was an intimidating sight; the valley was exposed, utterly open. And yet he must cross it.

And from here, now that there was no forest to soak up the noise, he could make out that great, mysterious roaring from the west. The remote noise sounded like the groaning cry of some huge, pained, angry beast, or like the thunderous hoofs of some great herbivorous herd. But when he looked to the west he could see no dust clouds, no black wash of animal bodies. There was nothing but the roaring, continuing just as it had all his life.

He began to clamber down the rocky slope, still heading south.

The ground became bare. Still trees clung to life here, their roots wormed into faults in the rock. But these pines were sparse, their leaves spiky, jealous of their water. He stopped under one of these trees. Its branches and leaves offered him virtually no shade. He could find no fruit, and the leaves he plucked were sharp and dry in his mouth. He made a grab for a small mouselike creature with long, levered hind legs; his mouth watered at the thought of biting into its soft wet body, its small bones crunching in his mouth. But here on this rocky ground he was clumsy and noisy, and the mouse thing evaded him easily.

Now the ground changed again, becoming a broad slope of broken stone that spread out before him, a road leading to the depths of the dry valley. The going got even harder as Capo slid and slipped on the loose rubble. Hot, thirsty, hungry, scared, he hooted his protest and threw bits of the rubble around, tramping and kicking it. But the land was not to be intimidated even by Capo's mighty displays.

Meanwhile the chasma watched the ragged group of anthropoids as they struggled down the uneven, treacherous slope.

She had never seen creatures like this before. With a predator's cold interest, she made unconscious calculations of their speed, strength, and meat yield, and began categorizing the individuals—here was one who seemed wounded and limped a little; here was an infant, clasped tightly to its mother's chest; here was a juvenile straying, foolishly, from the tight group.

This chasmaporthetes was actually a kind of hyena. But, long legged, slim, she looked more like a cheetah. She did not have all of the true cats' suppleness and speed, not quite; her kind had more adapting to do in the fleet conditions of this emerging world of grass. But her range was huge in this barren valley. She was the top predator here, and she was well equipped for her grisly work.

To her, the apes were new meat on the savannah. She waited, her eyes glowing like captive stars.

At last, exhausted, Capo gave up. He slumped to the ground. One by one, what was left of his troop joined him. By the time they had all arrived, the sun had started to set, filling the sky with fire and casting long, stark shadows along the floor of this gravel-littered bowl.

A kind of dull indecision raged within Capo. They shouldn't stay here, out in the open; his body longed to climb a tree trunk, to pull together branches to make a cozy, warm, safe nest. But there were no trees here, no security to be had. On the other hand they couldn't cross the valley floor in the dark. And they were all hungry, thirsty, exhausted.

He didn't know what to do. So he did nothing.

The troop began to disperse, following their own instincts. Finger picked up a cobble-shaped, palm-sized rock, perhaps hoping to use it in some future nut-cracking project. But a scorpion scuttled out from beneath the rock, and Finger fled, hooting.

Frond was sitting alone with his back to the rest of the group, assiduously working at something. Capo, suspicious, loped up as quietly as he could on this loose, scattered gravel.

Frond had found a termite mound. He was sitting before it, clumsily poking sticks into it. When he saw Capo he cowered, screeching. Capo delivered brisk, perfunctory blows to his head and shoulders, as Frond would have expected. He should have hooted to the rest on discovering this bounty.

Capo ripped open a shrub. All of its branches were spindly and bent, and when he stripped a branch by passing it through his mouth, the hard, spiky leaves hurt his lips. But it would have to do. He sat alongside Frond. He pushed his stick into a crevice in the mound, and worked it until it had slid in deep. It was not ideal; the stick was too short and bent to be truly effective, but it would have to do. He jiggled it around, waiting patiently. Then he withdrew the stick, centimeter by centimeter. To the stick clung soldier termites, sent to defend the colony from this invader. Capo took great care not to dislodge this cargo. Then he swept the stick through his mouth, enjoying a mouthful of sweet, moist flesh.

When they saw what was going on the rest of the troop crowded around, the older ones making their own fishing sticks. Very quickly a rough pecking order established itself, lubricated by kicks, punches, hoots, and sly grooming. The more senior male and females alike got closest to the mound while the young, who didn't understand what was happening anyhow, were excluded. Capo didn't care. He just concentrated on holding his own position close to the mound while working assiduously at the termites.

The termites were antique creatures whose complex society was the result of their own long evolutionary story. This mound was ancient, built of the mud that had pooled here when infrequent rainstorms caused temporary floods. Its rock-hard carapace protected the termites from the attentions of most animals, but not these apes.

Capo's use of tools—the termite-fishing sticks, the hammer-stones, the leaves he would chew to a sponge to extract water from hollows, even the fine toothpicklike sticks he sometimes used to perform crude dentistry—seemed sophisticated. He knew what he wanted to achieve; he knew what kind of tool he needed to achieve it. He would memorize the location of his favorite tools, like his hammer-stones, and made subtle decisions about using them—for instance trading off the distance he had to carry a hammer against its weight. And it wasn't a case of just picking up a handy rock, found by chance; he modified some of his tools, like this termite-fishing stick.

And yet he was not like a human craftsman. His modifications were slight: his tools, abandoned after use, would have been hard to distinguish from the products of the inanimate world. The actions he used to make the tools were part of his normal repertoire, like biting, leaf stripping, stone throwing. Nobody had invented wholly *new* actions, like a potter's clay throwing or a wood carver's whittling. He used each tool for one use, and one use only; it never occurred to him that a termite fishing-stick might also be used as a toothpick. He did not improve his tools, once he had found a design that worked. And if—by some chance—he had in the course of his life happened upon a new kind of tool, however successful a design it was, its use would have spread only very slowly through his community, perhaps taking generations to reach every member. Coaching, the notion that the contents of someone else's mind might be shaped by rehearsal and demonstration, had yet to be discovered.

So Capo's tool kit was staggeringly limited, and very conservative. Capo's ancestors, five million years gone, creatures of a different species, had used tools of only fractionally less sophistication. Capo wasn't even aware he *was* using tools.

And yet here was Capo, working assiduously, knowing what he wanted, selecting materials to achieve his goal, making and shaping the world around him, the cleverest so far of all of Purga's long line of descendants. It was as if a slow fire were smoldering in his eyes, his mind, his hands, a fire that would soon burn much more brightly.

As the sun slid beyond the horizon at the valley's end the apes huddled closer. Deeply unhappy, they pushed, jostled, and slapped, hooting and screeching at each other. This wasn't their place. They had no weapons to defend themselves, no fire to keep the animals at bay. They didn't even have the instinct to keep silent at sunset, the hour of predators. All they had was the protection of each other, of their numbers—the hope that another would be taken, not *me*.

Capo made sure he was right at the center of the band, surrounded by the burly bodies of the other adults.

The young male called Elephant didn't have as powerful an instinct for self-preservation. And his mother, lost somewhere in the middle of the huddle, was too concerned with her newest child, a female; right now Elephant was a low priority. He was unlucky to be just the wrong age: too old to be defended by the adults, too young to fight for a place at the center, away from the danger.

He soon found himself pushed out to the fringe of the group. Still, he tried to settle down. He found a place close to Finger, a cousin. This ground was hard and bony, unlike the soft roosts he was used to, but by squirming he managed to make himself a bowl-shaped hollow. He pressed his belly against Finger's back.

He was too young even to understand the danger he was in. He slept uneasily.

Later, in the dark, he was woken by a soft pricking at his shoulder. It was almost gentle, like a grooming. He squirmed a little, burrowing closer to Finger's back. But then he felt breath on his cheek, heard a purring growl like a rock rolling down a hillside, smelled a breath that stank of meat. Instantly awake, his heart hammering, he screeched and convulsed.

His shoulder was ripped, painfully. He found himself dragged backward, like a branch torn off a tree. He caught a final glimpse of the troop—they were awake, panicking, hooting, scrambling over each other to get away. Then a starlit sky whirled around him, and he was slammed into the ground hard enough to knock the breath out of him.

A form moved over him, sleek, silhouetted against the blue-black sky. He felt a hard-muscled chest press against his, almost lovingly. There was fur with a scent of burning, breath like blood, and two yellow eyes that shone over him.

Then the bites came, to his legs, over one of his kidneys. They were sharp, almost clinical stabs, and he convulsed with the fiery pain. He screeched and rolled, tried to run. But his legs collapsed, his hamstrings cut. Now came those prickings at his neck again. He was lifted up by the scruff, lifted right off the ground, and he could feel sharp teeth working *inside* his skin. At first he struggled, scrabbling at the gravel with his hands, but his efforts only brought more pain as the flesh at his neck was torn further.

He gave up. Hanging passively from the chasma's mouth, his head and damaged legs clattering against the uneven ground, his thoughts dissolved. He could no longer hear the hooting cries of his troop. He was alone now, alone with the pain and the iron stink of his own blood, and the steady, patient padding of the chasma's footsteps.

Perhaps he was unconscious for a while.

He was dropped on the ground. He did not land hard, but all his wounds flared with pain. Mewling, he pushed at the ground. It was littered with rubble like the place he had come from, but was covered in fur, and the stink of chasmas.

And now small shapes bounded around him, black on black, fast moving, a little clumsy. He felt the brush of whiskers on his fur, tiny nips at his ankles and wrists. They were chasma pups. He hooted his defiance, and swung a fist blindly. He connected with a hot little bundle that was knocked off its feet, yowling.

There was a short, barking roar: the mother chasma. In sudden panic, he tried to crawl.

The pups yapped excitedly as they completed their short chase. And now the biting started in earnest, digging into his back, buttocks, belly. He rolled onto his back, lifting his legs to his chest and flapping at the air. But the pups were fast, furious, and dogged; soon one of them had dug her teeth into his cheek, applying all her small weight to ripping open his face.

Again the mother roared, scattering the pups. Again Elephant tried to flee. Again the pups caught him and inflicted a dozen more tiny, debilitating wounds.

If not for her pups, the chasma would have killed Elephant quickly. She was giving them the chance to chase down a prey animal and knock it over. When they were older, they would be able to finish off prey themselves, ripping it apart; later still she would release some of her prey almost unharmed and allow the pups to finish the hunt. It was a kind of learning by opportunity. This was no more human-style teaching than what occurred among the apes: it was an innate behavior evolved in this clever carnivorous species to enable the young to acquire the skills they would need when hunting alone.

And as the lesson went on Elephant was still conscious, a spark of terror and longing buried in a broken shred of blood, flesh, and gristle. The boldest of the pups even fed on the tongue that dangled from his broken jaw.

But the pups were too young to finish off Elephant alone.

At last the mother took over. As her great jaw closed around his skull—as he felt a prickle of biting teeth around his scalp, like a crown of thorns—the last thing Elephant heard was that remote purring growl.

When the morning came, everyone knew that Elephant had been taken.

Capo peered with fascination at the scuffed, hair-strewn gravel patch where Elephant had briefly struggled, at the line of bloody paw marks, already dried to brown, that led away into the distance. He felt a vague regret at the loss of Elephant. It seemed baffling that he would never again see that clumsy youth with his stiff, awkward attempts at grooming, his clumsy fumbling as he tried to figure out how to get the flesh out of an oil palm nut.

But before the day was done, only Elephant's mother would remember him. And when she was dead in her turn, there would be nothing to say he had ever existed, and he would be gone into the final blank darkness that had swallowed up all of his ancestors, every one.

Elephant had paid the price of the troop's survival. Capo felt a cold relief. Without hesitation, without even performing the follow-me display, Capo moved down the slope and out onto the salt flats.

III

The next day they had to cross the salt. Under a washed-out blue-white sky the pan spread almost to Capo's horizon, where hills, trees, and marshes crowded. It was as if this gray sheet were a flaw in the world.

The salt, lying over hard, grayish mud, was broadly flat, but the surface had texture, streaked here and there by swooping concentric lines that crowded to central knots. In one place an underground spring had caused the salt to billow up in great blocks that the apes had to clamber over.

But nothing grew, here on the salt. There weren't even any tracks. Nothing moved save the apes, no rabbits or rodents, not even an insect. The wind moaned across this hard mineral stage, nowhere broken by the rustle of bushes and trees, the hiss of grass.

But still Capo kept on, for there was nothing else to do.

It took hours to cross the salt pan. But at last, his feet and hands aching, Capo found himself reluctantly climbing a ridge. At the crest of the ridge there was a belt of forest—even if it was a dense, uncomfortable-looking kind of forest.

Capo hesitated, facing the forest. He was overheated; his legs and feet were bleeding from a dozen small lesions. Then he pushed forward awkwardly and entered the forest's green gloom.

The ground was hidden by a tangle of roots, branches, moss, and leaves. Wild celery grew in clumps everywhere. Although it was around noon, the air here was cold, made damp by a faint mist like a morning fog. The tree trunks were clammy, and thick lichen and moss left uncomfortable green streaks on his palms. The dampness seemed to dig through his fur. But after the aridity of the salt pan he relished the close, comforting tangle of green around him, and he devoured the leaves, fruit, and fungi he was able to pluck from the ground around him. And he felt safe from predators. Surely there was nothing that could strike at the hungry, weary band in this green density.

But now he saw hulking brown-black shapes just ahead, dimly visible through the tangled green. He froze.

A huge arm reached out to a branch wider than Capo's thigh. Muscles worked in a great mound of shoulder, and the branch was snapped in two as easily as Capo might snap off a twig to clean his teeth. Giant fingers plucked leaves from the nearby branches and pushed them steadily into immense jaws. The whole head worked as the big animal chewed, heavy muscles working the skull and jaw together.

The nearest creature was an ape, as Capo was, a male—and yet unlike Capo. The big male watched the odd, scrawny little apes without curiosity. He looked powerful, threatening. But he didn't move. The male, and a small clan of females and infants, did nothing but sit around and feed on leaves and the wild celery that carpeted the forest floor.

This was a gorilla: a remote cousin of Capo's. His kind had split off from the broader lineages of apes a million years ago. The split had come in a period when another forest had fragmented, isolating the populations it supported. As their habitat shrank to the mountaintops, these apes had turned to a diet of leaves, endlessly abundant even here, and became huge enough to resist the cold—yet they remained oddly graceful, able to move silently through this dense forest.

Though populations of gorillas would later adapt back to lowland conditions, learning to climb trees and subsist off fruit, in a sense their evolutionary story was already over. They had become specialized in their environments, learning to eat food that was so well-defended—covered in hooks, spikes, and stings—that no other creatures competed for it. They could eat nettles, for example, with an elaborate maneuver that involved stripping leaves from a stem, folding in the stinging leaf edges, and popping the whole packet into their mouths.

Sitting in their montane islands, lazily eating their leaves, they would survive almost unchanged until human times, when the final extinction would overtake them all.

When he was sure the gorillas were no threat, Capo crept away, leading the others onward through the forest.

At last Capo emerged from the far side of the forested ridge.

They had at last clambered out of the arid lowland basin. When he looked south across the plateau he had reached, he faced a rocky, rubble-strewn valley that scoured its way down to lower ground. But there, beyond the valley, he could see the land he had hoped to find: higher than the plain he had left behind, but well watered, glistening with lakes, coated green by grass, and studded with pockets of forest. The shadowy forms of a great herd of herbivores—proboscideans, perhaps—drifted with stately grandeur across the lush plain.

With a hoot of triumph Capo capered, vaulted over rocks, drummed on the stony ground, and shit explosively, spraying the dry boulders with his stink.

His followers responded to Capo's display only listlessly. They were hungry and dreadfully thirsty. Capo was exhausted himself. But he displayed anyway, obeying a sound instinct that every triumph, however small, should be celebrated.

But now he had climbed so high that the remote, persistent growling from the west had grown louder. Dimly curious, Capo turned and looked that way.

From this elevated place he could see a long way. He made out a remote turbulence, a white billowing. It seemed to hover above the ground like a boiling cloud. He was actually seeing a kind of mirage, a very remote vision carried to him by refraction in the warming air. But the billowing steam clouds were real, though their suspension above the ground was not.

What he was glimpsing was the Strait of Gibraltar, where even now the mightiest waterfall in Earth's history—with the power and volume of a thousand Niagaras—was thundering over shattered cliffs and into an empty ocean basin. Once the plain from which Capo had climbed had been covered by water two kilometers deep, for it was the floor of the Mediterranean.

Capo had been born in the basin that lay between the coast of Africa, to the south, and Spain, to the north. In fact, he was not very far from the place where a clever dinosaur called Listener, long ago, had stood at the shore of Pangaea and gazed out on the mighty Tethys Sea. Now he had climbed out of the basin to reach Africa proper. But if Listener had seen the birth of the Tethys, Capo was witnessing something like its death. As the ocean levels dropped, this last fragment of the Tethys had become dammed at Gibraltar. Landlocked, the great ocean had evaporated—until at last it emptied, leaving behind a great valley in places five kilometers deep, littered with salt pans.

But as the climate oscillated, the sea level rose again, and Atlantic waters broke through the Gibraltar barrier. Now, the ocean was refilling. But Capo had nothing to fear of giant waves cascading from the west, for even a thousand Niagaras could not refill an ocean overnight. The

Gibraltar waters suffused the great basin more gradually, creating great rivers. The old seafloor turned slowly into sodden marshland, where the vegetation slowly died, before the waters rose so high they covered over the ground altogether.

But after each refilling the global ocean levels would drop again, and once again the Mediterranean would evaporate. This would happen as many as *fifteen times* over the million years bracketing Capo's brief life. The Mediterranean would be left with a complex seabed geology, with layers of silt sandwiching salt pans laid down in the successive dryings.

But this trapped ocean's dryings were having a profound effect on the area Capo lived in—and on Capo's kind. Before the great dryings, the Sahara region had been densely forested and well watered, and home to many species of apes. But with the climatic pump of the dryings, and in the lengthening rain shadow cast by the more remote Himalayas, the Sahara was becoming increasingly arid. The old forests were breaking up. And with them the communities of apes were splintering, each fragmentary population embarking on its own journey to a new evolutionary destiny—or extinction.

But the great rumbling, the blurred vision of Gibraltar, was too remote to have any meaning for Capo. He turned away, and stumbled down onto the plain.

At last Capo moved off bare rock on to vegetation. He relished the green softness of the grass under his knuckles as he loped forward. As the others tumbled after him they rolled and sprawled, pulling up the long grass around them, relishing the delicious contrast with the hard lifeless rock.

But they weren't home yet. A stretch of a few hundred meters of open savannah, studded with thorn bushes, separated them from the nearest forest clump—and the plain was not unoccupied.

A group of hyenas worked at a fallen carcass. Bulky, round, it might have been an infant gomphothere, perhaps felled by a chasma. The hyenas snapped and growled at each other as they worked at the scavenged meat, their heads buried in the creature's stomach, their sleek bodies writhing industriously.

As Capo cowered in the grass, Frond and Finger came up alongside him. They hooted softly, and gave Capo's backside a perfunctory groom, picking out bits of dust and rock. The younger males were cursorily acknowledging his authority. But Capo could tell they were impatient. Weary, thirsty, hungry, thoroughly spooked by the trek across the openness, they, like the rest of the troop, longed to reach the shelter and provision of the trees. And that was corroding Capo's hold on them. The tension between the three males was powerful, toxic.

But it was a confrontation conducted in near silence, as the three of them kept their presence concealed from the hyenas.

While Capo still hesitated, it was Frond who made the move. He took one, two tentative shuffles forward. He received a hefty clout on the back of his head from Capo for his defiance. But Frond just bared his teeth, and moved out of reach.

The tall grass stems waved languorously at Frond's passing, as if he were swimming through a sea of vegetation. And now Frond got up on to his hind legs, poking his head, shoulders, and upper torso out of the grass so he could see better. He was a slim shadow, upright, like a sapling.

The hyenas were still intent on their baby elephant. Frond ducked back into the grass and continued on his way.

At last he reached the nearest stand of trees. Capo, with a mixture of resentment and relief, saw him climb up a tall palm tree, his legs and arms working in synchrony, like components of a smoothly oiled machine. When Frond had reached the top of the palm he hooted softly, calling the others. Then he began plucking nuts from the palm and throwing them down to the ground.

One by one, led by Finger and the senior female, Leaf, the apes scurried through the grass toward the forest pocket.

They were not troubled by the hyenas, though many of the scavengers scented the vulnerable apes. They were fortunate that in the bloody calculations of the hyenas' small minds, the lure of the immediately available meat outweighed the attraction of attacking these dusty, ragged-looking primates.

Capo tried to make the best of it. He slapped and punched the other males as they loped along, as if the whole thing had been his idea, as if he were directing them in their short migration. The males submitted to his blows, but he sensed a tension about them, a subtle lack of deference that made him uneasy.

On entering the forest, the apes fanned out.

Capo pushed through a bank of slim young trees to find a marshy lake: flat green-blue water surrounded by the comforting green and brown of forest. He hurried down to the water's edge, pushed his muzzle into the cool liquid, and began to drink.

As the apes reached the water, some of them waded into it, walking upright until they were waist deep. They used their fingers to strain blue-green algae from the water and gobbled it down: a way of feeding that was another little gift of bipedalism. Several youngsters dove headlong into the water and started scraping the accumulated dust out of their fur; they made a terrific hooting and splashing. A flock of birds had been drifting in peace at the heart of the lake, but now they took fright, and clattered thunderously into the sky.

But some of the younger males had gathered together at the water's edge, Frond and Finger among them. Frond had found a cobble that might serve as a hammer-stone; he was toying with it experimentally. And every now and then the males cast sly glances toward Capo. Their body language was redolent of conspiracy.

Capo pursed his lips and blew a soft raspberry.

He was very smart at working through social problems. He knew what the younger males were thinking. He had brought them to safety, but that wasn't good enough: his performance as they had crossed that last grassy barrier had not convinced anyone. To restore his authority he was going to have to do some impressive displaying. He could rip down some branches and start stalking around the water's edge, for instance; the foliage, the water, and the light would make for a powerful show. And then there would be hard battles to be won.

But perhaps now wasn't the time.

He watched mothers gently bathing their infants, younger males wrestling almost politely as their limbs and skin recovered from the heat and aridity of the salt pan. Later. Let them get over the trek, before business as usual was resumed.

And besides, truth be told, he didn't feel up to a great new war right now. His limbs ached, his skin was sore and covered in scrapes and lesions, and his gut, used to a continual flow of food and water, rumbled at the stop-start treatment it had endured. He was *tired*. He rubbed his eyes and yawned, allowing himself an explosive belch. Time enough later for the hard work of life, of being Capo. For now he needed to rest.

With that excuse lodged in his mind, he turned away from the water and loped into the forest.

He quickly found a kapok tree filled with large ripe fruits. The kapok, though, was armed with long sharp thorns to defend its fruit. So he tore two smooth branches from the tree and placed one under each foot, gripping the branches with his toes. Then, clinging to the branches with his feet, he climbed the tree, marching over the thorns as if they didn't exist. The action of climbing made his limbs glow with the accustomed pleasure, their ancient design fulfilled; if he never took another step on the ground in his life he would have been content.

When he had reached a patch dense with fruit, he pulled off another branch and set it down over the thorns. Sitting on his impromptu saddle, he began to feed.

From here he could see that this forest clump had grown up around an oxbow lake, cast off by a river that wound its way back into the deeper country to the south, across this rich, vegetated Sahara. In the future this great Nile-like artery would be dislodged by tectonic shifting from its present course, and would curl around to the south, no longer crossing the Sahara. Eventually it would outflow into the Bight of Benin in western Africa, and humans would know it as the Niger. Even rivers were molded by time, as the land rose and fell, as the mountains grew and shrank away like dreams.

But for now this river was a great green corridor into the interior of the country. The troop could work that way, following the forest, penetrating deeper, moving away from the coast.

A piercing hoot echoed through the forest. It was a cry with only one meaning: *Danger is here.* Capo spat out a mouthful of fruit and scrambled down to the ground.

Before he got to the lake he knew what the problem was. He could *smell* them. And as he looked more carefully he could see the signs of their passing: bits of fruit skin, dumped even under this kapok, what looked like nests high in the taller trees.

Others.

They came swarming out of the trees and the undergrowth. There were many of them, bewilderingly many—fifty, sixty—more than Capo's troop had ever numbered. Their males came toward the water's edge. They were all displaying ferociously, fur bristling, drumming on roots and branches and hurling themselves through the low branches of the trees.

After all they had endured to get here, this patch of forest was not empty. Capo's heart sank, heavy with a sense of failure.

But Capo's troop was responding. Weak as they were, fur too damp to bristle effectively, nevertheless the males and even a couple of the older females were displaying as best they could. Capo threw himself forward to the front row of his troop and immediately began his own display, summoning up all his long experience to create as spectacular and intimidating a show as possible.

The two troops lined up; two walls of shrieking, posturing apes faced each other. They were the same species, and they looked indistinguishable, one from the other. But they could smell the differences between them: on the one hand the subtle, familiar savor of kin, and on the other the sharper stink of strangers. There was true xenophobic hatred in these displays, an authenticity in the threat they conveyed. Here was the other side of these clever animals' social bonds: If you were locked into a group, then everybody else became your enemy, just because they weren't *you.*

But Capo was scared. He quickly realized that these others were showing no signs of backing down. Indeed, their displays were becoming more ferocious, and those big lead males were steadily advancing on his troop.

Capo knew how it would go. It would not be an all-out war. The strongest would go first, the males and senior females; the infants would probably provide some sweet flesh for the bellies of these strangers. *One by one.* It would be a slow, bloody killing, but it would continue until it was complete. Such systematic slaughter was a horror new to the world, a horror only these apes, of all the Earth's animals, were smart enough to conceive of and see through.

They couldn't stay here, Capo knew. Maybe they could go on, resume the trek across the plain; maybe Capo could yet lead his troop somewhere empty, somewhere safe.

But in his deepest gut he intuitively knew the truth. In this world of shrinking forests, the surviving animals had already crammed themselves into all the remaining islands of the old vegetation. And that was why the others would fight so hard to exclude them. There were already too many of *them* for this dwindling patch—and they had nowhere else to go either.

There was nowhere safe to go, but no choice but to leave.

With much foot scuffing and branch waving, he began the subtle dance that indicated he wanted to lead his troop away from this place— back to the edge of the forest, back to the savannah. One or two of the females responded. Intimidated by these ferocious others, realizing how hopeless their situation was, Leaf and the others gathered up their infants and prepared to follow. Even Frond, one of the defiant young males, turned in confusion.

But Finger would not accept it.

He had been slamming a hammer-stone against an exposed root, adding its powerful noise to his display. Now, with a sudden, terrifying surge, he turned away from the others and launched a ferocious assault on Capo. He slammed into Capo's back, knocking him flat, and he pounded his leader's head with his fists. Then he rolled away and threw himself with equal vigor at the largest of the others' males. Suddenly the noise, already high, became cacophonous, and the air filled with the stink of blood and panic shit.

Capo rolled on to his back and sat up, his neck aching. The other males subtly moved away, even as they hooted and yelled.

Finger was not faring well. He had managed to pin the big male to the ground. But now more of the others were throwing themselves into the melee. Soon they had hold of Finger. They hauled him away from his opponent, holding his limbs and head as if he were a hunted monkey; already blood streamed from bite-inflicted gashes in his skin. And then they threw him to the ground. But his cries soon became gurgles, drowned in blood, and Capo heard the grisly rip of flesh, the cracking of bone, the snapping of ligaments.

But Finger's attack had had a profound effect. If anyone was going to attack these others, it should have been Capo. Capo knew he had already lost. He would be lucky to survive the day: If these others did not kill him, then his own former subordinates would.

Capo, though shamed and beaten, resumed his calling dance, trying to get his troop to come away. There was nothing else he could do.

They didn't all respond, even now. Some of them, spitting fear and defiance, dispersed into the forest to seek their own destinies. He would never see them again.

The young female Howl glanced at her troop with wide, fearful eyes—and then made directly for the others. She would suffer a beating at the hands of the females, but maybe she would be attractive enough to the other males to be allowed to live, especially if she managed to become pregnant quickly through the hard matings she would have to endure.

Those who remained with Capo at last began moving, back toward the fringe of the forest—but only when Frond echoed Capo's dance.

Capo understood, of course. They were following Frond, not him.

They came back to the fringe of the forest. They were not pursued, not for now. They picked at leaves and scraps of fruit, dismayed, uncertain.

Capo was depressed to be back where he had started. He could even see the corpse of that infant gomphothere, still lying on the ground. He clambered into a tree away from the others, and built an impromptu nest.

Now that Finger was dead, he wasn't sure who would emerge as his main challenger. Frond, perhaps? It was possible Capo could continue to maintain a powerful position by forming an alliance with one male against the other. He might no longer be the boss of bosses, but like a kingmaker his backing would be crucial, and he would continue to enjoy many of the privileges that came with power, notably mating privileges. Maybe he could even work his way back to the top that way. His subtle mind thought further, considering shifting alliances, treacheries . . .

His thoughts dissolved. He felt overwhelmed by the journey he had made, the crashing disappointment that had waited at the end of it.

Nothing seemed to matter anymore, not even the intricate political games that had won him so much in the past.

The others seemed to sense his mood. They avoided him, not coming to groom, not even looking at him. His gruesome defeat had been postponed by the death of Finger, but its sad process was still under way. Capo's day was done, his life nearly over. All his swagger was gone.

But now Leaf came to him. She clambered into his nest alongside him, and, gently, began to groom him, as she had when they were both young and the world was bright and rich and full of possibility.

Frond wasn't interested in Capo, one way or the other. He had something else on his mind.

He knuckle-walked a few paces out into the sunlit green. There he got to his hind legs once more. As always he was unsteady on his feet. But the elevation of his head gave him a platform from which to view the land, check on any predators or other dangers around.

Frond ducked back into the grass, and made his way cautiously to the gomphothere corpse. As he approached, carrion birds screeched their protest but flapped away. The scavengers had done their work well: The body looked as if it had exploded, with limbs and ribs lying scattered on the ground, bloody bone gleaming, and an eyeless, fleshless head peering back at him accusingly, spadelike tusks lying broken and gnawed. He rooted through the scraps of skin and bits of hyena-chewed flesh, but there was little to be had; the scavenging machinery of the savannah had worked thoroughly to consume the proboscidean's flesh. The hyenas had even destroyed the soft ribs. But he found a thigh bone, long, thick, terminating at either end in huge, bulging lumps. It was unbroken. He tapped it experimentally against another bone; it sounded hollow.

He found a cobble in the dirt, the right size to fit into his fist. He raised the cobble and smashed it into the bone. The bone split, and rich, delicious marrow began to leak out. It was a resource that had been beyond the reach of the dogs and carrion birds, beyond their teeth and beaks. But now it was not beyond Frond. He raised the bone and began to suck down the marrow greedily.

The others who had driven Capo and his troop out of the forest would stay there, clinging to what they had. Such groups would eventually give rise to the chimpanzees, who would differ little from this ancestral stock. They would survive, even prosper: As the desert spread and the forests retreated to their last redoubts around the equator, the great rivers would provide corridors for the chimps to use to migrate into Africa's interior.

But the descendants of Capo's troop were now marching toward a very different destiny. This unremarkable troop of apes, stranded by the disappearance of their forest, would find there was a way to make a living *out here*. But leaving an ecology to which they had been adapting for millions of years was hard: As long as the apes couldn't walk or run over long distances, while they couldn't sweat, while they couldn't even digest meat, many, many would die. But some would survive: just a few, but that was enough.

Frond had finished the marrow. But there were plenty more bones to be broken. He stood up again. He looked back to his troop, hooting to call them over.

Then he turned back to the savannah. He was bipedal, tool wielding, meat eating, xenophobic, hierarchical, combative, competitive—all of which he had brought from the forest—and yet he was imbued with the best qualities of his ancestors, with Purga's doggedness, Noth's exuberance, Roamer's courage, even Capo's vision. Full of the possibilities of the future, laden with the relics of the past, the young male, standing upright, gazed at the open plain.

TWO

humans

interlude

Alyce and Joan shuffled with the crowd of passengers toward the airport terminal. They had been out in the dense, smoky air for only a few minutes, and Joan was supported by the arm of Alyce Sigurdardottir. Still, she felt as if she were melting.

And when she had stepped off the plane the first thing Joan had felt was an earthquake. It was an extraordinary sensation, a dreamlike shifting, over almost before it had begun.

The quake had been caused by Rabaul, of course.

Beneath the island of Papua New Guinea, magma was stirring; molten rock, a thousand cubic kilometers of it. This great bleeding had been moving up through faults in the Earth's thin outer crust, up toward the huge, ancient caldera called Rabaul, at a rate of ten meters every month. It was an astounding pace for a geological event, a testament to the mighty energies. The rising mass had pushed up the overlying rock, putting the land under immense stress.

Rabaul had erupted cataclysmically many times before. Two such eruptions had been identified by human scientists, one some fifteen hundred years ago, the other around two thousand years before that. It would surely happen again sometime.

The other passengers, trooping through the smoky air to the airport's small terminal, seemed oblivious to the quake. Bex Scott had rejoined her mother, Alison, and her sister, who had golden eyes and *green* hair. Beneath a sky stained by remote fires, as the land shuddered beneath them unnoticed, the beautiful genriched children chattered brightly with their elegant mother. They had their silver earplugs still nestling in their small ears, Joan noticed. It was as if they walked around in a neon fog.

Joan remembered guiltily her bland assurance that Bex would have to be desperately unlucky for Rabaul to go pop just when she was in the vicinity. Out here, on this shuddering ground, such certainty seemed foolish. But she might still be right. The mountain might go back to sleep. One way or another, most people didn't think about it. It was a crowded world, with plenty of problems to worry about even more immediate than a grumbling volcano.

The walk to the terminal seemed endless. The airport apron was a dismal place despite the corporate logos plastered on every surface. The intermittent shuddering of the ground was a primeval disturbance, and the huge whining of the jet engines sounded like the groan of disappointed animals.

And now Joan heard a distant popping, like damp logs thrown on a fire. "Shit. Was that gunfire?"

"There are protesters at the airport fence," said Alyce Sigurdardottir. "I glimpsed them as we came in. A great ragged band of them, like a shantytown."

"Just for us?"

Alyce smiled. "You can't mount a respectable conference on globalization without the protesters jetting in. Come on, it's a tradition; they've been trashing these conferences so long the veterans have reunions. You should be flattered they're taking you seriously."

Joan said grimly, "Then we'll just have to work harder to persuade them that we have something new to offer. I sense you don't like Alison Scott."

"Scott's whole life, her work, is show business. Even her children have been co-opted—no, *created*—to be part of the performance. *Look* at them."

Joan shrugged. "But you can't blame her for genriching her children." She stroked her belly. "I don't think I would want it for Junior here. But people have always wanted to give their children the best chance: the best school, the best stone-tipped spear, the best branch in the fig tree."

That forced a smile from Alyce. But she went on, "Some genriching would be desirable, if *all* could afford it. There is nothing physiologically inevitable about our bodies' limited repair capabilities, for instance. Why can't we regrow amputated limbs like a starfish? Why can't we have several sets of teeth, instead of just two? Why don't we replace worn out and arthritic joints?

"But do you really think that's where Alison Scott has made her money? Look at her kids, their hair, teeth, skin. Innards are invisible. What's the point of spending money if you can't show off what you've got? *Ninety percent* of money currently spent on genriching goes on externals, on the visible. Those wretched kids of Scott's are nothing but walking billboards for her wealth and power. They didn't put the *rich* in *genrich* for nothing. I've never seen anything so decadent."

Joan put her arm around Alyce's waist. "Maybe so. But we have to be a broad church. We need Scott's contribution just as much as we need yours. You know, I feel like I have a boulder in my belly," she said breathlessly.

Alyce grimaced. "Tell me about it. I had three of them. But I went back to Iceland for them all. Ah, poor timing?"

Joan smiled. "An accident. The conference has been in the planning for two years. As for the baby—"

"Nature will take its course, as it always has, regardless of our petty concerns. The father?"

Another paleontologist, he had been caught in the middle of a meaningless brushfire war raging in the collapsed state of Kenya. He had been trying to protect hominid fossil beds from thieves; a bandit warlord had thought he was guarding silver, or diamonds, or AIDS vaccine. The experience, and the pregnancy that was its legacy, had hardened Joan's determination to make her conference a success.

But she didn't want to talk about it now. "A long story," she said.

Alyce seemed to understand. She squeezed Joan's arm.

At last they got inside the airport terminal. The coolness of the air-conditioning fell on Joan like a cold shower, though she felt a pang of guilt at the thought of the kilowatts of heat that must thereby be pumped out into the murky air somewhere else. A Qantas representative, an Aborigine woman, smoothly guided them to a reception lounge. "There's been some trouble," she said to the arriving passengers, over and over. "We're in no danger. There will be an announcement shortly. . . ."

Alyce and Joan made their way wearily to an empty metal couch. Alyce went to fetch them both some soda.

The walls of the lounge were smart, filled up with airline information, news bulletins, entertainment, phone facilities. Passengers were milling about. Many of them were conference attendees; Joan recognized their faces from the program booklet and their net sites. All obviously jet-lagged and disoriented, they looked either exhausted or hyper, or a mix of both.

A short, potbellied man in what might once have been called a Hawaiian shirt approached Joan shyly. Bald, perspiring heavily, with an apparently habitual grin on his face, he wore a button-badge that cycled images of Mars, the new NASA robot lander, an orange sky. Joan, as a small child, might have called him a nerd. But he was no older than thirty-five. A second-generation nerd, then. He held out his hand. "Ms. Useb? My name is Ian Maughan. I'm from JPL. Uh—"

"The Jet Propulsion Laboratory. NASA. I remember your name, of course." Joan struggled to her feet and shook his hand. "I'm delighted you agreed to come. Especially at such a time in your mission."

"It is going well, thank the great Ju-Ju," he said. He tipped up his button-badge. "These are live images, live net of the time delay from Mars, of course. Johnnie has already set up his fuel plant and is working on metal extraction."

"Iron, from that rusty Mars rock."

"You got it."

"Johnnie," the Mars lander, was officially named for John von Neumann, the twentieth-century American thinker credited with coming up with the notion of universal replicators, machines that, given the right raw materials, could manufacture anything—including copies of themselves. "Johnnie" was a technological trial, a prototype replicator. Its ultimate goal was, in fact, to make a copy of itself from the raw materials of the planet itself.

"He's proving an incredible hit with the public," Maughan said with a shy smile. "People just like to watch. I think it's the sense of purpose, of achievement as he completes one component after another."

"Reality TV from Mars."

"Like that, yeah. I can't say we planned for the ratings we're getting. Even after seventy years, NASA still doesn't think PR very well. But the attention's sure welcome."

"When do you think Johnnie will have, umm, given birth? Before my own attempt at replication?"

Maughan forced a laugh, unsurprisingly embarrassed at Joan's mention of her human biology. "Well, it's possible. But he's proceeding at his own pace. That's the beauty of this project, of course. Johnnie is autonomous. Now that he's up there, he doesn't need anything from the ground. Since he and his sons won't cost us another dime, this is actually a low-budget project."

Joan thought, *Sons?*

"But Johnnie is more an engineering stunt than science," said Alyce Sigurdardottir. She had returned with plastic cups of cola for herself and Joan. "Isn't that true?"

Maughan smiled, easily enough. Joan realized belatedly that despite his appearance he must actually be one of JPL's more PR-literate employees; otherwise he wouldn't be here. "I can't deny that," he said. "But that's our way. At NASA, the engineering and the science have always had to proceed hand in hand." He turned back to Joan. "I'm honored you asked me here, though I'm still not sure why. My grasp of biology is kind of flaky. I'm basically a computer scientist. And Johnnie is just another space probe, a hunk of silicon and aluminum."

Joan said, "This conference isn't just about biology. I wanted the best and brightest minds in many fields to come here and get in touch with each other. We've got to learn to think in a new way."

Alyce shook her head. "And for all my skepticism about this specific project, I think you underestimate yourself, Dr. Maughan. Think about it. You come into the world naked. You take what the Earth gives you—metal, oil—and you mold it, make it smart, and hurl it across space to *another world*. NASA's image has always been dismally poor. But what you actually do is so—romantic."

Maughan hid behind a weak joke. "Gee, ma'am, I'll have to invite you along to my next career review."

The lounge was continuing to fill up with passengers. Joan said, "Does anybody know what's happening?"

"It's the protesters," Ian Maughan said. "They are lobbing rocks into the airport compound. The police are pushing them back, but it's a mess. They let us land, but it's not safe for our baggage to be retrieved right now, or for us to leave the airport."

"Terrific," Joan said. "So we're going to be under siege all through the conference."

Alyce asked, "Who's involved?"

"Mostly the Fourth World." An umbrella group, based on a splinter Christian sect, that claimed to represent the interests of the global under-class: the so-called *Fourth World*, people with less visibility even than the nations and groupings that made up the Third World—the poorest and most excluded, beneath the radar of the rich northern and western nations. "They think Pickersgill himself is in Australia."

Joan felt a flickering of unease. British-born Gregory Pickersgill was the charismatic leader of the central cult; the worst kind of trouble—sometimes lethal—followed him around. Deliberately she put the worry aside. "Let's leave it to the police. We have a conference to run."

"And a planet to save," said Ian Maughan, smiling.

"Damn right."

In one corner of the terminal, there was a commotion as a large white box was wheeled in. It was like an immense refrigerator. Light flared, and cameras were thrust into Alison Scott's face.

"One piece of luggage that evidently couldn't wait," murmured Alyce.

"I think it's live cargo," Maughan said. "I heard them talking about it."

Now little Bex Scott came running up to Joan. Joan noticed Ian Maughan goggling at her blue hair and red eyes; maybe folk were a little backward in Pasadena. "Oh, Dr. Useb." Bex took Joan's hand. "I want you to see what my mother has brought. You, too, Dr. Sigurdardottir. Please come. Uh, you were kind to me on the plane. I really was frightened by all the smoke and the lurching."

"You weren't in any real danger."

"I know. But I was frightened even so. You saw that and you were kind. Come on, I'd love you to see."

So Joan, with Alyce and Maughan in tow, let herself be led across the lounge.

Alison Scott was talking to the camera. She was a tall, imposing woman. ". . . My field is in the evolution of development. Evo-devo, in tabloid-speak. The goal is to understand how to regrow a lost finger, say. You do that by studying ancestral genes. Put together a bird and a crocodile, and you can glimpse the genome of their common ancestor, a pre-dinosaur reptile from around two hundred and fifty million years ago. Even before the end of the twentieth century one group of experimenters was able to 'turn on' the growth of teeth in a hen's beak. The ancient circuits are still there, subverted to other purposes; all you have to do is look for the right molecular switch. . . ."

Joan raised her eyebrows. "Good grief. You'd think it was her event."

"The woman's work is show business," Alyce said with cold disapproval. "Nothing more, nothing less."

With a flourish, Alison Scott tapped the box beside her. One wall turned transparent. There was a gasp from the pressing crowd—and, beyond that, a subdued hooting. Scott said, "Please bear in mind that what you see is a generic reconstruction, no more. Details such as skin color and behavior have essentially had to be invented."

"My God," said Alyce.

The creature in the box looked like a chimp, to a first approximation. No more than a meter tall, she was female; her breasts and genitalia were prominent. But she could walk upright. Joan could tell that immediately from the peculiar sideways-on geometry of her hips. However, right now she wasn't walking anywhere. She was cowering in a corner, her long legs jammed up against her chest.

Bex said, "I told you, Dr. Useb. You don't have to go scraping for bones in the dust. Now you can *meet* your ancestors."

Despite herself, Joan was fascinated. Yes, she thought: *to meet my ancestors*, all those hairy grandmothers, that is what my life's work has really been all about. Alison Scott evidently understands the impulse. But can this poor chimera ever be real? And if not, what were they *really* like?

Bex impulsively grasped Alyce's hand. "And, you see?" Her crimson eyes were shining. "I did say you didn't have to be upset about the loss of the bonobos."

Alyce sighed. "But, child, if we have no room for the chimps, where will we find room for *her?*"

The mock australopithecine, terrified, bared her teeth in a panic grin.

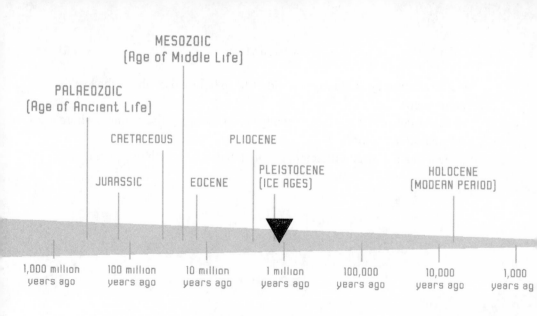

MESOZOIC
[Age of Middle Life]

PALAEOZOIC
[Age of Ancient Life]

CRETACEOUS   PLIOCENE

                              PLEISTOCENE
JURASSIC   EOCENE   [ICE AGES]   HOLOCENE
                                                    [MODERN PERIOD]

1,000 million   100 million   10 million   1 million   100,000   10,000   1,000
years ago   years ago   years ago   years ago   years ago years ago years ago

CHAPTER 9

the walkers

▼ Central Kenya, East Africa. Circa 1.5 million years before present.

I

She loved to run, more than anything else in her life. It was what her body was made for.

When she sprinted, she covered a hundred meters in six or seven seconds. At a more steady pace, she could finish a mile in three minutes. She could *run*. As she ran, her breath scorched in her lungs, and the muscles of her long legs and pumping arms seemed to glow. She loved to feel the sting of the dust where it clung to her bare, sweat-slick skin, and to smell the scorched, electric scent of the land's hot dryness.

It was late in the dry season. The day's most powerful heat lay heavy on the savannah, and the overhead sun skewered the scene with bright symmetry. Between the pillowlike volcanic hills the grass was sparse and yellow, everywhere browsed and trampled by the vast herds of herbivores. Their pathways, across which she ran, were like roads linking pastures and water courses. In this era the great grass eaters shaped the landscape; none of the many kinds of people in the world had yet usurped that role.

In the noon heat the grass eaters clustered in the shade, or simply lay in the dust. She glimpsed great static herds of elephant types, many species of them, like gray clouds in the distance. Clumsy, high-stepping ostriches pecked listlessly at the ground. Sleek predators slept lazily with their cubs. Even the scavengers, the wheeling birds and the scuttling feeders, were resting from their grisly chores. Nothing stirred but the dust that she kicked up, nothing moved but her own fleeting shadow, shrunk to a patch of darkness beneath her.

Fully immersed in her body, her world, she ran without calculation or analysis, ran with a fluency and freedom no primate kind had known before.

She was not thinking as a human would. She was conscious of nothing but her breath, the pleasurable ache in her muscles, her belly, the land that seemed to fly beneath her feet. But, running naked, she looked human.

She was tall—more than a hundred and fifty centimeters. Her kind were taller than any earlier people. She was lithe, lanky, and didn't weigh more than forty-five kilograms; her limbs were lean, her muscles hard, her belly and back flat. She was just nine years old. But she was at the cusp of adulthood, her hips broadening and her breasts small, firm, already rounded. And she was not done with growing yet. Though she would keep her slim body proportions, she could expect to grow to around two meters. Her sweat-flecked skin was bare, save for a curly black thatch on her head, and dark scraps at her crotch and armpits. In fact, she had as many body hairs as any other ape, but they were pale and tiny. Her face was round, small, and she had a fleshy, rounded nose, protruding like a human's, not lying flat like an ape's.

Perhaps her chest was a little high, a little conical; perhaps in the proportion of her long limbs she might have looked unusual. But her body was within the boundaries of human variation; she might have looked like a denizen of a desert country, like the Dinka of the Sudan, or the Turkana, or the Masai, who would one day walk the land she now crossed.

She looked human. Her head was different, though. Above her eyes ran a broad ridge of bone, which led back to a long, back-sloping forehead. From there, the bone ran with almost no rise to the back of her skull. The shape of her head was masked by her thick mass of hair, but it would have been impossible to mistake its flatness, the smallness of her cranium.

She had the body of a human, the skull of an ape. But her eyes were clear, sharp, curious. Nine years old, suffused with the joy of her body in this brief moment of life and light and freedom, she was as happy as it was possible for her to be. To human eyes, she would have been beautiful.

Her people were hominids—closer to humans than chimps or gorillas—and were related to the species one day tentatively labeled *Homo ergaster* and *Homo erectus*. But all across the Old World there were many, many variants, many subspecies based on the same overall body plan. They were a successful and diverse kind, and there would never be enough bones and bits of skull to tell their whole story.

Something darted out at her feet. She pulled up, startled, panting. It was a cane rat, a rodent; disturbed from its slow foraging it scuttled away, indignant.

And she heard a cry. "Far! Far!"

She looked back. Her people, a remote blur, had gathered on the rocky outcrop where they intended to stay for the night. One of them— her mother or grandmother—had clambered to the rock's highest point, and was calling to her through cupped hands. "Far!" It was a cry no ape could have made, not even Capo. This was a word.

The sun had begun to slide away from the zenith, and already the shadow at her feet had lengthened. Soon the animals would begin to stir; she would no longer be safe, no longer be shielded by the noon world's somnolence.

Alone, far from her people, she felt a delicious frisson of fear. Every day, every chance she got, she ran too far; and every day she had to be called back. She did not have a name. No hominid had yet given herself a name. But if she had, it would have been *Far*.

She turned back toward the rock and began to run again, at her steady, ground-devouring pace.

There were twenty-four people in the band.

Most of the adults were dispersed over the landscape near the eroded sandstone bluff. They moved like slim shadows across the dusty ground, seeking out nuts and small game, silent, intent, expert. Mothers had taken their youngest children along, clamped to their backs or scuttling at their feet.

Far's mother was working through a small stand of acacia trees that had been comprehensively destroyed by the passage of a herd of deinotheres. These ancient elephant types had used their downward-pointing tusks and stubby trunks to leave the trees broken and splintered, the ground churned up, and the roots hauled out. People weren't the only foragers here: warthogs and bushpigs grunted and squealed as they pushed their ugly faces into the churned-up earth. The destruction was recent. Far could see giant beetles at work burying fresh deinothere dung, and aardvarks and honey badgers rooting in the ground, seeking the beetles' larvae.

Such a place made for good foraging. A good strategy for finding food in an unfamiliar land was to seek out the leftovers of other animals, especially destructive types like elephants and pigs. In the smashed-up stand of trees, Far's mother would find food that would have otherwise been hidden or inaccessible. Among the broken trunks there were even ready-made levers, struts, and digging sticks to prize out roots from the ground, broken branches to shake to get at fruit, and slivers of palm to dig out pith.

Far's mother was a serene, elegant woman, tall even for her kind; she might have been called Calm. She walked with her two children, the sleeping baby cradled over one shoulder, and a son. The boy was half Far's age but already nearly as tall as she was, a skinny youth Far thought of as the Brat: irritating, clever, and much too successful at competing for their mother's attention and generosity.

Calm's own mother, Far's grandmother, was at her side. In her mid-forties now, the grandmother was too stiff to be of much help digging for food. But she assisted her daughter by keeping an eye on the youngest child. No human would have been surprised to see old people in this group; it would have looked very natural. But no previous types of primates had grown old; few had survived much past their fertile years. Why should their bodies continue to keep them alive when they could not contribute further to the gene pool? But now it was different; among Far's kind, old people had a role.

Panting, dusty, Far climbed the rock. It was just an outcrop a hundred meters across bearing nothing but strands of tough grass and a few insects and lizards. But for the people it was a temporary home base, an island of comparative sanctuary in this open savannah, this sea of danger. On the outcrop itself a couple of men were repairing wooden spears. They worked absently, eyes roving, as if their hands were working by themselves. Some of the older children played, rehearsing for the adulthood to come. They wrestled, chased, mock-stalked each other. Two six-year-olds were engaged in clumsy foreplay, fingering each other's nipples and bellies.

Far was neither an adult nor a child, and in this small band there was nobody close to her age. So she kept away from the rest and walked to the summit of the eroded sandstone lump. She found a bit of antelope jaw, deposited here by some scavenger, now scraped clean by hungry mouths and the patient work of insects. She cracked the bone into fragments on the rock, and used a sharp edge to scrape the sweat and dirt from her legs and belly.

From this vantage, the landscape was laid out, presenting a complex panorama. This was an immense valley. Huge geological anguish showed in a panorama of domes, lava flows, tiltings, and craters. To the east—and, beyond the horizon, in the west—the land had been uplifted, forming a plateau some three thousand meters high at its maximum, laden with fertile volcanic soil. The great plateau came to an end in a precipitate wall that plunged down into the valley.

This was the Rift Valley: a fracture between two separating tectonic plates. It ran for three thousand kilometers from the Red Sea and Ethiopia in the north down through Kenya, Uganda, Tanzania, and Malawi, terminating in Mozambique to the south. For twenty million years geological activity along the length of this great wound had created volcanoes, built highlands, and collapsed lowlands into valleys that channeled the waters into some of the continent's largest lakes. The land itself had been remolded, laid down as layer upon layer of volcanic ash, interspersed with broad beds of shale and mudstone. On the volcanic hills grew humid forests, and a complex mosaic of vegetation, from woodland to savannah to scrub, filled the floor. It was a crowded, jumbled, varied place.

And it was full of animals.

As the sun continued to roll down the sky, so the creatures of the savannah became more active: the hippos wallowing in the marshes, the herds of stately elephant types washing serenely across the grasslands. There were many species of elephant, in fact, subtly differing in the shape of their backs, skulls, trunks. They trumpeted shrilly to each other, sailing like dusky ships through the sea of dust they kicked up. As well as these large herbivores there were many other species directly dependent on the grass: hares, porcupines, and cane rats, rooting pigs. Predators upon the grass eaters—and themselves prey for still more dangerous animals—included jackals, hyenas, and mongooses.

The animals of the savannah would have looked startlingly familiar to human eyes, for they had already become finely adapted to savannah conditions. But the richness and variety of the life here would have astounded an observer used to the Africa of human times. This was the richest region on Earth in terms of the number of mammalian species, their diversity and abundance, and this was one of its most prolific periods. In this crowded, complicated place, plains creatures like antelopes and elephants lived close to forest dwellers like pigs and bats. The Rift provided a rich, sprawling landscape that presented opportunities for adaptation for many species of animals, like elephants, pigs, antelopes—and people. This, indeed, was the crucible from which Far's kind had emerged.

But they had not stayed here.

After Capo's time, liberated from the last ancestral ties to the forest, Far's people had become a wandering species. They had walked out of Africa: The first hominid footsteps had already been planted all along the southern coasts of the Asian landmass. Far's grandmothers, though, had unwittingly completed a great circuit to north, east, and south, over many generations returning here, to the place their kind had originated.

Sitting on her outcrop, Far surveyed the landscape with a professional, calculating eye. In their wanderings, the people mostly followed water courses. They had come to this place from the north, and she could see the streambed they had followed, a silver snake that slashed through the grass and scrub. Along the riverbank the land was silty, watered, and dense with nutrients, and a vigorous mix of trees, thicket, and grassland grew there, marked by pillars of termite mounds. To the east the ground rose, becoming dry and barren, and to the west the forest grew thicker, making an impassable belt. But if she looked south she could see possibilities for tomorrow, a great corridor of savannah with the mixture of grass, scrub, and forest patches that her people preferred.

Far was still young, still learning about the world and how best to use it. But she had a deep, systematic understanding of her environment. She was already capable of assessing an unfamiliar landscape like this and picking out sources of food, water, and danger, even spying out routes for onward migration.

It was a necessary skill. Committed to the open, Far's kind had been pushed by a harsh winnowing to develop a new kind of awareness of nature. They had been forced to understand the habits of game, the distribution of plants, the changes of seasons, the meanings of tracks—to solve the endless puzzles of the complex, unforgiving savannah. By comparison, her remote ancestor Capo, who had lived and died thousands of kilometers northwest of this place, had learned the features of his generous forest world by rote: Unable to read the land, to figure out new patterns, he had been endlessly baffled by the unfamiliar.

Now the adults and their infants were coming back to the rock, carrying food. They were naked, and they carried only what they could cram into their hands and cradle in their arms. Most of them came back with mouths still full and chewing. The people ate as fast as they could, helping themselves, feeding only close family members, not averse to stealing when they thought they could get away with it. And they ate silently save for belches, grunts of pleasure or disgust when a bit of rotten food turned up—and an occasional word. "Mine!" "Nut," "Break," "Hurt, hurt, hurt . . ."

They were simple nouns and verbs, possessives and challenges, one-word sentences with no structure, no grammar. But nevertheless it was a language, the words labels that referred to definite things—a system far advanced over the jabbering of Capo's time, and that of any other animal.

Here came Far's brother, the Brat. He was carrying the limp corpse of some small animal, maybe a hare. And her mother, Calm, had an armful of roots, fruit, and palm pith.

Far was suddenly hungry. She hurried forward, mewling, her hands held out and her mouth open.

Calm hissed at her, theatrically holding her armful of food away from her daughter. "Mine! Mine!" It was a rebuke, and it was backed up by glares from the grandmother. Far was getting too old now to be fed like an infant. She should have come to help her mother rather than waste her energy running purposelessly about the landscape. Why, here was her brother, the Brat, who had been hard at work and had even returned with his own scrap of meat. All of that was conveyed in a word.

Life was not as it had been in Capo's time. Nowadays the adults tried to coach the youngsters. The world had become too complex for children to be given the time to reinvent all the technology and techniques of survival from scratch; they had to be taught how to survive. And one of the roles of elders like Far's grandmother was to drive such wisdom home.

But Far held her hands out again, making piteous animal mewls. *Just once more. Just for today. I'll help tomorrow.*

"Graah!" Calm, as Far had known she would, dumped the food on the rock. She had gathered nuts, tsin beans, cowpeas, and asparagus bean tubers. She handed Far a fat tuber; Far bit into this quickly.

The Brat sat close to his mother. He was still too young to sit with the men, who were pawing through their own pile of food. The Brat had pulled apart his hare by main force, twisting off the limbs and head, and was using a chip of rock to lay open the chest. But as he performed this miniature butchery his gestures were tense, shivery.

None of his family knew it, but he was already gravely ill, through hypervitaminosis. A few days before one of the men had given him a few scraps of hyena liver, brought down in a brief battle over the remains of an antelope. Like that of most carnivorous predators, the liver had been full of vitamin A, and that subtle poisoning would soon become visible in the boy's body.

In a month he would be dead. In twelve, forgotten, even by his mother.

But for now Calm cuffed him, reasonably gently, and grabbed some of his hare away from him, making him share with his sister.

Since Capo's time the world had continued to cool and dry.

North of the equator, a great belt of taiga stretched right around the world, through North America and Asia, a forest of nothing but evergreen trees. And in the far north tundra had formed for the first time in three hundred million years. For the animals, the living offered by the taiga was meager compared to the old mixed deciduous and coniferous temperate forests. Similarly, the great grasslands continued to expand—grass was less thirsty than trees—but grass made arid plains, able to support only a much-reduced assemblage of animal species compared to the vanishing forests. As the slow desiccation continued, there were extinctions again.

But if the quality was diminished, the *quantity* of life was tremendous, astonishing.

The need to ride out periods of seasonal food shortages, and the need for guts able to process coarse diets all year round, favored the development of large herbivores. Giant mammals, a new "megafauna" on a scale not seen since the death of the dinosaurs, spread across the planet. Ancestral mammoths had already spread across northern Eurasia and, crossing the land bridges periodically exposed by the falling ocean levels, walked into North America. For now, living in equable climes, they were hairless and ate foliage rather than grass. They looked like typical elephants, but they had the high crowns and curling tusks of their woolly descendants.

Meanwhile there were giant camels in North America, and in Asia and Africa wandered the huge, mooselike sivatheres. A type of large rhino called an elasmotherium roamed across northern Eurasia. For a rhino it had long legs and a horn that could grow to two meters in length: It looked like a muscular unicorn.

And along with these huge packages of meat came new, specialized predators. The cats, freshly evolved, had perfected the technology of killing. They had side teeth like shears that could slice through skin, rip it aside, and get inside a body, where their incisors could nibble at the flesh. The saber-tooths were the acme. The saber-tooths would grow to twice the size of the lions of human times, becoming vast muscular predators built like bears, with short stocky limbs. They were built for power, not speed, and were ambush hunters, with mouths that could open hugely wide to crush prey. But all cats made even the dogs look like generalists by comparison; cats were perhaps the ultimate land predators.

But then, some half million years before Far's birth, a new and dramatic worsening of the climate began. For the world's creatures, the rules changed again.

There was a call from the plain. "Look, look! Me, look, me!" People stood up, gathering to see.

A man was approaching. He was tall, more heavily muscled than the rest, with a powerful, abnormally prominent browridge. This man, Brow, was dominant right now, the boss man in the tight, competitive world of the males. And he had a dead animal draped across his shoulder, a young eland.

The eight other adult men in the band began dutifully to whoop and yell, and they ran down the rocky slope. They slapped Brow on the back, stroked the eland respectfully, and ran and capered, kicking up a spectacular cloud of dust that hung, glowing, in the light of the descending sun. Together they hauled the eland up the slope and hurled it to the ground. The older children ran to see the eland, and began competing for its meat. The Brat was amongst them, but he was weaker even than others younger than himself, and he was easily pushed aside. Far could see a snapped-off wooden spear buried in the animal's chest. That was how Brow had killed his prey, probably after an ambush, and perhaps he had left the spear in there to show how he had achieved this feat.

Brow, meanwhile, had sprouted an impressive erection. The women, including Calm, Far's mother, made subtle signs of availability—a crooked hand here, thighs smoothly parting there.

Far, neither woman nor child, hung back from the rest. She nibbled on a root and waited as events unfolded.

Some of the adults had brought volcanic pebbles from the nearby stream. Now men and women began briskly to knap the pebbles, their hands working rapidly, their fingers exploring the stone. The tools emerged from the stone without real conscious effort—this was a skill that was already ancient, embedded in a self-contained section of a rigidly divided mind—and within a few minutes they had fashioned crude but serviceable choppers and cutting flakes. As quickly as each tool was finished its manufacturer fell on the eland.

The skin was sliced open from anus to throat, and pulled briskly off the carcass. The hide was discarded; nobody had thought up a use for animal skins, not yet. Now the carcass was briskly butchered, with the fine stone blades slicing into joints to separate the limbs from the body, through the rib cage to expose the soft, warm organs within, and then into the meat itself to separate it from the bone.

It was a fast, efficient, almost bloodless affair, a skillful butchering born of generations of ancestral learning. But the butchers did not work together. Though they deferred to Brow, allowing him to take the prime cuts and to extract the heart and liver, they competed as they scavenged the corpse, grunting and prodding at each other. Despite the tools in their hands, they worked at the eland like a pack of wolves.

Few of the women fought for the meat. Their unglamorous scavenging in the acacia grove and elsewhere had been successful today, and their bellies, and those of their children, were already full of figs, grewia berries, grass shoots, roots—fruits abundant in these dry lands that did not require much preparation before eating.

When most of the meat had been taken from the eland's bones, the bargaining began in earnest. Brow stalked among the men with a blade in one hand and a mighty slab of haunch in the other. He sliced off chunks of the meat and handed them to some of the men—and not to others, who turned away as if it were unimportant, but who would later try to snatch bits of the best meat from the rest. It was all part of the endless politicking of the men.

Then Brow walked among the women, handing out bits of meat like a visiting king. When he reached Calm, he paused, his erection proud, and sliced off a large and succulent slab of eland haunch. Sighing, she accepted it. She ate some of it quickly, then put the rest to one side, close to her infant, who was asleep in a nest of dead grass. Then she lay on her back and opened her thighs, and held up her arms to accept Brow.

Brow hadn't gone hunting primarily to bring food to his people. Large game provided maybe only a tenth of the group's intake; the vast majority of it came from the plants, nuts, insects, and small game foraged by the women and older children as much as by the men. Large game was a useful emergency food supply in hard times—drought or flood, perhaps, or in tough winters. But hunting was useful to the hunter in a whole range of ways. With his eland meat Brow was able to reinforce his political position among the men—and buy access to the women, which was ultimately the only purpose of his endless battle for dominance.

With their greater intelligence, tall, hairless bodies, and rudimentary language, these were the most *human* creatures yet to exist. But much of the way they ran their lives would have been immediately familiar to Capo. Brow's ancestors had fallen into this social pattern—of males fighting for dominance, of females linked along bloodlines, of hunting to buy favors—far back in time, long before Capo's fateful decision to leave his pocket of forest. There were other ways for primates to live, other kinds of societies that could be imagined. But once the pattern had been set, it was all but impossible to break.

Anyhow the system worked. The food was shared out; the peace was kept. One way or another, most people got fed.

When Brow was done Calm wiped her thighs with a leaf and returned to the meat. She used a discarded stone flake to slice it up, and handed some to her mother—who was too old to be of interest to Brow—and gave the rest to Far, who fell on it eagerly.

And later, as the light faded, Brow approached Far herself. She saw him as a tall, beefy silhouette against the sky's fading red purple. Most of his eland meat was gone now, but she smelled its blood on him. He carried a foreleg bone. He crouched down before her, sniffing her curiously. Then he slammed the bone against the rock, cracking it. She could smell its delicious marrow, and her mouth filled with saliva. Without thinking she reached for the bone.

He held it back, making her come closer.

As she approached she could smell him more clearly: the blood, the dirt, the sweat, and a lingering stink of semen. He relented and gave her the bone, and she pushed her tongue into the marrow, sucking at it eagerly. As she ate he put his hand on her shoulder and ran it down her body. She tried not to flinch when he explored her small breasts, pulling her nipples. But she squealed when his probing fingers parted her legs. He drew back his hand and sniffed her scent. Then, evidently deciding she had nothing to sell him, he grunted and moved away.

But he left her the marrow. Eagerly she devoured it, finishing most of it before the bone was stolen from her by an older woman.

The light leached quickly out of the sky. All across the savannah the predators called, marking their bloody kingdoms in their ancient way.

The people gathered on their island of rock. All of them felt a shiver of apprehension as they huddled together—children at the center, adults with their backs facing outward—and prepared to enter a long night of unbroken darkness. They ought to be safe here, in this inhospitable place: any ambitious predator would have to leave the ground and clamber up here, where it would face smart, large, and armed hominids. But there was no guarantee. There was a saber-tooth around called *dinofelis*, an ambush predator like a stocky jaguar, that specialized in killing hominids. Dinofelis could even climb trees.

As the darkness fell, the people went about their business. Some fed. Some tended to their bodies, digging dirt out of toenails or fingering blis-

ters. Some worked on tools. Many of these activities were repetitive, ritualistic. Nobody was truly thinking about what they were doing.

Some groomed: mothers with infants, siblings, mates, women, and
men reinforcing their subtle alliances. Far worked on her mother's dense
head hair, teasing out knots and pulling it into a kind of plait. Even now
hair needed a lot of work—it would tangle, mat, and attract lice, all of
which needed fixing.

These people were the only species of mammal whose heavy hair was
not self-maintaining; the spectacular tonsorial plumage of some monkeys,
for instance, just grew that way. Far's hair even needed cutting regularly.
But people's hair had developed that way because they needed something to groom. Out here on the savannah it paid to be part of a large
group, and the group needed social mechanisms to hold itself together.
There wasn't time now for the old ape ways, the elaborate full-body
grooming indulged in by Capo and his ancestors. Anyway you couldn't
groom skin that had become bare so it could sweat. But still, in this primitive hairdressing, they retained links with their heritage.

The grammar of the people as they went about their diverse activities
was not like that of a human group. In the gathering dark they huddled
together for protection, but there was no real sharing. There was no fire,
and nothing like a hearth, no central focus. They looked human, but their
minds were not like humans'.

Just as in Capo's time, their thinking was rigidly compartmented. The
main purpose of consciousness was still to help people figure out what
was in each others' minds: They were only truly self-aware in the human
sense when dealing with each other. The boundaries of awareness were
much more narrow than in human minds; there was much beyond, out in
the darkness, that they did essentially without thinking about it. Even
those making tools or working on food did so wordlessly, their hands
working impulsively, with no more conscious control than lions or
wolves. Their awareness at such times was rolling, fleeting. They made
tools as unconsciously as humans would walk or breathe.

However, human or not, a soft susurrus of language washed over the
group. The talking was among the mothers and infants, the groomers,
and the couples. There wasn't much information being passed on; much
of the talk was little more than sighs of pleasure, like the purring of cats.

But their words *sounded* like words.

People had had to learn to communicate with equipment designed for
other tasks—a mouth intended for eating, ears intended to listen for
danger—now jury-rigged for a new use. Their bipedalism had helped: the
repositioning of their larynxes and changes in the pattern of breathing

improved the quality of the sounds they could make. But to be useful, sounds had to be identifiable quickly and unambiguously. And the ways the hominids could achieve that were limited by the nature of the equipment they had to use. As people listened to each other, and imitated and reused useful noises, phonemes—the sound content of the words, the basis of all language—had selected themselves, driven by communicative necessity and engineering limitations.

But there was nothing yet like grammar—no sentences—and certainly no narratives, no stories. And the main purpose of talking right now wasn't to pass on information. Nobody talked about tools or hunting or food preparation. Language was social: It was used for commands and demands, for blunt expressions of joy or pain. And it was used for grooming: Language, even without much content, was a more efficient way to establish and reinforce relations than picking ticks out of pubic hair. It even worked to "groom" several people at once.

A lot of the evolution of language, in fact, had been driven by mothers and infants. Right now the ancestors of Demosthenes and Lincoln and Churchill spoke nothing much more than motherese.

And the children didn't talk at all.

The minds of the adults were about equivalent in complexity to a five-year-old human's. Their children were not capable of speech—nothing beyond chimplike jabbers—until they reached adolescence. It had only been a year or two since the adults' words had made any sense to Far, and the Brat, at seven, couldn't talk at all. The kids were like apes born to human parents.

As the light died, so the group settled toward sleep.

Far huddled against her mother's legs. The ending day became just one of a long chain that stretched back to the beginning of her life, days dimly remembered, only vaguely linked. In the darkness she imagined running in the blinding brightness of day, running and running.

She had no way of knowing that this was the last time she would fall asleep close to her mother.

II

A million years ago, tectonic drift, slow but relentless, had caused North and South America to collide, and the isthmus of Panama was formed.

In itself it seemed a small event, Panama an inconsequential sliver of land. But, as with Chicxulub, this region had once more become the epicenter of a worldwide catastrophe.

Because of Panama, the old equatorial flows through the Americas—the last trace of the Edenic Tethys current—had been cut off. Now the only Atlantic currents were the huge interpolar flows, great conveyor belts of cold water. The worldwide cooling intensified drastically. The scattered ice caps covering the northern ocean merged, and glaciers spread like claws over the northern landmasses.

The Ice Ages had begun. At their greatest extent the glaciers would cover more than a quarter of all Earth's surface; the ice would reach as far as Missouri and central England. Much was immediately lost. Where the glaciers passed, the land was scraped clean—down to the bedrock, which was itself pulverized and ground to dust—leaving a legacy of mountains with scored flanks, polished surfaces, scattered boulders, and gouged-out valleys. There had been no significant glaciation on Earth for two hundred million years; now a legacy of rocks and bones dating back deep into the age of the dinosaurs was comprehensively destroyed.

On the ice itself, nothing could live: nothing. Below the ice, great impoverished belts of tundra spread. Even in places far from the ice, like the equatorial regions of Africa, changes in wind patterns intensified the aridity, and vegetation shrank back to the coasts and river valleys.

The cooling was not a uniform trend. The planet tipped and bobbed in its endless dance around the sun, subtly shifting its degree of tilt, its inclination, and the fine-tuning of its orbit. And with each cycle the ice came and went, came and went; ocean levels fluctuated like the pumping of a heart. Even the land, compressed under kilometers of ice or released by its melting, rose and fell like a rocky tide.

Sometimes the climate shifts could be savage. Within a single year the amount of snowfall in an area could double, the average temperature fall by ten degrees. Faced with such chaotic oscillations, living things moved, or died.

Even the forests marched. Spruce proved a fast migrant, followed by pine, capable of marching at a kilometer every two years. The great chestnuts, massive trees with heavy seeds, could manage a pace of a hundred meters a year. Before the Ice Age the animals of the middle latitudes of the northern hemisphere had been a rich mixture of fleet grazers like deer and horses, giant herbivores like rhinos, and fast-running carnivores like lions and wolves. Now the animals were driven south in search of warmth. Populations of animals from different climatic zones were mixed up and forced to compete in fast-changing ecological arenas.

But some creatures began to adapt to the cold, to exploit the food supplies that still existed at the feet of the ice sheets. Many animals grew thick fur and layers of fat—large animals, like rhinos, and smaller animals, like foxes and horses and cats. Others began to take advantage of the huge temperature swings between the seasons. They migrated, moving north in the summer and south in the winter; the plains became a huge tidal wash of life, great mobile communities patiently stalked by predators.

There had been a catastrophe of mixing in the Americas. The two continents, north and south, had been separated since the shattering of Pangaea some one hundred and fifty million years ago. The fauna of South America had evolved in isolation, and was dominated by marsupial mammals and ungulates. There were marsupial "wolves" and saber-toothed "cats"; there were ungulate "camels" and trunked "elephants," and giant ground sloths that could weigh three tons and stood six meters tall when they stood up to browse on palm leaves. There were still glyptodonts, not so dissimilar from the huge armored beast that had terrified Roamer, and the top predators were giant flightless birds, just as in archaic times. This exotic assemblage had been left alone to develop—though it was supplemented from time to time by waifs, brought by rafting or temporary bridges, like Roamer and her hapless companions, whose children had populated the South American jungles with monkeys.

But when the Panama land bridge was closed there was a massive migration from north to south of insectivores, rabbits, squirrels, mice, and later dogs, bears, weasels, and cats. The natives of South America failed to compete with these new arrivals. The extinctions took millions of years, but the empire of the marsupials was done.

For all the difficulty and dying, this time of fast and savage changes was, perversely, a time of opportunity. In the entire four-billion-year history of the Earth there had been few times more propitious for diversification and evolutionary innovation. Amid much extinction there was wild speciation.

And right at the center of this ecological cauldron were the children of Capo.

The next morning dawned brightly, with a washed-out blue sky. But the air was very dry and smelled oddly sharp, and the heat was soon stifling. The animals of the savannah seemed subdued. Even the birds were quiet; the carrion eaters clung to their tree roosts like ugly black fruit.

With their bare, sweating skin, the people were as well equipped for this hot, open dryness as any other species here. But they too began their day listlessly. They milled about their island of rock, picking at what was left of yesterday's food.

This wasn't a particularly rich area. The people didn't discuss their plans—they never did, and anyhow they had no real plans—but it was obvious they shouldn't stay here. Before long some of the men started to set off toward the water course to continue their walk to the south.

But the Brat's condition had worsened overnight. The soles of his feet were cracked and oozing a watery pus, and when he tried to put his weight on them he cried out in pain. He wouldn't be walking anywhere today.

Calm, Far's grandmother, and most of the other women stayed close to the Brat. As for the men, the women just ignored their antics as they impatiently paced up and down the trail they had begun toward the south.

This conflict, all but wordless, over the day's course was hurtful for them all. It was a genuine dilemma. The savannah was not like the bountiful, reliable forest of earlier times; you couldn't just walk off in any random direction. Every day, in this sparse, changeable land, the people were faced with decisions about where to go to find food, water, what dangers to avoid. If they got it wrong, even once, the consequences were drastic. But the walkers had few children, and invested much effort in each one; you didn't abandon one lightly.

At last the men gave up. Some of them returned to the rock to laze in the light of the high, hot sun. A handful of others set off under Brow's leadership on the trail of an elephant herd, one of whose infants appeared to be limping. The rest of the men—and the women and older children—dispersed to the foraging sites they had explored yesterday.

The way these people were living—setting up a central home base, retrieving food, and sharing food and labor—was necessary. On the open plain the people had to work hard for food, and their slow-growing young extracted a high cost in care. They had to cooperate and share, one way or another. But there was no real planning. In many ways this was more like a wolf pack than any human community.

Far spent most of the morning in the same trampled thicket her mother had worked yesterday. The ground had already been thoroughly worked over, and to find new roots and fruit required much digging. Soon she was hot, dirty, and uncomfortable. She felt restless, confined, and her long legs, folded under her in the trampled dirt and debris, seemed to ache.

As noon approached, the desultory stillness of this strange, heavy day deepened. The savannah, open and free, beckoned Far, as it had done yesterday. As the emptiness in her belly diminished, the pressures of survival and familial duty were overcome by her longing to get *out* of here.

One spindly palm had survived the deinotheres' attention, and it had a cluster of nuts at its top. A young man shimmied up the tree with a grace that came from his body's deep-buried memory of earlier, greener times. Far watched his lithe torso working, and felt a peculiar ache at the base of her belly.

She came to a kind of decision. She dropped the last of the food, clambered out of the thicket, and just sprinted off to the west.

She felt a vast relief as her limbs worked, her lungs pumped, and she felt clean crisp dirt beneath her feet. For a time, as she ran without thinking, even the day's heat seemed alleviated as the breeze of her passing cooled her skin.

Then there was a deep, menacing rumble that echoed across the sky. She pulled up, crouched, and peered around fearfully.

The bright sunlight dimmed. Thick black clouds were pouring across the sky from the east. She was startled by a flash of purplish light that lit up the clouds from within. Almost immediately there was a shattering crash and a deeper, drawn-out rumble that seemed to roll around the sky.

Looking back at the rocky outcrop, which suddenly seemed very far away, she saw the people running, gathering up their infants. Her heart hammering, Far straightened up and began to head back.

But now rain lashed down from the blackening sky. The drops were heavy enough to sting her bare skin and unprotected scalp, and they dug small craters in the dirt. The ground rapidly turned to sticky mud that clung to her feet, slowing her down.

Light flashed again, this time a great river of it that briefly connected sky to ground. Dazzled, she stumbled and fell in the mud. Shattering noise pealed around her, as if the world were falling apart.

She saw that the tall palm at the center of the trampled clearing had been split in two, and it was blazing, the flames licking at the fronds that dangled forlornly from its tip. The fire quickly spread through the rest of the smashed thicket—and then the dry grass on the plain beyond began to catch.

A pall of gray-black smoke began to rise up before her. She got to her feet and tried to continue. But, despite the continuing rain, the fire spread quickly. The season had been exceptionally dry, and the savannah was littered with yellowed grass, dried shrubs, fallen trees ripe for burning. Somewhere an elephant trumpeted. Far glimpsed spindly forms fleeing through the murk: giraffes, perhaps.

The hominids were safe, though. The flames would lap harmlessly around their rocky outcrop. Though they would all suffer from the smoke and heat, nobody would die because of this. And if Far could reach the outcrop, she, too, would be safe. But she was still hundreds of meters away, and the screen of smoke and flame cut her off. The flames were leaping hungrily over the long, dry grass, each blade of which burned in an eye blink. The air turned smoky, making her cough. Bits of burning vegetation drifted through the air, blackened, still glowing. When they fell on her skin they stung.

She did the only thing she could do. She turned and ran: ran to the west, away from the fire, away from her family.

She didn't stop running until she came to a dense thicket of forest. Facing a blank, green wall, she hesitated for one heartbeat. Other dangers lurked here, but this place was surely invulnerable to the fire. She plunged inside.

Crouched close to the root of a tree fern, surrounded by damp cling-ing fronds, she peered out at the savannah. The fire still swept vora-ciously through the long grass, and smoke billowed, seeping into the dense forest. But this forest clump was indeed too dense and moist to be under threat. And the fire was quickly consuming its fuel; the rain was starting to douse the flames.

Soon she would be able to get out of here. She squatted down to wait it out.

A scuttling movement close to her foot drew her attention. At the base of the tree fern's textured root a scorpion moved with metallic preci-sion toward her foot. Without hesitation, but taking care to avoid the sting, she slammed the heel of her hand down on the scorpion. Carefully she picked up the scorpion between two fingers, and lifted it to her mouth.

Something rammed into her back. She was thrown forward onto her belly, with a mass on her back, hot, heavy, muscular. She was surrounded by screeching and hooting, and fists pounded at her back and head.

Winded, summoning up her strength, she rolled over.

A slim figure capered over her. It was not much more than half her height, with a skinny body covered with brown-black fur, long arms, an apelike head stuck over a narrow, conical chest, and a thin pink penis sticking out below its belly. Its fur was wet from the rain, and it stank, the smell musty and strong. And yet it—he—stood upright over her, like one of her own kind, like no ape.

This was a pithecine: an ape-man, a chimp-man, a representative of the first hominids of all, Far's remote cousin. And there were more of them in the jumbled branches above her, climbing down like shadows.

She turned to get up. But something slammed against her head, and she fell into blackness.

When she came to she was flat on her back. Her chest, legs, and buttocks ached.

Pithecines were all around her.

Some of them had clambered into pod mahogany trees in search of fruit. Others were digging in the ground, pulling out corkwood roots. They were active, foraging bipeds, working wordlessly. But, unlike her, they were short, hairy, their skin slack like chimps'.

Somebody was screaming. Far turned her head to see.

A pithecine was crouched in the dirt. It—she—was straining, her face contorted, her slack breasts heavy with milk. Far, blearily, saw a small solid mass emerge from her rump: mucus-covered, hairy, it was the head of a baby. This pithecine woman was giving birth.

Other females surrounded her, sisters, cousins, and her mother. Chattering and hooting softly, they reached between the new mother's legs. Gently they fumbled with the baby as, moistly, it was pushed out of the birth canal.

The new mother faced problems no earlier primate had endured, for the baby was being born facing away from her. Leaf, a female of Capo's time, would have been able to see her baby's face as it emerged, and would have been able to reach down between her legs to guide her baby's head and body out of her birth canal. If this pithecine were to try that she would bend the baby's neck backward and risk injuring its spinal cord, nerves, and muscles. She could not cope alone, as Leaf could have—but she did not have to.

When the baby's hands were free, it grabbed at its mother's fur and began to pull. Even now it was strong enough to aid in its own delivery.

It was all a consequence of bipedalism. A quadruped supported its abdominal organs with connective tissue hung from its backbone. The pelvis was just a connecting element that translated the pressure on the backbone down and outward to the hips and legs. But if you decided to walk upright your pelvis had to support the weight of your abdominal organs—and the weight of a growing embryo inside you. The pelvises of the upright pithecines had quickly adapted, becoming like a human's basin-shaped supporting structure. The central opening for the birth canal changed too, becoming larger side to side than front to back, an oval shape to match a baby's skull.

This pithecine mother's birth canal was narrower in comparison to her baby's head than any previous primate's. Her baby had entered the canal facing its mother's side, to let its head through. But then it had to turn so its shoulders lined up with the canal's widest dimension. Sometimes the baby would finish up in the easiest position, facing its mother, but more often than not it would turn away from her.

In the future, as hominid skulls increased in size to accommodate larger brains, still more elaborate redesigns of the birth passageways would be required, so that Joan Useb's baby would have to twist and turn in a complicated fashion as it headed for the light. But even in these deep times, the first bipedal mothers already needed midwives—and a new kind of social bond had been forged among the pithecines.

At last the baby emerged fully, falling to the leaf-strewn ground with a plop, its small fists closing. The mother fell to the ground with a gasp of relief. One older pithecine picked up the child, cleared plugs of mucus from its mouth and nose, and blew into its nostrils. At the hairy little scrap's first wail, the midwife peremptorily thrust the baby at its mother and loped away.

Suddenly Far felt strong hands around her ankles. She was jolted, leaves and dirt scraped under her back, and she lost sight of the mother and baby.

She was being dragged over the floor. Every time her head clattered on a rock or tree root pain exploded. Hooting, screeching creatures were all around her. These were all males, she saw now, with knotty pink genitals half-buried in their fur, and astonishingly large testicles that they would scratch absently. When they walked their gait was oddly awkward, the joints of their hips peculiar.

She realized dimly that they were hauling her deeper into the forest. But she seemed to have no strength, no will to fight.

Suddenly another bunch of pithecines came rushing out of the deeper green, howling angrily. The males who had taken Far rose to confront these newcomers.

For a time there was a festival of yelling, hooting, and displaying. The pithecines bristled their fur, making some of them look twice their usual size. The larger ones crashed through branches, ripped leaves from the trees, and leapt and slapped at the ground. One of Far's group sprouted an immense pink erection that he waggled at the interlopers. Another leaned back and pissed over his challengers. And so on. It was cacophonous, baffling, stinking, a skirmish between two groups of creatures who looked identical to a bewildered Far.

At last Far's captors drove off the intruders. Bristling with leftover aggression they hurled themselves around the trees, screeching and snapping at one another.

Now, calming, the pithecines began to forage on the ground, their long fingers raking through the debris of leaves and twigs. One of them found a chunk of black rock, a cobble of basalt. He quickly found another rock, and he turned the first over and over in his hands, his pink tongue comically protruding from his mouth.

At last he seemed satisfied. His eyes on the basalt rock, he set it on the ground, holding it precisely between thumb and forefinger. Then he slammed down his hammer-stone. Splinters sprayed away from the target rock, many of them so small they were barely visible. The pithecine rummaged in the dirt, rumbling his disappointment, then he turned back to his rock and started to turn it over in his hands once more. The next time he struck it, a thin black flake the size of his palm sheared off neatly. The pithecine hefted his flake in his hand, turning it around between thumb and forefinger while he studied its edge.

This stone knife was just a cracked-off splinter of stone. But its manufacture, involving an understanding of the material to be shaped and the use of one tool to make another, was a cognitive feat that would have been far beyond Capo.

The pithecine eyed Far. He was aware that Far was conscious, but he was going to begin his butchery anyhow.

His arm flashed out. The stone flake sliced into Far's shoulder.

The sudden sharpness of the pain, and the warm gush of her own blood, brought Far out of her passive shock. She screeched. The pithecine roared in response and raised his flake again. But, just as she had crushed the scorpion, Far slammed the heel of her hand into his face. She felt a satisfying crunch of bone, and her hand was covered in blood and snot. He recoiled, blood gushing.

The pithecines fell back, startled, hooting their alarm and slapping their big hands on the ground, as if reassessing the strength and danger of this large angry animal they had brought into their forest.

But now one of them bared his teeth and began to advance on her.

She forced herself to her feet and ran, deeper into the forest gloom.

She clattered against tree trunks, got lianas and roots wrapped around her legs, and pushed through dense knots of branches. Her long legs and powerful lungs, designed for hours of running over flat, open ground, were all but useless in this dense tangle, where she couldn't take a step without tripping over something.

And meanwhile the pithecines moved like shadows around her, chattering and hooting, climbing easily up trunks and along branches, leaping from tree to tree. This was their environment, not hers. When they had committed themselves to the savannah, Far's kind had turned their backs on the forest—which had, as if in revenge, become a place not of sanctuary but of claustrophobic danger, populated by these pithecines which, like the sprites they resembled, would inhabit nightmares long into the future.

Before long the pithecines had overtaken her on both sides, and began to move closer.

She stumbled suddenly into a twilight-dark clearing—where a new monster reared up before her, bellowing. She squealed and fell flat in the dirt.

For a heartbeat the monster stood over Far. Beyond it squat forms sat; broad faces turned toward her, incurious, huge jaws chewing.

The monster was another hominid: another pithecine, in fact, a robust form. This big male, with an immense swollen belly, was taller and much bulkier than the gracile types who had captured her. His posture, even when he stood erect, was much more apelike; he had a sloping back, long arms, and bent legs. His head was extravagantly sculpted, with high cheeks, an immense, rocklike jaw filled with worn, stubby teeth, and a great bony crest that ran down the length of his skull.

Exhausted, in pain, her shoulder bleeding heavily, Far curled up on the ground, expecting those immense fists to come slamming down on her. But the blows never came.

The blocky creatures on the ground behind the big male huddled a little closer together. They were all females, with heavy breasts over those giant bellies, and as they stared at Fur, they pulled their tubby infants toward them. But still they sat and ate, Far saw. One female picked up a hard nut—so hard Far would have had to use a rock to crack its shell—placed it between her teeth and, pushing up on her jaw with her hand, cracked it easily. Then she began to crunch it down, shell and all.

But now the skinny pithecines came hurtling into the clearing. When they saw Big Belly they clattered to a halt, stumbling over one another like clowns. Instantly they began to display, stalking to and fro with their fur erect; they slapped the ground and hurled twigs and bits of dried shit at their new opponent.

Big Belly growled back. The truth was this gorilla-man was a vegetarian, forced by the low quality of his diet to spend most of his day sitting still while his vast gut strove to process his food. But this immense brute with his stumps of teeth, powerfully muscled frame, and cowering harem seemed a much more intimidating proposition than the skinny pithecines. He dropped to a knuckle-walk posture with a slam that seemed to make the ground shake, his huge gut wobbling. He stalked back and forth before his little domain, his own fur bristling, roaring back at the impertinent graciles.

The pithecines backed away, hooting their frustration.

Far scrambled out of the way and blundered on, still deeper into the seemingly unending forest. This time, she wasn't pursued.

She couldn't see the sun, not directly; there was only a scattering of green-tinged dappled light to mark her way. She had no sense of how long she plunged on through the forest, how far she had come. The deep cut in her shoulder had crusted over, but still she lost blood. Her head ached from the slamming it had taken from the pithecine's rock, and her chest and back were just masses of bruises. And shock and bewilderment at losing her mother, and the small band of people who had made up her world, began to overwhelm her.

Exhaustion crept up.

At last she tripped over a root. She fell at the foot of a tree fern into soft, frond-littered loam.

She tried to push herself up, but her arms seemed to have no strength. She got to her hands and knees, but the color leached out of the world, its deep swallowing green turning gray. Then the ground seemed to tilt, the loamy ground swiveling up to slap into her face, hard.

The earth was cool under her cheek. She closed her eyes. The aches of her bruises and cuts seemed to fade, rattling into the distance like the storm's thunder. A clamor filled her head, monotonous and loud, but somehow comforting. She let herself sink into the noise.

After Capo had come the great divergence from the chimps. The new kinds of apes that followed were hominids—that is, closer to humans than chimps or gorillas.

In the grand drama of the evolution of the hominids, learning to walk upright had been the easy part. Millions of years of apelike tree-climbing had seen to that. Now, as Capo's descendants adapted to their new life on the interface between forest and savannah, to become more bipedal actually meant *less* body reorganization than needed to revert to all fours.

Their feet, no longer required to grip branches at odd angles, became simplified into compact pads that lost much of their flexibility, and their big toes no longer worked as thumbs—but their new arched feet served as shock absorbers that enabled them to walk long distances without injury. Knee joints and thigh bones were redesigned to absorb the new upright load. The uprights' spines became longer and curved to push their centers of gravity forward so it lay over their feet, and on the center line of their vertical bodies. New, specialized hip joints arose, a design that enabled them to lift one leg off the ground without losing their balance, as chimps would, so that they could walk without swaying. Their hands no longer had to combine manipulation with support and so became more flexible: their knuckles slimmed; their thumbs were freed up for more complex and delicate grasping. They became less strong, weight for weight, now that they didn't need to haul themselves through the trees all the time.

Bipedalism helped the new savannah apes by allowing them to walk or run long distances between scattered sources of food and shelter, and by enabling them to reach fruit and berries at higher levels. As time went on they became more upright and taller, succumbing to the same pressures that had shaped giraffes. Bipedalism was such a major advantage, in fact, that it had already evolved independently in other ape lineages— although all of those creatures would succumb to extinction long before true humans appeared.

The graciles, the skinny pithecines who had hunted Far, were like upright chimps. They were more upright than Capo or any ape. But their heads were like those of apes, with protruding muzzles, small brain pans, and flattened nostrils. Their posture, even when standing upright, was bent, the head thrust forward, and their arms were long, their grasping hands reaching almost to their knees. When they walked, they had to use more steps than Far would have done to cover the same ground, and they could not move so fast. But over the short distances they usually covered they were efficient and effective movers.

They had stuck to the forest fringe. But they had learned to exploit the resources of the savannah: especially the carcasses of the great herbivores laid low by predators. When the opportunity presented itself, they would rush out of the cover of their forest to a carcass, clutching their simple flake tools, and slice through tendons and ligaments. Stolen limbs could quickly be brought back to the safety of the forest for butchery and consumption, and hammer-stones could be used to crack the remnant bones for marrow.

All of this forced a selection for smartness. Hominids lacked the teeth of hyenas or the beaks of the carrion birds; if they were to scavenge effectively they needed better tools than Capo's rudimentary kit. Meanwhile their bodies had gotten better at processing meat. Many pithecine types had teeth capable of shredding uncooked flesh, and a more efficient digestive system able to tolerate such rich fodder.

Still they were marginal scavengers, at the bottom of the hierarchy of meat eaters; they had to wait their turn until the lions and hyenas and

vultures had taken what they wanted from the larger kills. And scavenging, and even their rudimentary hunting, wasn't the only pressure on the
savannah apes.

The savannah was predator hell. The leopards and bears of the forests
had been bad enough. Out on the savannah there were huge flesh-shearing
hyenas, and saber-tooths, and dogs the size of wolves. Small, slow, and
defenseless, the hominids, walking blinking out of their forests, were an easy
target for such creatures. Soon some of the predators, like the *dinofelis*,
even learned to specialize in taking hominids.

It was a ruthless attrition, a relentless pressure. But the hominids
responded. They learned to understand the predators' behavior, and how to
seek effective refuge. They learned to cooperate better with one another,
for there was safety in numbers, and they used tools to drive off their
assailants. Even the development of language was driven, in part, by these
pressures, as the specialized alarm cries that dated back to the forests of the
notharctus slowly morphed into more flexible words.

The savannah shaped the hominids. But they were not hunters; they
were the hunted.

The pithecines had their limitations. They needed the shelter of the
forest as their base, for they were not built to withstand long periods out
in the open. And they were tied to rivers, lakes, and marshes, for their
bodies had little fatty tissue and so were not resilient to long periods without water.

But as time went on, and Africa's climate and habitat range fluctuated, the forest-fringe environment the pithecines favored spread: In a
landscape of forest clumps, there was plenty of *edge*. The pithecine form
had proved effective and enduring, and there had been a great churning
of speciation events, a radiation of ape people.

The robust gorilla folk had abandoned the adventure of the forest
fringe and had taken to the deeper green. Here they had begun to exploit
a source of food for which there was little competition: leaves, bark, and
unripe fruit unfit for any other hominid type to digest, and nuts and seeds
too hard for other animals to crack. To adapt to this lifestyle they had, like
potbellies and gigantopithecines, developed huge energy-expensive guts
to process their low-quality food and heavily engineered skulls capable of
driving those huge jaws with their slablike teeth.

Their social lives had changed too. In the dense forest, where there
was always a supply of leaves and bark, stable groups of females came
together to live off a single patch of forest. Males became solitary, each
trying to maintain his hold over the females in his territory. So the males
became larger than the females, and there was a premium on brute

physical strength, so that each male could fight off those who would usurp him.

The gorilla-man's kind were among the least intelligent of the hominids of his day. That big gut was very energy expensive; to balance its budget his body, in the course of its adaptation, had had to make sacrifices elsewhere. Smarts weren't essential among the harems in the dim, stable gloom of the deep forest, and so the gorilla folk's big primate brains, very costly in blood and energy, had dissolved.

But because the gorilla-man could be sure of sexual access to his females, his testicles were small. By comparison the skinny pithecine chimp-men had to mate as often as possible with as many females as they could, and needed the large, pendulous balls they displayed so readily, to produce oceans of sperm.

Within these basic pithecine types, the gracile chimp folk and the robust gorilla types, there were many variants. Some enhanced their bipedalism. Some all but abandoned it. Some skinnies were smarter than others; some gorilla folk were dumber than the rest. There were skinnies who used tools even less advanced than Capo's, and gorilla types who used tools more sophisticated than the gracile pithecines' stone flakes. There were large and small, skulkers and runners, pygmies and giants, slim omnivores and pillar-toothed herbivores. There were creatures with protruding faces like a chimp's and others with delicate, flat features almost like a human's. And there was much crossbreeding among the types, a proliferation of subspecies and hybrids, ornamenting the carnival of hominid possibilities.

Baffled paleontologists of the future, trying to piece this diversity together from fragmentary fossils and stone tools, would devise elaborate family trees and nomenclatures, calling their imagined species *Kenyanthropus platypus*; or *Orrorin tugenenis*; or *Australopithecus garhi, africanus, afarensis, bahrelghazali, anamensis*; or *Ardipithecus ramidus*; or *Paranthropus robustus, boisei, aethiopicus*; or *Homo habilis*. But few of the names fit the reality. And besides, the boundaries between these categories of creature were very blurred. Out in the real world, of course, such labels did not matter; there were only individuals, struggling to survive and raise their offspring, as they always had.

Most of the diverse assemblage here would be lost in time, their poor bones swallowed up forever by the forest's voracious green. No human would ever know how it was to live in a world like this, crowded with so many different types of people. It was a bubbling evolutionary ferment, as many variants were spun off a fundamentally successful new body plan.

But none of this myriad of species had a future, for all these ape folk had clung to the forest. Their fingers and toes remained long and curved to help grab hold of tree trunks, and their legs were a peculiar compromise between the needs of knuckle-walking tree climber and those of biped. At night they would even make treetop nests like their forest-dwelling ancestors before them. And their brains never developed much beyond the size of Capo's, and those of their cousins, the ancestral chimps, because their low-quality diet could sustain nothing bigger.

For four million years the pithecines had been a wide, diverse, very successful flourishing of the hominid family. Once, in fact, the only hominids in the world had been ape-men. But their time of significant change was already over. They had been seduced by the shelter and protection of the forest, and this had robbed them of much possibility. The future lay with another group of hominids—descendants of pithecine stock themselves—but who, unlike any pithecine, had made the decisive break away from the forest.

The future lay with Far.

III

Reluctantly she opened her eyes. She saw a patch of dirty ground, tilted up under her face. When she raised her head she could see brightness filtering through the dense tree trunks.

She pushed at the ground, and got her body off the floor. Leaves and dirt stuck to her breasts and injured shoulder. She used a tree trunk to pull herself upright, and stood still until the pounding of her heart subsided. Then she began to stagger as best she could through the forest toward the light.

She stumbled out into the day. She raised her hand, shielding her eyes against a low, reddening sun. The land was scorched, the grass blackened, the ground cracked and dried. But beyond a low rise she saw the glint of water: a stream that rolled from eroded hills a little further away.

She didn't know this place. She had come right through the patch of forest, from east to west.

She stepped forward gingerly. The scorched ground was still hot—here and there tree stumps and bushes still smoked—and the crisped grass blades hurt her feet. Soon her lower legs, already filthy from her time in the forest, were coated with a deep black soot.

But she made it to the water. The stream was clear and fast moving. It ran over a bed of rounded volcanic cobbles, and bits of blackened vegetation skimmed over its surface. She plunged in her face and drank deeply. The dirt and dried blood washed off her skin, and the lingering stink of smoke in her nose and throat began to dissipate.

And then she heard a call. A voice. A word. But it wasn't a word she knew.

She scrambled out of the water and threw herself flat behind an eroded boulder. In her world, strangers were bad news. Like their pithecine cousins her nomadic people were fiercely xenophobic.

A man knelt on the ground, his hands nimbly exploring the scorched soil for any pickings the fire had left behind. He was young, his skin smooth, his hair thick.

He picked up a blackened lizard, stiff and immobile. With a kind of shaped stone—its form wasn't familiar to her—he scraped off the charred skin, exposing a morsel of pink flesh that he gulped down quickly. Now he found a snake, an adder, scorched to stiffness. Though he tried cutting through its burned skin it was too tough, and he threw the little corpse away.

Now the man found a real treasure. It was a tortoise, cooked in its shell. He picked it up and turned it over, muttering to himself. He took his handheld tool—it was a stone flake, but it was triangular, with each face worked, and a sharp edge all around it—and jammed it into the tortoise's neck entrance. With a little effort he cracked open the shell, and soon he was using the tool to slice up the meat. Tortoises were actually a favorite prey of pithecine hunters. They were one of the few savannah animals that were even smaller and slower than hominids, and the tortoises' habit of burrowing into the ground did not save them from clever animals able to dig them out with sticks and who had tools able to open up shells impervious to the teeth of lions and hyenas.

Far was fascinated by the young man's stone ax. With its finely worked edge and shaped faces, it was far beyond her own people's chopping stones and pithecine-like flakes. But she understood it immediately, at a deep somatic level; she had an impulse to reach out and take the stone teardrop, to try it out for herself.

As long as she knew him, she would associate this young man with the stone tool he wielded so expertly. She would think of him as Ax.

Suddenly Ax looked up, straight into Far's eyes.

She cowered back behind her boulder, but it was too late.

He growled and dropped the tortoise—its shell clattered on the sooty ground—and held up his stone ax.

She had nowhere to run. She stood up. She thought his gaze wandered over her body, her back and buttocks still wet from the stream. He lowered the ax and grinned at her. Then he went back to his tortoise and resumed carving it out of its shell.

Calls came floating from the distance.

She saw more people—folk like herself, adults and children, slim upright forms moving like shadows over the ash-strewn plain. They were exploring a miniature forest of blackened, twisted forms. It had been a birthing herd of antelopes; many of these unlucky creatures, straining over their last calves, had been unable to flee the flames. Now the people were slicing into this treasure with their marvelous stone axes, and even from here she could smell the delicious scent of cooked meat. Ax dropped the tortoise and ran off toward his people.

After a few heartbeats, torn between caution and ravening hunger, Far began to jog after him.

Night fell quickly, as it always did. The people gathered in a rocky hollow, which would give them some defense against the predators of the night.

Far, with nowhere else to go, followed them.

She couldn't spend a night on her own; she knew that. Even now she sensed cold yellow eyes tracking her, eyes that glowed with the knowledge that she was an outlier of this group—not quite embraced within its protection—*a target*, like the old, the very young, the lame.

The people didn't drive her away. They didn't exactly make her welcome, either. But when she tucked herself into a corner of the roomy hollow, huddled over a scrap of meat she had scavenged from one of the burnt carcasses, they tolerated her presence.

She watched a man knapping a bit of rock. The man was old—in his late forties—and skinny, with one eye almost closed by an ugly scar. Two children, a boy and a girl, sat at his feet. Not much younger than Far, they watched what Scar-face was doing, and with big stones held clumsily in their own small hands, they tried to copy him. The girl trapped her thumb, and squealed in pain. Scar-face wordlessly took the rock from her hands, turned it around and by guiding her hands showed her how to hold the cobble more effectively. But when he saw this the boy was jealous, and he pinched the girl, making her drop the rock. "Me! Me!"

As the darkness deepened, many of the people resorted to gentle, wordless grooming, the habit that had come with them from the ancestral forests. Mothers caressed infants, men and women alike played wordless politics as they cemented alliances and reinforced hierarchies. Sometimes the grooming turned to noisy sex.

Far, the stranger, was excluded from all this. But as she sank toward sleep, exhausted and battered, she was aware of Ax's eyes on her.

When she woke, the sky beyond the hollow was already very bright.

Everybody had gone, leaving behind a few scraps of food, patches of infant shit, damp urine marks.

She got to her feet quickly. The bruises on her back and chest seemed to have consolidated into a single mass of pain. But her young body was already throwing off the damage it had suffered yesterday, and her head was clear. She hurried out into the light.

The people had walked north, toward a lake. They were slim upright shadows, walking purposefully, their outlines softened by the shimmering heat haze. She ran after them.

The lakeshore was crowded. Far made out many kinds of elephants, rhinos, horses, giraffes, buffaloes, deer, antelope, gazelles, even ostriches. In the water there were crocodiles and turtles, and birds flapped over it noisily. The giant herbivores, concentrated around the water, had devastated the landscape. From this muddy arena, their wide, well-trodden avenues snaked off in every direction. On the hardpan around the lake nothing grew but a few hardy plant species distasteful to the elephants and rhinos and able to recover quickly from trampling.

The people moved down to the water. They picked a spot close to an elephant herd. Everybody knew that predators avoided elephants. The elephants ignored the people and continued with their own complex business. Some of them entered the water and were splashing and playing noisily; groups of cows rumbled mysteriously, and males trumpeted and clashed their huge tusks. These massive animals, the architects of the landscape, were slabs of muscle and power, with their own stately, flat-footed grace.

Most of the women were working the water's edge. Far saw that one of them had turned up the nest of a freshwater turtle; its long eggs were quickly cracked, their contents devoured. Other women were harvesting the mussels that grew abundantly in the shallow waters, especially freshwater clams.

Far saw that Ax, like most of the men, had waded into the water. He was carrying a wooden spear, and he stood very still, eyes fixed on the glimmering water's surface. After a few heartbeats he stabbed down with a powerful splash—and when he brought up the spear, a fish had been neatly skewered, its silver body wriggling. Ax hooted, pulled the fish off his spear, and threw it to the shore. Another man, a little further out, was creeping up on a water fowl that paddled complacently across the surface. The man leapt, but the bird got away, amid much comical splashing, squawking, and shouting.

Far joined the women.

She quickly found a horseshoe crab, crawling stiffly along a muddy channel. It was easy to catch. She held it upside down, and it waved its clawed legs feebly. She used a bit of stone to open up its head shield, which was the size of a dinner plate. Inside, near the front, there was a mass of eggs, like fat rice grains. She scooped them out with her fingers and gulped them down. The flavor was very strong, like oily fish. The rest of the crab's meat proved too tough to be worth digging out. She flipped away the smashed head shield, and moved on in search of more food.

Thus the day wore on, as the people foraged for their food, just another type of animal on this crowded savannah.

As midday approached, the hominids moved away from the water, relaxed, satiated.

But Ax struck out on his own. Far trailed after him. He gazed back at her. She knew he was aware she was following him.

Ax came to a dried-up streambed laced with worn cobbles. He walked up and down the bed, examining the rocks, until he found what he wanted. It was a cobble about the size of his fist, flattened and rounded. He sat squat in the streambed and rummaged around until he found a suitable hammer-stone. He had brought some dried brush that he spread over his crossed legs for protection. Then he went to work, tapping at the core he had selected. Soon flakes flew away, briskly rattling off the cobble.

Far sat ten meters away, her legs folded before her, hugging her knees, fascinated by his toolmaking. It was like nothing she had seen before.

In fact, Ax and Far had grown up in toolmaking traditions separated by millennia.

Once they had put the trees behind them and moved definitively out onto the savannah, a new range of possibilities had opened up for the walkers. They were more than merely mobile. They migrated. But it wasn't purposeful. For each individual, it was just a question of making a living. For people able to exploit new landscapes, it was often easier to walk to somewhere that looked a better place to live than to try to adapt to harsh conditions.

But as the generations ticked by the people covered thousands of kilometers. They even walked out of Africa, into lands where no hominid had set foot before. Before the great clamp of the glaciations tightened, equable conditions had spread well out of Africa into southern Europe, the Middle East, and southern Asia. Walking into these familiar surroundings the people followed the easy living of the coastlines, west around the Mediterranean and diffusing inland, at last colonizing Spain, France, Greece, Italy—as did animals later associated only with Africa, like elephants, giraffes, and antelope. To the east, they worked through India to the Far East, suffusing through what would become China, even working south to reach Indonesia.

It was not a conquest. Far's kind had become far more widespread than any other ape species. But other animals, like the elephants, spread much further. And there were fewer of them. Their numbers in any given area were less than lions, say. Despite their tools the people were still just big animals in a landscape on which they had minimal impact.

And the great wandering was not purposeful. One of Far's distant grandmothers had reached as far as Vietnam; now, in Far's time, chance and the endless walking had brought her lineage back to East Africa, to home.

But here, in the ancient homelands, the returning migrants encountered new pressures.

Some hominid populations had elected not to move, despite the climate's treacherous fluctuations. To survive they had been forced to become smarter. Better tools—crucially, the hand axes—had been the key to their survival. The ax's secret was its teardrop shape. A flattened bifaced shape gave a long cutting edge for minimal weight. Though they would still use simple pithecine-like flake tools if they needed to—the flakes, easy to make, were "cheap" and were actually better for some tasks, like tackling small prey—the hand axes were used not just for butchering meat, but for hacking sticks and clubs from branches, sharpening wooden spears, opening up beehives, digging into logs to get at larvae, peeling off bark, shredding pith, and opening the shells of tortoises and turtles. It was from a group of these stay-at-homes that Ax was descended.

Which was how Far, descendant of wanderers who had crossed southern Eurasia all the way to the Far East, now found herself confronted by the startlingly advanced technology of Ax and his kind.

Ax worked patiently. Her gaze wandering, Far noticed now that the dry bed here was littered with hand axes: many of the rocks she had assumed were just cobbles had actually been shaped. They all had the characteristic teardrop shape, and were all worked to a greater or lesser degree to give that fine edge all the way around the tool.

But these axes were strange. Some of the axes were tiny, the size of butterflies, while some were huge. Some of them were broken, some smeared with blood. But when she tried to pick up one of the larger axes, its edge cut into her fingers; it had hardly been used, if at all.

Someone walked up to her. She cowered back.

It was Scar-face, the man who had taught the children how to knap rock. He was looking at Far with a kind of hungry intensity. He had one of the huge axes in his hands. It was impractically large, too large to use to butcher. Still gazing at her he turned it over in his hands, and tapped at it with a hammer-stone, tidying up an edge. Then he scraped it over his leg, and removed a swath of the fine black hair that grew there. All through this he watched Far's face and body, his half-covered eye gleaming.

She had absolutely no idea what he wanted—none, that is, until she saw the erection poking out of his tuft of pubic hair.

Ax had more or less finished the blade he was making: hand-sized, utilitarian, rough and ready, it was clearly a functional tool, manufactured in minutes. But when he saw what Scar-face was doing he threw down his ax angrily. He got up, scattering his spill of flakes, and punched the man's shoulder. "Away! Away!"

Scar-face snarled back, his erection subsiding. At last Ax grabbed the huge gaudy ax out of his hands, and threw it to the ground. Part of its beautiful edge sheared off. Scar-face looked at the ax, at Far, and, with a final glare at Ax, walked away.

Far sat where she was, her knees tucked against her chest, fearful and baffled.

Ax stared at her. Then he stalked up and down the dry stream again, surveying the stones. At last he came across a big malformed volcanic block, so heavy it took two hands to lift it. He sat down again, picked up a few hammer-stones, scattered more brush over his legs.

He started to slam at the rock, displaying all his strength. Flakes and sheets of it began to fall away. But very quickly, thanks to his skill and strength, a crude hand ax teardrop shape emerged. Now he started to use a succession of smaller stones to shape the two lenticular surfaces, and to finish the edge to a fine blade.

Where his first effort had come easily, borne out of a rock that had already had the rough shape of the final ax, this rock was much more difficult. He couldn't have picked a tougher challenge—and he had chosen it deliberately. And all through this he made sure Far was watching him.

The walking folk had already been making tools more or less like this for two hundred thousand years. Over such an immense span of time, the axes had become more than mere tools, more than functional.

To Ax, this feat of toolmaking was a kind of courtship. He was displaying his fitness as a mate to Far. By making the tool he was showing her in one clear demonstration the strength of his body, the precision of his working, the clarity of his mind, his ability to conceive and see through a design, his skill for locating raw materials, his coordination of hand and eye, his spatial skills, his understanding of the environment around him. All of these were traits he expected she would want to pass on to her offspring—and that was why such displays had acquired a logic of their own, divorced from the utility of the hand axes.

Driven by lust and longing, men and boys would make dozens of axes, over and over. They would labor for hours over a single ax, seeking perfect symmetry. They would make tiny axes the size of their thumbnails, or they would make huge unwieldy affairs that would have to be held in two hands like an open book. They would, as Ax had, seek out particularly difficult raw materials and go ahead and carve out axes anyhow. Sometimes they would even throw away their axes, deliberately, to show how rich they were in strength and skill.

It was even worth trying to cheat, as Scar-face had done. It didn't work very often—women quickly learned they had to *see* the most impressive ax being made before them—but occasionally it paid off, and the liar got a chance to pass on his genes at very low cost.

This mixing up of toolmaking with sexual courtship would have a profound effect on the future. As no male could afford not to make axes just as his forefathers had done, it was a recipe for stultifying conservatism. These people would make the same tool to the same plan, over and over, across several continents, despite several glacial cycles, for a million years. Even the different *species* who followed them would continue with the same technology. It was a continuity and a consistency that no institution, no religion would ever match. Only sex had a strong enough hold on the human mind to have achieved such a vast freezing.

When he worked on his tools, Ax had to think, to some extent, like a human. Unlike the pithecine stone-slammer who would take whatever shape and size of flake his cobble offered him, Ax had to have an image of the final artifact in his mind. He had to select the raw materials and hammer-stones to match that vision, and he had to work systematically toward his goal. But his mind was divided as no human's could be. Ax made his tools like a human, but he attracted mates like a peacock or a bower bird.

When Ax was done, he turned the tool he had made over and over in his hands, showing her its fine faces, its smoothly finished edge. It was magnificent, if impractical.

Far, brought up in a subtly different culture, had no clear idea of what he was doing—and she was just as baffled by Scar-face's attempt to cheat. But she did sense Ax's interest in her, and a warmth in her belly spread in response. And a more calculating corner of her mind was aware that if she mated with Ax, if she became pregnant, then she would become part of this group, and her future would be secured.

But she had never had sex, not with anybody. Longing, fearful, she sat there at the edge of the streambed, her legs still tucked against her chest. She didn't know how to respond.

At length he dropped the beautiful ax, among so many others. Baffled, casting backward glances at her, he walked away.

Speciation—the emergence of a new species—was a rare event.

One species did not morph smoothly into another. Rather, speciation relied on a group of animals being isolated from the larger population and put under pressure to survive. The isolation could be physical—say, if a group of elephants was cut off by a flood—or it could be behavioral, if, for instance, one group of hominids that had adopted a particular way of scavenging was shunned by another group that hadn't.

Variation was implicit in the genome of every species. It was as if every species, at any given moment, was contained in a field, fenced off by the habitable limits of its environment. Every viable variation would come into play, to fill up every available corner of the field. An isolated group was stuck in a fenced-off corner of the field. But perhaps a little of the outer fence came down, opening up a new and empty field, into which they began, slowly, to diffuse. More variation might be necessary to fill the newly available space—and if the necessary variation wasn't available in the genome, perhaps it could be generated by mutation.

In the end, those who reached the furthest corner of the new range might have gone a great distance, genetically, from those who had remained in the old field. If the distance became too great for the old and new kinds to crossbreed, a new species was born. Later, when the isolating barriers came down, the evolved kind might interact with the parent type—perhaps to supplant them.

Some three hundred thousand years earlier, in another part of Africa, a group of nondescript forest-fringe pithecines had found themselves cut off from their home range by a lava flow, cast out of their forest once and for all.

There were many challenges to be met. The old pithecine habits of forest-fringe hunting had been a start, something to build on. But out on the savannah the food supply was very different from that in the forest. Whereas the forest had provided a steady supply of fruit, the main savannah food was meat. Meat was high-quality nutrition, but it came in packages scattered sparsely over an arid, inhospitable landscape, packages you had to be smart to spot, get hold of, and use. And stranded out on the savannah, away from the trees' shelter, a new kind of body was needed to cope with the aridity and the heat, new kinds of behavior needed to extract the resources needed from the new environment—and to survive in predator hell.

Within a mere few dozen generations Far's ancestors had adapted drastically.

The ancient primate body plan had been rebuilt, stretched tall almost to human proportions. Far's body was much bulkier than that of the ancestral apes. She was twice as heavy as an adult gracile pithecine. That bulk was an adaptation for openness: a larger body was more efficient at storing water, a key advantage on a plain where there could be many hours' walking between water sources.

And her metabolism had become efficient at creating and storing subcutaneous fat, for fat was a key fuel reserve. Ten kilograms of fat would be sufficient to see her through forty days without food, enough to ride out all but the most severe seasonal fluctuations. The fat had fleshed out her body, giving her swollen breasts, buttocks, and thighs, a much more *human* shape than the pithecines' chimplike slackness. But Far was not a round ball; instead she was tall and thin, so that her body was also an efficient radiator of waste heat, and when the sun beat down from above, comparatively little of her skin was directly exposed to its radiation.

More heat adaptations: Apart from her head, with its grooming patch of hair, her skin was all but bare. And she sweated, unlike Capo, unlike any other ape outside her species family, for bare, sweating skin was a better temperature regulator than hair for creatures destined to spend their lives in open tropical sunlight. Sweating was a paradox, for it meant Far lost water. So she had to be smart enough to find water sources to make up for that, and, unlike some of the true savannah creatures, her kind would always be tied to some extent to water courses and the coasts.

The most apelike characteristics of the pithecines—their grasping feet, long arms, and stooping gait—had soon been abandoned. Far's feet were best fit for running and walking, not climbing: her big toe was now a toe, not a thumb. But Far's rib cage was a little high, her shoulders a little narrow: even now her body still carried with it traces of its vanishing adaptation to the trees—as would modern humans', as would Joan Useb's.

Meanwhile her brain had grown to more than three times the mass of a pithecine's, the better to handle the puzzles of a difficult landscape and the intricacies of still more complex societies of large groups of savannah foragers. That big brain was very energy-hungry, but Far's diet was much richer than any pithecine's, with plenty of high-protein foods like meat and nuts, which in turn required greater intelligence to gather. Thus her smartness had been driven by a virtuous circle of development.

All these changes were drastic, and yet they had been achieved by an evolutionary strategy of remarkable economy. It had been heterochrony—*different timing.* Walker infants looked much as their more apelike ancestors had—as would human babies—with relatively large skulls, small faces and jaws. If you wanted to become Capo, you grew your jaw large and kept your brain relatively small. But Far's brain had grown large while her jaw had stayed small. Even the much larger size of her body had been achieved by stretching out growing phases: her body had something like the relative dimensions of a fetal Capo, inflated to adult size.

But that large body size and big brain came at a price. She had been born with her development incomplete, because that was the only way her head would have squeezed through her mother's birth canal. She had been born premature. Unlike the apes and even the pithecines, walker infants could not forage for themselves until long after weaning: aside from their physical immaturity, the ability to exploit food sources like hunted meat, clams, and heavy-shelled nuts was not innate in the newborn, and so had to be learned. But at the same time the children of the walkers were being born into the predator hell of the savannah. So, while they were young, kids needed a lot of care.

These costly, dependent children made it difficult for the walker types to compete with the fast-breeding pithecines, with whom they often shared the same habitats. And that was why the walkers began to live longer.

Most pithecine females, like the apes before them, died not long after their fertility ended—indeed, few long outlived their last birth. Walker women, and men, began to live for years, even decades after their reproductive career was apparently over. These grandmothers and grandfathers began to play a crucial role in shaping walker society. They helped with the division of labor: They helped their daughters care for the children, they helped gather food, they were essential in passing on the complex information required by the walkers to survive.

All this had required a new efficiency in body design. Walker bodies were much better than pithecines' at maintenance and longevity—all save their reproductive systems; a forty-year-old walker woman's ovaries were as badly degenerated as would be the rest of her body at age eighty, if she lived that long.

Crucially, the grandmothers' support meant their daughters could afford to have children more often. That was how the walkers outcompeted the pithecines and apes. Almost all walker children survived long after weaning. Almost all pithecine infants did not.

For the pithecines the emergence of this new form was a disaster. Walkers and pithecines were too close cousins to share the ecology easily. There were few direct conflicts between the types of people: Sometimes pithecines hunted walkers or walkers hunted pithecines, but they found each other too smart and dangerous a prey to be worth the trouble. But in ages to come the walkers—big-brained, flexible, mobile—would slowly drive their smaller-brained cousins to extinction.

Toolmaking and even consciousness were, ultimately, no guarantee of survival.

Of course it need not have happened. If not for the fluctuation of the climate, the chance isolation of Far's ancestors, there might have been no mankind: nothing but pithecines, upright chimps screeching and making their crude tools and waging their petty wars for millions of years more, until the forests disappeared altogether, and they succumbed to extinction.

Life always had been chancy.

Far spent the night alone, cold, drifting through an uneasy sleep.

The next day, as she tried to join in the group's activities, a woman, heavily pregnant, glared into her eyes, an ancient primate challenge. Was Far here to take food that might otherwise reach the belly of her unborn child?

Far felt more isolated than ever. She had no ties with anybody here. There was no reason why they should share their space, their resources with her. It wasn't as if this place was brimming with riches. And now even Ax seemed to be rejecting her.

As the afternoon wore on she was the first to return, alone, to the hollow in the sandstone outcrop. She tucked herself into the peripheral corner she had come to think of as her own.

But she noticed some lumps of crimson rock scattered deeper at the back of the hollow. She picked them up, turning them over curiously. Their redness was bright in the daylight, and they were soft. They were lumps of ocher, the iron red of ferric oxide. Someone had been attracted by their color and, on impulse, brought them here.

She saw scrapes of red on scattered basalt rocks at the back of the hollow: red the same color as the ocher, red like blood. Experimentally she pushed the ocher over the rock, and was startled to see more bloody streaks smear over the rock surface.

For long minutes she played with the bits of ocher, not really thinking, her clever fingers working by themselves to add their own meaningless scribbles to the scrawls on the rock.

Then she heard the hollers of the people as they started to drift back to their temporary base. She dropped the bits of ocher where she had found them, and made for her corner.

But the palms of her hands were bright red: red like blood. For an instant she thought she had cut herself. But when she licked her palms she tasted salty rock, and the scraping of ocher came away.

Red like blood. A tentative connection formed in her mind, a chink of light shining between her compartments of thought.

She went back to the bits of ocher. Now she tried scraping them over the back of her hands, where she made a hatchery of lines, and on the healing pithecine cut on her shoulder, which she made bright red again.

And she marked herself between her legs—marking her skin red like blood, as if she were bleeding, as she had seen her mother bleed.

She went back to her corner and waited until the light faded. As the people tended and crooned to each other, she huddled over and tried to sleep.

Someone approached: warm, breathing softly. It was Ax. She could smell the dusty scent of rock chippings on his legs and belly. His eyes were pits of shadow in the fading light. The moment stretched. Then he touched her shoulder. His hand was heavy and warm, but she shivered. He leaned toward her and sniffed quietly, scenting her just as had Brow before she had become separated from her family.

She opened her legs, so he could see the "blood" in the fading light. She sat tense, watching him.

Her life hung on his acceptance; she knew that. Perhaps it was that basic desperation and longing, a longing for him to see her as a woman, which had driven her to come up with this peculiar deceit.

Unlike his forest-dwelling ancestors, Ax was a creature of sight, not smell; the message from his eyes overrode the warning of his nose. He leaned forward. He touched her shoulder, her throat, her breast. Then he sat beside her and his strong fingers began to comb through her tangled hair.

Slowly she relaxed.

Far stayed with Ax and his people for the rest of her life. But as long as she could, whenever she could—as she grew in wisdom and strength, as her children grew until they gave her grandchildren to protect and mold in turn—she ran, and ran, and ran.

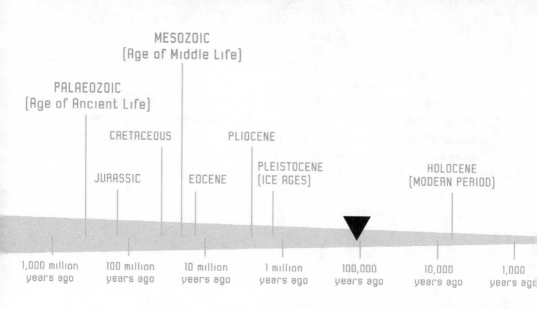

MESOZOIC
[Age of Middle Life]

PALAEOZOIC
[Age of Ancient Life]

CRETACEOUS

PLIOCENE

JURASSIC

EOCENE

PLEISTOCENE
[ICE AGES]

HOLOCENE
[MODERN PERIOD]

| 1,000 million years ago | 100 million years ago | 10 million years ago | 1 million years ago | 100,000 years ago | 10,000 years ago | 1,000 years ago |

CHAPTER 10

the crowded land

▼ **Central Kenya, East Africa. Circa 127,000 years before present.**

I

Pebble had found a yam vine. He bent and inspected it.

He was eight years old, naked save for smears of ocher on his barrel chest and broad face. He pulled out a little grass from around the yam's base. This was a spot for yam, not grass, and it was best to keep it that way.

People had been here before to dig out these tubers. Perhaps he had even been here himself. At eight years old he had already covered every scrap of his people's range, and he thought he remembered this spot, here between these eroded bluffs of sandstone.

He took his digging stick. This was a heavy pole shoved through a hole crudely bored in a small boulder. Despite the tool's weight, he lifted it easily, and he used the mass of the boulder to ram the digger's point into the hard ground.

Pebble was a solid slab of muscle built over a tough, robust skeleton. If Far, his long-dead, distant grandmother, had looked like a long-distance runner, Pebble might have been a junior shot-putter. His face was large, massive-featured, dominated by a great ridge of bone over his brow. He had a mountainous nose and large sinuses that gave his face an oddly puffed-out look. His teeth were flat-topped pillars of enamel. His skull, which would become considerably larger than Far's, housed a large and complex brain—in fact comparable in size to a modern human's—but it sat much more directly behind his face than a human's brain would have.

When he had been born, wet from the womb, Pebble's body had been sleek and round, inspiring an odd image in his mother's mind, a pebble worn by a stream. Names for people still lay far in the future—with just twelve people in Pebble's group there was no need for names—but nevertheless this boy's mother would often look on a glistening rock in a stream, and remember her child as he had been as a baby in her arms.

Pebble, then.

In this age there were many kinds of robust folk like Pebble's spread through Europe and western Asia. Those who inhabited Europe would one day be called Neandertals. But just as in Far's time, most of these new kinds of people would never be discovered, let alone understood, classified, linked to a hominid family tree.

His were a strong people, though. Even at eight years old, Pebble performed work essential to his family's survival. He wasn't yet up to joining the adults on the hunts, but he could dig out yams with the best of them.

The wind picked up a little, bringing him the delicious scent of wood smoke, of home. He went at his work with a will.

Already his digging had broken up the earth. He plunged his hands into the dry ground and began exposing a fat tuber that looked as if it might go down a long way, perhaps as deep as two meters. He went back to his digging stick. Bits of dust and rock flew up, sticking to his sweat-covered legs. He knew what to do with yams. When he had the tuber he would cut off the edible flesh, but then replace the tuber's stem and top in the ground so that it would regrow. His digging aided the yam in more subtle ways, too. He was loosening and aerating the soil, further fostering regrowth.

His mother would be pleased if he brought home three or four fat tubers, ready to be thrown onto the fire. And yams were useful in a lot of other ways besides eating. You could use them to poison birds and fish. You could rub their juice into your head to kill the lice that crawled there . . .

There was a crunching noise.

Startled, Pebble pulled back his digging stick. He leaned forward, shielding his eyes from the sun's brightness, trying to see what was down there in the hole. It could be some deep-burrowing insect. But he could see nothing but a scrap of rust brown, like a bit of sandstone. He reached down and, his clumsy fingers stretching, grabbed the scrap and pulled it to the surface. It was a ragged-edged dome, small enough to fit in the palm of his hand. When he held it up before his face two empty eye sockets peered back at him.

It was a skull. The head of a child.

That was no great horror. Children died all the time. This was a harsh place: There was little pity to spare for the weak and hapless.

But all the children who had died within Pebble's own short lifetime had been put in the ground close to the huts. Like all the dead, they were buried to keep the scavengers from harassing the living. Perhaps this child was long dead, then. Perhaps its people had buried it here before Pebble was born, where the yam clump grew now.

But the skull was oddly fine, light. Pebble weighed it in his hand. Its brow was a heavy lid of bone, from which a forehead sloped back almost horizontally. Pebble ran a hand over his own scalp and compared the slightly bulbous swelling of his forehead. There were tooth marks in the little cranium, he saw: precise puncture wounds inflicted by the teeth of a cat—but inflicted after the child was already dead, its body abandoned on the plain.

Pebble could not know that he was holding the remains of the Brat, brother of Far, who had lived and died not far from here. The Brat had succumbed to his infant vitaminosis and died while still a child, without issue. It would have been little comfort to the Brat if he could have known that one day, when his brief, forgotten life was already more than a million years gone, his small head would be cradled in the hand of a remote great-nephew.

And the Brat would have recognized little of this landscape, the place where he had once played.

The geological infrastructure of the Rift Valley—the plateau, the rocks, the volcanic mountains, the great sweep of the valley itself—had been left largely unchanged by time. But since Far's time this had become a sparse, dry place. Scattered stands of acacia, leadwood, and wild laurel had replaced the denser thickets and forest pockets of the past. Even the grasslands were subtly different, great swaths of them dominated by a handful of fire-resistant species. Meanwhile, the great animal communities of the past had imploded. There was not an elephant to be seen across this great dust bowl, not an antelope or giraffe. It was as if life had crashed here. The place was depleted. Far would have been startled by its impoverishment.

But the Brat's wretched remains had left their mark on the world: a scrap of moisture trapped in that buried, upturned skullcap had been enough to help establish the yam.

Incuriously Pebble closed his fist. The little skull was crushed to thin shards, and he let the dust fall back into the hole. He reached for his digging tool; there was still some root to be dug out.

That was when he glimpsed the strangers.

He crouched down behind a bluff, holding his breath.

They were hunters; he could see that immediately. They were following an old elephant track. Elephants walked to water, and where there was water, there would be many animals, including the medium-sized creatures like deer that people hunted by preference.

There were four of them, three men and a woman, all adults. As they walked the hunters' legs swung powerfully, with their torsos tipped a little forward. It was a gait built for strength, not elegance or speed: the hunters had none of the fleetness of Far. Thick beards hid the men's dark faces, and the woman had tied her long hair back with a bit of leather. Unlike Pebble this group wore clothes: just bits of hide, unsewn and tied around the body with strips of leather or plaited bark. Pebble could see the bite marks in the clothes. Leather was treated by chewing and stretching it with the teeth, and a major function of that big ridge of bone on Pebble's brow was to provide an anchor for the jaws that must do such mighty work.

And they carried weapons: narrow wooden throwing spears, and shorter, stubby thrusting spears, great logs of hardwood with slabs of stone stuck to the end with blobs of resin and leather ties. They were giants' weapons that a human would have had trouble lifting, let alone wielding in anger.

They were robust folk, people like Pebble's kind. But Pebble could see ocher markings scrawled on the skin of their faces, hands, and arms. Where Pebble's own adornment was made up of vertical lines—bars and stripes and bands, all pointing to the sky—these people wore a kind of clumsy crosshatch, sketched by thick fingers.

They were strangers. You could tell that by the markings. And strangers meant trouble. That was a law that worked as invariably as the rising of the sun, the waxing of the Moon.

Pebble waited until the newcomers had passed out of sight behind a stand of sparse acacia. Then, as silently as his slablike body would allow him, he began to run for home. The yam tubers he had dug up lay abandoned on the ground behind him—with his digging stick.

Pebble's home was a kind of village, with four large huts set roughly around a clearing. And yet it was not a village, for his people lived not quite as any humans ever would.

Pebble stood, panting, in the central clearing. Nobody was around. Close to the door of one hut a fire smoldered. The trampled ground was scattered with bone, vegetable debris, tools, mattresses of leaves and grass, trays of bark, pegs, wedges, a broken spear, discarded bits of leather. The place was a mess.

The huts were crude and ugly, but serviceable. They had been built of thick saplings set in rough circles in holes in the ground. The gaps between the saplings were filled with rattan cane split into switches, and overlapping leaves, bunches of rushes, bark. The saplings were bent over together and their ends pushed over and under each other. It was a kind of weaving that Capo would have recognized, for five million years earlier he had made his treetop nests in much the same way: Every innovation of necessity was built on what had gone before.

The huts were old. The people had lived here for generations. The dirt beneath Pebble's feet was thick with the bones of his ancestors. The people felt safe here. This was their place, their land.

But now, Pebble knew, all that might change.

He raised his head to the washed-out sky. "*U-lu-lu-lu-lu! U-lu-lu-lu-lu!...*" It was a cry of danger, of pain, the first cry any child learned after the feed-me yell.

Soon the people came running, from the huts, from the land beyond where they foraged and hunted. They gathered around Pebble in concern. There were twelve of them: three men, four women, three older children—including Pebble himself—and two infants in their mothers' frightened grasp.

He tried to tell them what he had seen. He pointed back to where he had seen the strangers, and ran a few paces back and forth. "Others! Others, others, hunters!" He began an elaborate performance, gesticulating, posturing, puffing himself up to walk like powerful hunters, even miming to show how they would smash in the people's heads with their mighty fists.

His audience were impatient. They turned away, as if eager to return to their foraging, or eating, or sleeping. But one man watched Pebble's performance more carefully. He was a squat man even more powerfully built than most, and his face was distorted by a childhood accident that had smashed the cartilage in his great fleshy nose. This man, Flatnose, was Pebble's father.

Pebble's language was sparse. It was just a string of concrete words with no grammar, no syntax. And, a million years after Far, talking was still basically a social skill, in fact used mainly for gossip. To convey detail or complex information, you had to repeat, use endless circumlocution—

and mime, gesture, perform. Besides, Pebble had to convince his audience. It was hard for the adults to accept what Pebble had to say. They
couldn't see the strangers for themselves. He might be lying or exaggerat-
ing: He was, after all, little more than a child. The only way they had to
gauge his sincerity was by the passion and energy he put into his performance.

It was always this way. To get anyone to listen, you had to shout.

At last Pebble gave up, panting, and sat squat in the dirt. He had done
his best.

Flatnose kneeled beside him. Flatnose believed his son: His performance had cost him too much to be lies. He rested his hand on his son's
head.

Reassured, Pebble touched his father's arm. There he found a series of
scars, long and straight, following the line of the forearm. These scratches
were the marks of no animal. Flatnose had inflicted them on himself, with
the sharp blade of a stone knife. When he was older, Pebble knew he would
join in the same game, the same silent, grinning self-mutilation: It was part
of what his father was, part of his strength, and Pebble found it reassuring
now to stroke those scars.

One by one the other adults joined them.

Then, the moment of silent acceptance over, Flatnose got to his feet.
There were no words now. Everybody knew what had to be done. The
adults and the older children—Pebble and a girl a little younger than
himself—started to move around the settlement, gathering weapons.
There was no particular order to the settlement, and weapons and other
tools lay where they had last been used, amid piles of food, debris, ash.

Despite the urgency the people moved sluggishly, as if even now
reluctant to accept the truth.

Dust, Pebble's mother, tried to soothe her squalling baby as she gathered up her gear. Her loose, prematurely grayed hair was, as always, full
of dry, aromatic dust, an eccentric affectation. At twenty-five she was
aging quickly, and she limped when she walked, the effect of an old hunting wound that had never healed right. Since then Dust had had to work
twice as hard, and the cumulative effect showed in her stooped posture
and careworn face. But her mind was clear and unusually imaginative.
She was already thinking of the difficult times ahead. Watching her face,
Pebble felt guilty at having brought this trouble down on her.

There was a soft sigh, a flash. Pebble turned.

In a dreamlike moment, he actually saw the wooden spear in flight. It
was hewn from a fine piece of hardwood, thickest near the point and
tapered back toward the other end, shaped to make it fly true.

Then it was as if time began to flow again.

The spear slammed into Flatnose's back. He was thrown to the ground, the spear sticking straight out of his back. He shuddered once, and a burst of shit cascaded from his bowels, and a black-red pool spread under him, soaking into the dirt.

For a heartbeat Pebble couldn't take this in—the thought that Flatnose had gone so suddenly—it was as if a mountain had suddenly vanished, a lake evaporated. But Pebble had seen plenty of death in his young life. And already he could smell the stink of shit and blood: meat smells, not person smells.

A stranger was standing between the huts, squat and powerful. He was wrapped in skins, and he held a thrusting spear. His face was daubed with crosshatched ocher marks. He was the one who had hurled the spear at Flatnose. And Pebble saw his own abandoned digging stick in the stranger's hand. They had seen him at the yam stand. They had tracked his footsteps. *Pebble had led them here.*

Full of rage, fear, and guilt, he hurled himself forward.

But he went clattering to the ground. His mother had grabbed his waist. Lame or not she was still stronger than he was, and she glared at him, jabbering, "Stupid, stupid!" For an instant sanity returned to Pebble. Naked, unarmed, he would have been killed in an instant.

A man burst out of the heart of the settlement. He was naked and he carried his own thrusting spear. He was Pebble's uncle, and he hurled himself at the killer of his brother. The stranger fended off the first blow, but his assailant closed in. The two of them fell to the dirt, wrestling, each trying to get in a decisive blow or thrust. Soon they had disappeared in a cloud of blood-spattered dust. They were two immensely muscled beings using all their mighty strength against each other. It was like a fight between two bears.

But more of the hunters came boiling out of the cover of the rock bluffs and trees. Men and women together, all armed with spears and axes; they were dirt-crusted, lean, hard-eyed. They had come hunting Pebble and his group, as if they were a herd of unwary antelope.

Pebble could see desperation in the eyes of the others. These newcomers were not nomads, not invaders by instinct, any more than Pebble's people would have been. Only a dire catastrophe of their own could have forced them to this plight, to make them come into a new and strange land, to wage this sudden war. But now that they were here, they would fight to the death, for they had no choice.

There was a howl. The hunter who had taken on his uncle was standing now. One arm dangled, bloody and broken. But he was grinning, his mouth a mass of blood and broken teeth. Pebble's uncle lay at his feet, his chest split open.

Already Pebble's folk had lost two of their three adult men, Flatnose and his brother. They had no chance of resisting.

The survivors ran. There was no time to grab anything, no tools or food—not even the children. And the hunters fell on them as they fled, using the butts of their spears to fell and disable. The third man was cut down. The hunters caught two of the women, and the girl younger than Pebble. The women were thrown to the ground, face first, and the young men pulled their legs apart, jostling for the right to be first.

The others ran, on and on, until the pursuers gave up.

Pebble looked back the way they had come. The hunters were pawing through the settlement, the ground that had been Pebble's ancestors' for time out of memory.

There were five of them left from the village, Pebble realized. Two women, including his mother, Pebble himself and a smaller girl, and one of the infants—not Pebble's sister. Just five.

Her face hard, Dust turned to Pebble. She laid a hand on his shoulder. "Man," she said gravely. "You."

It was true, he saw with horror. He was the oldest male left: of the five, only the squalling infant in the dirt at his feet was male.

Dust scooped up the motherless infant and held him close. Then she turned resolutely away from her settlement and began to stomp away to the north, her lame gait leaving uneven tracks in the dirt. She didn't look back, not once.

Bewildered, terrified, Pebble followed.

II

The Pleistocene, this era of ice, was an age of brutal climatic turbulence. Droughts and floods and storms were commonplace: in this age a "once-in-a-century" climatic disaster came around every decade. It was a time of intense variations, a noisy time.

This created an environment that was intensely challenging for all the animals who inhabited it. To cope with the changes many creatures got smarter—not just hominids, but carnivores, ungulates, and others. The average mammalian brain size would double across the two million years of the Pleistocene.

The great family of hominid species to which Pebble belonged had been born in Africa, as had so many others, far to the south of here. Smarter, stronger than Far's folk, they had pushed in a great arc out of Africa into Europe, south of the ice, and into Asia, as far as India. They had adapted their technology, their ways, and, over enough time, even their bodies to the disparate conditions they encountered.

And they had displaced the older forms of people. Elegant, skinny walkers like Far still survived in eastern Asia, but they clung on in Africa only in pockets. In Europe they were extinct altogether. As for the pithecine types, the last of them had succumbed long ago, squeezed out between the chimps and the new savannah folk. Still, the hominid range was narrow. There were still no people in the cold northern lands, none in Australia, and none in the Americas, none at all. But the Old World felt ever more full of them.

Meanwhile the land was growing poorer.

Once more there had been extinctions. And this time the people had had a lot to do with it. Under climate pressure, many of the larger, slow-breeding species of animals had found themselves increasingly tied to the water sources. They therefore became an easier target for increasingly clever hominid hunters, who, looking for the lowest-risk kills, selectively picked off the old, the weak—and, crucially, the very young.

The largest and least versatile species had been taken out first. In Africa, of the wide and ancient elephantid family, only the true elephants remained. Many varieties of giraffe, pig, and hippo had followed.

And then there was fire.

The harnessing of fire, not so many generations before Pebble's time, had been one of the most significant events in hominid evolution. Fire offered many advantages: warmth, light, protection from carnivores. It could be used to harden wood, and its heat could be used to make many plant and animal foods digestible. There was still no organized large-scale firing and ground clearing; that would come later. But already the daily use of fire had had, little by little, a profound impact on the vegetation, as those plants able to withstand fire were favored at the expense of less hardy cousins. And meanwhile, though true agriculture lay far in the future, hominids had begun to select those plant species they favored for their own purposes—just as Pebble had cleared grass from the yam stand.

Such small actions, repeated every day across hundreds of thousands of years, had an immense impact. Once the landscape had been shaped by the trampling of elephants: Far and her kind had been marginal. Not so now. This landscape had been made by people.

By now it was as if this bare landscape of fire-resistant trees and sparse grass-eaters were somehow natural, and had been here forever, for all time. It had been this way so long that no mind on Earth could remember how things might have been different.

Seal had caught a spider on the beach. He scampered over the sand and brought it to Pebble, grinning. "Spider web spider fish." Pebble tapped Seal on the head, warming to his infectious energy, and wishing he shared some of it.

Seal ran back to the clump of dune grass where he had found the spider. The web was built on a fan of strong radial lines, over which the spider had laid a spiral of continuous sticky web. Now—delicately, delicately, holding a small stick in his wide fingers—the boy lifted the spiral off its nonsticky guide ropes. He moved the rod spoke by spoke, twirling it so that the sticky stuff formed a dangling mass at the end of the rod. Then he hurried to a tidal pool, sheltered by lumpy, eroded rocks. He put his stick in the water, letting the sticky mass dance on the water's surface.

A tiny fish came to nibble the enticing lure. But with every bite its jaws got stuck more firmly in the web. At last it was glued to the stick and was easily scooped out of the water. Seal popped it straight into his mouth with a grin of triumph. Then he dipped his makeshift rod into the dead spider's glue sac and settled it back into the water.

Seal, brought out of the abandoned settlement in the arms of Dust eleven years back, was twelve years old now—seven years younger than Pebble himself. His early years had been quite different from Pebble's: They had been years on the move. But Seal didn't seem disturbed by his experiences. Perhaps he had got used to migrating, like one of the big grass-chewers that followed the seasons. And he had taken to the ocean. He was too heavy to swim—they all were—but whenever Pebble saw him in the shallow water close to the shore, he was reminded of a playful mammal of the sea.

But, eleven years after the trauma of the attack that had killed his father, Pebble had nothing in common with Seal's inventive playfulness.

At nineteen Pebble was fully mature, his frame as squat and powerful as his father's had been. But he was battered. His body bore old scars from ferocious, desperate hunting incidents. In a collision with a wild horse he had suffered a cracked rib that had never healed properly, and for the rest of his life he would suffer a diffuse pain every time he took a breath. And he bore the marks of wounds inflicted by people; too often he had had to fight.

Forced to grow up too quickly, he had become introspective. He hid his thoughts behind a mass of beard that, year after year, became more dense and knotted, and his eyes seemed to recede beneath their great browridge of bone.

And, like his father, on each of his arms he bore long, ragged scars.

With a sigh Pebble returned to his own gloomy inspection of the nets and lures he had strung out in the deeper water. This pebbly beach was protected from the sea by an outstretched arm of land, and a freshwater stream trickled down over the beach from the base of the bluffs. The sea was the Mediterranean: This was Africa's northern coast. Behind him, to the south, the land rose up in a series of bluffs. It was here that Pebble's refugee people had at last made their home, on the dry grassy dunes above the high-water mark, in a hut constructed from driftwood and saplings.

As far as he knew Seal, playing with spiders and their webs, had come up with his own miniature way of fishing. But then, on this dismal shore, they had all been forced to learn fast about the use of the sea. In the early days there had been much splashing around as hunters used to chasing down antelope had hurled themselves through the shallows after darting fish and dolphins that evaded them easily. They had gone hungry, and despaired.

They had got the right idea, in the end, from watching the spiders, and the birds and small animals that occasionally got tangled up in bushes or canes with sticky foliage, or in thickets with trailing vines.

Gradually they had figured out the use of nets and traps and snares, woven from bark and bits of leather. Their first attempts had failed more often than not. But they had slowly developed skills in exploiting natural cords and vines, and learned how to weave, repair, and tie fibers. And it worked. If you were lucky you could trap fish, octopus, and turtles. The deeper into the water you went, the better the catch would be.

Well, it had had to work. Otherwise they would surely have starved.

Ironically the land to the south, beyond these coastal bluffs, was rich, a mosaic of woodland and grass and fresh- and saltwater pools. And there were plenty of animals, beyond the marshes and on the higher ground: red deer, horse, and rhinoceros, and many smaller herbivores. Sometimes the animals would even come down to the beaches in search of salt.

If the land had been empty of people it might have been a paradise for Pebble's group. But the land was not empty, and that was the entire trouble.

On the horizon there was an island. His gaze was drawn there now. Though it was made misty blue by distance, even from here he could see how rich the island was, with lush vegetation running down every cleft of rock, almost to the ocean. And there were people there. He had seen them on clear days: skinny, tall people, who would run across their beaches and hilltops, pale flitting figures.

There he and his people would be safe, he thought. On an island like that, a scrap of land of their own, they could live forever, untroubled by strangers. If he could get there, perhaps he could fight those skinny folk for possession of their land.

If he could get there. But people could not swim like dolphins, and they could not walk over the water like insects. It was forever impossible.

So here they were, stuck.

They had never planned to come so far as this. None of them had planned any of this at all. They had just been forced to keep going, and going, while the years had worn away.

Pebble's kind were by nature sedentary; these robust folk had long lost the wanderlust of Far's day. It had stressed them hugely to be thrust into unfamiliar landscapes: For Pebble it was as if the great trek had been a long, slow breakdown, a time of madness and bewilderment.

During the journey the children had grown—Pebble himself had become a man—and their numbers had slowly risen, as more refugees from one disaster or another tagged along with them. And their numbers had grown in another way. Pebble had become a father; he had coupled with Green, the wistful woman who had come with them from the old settlement. But as they crossed a particularly harsh and dry land, the child had died.

And still they had found nowhere they could live. For the world was full of people.

Before the attack there had been twelve people in Pebble's close extended family. They were self-sufficient, and very sedentary. They did not trade, never traveled much further than could be reached in a day's walk.

But they had been aware of similar groups nearby, studded around the landscape, as immobile as trees.

In all there were over forty tribes in the larger clan of which Pebble's people were part, around a thousand people. Sometimes there would be exchanges as youngsters from one "village" sought mates in another. And there was occasional conflict as two parties found themselves competing over a rich foraging ground or the target of a hunt. But such incidents were usually settled with nothing much more than a slanging match, some inconclusive wrestling, and in extreme cases a spear in the leg, a maiming which had evolved as a ritual punishment.

And every one of this thousand-strong band, from the smallest baby to the most wizened thirty-five-year-old crone, was marked with the characteristic red or black vertical stripes that Pebble still wore on his face.

Far would have been astonished to see what had become of her innocent innovation with the bits of ocher. What had started out as a half-unconscious sexual deception had become, over immense stretches of time, a kind of looser celebration of fecundity. Women and even some men would mark their legs with the characteristic color of fertility. Slowly, dim minds and fumbling fingers had experimented with other forms of markings, new symbols.

By now, though, this crude scribbling had a purpose. Pebble's vertical markings were a kind of uniform, setting a boundary between his folk and others. You didn't need to remember everybody in your group personally—as Capo had had to when he had tried to lead his followers. You didn't need to know faces. All you needed was the symbol.

The symbols united the bands. In a way the symbols had become what they fought for. These crude stripes and body markings were the birth of art, but they were also the birth of nations, the birth of war. They would make possible conflicts that would transcend even the deaths of those who had started them. That was why hominid minds were becoming smarter at creating the symbols, with each new generation.

All across this landscape there were clans like this, clans of more or less the same size. They were all sedentary, all staying where they had been born, where their parents and grandparents had lived and died. Their languages were mutually incomprehensible. Indeed many of these communities were no longer even able to interbreed, so long had they been isolated. And there they stayed, until they were displaced by some natural catastrophe like a climate shift or a flood—or by other people.

Which was why the clans had formed in the first place, of course: to keep out the refugees.

It had been terribly hard for them. At last, after eleven years, they had come to this place, this beach, and they had been forced to stop, for here the land had run out.

Now Pebble heard a mournful cry from up the beach. "Hey, hey! Help, help!"

Pebble stood and peered that way. He saw two stocky figures staggering toward the hut. They were Hands and Hyena, the one characterized by his huge, powerful hands, the other by his habit, when hunting, of laughing like a scavenger. These two men had joined Pebble's group during their long odyssey. But now they were struggling. Hyena was leaning heavily on the powerful shoulders of his companion, and even from here Pebble could hear Hyena's wheezing gasps.

Dust came out of the hut. Pebble's mother, in her late thirties now, had grown gaunt and bent with the stresses her body had endured during the long walk, and her hair was white and wispy. But she was still doggedly alive. Now she began to hobble up the beach toward Hyena and Hands, and called out. "Stab, stab!"

Hyena collapsed to the beach, and Pebble could see a stone blade sticking out of his back. Hands struggled to get him to his feet again.

Muttering darkly Pebble stalked across the beach after his mother.

By the time they had brought Hyena back to the hut, the light was beginning to leave the sky.

Preparing themselves for the tasks of the night, the people moved around the hut. The men and women alike had immense bulging shoulder muscles that showed humplike through their leather wraps. Even their hands were huge, with broad spadelike fingertips. Their bones were thick-walled, capable of enduring great stress, and their joints were heavy and bony. These were massive people, solid, as if carved out of the Earth themselves.

They had to be strong. In a tough environment, they had to work very hard all their lives, making up in brute force and endless labor what they lacked in smarts. Few reached the end of their lives without the pain of old wounds and such problems as degenerative bone diseases. And hardly anybody lived beyond forty.

Hyena's wound was unremarkable. Even the fact that he had clearly been stabbed in the back by a hominid from a rival band beyond the bluffs did not arouse much interest. Life was hard. Injuries were commonplace.

Inside the low, irregular, poky hut there was no light save from the fire and whatever daylight leaked through the gaps in the plaited walls. There was little organization. At the back of the hut were piled up bones and shells, discarded after meals. Tools, some broken or just half-finished, lay where they had been dropped, as did bits of food, leather, wood, stone, unworked skin. On the floor could be spotted traces of the staples that the group relied on: bananas, dates, roots and tubers, a great deal of yam. The adults did dump their feces and urine outside, to keep out the flies, but the younger children had yet to learn that trick, and so the floor was littered with half-buried infant shit.

There weren't even any fixed places for the fires. The scars of old fires

were visible across the floor of the hut and outside in the blackened circles of scuffed pebbles and sand. When the wind changed or a part of the
hut collapsed, they would just move the embers from yesterday's fire to a
new place and start again.

A human would have found the hut dark, low, claustrophobic, cluttered, disorganized, and filled with an unbearable stench, the stench of
years of living. But to Pebble this was just the way things were, the way
they always had been.

There were actually two fires being tended tonight. Hands had turned
to the hot fire that had smoldered all day. He prowled around the settlement gathering bits of dried wood, and he carefully built up a pyramid of
wood and chips to make a more intense, hotter fire. He had stripped the
flesh off the head and limbs of a baby rhino, and now he would use his
fire to crack the bones and get at the rich marrow inside.

Toward the rear of the hut, Dust and the woman Green were working
on a second fire with Seal and Cry and some of the children. They had a
handful of stones which they knapped quickly to make knives and borers,
and with these they worked the food they had managed to gather during
the day within a few hundred meters of the hut. This included shellfish—
even a rat.

Soon, as they worked, smoke curled up into the plaited roof of the
hut. All this took place against a background of grunts, murmurs, belches,
and farts. Scarcely a word was spoken.

Cry was another survivor: She was the girl, younger than Pebble, who
had escaped the occupation of their old settlement. She had taken her
experiences hard. She had always been sickly and prone to weeping. Now
she was seventeen and a full woman, and Pebble, like Hands and Hyena,
had coupled with her more than once. But she had yet to fall pregnant,
and her body, skinny and comparatively lightly built, had given Pebble no
pleasure.

There was a peculiar economic arrangement among these people.
Men and women largely foraged separately, ate separately.

Those who foraged for vegetation, seafood, and small game close to
home—mostly women, but not exclusively—sat cooking it over their
warm fire, relying on tools quickly made of local resources to help them
eat. Those who roamed further to hunt—mostly men but not always—
would devour much of the meat they secured on the spot themselves.
Only if they had a surplus would they bring it home to share. The treat of
the bone marrow was always kept back for the hunters, after the bones
were cracked in the intense heat of their own fire.

Most of the time, the women's foraging actually supplied most of the groups' food, and in a way it subsidized the men's hunting. But hunting, as it had always been, was about more than acquiring food. There was still an element of peacocklike display in the male hunters' activities. In that, these people had not moved on much from Far's time.

Other things were different, though. The stone tools the women used to prepare their food were massive, but their surfaces and edges looked crudely finished compared to the exquisite hand axes Ax had been able to make more than a million years ago. But for all its beauty a hand ax was not really a great deal more useful for most tasks than a simple, large-edged flake. In harsher times, men and women had had to learn to make their tools as efficiently as possible to suit the task at hand. Under this pressure, the ancient grip of the hand ax template began to weaken. It had been a mental unfreezing. Though in some corners of the planet the hand ax makers still wooed with their tokens of stone, with the dead hand of sexual selection lifted there had been a burst of inventiveness and diversity.

Gradually, a new kind of toolmaking had been discovered. A core of stone would be prepared in such a way that a single blow could then detach a large flake of the desired shape, which could then be retouched and finished. The flakes came with the finest possible edges—sometimes just a molecule thick—all the way around. And with sufficient skill you could make a wide variety of tools this way: axes, yes, but also spear points, cutters, scrapers, punchers. It was a much more efficient way of making tools, even if they looked cruder.

But this new method involved many more cognitive steps than the old. You had to be capable of seeking out the right raw materials—not every type of stone was suitable—and you had to be able to see not just the ax in the stone, but the blades that would eventually flow from the core.

When the eating was finished, the people drifted to other tasks. The woman Green prepared a bit of antelope leather, biting on it and pulling it across her teeth. She was an expert at working animal skin, and her teeth, worn and chipped, showed their years of use. The smaller children were getting sleepy now. They gathered into a rough ring and began to groom each other, running their little fingers through the knotted hair on each other's heads. Hands was trying to tend to Hyena. He inspected the wound under its poultice, sniffed, and pushed the poultice back into place.

Dust, exhausted as she often was these days, had already lain down beside her fire. But she was awake, her eyes gleaming. Pebble understood. She was missing Flatnose, her "husband."

The people had paid a price for the increasingly large brains of their children. Pebble had been born utterly helpless, with much of his brain development still to come, a long period of growth and learning ahead of him before he could survive independently. The support of grandmothers was no longer enough. A new way of living had had to evolve.

Parents had to stick together, for the sake of their children: it was not monogamy, but it was close. Fathers had learned it was essential to stay around if their genetic inheritance was to go on to further generations. But women's ovulation was concealed, and they were almost continually sexually receptive. It was a lure: If a man was going to invest in raising a kid, he needed to be confident the kid really was *his*—and if he didn't know when his partner was fertile, the only way to ensure that was to stay around.

But it wasn't all compulsion. Couples preferred sex in private—or as much as was possible in such a close, small community. Sex had become a social cement that bound couples together. Relentless Pleistocene selection was shaping everything that would make up humanity. Even love was a by-product of evolution. Love, and the pain of loss.

But the shaping was not complete. The desultory talk in this crude hut was not much more than gossip. Toolmaking, food gathering, and other activities were still walled off from consciousness, in compartmented, if roomy, minds. And they still groomed like apes.

They were not human.

Pebble felt irritable, restless, confined. Gruffly he grabbed a slice of rhino belly from Seal, who protested loudly: "Mine, mine!" Then he went to sit, alone, in the doorway, facing the sea.

Close by, he could see the scrubby land where the people cleared away weeds from peas and beans and yams. But beyond that, looking north and west, a sunset towered into the sky, its purple-pink light painting the planes of his face. It was a magnificent Ice Age sunset. The glaciers, scouring across the northern continents, had thrown vast amounts of dust into the air; the sun's light was refracted through great clouds of ground-up rock.

Pebble felt stuck, like one of Seal's little fish glued to his blobs of spiderweb.

Barely conscious of what he was doing, he felt around on the ground for a sliver of rock. When he had found one sharp enough he lifted it to his right arm—he had to look for a patch that wasn't already scarred—and he pressed the stone to his flesh, relishing the delicious prickling pain.

He wished his father were here, so they could cut together. But the stone remained, the pain almost comforting as it pushed through his epidermis. He ran the stone blade down his arm, feeling the warmth of his own blood. He shuddered with the pain, but relished its cold certainty, knowing he could stop at any moment, yet knowing he would not.

Isolated, depressed, his life blocked, Pebble had turned in on himself, and a behavior that had once served to enable young men to compare their strength in a reasonably harmless way had become solitary and destructive. Pebble's kind were not human. And yet they knew love, and loss—and addiction.

In the darkness behind him, his mother watched, her bone-hooded eyes clouded.

Pebble was woken in the gray of the predawn—but not by the light or the cold.

A tongue lapped at his bare foot. It was almost comforting, and it penetrated his uneasy dreams. Then he woke enough to wonder what was doing the licking. His eyes snapped open.

A shaggy, muscular wolf stood on all fours before him, silhouetted against the dawn sky.

He yelped and dragged his legs back. The wolf whined, startled. Then it scampered away a few paces, turned and growled.

But a *person* stood beside the wolf.

She was at least a handbreadth taller than he was. Her body was slender, her shoulders narrow, her long legs elegant, like a stork's. She had narrow hips and shoulders, small high breasts, and a long neck. Her body was all stringy muscle: He could see the firm bulges of her arms and legs. She looked almost like a child, a great stretched-out child, her features unformed. But she was no child—he could tell that from the breasts, the thatches of hair under her arms, and from the fine lines that had gathered around her eyes and mouth.

The skinny folk on the island were just like this, from the neck down, anyhow. But from the neck up, Pebble had never seen anything like her.

Her chin stuck out into a kind of point. Her teeth were pale and regular—and unworn, like a child's, as if she had never used them to treat animal skin. Her face seemed flattened, her nose small and squashed back. Her hair was frizzy and black but hacked short. And the ridge over her eyes—well, there *was* no ridge. Her brow rose smoothly and *straight up,* and then her skull swept back into a great bulging shape like a rock, quite different from the turtle-shell shape of his own cranium.

She was a human—anatomically, a fully modern human. She might have stepped out of a tunnel through time from Joan Useb's chattering crowd in Darwin Airport. She could not have been a greater shock to heavy-browed Pebble if she had.

Her eyes flickered as she glanced from Pebble to the people—Hands, Cry, others—who had come out to see what was going on. She said something incomprehensible, and held out the harpoon at Pebble, point first.

Pebble stared, fascinated.

The harpoon's shaft was notched at the end, and in the notch, attached by resin and sinew thread, there was a carved point. It was a slim cylinder, not more than a finger's-width wide at the center. On one side fine barbs had been carved into the surface, pointing away from the direction in which the harpoon would be thrust. Its surface wasn't roughly finished like his own tools; it looked smooth as skin.

Her harpoon wasn't her only artifact, he saw now. She wore a scrap of some treated hide around her waist. A thing like a net, woven of vines, perhaps, was slung around her neck. Inside it nestled a collection of worked stones. They looked like flint. Flint was a fine stone, easy to shape, and he had encountered it several times during his trek out of Africa. But there was no flint to be found anywhere near this beach. So how had it got here? His confusion deepened.

But his attention was drawn back to that harpoon point. It was made of *bone*.

Pebble's people used bits of broken bone as scrapers or as hammers to finish the fine edges of their stone tools, but they did not try to shape it. Bone was difficult stuff, awkward to handle, liable to split in ways you didn't anticipate. He had never seen anything like this regularity, this finishing, this ingenuity.

In the future he would always associate her with this marvelous artifact. He would think of her as Harpoon. Unthinking, helplessly curious, he reached out with his long, broad fingers to touch the harpoon's point.

"*Ya!*" The woman backed off, grasping the harpoon. At her side, the wolf bared its teeth and growled at him.

Tension immediately rose. Hands had picked up heavy cobbles from the beach.

Pebble raised his arms. "No no no . . ." He had to work hard, gesturing and jabbering, to persuade Hands not to hurl his stones. He wasn't even sure why he did this. He ought to be joining Hands in driving her off. Strangers were nothing but trouble. But the dog, and the woman, had done him no harm.

And she was staring at his crotch.

He glanced down. An impressive erection thrust out. Suddenly he was aware of the pulse that beat in his throat, the hotness of his face, the moistness of his palms. Sex was a commonplace with Green or Cry, and it was usually pleasurable. But with this child-woman, with her flattened, ugly face and her harpoonlike body? If he were to lie on her, he would probably crush her.

But he had not felt like this since his first time, when Green had come to straddle him in the night.

The wolf growled. The woman, Harpoon, scratched the creature's ruff. "Ya, ya," she said gently. She was still looking at Pebble, her teeth showing. She was grinning at him.

Suddenly he felt ashamed, as if he were a boy who could not control his body. He turned and ran into the sea. When the water was deep enough to cover him he plunged forward face first. There, his mouth clamped closed, he grabbed at his erection and tugged it. He ejaculated quickly, the stringy white stuff looping in the water.

He kicked and stood up, gasping for breath. His heart still hammered, but at least the tension had gone. He stalked out of the water. The cuts he had made in his arm the night before had not yet healed, and red blood, diluted by salt water, dripped down his fingers.

The woman had gone. But he could see a trail of footsteps—narrow feet, delicate heels—that led off back the way she must have come, beyond the headland. The dog's clawed prints followed hers.

Hands and Cry were walking toward him. Cry was studying Pebble uncertainly. Hands called, "Stranger stranger wolf stranger!" He threw his cobbles down with a clatter, angry. He couldn't see why Pebble had reacted as he had, why he hadn't quickly driven off or killed this stranger.

Suddenly Pebble's dissatisfaction with his life came to a focus. "Ya, ya!" he snapped. And he turned away from the others and began to walk in the tracks the slender woman had made.

Cry ran after him. "No, no, trouble! Hut, food, hut." She even grabbed his hand and pulled it to her belly, and tried to slide it down to her crotch. But he shoved the heel of his hand into her chest, and she fell to the ground where she sprawled, staring forlornly after him.

III

He followed the tracks along the beach. His broad prints covered Harpoon's, obliterating them.

The shore was crusted with mussels and barnacles and the wrack of the sea: kelp, stranded jellyfish, and hundreds of washed up cuttlefish bones. Soon he was sweating, panting, his hips and knees aching subtly, a forerunner of the joint pains that would plague him as he grew older.

As he calmed down, his normal instincts began to reassert themselves. He remembered he was naked, and alone.

He cast around the beach until he found a large, sharp-edged rock that fit comfortably into his hand. Then, as he walked, he kept close to the water's edge. Even though the sand here was a soft, soggy mud that clung to his feet, at least there was only one side from which he could be approached.

Still those neat tracks, with the wolf's padding alongside, arrowed neatly through the softer sand. At last the tracks cut back up the beach. And there, in the shade of a clump of palms, he saw a hut.

He stood for long heartbeats, staring. Nobody was around. Cautiously he approached.

Set above the water's high-tide marks, the hut was built on a frame of saplings that had been thrust into the ground. The saplings had been woven together at their tops—no, he saw, they had been *tied*, not woven, tied up with fine bits of sinew. On this frame branches and fronds had been laid and tied into place. Tools and bits of debris, unidentifiable from this distance, lay around the hut's rounded opening.

The hut was nothing special. It was a little bigger than his own—perhaps big enough for twenty people or more—but that seemed to be the only difference.

His feet crunched softly over the debris on the trampled ground around the hut's entrance. He stepped inside the hut, eyes wide. There was a rich scent of ash.

It wasn't dark in here, but suffused by a warm brown light. He saw that a hole had been knocked in one wall, and a piece of hide, scraped thin, had been stretched over it, enough to shut out the wind but not the light. Briefly he inspected the bit of hide, looking for the marks and scrapes of teeth, but saw none. How could you prepare hide without using your teeth?

He looked around. There was dung on the floor: shit from children, what looked like spoor from wolves or hyenas. There was plenty of food litter, mostly clam shells and fish bones. But he also saw animal bones, some with scraps of meat still clinging to them. They were heavily worked, cut and gnawed. They were mostly from small animals, perhaps pigs or small deer, but even that stirred a vague envy. As far as he knew the ferocious folk of the interior kept the produce of the forests and grassy spaces to themselves.

He sat, legs crossed, and peered around, his eyes gradually adapting to the gloom.

He found the remains of a fire, just a circular patch of black on the ground. The ashes were hot, smoldering in places. He cautiously probed its edge with a finger. His finger sank into layers of ash. A pit had been dug into the ground, he saw, like the pits into which you would stick a dead person. But this pit had been made to contain the fire. The ash was thick, and he saw that many, many days and nights of burning had contributed to this dense accumulation. And on the side of the pit closest to the entrance, where the breeze was strongest, a low bank of cobbles had been built up.

It was a hearth, one of the first true hearths to be made anywhere in the world. Pebble had never seen anything like it.

Covering the ground, he saw, were sheets of some brown substance. He touched one of the sheets gingerly. It turned out to be bark. But the bark had been carefully stripped off its tree and somehow shaped, woven, and treated to make this soft blanket. When he lifted the bark blanket he saw a hole in the ground. There was food inside the hole: yams, piled up.

He found a heap of tools. A thick pile of spill showed that this was a place where stone tools were habitually made. He rummaged idly through the tools. Some were only half-finished. But there was a bewildering variety—he saw axes, cleavers, picks, hammer-stones, knives, scrapers, borers—and other designs he didn't even recognize.

Now he saw what looked like an ordinary ax, a stone head fixed to a handle of wood. But the head was bound by a bit of liana so tightly wound he couldn't unpick it. He had seen lianas strangle other plants. It was as if someone had put this ax head and its handle into the grip of a living liana, and then waited until the plant had grasped the artifacts, binding them more tightly together than any fingers could manage.

Here was a bit of netting like the one he had seen Harpoon wearing on the beach. It was a bag with tools of stone and bone inside it. He picked the bag up experimentally and lifted it to his shoulder, as he had seen Harpoon do. Pebble's kind did not make bags. They carried only what they could hold in their hands or sling over their shoulders. He teased at the stringy netting. He thought it might be creepers or lianas. But the fibers had been twisted tightly into a strong rope that was finer than any liana.

He dropped the bag, baffled.

It was like his hut, and yet it was not. For one thing it was strange to have everything *separated*. At home, you ate where you liked, made your tools where you liked. The space was not divided up. Here there seemed to be one place to eat, one to sleep, one to make the fire, one to work on tools. That was disturbing. And—

"Ko, ko, ko!"

A man had come in through the entrance. Silhouetted against the daylight he was tall, skinny like Harpoon, and had the same bulging dome of a head. There was fear in his weak face, but he raised a spear.

Adrenaline flooded Pebble's system. He got to his feet quickly, assessing his opponent.

The man, dressed in tied-on skins, was whip thin, with stringy muscles. He would be no match for Pebble's brute strength. And that weapon was just a spear of carved and hardened wood, light for throwing: It wasn't a thrusting spear, which was what was needed for fighting in this tight space. Pebble would be able to snap that scrawny neck easily.

But the man, frightened, looked determined. "Ko, ko, ko!" he yelled again. And he took one step forward. Pebble growled, bracing himself to meet the thrust.

"Ya ya." Here was Harpoon. She grabbed the man's arm. He tried to pull away. They began to argue. It was a conversation just as might have occurred in Pebble's hut: a string of words—none of which he could understand—with no structure or syntax, and only repetition, volume, and gesturing for emphasis. It took a long time, as all such arguments did. But at last the man backed down. He glared at Pebble, spat on the floor of the hut, and stalked out.

Cautiously Harpoon clambered into the hut. Watching Pebble, she sat on the trampled ground. Her eyes were bright in the gloom.

Slowly, Pebble sat before her.

At length Harpoon pushed her slim hand under a bark blanket and pulled out a handful of baobab fruit. She held it out to Pebble. Hesitantly he took it. For long heartbeats they sat in silence, representatives of two human subspecies, with not a word, not a gesture in common.

But at least they weren't trying to kill each other.

After that day Pebble felt increasingly uncomfortable in his home, with his people.

The stringy folk seemed to accept him. The tall man who had found him in the hut, Ko-Ko—for Pebble would always think of his cries of "Ko, ko!" "Get away!"—never quite trusted him, that was clear. But Harpoon seemed to take to him. They worked tools together, she showing off the subtle skills of her delicate fingers, he his immense strength. They peered across the sea at the rich island that still tantalized Pebble.

And they tried to work out each other's vocabulary. It wasn't easy.

There were many words, such as directional terms like "west," which Pebble's ancestors had never needed.

He even went hunting with her.

These newcomers were by preference scavengers or ambush hunters. With their lithe but feeble frames they used guile rather than brute strength to make their kills, and their weapons of choice were hurled, not thrust. But they grew to welcome Pebble's mighty contributions during the closing stages of a kill, when the prey had to be finished off at close quarters.

Meanwhile, the two kinds of people started a new kind of relationship. They did not fight, nor did they ignore each other, the only two ways people had had to relate to each other before.

Instead, they traded. In exchange for the fruits of the sea and some of their artifacts, such as their massive thrusting spears, Pebble's folk began to receive bone tools, meat from the interior, marrow, skins, and exotic items like honey.

Despite the obvious benefits of the new relationship, many of Pebble's folk felt uneasy. Hands and Seal had inquisitively explored the possibility of the new tools. Dust, aging quickly, seemed sunk in apathy. But Cry was unremittingly hostile to the new people—and to Harpoon in particular. *This wasn't the way things were done.*

These were, after all, an immensely conservative people, people who moved house only when forced to by an Ice Age. But they traded anyhow, for the advantages were undeniable.

Harpoon had been able to hold back Ko-Ko from killing Pebble because, to these people, a stranger wasn't necessarily a threat. You had to be able to think that way if you were going to trade.

For hominids, that was a brand-new way of thinking. But then Harpoon's kind was only five thousand years old.

There had been a band of people, not unlike Pebble's, who had lived on a beach, not unlike this one, on the eastern shore of southern Africa. The beach was crowded by thick, buff-colored sedimentary rocks. The vegetation was unique to that part of the world, an antique flora recalling Roamer's days, dominated by bushes and trees covered by big, thistly flowers. It was a rich place to live. The sea was productive, offering mussels, barnacles, fish, seabirds. In places the forest came right down to the shore, echoing with the calls of monkeys and birds, and in the grassy glades there was game in abundance: black rhinos, springboks, wild pig, elephant, as well as long-horned buffalo and giant horses.

Here Harpoon's ancestors had had a home base close to the sea. Like Pebble's folk, they had lived there for generations beyond counting, their bones lying thick in the earth. From here they would work across the landscape, never traveling more than a few kilometers from home.

But then, with terrible suddenness, the climate collapsed. The ocean rose, and flooded their ancestral home. Just like Pebble's group they had been forced to flee. And like Pebble's folk, lost in a crowded land, they had had nowhere to go.

Every step they took away from the lands they had known left them more baffled and confused. Many of them died. Many infants, in the arms of starving refugee mothers, failed to live much past birth.

At last, desperate, starving, they were forced along a riverbank. They reached the river's mouth, where mangroves grew thick. Here they could stay, because it was a place nobody else wanted. Much of the floor was covered with an oily brown water, through which slid crocodiles. Damp, fetid, unhealthy, it was a kingdom of lizards, snakes, and insects, many of which, even the marching ants, seemed to conspire to drive out the people.

There was food to be had: water lily roots, shoots, and stems. Even mangrove fruits were palatable to the starving. But there was scarcely any meat. And there was no stone anywhere with which to make tools. It was as if they were trying to live on a great soaked-through mat of vegetation.

Stranded out of their environment, the people might have died out within a generation, if they hadn't adapted.

It had started innocently. A woman, Harpoon's remote grandmother, had wandered as far as she could up the river valley and on to drier land. Here, on the floodplains and in the seasonal swamps, the well-watered, silty soil supported many annuals, herbs, legumes, vines, lilies, and arrow-roots. After years in the swamp she had grown adept at using crude wooden tools and her bare hands to harvest food from soggy, unpromising terrain. She had already filled her belly, and was gathering clumps of roots to take home to her children.

Then she came upon the stranger. The man, from another group further upriver, was using a knife of basalt to skin a rabbit. The two of them stared at each other, one with meat, the other with roots. They might have fled, or tried to kill each other. They did not.

They traded: meat for roots. And they went their separate ways.

A few days later the same women returned to the same spot. Again the man returned. Scowling, suspicious, their tongues mutually incomprehensible, they traded again, this time shellfish and barnacles from the river's mouth for a couple of basalt knives.

That was how it began. The people of the swamp, unable to find everything they needed to stay alive in the scrap of land they had inherited, exchanged the produce of the sea, the swamp, and the floodplain for meat, skin, stone, and fruit from the interior.

After a couple of generations they migrated out, and began a new kind of life. They became true nomads, following the great natural highways, the coasts and the inland water courses. And everywhere they went they traded. As they moved, so they fissured and spread, and tentative trading networks grew. Soon it was possible to find bits of shaped rock hundreds of kilometers from where they had been formed and seashells deep in the interior of the continent.

Living like this was a challenge, though. Trading meant building up a new kind of map of the world. Other people were no longer just passive features of the landscape, like rocks and trees. Now a track had to be kept of who lived where, what they could offer, how friendly they were—and how honest. There was a ferocious pressure on the swamp people to get smarter, fast.

The design of their heads changed drastically. Their skulls enlarged to make room for bigger brains. And changing diets and lifestyles had a dramatic effect on their faces. No longer used to chew tough, uncooked food or to treat leather, their teeth became more feebly rooted. As chewing muscles withered, the upper tooth row shrank back. The lower jaw was left jutting, and the face tilted back, so that these hominids lost the last trace of their ancient apelike muzzles. The declining muzzle and ballooning foreheads provided new anchoring surfaces for the muscles of the face, and the old projecting browridges disappeared.

Meanwhile, as they got smarter, they didn't need to be as strong. Their bodies shed much of the robustness of their immediate ancestors, and reverted to something like the graceful litheness of Far's people.

Pebble's first impression, that Harpoon had seemed childlike, was not accidental. With the proportions of their faces and their thinned bones these new people, compared to ancestral stock, were in some ways like children arrested in their growth. Once again, under ferocious selection pressure, the genes had reached for variations that could be implemented quickly: Adjusting the comparative growth rates of skeletal features was comparatively easy.

All of these changes had been essentially complete within a few millennia. After this process Harpoon, anatomically, was all but identical to a human of Joan Useb's time, even in her skull and the gross features of her brain. And it had been trading, a new way of dealing with other people, that had made them what they were.

But even Harpoon was not yet *human*.

There was a little more invention, a little more organization in her life. Her kind built hearths, for instance. But her tool kit was scarcely more advanced than that of Pebble and his ancestors. Her language was the same unstructured babbling. Much of the way she lived her life, like her sexuality, had been inherited with little change from the kinds of people who had gone before. There were still rigid barriers in her mind, a lack of connections in the neural wiring of her brain. A true human of Joan Useb's age, stranded in this age of her ancestors, would quickly have been driven crazy by the sameness, the routine, and ritual, the lack of art and language—the boring, drab poverty of life.

And, human form or not, these folk had not been dramatically successful. Though they had spread across Africa from their origins in that southeastern swamp, their lifestyle remained marginal. It was difficult to trade if there was nobody like you to trade with. Even now the new nomads' survival was chancy, and most extant groups, around the continent, would not survive.

The children of Harpoon were destined to pass through this bottleneck, but their genes would always bear the imprint of that narrow passage. In the future, the swarming billions who would spring from this unpromising seed would be virtually identical, genetically; every human would be a cousin.

Pebble's relationship with Harpoon came to a head during a hunt.

One day, Pebble found himself in a blind, upwind of a herd of giant horse who cropped the long grass peacefully. The blind was just a lean-to frame of saplings, loosely woven together and covered with palm fronds and grass. Here Pebble huddled, his thrusting-spear at his side, peering out at the big, lame animal that was their target. And Harpoon was at his side. He was tense, adrenaline pumping, and the heat of the day and the sweat scent of the horse filled his head.

Suddenly he felt her fingers on his face.

He turned. Her skin seemed to glow in the green gloom. She traced the vertical ocher stripes he still wore. And then her fine fingers moved to his arm, the long-healed cuts he had inflicted there. Her every touch was startling, as if her fingers were made of ice or fire.

He ran his fingers down her arm. His fist enclosed her forearm easily, as if it were a bird's leg. He felt he could snap the bone with a gesture. Suddenly it was just as it had been on the first day he had met her, on the beach. His mouth dried, his throat tightened.

He didn't understand his lust: the lust that had never gone away. He thought of the clever tools she made, her long, easy stride across the ground, the food she had brought his people—and that harpoon, the exquisite harpoon point, unimaginable before he had seen it that first day. There was something in her his body wanted; the longing was unbearable.

He rolled on his back. In the rustling shade of the blind, she straddled him and smiled.

IV

Each lump of flint was a miniature cemetery. In some long-vanished sea the corpses of crustaceans had settled into sediment, and minute glassy needles that had once formed the skeletons of sponges became the nuggets of flint embedded inside the gathering chalk seams.

Pebble had always loved the feel of flint. He turned the smooth-faced, brittle rock over in his hands, sensing its structure. Flint knappers got to know all of the stone's subtle properties. The more a flint was exposed to the elements the more likely it was to contain fractures, caused by frost or a battering by river or ocean currents. But this flint lacked the patina of exposure. It was fresh and clean. It had only recently been dug out of its chalk matrix, after a cliff had collapsed. You couldn't get such flint in this area, anywhere within the people's old range. Pebble had missed good flint, in the long years on this beach, before Harpoon had walked into his life.

These days he was never more content than when working stone—or, rather, he was never less discontented.

Seven years had elapsed since his first encounter with Harpoon. At twenty-six, his body was already declining, battered and scarred by the cumulative challenges of a life that continued to be very hard, despite his people's collaboration with the newcomers.

He had embraced Harpoon, and he had embraced the newness and changes she had brought—but those changes themselves had become bewildering. Pebble's mind was immensely conservative. And as he grew older he increasingly relished these moments alone with the stone, when he could retreat into the recesses of his roomy mind.

But this moment of peace didn't last.

"*Hai, hai, hai! Hai, hai, hai!*"

Here came his son and daughter, squat Sunset and spindly Smooth, running along the beach side by side, jabbering in the patois that had resulted as a merger of Pebble's tongue and Harpoon's. "Come, come, come here with us!" The children, naked, their skin crusted with salt and sweat, wanted him to come work on the logs that Ko-Ko and others were pushing into the sea.

He pretended not to hear them until they were almost on top of him. Then he grabbed them both with a roar, and all three of them rolled in the sand, wrestling. At last Pebble relented. He put aside his flint, got to his feet, and lumbered after the kids along the beach.

The morning was bright, the sun hot, and the air filled with the scent of salt and ozone. As the children flew ahead of his own lumbering gait, Smooth quickly outstripping her brother, Pebble felt briefly joyful at their youthful energy. This place would never be home to him, but it had its pleasures.

Ko-Ko, Hands, and Seal were making a kind of raft. Harpoon was here, her hands resting on a belly that was already showing a bump. She grinned fiercely as Pebble came up.

The men had cut down two stout palms from the inland forests, stripped them of their branches, and lashed them together with lianas and plaited vine. Now Hands and Seal were hauling this crude construction across the sand and down to the water. There was much straining and jabbering: "Push, push, push!" "Back back, no, back, back . . ." "*Hai, hai!*"

Pebble joined Hands and Seal at their task. Even with three of them it was hard work, and Pebble was soon sweating like the rest, his legs coated with stinging hot sand. Ko-Ko tried to help, but for sheer brute strength the robust folk had no match. And they were helped, and hindered, by the two children, and by Harpoon's wolf companion who ran around their legs, barking.

The wolf, raised from a captured cub, was all but feral. This was just the start of a relationship longer than any other between people and animals, a relationship that would ultimately shape both species.

Pebble had never forgotten his determination to reach the island. At last, as he sat brooding on his beach, he had watched skinny youngsters playing on bits of driftwood in the water—and a connection had closed in his mind.

In their mangrove swamp the ancestors of Harpoon, no better swimmers than Pebble, had been forced to find ways of crossing crocodile-infested water. After much trial and error—with every error punishable by maiming or death—they had hit on a way of using cut mangrove logs.

You could ride on such a log by lying flat on it and paddling with your hands. Through all their journeying, the skinnies had not forgotten that basic technique. And that was what Pebble had seen the children trying to do out on their bits of driftwood. At last he saw a way to get to the island.

But paddling a log across the still waters of a mangrove swamp was one thing. Mastering the choppy surface of an ocean channel was a different challenge.

After a few spectacular failures, Ko-Ko's inventive mind had come up with the notion of strapping two logs together. That way at least you got a little more stability. But these miniature rafts were still too vulnerable to tipping over.

At last they got the logs into the water. They floated, tied together to make a stable surface.

Ko-Ko and Hands threw themselves forward, splashing heavily. They both lay flat on the logs, legs stretched behind them, and began to paddle. Slowly they pulled away from the shore. But the waves tipped the logs up and down—and eventually over, pitching both men into the water. And then the logs' bindings came loose.

Hands came staggering back, spluttering and growling. With Ko-Ko, he hauled the logs back out of the water onto the beach.

Pebble knew that there had been no danger, for the water here was shallow enough to walk out to shore. But further away it deepened quickly—and that was where they must travel, if they were to reach the island.

So they kept working, trying different combinations, over and over.

Much had changed in Pebble's life in seven years.

Gradually those who had come with him from Flatnose's village faded out of the world. Hyena had never recovered from his stab wound, and they had put him in the ground. And not long after that they had had to put Dust in the ground too. Gradually Pebble's mother had seemed to have grown fond of Harpoon, this peculiar stranger who lay with her son. But at last her growing frailty overcame her strength of will.

But where life was lost, so new life was created. His two children were close in age—six and seven years old—but they were quite different.

Sunset was the younger, at six. The boy was the result of Pebble's reluctant union with Cry, who had continued to pursue him long after he had formed his bond with Harpoon. Sunset was squat, round, a ball of energy and muscle, and above a thick, shadowing browridge his hair was still the startling red it had been when he was born, Ice-Age-sunset red.

Sunset had brought poor Cry no pleasure, though. She had died in giving him birth, to the end protesting about the presence of the new people among them.

Pebble's other child, Smooth, had come from Harpoon. Though she had something of her father's chunkiness, she was much more like her mother's kind. Already she was taller than Sunset. Every time he saw her, Pebble was struck by Smooth's flat face, and the ridgeless brow that swept up above her clear eyes.

Pebble had had no reason to be surprised when his sexual contact with Harpoon had resulted in a child. Now, in fact, she was pregnant again. The changes between the ancestral stock and Harpoon's generation, though they were so striking, were not yet so fundamental that the two kinds of people could not crossbreed—and indeed their hybrid children would not be mules. They would be fertile.

Thus Harpoon's modified genes, and her new body plan and way of life, had begun to propagate through the wider population of robust folk. Thus the thread of genetic destiny would pass on through Smooth, child of human-form and robust, into the future.

As the long afternoon wore on, driven by Pebble's determination, they kept on trying to make the logs work.

It was frustrating. They had no way of discussing their ideas. Their language was too simple for that. And even the new folk were not particularly inventive with technology, for the compartment walls in their highly specialized minds denied them full awareness of what they were doing. They weren't able to think it through. It was something like trying to learn a new body skill, like riding a bicycle; conscious effort didn't help. And besides the work was uncoordinated, and only progressed when somebody was passionate enough to bully the rest.

But at last, quite suddenly, Ko-Ko hit on a solution. He splashed into the water. "*Ya, ya!*" With frantic yells and blows, he forced the swimmers to hold on to a single log and let it float. Then he went to the far end and, swimming strongly himself, guided the log out through the choppy inshore waves to the calmer waters beyond.

Pebble watched, amazed. It worked. Rather than riding the log, they used it as a float to help these nonswimmers swim. Soon the log was so far from the shore that all he could see was a row of bobbing heads and the black stripe of the log between them.

By clinging to the log and paddling for all they were worth even the robusts, too heavy to swim, were able to cross the water, far out of their depth. It was obvious to everybody that at last they had found a way to cross the strait that had baffled Pebble for years.

Pebble hollered his triumph. His sons ran to him. He picked up Smooth and whirled her, squealing, through the sunlit air, while Sunset pulled at his legs, clamoring for attention.

The raiding party landed on a little crescent of shell-strewn sand that nestled beneath walls of eroded blue-black rock. They staggered out of the water and lay gasping on the beach. Pebble saw immediately that everybody, robust and skinny alike, had made it to the shore.

The crossing had been harder than Pebble could have imagined. He would never be able to forget that awful sensation of being suspended over the blue-black depths where unknown creatures swam. But it was over now.

And already Ko-Ko was at work. Leading by example he was having the logs hauled to the shore. The warriors—a dozen robusts, a dozen skinnies—began to unpack their gear. Some of the weapons had been carried strapped to their backs or in pouches of netting, and some—the skinnies' long throwing spears, for example—had been tied to the logs themselves.

Harpoon stroked her belly and gazed out to sea, back the way they had come. She touched the vertical ocher stripes on Pebble's face, just as she had the first time they had coupled. But now she wore the same ferocious marking as he did—as did all the people, skinnies and robusts alike. He grinned, and she grinned back.

United by their symbols, two kinds of people prepared to make war on a third.

A woman cried out. Pebble and Harpoon whirled. A heavy basaltic rock had fallen onto the beach, pinning a skinny woman's leg. When the rock was pulled away, her foot was revealed, a smashed and bloody mess. She began to keen, tears streaking the ocher stripes on her cheeks.

People were jabbering, pointing at the cliffs. *"Hai, hai!"*

Pebble peered up, shielding his eyes. Something moved up there: a head, narrow shoulders. The rock had not fallen, Pebble realized. It had been pushed, or thrown.

So it had begun. He grabbed his thrusting spear and roared defiance, and ran along the beach. The people followed him.

A few hundred meters along, this sheltered beach gave way to a more open stretch of dunes and grassland. And on the open land Pebble saw a group of wraithlike hominids. There were more than twenty of them—women, men, children, infants. They had gathered around the carcass of a fallen eland. When they saw Pebble they stood up, their heads swiveling.

Pebble hurled himself forward, yelling.

Some of the hominids turned and ran—mothers with infants, some of the men. Others stood their ground. They picked up rocks and began to hurl them at the intruders, as if trying to drive off marauding hyenas. These people were tall, slender, naked, their bodies superficially similar to Harpoon's. But their heads were quite different, with squat forward-thrusting faces, strong browridges and flat crania.

They were a late variety of *Homo erectus*. This group had wandered on to this island when a glacial surge had lowered sea levels sufficiently for it to be joined to the mainland. When the sea had returned, they had survived while the rest of their kind had fallen, because nobody else had figured out how to cross the choppy strait to take the island from them.

Nobody until now, that is.

One male, more burly than the rest, grabbed a huge, heavy hand ax and came running toward Hands. The big robust roared in response, his heavy thrusting spear grasped in his fists. With blurring speed the male sidestepped Hands's charge and brought his hand ax slamming down on the back of Hands's neck. Blood gushed, and Hands faltered and fell face first. Still he fought. He twisted on to his back, his blood soaking into the dirt, and he tried to raise his thrusting spear. But the big male stood over him, ax raised.

Pebble, enraged, drove his own spear hard through the male's back. With this weapon Pebble was capable of piercing the hide and rib cage of a baby elephant, and he had little trouble driving his heavy spear point through hominid skin, ribs, heart. He raised the male's body high, like a speared fish. It flopped, blood spouting from its mouth and back, and sticky crimson gushed down the spear's shaft and over Pebble's arms.

When it was done Pebble knelt beside Hands. But the big man was unmoving, his massively muscled limbs splayed in the dirt. Grief spasmed in Pebble: another companion gone. He stood up, his hands and arms running with blood, seeking the next battle.

But the wraithlike naked ones were running. The skinnies were hurling their spears of fire-hardened wood, spears that rained down on the fleeing hominids.

Pebble shuddered, grateful that it was not him who these skinnies were pursuing with such deadly joy. But he picked up his thrusting spear and ran after his allies, abandoning Hands's body to the hyenas.

Systematic murder of one troop by another was common among many social and carnivorous species—ants, wolves, lions, monkeys, apes. In this, the behavior of the people was, as in many other things, no more than a derivation of deeper animal roots.

But among wolves, apes, pithecines, even the walkers, such campaigns had been inefficient. Without effective weapons, killings could be achieved only with overwhelming numbers, and it could take years for a war between two competing bands of thirty or forty pithecines to resolve itself. Even during the long age of the sedentary robusts, there had been little large-scale slaughter. Isolated strangers were killed, but there were no wars for lebensraum.

But now, as the genetic definition of Harpoon's new nomadic people continued to spread, that was starting to change. Harpoon's kind had accurate long-range weapons, and heads increasingly capable of systematic, orderly thinking; they were able to perform mass killing with unprecedented thoroughness. But there was a feedback effect. Warfare with other groups would force hominids to come together in increasingly large bands, with all the social complications that followed. The killing would shape the killers, too: If love was evolving, so was hate.

After cleaning out one particularly dense nest, Ko-Ko and the others had a kind of party. They dragged the bodies of the women, children, and men from the nest to an open space and piled them up—thirty, forty of them, all with ripped-open bellies, cleaved chests, smashed skulls. Then they began a fire, throwing burning branches onto the heap of bodies. Ko-Ko and the others danced around the burning corpses, whooping and hollering.

The skinny hunters dragged forward live captives. They were a mother and child, a spindly boy small enough to carry. The hunters had cornered her by a rock bluff where she had been trying to hide. Skinnies and robusts alike gathered around, hooting and yelling, and thrusting spears were raised before the mother's face.

To Pebble the mother seemed numbed. Perhaps there was a kind of guilt written on that slim, protruding face. She had survived while others had fallen around her, all save her small child, and she was unable to feel anymore.

Ko-Ko stepped forward. With a simple efficient thrust, he drove the point of his thrusting spear into the woman's chest. A black fluid burst from her skin. She convulsed—there was the too-familiar smell of death shit—and she slumped.

Still the infant lived. He was wailing, clinging to his mother and even trying to gnaw at her blood-streaked breast. But, just as a mother chasma had once pushed her pups toward hapless Elephant, so now Harpoon, her swollen belly proud before her, thrust Smooth toward the infant. Pebble's daughter carried a stone chopping tool. With a lithe body so like her mother's, she looked feverish, eager. And she raised the chopping stone over the infant's flat skull.

Though he never shirked the fighting, the killing, suddenly Pebble longed to be away from here, sitting on a beach under a tall sunset, or digging for yams to bring home to his mother.

By the next morning the fire was burned out. The hominids had been reduced to gaunt skeletons, their blackened bodies wizened into fetal postures. Ko-Ko and Smooth stalked amongst the smoking remains, smashing them to pieces with the butts of their heavy thrusting spears.

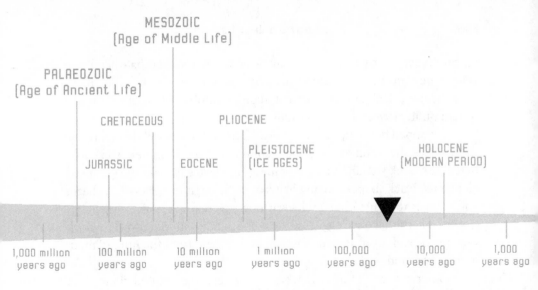

MESOZOIC
[Age of Middle Life]

PALAEOZOIC
[Age of Ancient Life]

CRETACEOUS   PLIOCENE

                            PLEISTOCENE   HOLOCENE
JURASSIC   EOCENE   [ICE AGES]   [MODERN PERIOD]

1,000 million   100 million   10 million   1 million   100,000   10,000   1,000
years ago   years ago   years ago   years ago   years ago   years ago   years ago

CHAPTER 11

mother's people

▼ **Sahara, North Africa. Circa 60,000 years before present.**

I

Mother walked alone, a slim, upright figure in a tabletop landscape. The ground was hot under her feet, the dust sharp and prickling. She came to a stand of Hoodia cactus. She crouched down, cut off a stem about the size of a cucumber, and munched on its moist flesh.

She went naked save for a bolt of eland leather tied round her waist. She had a shaped stone in one hand, but carried nothing else. Her face was fully human, her brow smooth and upright, her chin sharp. But her mouth was pinched and her eyes were sunken, her gaze darting suspiciously.

The savannah around her was arid, dismal. The empty shadowless flatness stretched away, dissolving into a ghostly heat haze that obscured the encircling horizon, a flatness broken only by an occasional drought-resistant bush or the remains of an elephant-trampled copse. There wasn't even any dung to be seen, for the great herbivores passed rarely now, and the beetles had long done their tidy and efficient work.

Clutching the cactus stem, she moved on.

She reached the edge of the lake—or where its edge had been last year, or perhaps the year before that. Now the ground was dry, a patina of dark, heat-cracked mud so hard it didn't crumble when she put her weight on it. Here and there scrubby grass, yellow white, clung to life.

She cupped her hands over her eyes. The water was still there, but far from where she stood, just a remote shimmer. Even from here she could detect the dank stench of stagnation. On the lake's far side she glimpsed elephants, black shapes moving like clouds through the glassy heat haze, and animals rooting in the mud—warthogs, perhaps.

But on the lake's clogged surface she made out waterfowl, a flock roosting peacefully at the center of the water, safe from the hungry predators of the land.

Mother smiled. The birds were just where she wanted them. She turned and walked back from the lake's barren muddy aureole.

At thirty years old, Mother's body was as lithe and upright as it had been in her youth. But her belly bore marks from the birth of her single child, her son, and her breasts sagged. Her buttocks were full; this was an adaptation to the long periods of drought, to help her store water in fat. Her limbs showed stringy muscles, and her belly showed none of the malnutritional swelling affecting many of the folk. She was evidently effective at the business of life.

But she couldn't remember a time when she had been happy. Not even as a child, when she had been clumsy, slow to talk, slow to fit in. Not even when her son had been born, healthy and wailing.

She *saw* too much.

This drought, for instance. The clouds had gone away, which enabled the sun to beat down all day, which dried the land and made the water vanish, which made the animals die, which made the people go hungry. So the people went hungry because of the clouds. What she couldn't figure out was what had made the clouds go away in the first place. Not yet.

This was what she had a talent for: seeing patterns and connections, networks of causes and effects that intrigued and baffled her. Her talent for spotting causal links brought her no comfort. It was more a kind of obsessive suspicion. But it did help her get through life sometimes—like today.

She came to a baobab tree, and studied its twisted branches. She knew what she wanted to make—a boomerang, a curved throwing weapon—and she inspected the branches and buttresses, looking for a place where the grain of the wood and its growth direction matched the weapon's final shape, as she could see it in her mind.

She found one slender branch that might work. With a brisk snap she broke it off close to where it joined with the tree. Then she sat down in the baobab's scrap of shade, took her stone tool, stripped off the bark, and began to carve the wood. She turned her stone blade over and over in her hand to bring favored edges into use. This tool—not quite an ax, or a knife, or a scraper—was her current favorite. Because any tool she couldn't make on the spot had to be carried, she had manufactured this one tool to do many jobs, and she had retouched it several times.

Soon she had produced a smoothly curved stick some thirty centimeters long, flat on one side and rounded on the other. She hefted the boomerang in her hand, assessed its balance and weight with a judgment born of long practice, and quickly scraped away a little excess.

Then she walked out of the baobab's shade and around the perimeter of the lake's muddy fringe. She found the place where she had stashed a net of plaited bark fiber a few days before. The net was undisturbed. She shook it clear of dust, and the beetles that gnawed its dry fibers.

She hung the net across two gaunt, conveniently placed baobabs so that it faced the lake. She had chosen this site, in fact, because of the baobabs.

Now she walked back around the lake, until she was sideways when compared to the position of her net. She took her throwing stick. Her tongue protruding, she hefted it, rehearsing the throw she would make. She would get only one shot at this, and she had to get it right.

Pain pulsed at her temples, distant, like thunder in remote mountains.

She lost her balance, and grimaced, annoyed at the distraction. The pain itself was trivial, but it was a precursor of what was to come. Her migraine was a relentless punishment she endured frequently, and there was nothing to be done about it—it had no cure, of course, not even a name. But she knew she had to get on with her task before the pain made it impossible. Otherwise she would go hungry today, and so would her son.

Ignoring the throbbing in her head, she set herself once more, hefted the stick, and hurled it with strength and precision. The whirling stick followed a sweet curving arc high into the air over the lake, its wooden blades whirling with a subtle whoosh.

The roosting waterfowl rustled and cawed irritably, and when the stick turned in the air and fell on them they panicked. With a clatter of ungainly wings the birds took to the air and fled from the lake—and the flock's low-flying outliers ran straight into Mother's net. Grinning, she ran back around the lake to claim her prize.

Connections. Mother threw the boomerang, which scared the birds, which flew into the net, because Mother had placed it there. As examples of Mother's causal-link thinking went, this had been elementary.

But with every step she took her headache worsened, as if her brain were rattling in her capacious skull, and her brief pleasure at her success was crowded out, as it always was.

Mother's people lived in a camp close to a dry, eroded channel that ran into a gorge. Shelters had been set up among the rocky bluffs, just lean-tos, sheets of hide or woven rattan propped up on simple frames. There were no permanent huts here, unlike the structures in Pebble's long-vanished encampment. The land wasn't rich enough for that. This was the temporary home of nomadic hunter-gatherers, people forced to follow their food supply. The people had been here for a month.

The site had its advantages. There was a stream, the local rock was good for toolmaking, and there was a clump of forest nearby, a source of wood for fires, and bark, leaves, liana, and vines for cloth, netting, and other tools and artifacts. And the site was a good place to ambush animals that came wandering foolishly toward the gorge. But the produce of the area here had not been good. The camp was poor, the undernourished people listless. They would probably move on soon.

Mother stumbled home, three waterfowl slung on bits of leather rope over her shoulder. The pain in her head had grown sharp now, and every surface seemed overbright and tinged with strange colors. The ballooning of the human brain, in the millennia before the birth of Mother's distant ancestor Harpoon, had been spectacular. This hasty rewiring brought unexpected benefits—like Mother's pattern-making ability—but costs, like her plaguing migraine.

"Hey, hey! Spear danger spear!"

She looked around dimly.

Two of the younger men were staring at her. They wore wraparound hides tied in place with bits of sinew. They both held wooden spears, crudely finished, their tips hardened by charring. They had been hurling their spears at an ox hide they had draped over the branches of a tree. Mother, distracted by the pain and the strange lights, had almost blundered into their path.

She had to wait while the spear throwers completed their contest. Neither of the two young men was particularly skillful, and their hide wraps were shabby. Only one of their spears had pierced the hide to embed itself in the tree; the rest lay scattered in the dirt.

But one of the hunters was at least hurling his spears with more power, she saw. This boy held the spear unusually far back along its shaft, and used the length of his bony arms to get a little more leverage. Tall for his age, whip thin, she thought of him as a sapling, drawn up by the sunlight. When Sapling threw the spear, it hissed through the air, oscillating slightly. The spear's movement was intriguing. But as her eyes tracked it, her head hurt even more.

When the spear throwers were done she blundered on, seeking the dark of the hide she shared with her son.

Inside Mother's hut was a stocky woman of thirty-five. She had ragged, graying hair and a habitually pinched, sour face. This woman, Sour, was using a pestle to grind a piece of root. She glared at Mother, her expression as hostile as usual. "Food, food?"

Mother waved a hand vaguely, caring nothing about Sour. "Birds," she said.

Sour put down her pestle and root, and went outside to see the birds Mother had hung up.

Sour was Mother's aunt. She had become embittered when she had lost her second child to some unknown illness a couple of days after childbirth. She would probably steal the birds, giving Mother and Silent a fraction of what Mother had brought home. But Mother, her head full of pain, felt too weary to care.

She tried to focus on her son. He sat with his back to the slanting woven roof, his knees tucked up to his chest. A sickly boy of eight, short and bony, he was using one bit of twig to push another around the dirt floor. Mother sat beside him and ruffled his hair. He looked up at her with heavy, sleepy eyes. He spent a lot of his time like this—silent, withdrawn from the rest, waiting for her. He took after his father, a short, unsuccessful hunter who had lovelessly coupled with Mother just once— and in that one coupling had succeeded in impregnating her.

Her experience of sex had been sporadic and not very pleasurable. She had met no man strong enough, or kind enough, to withstand the intensity of her gaze, her obsessiveness, her quickness to anger, and her frequent pain-driven withdrawals into herself. It was her great misfortune that the man who finally made her pregnant had quickly moved on to another—and that he had soon fallen to the ax blow of a rival.

The child was Silent, for that was his defining characteristic. And likewise, since it sometimes seemed that she had no identity in the eyes of other people here—no identity for anybody except the boy—she was Mother. She had little to give him. But at least he was spared the swollen-belly hunger that was already afflicting some of the other little ones in this time of drought.

At length the boy lay on his side and curled up, thumb in his mouth. She lay down herself on her pallet of bundled-together straw. She knew better than to try to fight the pain.

She had always been isolated, even as a child. She could not throw herself into the games of chase and wrestling and chattering that the other youngsters had indulged in, or their adolescent sexual experiments. It was always as if the others knew how to behave, what to do, how to laugh and cry—how to *fit in*, a mystery she could never share. Her restless inventiveness in such a conservative culture—and her habit of trying to figure out *why* things happened, *how* they worked—didn't make her any more popular.

As time had gone on she had come to suspect that other people were talking about her when she wasn't there, that they were plotting against her—planning to make her unhappy in ways she couldn't even understand. None of which helped her get along with her fellows.

But she had her comforts.

The headache would not go away. But it was during the headaches that she saw the shapes. The simplest were stars—but they were not stars, for they flared, bright and evanescent, before fading away. She would try to turn her head to follow them, hoping to see where the next came from. But the stars would move with her eyes, drifting like reeds in a lake. Then would come more shapes: zigzags, spirals, lattices, nested curves, parallel lines. Even in the deepest darkness, even when the pain blinded her, she could see the shapes. And when the pain faded, the memory of the strange, brilliant shapes stayed with her.

But even as she willed her body to relax, she thought of long-armed Sapling and his spear throwing, and little Silent pushing his bits of twig back and forth, back and forth . . .

Connections.

Sapling tried again.

A look of irritability on his face, he hooked the spear in the notch on the stick Mother had given him. Then, holding the stick in his right hand, he used his left hand to support the spear over his shoulder, point facing forward. He took a couple of hesitant steps forward, whipped his right arm forward—and the spear tipped up, its charred point gazing at the sky, before falling back to the dirt.

Sapling dropped the shaped stick and stamped on it. "Stupid, stupid!"

Mother, frustrated herself, slapped the back of his head. "Stupid! You!" Why couldn't he see what she wanted? She picked up the spear and the stick and thrust them into Sapling's hands, closing his fingers around the artifacts to make him try again.

She had been working at this all morning.

After that ferocious migraine Mother had woken with a new vision in her head, a peculiar mélange of Silent's indirect stick poking and Sapling's long, leverage-rich throwing arm. Ignoring her son, she had rushed to the clump of woods nearby.

Soon she had made what she wanted. It was a short, massy stick with a notch cut into one end. When she put the spear in the notch and tried to thrust the spear forward—yes, it was as she had thought; the stick was like an extension of her arm, making it longer even than Sapling's, and the notch was like a finger that grasped her spear.

There were very few people on the planet who could have thought this way, drawing an analogy between a stick and a hand, a natural object and a part of the body. But Mother could.

As always, when she had latched on to some project like this, she had become completely immersed in it, resenting the time she spent away from it to eat, drink, sleep, gather food—even to be with her son.

In her more lucid moments she was aware of her neglect of Silent. But Sour, her aunt, was around to take care of him. That was what aging female relatives were for, to share the burden of child rearing. Deep down, though, Mother was suspicious of Sour. Something had indeed soured inside her when she lost her second child; even though she had a daughter of her own, she took an interest in Silent that wasn't healthy. But Mother had no time to think about that, not while the spear throwing obsessed her.

She kept trying with Sapling, over and over, as the sun arced over the sky and the young man grew restive, hot, thirsty, his day's chores not even started. But every time he failed.

At length Mother started to see what the problem was. It wasn't a question of clumsy technique. Sapling didn't understand the principle of what she was trying to show him: that it was not his *hand* that would do the throwing, but the *stick*. And until he got that, he could never get the spear-thrower to work.

There were rigid compartment walls in Sapling's mind, almost as rigid as in Pebble's, his remote grandfather's. He was supremely intelligent socially; in his maneuverings, coalition-building, wooings and betrayals, he could rival Machiavelli. But he didn't apply that intelligence to other activities, like toolmaking. It was as if a different mind were switched on at such times, a mind no more advanced than Far's.

But it wasn't *quite* like that for Mother—and that was the source of her strangeness, and her genius.

She took the thrower from him, set the spear in its notch, and made as

if to throw. "Hand, throw, no," she said. Now she mimed the stick pushing the spear. "Stick, throw. Yes, yes. Stick. Throw. Spear. Stick throw
spear. Stick throw spear . . ."

Stick throw spear. It wasn't much of a sentence. But it had a rudimentary structure—subject, verb, object—and the honor of being one of the
first sentences spoken in any human language, anywhere in the world.

As she repeated her message over and over, it gradually sank in.

Sapling grinned and grabbed the spear and thrower from her. "Stick
throw spear! Stick throw spear!" Quickly he fitted the spear into its notch,
reached back, set the spear over his shoulder—and hurled with all his
might.

It was a lousy throw, that first time. The spear ended up skidding in
the dirt far short of the palm she had identified as a nominal target. But
he had gotten the idea. Excited, jabbering, he ran after the spear. With an
obsession that briefly matched Mother's own he tried over and over.

She had come up with this idea thanks to her peculiar ability to think
about the throwing stick in more than one way. It was a tool, yes—but it
was also like her fingers in the way it held the spear—and was even like a
person in that it could *do* things, it could throw the spear for you. If you
were capable of thinking of an object from more than one point of view,
you could imagine it doing all sorts of things. For Mother, consciousness
was becoming more than just a tool for lying.

Sapling probably would never have come up with this insight by himself. But once she had gotten through to him he had grasped the concept
quickly; after all his mind wasn't so much different from hers. As Sapling
hauled the throwing stick forward, the great force it applied to the spear
made it bend: the spear, flexing, actually seemed to leap away, like a
gazelle escaping a trap. Mother's mind spun with satisfaction and speculation.

"*Sick.*" The flat, ugly word cut through her euphoria. Sour, her aunt,
was standing outside the shelter they shared. She pointed inside.

Mother ran across the trampled dirt to the shelter. As soon as she
stepped inside she could smell the harsh stink of vomit. Silent was doubled
over, clutching his distended belly. He was shivering, his face sleek with
sweat, and his skin was pale. Vomit and shit lay smeared around him.

Standing in the bright light outside the shelter, Sour was grinning, her
face hard.

It took Silent a month to die.

It nearly destroyed Mother.

Her instinctive understanding of causality betrayed her. In this ultimate emergency, *nothing worked.* There were some illnesses you could treat. If you took a broken limb, pulled it back into shape and bound it up, very often it would set as good as before. If you rubbed dock leaves on insect bites, the poison could be drawn. But there was nothing she could do for this strange wasting away for which there wasn't even a *word.*

She brought him things he had loved—a tangled chunk of wood, bright bits of pyrite, even a strange spiral stone. In fact it was a fossilized ammonite, three hundred million years old. But he would just finger the toys, his eyes sliding, or he would ignore them completely.

There came a day when he didn't stir from his pallet. She cradled him and crooned wordlessly, as she had when he was an infant. But his head lolled. She tried to cram food into his mouth, but his lips were blue, his mouth *cold.* She even pressed those cold lips to her breast, but she had no milk.

At last the others came.

She fought them, convinced that if she only tried a little longer, wanted it a little more, then he would grin, reach for his bits of fool's gold, and get up and run into the light. But she had let herself grow weak during his illness, and they took him away easily.

The men dug a pit in the ground, outside the encampment. The boy's stiffening body was bundled inside, and the debris from the pit was hastily kicked back in, leaving a discolored patch of dirt.

It was functional—but it was a ceremony, of sorts. People had been sticking bodies in the ground for three hundred thousand years. Once it had been an essential way of disposing of waste: When you could expect to grow old and die in the same place you were born, you had to keep it clean. But now people were nomadic. Mother's folk would be gone from here soon. They could have just dumped the boy's body and let the scavengers take it, the dogs and birds and insects; what difference would it have made? And yet they still buried, as they always had. It had come to seem the right thing to do.

But no words were spoken, no marker was left, and the others dispersed quickly. Death was as absolute as it had always been, deep back down the lineages of hominids and primates: death was a termination, an end of existence, and those who had gone were as meaningless as evaporated dew, their very identities lost after a generation.

But it wasn't that way for Mother. No, not at all.

In the days that followed that brutal ending and efficient burial, she returned again and again to the patch of ground that held her son's bones. Even when the upturned ground began to fade in color, and the grass began to spread over it, still she remembered exactly where that hole's ragged edges had been, and could imagine how he must be lying, there deep in the earth.

There was no *reason* for him to have gone. That was what plagued her. If she had seen him fall, or drown, or be trampled by the herds, then she could have seen *why* he died, and perhaps could have accepted it. Of course she had seen disease afflict many members of the tribe. She had watched many people die of causes no one could name, let alone treat. But that only made things worse: If someone had to die, why Silent? And if blind chance had killed him—if someone so close could be taken so arbitrarily—then it could happen to *her*, at any time, anywhere.

It couldn't be accepted. Everything had a cause. And so *there must be a cause of Silent's death.*

Alone, obsessing, she retreated into herself.

II

Soon after the time of Pebble and Harpoon had come an interglacial, an interval of temperate climes between the long, icebound millennia. The bloated ice caps had melted, and the seas had risen, flooding the lowlands and deforming the coastlines. But, twelve thousand years after Pebble's death, this latest great summer drew to a close. A savage cooling cut in. The ice began to advance once more. As the ice sucked the humidity out of the air, it was as if the planet were drawing in a great, dry breath. Forests shrank, grasslands spread, and desertification intensified once more.

The Sahara, cupped in its mighty Himalayan rain shadow, was not yet a desert. Wide, shallow lakes lay across its interior—lakes, in the Sahara. These bodies of water waxed and waned, and sometimes dried out completely. But at their greatest extents they were full of fish, crocodile, and hippos. Around the waters gathered ostriches, zebra, rhinos, elephants, giraffes, buffalo, and various antelope—and animals that modern eyes would not have thought so characteristically African, like oxen, Barbary sheep, goats, and asses.

Where there was water, where there was game, there were people. This was the environment that cradled Mother's people. But it was a marginal place, the skim of life shallow. People had to work hard to survive.

And people were still scattered remarkably thin.

No humans had yet moved out of Africa. In Europe and across Asia, there were only the heavy-browed robusts and, in places, the older forms, the skinny walkers. America and Australia were still empty altogether.

Even in Africa people were thin on the ground. The more mobile, trade-based way of life that had been born with Harpoon and her kind had not been a uniform blessing. Ever since the move out of the forests, hominids had been vulnerable to trypanosomes—the parasites that caused sleeping sickness—carried by the clouds of tsetse flies that followed the savannah's ungulate herds. Now such diseases were spreading. The people's trading networks had proven very effective at exchanging goods, cultural innovations, and genes—but also at transmitting pathogens.

And, culturally, things weren't happening.

Pebble would have recognized almost everything in Mother's camp. People still split stone flakes off prepared cores, and still wrapped hide around their bodies, tied in place with bits of sinew or leather. Even their language was still a formless jabber of concrete words for things, feelings, actions, useless for transmitting complex information.

Across *seventy thousand years* these people—humans with as modern a body plan, even as modern a brain, as any twenty-first-century citizen— had scarcely made a single innovation in their technology or techniques. It had been a time of stupefying passivity, stunning stasis. After all this time, people were just another tool-using animal in the ecology, like beavers or bowerbirds, still little more than glorified chimps. And, bit by bit, they were losing their battle to survive.

Something was missing.

She could just walk off into the dust, alone.

Why live in a world without Silent?

But in the end she came out of the worst of her darkness.

Once again she started to gather food, eat, and drink. She had to: If she had not, she would have died. This was not a rich society. Though care was taken of the weak, the injured, and the elderly, there was little energy to spare for those who would not help themselves.

She had always been a skillful hunter and sharp-eyed forager. With the tools she invented, modified, or improvised, she was actually more effective than some of those younger and stronger than she was. She recovered rapidly. But the confusion in her head didn't dissipate.

She wasn't sure what first gave her the impulse to make the markings in the rock.

It wasn't even conscious. She was sitting beside an outcropping of soft, buttery sandstone, with a basalt scraper in her hand; she had been preparing a goat hide. And there, incised neatly into the rock, was a pair of zigzag lines, running crisply parallel to each other.

At first the marks puzzled her. But then she saw a scattering of sand grains under the scraping. She understood, the causal connections linking up as they always did. Without thinking, *she* had used the scraper; the scraper had made the markings. So *she* had made the markings.

What sparked her interest was that they were like the lines in her head.

Dropping the bit of leather she had been working, she knelt before the rock. She felt peculiarly excited. She turned the blunted scraper over to expose a fresh edge and dug it into the rock, tracing a line. She managed a neat spiral, circling to nothing at its center. It wasn't as clean and bright as the shapes in her head; it was clumsily scratched, the depth of line uneven, the curve angular and awkward.

So she tried again. She had always had a delicate skill when crafting tools from stone or wood or bone. This time the spiral was a little smoother, a little closer to the ideal inside her eyes. So she did it again. And again and again, until the unprepossessing lump of rock was covered in spirals, loops, whorls, and tracks.

It really was just like what she saw when she closed her eyes. It seemed miraculous to find that she was able to make the same shapes outside her head as she saw inside.

Later it occurred to her to try ocher.

People still used the red iron ore as a crayon to mark their skin with tribal scribbles, just as they had in Pebble's day. Now Mother experimented with the soft stuff, and found it much easier to use on rock than a scraper. And it could be applied to other surfaces as well. Soon her arms and legs—and the bits of skin she wore or draped over her shelter, and her tools and scrapers of stone and bone and wood—were all covered with loops and whorls and zigzags.

It was the flower that sparked the next stage of her peculiar development.

It was a kind of sunflower: not spectacular, its seeds neither edible nor poisonous, of no great interest. But its petals surrounded a neat spiral of yellow, twisting down toward a black central heart. She fell on the flower with a cry of recognition.

After that she started to see her shapes everywhere: the spirals of shells and cones, the lattices of honeycombs, even the spectacular zigzags of lightning that arced from the sky during storms. It was as if the contents of her dark skull were mapping themselves on to the world outside.

It was a girl who was the first to emulate her.

Mother saw her walking past, a rabbit over her shoulder—and a crimson spiral on her cheek, coiled under her eye. Next it was Sapling, with wavy lines on his long arms.

After that she started to see the lines and loops appearing everywhere, like a rash spreading over the surfaces of the encampment and the people's bodies. If she came up with some new design, a lattice or a nest of curves, it would quickly be copied and even elaborated on—especially by the young.

It was oddly satisfying. People were not avoiding her now. They were *copying* her. She became a kind of leader, in a way she never had been before.

But Sour was less pleased with Mother's new status. She kept her distance from Mother. In fact the two women had scarcely acknowledged each other's existence since the death of the boy.

Still, none of the designs, drawn by herself or others, came close to the glowing geometric perfection that came drifting silently through her head. It got to the point when she almost wished for the pain to return, so she could see them again.

At times, the changes in her consciousness scared her. What did this *mean?* She instinctively sought connections; that was her nature. But what connection could there be between a flash of light in her eyes and a towering storm in the sky? Did the storm cause the light in her head—or the other way around?

Life continued, the endless cycles of drawing breath, gathering food, the arcing of sun and Moon, the body's slow aging. And as the months wore by Mother sank deeper into the strangeness of her sensorium. She was beginning to see connections *everywhere*. It was as if the world were crisscrossed by causes like the threads of a vast, invisible spider's web. She felt as if she were dissolving, her sense of self dissipating.

But in all her inward wandering she clung to the memory of her son, a memory that was like an unending ache, like the stump of an amputated limb.

And gradually Silent's death began to seem to her the focus of all those causal tracks.

A wordless consensus was reached that the encampment should be broken up. The people prepared to move on.

Mother came with them. Sapling and others showed relief. Some had thought she might insist on staying beside the hole in the ground that contained the bones of her son.

After a long trek they reached a new camp, close to a mud-rimmed lake. They set up their hides and made their pallets. But as the dryness continued, life remained hard, and the children and old ones suffered.

One day Sapling brought Mother the head of a young ostrich. Its neck had been severed a hand's length below the jaw, and the head neatly punctured by a spear.

To bring down a fleet ostrich—to aim for the tiny head of a running bird, from fifty or seventy meters, and to bring it down—was a feat indeed. After months of practice Sapling and the other young hunters had learned to use the spear-thrower to hurl their weapons across unprecedented distances and with stunning accuracy. Mother's invention was a powerful one. With growing confidence the hunters had begun to penetrate further into the savannah, and soon the prey animals of the plains would learn to fear them greatly. It was as if the hunters had suddenly been given guns.

Today Sapling seemed bursting with the memory of his kill. Before the woman who had first showed him how to use the spear-thrower, he mimed how he had hurled the spear, how it had flexed and leapt, how it had flown to its precise target. "Bird fast, fast," he said, his feet paddling the ground. "Run fast." He pointed to himself. "I, I. Hide. Rock. Bird fast, fast. Spear . . ." He leapt out from behind his invisible rock and mimed hurling his triumphant spear once more.

Mother had little time for people these days. She was becoming increasingly absorbed in her own new perceptions. But she tolerated Sapling, who was the nearest thing to a friend she had. Absently she listened to his babbling.

"Wind carry smell. Smell touch ostrich. Ostrich run. Now, here. Stand, stand, hide. Wind carry smell. Ostrich here, wind there, wind carry smell *away* . . ."

His language was something like a pidgin. The words were simple, just nouns, verbs, adjectives with no inflectional endings. There was still much use of repetition and mime for emphasis. And with little real structure, there was a linguistic free-for-all: It didn't help communication that no two people, even brought up as siblings, ever talked quite alike.

But still, Sapling now occasionally used sentences. He had picked up the habit from Mother. Each sentence was a genuine subject-verb-object compound. The people's protolanguage was quickly developing around this seed of structure. Already the chattering people had had to invent pronouns—*you, me, him, her*—and different ways of expressing actions and their outcomes: *I did kill, I am killing, I did not kill.* . . . They were able to express comparatives and negatives, explore alternatives. They could consider going to the lake today, or not going to the lake, all in a universe of words, where before they would have had to pick one path or another, or split into factions.

It wasn't yet a full language. It wasn't even as rich as a creole. But it was a start, and it was growing fast.

And in a sense Mother had discovered, not invented, that basic sentence structure. Its central logic reflected hominids' deep apprehension of the world—a world of objects with properties—which reflected in turn a still deeper neural architecture common to most mammals. If a lion could have spoken, or an elephant, it would have spoken this way too. This central underpinning would be shared by almost all the myriad human languages that would follow in the ages to come, a universal template reflecting the essential causality of the world and the human perception of it. But it had taken Mother's dark genius to give that deep architecture expression, and to inspire the linguistic superstructure that rapidly followed.

And now it was time for another step.

Sapling said something that grabbed her attention. "Spear kill bird," he said excitedly. "Spear kill bird, spear kill bird. . . ."

She frowned. "No, no."

He stopped in midflow. Wrapped up in his performance he seemed to have forgotten she was there. "Spear kill bird." He mimed the spear's flight. He even picked up the ostrich's ragged head and arced his outstretched hand toward it just as his spear had flown, straight and true.

"No!" she barked. She got up and grabbed his hand. "*You* lift hand." She slapped the spear-thrower into his grip. "Hand push stick. Stick push spear. Spear kill bird."

He pulled back, baffled. "Spear kill bird." *Isn't that what I said?*

Irritated, she went through it again. "You lift hand. Spear kill bird. *You* kill bird." There was a causal chain, but the *intention* resided only in one place; in Sapling's head. She could see it clearly. *He* had killed the bird, not the spear. She slapped his head. *This is where the bird died, dummy. Inside your mind. The rest is detail.* They argued for a while, but Sapling grew increasingly confused, his simple boyish pleasure in his kill waning now that his boasting had degenerated into this peculiar philosophical discussion.

Then a bolt of pain stabbed through Mother's temples, as sharply and suddenly as Sapling's spear of hardened wood must have slammed through the head of that hapless ostrich. She stumbled to her knees, her fists pressed to her temples.

But now, suddenly, in that instant of pain, she could see a new truth.

She imagined the spear arcing through the air, like the bright lightning in her head, piercing the bird's skull and extinguishing its life. *She* knew that Sapling had thrown the spear. He had willed the bird dead, and everything else that followed was irrelevant.

But what if she *hadn't* seen Sapling throw the spear? What if he had been hidden by a rock, a tree? Would she have believed that the spear was the ultimate cause—that the spear itself had intended to kill the bird? No, of course not. Even if she couldn't see the whole causal chain, it must exist. If she saw the spear fly, she would *know* somebody must have thrown it.

Her peculiar vision of the world, the spiderweb of causes stretching across the world and from past to future, deepened further. If an ostrich fell, a hunter had willed it. And if a person died, another was to blame. As simple as that. She saw all this immediately, understood it on a deep intuitive level below words, as new connections opened in her complex, fast-developing consciousness.

The logic was clear, compelling. Appalling. Comforting.

And she knew how she had to act on this new insight.

She became aware that Sapling was kneeling before her, holding her shoulders. "Hurt? Head? Water. Sleep. Here. . . ." He took her arm, trying to help her stand.

But that flash of pain had come and gone in an instant, a meteor leaving a trail of shattered and remade connections in her mind. She stood up and pushed past him, stalking back toward the settlement. There was only one person she needed now, one thing she had to do.

Sour was in her shelter, a rough lean-to of palm fronds, sleeping off the heat of the day.

Mother stood over her. In her arms she held a massive boulder, the largest she could carry; she cradled it as once she had cradled Silent.

Mother had never forgotten the day when Silent had first fallen ill. On that day everything had changed for her, as if the land had pivoted around her, as if the clouds and rocks had exchanged places. It had been the start of the pain. And she hadn't forgotten Sour's half smile. *If I can't have a kid of my own,* she had been saying, *I'm glad you will lose yours.*

Now she saw everything clearly. Silent's death had not been random. Nothing happened by chance in Mother's universe: not anymore. Everything was connected; everything had meaning. She was the first conspiracy theorist.

And the first person she indicted was her closest surviving family member.

Mother didn't know *how* Sour had committed her crime. It might have been a look, a word, a touch—some subtle way, an invisible weapon that had brought the boy down as surely as a spear of carved wood—but *how* didn't matter. All that mattered was that Mother now knew who to blame.

She raised the rock.

In her last moment Sour woke, disturbed by Mother's movement. And she saw the rock falling toward her head. Her world ended, as thoroughly and suddenly extinguished as Cretaceous Earth's by the Devil's Tail.

The hominid brain, fueled by the need for increasing smartness, fed by the people's new fat-rich diet, had grown rapidly. It was more complex than any computer that humans would ever build. Inside Mother's head were a hundred billion neurons—interacting biochemical switches—a number comparable to the number of stars in the Galaxy. But each of those switches was capable of taking a hundred thousand variable positions. And this whole suite of complexity was bathed in a fluid laced with more than a thousand chemicals that varied with time, season, stress, diet, age, and a hundred other influences, each of which could affect the functioning of the switches.

Before Mother, people's minds were compartmented, with their subtle consciousness restricted to their social dealings while specialized modules dealt with such functions as toolmaking and environmental understanding, as well as more basic physiological functions such as breathing. The various functions of the brain had developed to some degree in isolation from one another, like separate subroutines not united into a master program.

It was all very jury-rigged, though. And this hugely complex biochemical computer was prone to mutation.

The physical difference between Mother's brain and those of the people around her was tiny, the result of a minor mutation, a small change in the chemistry of the fat in her skull, a slight rewiring of the neuronal circuitry that underpinned her consciousness. But that was enough to give her a new flexibility of thinking, a breaking-through between the different compartments of her intelligence—and a hugely different perception.

But the rewiring of so immensely complicated an organic computer inevitably had side effects—not all of them desirable.

It wasn't just the migraine. Mother was suffering from what might have been diagnosed as a kind of schizophrenia. Her symptoms had been triggered by the death of her son. Even in this first flowering of human creativity, Mother foreshadowed many of the flawed geniuses who would illuminate, and darken, human history in the generations that lay in the future.

There was no police force here. But random killers were not welcome in such a small, close-knit community. So they came to seek her out.

But she had gone.

Alone, she walked for days across the savannah, back to the place they had last camped, the place of the dry gorge. The patch of ground was now so weathered and overgrown that surely only she could have recognized it.

She cleared away the vegetation, grass, and scrub. Then she took a digging-stick and, like long-dead Pebble digging for yams, she began to beat her way into the earth.

At last, a meter or so deep, she glimpsed the white of bone. The first fragment she retrieved was a rib. In the harsh sunlight it gleamed white, utterly cleansed of flesh and blood; she was struck by the awful efficiency of the worms. But it wasn't ribs she wanted. She dropped the bone and dug her hands into the soil. She knew where to look, remembered every detail of that terrible day when Silent had been flung into this bit of ground, how he had fallen with head lolling back and limbs splayed, the stains of his death shit still showing on his thin legs.

Soon she closed her hands on his head.

She lifted the skull into the air, the gaping eyes facing her. A scrap of cartilage held the jaw in place—but then the rotting cartilage gave way, and the jaw creaked open, as if the fleshless child were trying to say something to her. But the gaping smile kept widening, grotesquely, and a fat worm wriggled where the tongue had been, and then the jaw fell off, back into the dirt.

That didn't matter. He didn't need a jaw. What were a few teeth? She spat on the cranium and polished it clean of dirt with the palm of her hand. She cradled the skull, crooning.

When she returned to the lake, the people were waiting for her. They were all here, all but the youngest children and the mothers with infants. Some of the adults carried weapons—stone knives, wooden spears—as if Mother were a rogue bull elephant who might suddenly turn on them. But as many of the group were dismayed as were overtly hostile. Here was Sapling, for instance, his spear-thrower slung over his back on a length of sinew, his pale eyes clouded as he watched the woman who had taught him so much. Many of them even wore the markings she had inspired on their flesh or clothes.

Sour's only surviving child was a girl, thirteen years old. She had always been prone to chubbiness, and that had gotten worse now that she was coming into womanhood; already her breasts were large, pendulous. And her skin was an odd yellow-brown color, like honey, the legacy of a chance meeting with a wandering group from the north a couple of generations back. Now this girl, Honey, Mother's cousin, stared at Mother with baffled anger, her dirty face streaked with tears.

Hostile, sad, pitying, or confused, they were all uncertain. When she recognized that uncertainty Mother felt a kind of inner warmth. Without yelling, without using violence, without so much as a gesture, she was in control of the situation.

She held up the skull and swiveled it so that its sightless eyes turned on the people. They gasped and flinched—but most looked more baffled than frightened. What use was an old skull?

But one girl turned away, as if the staring skull were looking at her accusingly. She was a skinny, intense fourteen-year-old with wide eyes. This girl, Eyes, had a particularly elaborate spiral design sketched on her upper arms in ocher. Mother made a mental note of her.

One man stepped forward. He was a huge fellow with a ferocious temper, like a cornered ox. Now Ox pointed back at Sour's shelter. "Dead," he said. He pointed his ax at Mother. "You. Head, rock. *Why?*"

For all the control she was exerting on the situation, Mother knew that what she said now would determine her entire future. If she was driven out of the camp she could not expect to survive long.

But she was confident.

She looked at the skull, and smiled. Then she pointed at Sour's body. "She kill boy. She kill *him.*"

Ox's black eyes narrowed. If that was true that Sour had killed the boy, then Mother's actions could be justified. Any mother, even a father, would be expected to avenge a murdered child.

But now Honey pushed forward. "How, how, how?" Struggling to express herself, her plump belly wobbling, she mimed stabbing, strangling. "Not kill. Not touch. How, how, how? Boy sick. Boy die. How, how?" *How is my mother supposed to have done this?*

Mother raised her face to the sun, which sailed through a cloudless dome of white-blue sky. "Hot," she said, wiping her brow. "Sun hot. Sun not touch. *She* not touch. *She* kill." *Action at a distance. It isn't necessary for the sun to touch your flesh for it to warm you. And it wasn't necessary for Sour to touch my son to kill him.*

There was fear in their faces now. There were plenty of invisible, incomprehensible killers in their lives. But the notion that a person could *control* such forces was new, frightening.

Mother forced herself to smile. "Safe. She dead. Safe now." *I killed her for you. I killed the demon. Trust me.* She held up the skull, stroking its cranium. "Tell me." And so it had been.

Ox glared at Mother. He growled and stamped, and pointed at her chest with his ax. "Boy *dead*. Not tell. Boy dead."

She smiled. She nestled the skull in the crook of her arm, like the head of a baby. And as they stared at her, half-believing, she could feel her power spread.

But Honey wouldn't accept any of this. Crying, jabbering meaninglessly, she lunged at Mother. But the women held her back.

Mother walked away toward her shelter. The people shrank back as she passed, eyes wide.

III

The dryness intensified. One hot, cloudless day gave way to another. The land dried quickly, the streams shriveling to brownish trickles. The plants died back, though there were still roots to be dug out with ingenuity and strength. The hunters had to range far in search of meat, their feet pounding over dusty baked-dry ground.

These were people who lived in the open, with the land, the sky, the air. They were sensitive to the changes in the world around them. And they all quickly knew that the drought was deepening.

Paradoxically, though, the drought brought them a short-term benefit.

When the dry period had lasted thirty days, the group broke up its encampment and trekked to the largest lake in the area, a great pool of standing water that persisted through all but the most ferocious dry seasons. Here they found the herbivores—elephant, oxen, antelope, buffalo, horses. Driven to distraction by thirst and hunger, the animals crowded around the lake, jostling to get at the water, and their great feet and hooves had turned the lake's perimeter into a trampled, muddy bowl where nothing could grow. But already some of them were failing: the old, the very young, the weak, those with the least reserves to see them through this harsh time.

The humans settled, watchful, alongside the other scavengers. There were other human bands here—even other kinds of people, the thick-browed sluggish ones you glimpsed in the distance sometimes. But the lake was big; there was no need for contact, conflict.

For a time the living was easy. It wasn't even necessary to hunt; the herbivores simply fell where they stood, and you could just walk in and take what you needed. The competition with other carnivores wasn't too intense, for there was plenty for everybody.

The people didn't even have to take the whole animal: The meat of a fallen elephant, say, was more than they could consume before it spoiled. So they took only the choicest cuts: the trunk, the delicious, fat-rich foot-pads, the liver and heart, the marrow of the bones, abandoning the rest to less choosy scavengers. Sometimes they would close in on an animal that wasn't yet dead, but was too weak to resist. If you let it live, the ravaged animal was a larder of fresh meat for those who preyed on it, as long as it survived.

So the animals fell and their meat was consumed, their bones were scattered and trampled by their surviving fellows, until the muddy margin that surrounded the shrinking lake glinted with shards of white.

But the drought wasn't a disaster for the people. Not yet.

Mother had moved to the lake with the people, of course; no matter what remarkable internal trajectory she was now following, she still had to eat, to stay alive, and the only way she could do that was as part of the group.

But life began to get subtly easier for her.

Nothing could grow close to this mud hole, and as the drought continued—and the elephants and other browsers demolished the trees over an increasingly wide radius—the people had to range further to gather raw materials for their fires, pallets, and shelters.

Mother got help with this chore. Eyes, the staring, intense girl who had been so impressed by Silent's stare, brought Mother wood, her skinny arms laden with the scratchy, dried-out stuff. Mother accepted this without comment. Later she let Eyes sit and watch as she made her markings in the dirt. After a time, shyly, Eyes joined in.

One of the younger men had been close to Eyes. He was a long-fingered boy, oddly fond of consuming insects. This boy, Ant-eater, jeered at Mother and tried to pull Eyes away. But Eyes resisted.

At length Mother took a long straight sapling trunk, thrust it into the ground, and set Silent's empty skull up on top of it. The next time Ant-eater came sniffing around Eyes, he walked straight into Silent's eyeless glare. Whimpering, he scuttled away.

After that, with the skull watching over her day and night, Mother's power and authority seemed to grow.

Soon it wasn't just Eyes who brought her wood and food, but several of the women. And if she walked down to the water's edge, even the men would grudgingly make way and let her have first cut of the drought's latest victim.

It was all because of Silent, of course. Her son was helping her, in his own subtle, characteristically quiet way. In gratitude she set his favorite toys out at the base of the post: the bits of pyrite, the twisted chunk of wood. She even took to leaving out food for him—elephant calf meat, well cooked and chewed by his mother, the way he had liked it as a small child. Every morning, the meat was gone.

She was no fool. She knew Silent wasn't alive in any brute physical sense. But *he wasn't dead.* He lived on in other, more subtle, dispersed ways. Perhaps he was in the animals who fed on the food she put out for him. Perhaps he was in the pallet that cushioned her when she slept. Perhaps he was working in the hearts of the people who gave her food. It didn't matter *how* he was here. It was enough that she knew now that death was just a stage, like birth, the sprouting of body hair, the withering of the aging. It was nothing to fear. The ache she had endured had gone. When she lay on her pallet, alone in the dark, she felt as close to Silent as she had when he was an infant snuggling at her breast.

She was certainly schizophrenic. Perhaps she was no longer sane. It would have been impossible to tell; in all the world, there were only a handful of people like Mother, only a few heads filled with such a light, and there was no meaningful comparison to make.

But, sane or not, she was happier than she had been for a long time. And, even in this time of drought, she was growing fat. From the point of view of simple survival, she was succeeding better than her fellows.

Her insanity—if it was insanity—was adaptive.

One day Eyes came up with something new.

Inspired by the carved ivory figurine Mother still kept at her side, Eyes began to make new kinds of marks on a bit of flattened-out elephant skin. At first they were very crude, just scribbles of ocher and soot on dusty hide. But Eyes persisted, struggling to replicate in ocher on skin what she could see in her head. Watching her, Mother recognized something of herself, the painful early times as she strove to get the strange contents of her head *out.*

And then she understood what Eyes was trying to do.

On this scrap of elephant hide, Eyes was drawing a horse. It was a crude picture, even infantile, the line poor, the anatomy distorted. But this was no abstract shape, like Mother's parallel lines and spirals. This was definitely a horse: There was the graceful head, the flowing neck, the blur of hooves beneath.

For Mother it was another thunderbolt moment, an instant when the connections closed and her head reconfigured once again. With a cry she fell to the ground, scrabbling for her own bits of ocher and charcoal. Startled, Eyes quailed back, fearful she had done something wrong. But Mother only grabbed a bit of hide and began to scratch and scribble as Eyes had done.

She felt the first sun-bright premonitory tingling of pain in her head. But she kept on working through the pain.

Soon Eyes and Mother had covered the surfaces around them, rocks and bone and skin and even the dry dust, with hasty images of leaping gazelles and towering giraffes, with elephants, horses, eland.

When they saw what Eyes and Mother were doing, others, immediately fascinated, tried to copy them. Gradually the new imagery spread, and throughout the little community ocher animals leapt and sooty spears flew. It was as if a new layer of life had entered the world, a surface of mind that changed everything it touched.

For Mother it was a new kind of power. When she had recognized that the shapes she saw in her head had matches in the world outside, she had begun to understand that *she* was at the focus of the global web of causality and control—as if the universe of people and animals, rocks and sky, was just a map of what lay inside her own imagination. And now, with this new technique of Eyes's, there was a whole new way to express that control, those connections. Taking the horse into her head and then transferring it, frozen, to a rock or a bit of skin was as if she owned it forever—no matter that the animal ran unimpeded across the dry plains.

Many people feared the new images and those who produced them. Mother herself had grown too strong to be challenged; few would meet the sightless gaze of that skull on the post. But Eyes, her closest acolyte, was an easier target.

One day she came to Mother, weeping. She was bedraggled and muddy, and the elaborate designs she had painted on her skin were smudged and washed away. Eyes's language skills remained poor, and Mother had to listen to a lot of her circumlocutory pidgin before she understood what had happened.

It had been Ant-eater, the boy who had shown interest in Eyes. He had pursued her again. When she had shown no desire for him he had tried to force himself on her. But still she resisted. So he carried her to the lake and threw her into the water, smeared her with mud, tried to destroy her skin markings.

Eyes looked at Mother as if she expected comfort, a hug, as if she were an upset child. But Mother merely sat before her, her face hard.

Then she went to her pallet and returned with a fine stone scraper. She made the girl rest her head in her lap—and Mother jabbed the stone into her cheek. Eyes cried out and pulled away, baffled; she touched her cheek and looked in horror at the blood on her fingers. But Mother coaxed her back, made her lie down again, and again punctured her cheek, this time a little below the first wound. Eyes struggled a little, but she submitted. Gradually, as the pain seeped through her, she went limp.

When Mother was done with the awl she wiped away the blood and took a piece of ocher, rubbing the crumbling rock deep into the wounds she had made. Eyes mewled as the salty stuff stung her damaged flesh.

Then Mother took her hand. "Come," she said. "Water."

She led the reluctant, baffled girl through the listless herbivores down to the lake. They splashed out into the water, their toes sinking into the clinging lake-bottom mud, until the water came up to their knees. They stood still until the ripples had settled, and the muddy water lay still and smooth before them.

Mother bade Eyes look down at her reflection.

Eyes saw that a vivid crimson spiral looped from her eye and over her cheek. Blood still seeped from the rudimentary tattoo. When she splashed water over her face the blood washed away, but the spiral remained. Eyes gaped and grinned—though the flexing of her face made her aching wounds hurt even more. She understood now what Mother had been doing.

The tattooing was a technique Mother had tried out on herself. It was painful, of course. But it was pain—the pain in her head, the pain of her loss of Silent—that had given birth to the great transformations of her life. Pain was to be welcomed, celebrated. What better way to make this child one of her own?

Hand in hand, the two of them walked back to the shore.

For day after relentless day the drought continued.

The lake became a dank puddle at the center of a bowl of cracked mud. The water was fouled by the droppings and corpses of the animals—but the people drank it nonetheless, for they had no choice, and many of them suffered diarrhea and other ailments. Among the animals the die back continued. But there was little fresh meat now, and there was ferocious competition from the wolves and hyenas and cats.

The bands, of skinny folk and bone-brows alike, stared at each other sullenly.

Among Mother's people, the first to die was an infant. Her little body had been depleted by diarrhea. Her mother keened over the little corpse, then she gave it up to her sisters, who took it away to put it in the ground. But the dirt was dry, hard packed, and the weakened folk had trouble digging into it. Next day another died, an old man. And two the next, two more children.

It was after that, after they had started to die, that the people began to come to Mother.

They approached her pallet, with the gleaming skull on its post. They would sit on the dusty ground, gazing at Mother or Eyes or the animals and geometric designs they had scratched everywhere. More of them began to copy Mother's practices, pasting spirals and starbursts and wavy lines on their faces and arms. And they would gaze into Silent's empty eye sockets, as if seeking wisdom there.

It was a matter of *why*. Mother had been able to tell them why her son had died, of an invisible illness nobody else had even been able to name; she had been able to pick out and punish Sour, the woman who had caused that death. Surely if anybody knew *why* this drought was afflicting them, it would be Mother.

Mother studied this rough congregation, her mind working relentlessly, ideas and interconnections sparking. The drought had a cause; of course it did. Behind every cause there was an intention, a mind, whether you could see it or not. And if there was a mind, you could negotiate with it. After all her people had already been traders, instinctive negotiators, for seventy thousand years.

But how was she to negotiate with the rain? What did she have to trade?

And overlaid on such musings was her suspicions about the people. Which of them could be trusted? Which of them talked about her when she wasn't present? Even now, as they gazed up at her in a kind of desultory hope, were they somehow communicating, sending secret messages to each other with gestures, looks, even scribbled marks in the dust?

In the end, the answer came to her.

Ox, the big short-tempered man who had challenged her after the death of Sour, came to join her rough congregation. He was weakened by diarrhea.

Mother stood abruptly and approached Ox. Sapling followed her.

Ox, weakened and ill, sat piteously in the dirt with the rest. Mother placed a hand on his head, gently. He looked up, bewildered, and she smiled at him. Then she beckoned him to follow her. Ox stood, clumsy, dizzy, stumbling. But he let Sapling guide him back to Mother's own pallet. There, Mother bade him lay down.

She took a wooden spear, its end charred, blood-soaked, hardened from use. She faced the people. She said, "Sky. Rain. Sky make rain. Earth drink rain." She glanced up at the cloudless bowl of the sky. "Sky not make rain. Angry, angry. Earth drink much rain. Thirsty, thirsty. Feed earth."

And, with a single fluid movement, she plunged the spear into Ox's chest. He convulsed, his fists grabbing the spear. Blood spewed from his wide-open mouth, and urine spilled down his legs. But with all her strength Mother twisted the spear, and felt it rip at the soft organs within. Flopping, Ox fell back on the pallet, and did not move again. Mother smiled and wrenched out the spear. Blood continued to spill onto the ground.

There was silence. Even Sapling and Eyes were staring, open-mouthed.

Mother bent and grabbed a handful of sticky, blood-soaked dust. "See! Dust drinks. Earth drinks." And she crammed the dust into the half mouth of her child; it stained its small teeth red. "Rain comes," she said gently. "Rain comes." Then she glared around at the staring people.

One by one they looked down, yielding before her gaze.

Honey, daughter of Sour, broke the spell. With a scream of despair she picked up a handful of cobbles and hurled them at Mother. They clattered uselessly on the ground. Then Honey ran away toward the lake.

Mother watched her go, eyes hard.

In her heart Mother believed everything she had said, everything she had done. The fact that it served a political purpose to have sacrificed poor Ox—for he was one of those who most openly opposed her—did not perturb her belief in herself and her actions. Ox's death had been expedient, but it would also mollify the rain. Yes, that was how it was.

Leaving Sapling to dispose of the corpse, she walked into her shelter.

Despite the sacrifice, the rain did not come. The people waited as day succeeded arid day, and not a cloud broke the washed-out dome of the sky. Gradually they grew restive. Honey, particularly, became more openly derisive of Mother, Eyes, Sapling, and those who clung to them.

But Mother simply waited, serene. She was convinced she was right, after all. It was just that Ox's death had not been sufficient appeasement for the sky, the soil. It was simply a question of finding the right trade-off, that was all. All she needed was patience—even though her own flesh was hanging on her bones.

One day Eyes came to her. She was led by Ant-eater. Gaunt as they were, Mother could see that they wanted to couple.

Ant-eater was not mocking now, but supplicating. And now it would be a kind of love, or pity, on the part of the young man, for the tattoo Mother had crudely carved into Eyes's face had become infected by the stagnant lake water. Its spiral shape was barely visible beneath a mass of swollen, leaking flesh that covered one half of the girl's face.

But Mother frowned. This match wouldn't be right. She stood and took Eyes's hand, prizing it away from the dismayed Ant-eater. Then she walked the girl through the scattered people until she found Sapling. He was lying on his back, gazing up at an empty sky.

Mother pushed Eyes into the dirt beside Sapling. He looked up at Mother, baffled. Mother said, "You. You. Fuck. Now."

Sapling looked at Eyes, obviously trying to mask his revulsion. Though they had spent much time in each other's company with Mother, he had never shown any sexual interest in Eyes, even before her face had become so badly disfigured, nor had she shown any in him.

But now, Mother saw, it was right that they should couple. Ant-eater would have been wrong; Sapling was right. Because Sapling *understood*. She stood over them until Sapling's hand had moved to the girl's small breast.

A full month after Ox's death, the people were woken by a wild, high-pitched keening. It was Mother. Bewildered, most of them already terrified of this disturbing woman in their midst, they came running to see what new strangeness was going to befall them.

Mother was kneeling beside the sapling trunk that had borne the skull of her child. But now the skull lay on the ground, broken into pieces. Mother pawed at the fragments, wailing as if the child had died a second time.

Eyes and Sapling hung back, unsure what Mother wanted them to do.

Mother, cradling the pathetic, broken bits of skull in her left hand, glared around at the people. Then her right hand shot forward, pointing. "*You!*"

People flinched. Heads turned, following her line. Mother was pointing at Honey.

"Here! Walk, walk here!"

The sagging jowls under Honey's chin shook with terror. She tried to pull back, but those around her stopped her. At last Sapling stepped forward, grabbed the girl by the wrist, and dragged her to Mother.

Mother threw the bits of skull in her face. "You! You throw stone. You smash boy."

"No, no. I—"

Mother's voice was hard. "*You stop rain.*"

Honey squealed, as terrified as if it might be true, and urine dribbled down her thighs.

This time, Mother didn't even have to perform the kill herself.

It did not start to rain that day. Or the next. Or the next after that.

But on the third day after Honey's sacrifice thunder pealed across a dry sky. The people cowered, an ancient reflex that dated back to the days when Purga had huddled in her burrow. But then the rain came at last, pouring out of the sky as if it had burst.

The people ran, laughing. They lay on their backs, mouths open to the water falling from the sky, or they rolled and threw mud at each other. Children wrestled, infants wailed. And there was a great round of coupling, an instinctive, lusty response to the end of the drought, this new beginning of life.

Mother sat beside her blood-soaked pallet and watched this, smiling.

As always she was thinking on many levels simultaneously.

Her sacrifice of Honey had once again been politically astute. Honey had not been a calculating opponent, but she was a focus of dissent; with her gone it would be easier for Mother to consolidate her power. At the same time the sacrifice had clearly been necessary. The sky and earth were appeased; mankind's first gods had relented, and let their children live.

But on still another level of calculation Mother knew that the storm would have come whatever she did. If the rain had not followed her sacrifice of Honey, she would have been prepared to continue, working through the people one by one—pushing her spear even into Eyes's heart if she had to.

She knew all these things simultaneously; she believed many contradictory things at once. That was the essence of her genius. She smiled, the water running down her face.

IV

Sapling walked slowly along the grassy river bank. He wore a simple skin wrap, and carried nothing more than a spear tied over his back and a net bag containing a few bone tools and artwork—no stone tools; if they were needed, it was easier to knap them on the spot than carry them.

In his thirties now—fifteen years after the deaths of Ox and Honey and the installation of Mother as the troop's de facto leader—Sapling had filled out, his face harder, his hair thinning and streaked with gray. But his body was as whiplash thin as ever. It wasn't possible to hide the tattoos that covered his arms and face, but he had been careful to rub dirt and mud over his skin to subdue their effect. Over the years the tattoos had proved alarming to strangers, and the barrier of mistrust was high enough anyhow.

He looked like a hunter, out exploring at random far from his troop, perhaps seeking to trade. But he was not alone; others watched every step, hidden in the foliage of the riverbank. His appearance was an elaborate lie. And his exploration was anything but random. He was scouting.

He was spotted first by a child, a chubby little girl playing with worn pebbles at the water's edge. Aged maybe five, she was naked save for a string of beads around her neck. She looked up, startled. He smiled at her, eyes wide and empty. She screamed and bolted down the riverbank, as he had expected her to do. He walked slowly after her.

The signs of settlement were soon apparent. The muddy ground underfoot was pocked with footprints, and he saw fishing nets strung across the river. After following a tight curve in the river's flow he came into view of the settlement itself. From a cluster of huts, roughly conical, threads of smoke curled up into the afternoon sky.

This was no temporary camp, he saw immediately. The huts had been built on sturdy logs driven deep into the ground. These river folk had been here for a while, and they evidently intended to stay.

A glance at the river showed why. Not far along the bank, the vegetation on both sides of the water had been trampled down, and he could see the glimmer of stones on the riverbed. This was a ford, where the migrating herds could cross the water. All the people had to do was wait here for the animals to come to them. And, indeed, he saw a great pile of bones, what looked like antelope, ox, even elephant, stacked up behind the huts.

But he was puzzled by the huts themselves. Their walls were solid, save for a break at each cone's apex to allow the smoke out, and there was no way for light to get in. Who would live in such darkness?

Two adults came running toward him—both women, he saw. They carried unremarkable wooden spears and stone axes, and wore straightforward skin wraps, much like his own. Their faces were daubed with crude but fierce-looking ocher designs, and they both had bits of bone pushed through their noses. One of the women raised her spear toward his chest. "*Fu, fu! Ne hai, ne, fu! . . .*"

He recognized none of the words. But he could tell that this crude jabber was like the pidgin he had grown up speaking, with none of the richness that had been steadily developing among Mother's people.

This was going to be easy.

He forced a smile. Then, moving slowly, he slid his bag from his shoulder and let it fall open. Watching the women, he produced a carved seashell. He put the shell on the ground before the women, and backed away, hands spread and empty. *I am a stranger, yes. But I am no threat. I want to trade. And this is what I have. See how beautiful it is . . .*

The women were disciplined. One kept her weapon aimed at his chest, while the other bent to inspect the shell.

The shell itself had last seen the sea a decade ago, and had since traveled hundreds of kilometers inland via tenuous, long-distance trading chains. And now it had been engraved with an exquisite elephant-head design by one of the people's best artisans, a young girl with long, delicate fingers. When the woman recognized the elephant's face, she gasped, childlike. She grabbed the shell and clutched it to her chest.

After that, the women beckoned Sapling to follow them toward the settlement. He walked easily, not looking back, confident his companions would remain concealed.

In the settlement of the river folk he created a stir. People glared as he passed, though they stared greedily at the carved shell. A couple of children, including the little girl who had first raised the alarm, tailed him, skipping, curious.

He was led into one of the huts. This was a typical living space, with an elaborate hearth, sleeping pallets, and food, tools, and skins stacked up. It looked as if ten or a dozen people lived here, including kids. But the family had cleared out, leaving only a couple of bearded men, at least as old as he was, and the women who had brought him here. The floor was well trampled and littered with the usual detritus of human occupation—bones, stone flakes from knapping, a few half-eaten roots and fruit.

The men sat before the smoldering embers in the hearth. They all had huge bones stuck through the septa of their noses. One of them gestured. "*Hora!*" The word was unfamiliar, the gesture unmistakable.

Sapling sat on the far side of the fire. He was offered a cooked root to eat and a drink of some thick liquid. As he laid out his goods he cast greedy looks around the hut. The hearth was elaborate—far more so than the simple holes in the ground made by Mother's people. And there was a pit nearby, skin-lined and filled with water and big flat riverbed boulders. He could immediately see how the water could be heated by dropping in fire-hot stones. There was a structure of clay bricks and straw that he failed to understand: He had never seen a kiln before. There were a few unusual artifacts, like well-made baskets—and a bowl made of what he thought at first was wood, but turned out to be a strange kind of hardened clay.

But most entrancing were the lamps.

They were just clay bowls of animal fat, with bits of juniper twig used as wicks. But they burned steadily, filling the hut with a clear yellow light. He could see now why these huts needed no windows—and his mind raced as he realized that with these lamps it would be possible to have light whenever it was wanted, even in the depths of night, even without a fire.

It was clear that these people were far ahead of his own in toolmaking. But their art was much more limited, although several of them wore strings of the beads he had spotted around the little girl's neck, beads that turned out to be made of elephant-tusk ivory.

So he wasn't surprised when the elders were stunned by the array of goods he was able to lay out before them. There were ivory and bone figurines of animals and humans, images, abstract and figurative, carved in relief into shell and bits of sandstone—and one of Mother's own more extraordinary figures, a creature with the body of a human but the head of a wolf.

It was a reaction he had seen many times before. The art of Mother's people had advanced hugely in the couple of decades since her own first uncertain fumblings. The people had been *ready* for it, with their big brains and nimble fingers; all it had taken was for somebody to come up with the idea—just as these river folk's roomy minds were ready for the art too. It was as if Mother had dropped a grain of dust into a supersaturated solution, and a crystal had immediately formed.

Sapling had no way of communicating with these river folk save for gestures and guessed-at words. But soon the parameters of the discussion were clear. There would be trade: Sapling's art for these sedentary strangers' advanced tools and artifacts.

By the time he left to rejoin his hidden companions, about midday the next day, he had a bag full of sample goods. And he had carefully memorized the location of every kiln, every elaborate hearth.

He had done all of this for Mother, as he had carried through so many other similar assignments. But Mother was not here, at his side, sharing the labor and the risks. In his heart he found, somewhat to his surprise, a dark particle of resentment.

Mother sat by the entrance to her shelter. Legs folded under her, hands resting on her knees, her face was in the sun, her back warmed by the remnants of last night's fire. She was growing old, gaunt, and she seemed to have trouble staying warm. But for now she was comfortable. Oddly satisfied.

Every square centimeter of her skin was covered with tattoos. Even the soles of her feet were adorned with lattice designs. She wore a skin wrap today, as she usually did, so much of her decoration was covered up, but the skin itself was alive with color and motion, leaping animals, darting spears, exploding stars. And on a wooden pillar beside her sat the skull of her long-dead child, stuck back together with a gum made of tree sap.

She watched the people come and go about their daily work. They would glance at her, sometimes nodding respectfully—or else they would turn away hurriedly, avoiding the stare of Mother and her eyeless son— but either way they were deflected, like planets drifting past the gravitational field of some immense black star.

After all, it was Mother who spoke to the dead, Mother who interceded with earth and sky and sun. If not for Mother, the rain would no longer fall, the grass would no longer grow, the animals would stay away. Even sitting here silently she was the most important person in the community.

The latest camp was a riot of color and shape. It was as if Mother had gradually taken the whole of this troop into her head, into her lightning-threaded imagination—and, in a sense, she had. The forms of animals, people, spears, axes—and strange beings that were mixtures of people and animals and trees and weapons—leapt from every surface, from rocks selected for their smooth workability, and from the treated hides that were draped over every shelter. And interlaced with these figurative forms were the abstract shapes that had always marked out Mother's domain, spirals and starbursts and lattices and zigzags. These symbols were invested with multiple meanings. The image of an eland could represent the animal itself—or people's knowledge of its behavior—or it could stand for the hunting activity that was required to bring it down, the toolmaking, planning, and stalking—or something more subtle yet, the animal's beauty, or the richness and joy of life itself.

Between the domains of Mother's mind—and in the minds of those who followed her—the ancient walls were coming down at last. No longer was her full awareness restricted to dealings with other people, while hands and legs and mouths worked independently of thought; no longer was consciousness restricted to its old function of a model of others' intentions. Now she could think about an animal as if it were a person, a tool as if it were a human to be negotiated with. It was as if the world were populated by *new kinds of people*—as if tools and rivers and animals, even the sun and the Moon were people, to be dealt with and understood as any other.

After millennia of stasis, consciousness had become a powerful multipurpose tool, reflected in the multiple layers and meanings of the art pieces, like mirrors of a new kind of mind. For the high-browed people this was a time of intellectual ferment.

And Mother wasn't the only catalyst. Scattered throughout the human range were many others like her. Each of these genius-prophets—if she were not quickly killed by her suspicious fellows—was similarly serving as the focus of a new kind of thinking, new ways of life, a new kind of fire. It was the beginning of an explosive change in the way people interacted with the world around them.

It was the instability of the climate that had driven the development of this new type of mind. The savagely fluctuating environment of this Pleistocene age, like nothing seen in later times, was an unforgiving filter: Only exceptional individuals survived the exceptional harshness, to pass on their genetic legacy. And, not only was the average mind improving, exceptional individuals like Mother were becoming more common—like the prescient technologists who had given the river folk their advanced tool kit. From the point of view of the species it was useful for the mind to be able to produce occasional geniuses. They might wither in the dirt—or they might invent something that would transform human fortunes.

And when such an innovation was made, the roomy heads of their fellows were ready for it. It was as if they longed for it. For seventy thousand years the people had had the necessary hardware. Now Mother, and others like her, supplied the software.

This new way of thinking about the world was already bringing Mother's people unprecedented new rewards. The encampment, save for its adornment, was the usual jumble of lean-tos. But this latest camp was large; there were twice as many people here now compared to the time before Mother's awakening. And it was a long time since anybody had suffered the sunken cheeks and swollen belly of hunger. Mother's ways were successful.

Mother saw the girl Finger sitting alone in the shade of a giant baobab. Finger, just fourteen, was working carefully at some new sculpture, whittling gently at a bit of ivory. She had her legs crossed and a scrap of leather over her lap; Mother's eyes, still sharp, could make out the gleam of waste bits of the ivory on the ground around her. It was she who had made the exquisite elephant-head shell carving Sapling had given to the river folk.

Finger wore the spiral-design cheek tattoo that had become the badge of those privileged to be closest to Mother: the insignia of her priesthood. But Finger was second generation. She was the daughter of Eyes—who was long dead now, killed by the infection of that first crude tattoo. Finger had been marked with the spiral insignia when she was still an infant; you could tell that by how much the tattoo had distorted and faded as she had grown, a mark of special honor.

But the girl was growing fast. Soon, Mother knew, she would have to find her a partner—just as she had selected partners for her mother, Eyes. Mother had several candidates in mind, boys and young men among her priesthood; she would trust her instincts to make the right choice when the time came.

A shadow passed across her. A woman approached Mother, hesitantly, gaze fixed on the dusty ground. She was young, but she walked stooped over. She had brought a haunch of deer meat; she laid this token on the ground before Mother. "Sore," said the woman feebly, her head downturned. "Back sore. Walk head up, back hurt. Lift baby, back hurt."

Mother knew she was only in her early twenties, but this girl had been plagued with problems with her back since foolishly engaging in a wrestling match with her brother—much older, much heavier—some years back.

Mother turned down almost all such requests. It would do her no good to be seen to grant miracles on demand, whether they worked or not. But today, having watched the small genius of Finger at work, warmed through by the sun, she was in an expansive mood. She snapped her fingers. She gestured for the girl to take off her skin wrap and kneel with her back turned.

The girl complied eagerly, bowing naked before Mother.

From the hearth behind her Mother took a handful of cold ash. She spat into it, making a thin, dusty paste, and she lifted it up to Silent's bony gaze for him to see. Then she rubbed the ash into the girl's back, muttering wordless jabber. The girl flinched as the ash touched her flesh, as if it were still hot.

When she was done Mother slapped the girl's backside and let her stand up. Mother waggled a finger. "Be strong. Think no bad. Say no bad." If the treatment worked, Mother would get the credit. If it failed, the girl would blame herself, for not being worthy. Either way Mother would garner a little more credit.

The girl nodded nervously. Mother let the girl go, satisfied. She took the meat and pushed it into her hut. Somebody would cook it and store it for her later.

All in a day's work.

Mother's crude treatment had given her patient a real sense of relief from the pain of her bad back. It was no more than what would one day be called the placebo effect: Because she *believed* in the power of the treatment, the girl felt better. But the fact that the placebo effect worked on the girl's mind rather than her body did not make it any less real, or less useful. Now she would be better able to care for her children—who would therefore have a better chance of survival than those of a comparable family with an unbelieving mother whose symptoms could *not* be relieved by a placebo—and so those children were more likely to go on to have children of their own, who would inherit their grandmother's internal propensity for belief.

It was the same for the hunters. They had begun to draw images of their prey animals on rocks and the hide walls of their shelters. They would stalk these images, spear them in the heart or the head, even reason with the animals about why they should lay down their lives for the benefit of the people. With these rituals the hunters' fear was anesthetized out of them. They were often wounded or killed for their recklessness—but their success rate was high, higher than those who did not believe they had any way of reasoning with their prey.

The emergent humans were still animals, still bound by natural law. No innovation in the way they lived would have taken root if it had not given them an adaptive advantage in the endless struggle to survive. An ability to believe in things that weren't true was a powerful tool.

And Mother was, half consciously, doing her very best to help this propensity for faith to take hold and spread. By selecting mating pairs among her believing followers, Mother was creating a new reproductive isolation. Thanks to this, the divergence of one kind of person from another—believers from those unable to believe—would be surprisingly rapid, leading to marked differences in brain chemistry and organization within a dozen generations. It was the beginning of a plague of thought that would quickly burn through the entire population.

And yet in the world beyond the human range, in northern Europe and the Far East, the older people, the robust beetle-brows and the lanky walkers, still made their simpler tools, even their ancient bower bird hand axes, and lived their simpler lives, just as they always had.

Later, Mother saw the girl again. She was walking more easily, her stoop much lessened. She smiled and even waved at Mother, who allowed herself to smile back.

At the end of the day Sapling returned from his expedition along the river, dusty, hot, thirsty. Of all the artifacts he had brought back he selected a single one to show Mother. It was a lamp, made of the miraculously hard-fired clay. He lit its bark wick and set it up inside her hut, illuminating the dark interior as the daylight faded. Mother nodded her head. *We must have this.* In terse sentences they began to make plans.

But Mother noticed an oddity in Sapling's behavior. Her closest lieutenant since the death of Eyes, he was as respectful as he had ever been toward her. However there was a certain impatience in his manner. But the sparkling light of the little lamp crowded such thoughts out of her head.

Sapling took his best hunters on scouting trips around the river folk's encampment.

He had explained how he wanted the attack to proceed. He drew sketchy maps in the dust, and set stones to serve as models of shelters and people. A talent for symbology had many uses. Social hunters had always had to coordinate their attacks. Wolves did it, as did the great cats, as had the raptors of vanished ages. But never before had planning been so meticulous and complete as in these clever hominids.

As the raiding party approached the river folk's base, they encountered few animals. The prey creatures were already learning to fear these clever new hunters with their far-reaching weapons and overwhelming intelligence.

And already some animals—some pigs, certain forest antelope—had become scarce in this area, exterminated by the humans.

This was, of course, like an advance echo of the future.

But for now, Sapling and his party were hunting people, not animals.

When the attack came, the river folk didn't stand a chance. It was not their weapons that gave the attackers their advantage, not their numbers, but their attitude.

Mother's people fought with a kind of liberating madness. They would fight on when their fellows were cut down around them, after suffering an injury that ought to have disabled them, even when it seemed inevitable that they would be killed. They fought as if they had a belief that they could not die—and that, in fact, was close to the truth. Had not Mother's child survived death, suffusing into the rocks and dirt and water and sky, to live with the invisible people who controlled the weather, the animals, the grass?

And just as they were able to believe that things, weapons or animals or the sky, were in some way people, it wasn't a hard leap to make to believe that some people were no more than *things*. The old categories had broken down. In attacking the river folk they weren't killing humans, people like themselves. They were killing objects, animals, something less than themselves. The river folk, for all their technical cleverness with fire and clay, had no such belief. It was a weapon they could not match. And this small but vicious conflict set a pattern that would be repeated again and again in the long, bloody ages to come.

When it was done, Sapling stalked through the remains of the encampment. He had most of the river folk men slaughtered, young or old, weak or strong. He tried to spare some of the children and the younger women. The children would be marked and trained to respect Mother and her acolytes. The women would be given to his fighting men. If they became pregnant, they would not be allowed to keep their babies unless they themselves had become acolytes. He had also identified some of those with an understanding of the kilns, the lamps, and the other clever things here, and they would be spared, if they were cooperative. He meant his people to learn the techniques of the river folk.

It was another successful operation, part of the long-term growth of Mother's community.

When she was shown the village of the river folk, Mother was pleased, and accepted Sapling's bowed obeisance. But again she saw a frown on Sapling's face. Perhaps he was growing discontented with obeying her instructions, she thought. Perhaps he wanted more for himself. She would have to consider, do something about it.

But it was too late for such plotting. Even as she surveyed this latest conquest, she had begun to die.

Mother never understood the cancer that devoured her from within. But she could feel it, a lump in her belly. Sometimes she imagined it was Silent, returned from the dead, preparing for a new birth. The pain in her head returned, as powerful as ever. Those sparking lights would flash behind her eyes, zigzags and lattices and stars bursting like pus-filled wounds. It got to the point where she could do nothing but lie in her shelter, smoky animal-fat lamps burning, and listen to the voices that echoed through her roomy cranium.

At last Sapling came to her. She could barely see him through the dazzle of patterns, but there was something she needed to tell him. She grabbed his arm with a hand like a claw. "Listen," she said.

He crooned softly, as if to a child, "You sleep."

"No, no," she insisted, her voice a rasp. "No *you*. No *I*." She raised her finger and tapped her head, her chest. "I, I. *Mother.*" In her language it was a soft word: *"Ja-ahn."*

Another connection had closed. Now she had a symbol even for herself: *Mother.* She was the first person in all of human history to have a name. And, though she was dying without a surviving child, she thought she was the mother of them all.

"Ja-ahn," Sapling whispered. *"Ja-ahn."* He smiled at her, understanding. He bent over her, covering her mouth with his lips. Then he pinched her nose shut.

As the gruesome kiss went on, as her weakened lungs pulled for air, the darkness quickly gathered.

She had suspected everyone in the group, at one time or another, of harboring malice for her. Everyone except Sapling, her first acolyte of all. How strange, she thought.

A growing belief that behind every event lay intention—be it an evil thought in the mind of another, or the benevolent whim of a god in the sky—was perhaps inevitable in creatures with an innate understanding of causality. If you were smart enough to make multicomponent tools, you eventually came to believe in gods, the end of all causal chains. There would be costs, of course. In the future, to serve their new gods and shamans, the people would have to sacrifice much: time, wealth, even their right to have children. Sometimes they would even have to lay down their lives. But the payback was that they no longer had to be afraid of dying.

And so now Mother was not afraid. The lights in her head went out at last, the images faded, even the pain soothed.

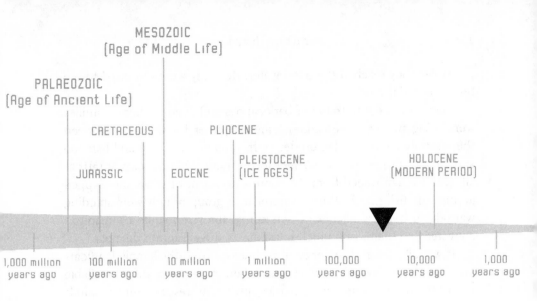

MESOZOIC
[Age of Middle Life]

PALAEOZOIC
[Age of Ancient Life]

CRETACEOUS   PLIOCENE

                                    PLEISTOCENE
JURASSIC   EOCENE   [ICE AGES]   HOLOCENE
                                                [MODERN PERIOD]

| 1,000 million years ago | 100 million years ago | 10 million years ago | 1 million years ago | 100,000 years ago | 10,000 years ago | 1,000 years ago |

CHAPTER 12

raft continent

I

▼ **Indonesian Peninsula, Southeast Asia. Circa 52,000 years before present.**

The two brothers pushed the canoe out from the riverbank. "Careful, careful—to my left. All right, we're clear. Now if we head to the right I think we can get through that channel." Ejan was in the prow of the bark canoe, his brother Torr in the stern. Aged twenty and twenty-two respectively, they were both small, slim, wiry men with nut dark skin and crisp black hair.

They maneuvered their boat through water clogged with reeds, tangled flood debris, and stranded trunks. The trees lining the banks were cheesewood, teak, mahogany, karaya, and tall mangrove. A tremendous translucent curtain of spiderwebs hung over the forest, catching the light and dimming the intensity of the green within. But the heat lay over the river like a great lid, and the air was drenched with light. Already Ejan was sweating heavily, and the dense moist air lay thick in his lungs.

It would have been hard to believe that this was the middle of the latest glaciation, that in the northern hemisphere giant deer roamed in the lee of ice caps kilometers' thick.

At last they reached the open water. But they were dismayed to see how crowded it was.

There was a dense traffic of bark canoes and dugouts. Some families were using two or three canoes lashed together for stability. Between these stately fleets scuttled cruder craft, rafts of mangrove and bamboo and reed. But there were also fisher folk working without boats or rafts at all. One woman waded from the shore with a pair of sticks she clapped around any fish that foolishly swam near. A group of girls were standing waist-deep, holding a series of nets across the river, while companions converged on them, with much splashing, to drive fish into the nets.

It was all a great divergence of technology from the simple log floats once used by Harpoon's people. Spurred on by the great riches available from the coasts, rivers, and estuaries, inventive, restless human minds had come up with a whole spectrum of ways to work the water.

The brothers maneuvered through this crowd.

"Busy today," growled Ejan. "We'll be lucky to eat tonight. If I was a fish I'd be far from here."

"Then let's hope the fish are even more stupid than you."

With a flick of his wooden paddle Ejan casually splashed his brother.

There was a cry from further down the river. The brothers turned and peered, cupping their eyes.

Through the murky cloud of sunlit insects that hovered over the water, they made out a raft of mangrove poles. Three men stood on this platform, slim dark shadows in the humid air. Ejan could see their equipment, weapons and skins, lashed to the raft.

"Our brothers," said Ejan, excited. He took a chance and stood up in the canoe, relying on Torr to keep the little craft stable, and waved vigorously. Seeing him, the brothers waved back, jumping up and down on their raft and making it rock. Today the three of them were going out into the open ocean on that raft, attempting a crossing to the great southern land.

Ejan sat down, his concern outweighing his evaporating elation at spotting his brothers. "I still say that raft is too flimsy," he murmured.

Torr paddled stoically. "Osa and the rest know what they are doing."

"But the ocean currents, the way the tide surges—"

"We killed a monkey for Ja'an last night," Torr reminded him. "Her soul is with them."

But, Ejan thought uneasily, it is *me* who bears the ancient name of the Wise One, not any of them. "Perhaps I should have gone with them."

"Too late now," said Torr reasonably. And so it was; Ejan could see that the three brothers had turned away and were paddling evenly downstream, toward the river's mouth. "Come, Ejan," Torr said. "Let's fish."

When they had reached an open stretch of deep water the brothers took their net of woven flax and slipped into the water. The brothers swam apart until the net was stretched out, then Ejan hooked his big toe into the net's lower margin to open it out vertically. They had turned the net into a fence across the current; it was about fifteen meters long. The brothers began to swim forward, sweeping the water.

Languidly flowing, the water was warm on Ejan's skin, muddy, murky with green life.

After about fifty meters they swam together, closing the net. Their haul was not great—the fish had indeed been scared off today—but there were a few fat specimens that they threw into the canoe. They took care to release the smallest, most immature fish; nobody would eat a morsel when he could wait and take a fat adult in a few months. They pulled the net taut and prepared to swim upstream once more.

But now a cry went up from the shore, an eerie wail.

Ejan turned to Torr. *"Mother."*

"We must go back."

They lodged their net over a tree stump; there it could wait. They scrambled back into the canoe, turned it, and thrust it back into the tangle of drifting debris that lined the riverbank.

When they got back to the encampment, they found their sisters trying to comfort their distraught mother. The three brothers hadn't even got out of sight of the shore before a tidal surge had smashed their fragile craft. None of them had been seen since; all of them had drowned.

Never again would Osa, Born, or Iner lash their canoes to Ejan's.

Ejan pushed his way through his siblings to his mother, and laid his hand on her shoulder. "I will make that journey," he said. "For Osa and the others. And *I* will not die trying."

But his mother, her graying hair ragged, her eyes blurred with tears, only wailed more loudly.

Ejan was a remote descendant of Eyes and Finger, acolytes of the original Mother of Africa.

After Mother, the progress of mankind was no longer limited by the millennial pace of biological evolution. Now language and culture were themselves evolving at the speed of thought, feeding back on themselves, becoming ever more complex.

Not long after Mother's death, a new exodus from Africa had begun, a great diffusion of people, in all directions. Ejan's folk had gone east. Following the ancient footsteps of Far's walker kind, they had worked their way along the southern fringe of Eurasia, following the coastlines and archipelagos. Now there were people strung out in a great strip from Indonesia and Indochina, through India and the Middle East, all the way back to Africa. And as the populations slowly grew, there had been a gradual colonizing push out of those beachheads along the inland waterways into the interior of the great continent.

Ejan and Torr were the product of the purest strand of coastal wanderers, those who had kept up their seashore migrations generation after generation. To exploit the riches of the rivers, estuaries, coastal strips, and offshore islands, these people had gradually honed their skills in boat-building and fishing.

But now they faced a quandary. On this archipelago, off the southwestern corner of the Asian landmass, they had traveled as far as they could go: They had run out of land. And the place was getting crowded.

There were opportunities to go further; everybody knew that.

Though the latest glaciation had yet to reach its deepest cold, the sea level had already dropped hundreds of meters. In the coastal reshaping that resulted, the islands of Java and Sumatra had been joined with Southeast Asia to form a great shelf, and much of Indonesia had become a long peninsula. Similarly Australia, Tasmania, and New Guinea had been merged into a single mighty mass.

In this unique, temporary geography, there were places where the Asian landmass was separated from greater Australia by only a hundred kilometers or so.

Everybody knew the southern land was there. Brave or unfortunate sailors, washed far from the coast and the offshore islands, had glimpsed it. Nobody knew its true extent, but over the generations enough travelers' tales had accumulated for everyone to be sure that this was no mere island: this was a new land, extensive, green, rich, with a long and abundant coast.

To get there would be quite a feat. The people had gotten this far by island-hopping, moving through reasonably equable seas from one scrap of land to another, each clearly visible, one from the next. Moving from this last island to the southern lands—passing out of sight of land altogether—would be a challenge of a different order.

But still, to open up a new world, all it would take was for somebody bold enough to attempt the crossing. Bold enough, smart enough—and lucky.

Ejan took many days to select the tree he wanted.

With Torr at his side he walked through the fringes of the forest, studying sterculias and palms. He would stand beneath the trees, eyeing the lines of their trunks, tapping on their bark with his fist to detect any inner defect.

At last he selected a palm—very fat, very true, its trunk a bulky unblemished pillar. But it was a long way from his band's settlement. Not only that, the palm was a long way from any riverbank; they wouldn't even be able to float it home.

Torr thought about complaining about this, but when he saw the set expression on Ejan's small face he kept his counsel.

First the brothers felled the palm with their stone axes. Then they briskly stripped the bark off the trunk. The exposed wood was perfect, as Ejan had hoped, and very hard under his hand.

They hiked back to the encampment to enlist help to bring back the trunk. Though there was a great deal of sympathy for the loss of their three brothers, nobody relished the prospect of such a long and difficult haul through the forest. In the end it was only family members—only Ejan, Torr, and their three sisters—who returned to the felled palm.

When he had gotten the palm back to camp Ejan immediately got to work. Sliver by sliver he hollowed out the stem of the trunk, taking care to leave the pith intact at stem and stern. He used stone axes and adzes— quickly blunted, yet equally quickly knapped.

Torr helped for the first couple of days. But then he drew away. As the oldest remaining sibling, responsibility now lay heavily on him, and he devoted himself to the basic chores of the family, to staying alive.

After a few days Ejan's youngest sister, Rocha, brought him a small net bag full of dates. He set the dates down on the stern platform he was carving into the wood, and absently pushed them into his mouth while he worked.

Rocha, fifteen years old, was small, dark, slim—a quiet, intense girl. She walked around the trunk, seeing what he had done.

The hollow now extended through much of the trunk's length. The trunk's broad base would be the prow, and Ejan was leaving a broad plat-form here on which a harpooner could stand. A smaller flat seat at the stern would accommodate the helmsman. It was remarkable to see a boat emerging from the wood. But the great notch Ejan was digging into the trunk was still heartbreakingly shallow, the surfaces rough and unfinished.

Rocha sighed. "You are working so hard, brother. Osa used to put together a raft in a day, two at most."

He straightened up. He wiped sweat from his brow with his bare arm, and dropped another worn ax blade. "But Osa's raft killed him. The ocean between us and the southern land is not like the placid waters of the river. No raft is strong enough." He ran his hand along the inside of the hollow. "In this canoe I will be tucked safely inside the craft. So will my belongings. Even if I capsize, I will not be harmed, for the boat will easily be righted. Look here." He rapped on the trunk's exterior. "This trunk is very hard on the outside, but the pith is light inside. The wood is so buoyant it cannot even sink. This is the best way to make the crossing, believe me."

Rocha ran her small hand along the worked wood. "If you must make a canoe, Torr says, you should use bark. Bark canoes are easy to make. He showed me. You can use a single sheet of bark that you hold open with lumps of clay fore and aft, or else you sew it together from strips, and—"

"And you spend the whole journey bailing, and before you have got halfway across, you sink. Sister, I don't have to sew my hull together, and it cannot rip; *my* canoe will not leak."

"But Torr thinks—"

"Too many think," he snapped. "Not enough *do*. I have finished the dates. Leave me now." And he bent to his work, scraping assiduously at the wood.

But she did not leave. Instead she clambered nimbly into the boat's rough interior. "If my words are of no use to you, brother, perhaps my hands will be. Give me a scraper."

Surprised, he grinned at her, and handed her an adze.

After that the work progressed steadily. When the canoe was roughly shaped Ejan thinned out the walls from the inside, making enough room for two people and their gear. To dry and harden the wood, small fires were lit carefully inside and outside the canoe.

It was a great day when brother and sister first took the canoe out onto the river, Ejan in the prow, Rocha in the stern.

Rocha was still an inexperienced canoeist, and the cylindrical craft would capsize at the slightest opportunity. But it would right itself just as easily, and Rocha learned to extend her sense of her own body's balance down through the canoe's center line, so that she and Ejan were able to keep the canoe upright with small muscular counteractions. Soon—at least on the still waters of the river—they were able to keep the canoe balanced without thinking consciously about it, and with their paddles they were able to generate good speed.

After the trials on the river Ejan spent more days working on the canoe. In places the wood had cracked and split as it dried. He caulked the flaws with wax and clay, and he applied resin to the inner and outer surfaces to protect against further splits.

When that was done, he judged the craft was ready for its first ocean trial.

Rocha demanded that she be allowed to accompany him. But he was reluctant. Although she had learned fast, she was still young, unskilled, and not as strong as she would eventually become. In the end, of course, he respected her opinion. Young or not, her life was her own to spend as she wished. That was the way of hunter-gatherer folk like these, and always would be: Their culture of mutual reliance bred mutual respect.

At last, for the first time, the canoe slid out of the river's broad mouth toward the open ocean. Ejan had loaded the canoe with boulders to simulate the cargo of food and water they would have to take with them for the real ocean crossing, which would likely be a journey of some days' duration.

As they passed, fisher folk on rafts and canoes stood up and yelled, waving their harpoons and fishing nets, and children ran along the bank, screaming. Ejan flushed with pride.

At first everything went well. Even when they had emerged from the river's mouth the water remained placid. Rocha gabbled excitedly about how easy the ocean was, how quickly they would make their crossing.

But Ejan was silent. He saw that the water around the canoe's prow was stained faintly brown, littered with bits of leaf matter and other debris. They were still in the river's outflow, where it pushed into the sea. If he tasted the water, probably it would be fresh. It was as if they had not yet left the river at all.

When they did hit the true ocean's currents, as Ejan had feared, the water suddenly became much more turbulent, and sharp, malevolent waves scudded across its surface. The simple cylindrical canoe rolled, and Ejan was immersed in cold, salty water. With practiced coordination they threw their bodies sideways to right the boat, and they came up gasping and soaked. But almost immediately the canoe capsized again. As the rolling went on, the bindings of their dummy cargo broke, and Ejan glimpsed the boulders he had stowed falling away into the deeper water.

When at last the boat stabilized he saw that Rocha had been thrown out. She quickly came up, spluttering and gasping.

He knew that the experiment was over. He dumped out the rest of the rocks, briskly paddled the canoe to his sister and hauled her out, and they began to make their way back to the river's mouth.

When they got back to their camp, their reception was subdued. Torr helped them berth the canoe, but he had little to say. Their mother was nowhere to be found. They had been close enough to the shore for their antics to be visible to everybody, painfully reminiscent of what had become of their brothers, Osa, Born and Iner.

Still Ejan was not put off. He knew that the crossing was possible in the canoe; it was just a question of skill and endurance—and he knew that determined as she was, poor Rocha did not yet have those qualities. If he was to reach the southern lands, he needed a stronger companion.

So he approached Torr.

Torr was working on a new canoe of his own, an elaborate construction of sewn bark. But he spent most of his time now gathering food and hunting. His back was bent from stooping over bushes and roots, and a great gash over his ribs, inflicted by a boar, was slow to heal.

Ejan thought his brother looked much older. In Torr he saw the solid, earthbound sense of responsibility that he took from the great-grandfather who had given him his name.

"Come with me," Ejan said. "It will be a great adventure."

"To attempt the crossing is not—necessary," Torr said awkwardly. "There is much to do here. Things are difficult for us now, Ejan. There are so few of us. It is not as it was." He forced a smile, but his eyes were flat. "Imagine the two of us out on the river in your magnificent canoe. How the girls will holler! And I pity any crocodile that breaks its teeth on our hull."

"I did not build the canoe for the river," Ejan said evenly. "I built it for the ocean. You know that. And to reach the southern land was the reason our brothers gave their lives."

Torr's face grew hard. "You think too much about our brothers. *They are gone.* Their souls are with Ja'an until they return in the hearts of new children. I have tried to help you, Ejan. I helped you bring back your log. I hoped all this work would clear your head of your troubled dreams. But now it has gotten to the point where you are prepared to let the ocean kill you, as it did our brothers."

"I have no intention of being killed," Ejan said, his anger burning deep.

"And Rocha?" Torr snapped. "Will you lead *her* to her death for the sake of your dream?"

Ejan shook his head, baffled. "If Osa were alive, he would come with me." He slapped the sewn hull of Torr's new canoe. "Two canoes are better than one. If this were Osa's canoe, he would strap it to mine and we would sail side by side across the ocean, until—"

"Until you both drowned!" Torr cried. "I am not Osa. And this is not his canoe." His anger and frustration were visible in his face now, Ejan saw, shocked—as was his fear. "Ejan, if we lose you—"

"Come with me," Ejan said evenly. "Strap your canoe to mine. We will defeat the ocean together."

Torr shook his head tightly, avoiding Ejan's eyes.

Sadly Ejan prepared to take his leave.

"Wait," said Torr softly. "I will not go with you. But you will take my canoe. It will ride alongside yours. My body will be here, digging roots." He grinned now, wistfully. "But my soul will be with you, in the canoe."

"Brother—"

"Just come back."

The use of Torr's canoe gave Ejan a new idea.

The second canoe, though it would be laden with food and other supplies, would not be manned. That meant it would not be as heavy as Ejan's, and to lash the canoes together side by side would not be the best solution for stability.

After a little thought and much experimentation, Ejan attached Torr's sturdy bark canoe to his own with two long crosspieces of wood. With this arrangement, the two canoes connected by an open framework of wood, it was almost as if he was building a kind of raft, founded on the canoes.

As his concept developed he became excited by the idea. Perhaps with this new way he could combine the best of the two designs. The rowers and their possessions would be tucked snugly inside the body of the dugout canoe, rather than being exposed on the surface of a raft, but the second canoe would give them the stability of a raft's wide platform.

With Rocha he took the new arrangement out for trials, in the river and skirting the ocean shore. The double-hull design proved more difficult to maneuver than a single canoe, but it was far more stable. Though they progressed farther out into the ocean than the first time they had tried out the dugout, they didn't capsize once. And because they didn't have to work constantly to keep the craft upright as they had the simple dugout, the journey was much less tiring.

At last Ejan felt he was ready.

He tried one last time to dissuade Rocha from coming with him. But in Rocha's eyes he saw a kind of hard restlessness, a rocky determination to meet this great challenge. Like Ejan's, her name had been handed down from the past; perhaps somewhere in the line of Rochas before her there had been another great traveler.

They loaded up the canoes with provisions—dried meat and roots, water, shells and skins for bailing, weapons and tools, even a bundle of dry wood to make a fire. They were trying to be prepared. They had no idea what they would find on that green shore to the south, no idea at all.

As they set off this time, there was no sense of celebration. People turned away, attending to their chores. Even Torr was not there to see the double canoe sliding smoothly out of the estuary. Ejan could not help but feel oppressed by their disapproval, even as he felt the smooth rocking of his craft as it cut through the deepening water.

But this modest expedition was the start of a great adventure.

All over the peninsula, Ejan's outrigger design was being derived independently. In some places the design evolved from double canoes, like Ejan's, with the eventual outrigger float descending from a degenerate second canoe. In some, the design was more like an opened-up raft. Elsewhere people were experimenting with simple poles lashed across a canoe's gunwales to improve its handling. Whatever its disparate origins, the outrigger design was a solution to the instability that before now had confined canoes to the rivers.

And in the generations to come the descendants of these folk in their outriggers would spread out across Australasia, the Indian Ocean, and Oceania. They would reach as far west as Madagascar off Africa's coast, east across the Pacific to Easter Island, north to Taiwan off the Chinese coast, and as far south as New Zealand, taking their language and culture with them. It was an epic migration: Indeed, it would take tens of thousands of years.

But in the end the children of these riverine folk would travel around more than two hundred and sixty degrees of the Earth's circumference.

Their smooth crossing of the strait to the new land was so easy as to be almost anticlimactic.

Ejan and Rocha followed an unknown coast. Eventually they reached a place where they could see a stream of what must be fresh water cutting out of the inland tangle of vegetation. They turned their craft to face the shore and paddled hard, until they felt the canoes' prows grinding into the bed of the shallowing sea. They had landed on a strip of beach, fringed by dense, tangled forest.

Rocha cried, "Me first, me first!" She leapt out of the dugout—or tried to; after a couple of days at sea, her legs gave way under her, and she slipped and fell on her backside in the water, laughing.

It wasn't a very dignified landing. Nobody made a speech or raised a flag. And there would be no monument here; in fact, in another thirty thousand years, this first landing site would be drowned by the rising sea. Nevertheless this was an extraordinary moment. For Rocha had become the first hominid ever to touch Australian soil, the first to set foot on the continent.

Ejan clambered out more carefully. Then, knee-deep in the warm, coastal water, they dragged their canoes until they were firmly grounded.

Rocha ran straight to the freshwater stream. She threw herself into it and rolled, sucking up great mouthfuls of it and scraping at her skin.

"Ugh, the salt! I am caked in it." With the exuberance of youth, she scrambled up the stream and into the fringe of forest, seeking fresh fruit.

Ejan took a tremendous drink of the cold, crisp water, and immersed his head for long heartbeats. Then, his legs trembling, he walked up the beach. He studied the jungle. He recognized mangroves, palms; it was much as it had been at home. He wondered how far this new island stretched. And he wondered if there were, after all, people here.

Rocha squealed softly. He hurried to her side.

Through the tangle of vegetation something was moving. It was massive, yet it moved all but silently. It had a terrible reptilian stillness about it that evoked deep primal fears in their hearts. And now it came slithering out of the undergrowth. It was a snake, Ejan saw immediately, but a snake of a size he had never seen before. It was at least a pace across, and seven or eight paces long. Brother and sister grabbed each other and hurried from the forest, back to the beach.

"Beasts," Rocha whispered. "We have come to a land of mighty beasts."

They stared into each other's eyes, panting, sweating. And then they started to laugh, their fear transmuting into exhilaration.

They limped back to the canoe to retrieve their wood and make a fire, the first artificial fire this huge land had ever seen.

But not the last.

II

▼ **Northwestern Australia. Circa 51,000 years before present.**

On a spit of rock-strewn beach, Jana had been gathering mussels. He was naked save for a belt from which dangled the net sacks containing his haul. His skin was deep brown, and his curly hair was piled on top of his head. At twenty-one he was slim, strong, tall, and very healthy—save for one slightly withered leg, the relic of a childhood brush with polio.

Sweating, he looked up from his work. To the west the sun was making its daily descent into the ocean. If he shaded his eyes he could make out outriggers, and silhouettes made gaunt by the light off the sea: people, out on the water. The day was ending, and the bags at Jana's waist were heavy.

Enough. He turned and made his slow way back along the spit. As he walked, he limped slightly.

All along the coast the people were returning home, attracted like moths to the threads of smoke that already climbed into the sky. People were crowded here, living in their dense little communities, feeding off the resources of the sea and the rivers.

It had already been some fifty generations since the first human footfalls in Australia. Ejan and Rocha had returned home, bringing news of what they had found, and more had followed. And their descendants, still largely keeping to their shore-based and riverine economy, had spread around the coast of greater Australia, and along the rivers into the crimson plains of the interior. But Ejan and Rocha had been the first. Still their spirits were handed down from generation to generation—Jana himself bore the name and housed the soul of Ejan himself—and still the story of their crossing, how they had flown over the water on a boat lined with gull feathers, and had battled giant snakes and other monsters on landing, was told by the shamans in the firelit dark.

Jana reached his home. His people lived in a cluster of lean-tos in the shelter of a heavily eroded sandstone bluff. The ground was crowded with the detritus of a seagoing folk: canoes, outriggers, and rafts had been hauled up on to the beach for the night, a dozen harpoons were stacked up against one another teepee-style, and nets, half-manufactured or half-repaired, lay heaped everywhere.

In the open space at the center of the settlement, a large communal fire had been built of eucalyptus logs. Smaller fires burned in the cobble-lined hearths of the huts. Cooking stones had been placed in the big fires, and men, women, and older children were busy scaling and gutting fish. Younger children ran everywhere, making trouble and noise as children always did, acting as a glue of good humor that bound everybody together.

But Jana couldn't see Agema.

Clutching his string bags, he made his way to the largest of the lean-tos. Agema shared this shelter with her parents—second cousins to Jana's own parents—and her wide brood of siblings. Jana took a breath at the darkened entrance to the hut, gathered his courage, and then stepped into the lean-to. Inside there was much activity and a rich mixture of scents, of wood smoke, cured meat, babies, milk, sweat.

Then he saw her. She was cleaning an infant, a tangle-haired little girl whose face was encrusted with snot.

Jana held up his net bag. The mussels within glistened. "I brought you these," he said. Agema looked up, and her mouth twitched in a smile, but she averted her eyes. The kid was staring at him, wide-eyed. Jana said, "They're the best, I think. Maybe we could—"

But now a foot shot out of the dark, catching his withered leg. It crumpled immediately, and he fell to the hard-trodden ground, spilling the mussels. He was surrounded by laughter. A strong hand grabbed his armpit and hauled him back to his feet.

"If you want to impress her you shouldn't try to walk, not with a leg like that. You ought to hop like a kangaroo."

Jana, his face burning, found himself staring into the deep, handsome eyes of Osu, Agema's brother. More of her siblings surrounded him. Jana tried to control his anger. "You tripped me."

When Osu made out the genuine anger in Jana's eyes his face clouded. "I didn't mean disrespect," he said gently.

His decency only made it worse. Jana bent to pick up the mussels.

Osu said, "Here, let me help."

Jana snapped, "I don't need your help. They're for—"

"Ah. For my sister?" Osu looked up at the girl, and Jana saw him wink.

Another of the brothers—Salo, impossibly tall, impossibly good-looking—stepped forward. "Look, fellow, if you want to impress her, *this* is what you ought to bring home." And he showed Jana a mussel shell—a huge one, so big he needed two hands to hold it.

Jana had never seen a mussel of such a size, not in a lifetime of gathering the mollusks—in fact nobody alive had seen such a giant. "Where did you find this?"

Salo nodded vaguely. "Along the beach, in an old midden. I'm thinking of using it as a bowl."

Osu nodded. "Giant mussels, eh? Ejan and Rocha must have eaten well in those days. All gone now, of course. Bring back one of those, little kangaroo, and Agema will open her legs faster than a mussel on the fire opens its shell."

More laughter. Jana saw that Agema was hiding her face, but her shoulders were shaking. Again that uncontrollable anger surged, and Jana knew he had to get out of there before he behaved like a child by displaying his anger—or, even worse, by striking one of these infuriating brothers.

He gathered up his mussels and got out with as much dignity as he could muster. But even as he left he could hear Osu's gently mocking voice: "I hear his dick is as bent as his leg."

Jana got very little sleep that night. But, as he lay awake, he knew what he had to do.

He rose before dawn. He gathered up his ropes, fire-hardened spears, bow, arrows, and fire tools, and crept out of the encampment.

Following the bank of a river, he worked his way inland.

As Jana stepped silently across the dead matter of the forest floor, he disturbed a cluster of scurrying, rodentlike creatures. They were a kind of kangaroo. They peered at him with large, resentful eyes before fleeing. He barely noticed them as he pushed on.

Many of the trees in the sparse riverbank forest were eucalyptus, wreathed by strips of half-shed bark. These peculiar trees, like much of the flora, were distant descendants of Gondwanaland vegetation, stranded when this raft continent had broken away from the other southern lands. And through the river water, shaded by the trees, cruised more relics of ancient times. They were crocodiles, rafted here like the eucalyptus—but unlike the trees, and like their cousins elsewhere, they were barely changed by time.

He came to a clearing.

A family of four-legged creatures the size of rhinos was working its way across the clearing. They had small ears, stubby tails, and they walked on flat feet, like bears. They were making a mess of the forest floor: With their tusklike lower teeth, they scraped steadily at the ground, seeking the salt bushes they favored. These herbivorous marsupials were diprotodons—a kind of giant wombat.

There were many kinds of kangaroo here. Some of the smaller kinds searched for grass and low vegetation on the ground. But the larger ones were much taller than Jana; these giants had grown so tall so they could browse at the trees' foliage. As they searched for food the kangaroos levered themselves forward using their forelegs, tails, and those powerful hind legs, a unique means of locomotion. They were slow and oddly graceful despite their size.

But now, from the forest on the far side of the clearing, there was a roar. The kangaroos, large and small, turned and fled, bouncing away with their extraordinary elastic leaps. The originator of the roar loped casually into the clearing. It looked like a lion, but it was not a close relation of any cat. It was a thylacoleo—another marsupial, like the diprotodons and the kangaroos—but this one was a carnivorous predator, molded into its leonine form by identical opportunities and roles. The catlike creature moved with silky stealth around the clearing, its cold eyes studying its prey.

Jana moved cautiously around the fringe of the clearing, eyeing the thylacoleo.

While in the rest of the world the placental mammals had become dominant, Australia had become a continent-sized laboratory of marsupial adaptation. There were carnivorous kangaroos that hunted in ferocious, high-bounding packs. There were strange creatures unlike any elsewhere: huge relatives of the platypus, giant tortoises the size of family cars, land-going crocodiles. And in the forests walked immense monitor lizards—related to the komodo dragons of Asia, but much larger—an eerie Cretaceous memory, one-ton carnivorous lizards big enough to take out a kangaroo, or a human.

Jana moved on, his thoughts far away.

Jana had known Agema all her life, as she had known him; here in this tight community everybody knew everybody else. But it was only in the last year, as she had passed seventeen, that he had become so attracted to her. Even now he could not have said what it was about her that had so enthralled him. She was not tall, not very shapely, with breasts that would always be small, hips and buttocks too wide, and her face was a wide moon of flesh with a small nose and downturned mouth. But there was about her a quietness, like the quiet of the sea when your canoe was far from land, a stillness masking depths and richness.

He had barely spoken to her of this. He had barely spoken to her at all, in fact, for a year, since becoming aware of her in this way.

What really hurt was that Osu and those other braying idiots were *right* to goad him, to point up his limping, his unsuitability as a husband for Agema. They were trying to protect their sister from a poor match. *He* knew that his damaged leg was no real impediment to his making a living, to his being able to help Agema raise the kids he wanted to share with her so badly, but what he had to do was convince her and her family of that.

And he was never going to do that by scraping mussels off rocks like a child. He was going to have to hunt, that was all. He was going to have to go out and bring home some big game—and he would have to do it alone, so he could prove to Agema and the rest that he was as strong, resourceful, and capable as any man.

The bulk of the people's food came from hunting small creatures or just simple foraging, in the sea, the river, and the coastal strip of forest: straightforward, low-risk, unspectacular stuff. Hunting bigger prey was pretty much a male preserve, a risky game that gave men and boys the chance to show off their fitness, just as it always had. And this ancient game was what Jana was going to have to play now.

Of course he wasn't foolish enough to take on anything too massive alone. The largest animals could be brought down only by a cooperative hunt. But there was one target that a solo hunter could bring home.

He kept walking, heading deeper into the forest.

At length he came to another clearing. And here he spotted what he wanted.

He had found a nest of roughly assembled foliage inside of which a dozen eggs had been carefully arranged. What made the nest extraordinary was its size—probably Jana himself could have laid down inside it—and some of those eggs were as big as Jana's skull. Purga, if she could have seen this tremendous structure, might have believed that the dinosaurs had indeed returned.

Jana laid his trap with skill. He scouted around the clearing until he spotted the mother bird's huge splay-footed tracks. He followed the tracks a little way into the forest. Then he strung ropes between the trees across the tracks, and he took his double-pointed spears and rammed them into the ground.

After that, it was time to set the fire.

It was quick work to gather bits of dry wood. To create a flame he used a tiny bow to rotate a stick of wood in a socket in a small log. He nursed the blaze with bits of kindling. When the fire had caught he thrust torches into the flames, and hurled them around the forest.

Everywhere the torches landed, flames blossomed like deadly flowers.

Birds rose with a shriek, fleeing the rising smoke, and ratty little kangaroos scurried at his feet, their eyes wide with alarm. By the time he had retreated to the clearing the flames were spreading, the separate pockets of fire joining up.

At last a huge bipedal form came screeching out of the forest. She bristled with dark feathers, her head held up on a long neck, and her muscular legs seemed to make the ground shake as she ran. She was a genyornis, a giant flightless bird twice the size of an emu. In fact she was one of the largest birds that would ever live. But she was terrified, Jana could see that: her eyes were wide; her startlingly small beak gaped.

And the bird's great feet caught in his rope. She plummeted forward toward the ground. Her own momentum skewered her neatly on Jana's spear. She did not die immediately. Trapped, the bloody spear protruding from her back, the genyornis flapped her feeble, useless wings. A deep part of her awareness experienced a kind of regret that her remote ancestors had given up the gift of the air. But now here was a capering, yelling hominid, and an ax that fell.

The flames were spreading. Jana was going to have to hurry his butchery and get out of here.

There had been fires in Australia before the arrival of humans, of course. They had come mostly in the monsoon season, when there were many lightning strikes. Some fire-resistant species of plants had developed in response. But they were not widespread or dominant.

But now things were changing. Everywhere they went the people burned, to encourage the growth of edible plants and to drive out game. The vegetation had already begun to adapt. Grasses, as hardy and prevalent as they were everywhere, were able to burn fiercely and yet survive. Candlebark eucalyptus trees had actually evolved to carry flame; bits of bark would break off and, borne by the wind, ignite new blazes tens of kilometers away. But for each winner there were many, many losers. The more fire-sensitive woody plants couldn't compete in the new conditions. Cypress pines, which had once been prevalent, were becoming rare. Even some plants prized by the people as food sources, like some fruiting shrubs, were extinguished. And as their habitats were scorched, animal communities imploded.

From Ejan's original pinprick landing site, people were diffusing out, generation by generation, along the coasts and river courses. It was as if a great wave of fire and smoke were spreading out from Australia's northwestern fringe, working across the interior of this vast red land. And before this front of destruction, the old life succumbed. The loss of the giant mussels had been just the first of the extinctions.

As Jana left the forest the fire still blazed, spreading rapidly, and great pillars of smoke towered into the sky. Uninterested, he did not turn back.

He could not carry the whole bird home, of course. But then, bringing back food wasn't really the point. And when Jana walked into his camp with the genyornis's head mounted on a spear, he was gratified by the slaps of approval from Osu and the others—and by the shy acceptance of his gifts by Agema.

III

▼ New South Wales, Australia. Circa 47,000 years before present.

The bark canoe sat motionless on the lake's murky water.

Jo'on and his wife, Leda, were fishing. Jo'on was standing up, holding his spear ready for the fish. The spear was tipped with wallaby bone, ground sharp and set in gum resin. Leda had made her line from pounded bark fiber, and had fitted it with a hook made from a bit of shell. But the hooks were brittle, the line weak, so Leda's intention was to lead in a hooked fish as gently as possible, while Jo'on stood ready to spear it.

Jo'on was forty years old. He was scrawny, but his wrinkled face was good-humored, though lined by a lifetime of hard work. And he was proud of his boat.

The canoe had been made by cutting a long oval of bark from a eucalyptus and tying up its ends to make bow and stern. The gunwale was reinforced with a stick sewn on with vegetable fiber, and shorter sticks served as spreaders. The cracks and seams were caulked with clay and gum resin. The canoe was unstable, though; low in the water it flexed with every ripple and leaked enthusiastically. But, leaky or not, with a little skill you could handle this canoe even in rough water. And if it was crudely finished, its main beauty was its simplicity; Jo'on had knocked it together in a day.

Jo'on's ancestors, starting with Ejan's very first landing, had walked right across Australia, from the northwest to this southeast corner, right across the continent's arid center. But they had never lost the knack for building a fine boat. Jo'on's canoe even had a fire, burning on a slab of wet clay sitting on the bottom, so they could cook the crayfish they caught.

Or could have, if they had caught any.

Jo'on didn't really care. He could have stood here in the seductive silence of his boat all day, whether the fish came to see him or not. Even the crocodiles that slid past, eyes glinting, failed to disturb his equilibrium. It was better than being back in the camp by the shore, where kids ran everywhere, men boasted, and women ground roots. Not to mention the yapping dingoes. In his opinion those half-wild dogs were more of a nuisance than they were worth, even if they did sometimes help flush out game.

Leda's patience snapped. With a snort of disgust she hurled her line into the water. "Stupid fish."

Jo'on sat down before her. "Now, Leda. The fish are just shy today. You shouldn't have thrown away your line. We'll have to—"

"And stupid, useless, leaking boat!" She kicked at the puddle of river water that lay in the flexing bottom of the boat, splashing him.

He sighed, fetched a bowl of carved wood, and began to bail. He kept his counsel, hoping to let her calm down.

Fish entrails were piled on Leda's head, slowly frying in the sun and leaking foul-smelling oil over her body and head. The oil kept away the mosquitoes that plagued the lake at this time of year. Her small nose was screwed up, her mouth a pucker. Only a year younger than Jo'on, as she aged she had become a heavy, nervous woman, quick to anger.

She had never looked uglier, he thought. And yet he knew he would never leave her. He remembered as if it were yesterday the day he had had to take her youngest child off her—he had smashed its head with a rock, then thrown its body on the fire—and the day only a few moons later when he had been forced to induce an abortion, thumping her belly until the child came out to see the world too early.

She had understood why he had had to take the children away. The people had been on the march, and she was already laden with a barely weaned toddler. She could not have afforded to bear another child. She had known all that. She had not even formed close bonds with either of her lost children; they had been taken too early for that. Yet those incidents had shaped her personality, set its pattern forever like the cracked mud of a dried-up lake bed. And, for the pain she suffered, she blamed Jo'on.

"We have to do better than this," she snapped now.

"Umm." He stroked his chin. "A thicker line? Or maybe—"

"I'm not talking about thicker lines, you crocodile turd. *Look* at this." She held up his spear with its bits of glued-on bone. "You are a fool. You fish with bits of bone, while Alli uses a harpoon pronged with *flint*. No wonder his children are growing fat."

He closed his eyes, suppressing another sigh. Alli, Alli, Alli: some days all he seemed to hear was the name of her older brother, so much smarter than Jo'on, not to mention better-looking, who lived life so expertly. "Shame you couldn't have your kids by him," he muttered.

She snapped like a dingo. "What did you say?"

"Never mind. Leda, be reasonable. We don't have any flint left."

"Then get some. Go to the coast and trade."

He restrained an impulse to argue. After all, stripped of the insults, her suggestion wasn't a bad one; the hundred-kilometer route to the sea was well trodden. "All right. I'll ask Alli to come with me—"

"No," she said, and now she looked away.

He frowned. "Why not? You spoke to your brother yesterday, before the dancing. What did you say to him?"

Her mouth pinched tighter. "We had words."

"Words. What about?" Now he was growing irritated. "About me? Have you been insulting me before your brother again?"

"Yes," she hissed now. "Yes, if you must know. So if you don't want to look like a foolish boy in front of everybody you should keep away from him. Go yourself."

"But such a journey . . ."

"*Go yourself.*" She grabbed a paddle from the bottom of the canoe. "Now we're going back."

He had no choice, in the end, but to prepare for a solitary walk to the coast. But before he left he found out the truth. When Leda spoke to Alli, she hadn't been attacking Jo'on, but *defending* him against her brother's mockery. He didn't say anything to Leda before he left, but he kept that little bit of warm truth close to his heart.

When he set off a couple of the dingoes followed him out of the encampment. He threw rocks at them until they backed off, snarling.

Away from the lake, he walked into silence. The ground was flat and red, littered with ghost-white spinifex grass. Nothing moved save his own puddle of shadow at his feet. There were no people, not as far as he could see, all the way to the horizon.

Australia would always be a marginal place to live. After five thousand years of human habitation there were less than three hundred thousand people in the whole continent—only one person for every twenty-five square kilometers—and most of them were concentrated around the coasts, the riverbanks, and lakes. And in the great red heart of the continent, the vast, ancient limestone plain and saltbush desert, less than twenty thousand people lived.

But humans, though sparse, had covered Australia in a thin web of their culture, in middens and hearths and shells, in images scrawled in the crimson rocks. And Jo'on had the confidence, even alone, even aged a creaky forty, to walk out naked into the red dust, armed only with his spear and woomera. He was confident because his family's knowledge was soaked into the landscape.

He was following the coiled trail of the ancestral snake: the first snake of all, which, it was said, had greeted Ejan on his first landing in his boat from the west. And every centimeter of the trail was laden with story, which he chanted to himself as he walked. The story was a codification of the people's knowledge of the land: It was a map story, very specific and complete.

The most important details concerned water sources. There was a tale attached to every category of waterhole and a variety of rock clefts and cisterns, hollow trees and dew traps. The first source he stopped at, in fact, was a slow seepage. Its particular story was of how in days gone by you would often see huge kangaroos gathered here, fascinated by the water and so easy to kill. But now the kangaroos were gone, leaving only the battered remnant of a eucalyptus as guardian of the water.

And so on. To Jo'on the land was as crammed with vivid detail as if it had been painted over with signposts and arrows—even though he had walked this way only once before in his life.

Such tales were the beginning of the Dreamtime. The tales would last as long as Jo'on's descendants kept their independent culture alive, mutating, growing steadily more elaborate—and yet always retaining a core of truth. It would always be possible to use the story of the ancestral snake to find water and food.

And no matter how far the people wandered, how deep into time they sank, it would always be possible to trace the Dreamtime trails back across the landscape, back to the northwest, to the place where Ejan and his sister had made their first footfalls.

Still, for all this oral wisdom, Jo'on could not know that this land was emptier, far emptier, than when his remote ancestor had first arrived here.

After a day's walking he reached a patch of forest, as he knew he would. Here he intended to do some hunting, to round out his store of trade goods with meat, before passing on to the coast. He moved silently into the forest.

He quickly found a treat: wild honey, retrieved from a hive hanging from a gum tree. As he dismantled the hive a blacksnake approached him, but he was able to grab its tail and crack it like a whip, easily smashing its head on a branch.

His greatest triumph that evening was spotting a goanna—a varanid lizard a couple of paces long. On seeing him the goanna took fright and hid in a hollowed-out log. But Jo'on had patience. As soon as the goanna had spotted him, he froze in midstride. Then he stood unblinking, as the sun sank further into the west, and the soil glowed still more brightly crimson. He saw the goanna's flickering tongue probing cautiously out of the log. Everybody knew goannas liked to taste the air to see if predators or prey were nearby. Still Jo'on stood still as a lump of rock; there was no wind, and his scent would not carry to the goanna.

At last, as he knew it would, the goanna's slow, patient brain forgot Jo'on was there. It scuttled out of the cover of its log. His spear got it in a single strike, pinning it to the ground.

At the foot of a eucalyptus, Jo'on made a fire with a rubbing stick. He briskly skinned and gutted the goanna, softened its flesh in the fire, and enjoyed a rich meal. Above him the sparks from the fire rose up into the towering dark.

When he woke in the dawn, the fire had subsided, but it was still alight. He yawned, stretched, voided briskly, and munched down a little more of the goanna.

Then he made a torch of dead wood, lit it in his hearth, and began to walk through the forest, setting fires. He looked especially for hollow trees that would burn well, and set alight the detritus at their roots.

After all this time the basic strategy of the forest hunters had not changed: to use fire to flush out game.

The smoke soon forced out possums, lizards, and marsupial rats from inside the trunks. They were small creatures all, but he managed to club some of them, and added their little corpses to the pile he accumulated close to his original hearth. But to impress the fisher folk by the sea he needed larger game than this. So he began to roam wider through the forest, setting alight more trees and undergrowth.

Gradually the flames spread and merged, self-organizing, feeding on each other's energy, generating draughts and winds that fed back to intensify the fires further. Soon the separate blazes were merging into a bushfire, a writhing wall of flame that moved forward faster than a human could run.

But Jo'on, by that time, was safely out of the forest. And as the tree-tops exploded into flame as if they were made of magnesium, he stood ready with his spear-thrower.

At last the animals started to rush out of the blazing forest pocket. There were kangaroos, possums, lizards, and many marsupial rats, all terrified. They ran in all directions. Some, blinded and bewildered, came dashing straight toward Jo'on. He ignored the small, fast-moving creatures. But here came two large animals, a pair of red kangaroos bounding with extraordinary speed toward him. He took his spear, lodged it in his grandfather's spear-thrower. He waited; he would get only one chance.

At the last moment the kangaroos saw him and veered away. His spear sailed uselessly into the smoky air.

Yelling his frustration he ran to retrieve his weapon. Cursing Leda's stubbornness and his own foolishness, he set his spear in the thrower and settled down to wait once more. But he knew that his best chance was already gone. He would have to make do with his pitiful pile of possums and lizards, because there were no large animals left to kill.

The goanna Jo'on had trapped was a relative of the giant lizard carnivores that had once stalked the red center of the continent. This hapless wretch had been a fraction of the size of those immense ancestors; the giants had all gone, hunted and burned to extinction. The red kangaroos he had tried to trap were similarly diminished echoes of mighty lineages. All the big ones had been killed off. Those that survived now were the small, fast-moving, fast-breeding creatures able to outrun fires and the hunters' spears.

Since Ejan's arrival, fifty-five species of large backboned animals had gone into the dark. Across the continent, in fact, every creature larger than a human had disappeared.

Eventually Jo'on reached the sea. He had come to the eastern coast of Australia, not far from the place that would one day be called Sydney. The light here, so much brighter than inland, dazzled his eyes, the stinks of salt and seaweed and fish overpowered his nose, and the restless grumbling of the sea filled his ears. After his trek across the dusty red center he wasn't accustomed to so much sensory clamor.

As he descended to the shore he made out people working the sea, in canoes and on rafts. In the bright light off the sea, they were slender upright figures working with their lines and nets and spears. These people stuck to the coast, and their main food resource was fish, which was why they were open to trading for meat from the interior.

Jo'on approached the people, his hands empty save for his bits of meat, yelling greetings in his few words of the local language.

The first locals he met were women with nursing infants. They were methodically eating their way through a pile of oysters. They watched him incuriously. As he walked toward them he found himself crunching over oyster shells, all broken open, a layer that grew thicker as he approached the women. Eventually, he saw with amazement, he was walking on top of a midden of shells taller than he was, the deposit of centuries of uninterrupted gathering. The midden was outside one of the scores of sandstone caves that lined the shores of this harbor. Some of the cave entrances were covered by crude sheets of woven bark. In the shade of the nearest cave, children played with heaps of ancient shells.

The women showed little interest in him. He walked on.

At last an elderly woman came limping out of one of the caves. Her hair was gray, and her naked skin hung on her like an empty sack. She said something incomprehensible, glanced at his wares dismissively, and beckoned him into the cave.

The floor was littered with flint chips, middens of shells, bone points, and charcoal. Where his feet disturbed this detritus he saw deeper layers of garbage beneath—even human turds, dried up and without odor. Like his own people, these fisher folk were not enthusiastic about tidying up their garbage, and would just walk away when a camp became unlivable, trusting in the invisible forces of nature to take care of the mess for them.

But he could see a great pile of flints piled up at the rear of this cave, an enviable treasure. It was said that there were caves on another coast to the south where you could just pry such flints out of the wall. But people of the interior like Jo'on understood little of the provenance of the valuable stones, and had to trade with those who did.

The fisher folk were hospitable enough, in the interest of future relations. They gave him food and water. In their mutually incomprehensible languages, they tried to talk over what he had seen on his journey, what new features of the land he had noticed. But they were not eager to trade. They took his ocher and what poor scraps of meat he had. But it was clear that this was valued at only a handful of flints. Better than noth-ing, he thought gloomily.

The fisher folk let him stay the night.

He lay down on a pallet of dried seaweed. It stank of salt and decay. He found himself peering by the dying firelight at paintings on the roof, pictures in charcoal, ocher, and a purplish dye that, it turned out, came from a sea creature. There were vivid images of wombats, kangaroos, and emus; the people shown hunting them loomed over the fleeing animals.

But—he peered more closely to see better—these pictures were laid over still stranger images: Giant birds, lizards, even kangaroos towered over the humans who hunted them. These images must be older than those he had first made out, he thought, because they lay underneath. But he was confused about what they showed. He supposed they meant nothing. Perhaps they had been drawn by a child.

He was wrong, of course. It was a peculiar tragedy that Jo'on's genera-tion had already forgotten what had been lost.

Jo'on lay down and closed his eyes, settling himself to ignore the noisy lovemaking of a couple in the corner, and waited for sleep. He wondered what Leda was going to say to him when he returned home with just a handful of flints. Meanwhile, over his head, the ancient, vanished birds, the giant kangaroos and snakes and diprotodons and goannas, all danced mournfully in the firelight.

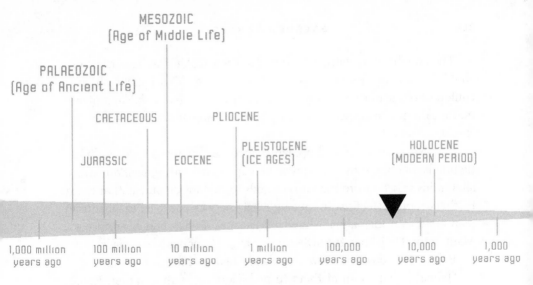

PALAEOZOIC
(Age of Ancient Life)

MESOZOIC
(Age of Middle Life)

CRETACEOUS

PLIOCENE

JURASSIC

EOCENE

PLEISTOCENE
(ICE AGES)

HOLOCENE
(MODERN PERIOD)

| 1,000 million years ago | 100 million years ago | 10 million years ago | 1 million years ago | 100,000 years ago | 10,000 years ago | 1,000 years ago |

CHAPTER 13

last contact

▼ **Western France. Circa 31,000 years before present.**

I

Hiding the carved mammoth in her fist, Jahna approached the bonehead
girl.

The sullen creature looked up at Jahna, baffled, dimly frightened. She
sat in the frosty dirt, filthy, ragged, doing nothing.

Jahna sat on her ankles and peered straight into the creature's eyes.
They were dark globes hidden under the great bony browridge that gave
her kind their name. Jahna was twelve years old—and so, as it happened,
was this bonehead cow. But the similarities ended there. Where Jahna
was tall, blond, slender, and supple as a young spruce, the bonehead was
short and squat and fat—strong, yes, but as round and ugly as a boulder.
And where Jahna wore close-fitting clothes of stitched leather and plant
fiber, with straw-stuffed moccasins, a fur-lined hood and woven cap, the
bonehead cow wore simple wraps of filthy, well-worn leather, tied on with
bits of sinew.

"Look, bonehead," Jahna said now, raising her fist. "Look. *Mammoth!*"
And she opened her fingers to reveal the little trinket.

The bonehead squealed and stumbled back, making Jahna laugh. You could almost see the cow's slow mind working. The boneheads just couldn't hold it in their heads that a bit of ivory could look like a mammoth; to them an object could only be one thing at a time. They were *stupid*.

Now Millo came running up. Jahna's brother, eight years old, was a little bundle of energy and noise, wrapped up in an ill-fitting sealskin coverall. On his feet he wore the skins of gulls turned inside out, so that their feathers kept his feet warm. Seeing what she was doing he grabbed the mammoth out of Jahna's hand. "Me, me! Look, bonehead. Look! Mammoth!" He jabbed the little carving at the bonehead cow's face.

Piss trickled down the cow's legs, and Millo squealed with delight.

"Jahna, Millo!" Both of them turned. Here came their father, Rood, tall and strong, arms bare despite the chill of this early spring day. Wearing his well-loved boots of mammoth skin, he was striding strongly. He looked exhilarated, excited.

Responding to his mood the youngsters forgot their game and ran to him. While Millo hugged his legs as he always did, Rood bent to embrace them. Jahna could smell smoked fish on his breath. He greeted them formally, according to their names. "My daughter, my mother. My son, my grandfather." Then he reached around Millo's waist and efficiently tickled his son; the boy squealed and writhed away. "Last night I dreamed of seals and narwhal," Rood said now. "I talked to the shaman, and the shaman cast his bones." He nodded. "My dream is good; my dream is the truth. We will go to the sea and hunt for fish and seals."

Millo jumped up and down, excited. "I want to ride the sled!"

Rood peered into Jahna's face, searching. "And you, Jahna? Will you come?"

Jahna pulled back from her father's embrace, thinking carefully.

Her father had not been flattering her in asking her approval. In this community of hunters, children were treated with respect from birth. Jahna bore the name, and hence the soul, of Rood's own mother, and so her wisdom lived on in Jahna. Similarly little Millo bore the soul of Rood's grandfather. People were not immortal—but their souls were, and their knowledge. (Jahna's name, of course, was doubly special. For it was the name not just of Jahna's grandmother but of *her* grandmother before her: It was a name that had roots thirty thousand years deep.) And besides the business of the names, how were children to grow into adults if they were not *treated* as adults? So Rood waited patiently. Jahna's judgment might not prevail, of course, but her reasoning would be listened to and tested.

She glanced at the sky, assessing the wind, the thin scattering of clouds; she probed at the frozen ground with her toe, estimating if it was likely to thaw significantly today. She had an odd sense of unease, in fact. But her father's enthusiasm was overwhelming, and she pushed down the particle of doubt.

"It is wise," she said seriously. "We will go to the sea."

Millo whooped and jumped on his father's back. "The sled! The sled!" Together the three of them headed back toward the village.

Throughout the exchange they had all ignored the bonehead cow, who lay huddled and quaking in the dirt, urine leaking down her legs.

At the village, the preparations for the hunt were already under way.

Unlike the boneheads' ugly shantytown, the village was an orderly grid of dome-shaped huts. Each hut had been erected over a frame of spruce saplings, brought from the forests to the south. Skin and tundra sod had been piled over the frame, and a doorway, windows, and chimney hole cut into the walls. The floors of the huts were paved, after a fashion, with riverbed cobbles. Even some of the open areas between the huts had been paved, to save the people from sinking into the mud of the fragile tundra loam.

Each hut was layered over with huge bones from mammoth or megaloceros antlers. These carapaces were there to help the huts endure the savage winds of winter and to obtain the animals' protection: The animals knew that human beings took their lives only when they had to, and in return they lent their great strength to the people's shelters.

Around these huts of bone, there was a hum of activity and anticipation.

One tall hunter—Jahna's aunt, Olith—was using a fine bone needle to repair her deerskin trousers. Others, in a small open area used as a workshop, were making nets and baskets and barbed harpoons of bone and ivory, and weavers were using looms to make cloth of vegetable fiber. Much of the clothing the people wore was made of animal skin for warmth and durability, but there were luxury items of woven cloth— skirts, bandeaus, snoods, sashes, and belts. This expertise in cordage dated back many tens of thousands of years, fueled by the need to find an alternative to animal sinew to strap together rafts and canoes.

Everybody wore decoration, pendants, necklaces, beads sewn into their clothing. And every surface, every tool of bone or wood or stone or ivory, was adorned with images of people, birds, plants, and animals: there were lions, woolly rhinos, mammoth, reindeer, horses, wild cattle, bears, ibexes, a leopard, even an owl. The images were not naturalistic— the animals leapt and pranced, their legs and heads sometimes a blur of movement—but they contained many precise details, captured by people who over generations had grown to know the animals on which they depended as intimately as they knew one another.

Everything so shaped was loaded with significance, for each element was part of the endless story by which the people understood themselves and the world they lived in. There was nothing with only one meaning, one purpose; the ubiquitous art was a testimony to the new integration of people's minds.

But even now ghosts of the old compartmentalism lingered, as they always would. An old man struggled to explain to a girl how she should use her flint blade to carve her bit of mammoth ivory just so. In the end it was easier for him to take the tool from her and just show her, letting his body's half-independent actions demonstrate themselves.

These people, as they went about their tasks, looked remarkably healthy: tall, long-limbed, confident, keen-faced, their skin clear and unlined. But there were very few children here.

Jahna passed the shaman's hut. The big, scary man was nowhere to be seen. He was probably sleeping off the exertions of last night, when once more he had danced and chanted his way into the trance world. Outside his hut was scattered a handful of broken shoulder blades, from deer and horses. Some of them had been mounted on slotted sticks and held in a fire. Even at a glance Jahna could read the fortunes told in their patterns of scorching; today would indeed be a good day for hunting by the water.

Though their language abilities were hugely advanced, the people were reaching out to distant and unknowable gods. And so they fell back on older instincts. As Pebble had once known, communication in a situation where you had no or limited language had to be simple, exaggerated, repetitious, unequivocal—that is, ritualistic. And, as Pebble had once tried to convince his father he spoke the truth about approaching strangers, so the shaman now labored to make his indifferent gods hear, understand, and respond. It was hard work. Nobody resented him sleeping late.

Millo and Jahna reached the hut they shared with their father, mother, infant sister, and aunts. Mesni, their mother, was here in the gloom. She was smoking megaloceros meat, scavenged from a lion kill a few days earlier.

"Mesni, Mesni!" Millo ran to his mother and grabbed her legs. "We're going to the sea! Are you coming?"

Millo hugged her son. "Not today," she said, smiling. "Today it's my turn to fix the meat. Your poor, poor mother. Don't you feel sorry for her?"

"Bye," Millo snapped, and he turned tail and ran out of the hut.

Mesni humphed, pulling a pretend-offended face, and continued patiently working.

Most of the megaloceros carcass had been stored in a pit dug into the permafrost. Mesni used a stone knife to slice the meat paper-thin, then hung it up on a wooden frame beside the hearth. In a few days' time the slices would be perfectly preserved; they were a source of protein that could be stored for many months. But Jahna's nose wrinkled at the smell of the meat. Only in the last month had the spring opened up enough to enable them to hunt and forage and to bring home fresh meat; before that, they had all endured a long winter consuming the dried remnants of last season, and Jahna had grown thoroughly sick of the leathery, tasteless stuff.

She stroked her mother's back. "Don't worry. I will stay with you and smoke meat all day while Millo rides the sled."

"I'm sure you would love that. You've done your duty by offering. Here." Mesni gave Jahna a bundle of meat wrapped in skin. "Don't let your father starve his wretched bonehead runners. You know what he's like. And I wouldn't trust him with *these*." She gave Jahna a handful of dried eulachon.

These were sardinelike fish, so rich in fat you could stand them on end and burn them like a candle. More parochially you could boil out the grease to use as a sauce, medicine, and even mosquito repellent—or in a pinch you could just eat the fish; the fatty flesh would sustain you for a long time. These precious items were an emergency kit.

Jahna took the fish solemnly and tucked them into a fold of her jerkin. It was quite a responsibility she had been given—but the soul of her grandmother, riding in her heart, gave her the confidence to accept that responsibility. She kissed her mother. "I'll look after everybody," she promised.

"I know. Now go help get ready. Go on."

Jahna grabbed her favorite harpoon and followed Millo out of the hut.

The hunting party briskly loaded up the sled with nets, harpoons, lines, sleeping bags made of reindeer hide, and other provisions. The sled was a sturdy affair, already ten years old, a wooden frame mounted on long runners of mammoth ivory. The lashing and lines were made from tough sealskin, and the reins that would control the bonehead haulers were made of mammoth leather. The sled was useful only in the early spring or late autumn, when the ground was frozen or snow-covered; in the late spring and summer, the ground grew too boggy for the sled's runners. Still, in a world where the wheel had yet to be invented and the horse yet to be tamed, this sled of wood and ivory was the height of transportation technology.

Meanwhile, Rood had stalked into the boneheads' camp, looking for haulers.

The camp was a shanty on the edge of the human village. The huts and shacks were as squat and misshapen as the boneheads themselves. They just sat on the tundra like huge turds, with adults and grotesque kids lumbering everywhere. In places like this, wherever they survived across the Old World, the robust boneheads made their simple tools and built their ugly huts—just as they had for half a million years, all the way back to the time of Pebble and long before. Unlike the cultural explosion of the humans, there had been no significant variation in the boneheads' industry across huge swaths of space and time.

With a tap of his whip handle Rood selected two powerful-looking young bucks. Passively the bucks followed him, and allowed themselves to be harnessed to the sled.

All too soon the sled was loaded. It took only a touch from Rood's whip to encourage the boneheads to begin their hauling. The first heave, to free the sled's runners from the hard earth, took some effort. Boneheads were bandy-legged and clumsy, their frames built for strength, not speed. But soon the two bucks had the sled hissing along at a little over walking pace. The hunters followed with whoops and hollering.

To the eerie wail of their bone flutes, the party crossed kilometer after kilometer of tundra. Rood sat on top of the bundles piled up on the sled, his whip of cured hide ready for the boneheads' backs. Millo sat up beside his father, hair streaming.

This was northern France. The hunting party, traveling southwest toward the Atlantic coast, would pass close to the eventual site of Paris. But the tree line—the latitude at which trees could grow tall—ran mostly many kilometers south of here. And not so far north of here lay the edge of the ice cap itself. Sometimes you could hear the wind howling off the ice, cold air that had spilled off the pole itself, a heavy, restless, relentless wind that had scoured clean a great chill desert at the feet of the glaciers.

The land was a patchwork of white and blue, with splashes of premature green. The sled's runners hissed as they ran over trees: they were dwarf willows and birches, flattened forests that clung to the ground, hiding from the wind. It was a shallow land, a skim of life-bearing soil over a deeper layer of permafrost. It was dotted with lakes, most of them still frozen, glimmering blue with the deeper ice that would not melt all summer. The ponds and lakes and marshes of summer were actually little more than transient lenses of meltwater pooled over the permafrost.

But spring was coming. In places the grass was growing already, and ground squirrel ran and foraged busily.

The tundra was a surprisingly productive place. The plants included many species of grass, sedges, small shrubs, and herbaceous plants like types of pea, daisy, and buttercup. The plants grew quickly and abundantly, whenever they could. And the various plants' short growing seasons did not overlap, so that for the animals that thrived here there was a long period of good feeding each year.

This complex, variegated mosaic of vegetation supported a huge population of herbivores. In eastern Europe and Asia there were hippos, wild sheep, and goat, red, roe, and fallow deer, boar, asses, wolves, hyenas, and jackals. In the west, here in Europe, there were rhinos, bison, boar, sheep, cattle, horses, reindeer, ibex, red and roe deer, antelope, musk oxen—and many, many carnivores, including cave bears and lions, hyenas, arctic fox, and wolves.

And—as Jahna saw, in the far south, as they worked across the snow-littered ground—mammoths.

There was a great herd of them—walking ponderously, in no hurry—a wall of bodies that stretched from one horizon to the other. They were not true migrants, but had spent the winter sheltering in valleys to the south, where immense herds would gather, channeled by geography. Their hair was a deep black-brown, but as they walked the curtains of guard hairs that hung from their trunks and flanks flowed and waved, shining golden in the low spring sunlight. They looked like boulders, bulky fur-covered boulders. But occasionally one would lift her head, and there would be a flash of trunk or curling tusk, and a thrilling, unmistakable trumpet. The woolly mammoths had become the most successful of all the ancient elephant lineages. They could be found throughout the great tundra belt that wrapped right around the planet's pole, making a giant herd that outnumbered by far any other proboscidean species that had ever lived.

On these great open lands, where such huge prey walked across open ground, the hunting was as easy for humans as it would ever be, in all their history. But already times were changing; soon the ice would begin its retreat once more. And already, whether they realized it or not, people had started to reshape the life and the land, just as in Australia.

They were thinly scattered, and life seemed hard. But in a sense humans had already reached the peak of their fortunes.

As they traveled the hunters pointed out the features of the land to each other, every bluff and ridge, every river and lake. Everything was named, even features off in the far distance, and everybody was listened to with respect as they shared and confirmed their knowledge. In this marginal land accurate information was at a premium; to know the land was to prosper, not to know it meant starvation, and experts were a lot more valuable than bosses.

They told stories, too, about the animals they glimpsed—how they lived, what they thought, what they believed. Anthropomorphism, attributing to animals personalities and characters, was a powerful tool for a hunter. A mammoth or a bird did not think about its foraging and movement in the same way as a human would, of course, but *imagining* that it did could be an excellent predictor of the animal's behavior.

So, as they traveled, they talked, and talked, and talked.

This land was Jahna's home, as it was Rood's, and his mother, Jahna's, before him. Her people owned it—but not as property that could be disposed of; they owned it as they owned their own bodies. Jahna's ancestors had always lived here, back through the generations, into the unending mists of time, when, so it was said, humans had sprung into existence from fire and trickery. Jahna could imagine living no place else.

At the precise midpoint of the journey, the party stopped.

Snow had drifted in the shelter of a sandstone bluff. Rood briskly cleared the snow with sweeps of his arms, and he dug out a large slice of narwhal skin, with subcutaneous fat still clinging to it. The meat had been there since last autumn, and much of it had been devoured by passing foxes, gulls, and ravens. But Rood cut off chunks with a fine stone knife, and soon they were all chewing. The tough, partially decomposed meat was a luxury. It had a name of its own, meaning something like meat-of-dead. It had been left here as an emergency cache in case a traveling party should find itself stranded.

The two bonehead bucks, panting, their hips and clumsy knees obviously aching, were allowed to rest awhile, chewing on bits of meat.

The hunters began to talk of the shaman's prophecies. Little Millo piped up. "I had a dream. I dreamed I was a big gull. I dreamed I fell in the sea. It was cold. A big fish came and ate me. It was dark. And then, and then—"

The hunters listened gravely, nodding.

Dreams were important. Each day the people faced decisions about what kind of gathering or hunting to attempt, what kind of animals to pursue, how the weather might behave. It was essential to make the correct call; a run of bad guesses could quickly starve your family. But their heads were crammed full of specific knowledge, about the land, the sea-

sons, the plants, the behavior of animals, acquired over a lifetime and dis-
tilled from the experience of generations. On top of that there was a mass
of daily data to absorb, on weather, animal marks. All this voluminous,
tentative, fast-changing data had to be processed to support rapid, firm
decision making.

The hunters' thinking was as a result much more intuitive than systematic and deductive. Dreams, in which the unconscious mind had a
chance to sort and explore all the data available to it, were an essential
part of that processing. And with their chants and dances, trances and rituals, the shamans were the most intense dreamers of all.

The convergence of the shaman's visions and fortune-telling and the
dreams of Rood and Millo was reassuring, a valid piece of information to
guide the hunters. It showed that their deep intuition about the nature of
the world was in accord.

Still, Jahna thought, Rood looked troubled. As he kicked the boneheads to their feet she approached him. "Father? Your face is long."

He glanced down at her, frowning. "It was just that dream of Millo's.
The water, the cold, the dark. Yes, it may be that he dreamed of hunting
in the sea, of catching fish. But . . ." He raised his head, sniffing the air.
"Millo's nose is smarter than yours or mine, daughter. Perhaps he smells
something we don't. But we are committed. Let us go and raid the sea."

With a smart slap on the buttocks of one of the buck boneheads, he
launched the sled off across the frozen ground once more. Millo, perched
on a pile of sleeping bags, squealed with joy.

When they reached the coast, Rood released the two boneheads and let
them forage on the cold ground. They wouldn't have the energy to run
off, or even the wit to imagine escape.

The ocean was frozen.

At this time of year only the coastal fringe was completely free of pack
ice. But the ice was broken by leads, huge open channels of black water
that radiated out from the tip of a headland. The hunters knew the leads
formed in this place every year because of the shape of the coast—and
that was why they had come here.

Eagerly, the hunters clambered on to the sea ice. Their bone harpoons in their mittened hands, Jahna and Millo hurried ahead of the others, hoping to be the first to get to the seals.

Jahna found herself surrounded by miniature mountain ranges,
hillocks of ice pushing four or five meters into the air. Wisps of ice crystals blew languidly, and gulls wheeled, seeking fish. As the sea swelled
impatiently, its skin of ice groaned and cracked; the air was full of sharp

noise. But the ice was rough: autumn storms and the tides around the headland had piled up heaps of huge fractured slabs.

Rood and a number of the others had gathered around the open water, and were calling excitedly. A narwhal had come up to breathe, and perhaps the hunters would make a spectacular kill.

But Millo, cawing like a gull, hurried ahead through the maze of ice. Jahna scampered after him. They came to a place where the water was crusted over by grayish new ice. But the ice was broken by circular holes, a pace or two across.

Millo and Jahna came to a hole and peered into it. In the chill waters, life teemed. Jahna could not make out the tiny plankton that crowded the waters, but she could see the tiny fish and shrimplike creatures that fed on them. In these cold, dry, windy times, dust eroded from the land was blown far out to sea, depositing iron salts; and the iron, always in short supply in the ocean, made life bloom.

But now Millo grabbed her arm and pointed. A little farther out to sea, close to a larger, slush-capped hole, seals lay on the ice. They were brown slabs of limp flesh, totally relaxed, frost sparkling on their fur. Seals were always attracted to such holes, so they could breathe or come up to bask.

Jahna thrilled at the opportunity here.

With immense care, making as little noise as possible, Jahna and Millo made their way across the ice. If one of the seals raised its head, they froze in place, crouching down against the ice, until the seal had relaxed again. Meanwhile, a moaning wind rose. Jahna welcomed it. She wasn't interested in the weather right now; she had eyes, ears for nothing but the seals. But the wind helped mask their crackling footsteps.

They were almost there, almost close enough to touch the nearest seals. They raised their harpoons.

Then, without warning, the wind howled like a wounded animal.

The seals woke up, startled. They looked around, honking, and with liquid grace and speed they slid into the water. Millo howled his frustration and hurled his harpoon anyway; it slid uselessly into the water and out of sight.

But Jahna had looked up. A wall of wind-driven snow was descending on them, turning the world white.

Jahna grabbed Millo's hand and dragged him into the shelter of an obtruding block of ice. They huddled up against the ice, knees tucked against their chests. The wind screamed through hollows and flutings in the ice, too loud for her to hear her own voice, too loud to think.

Then the snow was on them.

She could see nothing but white—no sea, no horizon, no sky. It was as if they had been thrust inside an egg, she thought, a perfect, closed-over egg, sealed off from the world.

Soon the snow was sticking to their furs and piling up against the ice wall. She knew there was a danger that the snow would drift, here in the lee of this boulder, and she tried to clear away the gathering layers of sharp white crystals.

But the storm went on, and on. And with every heartbeat that passed, the chances were that Rood and the others were getting farther and farther away.

Millo's patience ran out. He pushed her away and stood up, but the swirling wind almost knocked him off his feet. She pulled him back down.

"No!" he screamed through the wind, struggling. "We'll die if we stay here."

"We'll die if we leave," she yelled back. "Look at the snow! Listen to the wind! Think—which way is the land?"

He turned vaguely, his small round face battered by the snow.

"We already made a bad mistake," she said. "We didn't see the storm coming. What does your soul tell you to do? What does Millo, your great-grandfather, tell you?" She could probably have overpowered him, just forced him to stay, but that would have been wrong. She had to convince him to stay put. For if he chose to leave—well, that was his prerogative.

At last he relented. With tears freezing to his cheeks he dropped back to the ice and huddled up against his sister. She held him until the weeping was done.

She kept up her routine of clearing off the loose snow. But as darkness fell—as the bubble of white turned gray, then black, with no letup in the storm—she became increasingly weary, hungry, and thirsty.

At last she couldn't fight off the sleep any longer. Just for a while, she thought; I will rest just for a while, and wake before the snow gets too thick. She dreamed of rocking, as if she were an infant in her father's arms.

When she woke she felt the weight of her brother's head on her lap. The noise of the storm was gone. She was in darkness; but it was warm here, dark, warm, safe. She closed her eyes and settled back. It would surely do no harm to rest a little longer.

But now Millo gasped, as if struggling for air. She remembered his dream, of darkness and immersion and drowning. Maybe she was in the same dream now.

Darkness.

In sudden panic Jahna pushed Millo away. Reaching up, she felt a thick layer of loose snow above her. She forced herself to her feet, pushing her face through the clinging snow.

And found herself in dazzling light. She gasped in the sudden richness of the clean, cold air. The sky was a perfect deep blue dome through which the sun sailed. She gazed around at a landscape of jumbled ice blocks embedded in blue-gray pack ice, scattered with frost and snow drifts, all of it unfamiliar. She was waist-deep in snow. She had been lucky to wake when she did, she knew; the drifting snow had kept her warm, but had nearly suffocated her.

She reached down, pushing away the snow, until she found Millo's shoulders. She hauled him out into the air. Soon he was blinking in the light and rubbing his eyes. The snow where he had been lying had turned piss-yellow. "Are you all right?" She cleared the snow from his hair and face, took off his mittens and manipulated his fingers. "Can you feel your toes?"

"I'm thirsty," he said plaintively.

"I know."

"I want Rood. I want Mesni."

"I know." Jahna was furious with herself. Careless, careless again, to have fallen asleep like that. And it was carelessness that might yet cost Jahna her life and Millo his. "Let's get back to the headland."

"All right."

She put on her mittens and took his hand. They walked around the ice block that had sheltered them, back the way they had come yesterday. There was no headland. She could make out the land, but it was a low, worn-looking shore, blanketed by a crisp layer of unbroken snow.

Millo moaned, "Where's Rood?"

For a time Jahna struggled to accept what she was seeing. Everything had been made unfamiliar by the spring storm. And her knowledge of the land was not as deep as her father's. But still she could see that that was not the shore she had left before the storm. *Give me strength, Jahna, mother of my father.* "I think the pack ice must have broken up during the storm. We drifted over the sea—" she remembered now those dreams of languid rocking "—and finished up here."

"I don't recognize that place," Millo said, pointing to the land.

"We must have been carried a long way."

"Well," Millo said, businesslike, "that's where we've got to go. Back to the land. Isn't it, Jahna?"

"Yes. That's where we've got to go."

"Come on then." He took her hand. "This is the way. Watch your step."

She let him lead her.

They trekked along the coast. Blanketed by the snow, the land was silent. Hardly anything moved—just an occasional arctic fox, a bedraggled gull, an owl—and the quiet was eerie, unnerving.

It was difficult walking through the heaped-up snow, even close to the shore, especially for Millo with his shorter legs. They had no idea where they were, no idea how far the drifting ice might have carried them. They didn't even know if they were walking back the way they had come, toward the headland. At that they were lucky, Jahna reflected with a shudder, that the ice floe hadn't simply carried them out to sea, where, helpless, they would quickly have frozen to death.

They found a stream running fast enough to have stayed clear of this unseasonal snow. They bent to drink, up to their elbows in snow, their breath steaming. Jahna was relieved. If they had not found fresh water they might have been forced to eat snow. That would have quenched their thirst but it would have put out the fire that burned inside their bodies—and, as everybody knew, when that happened, you died.

Water, then. But they found no food, none at all. They walked on.

They stuck to the coast, feeling unwilling to penetrate that central inland silence. There were many dangers there—not the least of which were people.

As primates with bodies built for tropical climes strove to survive the rapidly changing extremes of the Pleistocene, they had built on the ancient traits they had inherited from the wordless creatures of the forests: on bonds of kinship and cooperation.

The clans scattered over Eurasia and Africa lived in almost complete isolation from one another. And the isolation went very deep. Fifty kilometers from Jahna's birthplace lived people who spoke a language more different from hers than Finnish would be from Chinese. In the days of Far and even Pebble, there had been a transcontinental uniformity; now there could be significant differences between one river valley and the next. Humans were capable of altruism so generous one would suffer injury, maiming, even death to save another—and yet they indulged in extreme xenophobia, even deliberate and purposeful genocide. But in a harsh land where food was short, it made sense for members of a community to support one another selflessly—and to fend off others, who might steal scarce resources. Even genocide had a certain horrible logic.

If the children were discovered by strangers, it was possible Jahna's life would be spared—but only so she could be taken for sex. Her best hope would be to fall pregnant, and win the loyalty of one of the men. But she would always be lowly, never one of the true people. Millo, meanwhile, would simply be killed, perhaps after a little sport. She knew this was so. She had seen it happen among her own kind. So it was best they remain undiscovered.

As the children plodded on, their hunger gnawed.

They crossed a low rocky ridge. In its lee a stand of spruce had grown—dwarfed. The trees were no taller than Jahna was, but in the rock's shelter they were at least able to lift up from the ground.

Suddenly Jahna grabbed Millo and unceremoniously dumped him to the ground. Their bodies concealed, they poked their heads over the ridge.

On a frozen pond beyond the ridge walked a small flock of ptarmigan. The birds were pecking at the ice, plunging their beaks into cracks and leads. They were brilliant white against the ice's steely blue gray. These early-arriving birds were invisible against the snow, but they would stand out brightly against the greens and browns of the later spring.

"Come on," she said. They turned and slithered down the ridge, back to the little stand of spruce.

Jahna selected a fine, supple young tree. With a stone ax from her pocket, she quickly felled it, a hand's breadth above the snow, and she lopped away its crown, leaving a length of trunk nearly as tall as she was. Now, with Millo's help, she made a notch in the trunk and drove in a wedge. The trunk split easily, leaving her with a thin, springy strip. She began to scrape it quickly. Meanwhile Millo peeled the bark off the rest of the trunk. He split it up into fibers and quickly wove it together into a length of string. The bow was so unfinished it had bits of string dangling where they had been hastily tied. Not perfect, she thought, but it would serve its purpose.

She turned hastily to splitting arrows off the remnants of the trunk. There was no fire to harden the arrows, of course—and, more seriously, no feathers to serve as flights. So she improvised; she took bits of peeled-off bark and jammed them in slits in her arrows.

They worked as fast as they could. But the sun had slid a little further down the sky by the time she was done.

She poked her head and shoulders above the ridge once more, wielding her bow. The birds were still there. She took aim, pulling back the bowstring.

The first arrow went so wide it didn't even disturb the birds. The second served only to startle them, and the birds took off, shrieking in protest, their shining wings rattling. She loosed off her last shot—a much more difficult attempt at a moving target—but one of the birds crumpled and fell out of the sky.

Whooping, brother and sister clambered over the ridge and ran down to the frozen pond. The bird lay sprawled on the ice, a splash of blood on its ragged feathers. The children knew better than to rush on to the ice. Millo found a length of spruce branch. They lay flat on their bellies on the firm land at the edge of the ice and used the branch to bring the bird to the shore.

In death the bird looked ugly, ungainly. But Jahna cupped its small head in her hands. She took a bit of snow, let it melt into her palm, and trickled the water into the bird's unmoving beak: a final drink. "Thank you," she said. It was important to pay this kind of respect to animals and plants alike. The world was bountiful—but only so long as you did not trouble it too much.

When the little ceremony was done, Jahna quickly plucked the bird, slit open its belly, and flensed it. She folded up the skin and put it in her pocket: she would make better arrows tomorrow, with the feathers the ptarmigan had given her.

They ate the meat raw, the blood trickling down their cheeks and making crimson spots in the snow beneath them. It was a moment of triumph. But Jahna's satisfaction at the kill did not last long. The light was fading, and the air was growing colder.

They would die without shelter.

Her bow on her back, the last of the bird's meat in her mouth, Jahna led Millo a little way inland. Soon they came to an open, snow-covered plain. Toward the center of the meadow, the snow came almost up to her knees.

Good enough.

She shaped blocks out of the snow around her. It was hard work; she had nothing to use but her hands and stone blades, and the upper layers of snow were soft and crumbled easily. But deeper down the snow was compressed and satisfyingly hard.

She began to pile the blocks in a tight ring around herself. Millo joined in with a will. Soon they were building a circular wall of snow blocks around an increasingly deep pit. With care they turned their spiraling lines of blocks inward, until they had made a neat dome shape. Jahna punched a tunnel into the wall through which they could come and go, and Millo smoothed over the dome's surface, inside and out.

The snow house was small, rough and ready, but it would do.

The light was fading fast now, and the first wolves' calls were already echoing. Hurriedly they dug themselves into their snow house.

We are more secure than last night, Jahna thought as they huddled together for warmth. *But tomorrow we must find more food.*

And we must build a fire.

II

The hunters returned from the sea. They dispersed among their families, bearing the food they had brought. There were no expressions of gratitude. These people had no words for *please* or *thank you*; among these hunter-gatherer folk there were no social inequalities that would have required such niceties. The food was simply shared out, according to need.

Of Jahna and Millo there was much quiet talk.

Mesni, mother of Millo and Jahna, visibly strove for self-control. She went about the tasks of the day, caring for her infant, gutting the fish and preparing the rest of the ocean harvest Rood had brought home. But sometimes she would put down her knife or her bowls and give way to open despair. She even wept.

She became insane with grief: that was how it seemed to Rood. The people prized themselves for their equanimity and control. To show visible anger or despair was to behave like a small child who knew no better.

As for Rood, he withdrew into himself. He stalked around the village, and out into the country, in his shame and sorrow struggling to keep his face expressionless. There was nothing he could do for Mesni. He knew she must adjust to her loss, must regain her own inner sense of calm and control.

But the loss was indeed terrible for the little community. There weren't that many of them to begin with. This little village of around twenty people consisted essentially of three large families. They were part of a more extended clan, who every spring would gather at the bank of a great river to the south of here for a great celebratory festival of trade, partner seeking, and storytelling. But, though they came from far away, there were never more than about a thousand at these gatherings: The tundra could support no higher a density of people than that.

In later times, archaeologists would find artifacts left behind by people like Rood's and wonder if some of them signified fertility magic. They did not. Fertility was never a problem for Rood's folk. Quite the opposite:

The problem was controlling their numbers. The people knew they must not overstretch the carrying capacity of the land that sustained them—and that they must stay mobile, in case of flood or fire or freeze or drought.

So they took care over the number of children they raised. They spaced their births by three or four years. There were a number of means to achieve this. Mesni had breast-fed both Jahna and Millo to advanced ages to suppress her fertility. Simple abstinence, or nonpenetrative sex, would do the trick. And, just as it always had, death stalked the very young. Disease, accident, and even predators could be relied upon to take away a good fraction of the weak.

If necessary—though Rood was grateful he had not gone through this himself—if a healthy child arrived for whom there really was no room, death could be given a helping hand.

As long as they met the basic constraint of numbers, even in this sparse landscape at the edge of the habitable world, Rood's people ate well, enjoyed much leisure and, with their nonhierarchical, respectful society, were granted great health in body and mind. Rood inhabited a boggy, half-frozen Eden—even if a price had to be paid in countless small lives snuffed out in the cold and regretful dark.

But none of this grim calculus applied to Millo and Jahna.

They had both arrived at a time when their parents had been able to cope with supporting them. They had survived the hazards of early childhood. They were growing healthy and intelligent. Jahna had even been approaching her menarche, so that Rood had been anticipating his first grandchild. Now, thanks to a freak spring storm and his own unforgivable carelessness, all of that investment in energy and love had been taken away from him.

Preoccupied, Rood had walked out of the settlement. He was approaching the crude shantytown of the boneheads.

The boneheads looked up dully as he passed. Some of them were gorging on scraps of narwhal skin. One cow had an infant clamped to her scrawny breast; she turned away from him, cowering. The boneheads had no place in this land owned by human beings. Indeed the boneheads would have starved if not for the largesse, and waste, of the people. Neither animal nor person, nothing about the boneheads was worthy of respect. The boneheads didn't even have *names*.

But they could be useful.

He came across one cow younger than the rest. In fact she was the cow whom Jahna had tormented not long before the disastrous expedition to the sea.

She looked up at him dully, her absurdly flat skull smeared with dirt. He knew this one was the same age as Jahna, but she was more advanced than his daughter; the boneheads grew up faster, lived harder, died younger. She sat in the dirt, dressed in an untied skin wrap, toying with a worn, broken pendant. The boneheads seemed to have enough mind to be fascinated by the artifacts of the people, yet not enough to make them for themselves: You could buy whatever you wanted from a bonehead for the sake of a mammoth-ivory bead or a carved bone harpoon.

On an impulse he didn't fully understand, Rood reached down and pulled the wrap away from the cow's body. If not for that pulled-forward face, that flattened head, her body wasn't so bad, he thought; she had yet to develop the full, bearlike stockiness of the adults.

He found an erection pushing out of his own wrap.

He knelt down, grabbed the cow's ankles, and twisted her onto her back. She complied easily, spreading her legs; evidently it wasn't the first time she had been used like this. Probing at her warm flesh he found her crotch and anus were crusted with filth. He scraped her clean with his fingers.

And then, with a single, savage thrust, he entered her. For a brief, oceanic time, he was able to forget that disastrous moment when the storm closed in and he realized he had lost Jahna and Millo on the ice.

But it was quickly over. Pulling away from the girl he felt a deep, stomach-churning sense of revulsion. He used a corner of his wrap to clean himself.

The girl, still naked, rolled on her back and held up her hands, pleading silently.

Around his neck he wore a pendant, the tooth of a cave bear. He ripped it off his neck, breaking its deerskin thong, and threw it in the dirt. The bonehead girl scrabbled for the pendant and held it up before her face, turning it over and over, peering into its endless mysteries. A trickle of blood seeped from her bruised thighs.

Jahna and Millo continued to follow the coast, still hoping to come across the headland where they had last seen their father and his companions. At night they built snow houses, if there was snow, or slept under hastily constructed lean-tos. Jahna's bow and Millo's fast reflexes kept them provided with some food; small animals and birds.

They could keep themselves fed, even build shelter. But already Millo had spent one agonizing night after unwisely eating a fish that had not been properly gutted. Worst of all they had failed, night after night, to make a fire, no matter how earnestly they rubbed sticks or smashed bits of rock together. And that was costing them dearly. The uncooked meat was beginning to make Jahna's teeth and stomach ache, and in the dead of night she imagined she would never be truly warm again.

The children plodded on; they had no choice. But they were losing weight, growing more tired every day, their clothing more ragged. They were slowly dying, Jahna knew. Though they were guided by the elder spirits within them, they did not yet know all they needed to know to keep themselves alive.

They came to a place where the tree line had strayed north, so they had to push through a scrap of forest. The trees, pines and spruce, grew sparse and tangled: gaunt and without leaves, they looked oddly frail. The path the children followed, worn by deer or goats, was soft with moss. It twisted through the trees, passing occasionally through more open glades.

As the light faded, ending another dismal day, the shadows of the trees striped over the ground, and the undergrowth turned black. Jahna and Millo were five million years removed from Capo, their last forest-dwelling ancestor, and to them the forest was a place well stocked with monsters and demons. They hurried forward anxiously.

At last they burst out of the trees. They found themselves on a scrap of snow-littered grassland where the yellow sward terminated in a ragged cliff edge. Beyond that blunt horizon the sea rolled, the pack ice distantly groaning and cracking, as it always did.

But the children faced a wall of flesh and antlers. It was a herd of megaloceros—creatures that would one day be called Irish elk. They walked massively, cropping at the new grass that poked hopefully through the scattered snow.

In the van was a huge male. He peered down his long nose at the children. His back bore a fleshy hump, a mound of fat to help sustain him through harsh times; in this early spring the hump was deflated. And his antlers, each twice as wide as a human was tall, were great heavy sculptures oddly like the open hands of a giant, with fingerlike tines branching off smooth palms.

There were thousands of deer in this herd alone, crowding out of the children's sight. Like many giant herbivores in this paradoxically rich time, the megaloceros flourished in vast migrant crowds, wandering all across the Old World from Britain to Siberia and China. And this vast herd was bearing down on Jahna and Millo. It was a slow-moving barrier, immense antlers clattering, stomachs rumbling. The air was full of the overwhelming stink of musk and dung.

The children needed badly to get out of the way. Jahna saw immediately that they couldn't evade the herd by running inland; it was too big, too widespread for that. The deer surely wouldn't penetrate far into the forest, but they would force the children back into that deepening darkness, which was a place she really didn't want to go back into.

On impulse she grabbed her brother's hand. "Come on. The cliff!"

They ran across the frozen grass. The cliff edge sloped away sharply beneath a lip of turf. Hastily the children scrambled down. The bow on Jahna's back caught on outcroppings of the rock, slowing her down. But they made it. They huddled on a narrow ledge, peering up at the ocean of black-brown fur that washed slowly along the cliff top.

The huge male looked on indifferently. Then he turned away, his burdened head dipping.

The antlers were heavy to carry, like weights held at arms' length, and the buck's neck had been redesigned to bear that load, with huge vertebrae and muscles like cables. The antlers were for sexual display—and for fighting; it was an awesome sight when two of these giant bucks clashed, heads down. But those great antlers would doom these animals. When the ice retreated and their habitat shriveled, there would be a selection pressure for smaller body sizes. While other species shrank to fit, the megaloceros would prove unable to give up their elaborate sexual displays. They had become overspecialized, their tremendous antlers overexpensive, and they would prove unable to cope with change.

The children heard a muffled growl. Jahna thought she saw a pale form, low-slung, stocky, move over the snow like a muscled ghost, trailing the deer. It might have been a cave lion. She shuddered.

"What now?" Millo whispered. "We can't stay *here*."

"No." Jahna cast around. She saw that their ledge led down the cliff face to a hollow a few body's lengths below. "That way," she said. "I think it's a cave."

He nodded curtly. He led the way, edging his way down the narrow ledge, clinging to the chalk. But he was more frightened than he was prepared to admit, she realized.

At last, the perilous descent over, they threw themselves into the hollow and lay panting on the rough floor. The cave, worn in the chalk, reached back into dark recesses. The floor was littered with guano and bits of eggshell. It must be used as a nesting ground, by gulls, perhaps. There were blackened patches scattered over the floor—not hearths, but obviously the sites of fires.

"Look," said Millo, his voice full of wonder. "*Mussels*."

He was right. The little shellfish were piled up in a low heap, surrounded by a scattering of flint flakes. A flicker of curiosity made her wonder how they had got there. But hunger spoke louder, and the two of them fell on the mussels. Frantically they tried to prize open the shells with their fingers and stone blades, but the shells were stubborn and would not yield.

"*Graah.*"

They both whirled.

The gravely voice had come out of the darkness at the back of the cave. A figure came forward. It was a burly man, dressed in a wrap of what looked like deer hide—no, Jahna thought, not a *man*. He had a vast, prominent nose, and powerful stocky legs, and huge hands. This was a bonehead, a massive bull. He glared at them.

The children backed away, clutching at each other.

He had no name. His people did not give themselves names. He thought of himself as the Old Man. And he was old, old for his kind, nearly forty years old.

He had lived alone for thirty of those years.

He had been dozing at the back of this cave, in the smoky, comforting glow of the torches he kept burning there. He had spent the early morning combing the beaches below the cliffs at low tide, seeking shellfish. With the coming of evening he would soon have woken up anyway; evening was his favorite time of day.

But he had been disturbed early by the noise and commotion at the cave's entrance. Thinking it might be gulls coming after his piles of shellfish—or something worse, an arctic fox maybe—he had come lumbering out into the light.

Not gulls, not a fox. Here were two children. Their bodies were tall and ludicrously spindly, their limbs shriveled and their shoulders narrow. Their faces were flat, as if squashed back by a mighty punch, their chins were pointed, and their heads bulged upward into comical swellings like huge fungi.

Skinny folk. Always skinny folk. He felt a vast weariness—and an echo of the loneliness that had once plagued his every waking moment and poisoned his dreams.

Almost without conscious thought he moved toward the children, his huge hands outstretched. He could crush their skulls with a single squeeze, or crack them together like two birds' eggs, and that would be the end of it. The bones of more than one skinny robber littered the rocky beach below this cave; and more would join them before he grew too old to defend this, his last bastion.

The children squealed, grabbed each other, and scurried to the wall of the cave. But the taller one, a girl, pushed the other behind her. She was terrified, he could see that, but she was trying to defend her brother. And she was holding her nerve. Though panic piss trickled down the boy's bare legs the girl kept herself under control. She dug into her jerkin and pulled out something that dangled on a string around her neck. *"Bonehead! Bonehead man! Leave us alone and I'll give you this! Pretty, pretty magic, bonehead man!"*

The Old Man's deep-set eyes glittered.

The pendant was a bit of quartz, a little obelisk, gleaming and transparent; its faces had been polished to shining smoothness, and one side had been painstakingly carved into a design that caught your eye and dazzled your mind. The girl swung the amulet back and forth, trying to draw his eyes, and she stepped forward from the wall. *"Bonehead man, pretty, pretty . . ."* The Old Man peered into blue eyes that stared straight back at him in that unsettling, direct way of the skinnies: a predator's gaze.

He reached out and flicked at the amulet. It flew around the girl's neck and smashed against the wall behind her. She yelped, for its leather string had burned her neck. The Old Man reached out again. It could be over in a heartbeat.

But the children were jabbering again, in their fast, complicated language. *"Make him go away! Oh, make him go away!"* *"It's all right, Millo. Don't be afraid. Your great-grandfather is inside you. He will help you."*

The Old Man let his huge hands drop to his sides.

He looked back at the mussels they had tried to take. The shells were scraped and chipped—one showed teeth marks—but not one was broken open. These children were helpless, even more so than most of their kind. They couldn't even steal his mussels.

It had been a long time since voices of any kind had been heard in this cave—any save his own, and the ugly cawing of gulls or the barking of foxes.

Not quite understanding why, he stalked off to the back of his cave. Here he stored his meat, his tools, and a stock of wood. He brought back an armful of pine logs, brought down from the forested area at the top of the cliff, and dumped them close to the entrance of the cave. Now he fetched one of his torches, a pine branch thick with resin and bound up with fat-laden sealskin. The torch burned steadily but smokily, and would stay alight all day. He set the torch on the ground and began to heap wood over it.

The children still cowered against the wall, eyes wide, staring at him. The boy pointed at the ground. *"Look. Where's his hearth? He's making a mess . . ."* The girl clamped her hand over his mouth.

When the fire was burning brightly, he kicked it open to expose red-hot burning logs within. Then he picked up a handful of mussels and threw them into the fire. The mussels' shells quickly popped open. He fished them out with a stick and scooped out their delicious, salty contents with a blunt finger, one after another.

The boy squirmed and got his mouth free. *"I can smell them. I'm hungry."*

"Hold still; just hold still."

When the Old Man had had his fill of the mussels he lifted his leg, let out a luxurious fart, and clambered painfully to his feet. He lumbered to the entrance to his cave. There he sat down with one leg folded under him, the other straight out, with his skin wrap over his legs and crotch. He picked up a flint cobble he had left there days before. Using a granite pebble as a hammer-stone he quickly began to shape a core from the flint. Soon waste flakes began to accumulate around his legs. He had seen dolphins today. There was a good chance one of those fat, lithe creatures might be washed up on the shore in the next day or two, and he needed to be prepared, to have the right tools ready. He wasn't planning, exactly—he wasn't thinking as a skinny might have thought—but a deep intuition of his environment shaped his actions and choices.

As he let his hands work—shaping this lump of compressed Cretaceous fossils, as the hands of his ancestors had worked for two hundred and fifty millennia—he gazed out to the west, where the sun was starting to set over the Atlantic, turning the water to a sheet of fire.

Behind him, unnoticed, Jahna and Millo crept to the fire, threw on more mussels, and gulped down their salty flesh.

As the days passed, the spring thaw advanced quickly. The lakes melted. Waterfalls that had spent the winter crusted with ice began to bubble and flow. Even the sea ice began to break up.

It was time for the gathering. It was a much-anticipated treat, a highlight of the year—despite the walk of several days across the tundra.

Not everybody could go: The very young, the old, and the ill could not make the journey, and some had to remain behind to look after them. This year, for the first time in many years, Rood and Mesni were freed of the burden of children—save for their youngest, still an infant small enough to be carried—and were able to travel.

Rood would not have chosen the situation; of course not. But he believed they must make the best of their damaged lives, and he urged Mesni to come with him to the gathering. But Mesni wanted to stay at home. She turned away from him, retreating into her dark sadness. So

Rood decided to walk with Olith, Mesni's sister, the aunt of his children. Olith herself had one grown boy, but his father had died of a coughing illness two winters ago, leaving Olith alone.

The party set off across the tundra.

In this brief interval of warmth and light, the ground underfoot was full of life, saxifrages, tundra flowers, grasses, and lichens. Clouds of insects gathered in the moist air above the ponds, mating frantically. Great flocks of geese, ducks, and waders fed and rested on the tundra's shallow lakes. Olith, taking Rood's arm, pointed out mallards, swans, snow geese, divers, loons, and cranes that looped grandly, filling the air with their clattering calls. In this place where the trees lay flat, many of these birds built their nests on the ground. When they stepped too close to a jaeger's nest, two birds dived at them, squawking ferociously. And, though most of the migrant herbivores had yet to return, the people glimpsed great herds of deer and mammoth, washing across the landscape like the shadows of clouds.

Yet how strange it was, Rood thought, that if he were to dig just a few arms' lengths anywhere under this carpet of crowded color and motion, he would find the ice, the frozen ground where nothing could live.

"It has been too long since I walked this way," said Rood. "I had forgotten what it is like."

Olith squeezed his arm and moved closer to him. "I know how you must feel—"

"That every blade of grass, every dancing saxifrage, is a torture, a beauty I do not deserve." Distantly he was aware of the scent of the vegetable oil she rubbed into her cropped hair. She was not like Mesni, her sister; Olith was taller, more stringy, but her breasts were heavy.

"The children are not gone," Olith reminded him. "Their souls will be reborn when you next have children. They were not old enough to have gathered wisdom of their own. But they carried the souls of their grandparents, and they will bring joy and exuberance to—"

"I have not lain with Mesni," he said stiffly, "since we last saw Jahna and Millo. Mesni is—changed."

"It has been a long time," Olith murmured, evidently surprised.

Rood shrugged. "Not long enough for Mesni. Perhaps it will never be long enough." He looked Olith in the eyes. "I will not have more children with Mesni. I do not think she will ever want that."

Olith looked away, but dipped her head. It was, he realized, startled, a gesture of both sympathy and seduction.

That night, in the crisp cold of the open tundra, under a lean-to hastily constructed of pine branches, they lay together for the first time.

As when he took the young bonehead cow, Rood felt relief from the guilt, the constant nagging doubts. Olith meant much more to him than any bonehead animal, of course. But afterward, when Olith lay in his arms, he felt the ice close around his heart once again, as if in the midst of spring he was still stranded in the depths of winter.

After four days' steady hiking, Rood and Olith reached the riverbank.

Already hundreds of people had gathered. There were shelters set up on the bank, stacks of spears and bows, even the carcass of a great buck megaloceros. The people had marked themselves with exuberant flashes of ocher and vegetable dye. Their designs had common elements, proclaiming the unity of the greater clan, and yet were elaborate and diverse, celebrating the identity and strength of their individual bands.

Probably around five hundred people would come to this gathering— not that anybody was counting. That would comprise about half of all the people on the planet who spoke a language even remotely resembling Rood's.

The group from home who had walked with Rood and Olith fanned out. Many of them were looking for partners: perhaps for a quick spring tumble, or perhaps with a view toward a longer-term relationship. This few days' gathering was the only chance you got to meet somebody new—or to check out if the skinny kid you remembered from last year showed signs of blossoming in the way you hoped he would.

Rood spotted a woman called Dela. Round, fat, with a booming laugh, she was a capable hunter of large game. In her younger days she had been a beauty with whom Rood had lain a couple of times. He saw that she had, typically, set up a large, flamboyant shelter of stretched hide painted gaily with designs of running animals.

Rood and Olith marched down the bank. Dela welcomed him with an embrace and a hearty back slap, and she served them bark tea and fruit. Though Dela eyed Olith, evidently wondering what had become of Mesni, she kept her counsel.

A huge fire already blazed on open ground before the shelter, and somebody was throwing handfuls of fish grease onto it, making explosions and crackles. It was Dela's folk who had brought in the megaloceros. Brawny young women were carving open the deer carcass, and the smell of blood and stomach contents filled the air.

Rood and Olith sat with Dela around a low fire. Dela began to ask Rood how this year's hunting had gone so far, and he responded in kind. They talked of how the season had unfolded this year, how the animals were behaving, what damage the winter storms had done, how high the fish were jumping, on a new way somebody had found to treat a bowstring so it lasted longer before it snapped, a way somebody else had found of soaking mammoth ivory in urine so you could straighten it out.

The purpose of this gathering was to exchange information, as much as food or goods or mates. Speakers did not exaggerate success or minimize failure. To the best of their ability they spoke with detail and precision, and allowed other participants in the discussion to ask questions. Accuracy was much more important than boasting. To people who relied on culture and knowledge to keep themselves alive, information was the most important thing in the world.

At last, though, Dela was able to move on to the subject that clearly fascinated her.

"And Mesni," she said carefully. "Has she stayed home with the children? Why, Jahna must be tall now—I remember how she caught the boys' eyes even last year—and—"

"No," Rood said gently, aware of Olith's hand covering his. Dela listened in silence as he described, in painful detail, how he had lost his children to the ice storm.

When he had finished Dela sipped her tea, her eyes averted. Rood had the odd sense that she knew something, but held it back.

To fill the silence, Dela recited the story of her land.

"... And the two brothers, lost in the snow, fell at last. One died. The other rose up. He grieved for his brother. But then he saw a fox, digging under a log, its coat white on white. The fox went away. But the brother knew that a fox will return to the same spot to retrieve what it has buried. So he set a snare, and waited. When the fox returned the brother caught it. But before he could kill it the fox sang for him. It was a lament for the lost brother, like this. . . ."

Like Jo'on's Dreamtime tales, though they were a blend of myth and reality, such stories and songs were long, specific, fact-heavy. This was an oral culture. Without writing to record factual data, memory was everything. If dreams and the shaman's trances were a means of integrating copious information to aid intuitive decision making, the songs and stories were an aid to storing that information in the first place.

Remarkably, the story Dela told was itself evolving. As the story passed from one listener to another, through error and embellishment its elements changed constantly. Most of the changes were incidental details that didn't matter, churning without effect, like the coding of junk DNA. The essentials of the story—its mood, the key nodes, its point—tended to remain stable. But not always: Sometimes a major adaptation would take place, by a speaker's intention or accident, and if the new element improved the story, it would be retained. The stories, like other aspects of the people's culture, had begun an evolutionary destiny of their own, played out in the arenas of the new humans' roomy minds.

But Dela's story was more than a mere tale, or aid to memory. With her story, by her setting out the narrative of her land and by her listeners' accepting it by hearing it, she was proclaiming a kind of title. Only by knowing the land well enough to tell its story truly could you affirm your right to that land. There were no written contracts here, no deeds, no courts; the only validity for Dela's claim came from the relationship of narrator to listener, reaffirmed at gatherings like this.

There was a ferocious sizzling noise, a great celebratory roar from outside the shelter. The first great slabs of the butchered megaloceros had been hurled on to the fire. Soon the mouth-watering smell of its meat filled the air. The festivities of the night began.

There was much eating, dancing, hollering. And at the end of the night, Rood was surprised when Dela approached him.

"Listen to me now, Rood. I am your friend. Once we lay together."

"Actually twice," he said with a rueful smile.

"Twice, then. What I say to you now I say out of friendship, and not to cause you suffering."

He frowned. "What are you trying to tell me?'

She sighed. "There is a tale. I heard it here, not two days ago; a group from the south told it. They say that in a stretch of worthless ground near the coast, a bonehead infests a cliff-top cave. Yes? And in that cave—so it is said, so a hunter claims to have seen—two children are living."

He didn't understand. "Bonehead cubs?"

"No. Not boneheads. *People*. The hunter, engrossed in his prey, saw all this from a distance. One of the children—so the hunter said—is a girl, maybe so high." She held up her hand. "And the other—"

"A boy," breathed Rood. "A little boy."

"I apologize for telling you this," said Dela.

Rood understood. Dela perceived that Rood had accepted his loss. Now she had ignited the cold pain of hope in his deadened heart once more. "Tomorrow," he said thickly. "Tomorrow you will show this hunter to me. And then—"

"Yes. But not tonight."

Later, in the deepest night, Olith lay with Rood, but he was restless.

"Morning will soon come," she whispered. "And then you will leave."

"Yes," he said. "Olith—come with me."

She thought briefly, then nodded. It was not wise for him to travel alone. She heard his teeth grind. She touched his jaw, felt the tense muscles there. "What is it?"

"If there is a bonehead buck, if he has harmed them—"

She crooned, "Your mind flies too far ahead; give your body a chance to catch up. Sleep now."

But for Rood, sleep proved impossible.

III

The bonehead returned to the cave. Jahna saw that he had a seal—the *whole animal*, a fat, heavy male—slung over one shoulder. Even now, after weeks in this cliff-top cave, his strength could surprise her.

Millo came running forward, his bonehead-style skin wrap flying. "A seal! A seal! We'll eat well tonight!" He hugged the bonehead's tree-trunk legs.

Just as he used to hug his father's. Jahna pushed the unwelcome thought out of her mind; it had no place here, and she must be strong.

The bonehead, perspiring from the effort of hauling such a weight up the cliff path from the beach, peered down at the boy. He made a string of guttural, grunting noises, a jabber that meant nothing . . . or at least Jahna didn't think it meant anything. Sometimes she wondered if he spoke words—bonehead words, what a strange idea—that she just couldn't recognize.

She walked forward and pointed to the rear of the cave. "Put the seal down there," she commanded. "We'll soon get it butchered. Look, I've built a fire already."

And so she had. Days ago she had dug out a pit to serve as a proper hearth, and had swept over the ugly ash stains that had randomly scarred the floor. Likewise she had sorted out the clutter of this cave. It had been a jumble, with food scraps and bits of skin and tools all mixed up with all sorts of waste. Now it almost seemed, well, habitable.

For a person, that is. It didn't occur to her to wonder what "habitable" might mean for the huge creature she thought of as the bonehead.

Right now the bonehead didn't seem happy. He was unpredictable like that. Growling, he dumped the seal on the floor. Then, sweating, filthy, his skin crusted with salt from the sea, he stamped off to the back of the cave for one of his naps.

Jahna and Millo fell to slicing open the seal carcass. It had been killed by a spear thrust to the heart, leaving a wide and ugly puncture, and Jahna quailed as she imagined the battle that must have preceded this killing strike. But with their sharp stone blades the children's small hands made efficient work of flensing and dismembering the big mammal. Soon the first slices of seal belly were on the fire.

The bonehead, as was his wont, woke up when the meat was ready. The children ate their meat well-cooked. The bonehead preferred his raw, or almost. He grabbed a big steak out of the fire, took it to his favorite spot by the entrance, and pulled at the meat with his teeth, facing the setting sun. He ate a *lot* of meat, about twice as much as Rood, say. But then he worked very hard, all the time.

It was an oddly domestic scene. But it had been like this for the weeks since Jahna and Millo had stumbled in here. Somehow it worked.

It had always hurt the Old Man to live alone; his kind were intensely social. But he had suffered more than just loneliness. His mind was of the old compartmented design. Much of what went on inside his cavernous skull was all but unconscious; it was as if his hands made his flint tools, not *him*. It was only when he was with people that he became truly alive, fully, intensely aware; it was as if without others he was in a dream, only half-conscious. To the Old Man's kind, other people were the brightest, most active things in the landscape. With no other people around, the world was dull, lifeless, static.

That was why he had tolerated the skinny children, with their jabber and their meddling, why he had fed and even clothed them. And why he would soon face death.

Jahna whispered, "Millo. Look." Watching to be sure the bonehead couldn't see, she brushed aside some dirt, and revealed a collection of blackened bones.

Millo gasped. He picked up a skull. It had a protruding face and a thick ridge over its gaping eyes. But it was small, smaller than Millo's own head; it must have been a child. "Where did you find them?"

"In the ground," she whispered. "At the front of the cave, when I was clearing up."

Millo dropped the skull; it clattered onto the other bones. The bonehead looked around dully. "It's scary," whispered Millo. "Maybe he killed it. The bonehead. Maybe he eats children."

"No, silly," Jahna said. Seeing her brother's fear was real, she put her arms around him. "He probably just put it in the ground when it was dead."

But Millo was shivering. She hadn't meant to scare him. She pushed the skull out of his sight and, to calm him, began to tell him a story.

"Listen to me now. Long, long ago, the people were like the dead. The world was dark and their eyes were dull. They lived in a camp as they do now, and they did the things they do now. But everything was dark, not real, like shadows. One day a young man came to the camp. He was like the dead too, but he was curious—different. He liked to go fishing and hunting. But he would always go deeper into the sea than anybody else. The people wondered why . . ."

As she crooned the story, Millo relaxed against her, sinking into sleep just as the sun sank into the ocean. Even the big bonehead was dozing, she saw, slumped against a wall, belching softly. Perhaps he was listening too.

Her story was a creation myth, a legend already more than twenty thousand years old. Such tales—which said that Jahna's group were the pinnacle of creation, that theirs was the only right way, and that all others were less than human—taught the people to care passionately about themselves, their kin, and a few treasured ideals.

But to the exclusion of all other humans, let alone such nonpeople as the Old Man's kind.

". . . One day they saw that the young man was with a sea lion. He was swimming in the waves with it. And he was making love to it. Enraged, the people drove out the young man, and they caught the sea lion. But when they butchered it they found a fish inside, in its womb. It was a fat fish." She meant a eulachon. "The fish had been fathered by the young man. He was neither person nor fish, but something different. So the people threw the fish-boy on their fire. His head burst into flames and made a bright light that dazzled them. So the fish-boy flew into the sky. The sky was dark, of course. There he sought the place where the light was hiding, because the fish-boy thought he could trick the light to come down to the dark world. And then . . ."

And then her father walked in.

The Old Man was a Neandertal.

His kind had endured in Europe, through the savage swings of the Ice Age, for a quarter of a million years. In their way the robust folk had been supremely successful. They had found ways to live here in the most marginal of environments, on the edge of the world, where the climate was not only harsh but could vary treacherously fast, where animal and plant resources were sparse and prone to fluctuate unpredictably.

For a long time they had even been able to resist the children of Mother. During warming pulses the new humans pushed into Europe from the south. But with their stocky bodies and big air-warming sinuses and heavily meat-tolerant digestion systems, the robusts were better able to withstand the cold than the moderns. And their bearlike builds made them formidable infighters: tough opponents for the humans, better technology or not. Then, when the cold intensified again, the moderns would retreat back to the south, and the robust folk could repopulate their old lands.

This had happened over and over. In southern Europe and the Middle East there were caves and other sites where layers of human detritus were overlaid by Neandertal waste, only to be reoccupied by humans again.

But during the last thaw the moderns had looked again to Europe and Asia. They had advanced, culturally and technologically. And this time the robusts hadn't been able to resist. Gradually the robusts were eliminated across much of Asia, and pushed back into their chill fortress, Europe.

The Old Man had been ten years old when skinny hunters had first stumbled on his people's encampment.

The camp had been constructed on a south-facing riverbank a few kilometers back from the cliff top, placed close to the trails of the great herds of migrant herbivores that washed over the landscape. They lived here as they had always lived, waiting for the seasons to bring the herds to their porch. The riverbank had been a good place.

Until the skinnies came.

It wasn't a war. The engagement had been much more complex, messy, and protracted than that.

At first there had even been a kind of trade, as the skinnies swapped sea produce for meat from the giant animals the people were able to kill with their thrusting spears and great strength. But the skinnies seemed to want more and more. And, as they came roaming over the land with their strange slender spears and the bits of wood that would hurl them far, the skinny hunters were just too effective. Soon the animals grew wary and changed their habits. No longer did they follow their old trails and gather at the lakes and ponds and rivers, and the robusts had to roam far in search of the prey that had once come to them.

Meanwhile, for the Old Man's folk, contact with the skinnies had inevitably increased.

There had been sex, willing and unwilling. There had been fights. If you got a skinny in close combat you could crush his or her spine, or smash that big bubble skull with a single punch. But the skinnies wouldn't close with you. They struck from a distance, with their hard-thrown spears and flying arrows. And the people could not strike back: even after tens of millennia of living alongside the skinnies the descendants of Pebble had failed to copy even their simplest innovations. Besides, as the skinnies ran around you hollering to each other in their birdlike voices—with their elaborately painted clothes and bodies, and with a restless blur of speed as if the world was too slow, too static for them—it was hard to even *see* them. You couldn't fight what you couldn't see.

Eventually there had come a day when the skinnies had decided they wanted the place where the Old Man's people lived, their riverbank home.

It had been simple for them. They had killed most of the men, and some of the women. They chased the survivors away, to forage for themselves as best they could. By the time the Old Man returned, from a solo expedition to the river, the skinnies were burning the huts and cleaning out the caves, places where the Old Man's grandmothers' bones lay a hundred generations deep.

After that, the people wandered aimlessly, sedentary creatures forced to be nomads. If they tried to set up a new base, the skinnies would quickly break it up again. Many of them starved.

At last, inevitably, they had been drawn to the camps of the skinnies. Even now, many of his kind still lived on, but they were like the bone-heads who followed Jahna's encampment, where they lived like rats on garbage, and even then only as long as the skinnies tolerated them. Their eventual fate was already obvious.

All save the Old Man. The Old Man had stayed away from the dismal skinny places. He was not the last of his kind. But he was the last to live as his ancestors had before the coming of the moderns. He was the last to live free.

When Mother had died, just sixty thousand years before the birth of Christ, there had still been many different kinds of people in the world. There had been Mother's humanlike people in parts of Africa. In Europe and western Asia lived robust folk like Pebble, like Neandertals. In eastern Asia there were still bands of the skinny, small-brained walkers, the *Homo erectus* types. The old hominid complexity had reigned still, with many variants and subspecies and even hybrids of the different types.

With the revolution started in Mother's generation, with the great expansion that had followed, all this changed. It was not genocide; it was not planned. It was a matter of ecology. The different forms of humans were competing for the same resources. All over the world there had been a wave of extinctions—human extinctions—a wave of last contacts, of regret-free good-byes, as one hominid species after another succumbed to the dark. For a time the last of the walkers had hung on in isolation on Indonesian islands, still living much as Far had, so long ago. But when the sea levels dropped once more, the bridges to the mainland were re-established, and the moderns crossed over—and for the walkers, after a long and static history spanning some two million years, the game was up.

And so on. The outcome was inevitable. And soon the world would be empty of people—empty, save for just one kind.

After he had lost his family the Old Man had fled from the skinnies, heading ever west. But here, in this coastal cave, the Old Man had reached the western shore of Europe, the fringe of the Atlantic. The ocean was an impassable barrier. He had nowhere left to go.

Jahna's encounter with the Old Man was the last contact of all.

Rood, silhouetted against the sunset, looked dusty, hot. At his side was Olith, Jahna's aunt. Rood's eyes were wide, as he took in what he saw in the cave.

For Jahna, it was like snapping awake from a nightmare. She dropped the bit of hide she had been working, ran forward across a cave floor that suddenly seemed filthy and cluttered, and hurled herself into her father's arms. There she wept like a very small child, while her father's hands hesitantly patted the crude bonehead wrap she wore.

The bonehead roused. The shadows of the two adults, cast by the setting sun, striped over him. He raised a hand to shield his eyes. Then, bleary with sleep, heavy with meat, he struggled to get to his feet, growling.

Rood pushed the children to Olith, who held them. Then he raised a cobble over the struggling bonehead's cranium.

Jahna cried, "No!" She struggled free of Olith and grabbed her father's hand.

Rood stared down at her. And she realized she had a choice to make.

Jahna thought about it for a heartbeat. She remembered the mussels, the seals, the fires she had built. And she looked at the ugly, lumpy brow of the bonehead. She released her father's arm.

Rood let his arm fall. It was a heavy blow. The bonehead fell forward. But bonehead skulls were thick. It seemed to Jahna that the Old Man could have got up, fought on even now. But he didn't. He remained in the dirt of his cave, on his hands and knees.

It took four, five blows before Rood had gotten through his skull. Long before the last blow Jahna had turned away.

They stayed in the cave one more night, with the fallen bonehead slumped on the floor, blood pooled beneath his shattered skull. In the morning they wrapped up what was left of the seal meat, and prepared to begin the journey back. But before they left Jahna insisted they dig a hole in the ground, wide but shallow. Into the hole she dropped the bones of the infant she had found, and the big carcass of the bonehead. Then she kicked the dirt back into the hole, and tamped it down with her feet.

After they had gone the gulls came. They pecked at the bits of seal meat, and the patch of dried blood in the entrance of the cave that faced the sea.

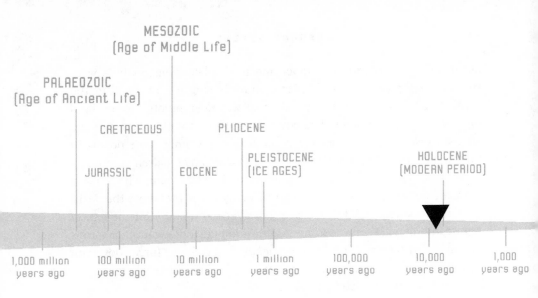

| PALAEOZOIC (Age of Ancient Life) | MESOZOIC (Age of Middle Life) | | | | | | |

CHAPTER 14

the swarming people

▼ **Anatolia, Turkey. Circa 9,600 years before present.**

I

The two girls, lying side by side, nibbled at their kernels of wild grain.

"So you like Tori better than Jaypee," said Sion.

Juna, at sixteen a year younger than her sister, flicked her hair out of her eyes. Her hair was a pale blond, strikingly bright. She said carefully, "Maybe. I think *he* likes *me* better than Jaypee does."

"But you said Tori was a runt. You said you liked the way Jaypee's hair falls when he runs, and those big thighs he has, and—"

"I know what I said," Juna said uncomfortably. "But Tori has a better—"

"Cock?"

"A better personality," Juna forced out.

Sion's pealing laughter billowed out over the empty space. A dog, slumbering in the shade of the men's hut, deigned to move one eye to check out the disturbance, then fell back asleep.

The girls were surrounded by the bare, trampled dust of the village. The place was dominated by the great slumped form of the men's hut, a ramshackle construction of timber and reeds. The women's huts were smaller satellites of this rude giant. Gravelly snoring from within the men's hut told the girls that the shaman was sleeping off another hard night of beer and visions. Nobody was moving: not the dogs, not the adults. Most of the men were out hunting; the women were dozing in their huts with their infants. There weren't even any children around.

Sion sprinkled a little more ground fennel on her grain. The fennel's aromatic oil was actually a defense evolved by the plant before the death of the dinosaurs, intended to make its leaves too slippery for the legs of boring, nibbling insects; now the result of that ancient evolutionary arms race flavored Sion's snack. "You are *joking*," said Sion. "Juna, I love you dearly. But you are the most shallow person I know. Since when has personality mattered a dried fig to *you*?"

Juna felt her face burn.

"Ah. There's something you aren't telling me." Sion studied Juna's face with a hunter's expert knowledge of her prey. "*Have you two lain together?*"

"No," Juna snapped.

Sion was still suspicious. "I didn't think Tori was lying with anybody yet. Apart from Acta, of course." Acta was one of the oldest of the men—not to mention the fattest—but he continued to prove his strength with his wily leadership of the hunts, and so he continued to assert his rights over the boys and young men. "I know Tori's getting sick of being poked with Acta's stinking dick; that's what Jaypee told me! Soon he's going to want to be with a woman, but not yet—"

Juna couldn't meet her sister's eyes—for the truth was, she *had* lain with Tori, just as Sion suspected. It had been out in the bush, with Tori boastfully full of beer. She didn't know why she'd let him do it. She hadn't even been sure he had done it right. She longed to tell her sister everything—how her bleeding had stopped, how she already felt the new life moving inside her—but how could she? Times were hard—times were always hard—and it wasn't a good time to be producing a baby by a feckless boy. She hadn't yet told Tori himself. She hadn't even told her mother, Pepule, who was herself expecting a child. "Sion, I—"

There was a hand on her arm, hot and heavy, a breath redolent with unfamiliar spices. "Hello, girls. Something on your mind?" Juna flinched away, pulling her arm free.

This was Cahl, the beer man. He was a big man, fatter even than Acta, and he wore strangely constraining clothes: a tightly sewn jacket and trousers, heavy leather shoes, a hat stuffed with straw. On his back was a heavy skin full of ale; it sloshed as he squatted down beside them. His skin was cratered, like soil after rain, and his teeth were ugly brown stumps. But his gaze, as he smiled at Juna, had a kind of predator's intensity.

Sion glared at him. "Why don't you go back where you came from? Nobody wants you here."

He frowned briefly, striving to translate what she had said. His language was different from theirs. It was a common speculation that Cahl's folk had come from somewhere far to the east, bringing their peculiar language with them. "Oh," he said at last, "*plenty* of people want me here. Some want me an awful lot. You'd be surprised what people will give me, in return for what I can give them." And he leered again, showing a mouthful of brown, rotten teeth. "Maybe we should talk about it, you and me," he said to Juna. "Maybe we should find out what we can do for each other."

"Keep away from me," Juna said tremulously.

But Cahl kept on staring at her, a snake's stare, hard and intense.

It was with relief that she heard the footsteps of the returning men, their bare feet grinding in the dirt. Their naked bodies were caked with dust, and they were obviously weary. Juna saw that once again the dozen men had returned home empty-handed save for a few rabbits and rats; bigger game was very rare.

Old man Acta had his fat arm draped over Tori's shoulders. Juna didn't want to meet the slim boy's gaze, and yet she longed to know what he was thinking. How would he react if she told him what had happened as a result of their foolish fumble?

Cahl broke away from the girls, stood up, and raised his sack of beer over his head. "Welcome the hunters!"

Acta strode up to him. His tongue hung out doglike, as if the pendulous sack contained the only drink in the world. "Cahl, my friend. I hoped you would be here. You are a better shaman than that old fool in the hut."

Sion gasped at that casual blasphemy.

Cahl handed over the beer sack. "You look like you need this."

Acta grabbed it and held it close. But a trace of his old wiliness showed in his deep, piglike eyes. "And the payment? You can see how we are. We have little enough meat for ourselves. But—"

"But," said Cahl evenly, "you will take the beer anyway. Won't you?" And he kept staring, until he had faced down Acta. Some of the men muttered uncomfortably at this show of weakness. But what Cahl said was obviously true. Cahl slapped Acta's shoulder amiably. "We can talk about it later. Go rest in the shade. And as for me—"

"Take her," Acta mumbled, gazing at the beer. "Do what you like." He shambled toward the men's hut. The other failed hunters dumped their meat outside the women's huts and followed Acta, eager for a share in the beer. Soon Juna heard the growling of the shaman, who was always quickly revived by the stink of ale.

Cahl came back to the girls. He shook his head. "In my home such a depraved oaf would be cast out."

Sion prickled at this new insult. "The boys live with the men, in the men's hut. It is a place of wisdom, where the boys learn to be men. And each man has a small house for his wife and his daughters and his infant sons. It is our way. It has always been our way."

"It might be your way, but it isn't mine," Cahl said bluntly.

Juna found her curiosity pricked by that.

The only thing anybody knew about the new people, save for their marvelous ability to make beer, was that there were many, many of them. Some of the women whispered that no baby was discarded among the strangers—not one, not ever. And that was why there was so many of them, though nobody had any idea how they fed themselves. Perhaps in their valleys and lowlands the animals still ran in great herds, just as they had in the days long gone, the days of legends.

"Who?" Sion asked softly.

"Who?"

"Acta said, 'Take her.' Who?"

"Why, his wife," Cahl said. "Pepule. Ah. I can see why you're interested. Acta isn't your father, *but Pepule is your mother*, isn't she?" He grinned, and gazed at Juna with that stone-hard intensity. "That will add spice. While I hump her I will think of you, little one."

Sion said coldly, "Pepule is with child."

"I know." He grinned. "I like them that way. Those big bellies, no?" Again his hard, calculating gaze turned on Juna. Then he took a pinch of ground corn from her mortar and strode away to their mother's hut.

Dissatisfied, vaguely afraid, Juna left the men to their drinking. She walked out into the country with her grandmother, Sheb. Sheb, nearly sixty, moved with caution, but in her long life she had avoided injury and serious illness and stayed limber.

The people lived on a high plateau. The land was dry, flat, all but featureless. Vegetation clung to the ground, deep-rooted, searching for water. There were streams and rivers, but they were trickles of waters that flowed between mighty banks; they seemed niggardly, starved, a relic of what had evidently passed away.

Naked, carrying lengths of rope and small stone-tipped spears, the women moved from place to place, setting and checking traps for the small game that provided the staple of the people's diet. They would have been astonished could they have glimpsed the mighty herds of giant herbivores that Jahna and her people had once followed, even though their folk tales talked of richer times in the past.

"Why do the men drink beer?" Juna fretted. "It makes them ugly and stupid. And they have to go to that slithery Cahl. If they must drink beer, they should make their own. They would be just as stupid, but at least Cahl would keep away."

Sheb sighed. "It isn't so simple. We can't make beer. Nobody knows how, not even the shaman. It is a secret Cahl's people keep to themselves."

"When the men are stupid they cannot hunt. All they think about is the beer. It is all they see."

Sheb shook her head. "I won't argue with you, child. My father never drank beer—we had never *heard* of beer in those days—and he was a fine hunter. Look, now. A rabbit is near."

Juna dutifully studied the bits of rabbit dropping, pressing them to see how fresh they were. She badly wanted to talk about Tori.

But Sheb had her own agenda. "I remember when I was your age," she was saying. "Once it rained as if the sky had split open, for day after day. The ground turned to mud, and we all sank in up to our knees. And water filled this valley here—not the muddy trickle you see now—all the way up the bank. See where the lip has been scoured?" And, yes, if she looked hard, Juna could make out how the bank had been eroded far above the current water level.

But so what? Absently Juna rubbed her belly. Her grandmother's tales of huge rain storms, a land turned to mud, the explosive blossoming of life that had followed, were like the fantastic visions of the shaman. They didn't mean anything to *her*. What did rain and rivers matter compared to the growing lump inside her?

Her grandmother slapped her head. Juna flinched, startled. Sheb scowled, making her wrinkles deepen. "It would pay you to listen to me, you foolish child. *I remember how it was,* the last time the rains came. I remember how we coped. How we moved to the higher ground. How we forded the river. All of it. Maybe I won't live to see the rains come again as they did before, but maybe you will. And then all that will keep you alive is what I have told you today."

Juna knew she had a point. Old people were cared for deeply: Before Sheb's own mother's death, Juna had seen Sheb chew her food until soft and spit it into a bowl for her. In this society without writing, old people were libraries of wisdom and experience. And now she was determined to make her granddaughter listen.

But today Juna was in no mood for a lesson in humility. She tried to stare back, defiant, resentful, but, before Sheb's ferocious glare, she broke down. "Oh, Sheb—" The weeping came suddenly and easily; she rested her head on Sheb's shoulder and let her tears fall to the arid ground.

"Tell me. What can be so bad?"

Sheb listened gravely to what she had to say. She asked specific questions: Who was the father, how he had approached her or she him, *why* she had chosen to conceive now. She seemed most dissatisfied with the news that it had all been a childish mistake. In response to Juna's agonized questions—"Sheb, what am I to do?"—for now, at least, Sheb would say nothing. But Juna thought she saw the shape of her future in the hard, sad lines of Sheb's set expression.

And then there was a keening wail from the village. Juna took her grandmother's arm and helped her to hurry home.

It turned out that Pepule, Juna's mother, Sheb's daughter, had gone into labor early.

As she entered the camp with Sheb, Juna saw the beer man, Cahl, walking away eastward, back toward his mysterious home. A sack of goods over his arm, he ignored the labor cries of the woman with whom he had lain only that morning, and Juna glared with futile hostility at his retreating back.

In Pepule's hut, Sion and other kinswomen had gathered. Juna hurried to Pepule's side. Pepule's bleary, pain-filled eyes turned toward her daughter, and she grasped Juna's hand. Juna saw a bruise the shape of a man's grip on her mother's shoulder.

As was their way, the women had set up a frame of wood to which Pepule clung, squatting. Meanwhile others were moistening the patch of earth under Pepule to soften it, and were digging a shallow hole nearby. There was a strong smell of vomit and blood.

Juna had witnessed and aided at many births before, but, bearing her own small burden within, she had never before shared so much pain herself.

At least this birth was quick. The baby dropped easily into the arms of one of Pepule's sisters. With a brisk, confident motion she cut the infant's umbilical and tied it off with a strip of sinew, and wiped off the birthing fluid with a bit of skin. Then the older women, including Sheb, clustered around the baby, examining it closely, picking over its limbs and face.

Juna experienced a sudden, unexpected surge of joy. "He's a boy," she said to Pepule. "He looks perfect. . . ."

Her mother gazed back at her, her face empty. Then she turned away.

Juna became aware that there was muttering from the women working on the baby; some of them glared up at Juna disapprovingly.

Now Juna saw what they were doing. They had put the baby on the ground, where he grasped at the air feebly. He had wisps of blond hair, Juna saw, stuck to his scalp by the fluids from the birth. Pepule's sister took a stick. She pushed the baby into the hole the women had dug, as if she was shoving away a bit of sour meat. Then the women started to fill in the hole. The first dirt fell on the baby's uncomprehending face.

"No!" Juna lunged forward.

Sheb, with surprising strength, took her shoulders and pushed her back. "It must be done."

Juna struggled. "But he is healthy."

"It," said Sheb. "Not *he*. Only people are *he*, and that baby is not yet a person, and never will be."

"But Pepule—"

"Look at her. *Look*, Juna. She is not hurt, not grieving. It is the way. She does not yet feel anything for the baby, not for these first few heart-beats when the decision must be made. If it were to live, to become a *he*, then the bond would grow firm, of course it would. But the bond is not there yet, and now it can never be."

On and on.

Pepule was coughing. She sounded exhausted—ill. Juna thought of Cahl lying with her mother just hours ago, and she wondered what filth he had brought with him.

Still Sheb was talking to her.

At last Juna dropped her head. "But the baby is healthy," she whispered. "He is healthy."

Sheb sighed. "Oh, child, don't you see? *We cannot feed it*, however healthy it is. This is not a time for a child—not for Pepule, anyhow."

"And me?" Juna raised her head and whispered. "What will become of me? What of *my* baby?"

Sheb's eyes clouded.

Juna twisted away and ran out of the hut, with its stink of shit and blood and useless milk.

The two sisters sat whispering in a corner of the small shelter they had constructed for themselves as children.

Juna had told Sion everything.

"I have to go," she said. "That's all. I knew it the moment they pushed the baby into that hole. Pepule is strong and experienced, where I am a child. And Acta, for all his drunken flaws, is beside her still. Tori doesn't even know my baby is his. If *her* baby is pushed into a hole, then what of mine?"

In the dusty dark, Sion shook her head. "You shouldn't speak like that. Sheb was right. It was not a person, not until it was named."

"They killed him."

"No. They could not let *it* live. For if all the babies were allowed to live, there wouldn't be enough to eat, and that would kill us all. You know the truth of it. There is nothing to be done."

It was ancient wisdom, drummed into them since birth, an echo of tens of millennia of human subsistence. Jo'on and Leda had had to face this. So had Rood's people. It was the price you paid. But for some in each generation, it was too high a price.

"I don't care," said Juna.

Sion reached for her sister's hand. "You can't leave. You must give birth here. Let the women come to you. And if they decide the time is not right—"

"But I'm not like Pepule," Juna said miserably. "*I won't be able to give it up.* I just know it." She looked into her sister's shadowed face. "Is there something wrong with me? Why am I not as strong as our mother? It feels as if I love my baby even now, as strongly as Pepule ever loved you or me. I know that if they take it from me, then I may as well follow it into the hole, for I could not live."

"Don't talk like that," said Sion.

"I will go in the morning," Juna said, trying to sound stronger. "I will take a spear. That is all I need."

"Where will you go? You can't live alone—and definitely not with a baby at your breast. And wherever you go the people will drive you off with stones. You know that. We would do the same."

But there is one place, Juna thought, where the people are at least *different*, where, perhaps, they do not murder their babies, where the people may not drive me off.

"Come with me, Sion. Please."

Sion, her eyes drying, pulled back. "No. If you want to kill yourself, I— I respect your choice. But I will not die with you."

"Then there is nothing more to be said."

Carrying nothing but a spear and a spear-thrower, wearing a simple shift of tanned goat hide, she jogged easily. She covered the ground quickly, despite the unaccustomed burden in her belly.

The land was so dry that Cahl's footsteps were crisp. Here and there she found his spoor—splashes of half-dried piss on rocks, a neatly coiled turd—hunting beer men, it seemed, was not hard. Even far from the village, farther than the hunters would usually roam, the land was empty.

After Jahna's time, once more the ice had retreated, brooding, to its Arctic fastnesses. The pine forests had marched north, greening the old tundra. And across the Old World people spread out from the refuges where they had survived the great winter, islands of relative warmth in the Balkans, the Ukraine, Spain. Quickly their children began to fill up the immense depopulated plains of Europe and Asia.

But things were not as they had been the last time the ice retreated.

In Australia, since Ejan's first footsteps, it had taken a mere five thousand years to achieve the grand erasing of the megafauna, the great kangaroos, reptiles, and birds. Now, everywhere people went, similar patterns unfolded.

In North America there had been ground sloths the size of rhinos, giant camels, bison with sharp-tipped horns that measured more than a man's arm span from tip to tip. These massive creatures were the prey of muscular jaguars, saber-toothed tigers, dire wolves with teeth able to crunch bone, and the terrible short-faced bears. The American prairies might have looked like Africa's Serengeti Plain in later times.

When the first humans marched from Asia into Alaska, this fantastic assemblage imploded. Seven in ten of the large animal species were lost within centuries. Even the native horses were destroyed. Many of the creatures that did survive—like the musk oxen, bison, moose, and elk—were, like the humans, immigrants from Asia, with a long history of learning how to survive in a world owned by people.

Similarly, in South America, once humans walked across the Panama land bridge, eight in ten of the large animal species would be destroyed. It happened across the great plains of Eurasia too. Even the mammoths were lost. All the large animals vanished like mist.

The damage was not always proportionate to the size of the territory occupied. In New Zealand, where there had been no mammals but bats, evolution had playfully filled the roles of mammals with other creatures, especially birds. There were flightless geese instead of rabbits, little songbirds instead of mice, gigantic eagles instead of leopards, and seventeen different species of moa, giant flightless birds, eerie avian parallels to deer. This unique fauna, like that of an alien planet, was wiped out within a few hundred years of human settlement—not always by humans themselves, but by the creatures they brought with them, especially the rats, which devastated the nests of the ground-dwelling birds.

All these animals had been under pressure from the fast-changing climate at the end of the glaciation. But most of these ancient lines had survived many similar changes before. The difference this time was the presence of humans. It was no great blitzkrieg. People were often pretty inept as hunters, and big game contributed only a fraction of their diet. Many communities, like Jahna's folk, actually believed they were touching the animals lightly. But by pressuring the animals at a time when they were most vulnerable, by selectively killing off the young, by disrupting habitats, by taking out key components of the food webs that sustained communities of creatures, they did immense damage. It was only in Africa, where the animals had evolved alongside humans and had had time to adapt to their ways, that something like the old Pleistocene diversity was maintained.

Rood's chill Eden had long gone. There had been a hideous shriveling, leaving an empty, echoing world, through which people walked as if bewildered, quickly forgetting that the great exotic beasts and different kinds of people had even existed.

People still lived by hunting and gathering, of course. But it turned out to be much harder to hunt deer and boar in the forests than it had been to ambush reindeer crossing rivers on the open steppe. After the extinctions, life was impoverished compared to what it had been in the past, with poorer quality food and less leisure time. Worldwide, people's culture actually devolved, becoming simpler.

Always, deep down, they would know that there was something wrong. And now they faced a new pressure.

Juna had been traveling only half a day when she caught up with Cahl. He had sprawled in the shade of a worn sandstone bluff, and he was eating a root. The meat and artifacts of shell and bone he had taken from the people had been dumped in the dirt at his side.

He watched her as she approached, his eyes bright in the shade. "Well," he said silkily. "Little *gold* head."

She didn't understand that word, "gold." She slowed as she approached, dismayed by his hard stare.

He got to his feet clumsily. His belly strained at his skin shirt. "What a frightened rabbit!" he said. "Look, *you* came all this way to find *me*, not the other way around. And I notice that no matter how repulsive I am, you aren't yet running off. So, why are you here?"

She stood frozen, staring at him. Her mind seemed flattened, as if a great rock had fallen on her, pinning her to the dirt. Although she had rehearsed this encounter—imagining herself taking control, making demands—this wasn't going remotely as she had planned.

He said, "No reply? Here's why. *You want something from me.*" He approached her, his gaze raking over her body. "That's how I make my living. Everybody wants something. And if I can figure out what that one thing is, then I can make anybody do whatever I like."

She forced herself to speak. "As Acta wants beer."

He grinned. "You follow. Good. So, just like Acta, you want something from me. But you're not going to get it, little girl, until you figure out what I might want from you." He walked around her, and let his fingertips slide over her buttocks. "You're skinny for my taste. Lean. All that chasing after wild goats, I suppose." He yawned, stretching, and looked off into the distance. "Frankly, child, I wore out my cock humping that fat mother of yours."

Impulsively she pulled up her shirt, exposing her belly.

Startled, he ran his hand over her skin, feeling the bump there. The flesh of his palm was oddly soft, without calluses. "Well," he said, breathing harder. "I knew there was something different about you. I must have good instincts. And as for you, you're getting the idea. My strange lust for pregnant sows; my one weakness—" He stroked his chin. "But I still don't know what *you* want. I can't believe it's the alluring thought of my fat belly on your back—"

"The baby," she blurted. "They killed it."

"What baby? Ah. Your mother's. They wouldn't let her keep her calf, eh? I know that's what you animals do, kill your young. Some say you feast on the tender little corpses." He continued to study her, calculating. "I think I see. If you have your baby, they'll take it away too. So that's why you came running after a greedy wretch like me—to save your unborn baby." Briefly his expression dissolved, and she thought she glimpsed sympathy.

She murmured, "They say—"

"Yes?"

"They say that in your place no babies are killed."

He shrugged. "We have a lot of food. We don't have to spend all of every day running after rabbits, as you people do. *That's* why we don't have to murder our children."

She wondered how this miracle could come about: Cahl's people must have a powerful shaman indeed.

But that brief lightening of Cahl's face had already dissipated, to be replaced by a kind of desperate greed. He approached her and grabbed her breast, pinching hard; she forced herself not to cry out. "If you come with me it will be hard for you. The way we live is—" he waved a hand at the open plain "—*different* from all this. More than you can imagine. And you will have to do as I say. That is our way."

She could smell his breath. She closed her eyes, shutting out his moonlike, pockmarked face. This was the decision point, she knew. She could still turn away, still run home. But her baby would be doomed. When Acta and Pepule found out they might even try to beat it out of her belly.

"I'll do what you say," she said hastily. What could be worse than that?

"Good," he said, his breath coming in short, hot gasps. "Now, let's get down to business. *Kneel down.*"

So it began, there in the dirt. She was grateful that nobody she cared about could see her.

II

He made her carry his load of meat, his bag of half-chewed roots, and his empty beer sack. He said it was the way, in his home. It wasn't heavy— the meat was nothing more than the spindly catch of small game brought back by the men the day before—but it seemed very strange to Juna to have to walk behind Cahl with meat piled on her shoulder while he strutted ahead, inexpertly brandishing *her* spear.

Soon they had walked far from her familiar range. It was deeply frightening to think that she was entering land where, probably, none of her ancestors had set a foot, not once; deep taboos, inspired by her well-founded fear of death at the hands of strangers, warred against her impulse to continue. But continue she did, for she had no choice.

They had to spend one night in the open. He brought her to the shelter of a bluff, a half cave he had evidently used before, for she saw more signs of his unpleasant spoor. He would not let her eat any of the meat, nor even hunt for more. Evidently he didn't trust her that far. But he gave her some of the thin, ill-tasting roots he had carried.

As darkness fell he used her again. The brutal coupling made her juvenile fumbling with Tori seem full of tenderness. But to her relief Cahl finished quickly—he had already spent himself that day—and when he rolled off her he quickly fell asleep.

She massaged her bruised thighs, alone with her thoughts.

In the morning they began to descend from the high, dry plateau into a broad valley. This was a greener land; grass grew thickly, and she could see the blue thread of a sluggish river, with trees clustered in a green ribbon along its bank. This would be a good place to live, she thought— better than the arid upper lands. There must be plenty of game here. But as they descended further she caught only fleeting glimpses of rabbits and mice and birds. There was no sign of the spoor of large animals, none of their characteristic tracks.

At last she made out a broad brown scar close to the bank of the river. Smoke rose from a dozen places, and she made out movement, a pale wriggling, like maggots in a wound. But the maggots were people, crowded, diminished by distance.

Gradually she understood. It was a town: a huge, sprawling settlement. She was astonished. She had never seen a human gathering on such a scale. Deepening dread settled in her stomach as they moved on.

Even before they got to the settlement they began to encounter people.

They all seemed short, dark, and bent, and they wore filthy clothes. And men, women, and children alike worked at patches of ground. Juna had never seen anything like it. In one place they were bent over, scratching roughly at the bare soil with stone tools mounted in wood. A little further on there was a meadow full of grass—nothing but grass—and the people here were pulling at the grass stems, plucking seeds to collect in baskets and bowls. Some of them peered up as she passed, showing a dull curiosity.

Cahl saw her staring. "These are *fields*," he said. "This is how we feed our children. See? You *clear* the ground. You *plant* the seed. You kill the *weeds* while the *crops* grow. You take your *harvest*."

She struggled to make sense of this; there were too many unfamiliar words. "Where is your shaman?"

He laughed. "We are all shamans, perhaps."

They passed another open area—another "field," as Cahl called it—where goats were penned by a fence of wooden stakes and bramble. When they saw Cahl and Juna approaching, the goats ran bleating to the fence, their heads lunging forward. They were hungry, Juna saw immediately. They had eaten all the grass in their enclosure, and they longed to be free, to go find food in the valley and the hills. She had no idea why the people kept them shut up like this.

They reached the valley bottom. The grass petered out, giving way to churned-up mud that was thick with shit and piss—human waste, just dumped here. It must be like living on a huge midden, she thought.

At last they reached the settlement itself. The huts were very solid and permanent, built on frames of tree trunks rammed into the muddy ground, and plastered over with mud and straw. They had holes in their roofs, from many of which smoke curled, even now in the middle of the day. Huts were huts. But there were many, many of them, so many she couldn't even count them.

And there were people everywhere.

They wore the strange, tightly sewn, all-covering clothes that Cahl favored. They were all smaller than she was, men and women alike, and their dark skin was pocked and scarred. Many of the women carried huge burdens. Here was one small woman bent over under a great sack; the sack was tied to her forehead, and it looked like it must weigh more than she did. By contrast the men seemed to carry little beyond what they could hold in their hands.

She had never seen so many people in her life, still less all crammed together in such a small space. Despite what she had glimpsed of the fields she still had no idea how such a dense knot of people could feed themselves; surely they must soon drive off all the game, devour all the edible vegetation in the area. And yet she saw butchered carcasses stacked outside one hut, grain baskets outside another.

And there were many children here. Several trailed after Juna, plucking at her shift and gazing at her shining hair. Then that much at least was true: There really were more children here than her own community could ever afford to support. But many of the children had bent bones and pocked skin and browned teeth. Some of them were scrawny, even displaying the ominous potbellies of malnutrition.

The men crowded around Cahl and Juna, jabbering in an incomprehensible language. They seemed to be congratulating Cahl, as if he were a hunter home with game. When the men leered at her she saw their teeth were bad, as bad as Cahl's.

Suddenly her nerve gave out. *Too many people.* She shrank back, but they followed her, pressing closer, and children plucked at her yellow hair, yelling. She found herself panicking, breathless. She longed for a glimpse of green, but there was no green, nothing but the shit brown of this dung heap of a place. The world spun around her. She fell, helplessly dumping Cahl's meat in the dirt. She was aware of Cahl's angry yell. But still children and adults clamored around her, prying, laughing.

She came to herself slowly, reluctantly.

She had been taken inside one of the huts. She was on her back, on the floor. She could see daylight poking through cracks and seams in the roof above her.

And Cahl was on her again, thrusting, heavy. She could smell nothing but the beer on his breath.

There were other people in the hut, moving in the dim dark, jabbering a language she couldn't understand. There were many children, of various ages. She wondered if they were all Cahl's. A woman came close. She was short, like the rest, scrawny, her face slack and lined, her black hair lying flat beside her face. She was carrying a bowl containing some liquid. She looked older than Juna—

Cahl's meaty hand clamped painfully around her jaw. "Watch me, you sow. Watch me, not her." And he continued his thrusting, harder than before.

At dawn the black-haired woman—whose name turned out to be Gwerei—came to rouse Juna with a kick to her backside. Juna climbed off the rough, filthy pallet she had been given, trying not to gag on air dense and laden with the stink of sweat and farts.

The woman jabbered at Juna, pointing at the hearth. Then, irritated at Juna's incomprehension, she stamped out of the hut. She returned with a fat day log that she threw on the fire. Pushing children out of the way, she uncovered a pit in the ground, which contained a mass of billowy white shapes. At first Juna thought they were fungi, perhaps mushrooms. But the woman bit into one of the masses, and broke up others, throwing handfuls to the clamoring children.

She threw a chunk of the white stuff to Juna. Juna tried it cautiously. It was bland, tasteless; it was like biting into wood. And it was gritty, with hard bits inside that ground against her teeth. But she had eaten nothing since her last stop with Cahl on the high plain, and hunger gnawed. So she devoured the food as readily as the children did.

It was her first mouthful of bread, though it would be many days before she learned its name.

While they ate, Cahl snored on in his pallet. It seemed strange to Juna that he should choose to stay with the women, but there seemed to be no men's hut here.

When they had eaten, Gwerei took her out of the town, up the valley, and to the open spaces on the far side. They walked in silence, since they shared not a word of common language: Juna was trapped in a bubble of incomprehension. But she was relieved just to get out of the great anthill of people that was the town.

Soon they were joined by more women, older children, a few men. They followed ruts worn into the ground by innumerable feet. Some of the women gazed at Juna curiously—and the men speculatively—but they seemed exhausted before their day had even started. She wondered where they were all going. Nobody was carrying any weapons, any spears or snares or traps. They weren't even looking for spoor, tracks or dung, any signifiers that animals had been here. They didn't even look around at the land they inhabited.

At last she came to the open spaces she had glimpsed yesterday, the *fields*. Gwerei led her into one of these fields, where people were already at work. Gwerei handed her a tool, and began to jabber at her, miming, holding her fists together and scratching imaginary gouges in the air.

Juna inspected the tool. It was like an ax, with a stone head fixed to a wooden handle by a binding of sinew and resin. But it was big, surely too heavy to use as an ax, yet the curved stone blade made it impractical to use even as a thrusting spear. As Gwerei yelled at her with increasing frustration, she just stared back.

At last Gwerei had to show her. She bent over the dirt, clasping the tool, and stuck the blade deep into the ground. Then she began to walk backward, legs stiff, bent over, dragging the blade through the earth. She had made a furrow a hand's length deep in the ground.

Juna saw that other people were doing just as Gwerei had, dragging their curved axes through the ground. She remembered seeing people do this yesterday. It was so simple a task a child could have done it, with enough strength. But it was hard work. After engraving furrows just a few paces long they were all grunting, their faces slick with sweat and dirt.

Still Juna had no idea why they were doing this. But she took the tool from Gwerei and rammed the blade into the ground. Then she bent as Gwerei had done and hauled the handle backward, until she had scraped a furrow just like Gwerei's. One woman clapped ironically.

Juna handed the tool back to Gwerei. "I've done that," she said in her own language. "Now what?"

The answer turned out to be simple. She had to do the same thing again, a little further on. And again after that. She, and the rest of the people here, had nothing to do but scrape these marks in the ground.

All day.

Where was the skill in this muck-scraping compared to even the simplest hunt, the setting of a rabbit snare? Did these people have no minds, no spirits? But perhaps this was part of the magic that the shamans here used to make their heaps of food, the abundance that allowed them to gather in great maggoty swarms and litter the ground with children. And besides, she reminded herself, she was a stranger here, and she must learn Gwerei's ways, not the other way around.

So she bent to her dull, repetitive work. But before the sun had risen much higher, she longed to get away from this tedium, to be running on the high plain. And after a day of forcing her body—a machine exquisitely designed for walking, running, throwing—to endure this repetitive hard labor, the aches became so overwhelming that all she wanted was for it to stop.

The next day, she was taken to another field, and put to the same dull plowing. And the next day was the same.

And the day after that.

It was agriculture: primitive, but agriculture. This new way of living had never been planned. It just emerged, step by step.

As far back as Pebble's time, even before true humans had emerged, people had been gathering the wild plants they favored and eliminating others that competed for resources. The domestication of animals had also begun accidentally. Dogs had learned to hunt with humans, and been rewarded for it. Goats had learned to follow human bands for the garbage they left behind—and the humans in turn learned to use the goats not just for their meat, but for their milk. For hundreds of thousands of years, there had been an unconscious selection of those plant and animal kinds most useful to humans. Now it had become conscious.

It had begun in a valley not far from here. For centuries the people there had enjoyed a steadily warming climate, and a rich diet of fruit, nuts, wild grains, and wild game. But then there had been a sudden drier, colder spell. The forests had shrunk back. The sources of wild food had begun to vanish.

So the people had focused their efforts on the grains they favored— the ones with big seeds that were easy to remove from the seed coats, and with nonshattering stalks that held all the seeds together—trying to ensure their growth at the expense of the less desirable plants around them.

Peas were another early success. The pods of wild peas would explode, scattering the peas on the ground to germinate. People preferred the occasional mutants whose pods failed to pop because they were easier to gather. In the wild such peas would fail to germinate, but they flourished under human attention. Similar nonpopping varieties of lentils, flax, and poppies were also favorites.

And so, by spreading the seeds of their preferred plants and eliminating those they did not favor, the people had begun to select. Very quickly the plants began to adapt. Within just a century, fatter-grained cereals, like rye, had begun to emerge. Some plants were favored for the large size of their seeds, like sunflowers, and others for the smallness of their seeds, like bananas, which became all fruit and no seed. Some genes that would once even have been lethal were now favored, like those for the nonpopping pea pods.

The first rye growers had not settled down immediately. For a time they had still collected their wild staples alongside their thin harvests.

The new fields had served as dependable larders, a hedge against starvation in difficult times: As with all innovations, farming had grown out of the practices that had preceded it.

But the new cultivation had proved so effective that soon they devoted their lives to it. Most of what grew wild was inedible; *nine-tenths* of what a farmer could grow could be eaten. That was how these people were able to afford so many babies; *that* was what fed the great anthill heaping of the town.

It was the most profound revolution in hominid living since *Homo erectus* had left the forest and committed themselves to the savannah. Compared to this phase shift, the advances of the future—even genetic engineering—were details. There would never be so significant a change again, not until humans themselves disappeared from the planet.

But the farming revolution did not make Earth a paradise.

Farming meant *work*: endless, bone-cracking drudgery every day. As the ground was cleared of everything except what people wanted to grow, humans had to do all the work that nature had once done for them: aerating the soil, fighting pests, fertilizing, weeding. Farming meant the sacrifice of your whole life—your skills, the joy of running, the freedom to choose what you would do—to the toil of the fields.

It was not even that the food they so laboriously scraped from the ground was rich. While the old hunter-gatherers had enjoyed a varied diet with adequate amounts of minerals, proteins, and vitamins, the farmers took most of their sustenance from starchy crops: It was as if they had exchanged expensive, high-quality food for nutrition that was plentiful but poor in quality. As a result—and because of the relentless hard work—they had become significantly less healthy than their ancestors. They had worse teeth, and were plagued by anemia. Women's elbows were wrecked by the constant work of grinding. Men suffered vastly increased social stress, resulting in frequent beatings and murders.

Compared to their tall, healthy ancestors, people were actually shrinking.

And then there were the deaths.

It was true that the mothers here did not have to sacrifice their babies. Indeed, the women were encouraged to have children as rapidly as possible, for children fulfilled the endless demand for more laborers for the fields: By the age of thirty, many of the women were exhausted by the endless drain of nursing and caring for weaned infants.

But where many were born, so did many more die. It did not take long for Juna to see it. Disease was rare among Juna's folk, but it was not rare here, in this crowded, filthy place. You could almost see it spreading, as people sneezed and coughed, as they scratched weeping sores, as their diarrhea poisoned the water supply of their neighbors. And the myriad afflictions targeted the weakest, the oldest and youngest. Many, many children died, far more than among Juna's folk.

And there was barely a handful of people her grandmother's age. Juna wondered what happened to all the wisdom when the old died so cheaply and so early.

The days wore by, identical, meaningless. The work was routine. But then everything here was a routine, the same thing, day after day.

Cahl continued to use her, most nights. He seemed to lack vigor, though. Sometimes he would come at her hard, pushing her down and ripping aside her shift, or pushing her on her face to take her from behind. It was as if he had to work himself up, to excite himself. But if he had taken too much beer, his pisser would not rise at all.

He was a weak man, she realized. He had power over her, but she did not fear him. In the end even his taking of her had become routine, just part of the background to her life. She was relieved, though, that she couldn't become pregnant with his brat—not while Tori's child continued to grow inside her.

One day, while she was straining to drag her stone plough across dry, rocky ground, sheep came blundering over a bluff, bleating noisily. Always ready for a break, the workers in the field straightened up to watch. They laughed as the sheep stumbled over the broken ground, nudging each other nervously and nuzzling in search of grass.

But now there was a frenzied barking. A dog came tearing over the bluff, chased by a boy wielding a wooden staff. As the workers laughed, clapped and whistled, the boy and the dog began to chase the sheep, with comical incompetence.

Gwerei was at Juna's side. She peered into her baffled face. Then, not unkindly, she pointed at the sheep. "*Owis. Kludhi.*" She picked out the sheep with her finger, one by one. "*Oynos. Dwo. Treyes. Owis.*" And she nudged Juna, trying to get her to respond.

Juna, her back aching, her hair matted, had had enough strangeness. "I'll never understand."

But Gwerei, remarkably, stayed patient. "*Owis. Kludhi. Owis.*"

And she began to speak to Juna, in her own tongue, but much more slowly and clearly than usual—and, to Juna's shock, with one or two words of Juna's language, presumably picked up from Cahl. She was trying to tell Juna something, something very important.

Juna subsided and listened. It took a long time. But gradually she pieced together what Gwerei was trying to tell her. Learn the language. Listen and learn. Because that is the only way you will ever get away from Cahl. Listen now.

Reluctantly she nodded. "*Owis*," she repeated. "Sheep. *Owis*. One, two, three—"

And so Juna learned her first words in the language of Gwerei and Cahl, these first farmers: her first words in the language that would one day be called proto-Indo-European.

As the days wore by, so her bump grew steadily. It began to hinder her work in the field, and her strength seemed drained. The other workers observed this, and some grumbled, though most of the women seemed to forgive Juna her slowing down.

But she worried. What would Cahl do when the child was born? Would he find her so attractive without a swollen belly? If he turned her out, she would be in as bad a position as if she had simply taken her chances on the high plain—worse, perhaps, after months of bad diet and backbreaking work, in a place she neither knew nor understood. The worry grew into a gnaw that consumed her mind, just as the growing child seemed to consume her body's strength.

But then the stranger with the shining necklace came to the town.

It was evening. She was shambling back from the fields as usual, mud-covered and exhausted.

Cahl was making his way to the hut of the beer maker. Juna had glimpsed the great wooden vats inside the hut, where the beer maker churned domesticated grasses and other unidentifiable substances to make his crude wheat ale. The beer seemed to have little effect on Cahl's people—not until they had consumed vast quantities of it—little, any-how, compared to what it did to Acta and the others. No wonder it was such a useful trade good for Cahl: cheap for him, priceless to Acta.

But this evening Cahl had with him a man—tall, as tall as she was, if not quite as lofty as some of the men of Juna's folk. His face was shaven clean, and his long black hair was tied in a knot at the back of his head. He looked young, surely not much older than she was. His eyes were clear, alert. And he wore extraordinary skins, skins that had been worked until they were soft, carefully stitched and decorated with dancing animal designs in red, blue, and black. She was frightened by the thought of the hours of work that had been invested in such garments.

But what most caught her eye was the necklace he wore around his neck. It was a simple chain of pierced shells. But in the central shell, below his chin, was fixed a lump of something that shone bright yellow, catching the light of the low sun.

Cahl was watching her. He let the young man go on ahead to the beer maker's hut. In her own tongue he said to her silkily, "Like him, do you? Like the gold around his neck? Think you'd prefer his slim cock to mine? He's called Keram. Much good that will do you. He's from Cata Huuk. You don't know where that is, do you? And you'll never know." He grabbed her between the legs and squeezed. "Keep yourself warm for me." And he pushed her away and walked off.

She had barely noticed his latest assault. *Keram. Cata Huuk.* She repeated the strange names to herself, over and over.

For she thought that—just for a moment, just before he turned his back to walk to the beer maker's—the young man had looked at her, and his eyes had widened in a kind of recognition.

It was three months before Keram traveled out from Cata Huuk to the town again.

He'd actually put off the call. As the youngest son of the Potus, he routinely got the worst jobs, and checking on the tribute collection from these outlying towns at the fringe of the city's hinterland was about as bad as it got.

"And this place," he told his friend Muti, "is the worst of them all. Look at it." The riverbank town was just a huddle of dung-colored huts, eroded to shapelessness by rain, stinking smoke curling up from their roofs. "You know what they call this place? *Keer.*" The word meant "Heart" in the language the two young men spoke, a language that was used throughout a wider belt of colonization spreading back from this place far to the east.

Muti grinned. "*Keer.* I like that. Can this be the heart of the world? Why does it look so much like its arsehole, then?" The two of them laughed together, their necklaces of shell and gold nuggets tinkling softly.

Cahl came up to them. The trader joined in with their laughter, his gaiety forced, his dim, piglike eyes darting from one to the other. The guards behind Keram moved subtly, showing their alertness, tilting the tips of their pikes.

Cahl said, "Master Keram. It is a pleasure to see you. How fine you look, how your clothes shine in the sunlight!" He turned to Muti. "And I don't believe—"

Muti introduced himself. "A second cousin of Keram. Cousin and ally."

Keram was amused to see the naked calculation in Cahl's eyes as the trader added Muti's name and position to the tentative map he was so obviously making of the power structures within Cata Huuk. Cahl began to flap and fuss as he led them into the town. "Come, come. Your tribute is ready, of course, piled in my hut. I have food and beer for you, fresh from the country. Will you stay the night?"

Keram said, "We have many more places to visit before—"

"But you must enjoy our hospitality. Your men too. We have girls, virgins, who are ready for you." He eyed Muti and winked. "Or boys. Whatever you desire. You are our guests, for as long as you choose to be with us."

As they walked delicately over the muddy, shit-strewn ground, Muti leaned closer to Keram. "What a repulsive fat slug."

"He's just trying his chances. He isn't even the chief of this little band of dirt-grubbers. And he has some interesting weaknesses, notably for fat women. Perhaps they remind him of the pigs who are no doubt his real loves. But he is useful. Easy to manipulate."

"Will he ever get to Cata Huuk?"

Keram snorted. "What do you think, cousin?"

Now they were approaching Cahl's hut—one of the grander in the town, but still a heap of mud in the eyes of the young men.

Keram asked Muti, "Do you want to stay awhile?" He nodded toward the four guards. "I usually let the dogs out of their pen for a while. And Cahl's usefulness does include digging out the more attractive sows from this sty. Sometimes their mud-hole desperation makes them—interesting. It's fun, in a strenuous sort of way. But you have to be prepared for a little filth—"

Muti, distracted, asked, "What's this?"

A girl had come out of Cahl's hut. She was quite unlike the dark, dumpy women of the town. Though scrawny and obviously careworn, she was tall—as tall as Keram, in fact—slender, and had blond hair that shone strikingly gold, despite the dirt tangled in it. She might have been sixteen or seventeen.

Cahl looked outraged at the girl's approach. He slammed his meaty fist into her temple, knocking her down in the dirt. "What are you doing? Get back in the hut. I will deal with you later." And he made to kick the girl as she lay helpless on the ground.

Smoothly, Muti grabbed Cahl's pudgy arm and twisted it behind his back. Cahl howled, but he quickly subsided.

Keram took the girl's hand and helped her to her feet. A bruise was already gathering on her temple. He saw now that her legs and arms were discolored by bruises. She was trembling, but she stood straight and faced him. He said, "What is your name?"

Cahl snapped, "Sir, don't talk to her—" Muti twisted his arm harder. "*Ow!*"

"Juna." Her accent was thick and unfamiliar, but her words were clear. "My name is Juna. I am from Cata Huuk," she said boldly. "I am like you."

Keram laughed at that, disbelieving—but his laughter died as he studied her. Certainly her height, her grace, her relatively good condition did not speak of a life with the pigs of Keer. He said carefully, "If you are from the city how did you end up here?"

"They took me as a child. These people, the people of Keer. They raised me with the dogs and the wolves, and so I don't speak as you. But—"

"She is lying," Cahl breathed. "She doesn't even know what Cata Huuk is. She is a savage from the tribes to the west, the animal people I have to deal with. Her mother is a fat slut who sells her body for beer. And—"

"I should not be here," Juna said steadily, her eyes on Keram. "Take me with you."

Uncertain, Keram and Muti exchanged glances.

Enraged, Cahl twisted away from Muti. "You want to lie with her? Is that it?" He ripped at Juna's simple shift, tearing it away from her swollen belly. "Look! The sow is full of piglets. Do you want to hump *that?*"

Keram frowned. "The child. Is it Cahl's?"

She trembled harder. "No. Though my belly excites him, and he uses me. The child is a man's from Cata Huuk. He came here. He used me. He did not tell me his name. He promised me—"

"She is lying!" Cahl raged. "She was with child when I found her."

"I am not for this place," said Juna, gazing at the town with faint disgust. "My child is not for this place. My child is for Cata Huuk."

Keram glanced again at Muti, who shrugged. Keram grinned. "I can't tell if you're speaking the truth, Ju-na. But you are a strange one, and your story will amuse my father—"

"No!" Again Cahl broke away. The troops moved forward. "You can't take her!"

Keram ignored him. He nodded to Muti. "Organize the collection of the tribute. You—Ju-na—do you have any possessions here? Any friends of whom you want to take your leave?"

She seemed to puzzle over his meaning, as if she wasn't quite sure what "possessions" were. "Nothing. And friends—only Gwerei."

Keram shrugged; the name meant nothing to him. "Make your preparations. We leave soon." He clapped his hands, and Muti and the troops proceeded to carry out his orders.

But Cahl, restrained by a guard, continued to beg and plead. "Take me! Oh, take me!"

III

It would take them three days to cover the ground to Keram's mysterious home, to Cata Huuk.

The grain and meat, what Keram called the "tribute," was briskly collected. Juna had no idea why the townsfolk—hardly well-off themselves—should wish to hand over so much of their provisions to these strangers. They didn't even get beer back in return.

But now was not the time for her to inquire into such matters. The speech she had rehearsed for so long, since first seeing Keram, had paid off. Now was the time for her to keep quiet and follow where she was led.

The party formed up into a loose line. Keram and Muti took the lead. Their four squat guards followed, two of them with hands free to deploy weapons, the others loaded up with the tribute. Juna, carrying nothing but the spear with which she had arrived here, approached one of the guards, expecting to be given a share of the load.

Keram rebuked her. "Let them do their job."

Juna shrugged. "In Cahl's town, it would be my job."

"Well, I am not Cahl. You must do as we do, girl. It is our way."

"I was taken as a child from—"

"I remember what you told me," Keram said, his eyebrows raised in good humor. "I'm not sure I believe a word of it. But listen now. In Cata Huuk, the word of the Potus is law. I am the son of the Potus. You will obey me. You will not question me. Do you understand?"

Juna's folk were egalitarian, like most hunter-gatherer folk; no, she didn't understand. But she nodded dumbly.

They set off. The young men, unburdened, strode ahead easily enough—as did Juna, despite her pregnancy and the four months she had endured of poor diet and hard labor. But the guards puffed and complained of their weary feet.

It was a great relief for Juna to be out of the squalid town and in the open country once more, a great relief to be *walking* rather than bending her back over some dusty field—even if, as they headed steadily east, she was entering countryside that was increasingly remote from the place where she and her ancestors had always lived.

They stopped each night in small towns, no more or less impressive than Cahl's had been. The guards were plied with beer and girls. Keram and Muti kept themselves to themselves, spending their nights quietly in huts. They let Juna stay with them, huddled in a corner.

Neither of them touched her. Perhaps it was her pregnancy. Perhaps they were just not sure of her. Part of her, glad to be free of the grubby attentions of Cahl, relished not having to share her body with anybody else. But part of her, more calculating, regretted it. She had no real understanding of what this place, this Cata Huuk, would be like. But she suspected her best chance of surviving was to bind herself to Keram or Muti.

So she made sure that each evening and morning, as she cast off her shift, she showed them her body; and she was aware of how, when he thought she was not looking, Keram's gaze followed her.

As they walked on, the landscape became more crowded with fields and towns. No trees grew here, though there were stumps and patches of burned-out forest. There was no open land at all, in fact, save for worthless rocky land or marshes. There were only fields, and patches of land that had clearly once been plowed but were now abandoned, useless, exhausted. Soon there was scarcely a footfall she could make without stepping into the track of somebody who had been here before. The extent to which these swarming people had remade the world oppressed her.

And at last they reached Cata Huuk itself.

The first thing Juna saw was a wall. Made of mud bricks and straw, it was a great circular barrier that must have been as high as three people standing on each other's shoulders, and it bristled with spikes. Outside the wall there was a great ring of shabby huts and lean-tos made of mud and tree branches. The wall was so wide it seemed to cut the land in half.

A broad, well-trodden path led up to the wall itself, a path which Keram's party followed. But as they approached people came boiling like wasps out of the huts, yelling, plucking at Keram's robes, holding up meat and fruit and sweetmeats and bits of carved wood and stone. Juna shrank back. But Keram assured her that there was nothing to be concerned about. These people were simply trying to *sell* things; this was a *market*. The words meant nothing to her.

A great gate made of wood had been set in the wall. Keram called out loudly. A man on top of the wall waved, and the gate was hauled open. The party walked through.

As she walked into strangeness, Juna found herself trembling.

The huts: that was the first thing that struck her. There were many of them, tens of tens, strewn in great masses across the kilometers-wide compound inside the walls. Most of them were no better than Cahl's dwelling, simple slumped mounds of mud and wood. But some, toward the center of the city, were grander than that, tottering structures of two or three stories, their frontages walled with woven yellow grasses that shone in the sun. The clusters of huts were cut through by lanes that sliced this way and that, like a spider's web. Smoke hung in a great gray cloud everywhere. Sewage ran down channels cut into the center of each street, and flies buzzed in great linear clouds over the sluggishly flowing waste.

And people swarmed, the men walking together, the children running and yelling, the women burdened with heavy loads on their heads and backs. There were animals, goats and sheep and dogs, crowded in as tightly as the people. The noise was astonishing, an unending clamor. The smells—of shit, piss, animals, fires, greasy cooked meat—were overwhelming.

This was Cata Huuk. With ten thousand people crammed within its walls, it was one of Earth's first cities. Even Keer had been no preparation for this. To Juna, it was like looking into a great murky sea full of people.

Keram smiled at her. "Are you all right?"

"What trickster god made this teeming pile?"

"No god. *People*, Juna. Many, many people. You must remember that. No matter how strange all this appears, it is the work of people, like you and me. Besides," he said with mock innocence, "this is where you were born. This is where you belong."

"This is where I was born," she said, unable to project much conviction. "But I am afraid. I can't help it."

"I'll be with you," he murmured.

With calculation she slid her hand into his. She caught Muti's eye; he was smirking, knowing.

They walked down a radial avenue toward the great structures at the center of the city. Now Juna was truly stunned. Three stories high, these buildings were great blocks that loomed like giants over the rest of the city. The buildings were set in a loose square around a central courtyard, where grass and flowers grew thickly. Men armed with barbed pikes stood at every entrance, glaring suspiciously. Women moved with bowls of water, which they sprinkled on the grass.

Muti grinned at Juna. "Again she is staring. What is so strange now?"

"The grass. Why do they throw water on it?" She struggled to express herself. "Rain falls. Grass grows."

Muti shook his head. "Not regularly enough for the Potus. I think he would command the weather itself."

They walked into the largest of the buildings. Juna had never been in such a huge enclosed space. Stairways and ladders connected the mezzanine-like floors above. Despite the brightness of the day, torches burned smokily on the walls, banishing shadows and filling the palace with yellow light. People dressed in shining clothes walked through all the levels, and some of them waved down to Keram and Muti as they went by. It was like looking up into the branches of a great tree. Even the floor was extraordinary, made of wood cut so smoothly it felt slippery under her feet, and oil or grease had been worked into it until it shone.

They came to the very center of the building. Here was a platform, raised to shoulder-height above the ground. And on the platform, sitting on an ornately carved block of wood, was the fattest man Juna had ever seen. His breasts were larger than a nursing mother's. His belly, glistening with oil, was like the Moon. And his head was a ball of flesh, completely devoid of hair; his scalp was shaved, and he had no beard, moustache, or even eyebrows. He was naked to the waist, but he wore finely stitched trousers.

This fat creature was the Potus, the Powerful One. He was one of mankind's first kings. He was talking to a skinny corpselike man at his elbow, who thumbed through lengths of knotted string with intense concentration.

Keram and Muti waited patiently until the Potus's attention was free.

Juna whispered, "What are they doing with the string?"

"Tallies," Muti whispered. "They record, umm, the workings of the city and the farms: how many sheep and goats, how much grain can be expected from the next harvest, how many newborn, how many dead." He smiled at her wide-open eyes. "Our stories are told on those bits of string, Juna. This is how Cata Huuk works."

Keram nudged him. The man with the string had withdrawn. The Potus's great head had swiveled toward them. Keram and Muti immediately bowed. Juna just stared, until Keram dragged her down.

"Let her stand," said the Potus. His voice was like riverbed gravel. His eyes on Juna, he beckoned her.

Hesitantly Juna walked forward.

He leaned over her. She could smell animal oil on his skin. He pulled at her hair, hard enough to make her yowl. "Where did you get her?"

Keram quickly explained what had happened at Keer. "Potus, she says she was born here—here, in Cata Huuk. She says she was stolen as a baby. And—"

"Take your clothes off," the Potus snapped at Juna.

She glared back, repulsed by his smell, and did not obey. But Muti hastily ripped her skin shift from her, until she stood naked.

The Potus nodded, as if appraising a hunter's kill. "Good breasts.

Good height, good posture—and a pup in the belly, I see. Do you believe her, Keram? I never heard of a child like this being stolen—what, fifteen, sixteen years ago?"

"Nor I," said Keram.

"They say the wild ones beyond the fields grow like this: tall, healthy-looking, despite their appalling way of life."

"But if she is wild, she is a clever one," Keram said carefully. "I thought her tale would amuse you."

Juna said, "It is the truth!"

The Potus barked laughter. "It speaks."

"She speaks well. She is clever, sir, with—"

"Dance for me, girl." When Juna stared back at him, mute, the Potus said with a quiet hardness, "Dance for me, or I will have you dragged from here now."

Juna understood little of what was happening, but she could see that her life depended on how she responded now.

So she danced. She recalled dances she and her sister Sion had made up as children, and dances she had joined as an adult, following the capering of the shaman.

After a time, the Potus grinned. And then he, as well as Keram and Muti, began to clap to the rhythm of her bare feet as they slapped against the floor of polished wood.

Naked, stranded in strangeness, she danced, and danced.

From the beginning Juna saw very clearly that if she wished to remain healthy, well-fed—and free of the scourge of endless, repetitive, back-breaking work—then she had to stay as close to the Potus as she could.

And so she made herself as interesting as possible. She rummaged through her memories for skills and feats that had been commonplace among her own people, and yet would seem marvelous to these hive dwellers. She organized long-distance races, which she won with stunning ease, even heavily pregnant. She made spear-throwers, and showed her skill at hitting targets so small and distant most of the Potus's court couldn't even see them. She would take random bits of stone, wood, and shell, and, starting with no tools at all, knap out blades and carve ornaments, a process that seemed charming and miraculous to these people, so remote were they from the resources of the Earth.

Her baby was born. He was a slender boy, who might grow up to look like Tori, his now-lost father. As soon as she could she began to train him to run, to dance, to throw as she could.

And when at last she coaxed Keram into her bed—when he forgave her the lies she had told to persuade him to bring her here—and when a year later, wearing his gold-studded shell necklace, she gave birth to his child, she felt her place at the heart of this nest of people was secure.

As for the city, it didn't take Juna long to see the truth about this cramped hive.

This was a place of layers, of rigidity and control. The mass of the people here slaved their days away to feed the Potus, his wives, sons, daughters, and relatives, and those who served him, and the priesthood, the mysterious network of shamanlike mystics who seemed to live an even grander life than the Potus himself.

It had to be this way. With the taming of the plants, the land had become much more productive. The natural checks that had held back the growth of populations were suddenly removed. Human numbers exploded.

Suddenly people no longer bred like primates. They bred like bacteria.

The new, dense populations made possible the growth of new kinds of communities: large centers of population, towns, cities, fed by a steady flow of food and raw materials from the countryside.

There had never been such numbers before, never such an elaboration of human relations. The cities, of necessity, shook themselves down into a new form of social organization. In communities like Juna's, decision making had been communal and leadership informal, since everybody knew everybody else. Kinship ties had been sufficient to resolve most conflict. In slightly larger groups, chiefs would gather central control in order to manage affairs.

Now it was no longer possible for everybody to participate in every decision. It was no longer efficient for each family to grow and gather its own food, to make its own tools and clothing, to trade one-on-one with its neighbors. And day by day people could expect to meet perfect strangers—and have to get along with them, rather than just drive them away or kill them, as in the old days. The old inhibitions of kinship were no longer enough: Policing of some kind was required to keep order.

Central control rapidly asserted itself. Power and resources were increasingly concentrated in the hands of an elite. Chiefs and kings arose, with monopolies on decision making, information, and power. A new kind of redistributive economy was developed. There was political organization, rapidly advancing technology, record keeping, bureaucracy, taxation: an explosion of sophistication in the means by which human beings dealt with one another.

And, for the first time in hominid history, there were people who didn't have to work for food.

For thirty thousand years there had been religion, art, music, story-telling, war. But now it became possible for the new societies to afford specialists: people who did nothing but paint, or perfect melodies on flutes of bones and wood, or speculate on the nature of a god who had given the gifts of fire and agriculture to an unworthy mankind, or kill. Out of this tradition would eventually emerge much of the beauty and grandeur implicit in human potential. But so would emerge armies of professional, dedicated killers, of whom Keram's guards were a prototype.

And almost everywhere, right from the beginning, the new communi-ties were dominated by men: men competing with each other for power, in societies where women were treated more or less as a resource. During the days of the hunter-gatherers humans had briefly thrown off the ancient prison of the primate male hierarchies. Equality and mutual respect had not been luxuries: Hunter-gatherer communities were innately egalitarian because to share food and knowledge was self-evidently in the interests of everybody. But those days were vanishing now. Seeking a new way to organize their swelling numbers, humans were slipping comfortably into the ways of a mindless past.

The new urban concentrations appeared to be an utterly new way of living. No hominids—indeed no primates—had ever lived in such dense heapings. But in fact they were a throwback to a much more ancient form. The new cities had less in common with the hunter-gatherer com-munities of their immediate past than with the chimpanzee colonies of the forest.

Juna's interval of security lasted no more than four years.

In the dark of night, Keram shook her awake. "Come. Get the chil-dren. We have to leave."

Juna sat up, bleary-eyed. The previous evening they had thrown a party, and Juna had drunk too much mead, honey liqueur, than was good for her. Only in farmed lands were alcoholic drinks possible, for they needed cultivated grain for their manufacture—one of the key advan-tages of the farmers over the hunters, who had grown dependent on beer but could never learn to manufacture it for themselves. As for Juna, it was a luxury she still had to get used to.

She looked around, trying to wake up and cut through her confusion. The room was in darkness, but there was light outside the window. Not the light of day, but of fire.

And now she could hear the shouting.

She slipped out of bed and pulled on a simple, functional shift. She went to the next room and collected the children. The two boys were grumpy at being disturbed, but they settled to sleep again in her arms. She went back to Keram, who was cramming weapons and valuables into a sack. "I'm ready," she said.

He looked at her, standing waiting for him with their children held in her arms. He ran to her and kissed her hard on the lips. "I do love you, by the Potus's balls. If he has any left."

She was puzzled by the non sequitur. "Any what?'

"This is a bad night for Cata Huuk," he said grimly. "And for us, unless we are lucky." He turned and made for the door, lugging his sack. "Come on. We'll leave by the back gate."

They slipped out of their house. Now she could see the source of the fire. The great yellow palace of the Potus was burning, the flames and sparks rising high into the air. Juna heard screams from within the palace itself, and glimpsed people running.

The streets were full of people. Skinny, filthy, many dressed in ragged skins or rags of vegetable fiber, they swarmed like hungry rats. To Juna the merged voices of the mob were not human: They were like the roaring of thunder or the growling of a rainstorm, something beyond human control. Clutching her children, she tried to control her fear. "It is the hunger," she said.

"Yes."

Famine: It was another word Juna had been forced to learn. A blight had affected the main wheat crop of the farms in the area. Nobody understood it; nobody could cure it. When the harvest had failed, the hunger had spread rapidly. The first signs of unrest had been the murder of tribute collectors, trying to gather what was rightfully the Potus's. And now it had come to this. Juna's folk fed on many wild plants; no blight would destroy them all, as it could wipe out a single vital crop. Famine: another ambiguous gift of the new way of living.

The family kept their heads down. They avoided the main avenues, and made their way zigzag fashion toward the main gate.

Keram said, "There is a new settlement west of here, by the coast. The farmland is rich, and the resources of the sea are bountiful. It is many days' travel, but—"

"We will make it," she said firmly.

He nodded curtly. "We have to."

At last they reached the open gate. Here Muti waited for them. The three of them, cradling the children, slipped into the night.

As they headed east, everywhere they traveled, they walked through lands transformed by farmers and city builders. Even the land Juna had once crossed, fleeing with Cahl from her home, was now changed beyond recognition, so rapid had been the expansion.

The expansion happened because farmed lands soon became over-crowded. Sons and daughters wanted to own their own slice of the world, to master it as their parents had. This was easily achieved. The farmers' knowl-edge was not tied to a particular patch of land, as the hunter-gatherers' had been. Their thinking was systematic: They knew how to transform the land to make it the way they wanted it—*any* piece of land. They did not have to accept it as it was. For farmers, colonization was easy.

And so, from the first humble scratched farms in the east of Anatolia, the great expansion began. It was a kind of slow war, waged on the Earth itself, as it was transformed to suit the needs of the growing crowd of human bellies. It became an expansion that would soon outstrip geo-graphically the diffusion of *Homo erectus* and earlier generations of humans, an expansion that would proceed with astonishing speed.

But the expansion did not occur into a vacuum, but into land already occupied by the ancient hunter-gatherer communities.

It was not possible to share, of course. This was a conflict between two fundamentally different views of the land. The hunters saw their land as a place to which they were attached, like the trees that grew from it. To the farmers, it was a resource to own, to buy, sell, subdivide: Land was property, not a place. There could be only one outcome. The hunter-gatherers were simply outnumbered: Ten malnourished, runtish farmers could always overcome one healthy hunter.

After three days' traveling, they reached a kind of shantytown, a rough huddle of shelters and lean-tos. Juna peered around, tense, uninter-ested. "Why have we come here? We should move on before it grows dark—"

Keram placed a kindly hand on her arm. "I thought you would want to stop here. Juna, don't you recognize this place?'

"You should," came a woman's voice, oddly familiar.

Juna turned around. A woman was limping toward her, an ancient piece of skin thrown over her head. Juna's mind whirled. The words had been strange, yes—*because they were in Juna's birth language*, a tongue she had not heard since the day she had followed Cahl out of her village.

Now Juna could see the woman's face. It was Sion, her older sister. An unidentifiable longing came rushing back. "Oh, Sion—" She stepped for-ward, arms outstretched.

But Sion drew back. "No! Keep away." She grimaced. "The sickness did not murder me, as it murdered so many others, but I may carry it yet."

"Sion. Who—"

"Who died?" Sion barked a bitter laugh. "It would be better for you to ask who survived."

Juna glanced around. "And is this truly where we lived? Nothing is the same."

Sion snorted. "The men drink beer and mead. The women labor in the farms of Keer. Nobody hunts now, Juna. The animals have been driven off to make room for fields. We get by. Sometimes we sing the old songs for the farmers. They give us more beer."

"Who is shaman now?"

"Shamans are not allowed. The last of them drank himself to death, the fat fool." She shrugged. "It makes no difference. Nothing the shaman could tell us would help us now. It is not the shaman who knows how the wheat grows, nobody but the farmers, and their masters from the city with their bits of string and narrow eyes that peer at the sky."

The disease, as it happened, had been measles.

Mankind had always been prey to some diseases, of course: leprosy, yaws, and yellow fever were among the most ancient blights. Many of them were caused by microbes that would maintain themselves in the soil, or in animal populations—as yellow fever was carried by African monkeys. But people had had time, evolutionary time, to adapt to most such diseases and parasites.

With the coming of the new, dense communities had come new plagues—crowd diseases, like measles, rubella, smallpox, and influenza. Unlike the older illnesses, the microbes responsible for these diseases could only survive in the bodies of living people. Such diseases could not have evolved in humans until there were sufficiently dense and mobile crowds to allow them to spread.

But, if they infected crowds, they must have come from crowds. And so they had: crowds of animals, the heavily social herd creatures people now lived close to, animals in which the diseases had long been endemic. Tuberculosis, measles, and smallpox crossed to humans from cattle, influenza from pigs, malaria from birds. Meanwhile, with the building of grain stores, the vectors of infectious diseases—rats and mice and fleas and bugs—reached populations of unprecedented density. Still, those who survived developed resistance of some kind, though some of these mechanisms were clumsy, with damaging side effects. The mechanisms of adaptation operated too slowly, compared to the frenzied rate of change of human culture, to iron out the deficiencies.

But the hunter-gatherers at the farms' expanding borders had no resistance. They were devastated, even as their lands were overwhelmed by their farmer neighbors.

This transition, from the old way of living to the new, was a crucial moment in human history. A mass, unconscious choice was being made between limiting population growth to match the resources available, as the hunter-gatherers of the past had done, or trying to increase food production to feed a growing population. And once that choice had been made, the farmers' expansion could only accelerate. Henceforth the folk following the older ways would survive only in the most marginal environments, the fringes of deserts, the mountain peaks, the densest jungles—places the farmers could not tame.

It would happen in Africa, where Bantu farmers equipped with iron weapons would spread out of the western Sahara, overwhelming peoples like the pygmies and the Khoisan—ancestors to Joan Useb—at last marching all the way to the east coast of South Africa. It happened in China, where farmers from the north, aided by China's interconnected geography, would march south to repopulate and homogenize much of tropical southeast Asia, driving existing populations ahead of them in secondary invasions that hit Thailand and Burma.

And the great east-west span of Eurasia proved especially conducive to expansion. Farmers spread easily along lines of latitude, moving into places with a similar climate and length of day to their origin, and so suitable for their crops and beasts. With their cattle and goats and pigs and sheep, their highly productive wheat and barley, and their swelling numbers, the descendants of the farmers of Cata Huuk would build a mighty dominion of wheat and rice. The pyramids of Egypt would be built by workers fed by crops whose ancestors had been native to southwest Asia. They would take their Indo-European language with them, but it would splinter, mutate, and proliferate, generating Latin, German, Sanskrit, Hindi, Russian, Welsh, English, Spanish, French, Gaelic. At last they would colonize a huge east-west band stretching from the Atlantic coast to Turkestan, from Scandinavia to North Africa. One day they would even cross the oceans, in boats of wood and iron.

All across this immense span of cultivated land cities would burgeon, and empires would flourish and decay, like mushrooms. And everywhere the farmers went they carried the great diseases with them, a vicious froth on a tide of language, culture, and war.

Juna said impulsively, "Sister, come with us."

Sion glanced at Keram and Muti, and laughed. "That will not be possible." With an expression of anguish, she peered at Juna's children, who slept in the arms of Muti and Keram. Then she whispered, "Good-bye," and hurried back to the huts.

Juna made to call good-bye after her, but, she thought, that would be the last word I will ever speak in my own tongue. For I will never come back here. Never.

So, without speaking, she turned her face away and, with her children, resumed her steadfast walk to the west, and the new city on the coast.

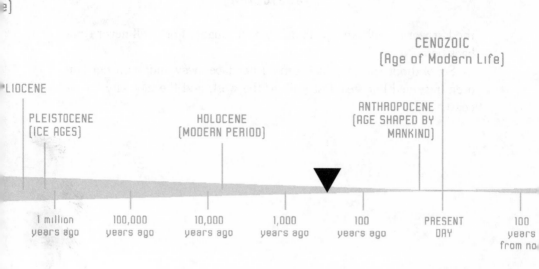

e]

LIOCENE

PLEISTOCENE
(ICE AGES)

HOLOCENE
(MODERN PERIOD)

CENOZOIC
(Age of Modern Life)

ANTHROPOCENE
(AGE SHAPED BY
MANKIND)

1 million
years ago

100,000
years ago

10,000
years ago

1,000
years ago

100
years ago

PRESENT
DAY

100
years
from no

CHAPTER 15

the dying light

▼ **Rome. Common Era (CE) 482.**

I

In Rome, the sun was bright, and the Italian air felt liquid to men used to the milder climes of Gaul. Everywhere lingered the immense stenches of the city: of fires, of cooking, and, above all, of sewage.

When Honorius led him into the Forum, Athalaric tried not to be overwhelmed.

Gaunt old Honorius stumbled forward, his threadbare toga wrapped around him. "I had not expected the strength of this sun. The light must have molded my ancestors, filled them with vigor. Oh! How I have longed to see this place. This is the Sacred Way, of course. There is the Temple of Castor and Pollux, there the Temple of the Deified Caesar with the Arch of Augustus beside it." He made his way to the shade of a statue—a horseback hero done in bronze, whose plinth alone towered ten to twelve times Athalaric's height—and he leaned against the marble, wheezing. "Augustus said he found Rome a city of brick and left it one of marble. The white marble, you see, comes from Luna, to the north, and the colored marbles from northern Africa, Greece, and Asia Minor—not so exotic destinations as they are today—"

Athalaric listened to his mentor, keeping his face expressionless.

This was the heart of Rome. It was here that the business of the city had been done even in Republican times. Since then, leaders and emperors as far back as Julius Caesar and Pompey had sought prestige by embellishing this ancient place, and the area had become a maze of temples, processional ways, triumphal arches, basilicas, council halls, rostra, and open spaces. The imperial residences on Palatine Hill still loomed over it all, a symbol of brooding power.

But now, of course, the emperors, like the Republicans before them, had gone.

Today Athalaric had chosen to wear his best metalwork, his belt buckle of bronze with fine lines of silver and gold hammered into its engraved pattern and the bow brooch of gold with silver filigree and garnets that held his cloak in place. His *barbarian* jewelry, so sneered at by the Romans, caught the light of the fierce Italian sun, even here in the ancient heart of their capital. And to remind himself of where he had come from, around his neck Athalaric wore the tag of beaten tin that had marked his father out as a slave.

He was proud of who he was, and who he might become. And yet, and yet . . .

And yet the sheer scale of it all, to eyes accustomed only to the small towns of Gaul, was astonishing.

Much of Rome was a city of mud brick, timber, and rubble-work; its predominant color was the bright red of the roofing tiles that covered so many of the residential buildings. The population had long overflowed the fortifications of the ancient city, and even the more extensive walls erected under the threat of barbarian invasion two centuries ago. It was said that at one time a million people had lived in this city, which had ruled an empire of a *hundred* million. Well, those days were gone—the burned-out and abandoned outer suburbs attested to that—but even in these straitened times, the sheer *numbers* of the place were stunning. There were two circuses, two amphitheaters, eleven public baths, thirty-six arches, nearly *two thousand* palaces, and a thousand pools and fountains fed with Tiber water by no less than nineteen aqueducts.

And at the heart of this sea of red tile and swarming people, here he was in an immense island of marble: marble used not just for columns and statues, but for the veneers of the walls, even for paving.

But, though the great spaces of the Forum were thronged with market stalls, Athalaric thought he sensed a great sadness here. Today the city was no longer even under Roman rule. Italy was now governed by a Scirian German called Odoacer, placed there by rebellious German troops, and Odoacer used Ravenna, a northern city lost in marshland, as his capital. Rome itself had been sacked twice.

Athalaric, motivated by a mild cruelty that puzzled him, began to point out evidence of damage. "See where the plinths are empty; the statues have been stolen. Those columns have tumbled, never to be repaired. Even some of the marble from the temples' walls has been taken! Rome is decaying, Honorius."

"Of course it is decaying," Honorius snapped. He shifted to stay in the shade of the plinth. "Of course the city decays. *I* decay." He held up his liver-spotted hand. "As do you, young Athalaric, despite your arrogance. And yet I am still strong. *I am here,* am I not?"

"Yes, you are here," Athalaric said more kindly. "And so is Rome."

"Do you believe that nature is running down, Athalaric? That all life-forms are diminishing with successive generations?" Honorius shook his head. "Surely this mighty place could only have been constructed by men with the most tremendous hearts and minds, men one will not find in the present world of squabbling and fracture, men who have evidently, tragically, become extinct. And if so it behooves us to conduct ourselves as did those who came before—those who built this place, rather than those who would tear it down."

Athalaric was moved by these words. But they subtly excluded him. Athalaric knew he was a good student, that Honorius respected him for his mind. Athalaric had reason to feel protective of the old man, even fond, of course; else he would not have accompanied him on this hazardous jaunt across Europe in search of ancient bones. And yet Athalaric was aware, too, that there were barriers in Honorius's heart every bit as solid and enduring as these great walls of white marble around him.

It was Honorius's ancestors who had built this mighty place, not Athalaric's. To Honorius, whatever he did, Athalaric would always be the son of a slave—and a barbarian at that.

A man approached them. He was dressed in a toga every bit as grand as Honorius's was threadbare, but his skin was as dark as an olive's.

Honorius pushed himself away from the plinth and stood up. Athalaric shifted his robe so that the weapon at his waist was visible.

His hands hidden in a fold of his toga, the man appraised them coolly. In clear but highly accented Latin, he said, "I have been waiting for you."

"But you do not know us," Honorius said.

The newcomer raised his eyebrows and glanced at Honorius's travel-stained toga, Athalaric's gaudy jewelry. "This is still Rome, sir. Travelers from the provinces are usually easily recognized. Honorius, I am the one you seek. You may call me Papak."

"A Sassanian name—a famous name."

Papak smiled. "You are learned."

As Papak smoothly questioned Honorius about the difficulty of their journey, Athalaric appraised him. The name alone told him much: Papak was evidently a Persian, from that great and powerful state beyond the borders of the remnant empire in the east. And yet he was in fully Roman attire, with not a trace of his origin save for the color of his skin and the name he bore.

Almost certainly he was a criminal, Athalaric thought. In these times of disintegrating order, those who worked in the shadows thrived, trading on greed and misery and fear.

He interrupted Papak's easy conversation. "Forgive my poor education," he said silkily. "If I remember my Persian history, *Papak* was a bandit who stole the crown from his sworn ruler."

Papak turned to him smoothly. "Not a bandit, sir. A rebel priest, yes. A man of principle, yes. Papak's life was not easy; his choices were difficult; his career was honorable. His is an honored name I am proud to bear. Would you like to compare the integrity of our lineages? Your German forebears chased pigs through the northern forests—"

Honorius said, "Gentlemen, perhaps we should cut to the heart of the matter."

"Yes," Athalaric snapped. "*The bones,* sir. We are here to meet your Scythian, and see his bones of heroes."

Honorius laid a placating hand on his arm. But Athalaric could sense his intensity as he waited for Papak's answer.

As Athalaric had half expected, the Persian sighed and spread his hands. "I did promise that my Scythian would meet you here, in Rome itself. But the Scythian is a man of the eastern desert. Which is why he is so difficult to work with. But his rootlessness is why the Scythian is so useful, of course." Papak rubbed his fleshy nose regretfully. "In these unfortunate times travel from the east is not so secure as it once was. And the Scythian is reluctant—"

To Athalaric's irritation, the ploy worked.

"It has always been thus," Honorius said sympathetically. "It was always easier to deal with farmers. Coherent wars can be fought with those who own land; if deals are struck all understand the meaning of the transactions. But nomads make for a much stiffer challenge. How can you *conquer* a man if he does not understand the meaning of the word?"

"We had an arrangement," Athalaric snapped. "We engaged in extensive correspondence with you, on receipt of your catalog of curiosities. We have traveled across Europe to meet this man, at great expense and not insignificant danger. We have already paid you half of the fee we agreed, let me remind you. And now you let us down."

Athalaric, despite himself, was impressed by Papak's display of hurt pride—the flaring nostrils, the trace of deeper color in his cheeks. "I have a reputation that spans the continent. Even in these difficult days there are many connoisseurs, like yourself, sir Honorius, of the bones of the heroes and beasts of the past. It has been a tradition across the old empire for a thousand years. If I were to be found out a cheat—"

Honorius made placatory noises. "Athalaric, please. I am sure our new friend did not mean to deceive us."

"It simply strikes me as remarkable," Athalaric said heavily, "that as soon as we meet, your promises evaporate like morning dew."

"I do not intend to renege," Papak said grandly. "The Scythian is—a difficult man. I cannot deliver him like an amphora of wine, much though I regret the fact."

Athalaric growled, "*But?*"

"I can propose a compromise."

Honorius sounded hopeful. "There, you see, Athalaric; I knew this would come good if we have patience and faith."

Papak sighed. "I am afraid it will demand of you further travel—"

"And expense?" Athalaric asked suspiciously.

"The Scythian will meet you at a rather more remote city: ancient Petra."

"Ah," said Honorius, and a little more of the life went out of him.

Athalaric knew Petra was in Jordan, a land still under the protection of Emperor Zeno in Constantinople. In such times as these, Petra was another world away. Athalaric took Honorius's arm. "Master, enough. He is applying storekeepers' tricks. He is merely trying to draw us more deeply into—"

Honorius murmured, "When I was a child my father ran a shop from the front of our villa. We sold cheese and eggs and other produce from the farms, and we bought and sold curiosities from all across the empire and beyond. That was how I got my taste for antiquities—and my nose for business. I am old but no fool yet, Athalaric! I am sure Papak senses further profit for himself in this situation—and yet I do not believe he is lying about the fundamentals."

Athalaric lost patience. "We have much work waiting for us at home. To be hauled across the ocean for a handful of decayed old bones—"

But Honorius had turned to Papak. "*Petra,*" he said. "A name almost as famous as Rome's itself! I will have many colorful adventures to recount to my grandchildren on my return to Burdigala. Now, sir, I suspect we must begin to discuss the practicalities of the journey."

A broad smile spread across Papak's face. Athalaric studied his eyes, trying to assess his honesty.

It took Honorius and Athalaric many weeks to reach Jordan, much of it consumed by the bureaucracy required to deal with the eastern empire. Every official they met proved deeply suspicious of outsiders from the broken remnants of the western empire—even of Honorius, a man whose father had actually been a senator of Rome itself.

It was Athalaric's self-appointed duty to care for Honorius.

The old man had once had a son, a childhood friend of Athalaric's. But Honorius had taken his family, with Athalaric, to a religious festival in Tolosa, to the south of Gaul. The party had been set upon by bandits. Athalaric had never forgotten his feeling of helplessness as, just a boy himself, he had watched as the bandits had beaten Honorius, molested his daughters—and so carelessly killed the brave little boy who had tried to come to his sisters' aid. *A fine Roman citizen! Where are your legions now? Where are your eagles, your emperors?*

Something had broken in Honorius that dark day. It was as if he had decided to detach himself from a world in which the sons of senators needed the patronage of Goth nobles, and bandits freely roamed the interior of what had been Roman provinces. Though he had never neglected his civic and family duties, Honorius had become increasingly absorbed by his study of relics of the past, the mysterious bones and artifacts that told of a vanished world inhabited by giants and monsters.

Meanwhile Athalaric had developed a deepening loyalty to old Honorius—it was as if he had taken the place of that lost son—and he had been pleased, though not surprised, when his own father had agreed that he should serve as Honorius's pupil in the law.

Honorius's story was only one of a myriad similar small tragedies, generated by the huge, implacable historical forces that were transforming Europe. The mighty political, military, and economic structure built by the Romans was already a thousand years old. Once it had sprawled across Europe, northern Africa and Asia: Roman soldiers had come into conflict with the inhabitants of Scotland in the west and the Chinese to the east. The Empire had thrived on expansion, which had bought triumphs for ambitious generals, profits for traders, and a ready source of slaves.

But when expansion was no longer possible, the system became impossible to sustain.

There came a point of diminishing returns, in which every *denarius* collected in taxes was pumped into administrative maintenance and the military. The empire became increasingly complex and bureaucratic— and so even more expensive to run—and inequality of wealth became grotesque. By the time of Nero in the first century, all the land from the Rhine to the Euphrates was owned by just two thousand obscenely rich individuals. Tax evasion among the wealthy became endemic, and the increasing cost of propping up the empire fell ever more heavily on the poor. The old middle class—once the backbone of the empire—declined, bled by taxes and squeezed out from above and below. The empire had consumed itself from within.

It had happened before. The great Indo-European expansion had spun off many civilizations, high and low. Great cities already lay buried in history's dust, forgotten.

Although the west had been the origin of the sprawling empire, the east had eventually become its center of gravity. Egypt produced three times as much grain as the west's richest province in Africa. And while the west's long borders were vulnerable to attack by land-hungry Germans, Hunni, and others, the east was like an immense fastness. The constant drain of resources from east to west had caused a growing political and economic tension. At last—eighty years before Honorius's visit to Rome—the division between the two halves of the old empire was made permanent. After that the collapse of the west had proceeded apace.

Constantinople still used Roman law, and the language of the state remained Latin. But, Athalaric found, its bureaucracy was difficult, entangling, altogether more *eastern*. Evidently Constantinople's engagements with the mysterious nations that lay beyond Persia in the unseen heart of Asia were influencing its destiny. At last, however, all the paperwork was arranged—even though Honorius's dwindling supply of gold was diminished further in the process. They joined a boatload of pilgrims, mostly minor Roman aristocracy from the western lands, bound for the Holy Land. After that they traveled by horseback and camel into the deeper interior.

But as the days of their journey wore on, and Honorius grew visibly more frail and exhausted. Athalaric felt increasingly regretful that he had not, after all, persuaded his mentor to turn back at Rome.

Petra turned out to be a city of rock.

"But this is extraordinary," Honorius said. He dismounted hastily and strode toward the giant buildings. "Quite extraordinary."

Athalaric clambered down from his horse. Casting a glance at Papak and his porters as they led the horses to water, he followed his mentor. The heat was intense, and in this dry, dusty air Athalaric did not feel protected at all by the loose, bright white local garment Papak had provided for him.

Huge tombs and temples thrust out of a steppe so arid that it was all but a desert. It was still a bustling city, Athalaric could see that. An elaborate system of channels, pipes, and cisterns collected and stored water for orchards, fields, and the city itself. And yet the people looked somehow dwarfed by the great monuments around them, as if they had been shrunken by time.

"Once, you know, this place was the center of the world," Honorius mused. "There was a battle for ascendancy between Assyria, Babylon, Persia, Egypt—all centered on this region, for under the Nabataeans Petra controlled the trade between Europe, Africa, and the east. It was an extraordinarily powerful position. And under Roman rule Petra grew even richer."

Athalaric nodded. "So why did Rome come to rule the world? Why not Petra?"

"I think you see the answer all around," Honorius said. "*Look.*"

Athalaric could see nothing but a few trees struggling for life among the shrubs, herbs, and grasses. Goats, tended by a ragged, wide-eyed boy, nibbled low branches.

Honorius said, "Once this was woodland, dominated by oak and pistachio trees: so say the historians. But the trees were felled to build houses, and to make plaster for the walls. Now the goats eat what remains, and the soil, overfarmed, grows dry and blows away into the air. As the land has grown poor, as the water is pumped dry, so the population flees—or starves. If Petra did not exist here already, it could never be sustained by such a poor hinterland. In another few centuries it will be abandoned altogether."

Athalaric was struck by an oppressive feeling of waste. "What is the purpose of these magnificent heapings of stone—all the lives that must have been consumed in their construction—if the people are to eat themselves to barrenness and ruin, and all is to decay to rubble?"

Honorius said grimly, "It may be that one day Rome itself will be a place of shells, of fallen monuments, inhabited by filthy people who will herd their goats along the Sacred Way, never understanding the mighty ruins they see all around them."

"But if cities rise and fall, a man may be master of his own destiny," Papak murmured. He had come up to them and was listening intently. "And here is one such, I think."

A man was striding out of the city toward them. He was remarkably tall, and he wore garments of some black cloth that clung tightly to his upper body and legs. A crimson swatch enclosed his head and covered much of his face. The dust seemed to swirl around his feet. It seemed to Athalaric that he was a figure of strangeness, as if from another time.

"Your Scythian, I take it," Honorius murmured.

"Indeed," said Papak.

Honorius drew himself up and reached for the fold of his toga. Athalaric felt a flicker of pride, complicated by a sense of envy, or perhaps inferiority. No matter how imposing this stranger was, Honorius was a Roman citizen, afraid of no man on Earth.

The Scythian unwrapped the cloth over his face and head, scattering more dust. His face was sharp-nosed, a thing of weather-beaten planes. Athalaric was startled to see that his hair was quite blond, as yellow as a Saxon's.

Honorius murmured to Papak, "Bid him greetings, and assure him of our best intentions to—"

Papak cut him short. "These fellows of the desert have little time for niceties, sir. He wants to see your gold."

Athalaric growled, "We've come a long way to be insulted by a sand flea."

Honorius looked pained. "Athalaric, please. The money."

Glaring at the Scythian, Athalaric opened his wrap to reveal a sack of gold. He tossed a piece to the Scythian, who tested it with his teeth.

"Now," whispered Honorius. "*The bones.* Is it true? Show me, sir. Show me—"

That needed no translation. The Scythian drew a bundle of cloth from a deep pocket. Carefully he began to unwind the cloth, and he spoke in his own liquid tongue.

"He says this is a treasure indeed," Papak murmured. "He says it comes from beyond the desert with the sand of gold, where the bones of the griffins—"

"I know about griffins," said Honorius tightly. "I do not care about griffins."

"From beyond the land of the Persians, from beyond the land of the Guptas—it is hard to translate," Papak said tightly. "His sense of who owns the land is not as ours, and his descriptions are lengthy and specific."

At last—with a shopkeeper's sense of timing, Athalaric thought cynically—the Scythian began to open up the wrapped bandages. He revealed a skull.

Honorius gasped and all but fell on the fragment. "*It is a man.* But not as we are—"

In the course of his education Athalaric had seen plenty of human skulls. The flat face and jaw of this skull were very human. But there was nothing human about the thick ridge of bone over the brow, or that small brain pan, so small he could have cupped it in one hand.

"I have longed to study such a relic," Honorius said breathlessly. "Is it true, as Titus Lucretius Carus wrote, that the early men could endure any environment, though they lacked clothing and fire, that they traveled in bands like animals and slept on the ground or in thickets, that they could eat anything and rarely fall ill? Oh, you must come to Rome, sir. You must come to Gaul! For there is a cave there, a cave on the coast of the ocean, where I have seen, I have seen—"

But the Scythian, perhaps mindful of the gold that still lay out of his reach, was not listening. He held up the fragment like a trophy.

The *Homo erectus* skull, polished by a million years, gleamed in the sunlight.

II

Under Honorius's pressure, the Scythian eventually agreed to come to Rome. Papak came along too, as a more or less necessary interpreter— and, to Athalaric's further dismay, so did two of the porters they had used in the desert.

Athalaric confronted Papak during the sea crossing back to Italy. "You are milking the old man's purse. I know your kind, Persian."

Papak was unperturbed. "But we are alike. I take his money, you empty his mind. What's the difference? The young have always fed off the wealth of the old, one way or another. Isn't it so?"

"I have pledged that I will bring him home safely. And that I will do, regardless of your ambitions."

Papak laughed smoothly. "I mean Honorius no harm." He indicated the impassive Scythian. "I have given him what he wants, haven't I?" But the Scythian's demeanor, as he coldly watched this exchange, made it clear to Athalaric that he was not to be regarded as anybody's property, however temporarily.

Still, even Athalaric's curiosity was pricked when this desert-dwelling nomad was brought to the greatest city in the world.

On the outskirts of Rome, they spent a night in a villa rented by Honorius.

Set on a slight rise on the edge of the city proper, this was a typical imperial-period home, its design drawn from Greek and Etruscan influences. The house was built on a series of bedrooms grouped around three sides of an open atrium. At the back were a dining room, offices, and utility rooms. Two street-facing rooms had been given over to shops. Honorius told him this had not been uncommon in the days of the empire; he reminded Athalaric of the shop his own family had once run.

But, like the city it overlooked, the villa had seen better days. The little shops were boarded up. The *impluvium*, the pool at the center of the atrium, had been crudely dug out, apparently to get at the lead piping that had once collected rainwater.

Honorius shrugged at this decay. "The place lost a lot of its value when the sackings came—too hard to defend, you see, so far out of the city. That is how I was able to rent it so cheaply."

That night, amid this battered grandeur, they ate a meal together. Even the mosaic on the floor of the dining room was badly damaged; it appeared that thieves had taken any pieces that showed traces of gold leaf.

The food itself was a signature of the great pan-Eurasian mixing that had followed the expansion of the farming communities. The staples were wheat and rice from the original Anatolian agricultural package, but supplemented by quince originally from the Caucasus, millet from Central Asia, cucumber, sesame, and citrus fruit from India, and apricots and peaches from China. This transcontinental diet was an everyday miracle, unremarked on by those who ate it.

The next day they took the Scythian into the old city itself.

They walked to the Palatine, the Capitol, the Forum. The Scythian gazed around him with his horizon-sharp eyes, assessing, somehow measuring. He wore his desert garb of black clothing with scarlet wrap around his head; it must have been uncomfortable in Rome's humid air, but he showed no signs of discomfort.

Athalaric murmured to Papak, "He doesn't seem very impressed."

Now the Scythian snapped out something in his terse, ancient language, and Papak translated automatically. "He says he understands now why the Romans had to take slaves and gold and food from his land."

Honorius seemed obscurely pleased. "A savage he may be, but he is no fool—and he is not intimidated, not even by mighty Rome. Good for him."

Away from the monumental areas, central Rome was a clotted network of streets and alleys, narrow and gloomy, the product of more than a thousand years' uncontrolled building. Many of the residences here were five or six stories tall. Raised by unscrupulous landlords determined to get as much income as possible out of every scrap of precious land, they towered unsteadily. Walking through sewage-littered, unpaved streets, with buildings crowded so closely they almost touched above their heads, it seemed to Athalaric that he was passing through an immense network of sewers, like one of the famous *cloacae* that ran beneath Rome to the Tiber.

The crowds in the streets wore masks over their mouths and noses, gauze soaked in oil or spices. There had been a recent outbreak of smallpox. Disease was a constant threat: People still talked of the mighty Plague of Antoninus of three centuries earlier. In the millennia since the death of Juna, medical advances had barely slowed the march of the mighty diseases. Immense trade routes had united the populations of Europe, northern Africa, and Asia into a single vast resource pool for microbes, and the increased crowding of people into cities with little or no sanitation had exacerbated the problem. Throughout Rome's imperial period it had been necessary to encourage a constant immigration of healthy peasants into the cities to replace those who died, and in fact urban populations would not become self-sustaining until the twentieth century.

This swarming place was a pathological outcome of the farming revolution, a place where people were crowded like ants, not primates.

It was almost a relief when they reached an area that had been burned out during one of the barbarian sackings. Though the destruction was decades past, this scorched, shattered area had never been rebuilt. But at least here among the rubble Athalaric could see the sky, unimpeded by filth-strewn balconies.

Honorius said to the Persian, "Ask him what he thinks now."

The Scythian turned and surveyed the rows of heaped-up residential buildings. He murmured, and Papak translated. "How strange that you people choose to live in cliffs, like gulls." Athalaric had heard the contempt in the Scythian's voice.

When they returned to their villa Athalaric found that the purse he carried around his waist had been neatly slit open and emptied. He was angry, with himself as much as the thief—how was he supposed to be looking after Honorius if he couldn't even watch over his own purse?— but he knew he should be grateful that the invisible bandit had not slit open his belly in the process and robbed him of his life as well.

The next day Honorius said he would take the party out into the country, to what he called the Museum of Augustus. So they piled into carts and went clattering over metaled but overgrown roads, out through the farms that crowded around the city.

They came to what must once have been an exclusive, expensive small town. An adobe wall contained a handful of villas and a cluster of meaner dwellings that had housed slaves. The place was obviously abandoned. The outer wall had been broken down, the buildings burned out and looted.

Honorius, with a scrawled map in his hand, led them into the complex, muttering, turning the map this way and that.

A thick layer of vegetation had broken through the mosaics and floor tiles, and ivy clung to fire-cracked walls. There must have been agony here, Athalaric thought, when the strength of the thousand-year empire had failed at last and its protection was lost. But the presence of the new vegetation in the midst of decay was oddly reassuring. It was even comforting to imagine that after another few centuries, as the green returned, nothing would be left of this place but a few hummocks in the ground, and oddly shaped stones that might break an unwary farmer's plow.

Honorius brought them to a small building at the center of the complex. It might once have been a temple, but it was as burned out and ruined as the rest. The porters had to haul aside a tangle of vines and ivy. Honorius rummaged over the ground. At last, with a cry of triumph, he retrieved a bone, a great scapula the size of a dinner plate. "I knew it! The barbarians took the petty gold, the shiny silver, but they knew nothing of the true treasures here."

At the sight of Honorius's spectacular find, the others began to root in the dirt and vegetation with the enthusiasm of prospectors. Even the doltish porters seemed fired by intellectual curiosity, perhaps for the first time in their lives. Soon they were all unearthing huge bones, tusks, even misshapen skulls. It was an extraordinarily exciting moment.

Honorius was saying, "This was once a bone museum, established by Emperor Augustus himself! The biographer Suetonius tells us that it was first set up on the island of Capri. In later times one of Augustus's successors imported the best of the pieces here. Some of the bones have crumbled away—look at this one—they are clearly very ancient, and have been subject to grievous misuse."

Now Honorius found a heavy slab of red sandstone, with startling white objects embedded within it. It was the size of a coffin lid and much too heavy for him, and the porters had to help him raise it. "Now, sir Scythian. No doubt you will recognize this handsome fellow."

The Scythian smiled. Athalaric and the others crowded around to see.

The white objects, suspended in the red matrix, were bones: the skeletal remains of a creature embedded in the rock. The creature must have been as long in its body as Athalaric was tall. It had big hind limbs, clearly visible ribs suspended from its spine, and short forearms, folded before its chest. Its tail was long, something like a crocodile's, Athalaric thought. But its most surprising feature was its head. The skull was massive, with a great hollow crest of bone, and a huge, powerful jaw hinged under what looked like a bird's beak. Two empty eyes stared out of time.

Honorius was watching him, rheumy eyes glittering. "Well, Athalaric?"

"I have never seen such a thing before," Athalaric breathed. "But—"

"But you know what it is."

It must be a griffin: the legendary monsters of the eastern deserts, four-footed, and yet with a head like a great bird's. The images of griffins had permeated paintings and sculpture for a thousand years.

Now the Scythian began to talk, rapidly, fluently, and Papak scrambled to keep up his translation. "He says that his father, and his father before him, prospected the great deserts to the east for the gold that washes down from the mountains. And the griffins guard the gold. He has seen their bones everywhere, peering out of the rocks, just like this."

"Just as Herodotus described," Honorius said.

Athalaric said, "Ask him if he has seen one alive."

"No," the Scythian said through Papak, "but he has seen their eggs many times. Like birds they lay their eggs in nests, but on the ground."

Athalaric murmured, "How did the beast get into the rock?"

Honorius smiled. "Remember Prometheus."

"Prometheus?"

"To punish him for bringing fire to humans, the old gods chained Prometheus to a mountain in the eastern deserts—a place guarded by mute griffins, as it happens. Aeschylus tells us how landslides and rain buried his body, where it was trapped for long ages until the wearing of the rock returned it to the light. Here is a Promethean beast, Athalaric!"

On they talked, rummaging among the bones. They were all strange, gigantic, distorted, unrecognizable. Most of these remains were actually of rhinos, giraffes, elephants, lions, and chalicotheres, the huge mammals of the Pleistocene brought to light by the tectonic churning of this place, where Africa drove slowly north into Eurasia. As in Australia, as all over the world, so here; people had even forgotten what they had lost, and only distorted trace memories of these giants remained.

And as the men argued and pried at the fossil, the skull of the protoceratops—a dinosaur trapped in a sandstorm only a few centuries before the birth of Purga—peered out with the sightless calm of eternity.

"... These are accounts written down by Hesiod and Homer and many others, but handed down by generations of storytellers before them.

"Long before the existence of modern humans, the Earth was empty. But the primordial ground birthed a series of Titans. The Titans were like men, but huge. Prometheus was one of them. Kronos led his sibling Titans to slay their father, Uranos. But his blood produced the next generation, the Giants. In those days, not long after the origin of life itself, there was much chaos in the blood, and generations of giants and monsters proliferated."

They sat in the half-ruined atrium of the rented villa. The air had remained hot and still as the evening had drawn on, but the wine, the hum of the insects, and the luxuriant, unlikely greenery draped around the atrium made this place somehow welcoming.

And in this decayed place, over glass after glass of wine, Honorius tried to persuade the man from the desert that he must travel with him much further: back across the wreckage of the empire, all the way west to the fringe of the world ocean itself. And so he told him stories of the birth and death of gods.

Another generation of life had passed, and more new forms evolved. The Titans Kronos and Rhea gave birth to the future gods of Olympus, the Romans' Jupiter among them. Eventually Jupiter led the new, human-form gods against a coalition of the older Titans, Giants, and monsters. It was a war for the supremacy of the cosmos itself.

"The land was shattered," Honorius whispered. "Islands emerged from the deep. Mountains fell into the sea. Rivers ran dry, or changed course, flooding the land. And the bones of the monsters were buried where they fell.

"Now," Honorius went on, "the natural philosophers have always countered the myths—they seek natural causes that conform to natural laws—and perhaps they are right to do so. But sometimes they go too far. Aristotle holds that creatures always breed true, that the species of life are fixed for all time. Let him explain the giants' bones we dig out of the ground! Aristotle must never have seen a bone in his life! The thing embedded in the rock in the museum may or may not be a griffin. But is it not clear the bones are *old*? How long can it take for sand to turn to rock? What is that great slab but evidence of *different times* in the past?

"Look beyond the stories. Listen to the essence of what the myths tell us: that the Earth was populated by different creatures in the past—

species that sometimes bred true, and sometimes produced hybrids and monsters radically different from their parents. Just as the bones show! Whatever the precise facts, is it not clear that *the myths hold truth,* for they are the product of a thousand years of study of the Earth, and contemplation of its meaning. And yet, and yet—"

Athalaric laid a hand on his friend's arm. "Calm yourself, Honorius. You are speaking well. There is no need to shout."

Honorius, trembling with his passion, said, "I contend we cannot ignore the myths. Perhaps they are memories, the best memories we have, of the great cataclysms and extraordinary times of the past, witnessed by men who might have comprehended little of what they saw, men who might have been only half men themselves." He caught Athalaric's frown. "Yes, half men!" Honorius produced the skull that the Scythian had given to him, with its human face and apelike cranium. "A human, but not a human," he murmured. "It is the greatest mystery of all. *What came before us?* What can answer such a question? What but the bones? Sir Scythian, you told me that this skullcap comes from the east."

Papak translated. "The Scythian cannot say where it originated. It passed through many hands, traveling west, until it reached you."

"And with each transaction," Athalaric murmured almost genially, "no doubt the price increased."

Papak raised his thin eyebrows at that. "It is said that in the land of the people with the pale skin and narrow eyes, far to the east, such bones are commonplace. The bones are ground up for medicine and charms, and to make the fields rich."

Honorius leaned forward. "So in the east we now know that there once lived a race of men of human form but of small brain. *Animal men.*" His voice was trembling. "And what if I were to tell you that in the furthest west, at the edge of the world, there was once *another* race of pre-men— men with bodies like bears and brows like centurions' helmets?"

Athalaric was stunned; Honorius had told him nothing of this.

The Scythian began to talk. His smooth vowels and subdued consonants sounded like a song, barely perturbed by Papak's clumsy translations, a song from the desert that soared up into the humid Italian night.

"He says there were once many kinds of people. They are all gone now, these people, but in the deserts and the mountains they linger on in stories and songs. We have forgotten, he says. Once the world was full of different men, different animals. We have forgotten."

"Yes!" Honorius cried, and he suddenly stood up, flushed. "Yes, yes! We have forgotten almost everything, save only distorted traces preserved in myth. It is a tragedy, an agony of loneliness. Why, you and I, sir Scythian, have almost forgotten how to talk to each other. And yet you understand, as I do, that we float, like sailors on a raft, over a great sea of undiscovered time. Come with me—I must show you the bones I have found—oh, come with me!"

III

Athalaric and Honorius came from Burdigala, a city of the thirty-year-old Gothic kingdom that now spanned much of what had once been the Roman provinces of Gaul and Spain. To get home, they were forced to travel back through the patchwork of territories which had emerged as Roman dominion had broken down across western Europe.

The relationship between Rome and the clamoring German tribes of the north had long been problematic, as the Germans pressed down hard on the old empire's long, vulnerable northern border. For centuries some Germans had been used as mercenaries by the empire, and at last whole tribes had been allowed to settle inside the empire on the understanding that they fought as allies against common enemies beyond the border. So the empire had become a kind of shell, inhabited and controlled not by Romans but by the more vigorous Germans, Goths, and Vandals.

As the pressure on the border increased—an indirect result of the mighty expansion of the Huns out of Asia—the last elements of Roman control had melted away. The governors and their staff had disappeared, and the last Roman soldiers left clinging to their posts, ill-paid, badly equipped, and demoralized, had failed to prevent the breakdown of order.

Thus the western empire had fallen, almost unremarked. New nations emerged amid the political rubble, and slaves became kings.

And so, from the kingdom of Odoacer, covering Italy and the remnants of the old provinces of Raetia and Noricum to the north, Athalaric and Honorius passed through the kingdom of the Burgundians, which spanned much of the hinterland of the Rhone to the east of Gaul, and the kingdom of the Soissons in northern France, before returning at last to their western Gothic kingdom.

Athalaric had feared his jaunt into the failing heart of the old empire might leave him overwhelmed by the inferiority of his people's meager achievements. But when he at last got home he found the opposite seemed to be true. After the crumbling grandeur of Rome, Burdigala indeed seemed small, provincial, primitive, even ugly. But Burdigala was expanding. Large new developments were visible all around its harbor area, and the harbor itself was crowded with ships.

Rome was magnificent, but it was dead. *This* was the future—his future, his to make.

Athalaric's uncle Theodoric was a remote cousin of Euric, the Goth king of Gaul and Spain. Theodoric, who nursed long-term ambitions for his family, had set up a kind of satellite court in an old, expansive Roman villa outside Burdigala. When he heard about the exotic visitors brought back by Honorius and Athalaric, he insisted they stay in his villa, and he immediately began to plan a series of social occasions to show off the visitors, as well as the accomplishments and travels of his nephew.

At these occasions, Theodoric was to entertain members of the new Goth nobility—and also Roman aristocrats.

If political control had been lost, the culture of the thousand-year-old empire persisted. The new German rulers showed themselves willing to learn from the Romans. The Goth king Euric had had the laws of his kingdom drawn up by Roman jurists and issued in Latin; it was this body of law which Athalaric had been assigned to Honorius to study. And meanwhile the old landed aristocracy of the empire continued to live alongside the newcomers. Many of them, with centuries of acquisition behind them, remained rich and powerful even now.

Even after visiting Rome itself, Athalaric found it ironic to see these toga-clad scions of ancient families, many of them still holding imperial titles, among leather-clad barbarian nobles, gliding effortlessly through rooms whose genteel frescoes and mosaics were now overlaid with the cruder imagery of a warrior people, horseback warriors with their helmets, shields, and lances. It could be argued—Honorius *did* argue—that with their systematic greed, practiced over centuries, these exquisite creatures had destroyed the very empire that created them. But for these aristocrats, the replacement of the vast imperial superstructure with the new patchwork of Gothic and Burgundian chiefs had made no significant difference in their own gilded lives.

In fact, for some of them, it seemed that the collapse of the empire had actually opened up business opportunities.

As a trophy guest the Scythian proved less than satisfactory for Theodoric. The man from the desert seemed revolted by the elaborate atrium, gardens, and rooms of the villa. He preferred to spend his time in the room Theodoric had granted him. But he ignored the bed and the rest of the furniture in the room, spread the rolled blanket he carried on the floor, and set up a kind of tent of sheets. It was as if he had brought the desert to Gaul.

If the Scythian was a social disappointment, Papak was a success, as Athalaric had sourly expected. Bringing a whiff of the exotic, the Persian moved smoothly among Theodoric's guests, barbarian and citizen alike. He flirted outrageously with the women, and captivated the men with his tales of the peculiar dangers of the east. Everyone was charmed.

One of Papak's most popular innovations was chess. This was a game, he said, recently invented to amuse the court of Persia. Nobody in Gaul had heard of it, and Papak had one of Theodoric's craftsman carve a board and pieces for him. The game was played on a six-by-six grid of squares, over which pieces shaped like horses or warriors moved and battled. The rules were simple, but the strategy was deceptively deep. The Goths—who still prided themselves on their warrior credentials, even though many of them had not been near a horse in twenty years—relished the sublimated combat of the new game. Their first tournaments were fast and bloody affairs. But under Papak's tactful tutelage, the better players soon grasped the game's subtleties, and the matches became drawn out and interesting.

As for Honorius himself, he was irritated that the parlor games of a Persian were so much more compelling than his tales of old bones. But then, Athalaric thought with exasperated fondness, the old man never had been much of a one for social niceties, and still less for the intricacies of court life. Honorius insisted on sticking to his usual games of backgammon, played with his cronies from the old landed aristocracy—"the game of Plato," as he called it.

After a few days of the stay, Theodoric called his nephew into a private room.

Athalaric was surprised to find Galla here. Tall, dark-haired, with the classical prominent nose of her Roman forebears, Galla was the wife of one of the more prominent citizens of the community. But at forty she was some twenty years younger than her husband, and it was well known that she was the power in his household.

A grave expression on his bearded face, Theodoric placed his hand on his nephew's arm. "Athalaric, we need your help."

"You have a job for me?"

"Not exactly. We have a job for Honorius—and we want you to persuade him to take it. Let us try to explain why—"

As Theodoric talked, Athalaric was aware of Galla's cool eyes appraising him, the slight opening of her full mouth. There was a myth among some of these last Romans that the barbarians were a younger, more vigorous race. Galla, in exploring intimacy with men she saw as little better than savages, might be seeking a muscular excitement she must lack in her own marriage to an etiolated citizen.

But Athalaric, a mere five years older than Galla's own twin children, had no desire to be the toy of a decadent aristocrat. He returned her gaze coolly, his face impassive.

This subtle transaction was played out completely beneath the attention of Theodoric.

Now Galla said smoothly, "Athalaric, a mere three decades ago, as even I can remember, this kingdom of Euric's was still a federate settlement within the empire. Things have changed rapidly. But there are strict barriers between our peoples. Marriage, the law, even the Church—"

Theodoric sighed. "She is right, Athalaric. There are many tensions in this young society of ours."

Athalaric knew this was true. The new barbarian rulers lived by their traditional laws, which they saw as part of their identity, while their subjects clung to Roman law, which for their part they saw as a set of universal rules. Disputes over differing rulings made under the two systems were common. Meanwhile, intermarriage was forbidden. Though all parties were Christian, the Goths followed the teachings of Arius and were met with hostility by their mostly Catholic subjects. And so on.

All of this was a barrier to the assimilation the imperial Romans had practiced so successfully for so many centuries—an assimilation that had led to stability and social longevity. If this place were still under Roman rule, then Theodoric would have had an excellent chance of becoming a full Roman citizen. But the sons of Galla were forever excluded from being accepted as equals by the Goths, forever denied true power.

Athalaric listened gravely to all of this. "It is difficult, but Honorius has taught me nothing if not that time is long, and that in time everything changes. Perhaps these barriers will ultimately melt away."

Theodoric nodded. "I myself believe it is so. I sent you to study in a Roman school, and later with Honorius." He chuckled. "*My* father would never have allowed such a thing. He didn't believe in schools! *If you learn to fear a teacher's strap now, you will never learn to look on a sword or javelin without a shudder.* To him, we were warriors before anything else. But we, these days, are a different generation."

"And the better for it," said Galla. "The empire will never come back. But I truly believe that some day, out of the union of our peoples here and across the continent, new blood will arise, new kinds of strength and vision."

Athalaric raised his eyebrows. Something in her tone reminded him unfortunately of Papak, and he wondered what she was trying to sell his uncle. He said dryly, "But in the meantime, before that marvelous day comes to pass—"

"In the meantime I am concerned for my children."

"Why? Are they in peril?"

"In fact, yes," Galla said, letting her irritation show. "You have been away too long, young man, or else you have your head too firmly buried in Honorius's teachings."

"There have been attacks," Theodoric said. "Property damage, fires, thefts."

"Directed against the Romans?"

"I am afraid so." Theodoric sighed. "I, who remember how it was, would like to preserve what was best about the empire—stability, peace, learning, a just system of law. But the young know nothing of this. Like their forefathers who lived simpler lives on the northern plains, they hate what they know of the empire: power over the land, the people, riches from which they were excluded."

"And so they wish to punish those who remain," said Athalaric.

Galla said, "*Why* they behave as they do scarcely matters. What is important is what must be done to stop them."

"I have raised militia. The disturbances can be quelled, but they erupt again elsewhere. What we need is a solution for the long term. We must restore the balance." Theodoric smiled. "It is a paradox that I should come to believe it is necessary to make our Romans strong again."

Athalaric snorted. "How? Give them a legion? Raise Augustus from the dead?"

"Simpler than that," Galla said, unmoved by his mockery. "We must have a bishop."

Now Athalaric began to understand.

Galla said, "Remember, it was Pope Leo who persuaded Attila himself to turn back from the gates of Rome—"

"So that's why I'm here. You want Honorius to become a bishop. And you want me to persuade him to do it."

Theodoric nodded, pleased. "Galla, I told you the boy is perspicacious."

Athalaric shook his head. "He will refuse. Honorius is not—worldly. He is interested in his old bones, not in power."

Theodoric sighed. "But there is a shortage of candidates, Athalaric. Forgive me, madam, but too many of the Roman gentry have proved themselves fools—arrogant, greedy, overbearing."

"My husband among them," Galla said evenly. "There is no offense to be given by the truth, my lord."

Theodoric said, "It is only Honorius who commands true respect—perhaps *because* of his lack of worldliness." He eyed Athalaric. "If it had not been so I would never have been able to release you to his tutelage."

Galla leaned forward. "I understand your misgivings, Athalaric. But will you try nevertheless?"

Athalaric shrugged. "I will try, but—"

Galla's hand shot out and grabbed his arm. "As long as he lives, Honorius is the only candidate for the position; no other can fill the role. *As long as he lives.* I trust you will try very hard to persuade him, Athalaric."

Suddenly Athalaric saw power in her: the power of an ancient empire, the power of an angry, threatened mother. He pulled himself free of her grip, disturbed by her intensity.

Honorius prepared for the last leg of the epic journey he had first conceived on meeting the Scythian on the edge of the eastern deserts.

A traveling party formed up. The core was Honorius, Athalaric, Papak, and the Scythian, just as it had been before. But now some of Theodoric's militia traveled with them—away from the towns, the country was far from safe—along with a handful of the more inquisitive young Goths and even some members of the old Roman families.

So they journeyed west.

As it happened they were all but retracing the steps taken by Rood's hunting party, some thirty thousand years earlier. But the ice had long retreated to its northern fortresses—so long ago, in fact, that humans had forgotten it had even come this way. Rood would not have recognized this rich, temperate land. And he would have been astonished at the great density of people living here now—just as Athalaric would have been astounded if he could have glimpsed Rood's mammoth herds gliding across a land empty of humans.

At last the land ran out. They came to a chalk cliff. Eroded by time, the cliff looked out over the restless Atlantic. The grassy plateau at its top was windswept and barren, save for a skimming of grass littered by rabbit droppings.

As the porters unpacked the party's belongings from their carts, the Scythian walked alone to the edge of the cliff. The wind caught his strange blond hair, whipping it about his brow. Athalaric thought it a remarkable sight. Here was a man who had peered into the great sand ocean of the east, now brought to the western fringe of the world. Silently he applauded Honorius's vision; whatever the Scythian made of Honorius's enigmatic bones, the old man had already crafted a remarkable moment.

Though the members of the party were wearied by the long journey from Burdigala, Honorius was impatient to conclude the jaunt. He would allow them only a brief respite for meat, drink, and the necessary attention to their bladders and bowels. Then, capering gauntly, Honorius led them toward the cliff face. The rest of the party followed—all but Papak's two porters, Athalaric saw, who seemed intent on making a trap for the rabbits that infested this chalky cliff top.

As they walked together, Athalaric tried to reason with Honorius again about the offer of the bishopric.

It made a certain sense. As the old civil administration of the empire had broken down, the Church, enduring, had proven a bastion of strength, and its bishops had acquired status and power. Very often these churchmen had been drawn from the landed aristocracy of the empire, who had learning, administrative experience drawn from running their great estates, and a tradition of local leadership: their theology might be shaky, but that was less important than shrewdness and practical experience. In turbulent times these worldly clerics had proved able to protect the vulnerable Roman population by pleading for the protection of towns, directing defenses and even leading men into battle.

But, as Athalaric had expected, Honorius refused the offer flat. "Is the Church to swallow us all?" he railed. "Must its shadow extinguish everything else in the world, everything we have built up over a thousand years?"

Athalaric sighed. He had very little idea what the old man was talking about, but the only way to talk to Honorius was on his terms. "Honorius, please—this has nothing to do with history, nor even theology. This is all about temporal power. And civic duty."

"Civic duty? What does that mean?" From a bag he fished out his skull, the antique human skull that the Scythian had given him, and he brandished it angrily. "Here is a creature half human and half animal. And yet it is clearly *like us*. What, then, are we? A quarter animal, a tenth? The Greek Galen pointed out two centuries ago that man is nothing more than a variety of monkey. Will we ever walk out of the shadow of the beast? What would *civic duty* mean to a monkey, what but a foolish performance?"

Hesitantly Athalaric touched the old man's arm. "But even if that is true, even if we are governed by the legacy of an animal past, then it is up to us to behave as if it were not so."

Honorius smiled bitterly. "Is it? But everything we build passes, Athalaric. We are *seeing* it. In my lifetime a thousand-year-old empire has crumbled faster than the mortar in the walls of its capital buildings. If all passes but our own brutish natures, what hope do we have? Even beliefs wither like grapes left on the vine."

Athalaric understood; this was a concern Honorius had rehearsed many times. In the last centuries of the empire, educational standards and literacy had fallen. In the dulled heads of the masses, distracted by cheap food and the barbaric spectacles of the coliseums, the values on which Rome had been founded and the ancient rationalism of the Greeks had been replaced by mysticism and superstition. It was—Honorius had explained to his pupil—as if a whole culture was losing its mind. People were forgetting how to think, and soon they would forget they had forgotten. And, to Honorius's thinking, Christianity only exacerbated that problem.

"You know, Augustine warned us that belief in the old myths was fading—even a century and a half ago, as the dogma of the Christians took root. And with the loss of the myths, so vanishes the learning of a thousand years, which are codified in those myths, and the monolithic dogmas of the Church will snuff out rational inquiry for ten more centuries. *The light is fading,* Athalaric."

"Then take the bishopric," Athalaric urged. "Protect the monasteries. Establish your own, if you must! And in its library and *scriptorium* have the monks preserve and make copies of the great texts, before they are lost—"

"I have seen the monasteries," Honorius spat. "To have the great works of the past copied as if they were magical spells, by dolts with their heads full of God—pah! I think I would rather burn them myself."

Athalaric suppressed a sigh. "You know, Augustine found comfort in his faith. He believed that the empire had been created by God to spread the message of Christ, so how could he allow it to collapse? But Augustine concluded that history's purpose is God's, not man's. Therefore in the end the fall of Rome did not matter."

Honorius eyed him wryly. "Now, if you were a diplomat, you would point out to me that poor Augustine died just as the Vandals swept through northern Africa. And you would say that if he had devoted more attention to worldly matters than spiritual, he might have lived a little longer, and managed a little more studying. *That* is what you should say if you want to persuade me about your wretched bishopric."

"I am glad your mood is improving," said Athalaric dryly.

Honorius tapped his hand. "You are a good friend, Athalaric. Better than I deserve. But I will not take your uncle's gift of a bishopric. God and politics are not for me; leave me to my bones and my maundering. We are nearly there!"

They had reached the cliff's edge.

To Honorius's frustration the path he remembered was overgrown. It was anyhow little more than a scratch in the cliff's crumbling face, perhaps made by goats or sheep. The militiamen used their spears to clear some of the weeds and grass. "It is many years since I came here," Honorius breathed.

Athalaric said sternly, "Sir, you were younger when you were here—much younger. You must take care as we descend."

"What do I care of the difficulty? Athalaric, if the path is overgrown it has not been used since I was last here—and the bones I found are undisturbed. What matters compared to that? Look, the Scythian has already started his descent, and I want to see his reaction. Come, come."

The party formed up into a line and, one by one, they stepped with care down the crumbling path. Honorius insisted on walking alone—the path was scarcely wide enough to allow two to walk side by side—but Athalaric went first, so at least he would have a chance of saving the old man if he fell.

They reached a cave, eroded into the soft chalk face. They fanned out, the militiamen probing at the walls and ground with their spears.

Athalaric stepped forward carefully. The floor near the entrance was stained almost white by guano and littered with eggshells. The walls and floor were worn butter smooth, as if many creatures, or people, had been here before. Athalaric detected a strong animal scent, perhaps of foxes, but it was stale. Save for the seabirds, it was evident nothing had lived here for a long time.

But it was here that a younger Honorius had found his precious bones.

Honorius hobbled around the cave, peering at anonymous bits of the floor, kicking aside dried leaves and bits of dead seaweed. Soon he found what he was looking for. He got to his knees and cleared away the debris, carefully, using only his fingertips. "It is just as I found it—and left it—for I did not want the bones to be disturbed."

The others crowded around. Athalaric absently noticed that one of the young Romans, a man of Galla's entourage, was pressing peculiarly close behind Honorius. But there seemed no harm, nothing but eagerness in the boy.

And everyone was impressed when Honorius gently lifted his osteoid treasure from the dirt. Athalaric could immediately see that it was the skeleton of a human—but this must have been a particularly stocky human, he thought, with heavy limb bones and long fingers—and that the skull was distorted. In fact, it appeared to have been broken from behind, perhaps by a blow. Beneath the bones was a litter of shells and flint flakes.

Honorius pointed to features of his find. "Look here. You can see where he has eaten mussels. The shells are scorched; perhaps he threw them on a fire to make them open. And I believe these flint chips are waste from a tool he made. He was clearly human, *but not as we are.* Consider that skull, sir Scythian! Those massive brows, the cheekbones like ledges—have you ever seen its like?" He glanced at Athalaric, his rheumy eyes shining. "It is as if we have been transported back to another day, lost unknown centuries in the past."

The Scythian bent down to scrutinize the skull.

That was when it happened.

The young Roman behind Honorius took one step forward. Athalaric saw his flashing arm, heard a soft crunch. Blood splashed. Honorius fell forward over the bones.

The people, startled, scrambled out of the way. Papak squealed like a frightened pig. But the Scythian caught Honorius as he fell and lowered him to the ground.

Athalaric could see that the back of Honorius's head had been smashed. He lunged at the young man who had stood behind Honorius, and grabbed his tunic. "It was you. I saw it. *It was you.* Why? He was a Roman like you, one of your own—"

"It was an accident," the young man said levelly.

"Liar!" Athalaric slapped his face, drawing blood. "Who put you up to this? Galla?" Athalaric made to strike the man again, but strong arms wrapped around his waist and pulled him away. Struggling, Athalaric gazed around at the others. "Help me. You saw what happened. The man is a murderer!"

But only blank stares met his entreaties.

It was then that Athalaric understood.

It had all been planned. Only the terrified Papak, and, Athalaric presumed, the Scythian, had known nothing of the crude plot—aside from Athalaric himself, the barbarian too unschooled in the ways of a mighty civilization to be able to imagine such poisonous plotting. With his refusal to accept the bishopric, Honorius had become an inconvenience to Goth and Roman alike. The planners of this foolish, vicious conspiracy had cared nothing for Honorius's miraculous old bones; this jaunt to the remote seashore had been seen merely as an opportunity. Perhaps poor Honorius's body would be dumped in the sea, not even returned for inconvenient inspection to Burdigala.

Athalaric struggled free and hurried to Honorius. The old man, his ruined head still cradled in the Scythian's bloodstained arms, was still breathing, but his eyes were closed.

"Teacher? Can you hear me?"

Remarkably Honorius's eyes fluttered open. "Athalaric?" The eyes wandered vaguely in their sockets. "I could hear it, an immense crunch, as if my head were an apple bit into by a willful child. . . ."

"Don't talk—"

"Did you see the bones?"

"Yes, I saw."

"It was another man of the dawn, wasn't it?"

To Athalaric's shock, the Scythian spoke in comprehensible but heavily accented Latin. "Man of the dawn."

"Ah," Honorius sighed. Then he gripped Athalaric's hand so hard it was painful.

Athalaric was aware of the silent circle around him, the men from the east, the Goths, the Romans, all save the Scythian and the Persian complicit in this murder. The grip slackened. With a last shudder, Honorius was gone.

The Scythian carefully laid Honorius's body over the bones he had discovered—Neandertal bones, the bones of a creature who had thought of himself as the Old Man—and the pooling blood soaked slowly into the chalky ground.

The wind changed. A breeze off the sea wafted into the cave, laden with salt.

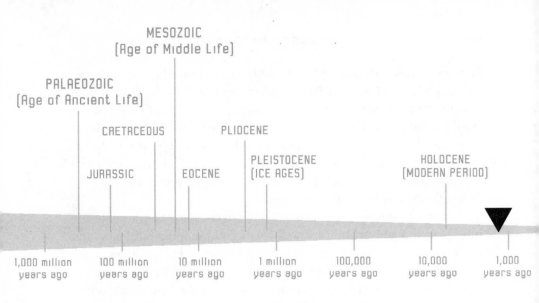

MESOZOIC
[Age of Middle Life]

PALAEOZOIC
[Age of Ancient Life]

CRETACEOUS   PLIOCENE

                    PLEISTOCENE   HOLOCENE
JURASSIC   EOCENE   [ICE AGES]   [MODERN PERIOD]

1,000 million   100 million   10 million   1 million   100,000   10,000   1,000
years ago   years ago   years ago   years ago   years ago   years ago   years ago

CHAPTER 16

an entangled bank

▼ Darwin, Northern Territory, Australia. CE 2031.

I

At Rabaul, the sequence of events followed an inevitable logic, as if the great volcanic mountain and its pocket of magma beneath were some vast geological machine.

The first crack opened up in the ground. A vast cloud of ash towered into the smog-laden sky, and red-hot molten rock soared like a fountain. With the bulk of the rising plume of magma still some five kilometers underground, the stress on Rabaul's thin upper carapace had proved too great.

In Darwin, the quakes worsened.

It was the end of the first day of the conference. The attendees, returning from their disparate dining arrangements, filed into the hotel bar. Sitting on a sofa with her feet up on a low stool, Joan watched as people got their drinks and reefers and pills and gathered in little clusters, chattering excitedly.

The delegates were typical academics, Joan thought with exasperated fondness. They were dressed every which way, from the bright orange jackets and green trousers that seemed to be favored by Europeans from Benelux and Germany, to the open sandals, T-shirts, and shorts of the small Californian contingent, to even a few ostentatiously worn ethnic costumes. Academics tended to joke about how they never planned what they wore, but in their "unconscious" choices they actually displayed a lot more of their personalities than blandly dressed fashion victims—the Alison Scotts of the world, for example.

The bar itself was a typical slice of modern consumerist-corporate culture, Joan thought, with every wall smart and pumping out logos, ads, news, and sports images, and everybody talking as loud as they could. Even the coasters on the table in front of her cycled through one animated beer commercial after another. It was as if she had been plunged into a clamorous bath of noise. It was the environment she'd grown up in all her life, save for the remote stillness of her mother's field digs. But after that eerie interval on the airport apron—the whining of the jets, the distant popping of guns, grim mechanical reality—she felt oddly dislocated. This continuous dull roar was comforting in its way, but it had the lethal ability to drown out thought.

But now the images of the worsening eruption at Rabaul filled the bar's smart walls, crowding out the sports and news channels, even a live feed of Ian Maughan's toiling Martian probe.

Alyce Sigurdardottir handed Joan a soda. "That young Aussie barman is a dish," she said. "Hair and teeth to die for. If I was forty years younger I'd do something about it."

Sipping her soda, Joan asked Alyce, "You think people are scared?"

"Of what, the eruption, the terrorists? . . . Excited-scared right now. That could change."

"Yeah. Alyce, listen." Joan leaned closer. "The Rabaul curfew the police imposed on us"—officially the line was that the ash from Rabaul, mixed with forest fire debris from further away, was mildly toxic—"it's not the full story."

Alyce nodded, her lined face hard. "Let me guess. The Fourth Worlders."

"They have planted smallpox bombs around the hotel. So they claim."

Alyce's face showed exquisite disgust. "Oh, Jesus. It's 2001 all over again." She sensed Joan's hesitant mood. "Listen to me. We can't give up because of those assholes. We have to go on with the meeting."

Joan glanced around the room. "We're already under pressure. It took an act of courage for most of the participants to come here at all. We were under attack even at the airport. If the attendees get wind of this smallpox scare . . . Maybe the mood is too flaky for, you know, the Bull Session to start tonight."

Alyce covered Joan's hand with her own; her palm was dry and callused. "It's never going to get any easier. And your Bull Session is the whole point, remember." She reached out and took Joan's soda away from her. "Get up. Do it now."

Joan laughed. "Oh, Alyce—"

"On your feet."

Joan imagined Alyce jollying some timid student of chimps or baboons into the dark dangers of the bush, but she complied. She kicked off her shoes. And, with Alyce's help, she clambered on to a coffee table.

She was overwhelmed by a self-conscious absurdity. With her conference literally under attack, how could she think she could get up on her hind legs and lecture an audience of her peers about how to save the planet? But here she was, and people were already staring. She clapped her hands until a quorum was turned her way.

"Guys, I apologize," Joan began, hesitantly, "but I need your attention. We've worked hard all day, but I'm afraid I'm not going to let up on you now.

"We're here to discuss mankind's impact on the world against the background of our evolutionary emergence. We've assembled here a unique group, cross-disciplinary, international, influential. Probably nobody alive knows more about how and why we got into this mess than we do, here tonight. And so we have an opportunity—maybe unique, probably unrepeatable—to do something more than just talk about it.

"I've had an additional purpose, a covert purpose, in calling you together. I want to use this evening as an extra session—an unusual session—if it goes the way I hope, a session that may spark off an entirely new thread. A new hope." She felt embarrassed at this unscientific language, and there were plenty of pursed lips and raised eyebrows. "So charge your glasses and vials and tubes, find somewhere to sit, and we'll begin."

And so, in this nondescript hotel bar, as the conference attendees settled on dragged-over chairs, stools, and tabletops, she began to talk about mass extinction.

Joan smiled. "Even paleontologists, like me, understand cooperation and complexity. Papa Darwin himself, toward the end of *Origin of Species*, came up with a metaphor that sums up the whole thing." Feeling awkward, she read from a scrap of paper. "*It is interesting to contemplate an entangled bank, clothed with many plants of many kinds, with birds singing on the bushes, with various insects flitting about, and with worms crawling through the damp earth, and to reflect that these elaborately constructed forms, so different from each other, and dependent on each other in so complex a manner, have all been produced by the laws acting around us . . ."*

She put down the paper. "But right now that entangled bank is in trouble. You don't need me to spell it out for you.

"We are undoubtedly in the middle of a mass extinction. The specifics are heartbreaking. In my lifetime the last wild elephants have disappeared from the savannahs and forests. No more elephants! How will we ever be able to justify *that* to our grandchildren? In my lifetime, we have *already* lost a quarter of all the species extant in the year 2000. If we keep going at the current rate, we will destroy some *two-thirds* of the species extant in 1900 by the end of this century. The event's severity already puts it up there with the previous big five of Earth's battered history.

"Meanwhile human-induced climate change has already turned out to be much more severe than any but a few scientists predicted. Africa's major coastal cities, from Cairo to Lagos, have been partially or completely flooded, displacing tens of millions of people. Bangladesh is almost totally inundated. If it wasn't for billion-dollar flood defenses, even Florida would be an archipelago. And so on.

"The fault is all ours. We have become overwhelming. About one in twenty of all the people who have ever existed is alive today, compared to just one in a *thousand* of other species. As a result we are depleting the Earth.

"But even now the question is still asked: Does it really matter? So we lose a few cute mammals, and a lot of bugs nobody ever heard of. So what? *We're* still here.

"Yes, we are. But the ecosystem is like a vast life-support machine. It is built on the interactions of species on all scales of life, from the humblest fungi filaments that sustain the roots of plants to the tremendous global cycles of water, oxygen, and carbon dioxide. Darwin's entangled bank, indeed. How does the machine stay stable? We don't know. Which are its most important components? We don't know. How much of it can we take out safely? We don't know that either. Even if we could identify and save the species that are critical for our survival, we wouldn't know which species *they* depend on in turn. But if we keep on our present course, we will soon find out the limits of robustness.

"I may be biased, but I believe it will matter a great deal if we were to die by our own foolishness. Because we bring to the world something that no other creature in all its long history has had, and that is conscious purpose. We can think our way out of this.

"So my question is—consciously, purposefully, what are we going to do?"

She ground to a halt, impassioned, uncertain, standing on her coffee table.

Some people were nodding. Others were looking bored.

Alison Scott was the first to stand up, long legs unfolding languidly. Joan held her breath.

"You aren't telling us anything new, Joan. The slow death of the biosphere is—ah—banal. A cliché. And I have to point out that what we have done is in fact inevitable. We are animals, we continue to behave like animals, and we always will." There was a grumble of dissent. Scott plowed on, "Other animals have been known to eat themselves to extinction. In the twentieth century reindeer were introduced to a small island in the Bering Sea. An initial population of twenty-nine ballooned to *six thousand* in twenty years. But their food was slow-growing lichens, which had no time to recover from their intensive grazing."

"But," somebody shouted out, "reindeer don't know anything about ecology."

Scott said smoothly, "We've done this throughout history. The example of the Polynesian islands is well known. The Mideast city of Petra—"

As Joan had hoped, the group broke up into arguing clusters.

". . . those people of the past who failed to manage their resources were guilty simply of failing to solve a difficult ecological problem . . ."

"We are already handling energy and mass flows on a scale that rivals natural processes. Now we have to use those powers consciously. . . ."

"But the risks of tinkering with the fundamentals of an overcrowded planet . . ."

"All these technological measures would themselves *cost* energy, and so would actually add to the planetary burden of waste heat. . . ."

"Our civilization has no common agenda. How would you propose to resolve the political, legal, ethical, cultural, and financial issues implicit in your proposals? . . ."

"I've been listening to this kind of technocratic horseshit all my adult life! What is this, a NASA funding pitch?"

"I say fuck the ecosystem. Who needs horny-backed toads anyhow? Let's go for a drastic simplification. All you've got to do is soak up cee oh two, pump out oxygen, and regulate the heat. How hard can it be?"

"So, madam, you really want to live in *Blade Runner* world?"

Joan had to intervene again to pull the group back together. "We need a unity of will, a mobilization we haven't seen before. But maybe we haven't yet hit on the solution we should be reaching for."

"Precisely," said Alison Scott, and she stood up again. She rested her hands on the shining hair, blue and green, of her two daughters. "Big engineering is a defunct dream of the twentieth century. The solution is not out there; it will be found *in us*."

More hostility greeted these pronouncements. "She means engineering babies, like her own two little freaks."

"I'm talking about evolution," Scott snapped. "That's what happens to a species when the environment changes. Throughout our history we have proved to be a remarkably adaptable species."

A woman stood up, sixtyish, black. Joan knew her. Evelyn Smith was one of the premier evolutionary biologists of her time. Smith said coldly, "Natural selection has not been operating on human populations for some tens of millennia. Claims that it has show a lack of understanding of the basic mechanism. We fend off the winnowing processes that drive selection: Our weapons have eliminated predators, agricultural development has beaten back starvation, and so on. But this will change if the imminent collapse occurs. In that case, selection will return. This is the subject of my paper in Session Three, incidentally."

There were some protests.

". . . what 'imminent collapse'?"

". . . for all its surface brilliance, our society shows symptoms of decline: growing inequality, declining returns from economic expansion, collapsing educational standards and intellectual achievement."

". . . yes, and spiritual death. Even we Americans pay only lip service to totems—the flag, the Constitution, democracy—while we surrender power over our lives to the corporations and comfort ourselves with mysticism and muddle. It's happened before. The parallels with Rome especially are very clear. . . ."

". . . except that now we're all joined up, all over the world. If we do collapse, there might be nothing much left to un-collapse out of."

". . . absurdly pessimistic. We're resilient—we achieved great things before . . ."

"We dug out all the easy ores and burnt all the easy oil and coal; if we did fall, we'd have nothing to build from. . . ."

"My point," said Smith doggedly, "is that we may not have much time."

These words, softly spoken, briefly silenced everybody, and Joan saw her opportunity.

She said dryly, "So I guess that if we don't want to go back to the bad old days of being just another animal in the ecology, we need to get a hold of this mess. But I think there's a way we can do that." Absently stroking her belly, she smiled. "A new way. But a way we've known about all along. A primate way."

And she began to outline her vision.

Human culture, Joan said, had been an adaptation to help people live through the wild climate swings of the Pleistocene. Now, in a savage millennial irony, that culture was feeding back to cause still more drastic environmental damage. Culture, which had once been so profoundly adaptive, had become *maladaptive,* and would have to change.

"Life isn't just about competition," she said. "It's also about cooperation. Interdependence. It always has been. The first cells depended on the cooperation of simpler bacteria. So did the first ecologies, the stromatolites. Now, our lives are so interdependent that they must, in the future, develop with a common purpose."

"You're just talking about globalization. What corporation is sponsoring you?"

"We're back to Gaia and other Earth goddesses, aren't we?"

Joan said, "Our global society is becoming so highly structured that it is becoming something akin to a holon: a single, composite entity. We have to learn to think of ourselves in that way. We have to build on the other half of our primate natures—the part that *isn't* about competition and xenophobia. Primates cooperate a lot more than they compete. Chimps do; lemurs do; pithecines and *erectus* and Neandertals must have; *we* do. Human interdependence comes from our deepest history. Now, without anybody planning it, we have engulfed the biosphere, and we have to learn to manage it together."

Alison Scott stood again. "What exactly is it you *want,* Joan?"

"A manifesto. A statement. A cosigned letter to the UN, from all of us. We have to give a lead, start something new. We have to start showing the path to a sustainable future. Who else but us?"

"Hoorah, we can save the world . . ."

"She's right. Gaia will be not our mother, but our *daughter.*"

"What makes you think anybody with power will listen to a bunch of scientists? They never have before. This is pie in the sky . . ."

Evelyn Smith said, "They'll listen if they are desperate enough."

Alyce Sigurdardottir stood up. "Confucius said, 'Those who say it cannot be done need to get out of the way of the people who are doing it.' " She raised her thin fist in a power salute. "We're still primates—only more so. Right?"

Despite a few catcalls, Joan thought she saw a warmer response in the faces ranked before her. It's going to work, she thought. It's just a start, but it's going to work. We can *fix* this. She stroked her belly.

In fact she was right; it might have worked.

The political and economic pressures might indeed have induced a receptivity in the global power brokers that hadn't existed before. Joan Useb's ideas could indeed have shown how to ally the interconnections offered by technology with older primate instincts of cooperation. And it might have gone beyond mere ecological management. After all no species before had had the potential to be linked globally, not in four billion years of life on Earth. Given time, Joan's approach might have inspired a cognitive breakthrough as significant as the integration of Mother's generation.

Humans had become smart enough to damage their planet. Now, just given a little more time, they might have become smart enough to save it.

Just a little more time.

But now the lights went out. There were explosions, like great footfalls. People screamed and ran.

Meanwhile, over Rabaul, the earthquakes had gotten increasingly severe. At last they cracked the seabed above Rabaul's magma chamber. The magma was rising to the surface through great tunnels, some of them three hundred meters wide. Now seawater rushed into the tunnels and flashed instantly to steam. Meanwhile, other gases, carbon dioxide and sulfur compounds that had been kept dissolved in the magma by the higher pressure of the depths, like the carbon dioxide in a bottle of soda. But now the bottle was cracked, and the gases came bubbling out.

In the rock chambers, the pressure escalated exponentially.

II

Emergency lights came on, filling the room with a cold glow.

The false ceiling had broken up into polystyrene shards that hailed down on the fleeing attendees. Joan saw Alison Scott grab her two girls and huddle with them in a corner. The exposed roof space, filled with insulation-lagged ducts and cables, was cavernous, dark, dirty.

Fine nylon ropes tumbled down through air thick with polystyrene dust. She glimpsed black-clad shapes that moved, spiderlike, through the roof space, and slid down to the bar's littered floor. They wore skintight black coveralls and balaclava hoods with silvery eye visors. She counted five, six, seven of them. She couldn't tell if they were male or female. They all carried slim automatic weapons.

Alyce Sigurdardottir was tugging at her arm, trying to make her climb down from her table. But she resisted, aware that she was still the center here; she felt, maybe irrationally, that things would get even worse if she gave in to the chaos.

One of the invaders looked to be in command. On the floor, the others gathered around him as he surveyed the situation. He, she? No, *he*, Joan thought; in a group like this, it will be a he. Two of the intruders stayed with the leader. The other four made for the doors. With their backs to the walls they trained their weapons on the delegates, who herded, sheeplike, toward the center of the room.

There was only one hotel staff member here: the barman, the young Australian who had caught Alyce's eye. He was slim, with curly black hair—at least part Aborigine, Joan thought—and he wore a bow tie and sparkling vest. Now, with great courage, he stepped forward, hands spread. "Listen," he began. "I don't know what you want here. But if you will let me call—"

The gun's sound was quiet, oddly like a leopard's cough, Joan thought absently. The boy fell, twitching. There was a sudden stink of death shit, a smell she hadn't encountered since Africa. The delegates screamed, fell back, froze, as they each in their separate ways sought not to attract the attention of the murderers.

Beyond all this, incongruously, the smart walls continued to cycle, showing meaningless images of the New Guinea volcano, the toiling robot factories on Mars, ads for beer and drugs and technological trinkets.

As Joan had expected, the leader, his symbolic killing done, approached her. His gun was at his side, presumably still hot. His visor had been sewn into the balaclava. It was stylish, almost chic.

Before he could speak, she snapped, "Are you afraid to show me your face?"

He laughed and pulled off his balaclava—*he*, yes, she had been right. His head was shaven. He was white, with brown eyes. He was maybe twenty-five, surely not much older than the barman he had just killed. He eyed her, measuring her unspoken challenge.

His followers peeled off their balaclavas. They all had ostentatiously bare scalps. There were four men, including the leader, and three women.

Joan asked, "Are you Pickersgill?"

The leader laughed. "Pickersgill doesn't exist. The global police state chases a chimera. Pickersgill is a pleasing joke, and useful." His accent was Midwestern American, but with a faint exotic burr; such was the worldwide dominance of American English nowadays, this boy could have come from anywhere.

"So who are you?"

"*I* am Elisha."

"Elisha, tell me what you want," Joan said carefully.

"You are not setting the agenda now," the boy said. "I will tell you what we have *done*. Dr. Joan Useb, we have released the disease."

Joan's skin prickled.

"You are all infected. *We* are infected. Without treatment, in a few days most of us will die. If this situation is resolved to our satisfaction, perhaps we will all survive. But *we* are prepared to die for what we believe. Are you?"

Joan considered. "Do you want the table?"

He stalked up and down before the coffee table, thinking it over. The absurd little table was the focus of power in this room: Of course he wanted it. "Yes. Get down."

With Alyce's help, she clambered down to the floor. Elisha leapt with some agility on to Joan's improvised podium and began to bark commands in what sounded like Swedish to his colleagues.

"Classic primate behavior," Alyce murmured. "Male dominance hierarchies. Paranoia. Xenophobia verging on schizophrenia. That's what's going on here, under the horse feathers."

"But it's only dealing with the horse feathers that is going to get any of us out of here—"

She was drowned out by a huge flapping noise, as if some vast pterosaur were coming in to land on the roof of the hotel. It was a helicopter, of course, suspended in the sky beyond the roof. And now an amplified voice boomed through the walls, announcing itself as the police.

The terrorists blasted their weapons at the roof, bringing down even more of the ceiling. The conference delegates cowered and screamed— thereby adding to the din the bad guys wanted to create, Joan thought, her hands pressed to her ears. When the police stopped trying to communicate, the guns were shut down.

Joan stood up carefully, brushing away dust. She was oddly unafraid. She looked up at Elisha, who stalked his coffee table podium, flushed, breathing hard, his gun resting on his shoulder. "You haven't a chance of getting what you want, whatever it is, unless you let them speak to you."

"But I don't need to speak to police, or their mind-twisting psychological advisors. Not when I have you here—you, the self-styled head of the new globalization, this *holon*."

Alyce sighed. "Why do I get the feeling that such an innocent word is suddenly going to become the name of a new demon?"

"We listened to your grandiose speech in the ceiling space, excluded from the light—how fitting!"

Joan said, "You really—" *You really don't understand.* Wrong words, Joan. "Please. Tell me your concerns."

He eyed her. Then he clambered down off his table. "Listen to me," he said more quietly. "I heard what you said about the global organism into which we must soon be submerged. Very well. But any organism must have a boundary. What about those beyond the boundary? Doctor Joan Useb, the three hundred wealthiest people on the planet own as much as do the poorest three *billion* of their fellow human beings. Beyond the bastions of the elite, some poor regions are effectively enslaved, the people mined for their labor and bodies—or body parts. How is your global nervous system to be made aware of *their* misery?"

Her mind raced. Everything he said sounded rehearsed. Of course it did: This was his moment, the crux of his life; everything she did had to be governed by understanding that. Was he a student? If he was some kind of latter-day cultural colonial type on a guilt trip, maybe she could find weak spots in his commitment.

But he was a murderer, she reminded herself. And he had killed so casually, with not a moment's hesitation. She wondered what drug regime he was using.

"Excuse me." A new voice. It turned out to be Alison Scott. She was standing before Elisha, her two terrified daughters at her side, their hair of blue and green shining in the meaningless, flickering light of the walls.

Joan felt a stab of pain in her lower belly, hard enough to make her gasp. She had a sense of things escalating out of control.

Bex was staring at her accusingly.

"Bex, are you OK?"

"You said Rabaul wasn't going to hurt us. You said it was so unlikely, while we were here. You said we were safe."

"I'm sorry. Really. Alison, please go sit down. There's nothing you can do here."

Scott ignored her. "Look, whoever you are, whatever you want, we are hot, we are tired, we are thirsty, we are already starting to feel sick."

"That's ridiculous," Elisha said evenly. "Psychosomatic. You're being neurotic."

Scott actually snarled. "Don't you psychoanalyze me. I demand—"

"You demand, you demand, yammer, yammer, yammer." He approached Scott. She held her ground, her arms tightly wrapped around her girls. Elisha lifted Bex's aquamarine hair, tugged it gently, rubbed it between his fingers. "Genriched," he said.

"Leave her alone," Scott hissed.

"How beautiful they are, like toys." He ran his hand down Bex's hair to her shoulder, then squeezed her small breast.

Bex yelped, and Scott pulled her away. "She's fourteen years old—"

"You know what they do, Dr. Joan Useb, these genetic engineers? They stuff a whole extra chromosome into their kids, an extra chromosome full of desirable genes. But, aside from the hair and the teeth, do you know what that extra chromosome does? It stops those perfect kids breeding with us old-style unenhanced *Homo sapiens.* Now, what higher exclusion barrier can you imagine than that? Today, the rich even set themselves up as a separate *species.*" As if absently, like pulling a fruit from its branch, he pulled Bex away from her mother's grasp. One of the female terrorists held back Scott. Elisha ripped open the girl's blouse, exposing her light, lacy brassiere. Bex closed her eyes; she was muttering to herself, a song or a rhyme.

"Elisha, please—" Now there was another stab of pain in Joan's belly, a liquid surge. She found herself bent double. Oh, Christ, not now, she thought. Not now.

Suddenly Alyce was here. "Take it easy. Sit down."

The wall images were changing, Joan saw. Her vision was misted, but there seemed to be a lot more orange, black, gray.

Alyce was grinning, a humorless grimace, like a skull's. "That's Rabaul going up. Great timing."

Elisha had gotten hold of the girl's wrists and pushed her arms over her head.

Joan said quickly, "Come on, Elisha. You aren't here for this."

"Aren't I?"

Scott said grimly, "If all you want is something to fuck, *take me.*"

"Oh, but there would be no point," Elisha said. "It's not the act but the symbolism, you see. This is the first time since the extinction of the Neandertals that there have been two distinct human species in the world." He stared down at the girl. "Is it rape, if the act occurs between different species?"

The doors blew in.

There was screaming, running, the crackle of gunfire. Small black pellets were hurled through the open doors and burst. White smoke began to fill the air.

Joan looked for the terrorists, trying to count. Two of them had fallen when the doors were charged. Another two, running and firing, fell as she watched, suddenly turned into tumbling puppets. Most of her delegates were on the floor or cowering under the furniture. Two, three, four looked as if they might be hurt: She saw inert shapes in the smoke, splashes of bloodred in the gray murk.

A new ripple of pain passed over Joan's abdomen.

Elisha stood before her. He was smiling. He had hold of a length of black cord that extended from his waistband.

At least Bex had been released; the girl, in the arms of her mother, was backing away.

"Elisha. You don't have to die."

His smile broadened. "All over the planet, five hundred of us are poised to make the same statement."

Alyce half reached for him. "Don't do it, for God's sake—"

"You won't be harmed," he said. He pulled his balaclava back over his head. "I die as I lived. Faceless."

Joan screamed, "Elisha!"

He tugged on the cord, as if starting a gasoline engine. There was a flash around his waist, a belt of transient light. Then the upper half of his body tipped away from the lower. As the pieces of him fell, neatly bisected, there was a stink of blood, the acid stench of stomach contents.

Alyce clung to Joan. "Oh, God, oh, God."

The smoke was thickening, blinding, and Joan was coughing like a lifelong smoker. Now the pain came again, washing through her abdomen and back. She held on to Alyce. "Has it ever struck you how maladaptive group suicide is?"

"For God's sake, Joan—"

"I mean, individual suicide can sometimes be justified, from a biological point of view. Perhaps a suicide is removing a burden from her kin. But what biological rationale can group suicide ever have? The capacity to believe in cultural dictates has been adaptive. It must have been or we wouldn't have it. But sometimes the mechanism goes wrong—"

"We're crazy. Is that what you're trying to say? We're all crazy. I agree."

"Ma'am, please come with me." A shadow before her. It looked like a soldier in a space suit, reaching for her.

Pain rippled through her again, an extinction of purposeful thought. She crumpled against Alyce Sigurdardottir. She heard another explosion. She thought it was just another part of the military or police operation.

She was wrong, as it happened. That had been Rabaul.

Once the sea had penetrated the magma chamber, the explosion became inevitable.

Shreds of molten magma flew into the air faster than sound, reaching heights of fifty kilometers. They broke up into solidifying fragments, ranging from tiny ash particles to chunks a meter wide. Mixed in with all of this were chunks of the shattered mountain itself. These bits of rock had been hurled far above the weather, far above aircraft and balloons, above even the ozone layer, fragments of Rabaul mingling with the meteorites, burning brightly and briefly. It was a sky full of rock.

And on the ground, the shock wave moved out from the shattered caldera at twice the speed of sound. Silent until it hit, it leveled everything in its path, houses, temples, trees, bridges. Where it passed energy poured into the air, compressing it and raising it to enormous temperatures. Anything combustible burst into flames.

People could see the shock was coming, but they could not hear it and they certainly could not flee it. They just popped into flame and vanished, like pine needles on a bonfire. This was just the beginning.

Space suited soldiers bundled Joan out of the smoke-filled bar, out of the hotel, and into fresh air. She was put on to a stretcher that was hauled away at running speed. All around her was a blizzard of movement, people running, cars rushing, tarmac beneath, helicopters flapping through an orange sky.

Now they were bundling her into the back of a van. An ambulance? *One, two, three, lift.* The stretcher slid inside the vehicle, alongside a kind of narrow bunk bed. There was anonymous equipment on the walls, none of it bleeping or humming, nothing like the equipment in the medical soaps she had once been addicted to.

She waved her hand through the air. "Alyce."

Alyce grabbed her hand. "I'm here, Joan."

"I feel like an amphibian, Alyce. I swim in blood and piss, but I breathe the air of culture. Neither one thing nor the other—"

Alyce's drawn face was above her, distracted, fearful. "What? What did you say?"

"What time is it?"

"Joan, save your breath. Believe me, I've been through this; you're going to need it."

"Is it day or night? I lost track. I couldn't tell from the sky."

"My watch is broken. Night, I think."

Somebody was working on her legs—cutting away her clothes? The ambulance lurched into motion, and she heard the remote wail of a siren, like some animal lost in the fog. All she could see was the bare, gloomily painted roof of the vehicle, those meaningless bits of equipment, and Alyce's thin face.

"Listen, Alyce."

"I'm here."

"I never told you my family's true history."

"Joan—"

She said sharply, "If I don't make it out of this, tell my daughter where she came from."

Alyce nodded soberly. "You came to America as slaves."

"My great-grandfather worked out the story. We came from what is now Namibia, not far from Windhoek. We were San, what they called 'bushmen.' We nearly got wiped out by the Bantu, and in colonial days we were killed as vermin. But we kept some cultural identity."

"Joan—"

"Alyce, gene frequency studies show that female-line DNA among San women is more diverse than anywhere else on Earth. The implication is that San genes have been around in southern Africa much longer than any genes anywhere else on Earth. People of San ancestry are about the closest we'll ever get to the direct line of descent from our common grandmother, our mitochondrial Eve—"

Alyce nodded soberly. "I understand. So your child is one of the youngest people on the planet—and the oldest." Alyce covered her hand. "I promise I'll tell her."

The pain came in waves now. She felt as if her mind were dissolving; she struggled to think. "You know, normal human births are statistically likely to happen at night. An ancient primate trait. It's as well to bear your child in the safety of your treetop nest."

"Joan—"

"Let me talk, damn it. Talking makes the pain go away."

"*Drugs* make the pain go away."

"*Ow!* That one felt different. Is there a midwife in this damn van?"

"They're all trained paramedics. You've got nothing to be afraid of."

"I think my daughter is keen to see the inside of this scruffy ambulance."

"You've done your classes. Breathe. Push."

She began to breathe in gasping snatches, *Oof, oof, oof.*

Alyce kept glancing down toward the business end. "You're doing fine."

"Even if I do have the pelvis of an australopithecine."

"You really are full of shit, Joan Useb."

"Not anymore, I fear."

"She's coming. She's *coming,*" Alyce said.

The baby's skull bones and their junctions were soft, able to mold under the pressure of being squeezed through the birth canal. And she was able to withstand oxygen deprivation up to the moment of birth.

These last moments were the most extreme physical transformation she would suffer up until the moment of death itself. But the baby's body was flooded with natural opiates and analgesics. She was feeling no real pain, just a continuation of the long womb dream out of which her self, her identity, had gradually coalesced.

A space suited paramedic took Joan's child, blew into its nose, and slapped its backside. A satisfying wail filled the ambulance. The soggy little scrap of flesh was hastily wrapped in a blanket and handed to Joan.

Joan, exhausted, wondering, touched her daughter's cheek. The child turned her head, and her mouth worked, seeking something to suck.

Alyce was smiling down, sweating and exhausted herself, like any proud aunt. "By God, look at her. She's already communicating with us, in her way. She's already human."

"I think she wants to suckle. But I don't have any milk yet, do I?"

"Let her suckle anyhow," Alyce advised. "It will stimulate your body to release more oxytocin."

Now Joan remembered her classes. "Which will cause my uterus to contract, reduce the bleeding, help expel the placenta—"

"Don't worry about that," said a space suit. "We injected you already."

Joan let the child lick her nipple. "Look at that. She's making grasping motions. And it's like she's stepping. I can feel her feet."

"If you had a hairy chest she could probably support her weight, and maybe crawl over you. And if you moved suddenly, she'd grab even harder."

"In case I go bounding off through the trees. Look, she's calming."

"Give her twenty more minutes and she'll be pulling her tongue at you."

Joan felt as if she were floating, as if nothing was real but the fragile warm bundle in her arms. "I know it's all innate. I know I'm being reprogrammed so I don't shuck off this damp little parasite. And yet, and yet—"

Alyce laid her hand on Joan's shoulder. "And yet it's what your life has been all about, but you just never knew it before."

"Yes."

There was a bleep. Alyce pulled a mobile out of her pocket. Its face lit up with bright images, flickers of movement.

A space suit murmured to Joan. "We're approaching the hospital. You're not to be afraid. They have a secure, enclosed entrance."

Joan cradled her baby. "So Lucy, having just passed through one long dark tunnel, is about to enter another."

The space suit hesitated. "Lucy?"

"What better name for a primate gal?"

Alyce managed a smile. "Joan, you aren't the only new parent."

"Huh?"

"Ian Maughan's robot worker on Mars has managed to build a fully working replica of itself. It has managed to reproduce. From the tone of this text, he is very happy."

"He texted you about *that*?"

"You know guys like that. The rest of the world can go to hell as long as their latest gadget does what it's supposed to. Oh. The Fourth Worlders killed Alison Scott's pithecine chimera. I imagine they believed she was an abomination. I wonder what *she* believed."

"I suppose she only wanted security, as we all do."

Joan gazed down at her new baby. One world had begun, just heartbeats ago, while another was ending.

"We came close, didn't we, Alyce? The conference, the manifesto. It could have worked, couldn't it?"

"Yes, I believe so."

"We just ran out of time, is all."

"Yes. That, and luck. But we must be hopeful, Joan."

"Yes. We must always be that."

The ambulance rattled to a halt. The doors banged open and cooler air gushed in. More space suits swarmed around, pushing Alyce out of the way, seeking to get Joan on a stretcher. They tried to take her baby off her, but she wouldn't let them.

The geologists had long known that Earth had been overdue for a major volcanic incident.

Rabaul 2031 was not the worst eruption known—not even the worst in the historical record. Still, Rabaul had been far more severe than the 1991 eruption of Pinatubo in the Philippines, which had cooled the Earth by half a degree. It was worse than the explosion of Tambora in Indonesia in 1815, which had caused the "year without a summer" in America and Europe. Rabaul was the largest volcanic event since the sixth century after Christ, and one of the largest of the previous fifty thousand years. Rabaul was respectable.

Changes in climate were not always smooth and proportional to their causes. Earth was prone to sudden and drastic alterations in climate and ecology, flips from one stable state to another. The effects of even small perturbations could become magnified.

Rabaul was such a perturbation. But it was not going to be a small one.

It wasn't really Rabaul's fault. The volcano was just the final straw.

Everything had been stretched to the breaking point anyhow by the humans' extraordinary growth. It wasn't even bad luck. If it hadn't been Rabaul, it would have been another volcano or a quake or an asteroid, or some damn thing.

But as the natural systems of the planet broke down, humans would discover conclusively that they were still, after all, just animals embedded in an ecosystem; and as it died back, so did they.

Meanwhile, on Mars, the little robots worked on. Patiently they turned the wan sunlight and the red dust and the carbon dioxide air into little factories, which in turn produced copies of the robots themselves, with jointed legs and solar cell carapaces and little silicon brains.

The robots transmitted news of their endeavors back to their makers on Earth. No reply came. But they kept working anyway.

Under the burnt orange sky of Mars, generations passed quickly.

Of course no replication, biological or mechanical, could ever be perfect. Some variants worked better than others. The robots were actually programmed to learn—to retain what worked, to eliminate what didn't. The weaker ones died out. The stronger survived, and carried forward their design changes to the next metallic generation.

Thus variation and selection had begun to operate.

On and on the robots toiled, until the ancient seabeds and canyons glistened, covered by insectlike metal carapaces.

THREE

descendants

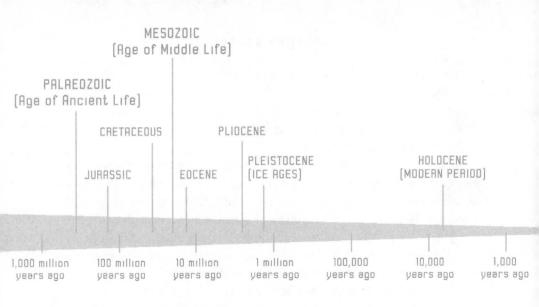

MESOZOIC
[Age of Middle Life]

PALAEOZOIC
[Age of Ancient Life]

CRETACEOUS   PLIOCENE

                                    PLEISTOCENE   HOLOCENE
JURASSIC   EOCENE   [ICE AGES]   [MODERN PERIOD]

| 1,000 million | 100 million | 10 million | 1 million | 100,000 | 10,000 | 1,000 |
| years ago | years ago | years ago | years ago | years ago | years ago | years ago |

CHAPTER 17

a long shadow

▼ Place and time unknown.

I

Waking from a cold sleep wasn't at all like a normal waking, in your own bed, with your wife beside you. It was more like surfacing from a deep dunking in a tank of some clinging, deadening fluid.

But now here was a break in the murk, a widening circle of light centered on a blurry face. The face belonged to Ahmed, the splot—the senior pilot—and not to the CO. That was Snowy's first indication that something was wrong.

Ahmed was repeating, "OK? Are you OK?"

Before submitting to the injections Snowy had rehearsed how he was going to respond to his wake-up call. He smiled and raised the middle finger of his right hand. "Any landing you walk away from is a good one." His voice was a rasp, and his mouth was desert dry.

"You aren't walking yet, smart arse," Ahmed said grimly.

"Where's Barking?" Robert Madd, blessed with one of the Royal Navy's less imaginative nicknames, was the unit's CO.

"Later," said Ahmed. He withdrew, letting Snowy see the metal walls of the Pit. He threw a ration pack on the bed. "Get out of there. Help me with the others."

Snowy—Robert Wayne Snow, age 31—was a lieutenant in the British Royal Navy, which had given him at least an inclination to follow the odd order. So he struggled to sit up.

The Pit was just a cylinder of gunmetal gray, the walls unadorned save for instrument and sensor consoles. The light came from low-energy fluorescents that cast a sickly glow over everything. The instruments were all dead, just blank screens. It was like being inside an oil tank. And the Pit was full of bunk beds, twenty of them, stacked up. Plastic carapaces lay over the beds. Ahmed was working his way around the room, opening the carapaces one by one, and reclosing most of them.

Snowy was stark naked, but he wasn't cold. He picked up his ration pack. It was a clear vacuum-packed bag containing dried banana, chocolate, and other goodies. He ripped into it with the only tool available to him, his teeth. The bag popped and air hissed. He dumped out the goodies on his bed and crammed some banana into his mouth. He felt like he'd been running a marathon. He'd been through cold sleep twice before, for training and evaluation purposes, just a week at a time. It was a peculiarity of the process that at no time did you feel cold, but you always woke up ravenous: something to do with your body slowly absorbing its stores to keep itself alive, according to the medicos.

But something was wrong with his bunk. He could see where he had been lying, his body had left a very clear imprint, like the gruesome dead-mother's-bed scene in *Psycho*. He probed at the mattress. It was lumpy and hard. And the sheets on which he had been lying crumbled as he poked at them, like a mummy's wrappings.

He felt a gathering sense of dread.

Ahmed was helping a girl from one of the upper bunks. Her name was June, so, naturally, she was known as Moon. She was a cutie, in or out of her clothes; but now, naked, she looked fragile, even ill, and Snowy felt nothing but an impulse to help her as she clambered awkwardly down from her bunk, flinching as her bare flesh brushed against the metal.

With Moon awake, Snowy started to feel self-conscious. He reached under his bunk, looking for his clothes.

But the floor seemed to be on a tilt. He straightened up, expecting his head to clear. But still the bare floor seemed askew, the vertical lines of the bunk frames leaning like drunks. Not good, Snowy thought. He could think of nothing reassuring that would tip up this hundred-ton emplacement.

He reached under his bed again. The cardboard box that had contained his clothes was gone. His clothes were still there, in a heap. But
when he grabbed them the cloth just crumbled, like the sheets on his bed.

"Forget it," Ahmed called, watching him. "Get your flight suit. They
seem to have lasted."

"Lasted?"

"It's the plastic, I think."

Snowy complied. He found his boots were still intact too, made of
some imperishable artificial material. But he had no surviving socks, none
at all; that might be a problem.

Snowy helped get some food inside Moon, while Ahmed continued
his patroling.

The woken gathered in a circle, sitting on the lowest tier of the bunks.
But there were only five of them, five out of the twenty who had been
stored here. The five were Snowy, Ahmed, Sidewise, the girl Moon, and a
young pilot called Bonner.

For a time they were silent, as they tucked into banana and chocolate
and drank vials of water. Snowy knew that was a good idea. If you were
dropped into some new situation it always paid to give yourself time to
just sit and listen and think, and adjust to the new situation.

Snowy had pressed Ahmed about the CO. Ahmed showed him.
Barking Madd's body was shriveled and shrunken, literally mummified,
just hardened flesh over the bone. The rest, the other fourteen, were the
same.

Sidewise, predictably, couldn't keep his mouth closed. Sidewise was
an air warfare officer. He was a thin, intense man, and he had earned his
handle for his habit of making sideways crablike moves whenever he got
on a dance floor. Now he glanced around at the little group. "Fucking
hell," he said to Snowy. "So much for the safety margins."

"Shut it," Ahmed snapped.

Bonner asked Ahmed, "So what was the tally?"

Tally, for tally-ho, was the slang for a wake-up call. "There wasn't
one," Ahmed said bluntly.

"So if not a tally, what woke us up?"

Ahmed shrugged. "Maybe the Pit has an automatic timer. Or maybe
something just failed and it pitched us out."

Bonner was a good-looking kid, though one of the gen-enged plagues
had left him hairless from head to toe. Now he ran his hand over his bare
scalp. His accent was faintly Welsh. "Maybe we just pushed it too hard.

The Pit was supposed to be a cryostore for seeds and animal embryos and stuff. Insurance against the mass extinction. Not for humans—"

"Especially not humans like you, Bonner," Snowy said. "Maybe your farts blew the gaskets."

The bit of low humor seemed to relax the group, as Snowy had hoped.

Ahmed said, "This Pit might have been originally built for elephant embryos or whatever, but it was man rated. We all saw the lectures on the safety parameters, the reliability of the systems."

"Sure," Sidewise said. "But *any* system will fail, no matter how well it's designed and built, if you give it enough time." That silenced them. And Sidewise said, "Anybody noticed the clock?"

Most of the Pit's instruments were dead. But there had been a backup mechanical clock that had drawn on a trickle of thermal energy from deep roots planted in the earth below. Before they submitted to the cold sleep they had all been shown the clock's working—the cogs made of diamond that would never wear out, the dials that spanned the unthinkable time of fifty years, and so on. It had been a not-so-subtle psychological ploy to reassure them that no matter how long they were in the ground, no matter what became of the outside world, no matter what else failed in the Pit, they would know the date.

But now Snowy saw that the clock's hands had jammed against the end of their dials.

Snowy thought of his wife, Clara. She had been pregnant when he had gone into cold sleep. *Fifty years?* The kid would be born, grown, with kids of its own. Maybe even *grandkids*. No. He rejected the thought. It made no sense; you couldn't have a human life with a gap of fifty years in the middle of it.

But Sidewise was still talking. "*At least* fifty years," he said relentlessly. "How long do you think it would take for Barking's body to mummify like that, for all our clothes to rot away?" That was the trouble with Sidewise, Snowy thought. He was never shy of saying what everybody else didn't even want to think about.

"Enough," Ahmed snapped. He was short, stocky, squat. "Barking is dead. I'm senior here. I'm in charge." He glared around at them. "Everyone happy with that?"

Moon and Bonner seemed to have withdrawn into themselves. Sidewise was smiling oddly, as if he knew a secret he wasn't sharing.

Snowy shrugged. He knew Ahmed had served as a watch chief—the navy equivalent of a sergeant major. Snowy thought of him as competent, oddly thoughtful, but inexperienced. And, incidentally, not popular enough for a nickname. But there wasn't anybody better qualified here, regardless of rank. "I suggest you get on with it, sir."

Ahmed gave him a look of gratitude. "All right. Here's the deal. We've had no tally. In fact, no contact from the outside. I can't even tell how long since we last got a contact of any sort. Too many of the systems are down."

Moon said, "So we don't know what's happening out there?"

Snowy said briskly, "Tell us what we do."

"We get out of here. We don't need protective gear. Enough of the external sensors are working to tell us that."

That was a relief, Snowy thought. He wouldn't have welcomed relying for protection on his NBC suit—nuclear-biological-chemical—if it had been subject to the same ferocious aging as his other clothes.

Ahmed hauled a steel trunk out from under one of the bunks. Inside were pistols, Walther PPKs, each packed in a plastic bag filled with oil. "I checked one already. We can test fire them outside." He handed them around.

Snowy cracked the bag, wiped clean his pistol on crumbling bits of sheet, and tucked its reassuring mass into his belt. He rummaged through more of his surviving kit: helmets, life jackets, survival vests—a pilot's equipment. The plastic components seemed more or less intact, but the cloth and rubber had failed. He took what he thought he would need. He regretted leaving behind his helmet, his venerable bone-dome, even if it was painted United Nations blue. Still, he somehow doubted he would be doing much flying today one way or another.

They clustered before the exit. The door to the facility was heavy, round-edged, and airtight, and operated by a wheel; it was like a submarine's hatch. Ahmed began to break its seals.

They were all shitting themselves, Snowy realized, even if none of them wanted to show it to the rest.

"So what do you think we'll find?" whispered Sidewise. "Russians? Chinese? Bomb craters, two-headed kids? Everybody wearing monkey masks, like *Planet of the Apes*?"

"Fuck off, Side, you twat."

With an uncompromising motion Ahmed turned the wheel. The last seal broke with a crack. The door swung back.

Green light flooded in.

Cryobiology was actually a venerable industry.

The key to its utility was that far below the freezing point of water, molecules slowed the frenetic pace that permitted chemical reactions to proceed. So red blood cells could be stored for a decade or more. You could freeze, thaw, and reuse corneas, organ tissue, neural tissue. You could even freeze embryos. The cold was as much an enemy as an ally, of course; expanding crystals of ice had an unpleasant habit of destroying cell walls. So the medicos infused tissues with cryoprotective agents like glycerol and dimethyl sulfoxide.

Still, freezing and reviving a complex mature organism—such as a hundred kilograms of blasphemous Royal Navy pilot—presented more of a challenge. In Snowy's body there were many different types of cells, each requiring a different freeze-thaw profile. In the end, a little subtle genetic engineering had done the trick. Snowy's cells had been given the ability to manufacture natural antifreeze—in fact, glycoproteins, a trick borrowed from some species of polar fish—and the freezing was regulated at the level of the cells themselves.

Obviously it had worked. Snowy had come out of the process alive and functioning. After half an hour he barely felt a thing.

Of course he had been intended to come out fighting.

Officially this unit was under the command of UNPROFOR, the UN Protection Force. But everybody knew that was only a cover. The strategy had become known as *sowing dragon's teeth.* As the intensity of global conflict had rapidly increased, post-Rabaul, new forms of deterrence had been devised. The idea was that it would be futile for any power to attempt an invasion if it knew that the ground was salted with groups of highly trained military personnel, fresh and fully equipped, ready to resume the battle. From these scattered teeth the dragon would regrow. That was the theory.

There were drawbacks, of course. The cold sleep process itself brought a risk of injury or fatality (but low, not 75 *percent*). And you never knew where you would be stationed; the freezing had been done at huge central depots, the subjects transported and deposited, all unconscious, at selected sites around the country, even abroad. But Snowy had known that his unit of Navy flyers would be kept together, which was more than reassuring.

And there were worse assignments. The tour of duty was limited to two years. For sure it was safer than being posted on a carrier to one of the world's oceanic hellholes, the Adriatic or the Baltic or the South China Sea. In all, it was odd but it was just another posting.

Snowy had been happy to go along with it, even though it meant being locked away from his wife. He had expected to come out of the hole healthy and happy, a lot richer with the back pay he hadn't been able to spend. Or, failing that, the grimmer possibility would be that he would have to come out fighting. But that was what he was trained for. Even then, he had expected to emerge into the middle of an ongoing high-tech war, to find a chain of command, everything basically functioning, to find something to *fly*. That was why they had salted away pilots in the first place. He hadn't expected that they would be cracking the door cut off from any chain of command, completely ignorant of conditions outside—ignorant even of where he *was*. But that was what he faced.

Snowy took the lead. He stepped through the hatch.

Beyond the hatch, a stairwell was cut into concrete. The well led up to a rectangle of bright green light: leaves, traces of blue-white sky beyond. A forest?

The stairwell's concrete, where it was exposed, was stained brown where metal fittings had rusted away. And when Snowy put his weight too close to the edge of a step, the concrete just crumbled. The stairs themselves were barely visible under a tangle of moss, leaves, debris of all kinds. Snowy wasted a little energy trying to clear this stuff off, but found that much of it was actually growing here, out of a layer of mulch over the concrete.

Ignoring the mess, he stepped up and just pushed his way out of the well.

At last he found himself standing on leaf-covered ground. He was panting hard. Evidently the cold sleep had taken more out of him than he had expected. The others followed him, one by one, brushing dead leaves and moss and mulch off their clothes.

The forest was built of tall trees, with low branches, heavy, spreading leaves. Oak, perhaps. Wind rustled, bringing warm air to Snowy's face. It felt like late spring or early summer. The air smelled fresh, of nothing but forest, green and mulchy.

The Pit was set in the ground, half-concealed by a great concrete lid. But the lid was tilted askew and cracked, and plants were growing out of its surface.

Ahmed had a small black backpack. This contained a clockwork radio transceiver—which, like the pistols, had been stored in oil. Now he turned this on, wound it up, extended its aerial and began to walk around the little clearing.

Both Moon and Bonner looked very young and scared, lost in the green shade.

Sidewise stood by Snowy. Moodily he kicked the concrete carapace. "It's amazing the power supply kept going as long as it did."

Snowy said, "It's like we just clambered out of Chernobyl."

"I don't think Chernobyl is a problem anymore."

"What?"

"Snow, just how long do you think we've been stuck down that hole?"

Snowy braced himself. "More than fifty years?"

Sidewise grunted. "Look around you, pal. Those trees are *oak*. And look at this." He led Snowy to a fallen tree. The trunk had snapped off maybe a meter above the ground. Much of the fallen trunk was coated with greenery, and fat, platelike fungi adhered to the upright stub of trunk, like disks stuck into the wood. "Snow," said Sidewise, "you are surrounded by a mature forest. These are *old* trees. This one got so old it died without being felled. Come on, Snow. You remember those eco classes in training. What happens if you let a forest clearing recover?"

The grasses and herbs would be first to colonize the empty space. Within a year or so there would be Scots pine seedlings, birches, other deciduous trees sprouting from seeds left in the ground, or from stumps. Once there was some protection from the frost, Norway spruce and chestnut might take hold. Then, as conditions changed, different species would compete for light and space. After maybe fifty years, as the recovering forest darkened, the grasses on the floor would make way for shade-tolerant vegetation like bilberry and mosses. And after *that*, the oaks would return.

Snowy hadn't paid a great deal of attention to this kind of stuff, at school, during his training, or later. Eco was always too depressing, nothing but lists of dead creatures. But—*how long?*

Sidewise poked at the grounded trunk. "Look at these bryophytes—the mosses and liverworts—and the lichens, fungi, insects burrowing away. You know, in our day a sight like this dead trunk was as rare as a wolf."

"*In our day?*"

Ahmed had given up his stroll around the clearing. "Nothing," he said. "Not a peep on any frequency. Not even GPS."

"Maybe the radio's out," Moon said.

Ahmed pressed a green button on the set. "The self-test is okay."

"Then," said Bonner, "what do we do?"

Ahmed straightened up. "We keep ourselves alive. We get out of this damn forest. And we find somebody to report to."

Snowy nodded. "Which way?"

"The maps," said Bonner immediately.

Their training asserted itself, and they hurried back to the Pit.

The Pit had been equipped with external stores of paper maps, in case of the eventuality that a troop found itself revived like this without external direction or orientation. The maps were supposed to be contained in weatherproof boxes on the exterior of the Pit. The maps would also come with spins—specific instructions. Snowy knew they would all be reassured to find something to tell them what to do, maybe a clue as to what was going on.

But, try as they might, they couldn't even find a trace of the map boxes. There was nothing but a surface of corroded, crumbling concrete, heavily colonized by mosses and grass.

Sidewise helped with the search, but Snowy could tell that his heart wasn't in it. He had *known* the maps wouldn't be here. Snowy began to feel vaguely scared of Sidewise, because he was so far ahead of the game; he really didn't want to know what Sidewise had already figured out.

They gave up on the maps. Still Ahmed tried to take a lead, to be decisive, and Snowy admired him for that. Ahmed sniffed the air, looked around, and pointed. "The land is rising that way. So that's the way we'll go. If we're lucky, we'll break out of these woods. Agreed?"

He was rewarded by shrugs and nods.

II

There wasn't much to take from the Pit—nothing but what they could plunder from the dead: all the weapons and ammo they could find, spare clothing, ration packs. They made backpacks from spare flight suits, and loaded up their gear.

They set off in the direction Ahmed had chosen. The sun looked to be setting, and that meant, Snowy thought, that they had to be traveling roughly north. Unless even *that* had gotten itself screwed up in the years they had lost in the Pit.

The forest was dominated by the great oaks, though they were interspersed with other species like sycamore, Norway maple, and conifers. There were plenty of birds—mostly starlings, it seemed to Snowy—but he was startled to see a rattle of green and yellow wings pass across the sun. Occasionally they saw animals—rabbits, squirrels, small, timid-looking deer, even what looked like a wolf, which had them all fingering their pistols.

After maybe an hour they came to a neat round hole in the ground. It was full of debris, but was obviously man-made. The bit of human design drew them insistently. They gathered around, sipping water from the small vials they carried.

Snowy said to Sidewise, "Did you see those green birds? They looked like—"

"Budgerigars. The descendants of escaped pets. Why not? There are probably parakeets and parrots too. Some of those deer looked like muntjac to me. Out of zoo stock, maybe. Even some of the trees look like imports—like that turkey oak back there. Like they taught us: Once you disturb the balance of nature, once you start importing species, it never goes back the way it used to be."

Snowy said, "There was a wolf."

"You sure it was a wolf?" Sidewise said sharply. "Didn't it look too low, too fast?"

Come to think of it, Sidewise was right. It had looked a little furtive, low-slung. Rodentlike.

Bonner said, "All right, two-brains, what about this hole in the ground? Somebody's removed a tree stump here, and done it deliberately."

"Maybe," said Sidewise coldly. "But holes in the ground last a long time. You can still find holes dug by hunter-gatherers tens of thousands of years ago. All this tells us is there hasn't been another Ice Age yet."

Ahmed glared at him. "You aren't doing much for morale, Sidewise."

Sidewise shot back, "And what about my morale? It does me no damn good to ignore what's blindingly obvious all around us."

There was a moment of strained silence. For a minute Snowy glimpsed Sidewise's past, a past he never talked about: the too-brainy kid at school, impatient of the rest, constantly bullied back into line by his fellows.

"Let's move on," Bonner said gruffly. Ahmed nodded and led the way.

Soon they came to what looked like a track. It was nothing but a winding ribbon of earth, almost invisible, crooked and devious. But the vegetation here grew a little sparser, and Snowy could feel how the ground did not give under his feet as it did elsewhere. A track, then—and surely a human-made track, not animal, if the ground had been compacted as much as it felt.

They didn't say anything. Nobody wanted this little bit of hope to be punctured by another lecture from Sidewise. But they all followed the track, walking single file, moving that much more briskly up the shallow slope.

Snowy already felt exhausted, strung out.

He found he wasn't thinking of his wife, his buddies back home, the life that seemed to have vanished forever. Everything was too strange for that. But he longed, absurdly, for the snug safety of his cold-sleep bed, with its enclosing carapace and humming machines. Out here he felt very exposed—his PPK didn't add up to much protection—and he was very aware that when darkness fell in this strange, transformed place they were going to be very vulnerable.

We have to find some answers before then, he thought.

After maybe another hour the trees thinned out, and with relief Snowy found himself walking out in the open. But he still couldn't see much. He was on the breast of a broad shallow rise, its summit hidden over the nearby horizon. The ground was chalky, he saw, and the soil thin and heavily eroded. Nothing much grew here but heather, and shoulders of bare rock stuck out of the ground.

The sky was clear, save for a scattering of thin, high cloud. The setting sun cast long shadows on the ground. It was so low that Snowy would have expected the sunset to have started already, a tall Rabaul-ash light show. But there was no redness in the western sky; the sun shone bright and white. Was the ash gone?

Moon yelped. "Tracks! Vehicle tracks!" She was pointing a little way down the slope to their right, jumping up and down with excitement.

They all ran that way, their improvised packs bouncing on their backs.

She was right. The tracks were quite unmistakable. They had been made by some off-road vehicle, and they ran at an angle down the slope.

The mood was suddenly exultant. Bonner was grinning. "So there's somebody around. Thank Christ for that."

"All right," Ahmed said. "We have a choice. We can keep on heading for the high ground, looking for a viewpoint. Or we can follow these tracks back downhill and find a road."

The high ground would probably have been the smarter move, Snowy thought. But in the circumstances none of them wanted to let go of these traces of human activity. So they started downhill, following the twin scars in the hillside.

Sidewise walked beside Snowy. "This is dickheaded," he muttered.

"Side—"

"Look at it. These are vehicle tracks, all right. But they have turned into gullies. Look over there. They've eroded right down to the bedrock. Snow, in an area like this, above the treeline, it can take centuries for a covering of soil and vegetation to re-establish itself once it's removed. *Centuries.*"

Snowy stared at him. His thin face was gray in the fading light. "These tracks look like they were made yesterday, as if somebody just drove by."

"I'm telling you they could be any age. I don't fucking *know*." He looked as if he was dying for a cigarette.

The tracks wound down the hillside, eventually leading them into a broad valley that cupped the silvery streak of a river. The tracks veered off the rough ground onto what was unmistakably a road following the valley wall, a neat flat shelf carved almost parallel to the valley's contours.

The group clambered into the road surface with relief. They started to hike down the road, along the valley toward the lower ground, their mood staying high despite their fatigue.

But the road was in bad shape, Snowy saw. It was overgrown. There was still some asphalt—he could see it as black fragments in the green— but it had aged, becoming cracked and brittle. Plants and fungi had long since broken through the surface, and in fact as he walked he sometimes had to push through thickets of birch and aspen seedlings. It was less like walking along a road than over a sparsely vegetated ridge.

Sidewise was walking alongside him again. "So what do you think? Where are we?"

They had all been trained up in the basic geographical features of Europe and North America. "The valley isn't glaciated," Snowy said reluctantly. "So if we're in Europe, we aren't too far north. Southern England. France maybe."

"But it's been a long time since anybody maintained this road. And look down there." Sidewise pointed to a line etched in the side of the far valley wall, just bare rock.

"So what?"

"See how level it is? I think this valley was flooded once. Dammed. At the water's surface you get a lot of erosion—you get horizontal cuts like that—because when the flow is managed, the water levels fluctuate fast."

"So where's the dam?"

"We'll come to it," said Sidewise grimly.

After another hour of walking, they did.

They turned around a breast of the valley, and there it was. A branch of this roadway actually led down to the dam, and must have run over it to the valley's far side.

But the dam was gone. Snowy could make out the piers that still clung to the shore, heavily eroded and overgrown with greenery. Of the central section, the great curving wall and gates and machinery that had once tamed the river, there was nothing left but a hummocky arced line on the valley floor, a kind of weir that barely perturbed the river as it ran over it.

Moon said, "Maybe somebody blew it up."

Sidewise shook his head. "Nothing is impervious. There are always cracks and weaknesses, places the water can get into. And if you don't do anything about it, the leaks get worse, until . . ." He fell silent. "All you need is time," he finished lamely.

"Fucking hell," growled Bonner. "Fucking buggering hell."

It seemed to Snowy that the unavoidable truth was starting to sink into them all. Even Sidewise didn't need to say any more to make it so.

Ahmed strode ahead a few paces, and peered further down the valley. He was a pilot; like them all, he had good eyes. He pointed. "I think there's a town down there."

Maybe, thought Snowy. It was just a splash of greenish gray. He could see no movement, no car windshields or windows glinting, no smoke rising, no lights. But they had nowhere else to go.

Before they left the higher ground Ahmed fired off a couple of the search-and-rescue flares he had retrieved from the shelter. There was no reply.

They followed Ahmed as he made bold, defiant strides along the grassed-over roadway, down the valley toward the town. The light began to fade. Not a single light came on in the town they approached; it was a well of darkness and silence.

In some places the river's banks had reverted to marsh, with low, green-clad hummocks marking what might once have been buildings. Elsewhere the banks were lined with elder and graceful willows—*old-looking* willows, Snowy thought reluctantly—and the floodplain beyond was covered by a forest of poplar and ash. Beyond, he could see arms of the oak forest spreading over the low hills.

Long before they reached the center of the town they had to abandon the grown-over road, as it slipped under the surface of the broadening river. Further out into the river, Snowy could make out shapes, lines, under the shallow water.

"If you build around a river," said Moon slowly, "you reclaim the land to either side. Right? But when you abandon the town, the water table is going to rise because you're no longer pumping out groundwater for industrial use, and you'll get flooded out."

Nobody commented. They walked on, skirting the river and its marshy fringe.

At last they came to the town itself. There was a layout of streets here, you could see that, a roughly rectangular grid laid out over shallow slopes. But the roads were as ruined as the one they had followed here. The buildings themselves were just patterns of mounds and hummocks draped with green, most of them no more than waist height. The whole place looked like an overgrown graveyard. Snowy thought they could have passed by any of these heaps of green-clad rubble in the forest and thought it just another extrusion of rock, the product of nature's mindless churning. Even the vegetation was much the same as in the open land beyond the town. It was only the patterns that told you that hands had built this place, that minds had planned it.

Here and there, though, more enduring fragments poked out of the drowning green. There was one looming, circular hill, as green clad as the rest. Snowy wondered if this might be a keep, the base of one of the Normans' great castles, erected to enforce their occupation of England in the eleventh century. If so, it had lasted where much else had failed. They came across a row of columns, worn to stubs, that looked as if they had been clad in marble. They might have been the grandiose frontage of a bank or town hall.

And here was a statue, fallen on its back. Its face, pocked by lichen and eroded beyond recognition, peered up at the sky from an ocean of green. But the statue bore traces of charring, Snowy saw. He searched for a date, but couldn't find one.

When he dug into the greenery that blanketed other anonymous mounds, he found more traces of fire, of soot and scorching. This place had burned, then, before it had been broken up. He was walking on tragedy, on overgrown horror. He wondered how deep he would have to dig before he found bones.

They came to a comparatively open space. This must have been a central square, maybe a marketplace. Ahmed called a halt. They dropped their packs, drank their water, and peered around. In the lengthening shadows of evening the ruined town was an eerie place, Snowy thought, neither quite natural nor human, neither one thing nor the other.

A little ratty creature scuttled from under Snowy's feet, crisply pattering over the broken asphalt surface and disappearing into the richer green away from the square. It looked like a vole. And, following its tracks, Snowy made out the upright, wary form of a hare. With bewildering speed it turned and scuttled away.

"Voles and hares," he muttered to Sidewise. "I thought we'd see cats and dogs."

Sidewise shrugged, sweat and grime coating his face. "People have gone, right? Civilization has fallen, blah, blah, blah. Cats and dogs were pampered, domesticated, all the genetic variation bred out of them. They wouldn't have lasted long without us."

"I'd have thought cats would survive. Even little kittens used to go hunting."

"Wild cats were perfect killing machines. But the domestic variety had smaller teeth, jaws, brains than their wild ancestors, because old ladies liked them better that way." Sidewise winked. "I always thought cats were faking it. They weren't so tough. Just a pain in the arse."

"Where are the cars?" Moon asked. "I mean, I see the buildings, what's left of them. What about the cars?"

"If you dig in the greenery you might find a few patches of rust, or bits of plastic." Sidewise glared at Ahmed. "What, are you going to chew me out for lowering morale again? I'm only pointing out the bleeding obvious."

"But we don't have to deal with that right now," Ahmed said, with an evenness Snowy admired. "What we need to *do* is obvious too."

Snowy nodded. "We have to find shelter."

Bonner clambered up onto a low mound that might once have been a wall. Now he pointed, roughly west. "That way. I can see walls. I mean, standing walls. Something that isn't all covered in shit."

With an unreasonable spark of hope, Snowy got to his feet. It was a church, he saw. A medieval church. He could make out the tall, narrow windows, the high doorway. But the doors and roof had long gone, leaving the building open to the sky. He felt disappointment—and yet a stab of admiration.

Sidewise seemed to share his thought. "If you're going to build, build out of stone."

"Where do you think we are? England, France?"

Sidewise shrugged. "What do I know about churches?"

Ahmed picked up his pack. "All right. There's no roof, so we'll have to make lean-tos. Bonner, Snowy, come with me and we'll fetch some branches. And we'll need a fire. Moon, Sidewise, you attend to that." He looked around at their faces, which were shining like coins in the gathering dark. This would be the first time they had been out of each other's sight since they had woken up, and even Snowy felt a pang of uncertainty. "Don't go too far," Ahmed said gently. "We're alone here. There doesn't seem to be anybody to help us. But we'll be fine so long as we're careful. If anything goes wrong—anything—shout or use your pistol, and the rest of us will come running. All right?"

They nodded and murmured. Then they moved off into the gathering dark, purposefully pursuing their allotted tasks.

The interior of the church was just another patch of greenery. There was a mound at one end that might once have been an altar, but there was no sign of pews or crucifixes, prayer books or candles. The roof was gaping open to the sky, not a trace left of the wooden construction that must once have spanned these slender, sturdy walls.

Under their lean-tos, on pallets of brush, with leaves for blankets, it wasn't going to be such an uncomfortable night. They had all had plenty of survival training; this wasn't so bad compared to that.

They stuck to their survival packs, munching on dried bananas and beef jerky. They didn't eat any of the fruit from the forest. It was a little superstitious, Snowy thought, as if they wanted to cling to what was left of the past as long as possible, before committing themselves to this peculiar new present. But it was OK to take it slow. Ahmed was showing a good grasp of psychology in allowing that. It certainly wouldn't make any difference in the long run.

They were all pretty exhausted after a walk of many klicks on their first day out of the Pit. Snowy wondered how they would have got on if they'd really had to fight; maybe this strategy wouldn't have worked as well as the planners had imagined. And they all had trouble with their feet, with blisters and aches. It was the lack of socks that was the problem. Snowy worried about using up their limited supplies of ointments too fast. They would have to do something about that tomorrow.

But it was comforting to shelter in this relic of human construction, as if they were still cradled by the civilization they had come from. Still, they would keep their fire burning all night.

Snowy was relieved to find he was too tired to think too hard. Still, he woke.

He rolled on his back, restless. The air was hot—too damn hot for an English spring; maybe the climate had changed, global warming gone crazy or somesuch. The sky framed by the open roof was littered with stars, obscured here and there by cloud. There was a crescent moon, too narrow to banish the stars, as far as he could see unchanged from the patient face that had watched over his boyhood. He had learned a little astronomy, during training exercises in the desert, for navigation purposes. He picked out constellations. There was Cassiopeia—but the familiar W shape was extended by a sixth star. A hot young star, maybe, born since he had gone into the Pit. What a strange thought.

"I can't see Mars," Sidewise whispered, from out of the dark.

That startled Snowy; he hadn't known Sidewise was awake. "What?"

Sidewise pointed to the sky, his arm a silhouette. "Venus. Jupiter. Saturn, I think. Where's Mars?"

"Maybe it set already."

"Maybe. Or maybe something happened to it."

"This is bad shit, isn't it, Side?"

Sidewise didn't reply.

"Once I saw some Roman ruins," Snowy whispered. "Hadrian's Wall. It was like this. All grown over, even the mortar rotted away."

"This was a different scale," Sidewise murmured. "Even from Rome. We had a global civilization, a crowded world. Everything was linked up."

"What do you think happened?"

"I don't know. That fucking volcano, maybe. Famine. Disease. Refugees everywhere. War in the end, I guess. I'm glad I didn't live through it."

"Shut up, you two," Ahmed murmured.

Snowy sat up. He peered out through a glassless window frame in the wall of the church. He could see nothing. The land was just a blanket of dark, no glimmer of lights, no glow of streetlights on the horizon. Maybe everywhere was dark like this. Maybe their fire was the *only* light in England—on the whole damn planet. It was a stupendous, unbelievable, unacceptable thought. Maybe Sidewise could grasp it properly, but Snowy sure couldn't.

Some kind of animal howled, out in the night.

He threw a little more wood on the fire, and buried himself deeper in his mound of greenery.

Sidewise had been right. Mars was missing.

The replicators, Ian Maughan's robot probes, had survived. The program had been designed as a precursor to human colonization of the planet. The replicating robots would have been instructed to build homes for human astronauts, to make them cars and computers, to assemble air and water, even grow food for them.

But the humans never came. Even their commands ceased to be received.

That wasn't troubling, for the replicating robots. Why should it be? Until they were told otherwise, their only purpose was to replicate. Nothing else mattered, not even the strange silence from the blue world in the sky.

And replicate they did.

Many modifications were tried, incorporated, abandoned. It did not take long for a radically better design to converge.

The replicators began to incorporate the factory components within their bodies. The new kind looked like tractors, pilotless, trundling over the impassive red dust. Each weighed about a ton. It took each one a year to make a copy of itself—a much shorter reproduction time than before, because they could go where the resources were.

After a year, one of the new replicator types would become two.

Which after another year had made two more copies, a total of four. And in another year there were eight. And so on.

The growth was exponential. The outcome was predictable.

Within a century the factory-robots were everywhere on Mars, from pole to equator, from the peak of Mons Olympus to the depths of the Hellas crater. Some of them came into conflict over resources: There were slow, logical, mechanical wars. Others began to dig, to exploit the deeper materials of Mars. If you mined, there was still plenty of resources to go around—for a while, anyhow.

The mines got deeper and deeper. In places the crust collapsed. But still they kept digging. Mars was a cold, hard world, rocky for much of its interior. That helped the mining. But as they dug deeper and encountered new conditions, the replicators had to learn quickly, adapt. They were capable of that, of course.

Still, the penetration of the mantle presented certain technical challenges. The dismantling of the core was tricky too.

Mars weighed one hundred billion billion times as much as any one of the tractor-replicators. But that number was small in the face of the doubling-every-generation rule. Because of the continuing conflicts, the pace of growth was a little slower than optimal. Even so, in just a few hundred generations, *Mars had gone,* all but a trace of its substance converted to the glistening bulks of replicators.

With the whole planet transformed to copies of themselves—using solar sails, fusion drives, even crude antimatter engines—the swarm of replicators had moved out through the solar system, seeking raw material.

The next day, roaming into the country around the town, Snowy saw birds, squirrels, mice, rabbits, rats. Once he thought he saw a goat; it fled at his approach.

Not much else. There didn't even seem to be many birds around. The place was silent, as if all the living things had been collected up and removed.

Some of the rats were huge, though. And then there were the rat-wolves he thought he had glimpsed. Whatever they were, they fled at his approach.

Rodents had always been in competition with primates, Sidewise said. Even at the peak of their technical civilization, people had had to be content with keeping rodents out of sight, and out of the food. Now, with people out of the picture, the rats were evidently flourishing.

It was easy to hunt, though. Snowy set a few snares, in a spirit of experimentation. The snares worked. The hares and voles seemed peculiarly tame. Another bad sign if you thought about it, because it meant they hadn't seen humans for a while.

At the end of the second day, Ahmed had them sit in the ruins of the church, in a rough circle on corroded stone blocks.

Snowy was aware of subtle changes in the group. Moon was looking down, avoiding everybody's eyes. Bonner, Ahmed, and Sidewise were watching each other, and Snowy, with calculation.

Ahmed held up an empty ration packet. "We can't stay here. We have to plan."

Bonner shook his head. "The most important thing is finding other people."

"We're going to have to face it," Sidewise said. "There *are* no other people—nobody who can help us, anyhow. We haven't seen anybody. We've seen no sign that anybody has been in this area recently."

"No contrails," Ahmed said, pointing to the sky. "Nothing on the radio, on any frequency. No satellites. Something went wrong—"

Moon laughed hollowly. "You can say that again."

"We can't know how events unfolded. Before the end it must have become—chaotic. We were never recalled. Eventually, I suppose, we were forgotten. Until we were revived by chance."

Snowy forced himself to ask the question. "How long, Side?"

Sidewise rubbed his nose. "Hard to say. If we had an astronomy almanac I guess we could figure it out from the changed positions of the stars. Failing that, your best guess is based on the maturity of the oak forest."

Bonner snapped, "You're so full of shit, you scrawny bastard. How fucking *long*? Fifty years, sixty—"

"Not less than a thousand years," Sidewise said, his voice tight. "Maybe more. Probably more, actually."

In silence, they let that sink in. And Snowy closed his eyes, imagining he was plunging off the deck of an aircraft carrier into the dark.

A *thousand years*. And yet it meant no more than the fifty-year gulf that he thought had separated him from his wife. Less, maybe, because it was just unimaginable.

"Some future this is," Bonner said edgily. "No jet cars. No starships, no cities on the Moon. Just shit."

Ahmed said, "We have to assume we are not going to find anybody else. That we're alone. We have to plan on that basis."

Sidewise snorted. "Civilization has collapsed, everybody is dead, and we're stuck a thousand years in the future. How are we supposed to *plan* for that?"

"That river is probably clean," Snowy said. "All the factories must have shut down centuries ago."

Ahmed nodded gratefully at him. "Good. At last, something we can actually build on. We can fish, we can hunt; we can start that tomorrow. Sidewise, why don't you use that brain of yours for something useful and think about the fishing? Figure out how we can improvise lines, nets, whatever the hell. Snowy, you do the same for the hunting. Further down the line, we're going to have to find somewhere to live. Maybe we can find a farm. Start thinking about clearing the ground, planting wheat." He glanced at the sky. "What do you think the season is? Early summer? We're too late for a harvest this year. But next spring—"

Sidewise snapped, "Where do you think you're going to find wheat? Do you know what happens if you leave corn or wheat unharvested? The ears fall to the ground and rot. Cultivated wheat needed *us* to survive. And if you leave cows unmilked for a few days, they just die of udder bursts."

"Take it easy," Snowy said.

"All I'm telling you is that if you want to farm, you'll have to start from scratch. The whole damn thing, agriculture and husbandry, all over again from wild stock, plants and animals."

Ahmed nodded stiffly. "We, Side. Not *you*. We. We all share the problems here. All right. So that's what we'll do. And in the meantime we gather, we hunt. We live off the land. It's been done before."

Moon fingered her clothing. "This stuff won't last forever. We'll have to find out how to make cloth. And our weapons will be pretty useless once the ammo is gone."

Bonner said, "Maybe we can make more ammo."

Sidewise just laughed. "Think about stone axes, pal."

Bonner growled, "I don't know how to make a fucking stone ax."

"Neither do I, come to think of it," Sidewise said thoughtfully. "And you know what? I bet there aren't even any books to tell us how. All that wisdom, painfully acquired since we were buck naked *Homo erectus* running around in Africa. All gone."

"Then we'll just have to start that again too," Ahmed said firmly.

Bonner eyed him. "Why?"

Ahmed looked up at the sky. "We owe it to our children."

Sidewise said simply, "Four Adams and one Eve."

There was a long, intense silence. Moon was like a statue, her eyes hard. Snowy noticed how close her hand was to her PPK.

Ahmed got to his feet. "Don't think about the future. Think about filling your belly." He clapped his hands. "Let's move it."

They dispersed. The crescent moon was already rising, a bonelike sliver in the blue sky.

"So," Sidewise said to Snowy as they moved off, "how are you finding life in the future?"

"Like doing time, mate," Snowy said bitterly. "Like doing fucking time."

III

Maybe five kilometers from the base camp, Snowy was trying to build a fire.

He was in what must once have been a field. There were still traces of a dry stone wall that marked out a broad rectangle. But after a thousand years it was pretty much like any patch of land hereabouts, choked by perennial herbs and grasses, shrubs and deciduous seedlings.

He had made a fire board about the length of his forearm, with a dish cut into its flat side. He had a spindle, a stick with a pointed end; a socket, a bit of rock that fit neatly into his hand; and a bow, more sapling with a bit of plastic shoelace tied tight across it. A bit of bark under the notch served as a tray to catch the embers he would make. Nearby he had made a little nest of dry bark, leaves, and dead grass, ready to feed the flames. He knelt on his right knee, and put the ball of his left foot on the fire board. He looped the bow string and slid the spindle through it. He lubricated the notch with a bit of earwax, and put the rounded end of the spindle into the dish of his fire board, and held the pointed end in the hand socket. Then, pressing lightly on the socket, he drew the bow back and forth, rotating the spindle with increasing pressure and speed, waiting for smoke and embers.

Snowy knew he looked older. He wore his hair long now, tied back in a ponytail by a bit of wire. His beard was growing too, though he hacked it back with a knife every couple of days. His skin was like tough leather, wrinkled around the eyes, the mouth. Well, I am older, he thought. A thousand years older. I should look the part.

It was hard to believe that it was only a bit more than a month since they had come out of the Pit.

They didn't need to do this kind of thing yet, this fire building from scratch. They still had plenty of boxes of waterproof matches, and a supply of trioxane packs—a light chemical heat source much used by the military. But Snowy was looking ahead to the day when they wouldn't be able to rely on what had come out of the Pit. In some ways he was "cheating," of course. He had used his thousand-year-old finely manufactured Swiss Army knife to make the bow and the fire board; later he would have to try out stone knives. But one step at a time.

This ancient field was close to an arm of the vast oak forest which, as far as they had scouted, dominated the landscape of this posthuman England. It was on a slight rise. To the west, further down the hill, a lake had gathered. Snowy could see traces of stone walls disappearing under the placid water. But the lake was choked with reeds and lilies and weeds, and on its surface he could see the sickly gray-green sheen of an algal bloom. Eutrophication, said Sidewise: Even now, artificial nutrients—notably phosphorus—were leaching out of the land into the lake and overstimulating the miniature ecology. It seemed incredible to Snowy that the shit long-dead farmers had pumped into their land could still be poisoning the environment around him, but it seemed to be true.

It was a strangely empty landscape. Silence surrounded him. There wasn't even birdsong.

Some creatures had probably bounced back quickly once human hunting, pest control, and land use had ceased—hares, rabbits, grouse. Larger mammals reproduced so slowly that recovery must have taken longer. But there seemed to be various species of deer, and Snowy had glimpsed pigs in the forests. They'd seen no large predators. Even foxes seemed rare. There were no birds of prey either—apart from a few aggressive-looking starlings. Sidewise said that as their food chains had collapsed, the specialized top predators would have died out. In Africa there were probably no lions or cheetahs either, he said, even if they had escaped being eaten by the last starving human refugees.

Maybe, Snowy thought. He wondered about the rats, though.

Balance would return in the long run, of course. Variation, adaptation, and natural selection would see to that; the old roles would be filled one way or another. But it might not be anything like the community that had gone before. And, said Sidewise, since the average mammalian species lasted only a few million years, it would correspondingly be millions of years—ten, twenty maybe, *twenty million years*—before there would again be assembled a world of the richness it had enjoyed. So even if humans recovered and lasted, say, five million years, they wouldn't see anything like the world Snowy had known as a kid.

Snowy was not a tree hugger, definitely. But there was something deeply disturbing about these thoughts. How strange it was to have lived to see it come about.

Still no smoke, still the damn embers hadn't caught. He continued to work the bow.

The main problem with fire making was that it gave him too much time to think. He missed his friends, the camaraderie of navy life. He missed his work, even the routine bits—maybe the routine most of all, since it had given his life a definition it lacked now.

He missed the *noise*, he found, though that was harder to pin down: TV and the web and music, movies and ads, the logos and jingles and news. The one thing about the new world that would drive him crazy in the end, he suspected, was the *silence*, the huge, inhuman, vegetable silence. It gave him the shivers to imagine how it must have been in the last days, when all the machines had died, the winking logos and neon tubes and screens flickering and dying, one by one.

And he missed Clara. Of course he did. He had never known his kid, never even seen him, or her.

At the beginning he had been plagued by spasms of guilt: guilt that he was still alive where so many had gone into the dark, guilt that there was nothing he could do for Clara, guilt that he was eating and breathing and pissing and taking shits and covertly studying Moon's butt while everybody he had ever known was *dead*. But that, mercifully, was fading. He had always been blessed, as Sidewise had once told him, by a lack of imagination.

Or maybe it was more than that.

In the clear light of this new time it seemed like it was his old life, in the crowded, murky England of the twenty-first century, which was the dream. As if he were dissolving into the green.

There was a rustle in the waist-high foliage, a dozen paces away. He turned that way, still and silent. A single grass stem, laden with seeds, nodded gracefully. He had set a snare over there. Was there something in the foliage—a curve of shoulder, a bright, staring eye?

He put down the bow and spindle. He stood, stretched, and casually walked toward the place he had seen the rustle. He slid his bow from his back, scooped an arrow from his rabbit-skin quiver, notched it carefully.

There was no movement in the foliage—not until he was almost on it—and then there was a sudden blur, a lunge away from his approach. He glimpsed pale skin flecked with brown, long limbs. A fox? But it was *big*, bigger than anything he'd seen here so far.

Without hesitating further he ran up to the thing, lodged his boot in the small of its back, and raised his arrow toward its head. The creature squirmed onto its back. It yowled like a cat, put its hands over its face.

He lowered the bow. *Hands.* It had hands, like a human, or an ape.

His heart thumping, he dropped the bow. He knelt over the creature, trapping its torso, and got hold of its wrists. It was spindly, lithe, but very strong; it took all of his power to force those hands away from the face. Still the creature spat and hissed at him.

But its face—no, *her* face—was no chimp's, no ape's. It was unmistakably human.

For long seconds Snowy sat there, astounded, astride the girl.

She was naked, and though her pale skin showed through, she was covered by a loose fur of straggling orange-brown hairs. The hair on her head was darker, a tangle of filthy curls that looked as if they had never been cut. She was not tall, but she had breasts, sagging little sacks with hard nipples protruding from the hair, and beneath the triangle of darker fur at her crotch there was a smear of what might be menstrual blood. And she had *stretch marks.*

Not only that, she stank like a monkey cage.

But that face was no ape's. Her nose was small but protruding. Her mouth was small, her chin V-shaped with a distinct notch. Over blue eyes, her brow was smooth. Was it a little lower than his?

She looked human, despite her hairy belly. But her eyes were—cloudy. Frightened. Bewildered.

His throat tight, he spoke to her. "Do you speak English?"

She screeched and thrashed.

And suddenly Snowy had an erection like an iron rod. Holy shit, he thought. Quickly he rolled off the girl, reaching for his bow and his knife.

The girl couldn't get up. Her right foot was trapped by his snare. She scrabbled over the moist ground until she was hunched over her foot. She rocked back and forth, crooning, obviously scared out of whatever wits she had.

Snowy's spasm of lust faded. Now she looked like a chimp in her gestures, in her mindless misery, even though her body had felt like a woman's under his. (Clara, forgive me, it's been a long time. . . .) The scrapings of shit on her legs, the puddles of droppings where she had been lying, put him off even more.

He rummaged in a pocket of his flight suit, and pulled out the remains of a ration pack. It still contained a handful of nuts, a bit of beef jerky, some dried banana. He pulled out the banana and held it out, a handful of curling flakes, toward the girl.

She shied back, pulling as far as she could on the wire.

He tried miming, putting a flake or two into his own mouth and exaggeratedly devouring it with every expression of enjoyment. "Yum, yum. Delicious."

But still she wouldn't take the food from his hand. Then again, neither would a deer or a rabbit, he thought. So he put the flakes on the ground between them and backed away.

She grabbed a couple of the flakes and crammed them into her mouth. She chewed and chewed at the bits of banana, as if extracting every bit of flavor from them, before finally swallowing them. She must never have tasted anything so sweet, he thought.

Or maybe it was just that she was starving. He had set the trap a couple of days before; she might have been here for forty-eight hours already. All the shit and piss, the way the fur on her legs was matted and stained, indicated that too.

As she ate he got a good look at the foot that had been caught in the snare. It was a simple loop snare, meant for the heads of rabbits and hares. In her efforts to get free she had pulled the snare tighter—it had worked just as it had been designed—and it had cut so deeply into her leg that it had made a grisly, bloody mess of her flesh, and he thought he could see the white of bone in the wound.

What now? He could slug her and take her back to the base camp. But this wasn't a prey animal, a rabbit or a hare; it wasn't some interesting specimen, like the huge half-way-flightless parakeet Sidewise had caught stalking the fringe of a stagnant pond. This was a *person*, no matter what she looked like. And, he reminded himself, those stretch marks told him she had at least one kid out there waiting for her.

"Did I come all this way, across a thousand fucking years, to make the same mess of your life as I've made of mine? I don't bloody think so," he muttered. "Pardon me." And without hesitating he leapt on her.

It was another wrestling match. He got her pinned to the ground, face down, her arms under her, his buttocks in the small of her back. He used his Swiss Army knife to cut the snare wire, and prized the loop out of the bloody gouge it had dug. Then he used up more of his precious supplies to clean away the dirt and dried blood and pus with antiseptic fluid—he had to pick strands of brown hair out of the scabs—and to apply sealant and cream to the wound. Maybe she would leave the stuff on long enough for the wound to get itself disinfected.

The moment he released her she was gone. He glimpsed a figure, upright and lithe, shimmering through the long grass toward the trees, limping but moving fast even so.

It was already late afternoon. They weren't supposed to be alone in the dark, away from base: Ahmed's standing orders. He longed to follow the girl into the green mysteries of the denser forest. But he knew he must not. Regretfully he gathered up his gear and set off back to the base camp.

Snowy was the last to join the group that evening.

They had decided to settle close to a lake a few kilometers from the ruined town. The site was in the lee of a compact, cone-shaped hill—apparently artificial, maybe an Iron Age barrow, or maybe just a spoil heap of some kind.

Ahmed made them gather round the stump of a fallen tree, where he sat, a bit grandly. Snowy wanted to tell the others of his encounter, of what he had found. But the mood wasn't right. So he just sat down.

Moon had grown increasingly withdrawn as the weeks had worn away; now she just sat cross-legged before Ahmed, her eyes averted. But she was the center of everything, as always, all the wordless maneuvering. Sidewise had his usual detached dreaminess, but he was sitting facing Moon, and Snowy saw how his gaze strayed over the curve of her hip, the centimeters of calf she showed above her boot. Ahmed himself sat beside the girl, raised up on his tree stump, as if he owned her.

Bonner was the one whose lust for Moon showed most nakedly. He sat awkwardly, muscles tensed, with a great stripe of mud splashed across his face, a hunter's camouflage marking. He looked like an animal himself, Snowy thought, as if the last bits of his training were barely holding him together.

They were breaking up, Snowy saw, drifting apart, with great fault lines running through their intense little set of relationships. There was hardly anything left of the timid group of Navy fliers who had huddled in the ruined church that first night, chomping on their rations. They might kill each other over Moon, if Moon didn't kill them first.

And Ahmed, their leader, was aware of none of this. Ahmed, in fact, was smiling. "I've been thinking about the future," he said.

Sidewise gave a muffled groan.

"I mean, the further future," Ahmed said. "Beyond the next few months, even the next few years. However we get through the next winter, times are going to be hard for our children."

At the talk of children, Snowy cast a glance at Moon. She was glaring at her hands, her nested fingers.

Ahmed said that during the industrialized period—and especially during the last few insane decades—mankind had used up all its accessible supplies of fossil fuels: coal, gas, oil. "The fossil fuels are probably forming again even now. We know that. But incredibly slowly. The stuff we burned up in a few centuries took around four hundred and fifty *million* years to form. But there will always be fuel for our descendants," he said. "*Peat.* Peat is what you get when bog mosses, sedges, and other vegetation decompose in oxygen-starved wetlands. Right? And in some parts of the world peat-cutting for fuel continued right until the middle of the twentieth century."

"In Ireland," Sidewise said. "In Scandinavia. Not *here.*"

"Then we go to Ireland, or Scandinavia. Or maybe we'll find it here. Conditions have changed a lot since we went into the cold sleep. Anyhow, if we don't find peat we'll find something else. We've inherited a burned-out world." He tapped his temple. "But we still have our minds, our ingenuity."

"Oh, for God's sake," Sidewise said explosively. "Ahmed, don't you get it? We're just a bunch of castaways—that's it—castaways in time. For Christ's sake, man, we only have one womb between us."

"My womb," said Moon now, without looking up. "*My* womb. You insufferable prick."

"Bog iron," Ahmed said smoothly.

They all stared.

Ahmed said, "You get iron oxide forming in bogs and marshes. When iron-rich groundwater comes into contact with the air, well, it rusts. Right, Sidewise? The Vikings used to exploit that stuff. Why don't we?"

As the bickering went on, Snowy's gaze was drawn to the nearby woods, the shadowed green. Sidewise is right, he thought. We are here by accident, just a kind of echo. We are just going to fall apart, and get pulled down by the green like all the ruined buildings, and just disappear, adding our bones to the billions already heaped in the ground. And it won't matter a damn. If he hadn't known it before, known it in his gut, he was convinced of it now, having encountered the ape-girl. *She* is the future, he thought; she, with her bright lion's gaze, her naked little body, her nimbleness and strength—her wordless silence.

As they dispersed, Snowy took Sidewise to one side, and told him about the feral woman.

Sidewise asked immediately, "Did you fuck her?"

Snowy frowned his disgust. "No. I felt like it—I got a hell of a rod—but when I saw what she was really like, I couldn't have."

Sidewise clapped him on the shoulder. "No reflection on your manhood, pal. Weena is probably the wrong species, that's all."

"Weena?"

"An old literary reference. Never mind. Listen. No matter what El

Presidente over there says, we ought to find out more about these crit-
ters. That's a hell of a lot more important than digging peat. We need to
figure out how they are surviving here. Because that's the way we are
going to have to live too. Go find your girlfriend, Snowy. And ask her if
she'd like a double date."

A couple of days after that, before Ahmed could implement his plans for
rebuilding civilization, he fell ill. He had to retreat to his lean-to, dependent on the food and water the others brought him.

Sidewise thought it was mercury poisoning, from the spoil heap by the
camp. Mercury had been used for centuries in the making of everything
from hats to mirrors to bug-control potions to treatments for syphilis. The
ground was probably saturated with it, relatively speaking, and even now, a
thousand years later, it was still leaching by various slow-dispersal routes
into the lake, where it worked its way up the food chain to maximum concentration in the bodies of fish, and the mouths of the people who ate them.

Sidewise seemed to think all of this was funny: that Ahmed, the great
planner—the one who, among them all, had clung the longest and hardest to the expansionist dreams of the long-gone twenty-first century—had
succumbed to a dose of poison, a lingering legacy of that destructive age.

Snowy didn't much care. There were far more interesting things in
the world than anything Ahmed said or did.

Like Weena, and her hairy folk of the forest.

Snowy and Sidewise built a kind of blind, a lean-to liberally sprinkled
with grass and green leaves, not far from where Snowy had first encountered the ape-girl Sidewise had christened Weena.

Snowy glanced at Sidewise, stretched out in the blind's shade. In the
dense heat of this un-English summer, both of them had taken to going
naked save for shorts, an equipment belt, and boots. Sidewise's skin,
brown and smeared liberally with dirt, was as good a camouflage as anything invented by the hand of man. Only five or six weeks out of the Pit
he was unrecognizable.

"There," hissed Sidewise.

Slim gray-brown figures—two, three, four of them—coalesced out of
the shadows at the edge of the forest. They took a few cautious steps out
onto the open ground. They were naked, but they were slim and upright,
and they carried something in their hands, probably their usual crude
stone hammers and knives. Standing in a loose circle, their backs to each
other, they peered around with sharp jerks of their heads.

Sidewise being Sidewise, he had developed a story about where these
diminutive hairy folk had come from. "Sewer kids," he had said. "When

the cities fell, who was going to last the longest? The scrubby little kids who were already in the drains and the sewers and living off the garbage. It might have been years before some of them even noticed anything had changed—"

Now the hairies ran across the grassy meadow toward a slumped, fallen form. It was a deer, a big buck, that Snowy and Sidewise had brought down with a slingshot and dumped here in the hope of attracting the hairies out of their forest cover. The hairies converged on the carcass. They began to hack away at the joints where the hind legs were attached to the lower body. And as they worked in their intent silence, one of them was always on her feet, peering around, keeping guard.

"That's their way of working," murmured Snowy. "Taking the legs—see?"

"Quick and easy," said Sidewise. "About the easiest bit of butchery you can do. Hack off a leg, then beat it back to the forest cover before something with bigger teeth than you comes along to make a contest of it. They are coordinated, even if they don't speak. See the way they are taking turns to be look-out? They are pack hunters. Or scavengers anyhow."

Snowy wondered how come they were so cautious if Sidewise was right about there being no big predators around.

"They look human but they don't act it," Snowy whispered. "You see what I mean? They aren't like a patrol. They're looking around like cats, or birds."

Sidewise grunted. "Those sewer kids must have had no culture, no learning. All they would have known was the sewers. Maybe that was why they stopped talking. In the sewers, maybe the cover of silence was more important than language."

"They lost *language*?"

"Why not? Birds lose their flight all the time. To be smart *costs*. Even a brain the size of yours, Snow, is expensive; it eats a lot of energy from your body's supply. Maybe this isn't a world where being smart pays off as much as, say, being able to run fast or see sharply. It probably didn't take much rewiring for language, even consciousness, to be shut down. And now the brains are free to shrink. Give them a hundred thousand years and they'll look like australopithecines."

Snowy shook his head. "I always thought men from the future would have big bubble heads and no dicks."

Sidewise looked at him in the dark of the blind. "Being smart didn't exactly do us a lot of good, did it?" he said sourly. He peered out at the hairies, rubbing his face. "Makes you think, looking at them, how brief it all was. There was a moment when there were minds there to understand:

to change things, to build. Now it's gone, evaporated, and we're back to *this*: living as animals, just another beast in the ecology. Just raw, unmediated existence."

They watched a little longer, as the hairy, naked folk tore the limbs off the fallen deer and, cooperating and squabbling in turns, hauled the haunches back to the shelter of the forest.

Then they returned to their base camp.

Where they found that Bonner was ripping up the place because Moon had disappeared.

"Where the fuck is she?"

Moon had set up her own little lean-to, more solidly built and private than the others. Snowy had always thought that if she could have put on a door with a padlock she would have. Now everything was gone—the backpack Moon had made from a spare flight suit, her tools and clothes, her homemade wooden comb, her precious store of washable tampons.

Bonner was rampaging through what was left, smashing apart the walls of the lean-to. Naked save for now-disintegrating shorts, with his bulked-up muscles and mud smeared over his face and chest and in his spiky hair, Snowy thought there was very little left of the timid young pilot he remembered looking after when they had first met, on assignment to a carrier in the Adriatic.

Ahmed came out of his own lean-to, wrapped in a silvered survival blanket. "What's going on?"

"She's gone. She's fucking gone!" Bonner raged.

Sidewise stepped forward. "We can all see she's gone, you moron—"

Bonner hit at him with a slashing blow. Sidewise managed to duck out of the path of the young pilot's fist, but he was caught on the temple and knocked flat.

Snowy ran forward and grabbed Bonner's arms from behind. "For Christ's sake, Bon, take it easy."

"That two-brained bastard has been fucking her. All the time he was fucking her."

Ahmed seemed utterly dismayed—as well he might, thought Snowy, for if Moon was gone, taking their only hope of procreation with her, all his grandiose plans were ruined before they had started. "But why would she go?" he moaned. "Why be alone? What would be the *point*?"

Snowy said, "What's the point of any of it? We're all going to die here. It was never going to work, splot. All the bog iron in the world wouldn't have made any difference to that."

Sidewise managed a grin. "I don't think Bonner is worried about the destiny of mankind right now. Are you, Bon? All he cares about is that the only pussy in the world has vanished, without him getting any of it—"

Bonner roared and swung again, but this time Snowy managed to hold him back.

Ahmed sloped back to his shelter, coughing.

When relative calm was restored, Snowy went to the rack where they had hung a row of skinned rabbits, and started preparing a meal.

Before the first rabbit kebab was cooked over the fire, Bonner had made up a pack. He stood there, in the gathering twilight, facing Sidewise and Snowy. "I'm pissing off," he said.

Sidewise nodded. "You going after Moon?"

"What do you think, shithead?"

"I think she has good land craft. She'll be hard to track."

"I'll manage," Bonner snarled.

"Wait until morning," Snowy said reasonably. "Have some food. You're asking for trouble, going off in the dark."

But the reasoning part of Bonner's head seemed to have switched off for good. He glared at them out of his mask of mud, every muscle tense. Then, his clumsy pack bumping on his back, he stalked away.

Sidewise put another bit of rabbit on the fire. "That's the last we'll see of him."

"You think he'll find Moon?"

"Not if she sees him coming." Sidewise looked reflective. "And if he tries to force her, she'll kill him. She's tough that way."

The rabbit was nearly done. Snowy pulled it off the fire, and began to push bits of it off the spit and onto their crude wooden plates. Every night he had divided up their food into five portions. Now, with Bonner and Moon gone, he divided it into three.

He and Sidewise just looked at the three portions for a while. Ahmed was back in his shelter. Out of sight, out of mind. Snowy picked up the third plate and, with the blade of his knife, scraped off the meat onto the other two plates. "If Ahmed gets better, he can look after himself. If not, there's nothing we can do for him."

For a time they chewed on their rabbit.

"I'll leave tomorrow," Snowy said eventually.

Sidewise didn't reply to that.

"What about you? Where will you go?"

"I think I'd like to explore," Sidewise said. "Go see the cities. London.

Paris, if I can get across the Channel. Find out more about what's happened. A lot of it must have gone already. But some of it must be like the ruins of the Roman Empire."

"Nobody else will ever see such sights," Snowy said.

"That's true."

Hesitantly, Snowy said, "What about after that? I mean, when we get older. Less strong."

"I don't think that is going to be a problem," Sidewise said laconically. "The challenge will be to pick how you want to go. To make sure you control at least that."

"When you've seen all you want to see."

"Whatever." He smiled. "Maybe in Paris there will be a few windows left to smash. Thousand-year-old brandy to drink. I'd enjoy that."

"But," Snowy said carefully, "there will be nobody to tell about it."

"We've always known that," Sidewise said sharply. "From the moment we clambered out of the Pit into that ancient oak forest. It was obvious even then."

"Maybe to you," Snowy said.

Sidewise tapped his temple, where a healthy bruise was developing from Bonner's punch. "That's my big brain working. Churning out one useless conclusion after another. And all of it making no damn difference, none at all. Listen. Let's make a pact. We'll pick a meeting place. We'll aim to rendezvous, every year. We may not make it every time, but you can always leave a message, something."

They picked a site—Stonehenge, on the high ground of Salisbury Plain, surely still unmistakable—and a time, the summer solstice, easy to track with the timekeeping discipline Ahmed had instilled in them. It was a good idea. Somehow it was comforting to Snowy, even now, to think that his future would have a little structure.

When they had done eating, the dark was closing in. It wasn't cold, but Snowy fetched himself a blanket of crudely woven bark and wrapped it around his shoulders. "Hey, Side. Was he right?"

"Who?"

"Bonner. Did you pork Moon?"

"Too right I porked her."

"You fucking dark horse. I never knew. Why you?"

"Atavistic urges, mate. I think she was responding to my smarter than the average brain."

Snowy mulled over that. "So our big brains are good for one thing, then."

"Oh, yes. They were always good for that. Probably what they were for in the first place. All the rest was bullshit."

"You fucking dark horse."

IV

Snowy followed the ape people.

He didn't live as they did. He used his snares to trap game up to the size of pigs and small deer, and used knives and fires and lean-tos for protection and butchery. But he walked where they walked.

They wandered impressively widely, through the great forests that blanketed southern England, forests that concealed the ruins of cities and cathedrals, palaces and parks. He became concerned if he lost sight of Weena, reassured when he found her again. He grew to know all the individuals in the little group—he gave them names, like Grandpa and Shorty and Doc—and he followed their lives, their triumphs and tragedies, as if he were watching a small soap opera.

They were frightened of the rats—the big ones, the rat-wolves that seemed to hunt in packs. He found that out quickly.

He wondered how he must seem to them. They were clearly aware of him, but he didn't interfere with them or the food they gathered. So they let him be, unremarked. He was like a ghost, he thought, a ghost from a vanished past, haunting these new people.

After a few months, with the long, long summer of these late times at last drawing to a close, they came to a beach. Snowy thought he was somewhere on the Sussex shore, on Britain's south coast.

The hairies did a little foraging at the fringe of the forest, ignoring Snowy as usual.

Snowy wandered along the beach. The forest washed right down to the shore, as if this were a Robinson Crusoe tropical island, not England at all. He found a place to sit, facing the crashing waves.

He picked up a handful of sand. It was fine and golden, and ran easily through his fingers. But there were black grains in there, he saw, and some bits of orange and green and blue. The multicolored stuff must be plastic. And the black stuff looked like soot—soot from Rabaul, the killer volcano, or from the fires that had swept the world as everything went to shit.

It's all gone, he thought wonderingly. It really has. The sand was a kind of proof. Moon rock and cathedrals and football stadiums, libraries and museums and paintings, highways and cities and shanties, Shakespeare and Mozart and Einstein, Buddha and Mohammed and Jesus, lions and elephants and horses and gorillas and the rest of the menagerie of extinction—all worn away and scattered and ground down, mixed into this sooty sand he trickled through his fingers.

The hairies were leaving. He could see their slim forms sliding silently into the deeper forest.

He stood up, brushed the sand off his palms, shifted the pack on his back, and followed them.

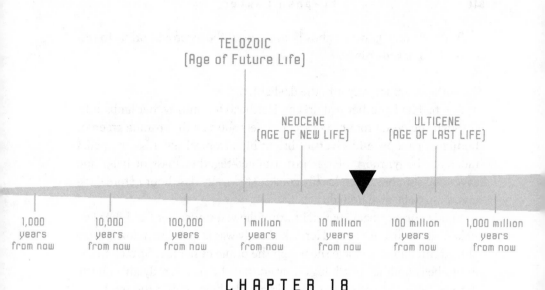

TELOZOIC
[Age of Future Life]

NEOCENE
[AGE OF NEW LIFE]

ULTICENE
[AGE OF LAST LIFE]

| 1,000 years from now | 10,000 years from now | 100,000 years from now | 1 million years from now | 10 million years from now | 100 million years from now | 1,000 million years from now |

CHAPTER 18

the kingdom of the rats

▼ **East Africa. Circa 30 million years after present.**

I

The asteroid had once been called Eros.

Eros had its own miniature geography. Its ground was covered by impact craters, scattered rubble and debris, and strange pools of very fine, bluish dust, electrically charged by the relentless sunlight. Some three times as long as it was wide, it was like Manhattan Island hurled into space.

Eros was as old as the Devil's Tail. Like the Chicxulub comet it was a relic of the formation of the solar system itself. But unlike the comet the asteroid had coalesced well within the clockwork of the inner system—inside the orbit of Jupiter, in fact. In the early days there had been mass destruction as the young asteroids, following their careening orbits, had smashed helplessly into each other. Most were shattered into clouds of dust, or thrown into the great maw of Jupiter, or into the crowded and dangerous inner system. The survivors, in their depleted swarms, followed orderly orbits around the brightening sun.

But even now gravity's ghostly tug caused the asteroids' orbits to resonate like plucked strings.

She surfaced reluctantly into the daylight.

She had had another bad dream. Her head felt muzzy, her limbs stiff. Through the crude roof of her treetop nest she saw the rustling green of the higher canopy, and slivers of bright blue tropical sky. Like the pallet under her body, the roof was just a pulled-together mass of twigs and leaves and slim branches, hastily constructed in the last hour before darkness, soon to be abandoned.

She lay on her back, her right arm pillowed under her head, her legs tucked up against her belly. Her naked body was covered with fine golden hair. At fifteen years of age she was in the prime of her life. Stretch marks on her belly and her small dugs showed that she had already given birth. Her eyes, crusted with sleep, were large, black, watchful: the mark of a slow readaptation to nocturnal living. Behind them a shallow brow led to a small, neat brainpan, its modest outline obscured by a thatch of curly dark hair.

A part of her never slept soundly, no matter how well she constructed her nests. Her dreams were always troubled by the huge spaces beneath her, into which she might fall. Since the treetops were the only safe place for her people to live, this didn't make sense, but there it was. It was going to take more time yet for people to get used to their return to the trees.

It didn't help, of course, that her only child so far had been taken by those spaces beneath her, his grip loosened from her fur by rain, his little body tumbling into the green depths.

She had never discussed this with anyone. In fact nobody discussed anything anymore. The days of endless talking were long gone, the larynxes and cognitive capacities of a loquacious folk put aside, irrelevant to life in the trees.

She didn't even have a name. But perhaps something in her retained a deep memory of vanished, different days. Call her Remembrance.

She heard a rustling in the layers of vegetation beneath her, a trickle of discarded fruit husks falling through the leaves, the first tentative hooting pants of the males.

She rolled on to her belly and pressed her face into her bed of twigs. She could just make out the colony itself, a dark, pendulous mass in the deeper layers of the canopy, like a wooden submarine somehow lodged high in the green. All around the colony slim figures were moving, working, bickering. The business of the day was starting. And it didn't pay to be a late arrival.

Remembrance stood upright and broke open her nest, like a bird bursting from its egg. With her small head raised to her full meter-tall height above the branch, she peered around at her world.

Everywhere the forest lapped in great green layers of life. The highest canopy was a roof far above her own elevation. To north, west, and east, beyond the trees, Remembrance could make out a blue, sparkling glimmer. The light off the ocean had always intrigued her. And though she could not make out the southern shore, she had a correct intuition that the ocean continued even there, making a great belt around the land: she knew that she lived on a vast island. But the ocean was another irrelevance, too far away for her to be troubled with.

This particularly dense pocket of forest had sprouted from a gorge cut deep into the bedrock. Sheltered by walls of hard rock, fed by streams that ran along the base of the gorge, this was a crowded, vibrant place, full of life—though here and there were bare patches cleared by borametz trees and their servants, a new kind of life.

But the gorge itself wasn't natural. Long ago blasted out of ancient bedrock, it was the result of human road building. Erosion had taken its toll: When the drainage ditches and culverts were no longer maintained, the cutting slopes had collapsed. But nevertheless a patient geologist could have detected a fine dark layer in the sandstone that had slowly gathered at the bottom of the gorge. The dark layer was metamorphosing bitumen, a stratum still sprinkled here and there with fragments of the vehicles that had once come this way.

Even now the passing of humans left its mark.

A shadow flickered over the leaves that rustled around her, fast-moving, silent, cast by the low sun. Hastily she ducked down, seeking the safety of the green's cover. It had been a bird, of course. The predators of the upper canopy had already started their day, and it did not do to be too visible.

With a last glance at the remains of her nest—littered by bits of shit and discarded hair, stained by her urine, soon to be forgotten—she began to clamber down.

As the tropical day brightened, the people had already spread out through the trees, lithe and graceful, beginning the day's relentless search for fruit, bark-burrowing insects, and leaf-cupped water.

Remembrance, still listless, hung back, watching.

There were males and females alike, some of the women laden with clinging infants. The males also did a great deal of displaying, hooting, aggressive leaping to and fro. Here was something that had not changed down the long years: the structure of primate society was still the same, a flashy male-hierarchy superstructure imposed on top of a network of patient female clans.

In these middle layers of the canopy the taller trees thrust upward past the crowns of their smaller brethren. In this intermediate place, neither low nor high, the people were relatively safe from threats from above and below. And it was here, surrounded by the tall, slim stripes of the great trees' trunks, that they had built their colony.

It was a ball some ten meters across. Its thick wall was made of twigs and dead leaves, crudely crammed together. The leaves had been softened by chewing before being pressed into gaps in the structure. The whole thing was neatly lodged in the crooks of the robust branches of the tree, in which it had been constructed over generations. And it was lived in: A thin stream of shit and piss slid down the tree's great trunk, sewage trickling out of the openings that pocked the colony's base.

This ball of spittle and twigs was the most advanced construction any posthumans were now capable of. But it was the result of instinct, not mind, as empty of conscious planning as a bower bird's nest or a termite mound.

Remembrance could see small faces peering out timidly through gaps in the colony's crude wall. She remembered her time with her own child inside those dank, ill-smelling walls. The colony's basic purpose was to shelter the most vulnerable from the forest's predators: at night the prepubescent young, the old and sickly would cram within its walls. But only the smallest infants and their mothers were allowed to stay in its shelter during the day while the rest risked the open spaces to forage.

And, as stray canopy-filtered rays of sunlight caught the colony, the walls sparkled. Embedded in the packed-together twigs and leaves were bright stones gathered from the forest floor. There were even bits of glass. Across millions of years glass was unstable, becoming opaque as tiny crystals formed within it—but nevertheless these fragments had retained their shapes, bits of windshields or taillights or bottles, now retrieved and gathered to adorn the walls of this shapeless building.

It looked like decoration, but it was not. The glass and bright stones were meant for defense. Even now predators on these postpeople could be deterred by the remnants of buildings, by glittering stones and shining glass, haunted by deep-buried instincts developed in the time of the most dangerous killers who had ever walked the Earth. So Remembrance's folk aped the structures of their ancestors, not even capable of imagining what they were imitating.

Once, of course, the trees had been the domain of primates, where they had been able to roam with little fear of predation. Monkeys and chimpanzees had not needed fortresses of leaf and twig. Times had changed.

As Remembrance lingered, a young male hissed at her. He had a bizarre white patch of fur on his backside, almost like a rabbit's. She knew what he was thinking: He suspected she might be after the patch of bark he was working with his mother and siblings. People's minds were not what their ancestors' had been, but Remembrance was still capable of working out the beliefs and intentions of others.

But White-patch's troop had been weakened today. Since the last time Remembrance had seen them, their elder son had gone. He might have left to seek some other colony, suspended somewhere in the forest's green depths. Or, of course, he might be dead. The family members themselves showed they were still aware of the lost one's absence in the way they looked over their shoulders at nobody, or left a space for a big male who never came. But soon their memories would heal over, and the brother would vanish into the unremembering mists of the past, as lost as had been all the children of man since the construction of the last tombstone.

Remembrance herself would never learn what had become of the other son. This was not an age of information. Nobody told anybody else anything anymore. All she knew for sure was what she saw for herself.

For Remembrance, though, this was an opportunity. She could probably fight this weakened group for a place on their tree. But her poor sleep had left her feeling brittle, restless. It was a mood that had plagued her since the loss of her child. The child's death had been more than a year ago, but so sharp was the pain, so vivid was it still in her kaleidoscopic, unstructured mind, that it might have been yesterday. Like all her kind, Remembrance was a creature not of purposeful planning but of impulse. And today her impulse was not to fight these squabbling folk for the privilege of a place on their crowded branch, to peel back a bit of bark in search of grubs.

She turned away and began to make her way through the tangled levels of trees.

As she swung, clambered, and leapt her way from branch to branch, she began to feel better. The stiffness quickly worked out of her muscles, and it was as if she were coming fully awake. She even forgot, briefly, the loss of her child. She was still young; her kind often lived beyond twenty-five or even thirty years. And, long after a remote ancestor had crawled, baffled, out of a sewer into the greening daylight, her body was well adapted to her way of life, if not yet the deepest chapels of her mind.

So, as she worked in a blur of speed through the trees, she felt a kind of joy. Why not? Much had been lost, but that made no difference to Remembrance. Her brief moment in the light was here, now, and was to be cherished. As she soared through the dense twilight of the forest layers, her lips drew back from her teeth, and she laughed out loud. It was a reflex the children of man had never lost—even though, across Earth's healing face, thirty million summers had flickered and gone.

Remembrance's tropical forest was part of a great belt wrapped around the waist of the planet, a belt broken only by oceans and mountains. The forests were luxuriant—although they had taken thousands of years after the cessation of man's ferocious logging to attain something like their former richness.

The reassembled world, engulfed by forest, had left little room for the descendants of mankind. And so Remembrance's ancestors had left the ground and taken once more to the green womb of the canopies. There had already been primates here: monkeys whose ancestors had evaded the starving humans in the final days, survivors of the great extinction event. At first the posthumans were clumsier than the monkeys. But they were still smart, relatively—and they were desperate. Soon they completed the extinction that their forefathers had begun.

After that they had begun to proliferate. But the pressures that had driven them off the ground continued to pursue them.

Remembrance knew nothing of this. And yet she carried within her a molecular memory, a continuing unbroken line of genetic inheritance that stretched back to the vanished folk who had carved the mighty roadway out of the rock—and back, back far beyond them, to still more distant times when creatures not unlike Remembrance had clambered in trees not unlike this one.

She stopped at a branch laden with fat red fruit. She sat squat on the branch and began to feed briskly, shelling the fruit and sucking down the soft contents, letting the drained husks fall into the darkness below. But as she ate she kept her back to the trunk, her gaze darted fearfully around the shadows, and her motions were fast, furtive.

Despite her watchfulness, she was startled when the first chunk of rind hit her on the back of the head.

Cowering against the trunk, she looked up. Now she saw that the branches above her were heavy with what looked like fruit: fat, dark, pendulous. But those "fruit" were sprouting arms and legs and heads and glittering eyes, and clever hands that hurled rinds and bits of bark and twig down at her. They had probably lain in wait as she approached, and then just as silently converged on her position. They even threw lumps of warm shit.

And now the chattering began. It was a screaming, meaningless jabber that filled her head, disorienting her—as was its purpose. She huddled in the crook of the branch, her hands clapped over her ears.

The Chattering Folk were cousins of Remembrance's kind. They used to be humans too. But the Chatterers lived differently. They were cooperative hunters. All of them, from barely weaned young upward, would work with a cold, instinctive discipline to bring down any prey, or battle any predator. The strategy worked: Remembrance had seen more than one of her kind fall before this treetop army.

Despite their different ways of living, up to a couple of million years ago the two kinds of people could still have crossbred, though their off-spring would have been infertile. By now that was impossible. It had been a speciation, one of many. To the Chattering Folk, Remembrance was not kin, nothing but a potential threat—or perhaps, a meal.

She was cut off. There seemed to be a Chatterer on every branch. She could never get past them and reach the sanctuary of another tree. She had only one way off this bare trunk: across the ground itself.

She didn't hesitate. Skittering down the trunk—letting herself fall for long distances, trusting on her reflexes to grab at branches and slow her descent—she escaped toward the deeper gloom of the forest floor.

At first the Chatterers followed her, and their bits of fruit and shit hailed around her, splattering against the bark. She heard them spread out through the tree from which they had ousted her, chattering and screaming their useless triumph.

At last she slid off the trunk. She intended to make for another great tree trunk a couple of hundred meters away, which might be far enough away from the Chatterers to give her a safe passage back to the canopy.

She stepped forward, her eyes wide and alert, walking upright.

Remembrance had narrow hips and long legs, relics of the bipedal days of ground-dwelling savannah apes. She was more upright than any chimp had ever been, more upright than Capo's folk. But even upright, her legs remained slightly bent, her neck sloped forward. Her shoulders were narrow, her arms long and strong, and her feet were long and equipped with opposable toes—all good equipment for climbing, cling-ing, leaping. Arboreal life had reshaped her kind: Selection had reached back to ancient designs, much modified, their templates never aban-doned.

She wasn't comfortable here on the ground. When she looked up she saw layers of foliage, trees competing for the energy of the sun, cutting out all but the most diffuse light. It was like looking up at another world, a three-dimensional city.

By contrast the forest floor was a dark, humid place. Shrubs, herbs, and fungi grew sparsely in the endless twilight. Though leaves and other debris fell in a continual slow rain from the green galleries above, the ground cover was shallow: the ants and termites, whose mounds stood around the floor like eroded monuments, saw to that.

She came to a huge mushroom. She stopped and began to cram its tasty white meat into her mouth. She had eaten little so far that day, and she had used up a lot of energy in fleeing the Chatterers.

Beyond a stand of spindly saplings something moved through the shadows: huge shapes, grunting, snuffling at the dirt. Remembrance ducked behind the mushroom.

The creatures emerged from the shadows, dimly outlined in the gray-green twilight. They had bulky, hairy bodies, stocky heads, and short trunks that scraped at the ground and plucked foliage and fruit from the trees' lower branches. A couple of meters tall at the shoulder, they looked like forest elephants, though they were tuskless.

These browsers' small pointed ears and oddly curling tails gave away their ancestry. They were pigs, descended from one of the few species domesticated by mankind to survive the great destruction, and now shaped into this efficient form. The last true elephants, in fact, had gone with humans into extinction.

More large, hairy creatures shouldered their way into Remembrance's view. They were elephantine forms too, the same size and shape as the pigs. But where the pigs had trunks but lacked tusks, these animals had no trunks, but carried great sweeping horns that curled before them and served as elephants' tusks once had, clearing the ground and upturning roots and tubers. More skittish and aggressive than the pigs, these animals were descended from another generalist survivor of human farmyards, the goats.

The two kinds of browser, pig- and goat-elephants, worked the shallow ground, different enough to be able to share this space, loftily ignoring each other's presence. Remembrance cowered, waiting for a chance to get away from these much-evolved descendants of farm animals.

And then she smelled a breath on her neck: the faintest trace of warmth, the putrid stink of meat.

Immediately she hurled herself forward. Ignoring the elephantine pigs and goats, she ran until she reached a tree trunk and swarmed up, clinging to crevices in the bark. She didn't hesitate for a moment, not even to look back to see what it was that had so nearly crept up on her.

She caught glimpses, though. It was a creature the size of a leopard, with red eyes, long limbs, grasping paws, and powerful incisors.

She knew what it was. It was a rat. When you smelled rat, you ran.

But the rat followed.

To pursue its climbing prey, the rat-leopard's kind had learned to climb too. The rat-leopard had claws, opposable fingers to grasp branches, forelimbs that could swing wide to allow it to hurl itself from branch to branch, even a prehensile tail. It wasn't as good a climber as the best of the primates, like Remembrance. Not yet. But it didn't need to be as good as the best. It only needed to be better than the worst, the weak and the ill—and the unlucky.

And so Remembrance climbed, on and on, ascending into the pale green light of the upper canopy, faster and faster, ignoring the bursting pain in her lungs and the ache in her arms. Soon she was dazzled by the light. She was reaching the upper reaches of the canopy. But still she climbed, for she had no choice.

Until she burst into open daylight.

She almost stumbled, so suddenly had she erupted out of the green. She clung to a narrow branch that swayed alarmingly under her, bright with leaves that, green and lush, drank in the sunlight.

She was perched right on top of the giant tree's uppermost branch. The canopy was a blanket of green that stretched away to the ocean. But she could make out the rocky shoulders of the gorge within which her dense pocket of forest grew, the ancient roadway of her ancestors. She had nowhere to go. Panting, exhausted, her depleted muscles trembling, she could only cling to this spindly branch. The sun beat down, too hot. Unlike her remote ancestors she was not built for the open: Her kind had given up the ability to sweat.

But the rat did not follow her. She thought she glimpsed its red-rimmed eyes, glittering, before it descended back into the gloom of the forest.

For a heartbeat she exulted. She threw back her head and whooped her joy.

Perhaps it was that that gave her away.

She felt a breeze first. Then came an almost metallic rustle of feathers, a swooping shadow over her.

Claws dug deep into the flesh of her shoulders. The pain was immediately agonizing—and grew worse as she was lifted by those claws, her whole weight suspended from scraps of her own flesh. She was *flying*. She glimpsed the land wheeling beneath her—scraps of forest, swaths of green grassland and brown borametz groves, all laid over a broken, eroded volcanic landscape, and that belt of glimmering sea beyond.

In Remembrance's world there were ferocious predators both above and below, like red mouths all around you, waiting to punish the slightest mistake. In escaping from one peril, she had run straight into the grasp of another.

The bird was like a cross between an owl and an eagle, with a fierce yellow beak and round forward-facing eyes, adapted for its forays into the gloom of the forest canopy. But it was neither owl nor eagle. This ferocious killer was actually descended from finches, another widespread generalist survivor of the human catastrophe.

The finch was hauling her toward a high complex of volcanic plugs, the eroded core of ancient volcanoes. The debris-littered ground nearby was green with grass, here and there browned by groves of borametz trees. And, tucked into the high ledges, Remembrance glimpsed nests: nests full of pink, straining mouths.

She knew what would happen if the finch succeeded in getting her to its nest.

She began to scream and struggle, pounding her fists against the legs and underbelly of the bird. As she fought, the hooked flesh in her shoulder ripped, sending blood streaming down her fur, but she ignored the pulses of agonizing pain.

The finch cawed angrily and flapped its wings, great tents of oily feathers that hammered at her head and back. She could smell the iron staleness of its blood-caked beak. But she was a big piece of meat, even for this giant bird. As she fought they spun toward the ground, hominid and bird tied up in their clumsy midair battle. At last she got her teeth into the softer flesh above the bird's scaly talons. The bird screamed and spasmed. Its claws opened.

And she was falling through sudden silence. The only noise was her own ragged breathing, the buffeting of the air, like a wind. She could still see the bird, a wheeling shadow above her, fast receding. She reached for branches or rocks, but there was nothing to grab.

Oddly, now that she was lost in her own deepest nightmare of falling, she was no longer afraid. She hung limp, waiting.

She smashed into a tree. Leaves and twigs clutched painfully at her skin as she crashed through them. But the foliage slowed her, and she plummeted at last to the grassy ground. Battered, torn, bruised, she was only winded. For a few heartbeats she could not move.

A human's shock would have been deeper. Who was to blame for this sequence of calamities? The rat, the bird of prey, a spell-casting enemy, a malevolent god? Why had this happened? *Why me?* But Remembrance asked herself no such questions. For Remembrance, life was not something to be controlled. Life was episodic, random, purposeless.

That was how things were now, for people. You didn't live long. You didn't get to shape the world around you. You barely understood much of what happened to you. All you thought about was *now*: drawing another breath, finding another meal, evading the next random killer.

Seeing what happened next.

When she had got her breath back she rolled to all fours and scuttled into the shade of the tree that had broken her fall.

II

Remembrance's time might have been called the Age of the Atlantic.

Since the fall of man the continents' chthonic dance had continued. That great ocean, born as a crack in Pangaea over two hundred million years ago, was continuing to widen as new seabed erupted endlessly along the line of the midocean ridge. The Americas had drifted westward, and South America had broken away from North to resume its interrupted career as an island continent. Meanwhile the cluster of continents around Asia had drifted east, so that the Pacific was slowly closing up. Alaska had reached out to Asia, rebuilding the Bering Strait bridge that had been made and undone repeatedly by the Ice Age glaciations.

There had been tremendous, protracted collisions. Australia had migrated north until it rammed itself into southern Asia, and Africa had crashed into southern Europe. It was as if the continents were crowding into the northern hemisphere, leaving the south abandoned save for lonely, icebound Antarctica. But Africa itself had fragmented, as the mighty wound of the ancient Rift Valley had deepened.

Where continents met, new mountain ranges were stitched. Where the Mediterranean had been there was now a mighty mountain range that reached eastward toward the Himalayas. It was the final extinction of the ancient Tethys. No trace of Rome had survived: the bones of emperors and philosophers alike had been crushed, melted, and gone swimming into the Earth itself. But while mountains were built, others evaporated like dew. The Himalayas were eroded to stumps, opening up new migration routes between India and Asia.

Nothing mankind had done in its short and bloody history had made the slightest bit of difference to this patient geographical realignment.

Meanwhile the Earth, left to its own devices, had deployed a variety of healing mechanisms, physical, chemical, biological, and geological, to recover from the devastating interventions of its human inhabitants. Air pollutants had been broken up by sunlight and dispersed. Bog ore had absorbed much metallic waste. Vegetation had recolonized abandoned landscapes, roots breaking up concrete and asphalt, overgrowing ditches and canals. Erosion by wind and water had caused the final collapse of the last structures, washing it all into sand.

Meanwhile the relentless processes of variation and selection had worked to fill an emptied world.

The sun climbed higher. Despite all that had happened to Remembrance, it was not yet midday.

She was stranded on a grassy plain, with purple volcanic hills in the distance, a few sparse stands of trees and shrubs, and a brown patch of borametz, the new kind of tree. Here, in the rain shadow of those purple hills, the rainfall was intermittent and erratic. The soil was habitually dry, and in such conditions trees were unable to establish themselves, and the grasses continued their ancient dominion—almost. Even vegetable communities evolved. And now the grasses had new competitors, in the borametz groves.

The tree that had saved her from the fall was barren of fruit, parched, clinging to life in the dry soil of this grassland. There was nothing to eat here—nothing but the scorpions and beetles that squirmed from beneath the rocks, bugs she popped into her mouth.

She made out a belt of forest, huddled against those remote purple hills, shimmering in the heat haze. Vaguely she realized that if she could get there she would be safer, she might find food, even people of her own kind.

But the forest was far away. Remembrance's distant grandmothers would have easily walked across this stretch of open savannah. But not Remembrance. She was too clumsy a walker. And like Capo, a chimplike ape of a different time, her kind had regrown their hair and forgotten how to sweat.

So she sat there, her mind empty of plans, waiting for something to turn up.

Suddenly a slim head swooped down from the washed-out sky. Remembrance chattered and flinched back against the tree trunk. She saw black round eyes, wide with surprise, set in a slender, fur-covered face, and two long ears that swept back against an elegant neck. It was a rabbit's head—but it was large, as large as a gazelle's.

The rabbit-gazelle evidently decided that the cowering hominid was no particular threat to her. She proceeded to crop at the grass that grew thinly in the shade of the tree.

Cautiously Remembrance crept forward.

Her visitor was one of a herd, she saw now, scattered over the plain and grazing patiently on the grass. They were tall, some twice as tall as she was. Slim, graceful, they looked like gazelles—but they were indeed descended from rabbits, as their long ears and small white tails clearly demonstrated.

The legs of these animals were like gazelles', too. Their forelegs were straight, and could be locked into position to support the animal with little effort. But halfway down their hind legs these rabbits had backward-bending joints that were in fact ankles. The lower leg was like an extended foot—balanced on two hooflike toes—and the knee was up near the torso, hidden in fur. Their back legs held in a permanent sprinter's crouch, the rabbit-gazelles were constantly ready for flight, the most critical task in their lives. As they grazed, the youngest scuttling at the feet of their elders, the herd remained compact, and there was never a time when at least one of the adults was not scanning the grass.

The reason for all of this soon became apparent. One of the bigger bucks startled, went rigid, fled. The rest of the herd followed immediately, in a blur of speed and dust.

From the cover of a bluff of rocks a slim black form darted forward. It was another rat, this one shaped to run with the low-slung power of a cheetah. The rat-cheetah disappeared into the dust, pursuing the rabbit herd.

Stillness resumed. For a time, nothing moved over the grass-covered plain, nothing but the shimmer of the air. The sun slid away from its height. But the heat did not lessen, and thirst clawed at Remembrance's throat.

She crept out of her hiding place. Her very human face, with straight nose, small mouth and chin, wrinkled in the bright afternoon light. She raised herself to her full height and sniffed. She heard a lowing, a clattering of tusks that sounded as if it were coming from the east, away from the sun. And she smelled the tang of water.

She began to run that way. She moved in scurries, hurrying from one patch of covering shade to the next, with frequent drops to an all-fours lope. This daughter of mankind ran like a chimp.

At last she crested a shallow bluff of eroded sandstone. She found herself facing a broad lake. It was fed by streams that snaked from more distant hills, but she could see that it was choked with reeds and fringed by a broad mud pan. She found an acacia to shelter under, and peered out, trying to find a way to get to the water.

Here, just as they always had, the herbivores had gathered to drink.

She saw more rabbits. There were skittish gazellelike creatures of the kind she had seen before. But there were also heavier-built, bisonlike powerhouses—and, running around their feet, smaller creatures that hopped and jumped. The rabbits, widespread and fast breeding, had, after the fall of man, radiated and adapted quickly. But not all of the new species had abandoned the ancient ways. There were still smaller browsers, especially in the forests where small beasts kicked and leapt and hopped as their ancestors always had.

Meanwhile warthogs snuffled and snorted in the muddy fringe of the lake, left all but unchanged by time. If there was no need to adapt, nature was conservative. And Remembrance made out huge, slow-moving creatures, marching serenely through the shallow water. They were related to the goats she had encountered in the forest, but these were giants, with tree trunk legs and horns that curled like mammoth tusks. They lacked trunks—none of these ruminants had evolved that particular anatomical trick—but, giraffelike, they had long necks that let them reach the succulent leaves growing on low-hanging tree branches, or the water of the lake.

A herd of different goat descendants stood knee-deep in the water. They had webbed feet that kept them from sinking in soft mud and sand. Each had a broad bill-like mask before its face. Sculpted from horns, these bills were used for browsing on the soft weeds found at the edge of the lakes. Sucking peacefully at the lakeside vegetation, these goats were like nothing so much as the hadrosaurs, the long-vanished duck-billed dinosaurs.

And, just as the hadrosaurs had been the most diverse group of dinosaurs before the comet fell, so this rediscovery of an ancient strategy was enabling a new radiation. Already many species of the duck-billed goats, subtly distinguished by differences in horn design, size, and diet preferences, were to be found at many of the water courses of the world's tropical regions and elsewhere.

Meanwhile, all around this scene of relatively peaceful herbivorous thirst-quenching—just as there had always been—intent predatory eyes watched the herbivores at work.

Watching this scene with half-closed eyes it would not have been impossible to imagine that the animals obliterated by human action had been restored. But on this new African savannah the familiar roles had been taken up by new actors, descended from creatures that had best survived the human extinction event. These were those that had resisted all of mankind's attempts at extirpation: the vermin, especially the generalists—starlings, finches, rabbits, squirrels—and rodents like rats and mice. Thus there were rabbits morphed into gazelles, rats become cheetahs. Only subtleties were changed—a nervous twitchiness about the rabbits, a hard-running intensity about the rats that had replaced the cats' languid grace.

There was a sudden flurry of activity, a great clash like a bone breaking. Two of the great goat-elephants, males, had begun a dispute. Their heads bobbed and swayed atop long giraffelike necks, and their horns, elaborately curling before their faces, clashed like baroque swords.

Remembrance cowered deep into the shade of her acacia. As the great herbivores began to mill around her, disturbed by the battle, she wasn't so safe. This tree, trunk and all, could be smashed up and devoured in a few heartbeats.

And now the watchful predators took advantage of the confusion.

A pack of them erupted from cover. Lean and vulpine, with long, powerful shanks and thickly padded feet, they were more rats. Working closely together, they moved wedgelike to separate one older goat-elephant from the rest of the herd. His huge horn-tusks chipped and scarred by a lifetime of battles, this big male bellowed his rage and fear and began to run. The rats settled into the pursuit, running closely together.

These rat derivatives were like dogs, yet they were not dogs. Their characteristic rodents' incisors had been subtly modified from teeth designed for processing seeds and insects into blades with stabbing points. Their rear molars were like shears, well equipped for shredding meat. And they moved more closely than any dog pack had ever run, with a liquid, slithering power. But, like a dog pack, their basic strategy was to chase the goat-elephant until he was exhausted.

Soon the prey and his pursuers had passed out of sight.

The goat-elephants settled down once more to their drinking and fighting—though some of them turned their great heads to the place where the old one had stood, remembering his absence.

Remembrance took the opportunity to creep forward.

The water was scum laden. But she scooped it up in her hands and let it trickle into her mouth, leaving her palms and fingers coated with fine green slime.

From the water, two yellow eyes watched her with abstract instinct. It was a crocodile, of course. These ancient survivors had ridden out the human apocalypse as they had survived so many before: by living off the gruesome brown food chain of the dying lands, by burrowing into the welcoming mud in drought. And even now no animal, no pig or rabbit or primate, no fish or bird, reptile or amphibian—not even the rodents—had managed to dislodge the crocodiles from their watery kingdom.

Remembrance shuddered, and backed off from the water's edge.

A new predator stalked over the bluff toward the lake. Again Remembrance scurried for cover, screened by the huge, impassive bodies of a herd of duck-billed goats.

This predator was more rodent stock; in fact it came from a kind of mouse. But its behavior was not like any dog or cat's. It came to the edge of the water, and lifted itself up on its massive hind legs. The herbivores at the water's edge cowered away. But the mouse-raptor had no interest in the creatures milling before it. With lordly dismissal it dipped its ferocious muzzle to taste the water. Then it stalked back to dry land where it used its small, feeble-looking hands to pluck at the grass, as if testing it.

It looked like one of the great carnivorous dinosaurs of the Cretaceous days. Its forearms were small, its tail was thickened for balance, and its hind legs were awesomely powerful machines of muscle and bone. Its incisors had developed into ferocious slashing weapons, to be deployed by thrusts of the heavy head. The mouse-raptor was a land shark, like a tyrannosaur, a body design rediscovered and made devastatingly effective. And yet this arrogant creature retained the small ears and brown fur of the diminutive rodents from which it had derived.

The mouse-raptor seemed satisfied with the water and the grass. It squealed, spat, and drummed its tail on the ground. From the distance there was a series of answering calls, drums, and cries.

More mouse-raptors approached the lake. They fanned out over a swath of grassland, sniffing the air. A few kits ran around the legs of the adults, wrestling and nipping at each other with the ancient playful curiosity of predators.

When they had gathered, the adult mouse-raptors turned, opened their throats, and set up a kind of synchronized wailing. In response, a herd of another kind of animal came lumbering toward the water.

These were big creatures, as big as the goat-elephants. Nervously they huddled together, querulously jostling. But even as they stumbled toward the water, under the apparent guidance of the mouse-raptors, they cropped hastily at the grass under their feet.

Their bodies were coated with sparse fur. Their heads were crested, their skulls shaped to allow anchorage for the tremendous cheek muscles that worked their immense lower jaws: Their heads looked rather like those of robust pithecines, in fact. Their ears, plastered back over their massive skulls, were huge and veined, great radiator fins designed to extract waste heat from their huge bodies. Though their hind legs were massive, enabling them to support their weight, they had the peculiar wrong-way-bending look of the rabbit-gazelles: legs meant for fleeing.

These animals were ugly, elephantine. But they had not descended from goat or pig. They had forward-looking eyes under heavy browridges, huge dark eyes that peered at the world, baffled and fearful. They walked on all fours, but they supported themselves on the folded knuckles of their hands, a posture that had once been called knuckle-walking.

Like Remembrance, their ancestors had once been human.

Remembrance waited until the big dull animals had settled to their drinking, jostling querulously, their ears spreading in the cooling air of the afternoon. Then she crept away.

It had taken millions of years for the great rebound of life to be completed.

Today, to the north of Remembrance's tropical forest, a great band of temperate woodland and grassland marched around the Earth, stretching from Europe-Africa across Asia to North America. Here more rabbit types browsed the cool foliage, while things like hedgehogs and pigs worked the undergrowth. In the trees there were birds and squirrels—and many, many bats. This diverse group of mammals had continued to proliferate and diverge, and now there were some nocturnal flyers who had lost their eyes altogether, others who had learned to compete with the birds for the richer pickings of the day.

Further north still, coniferous forests grew, evergreen trees whose spiky leaves were always ready to take advantage of the sun's thin ration of light. Browsing animals lived on the young twigs and needles in the summer, and on bark, mosses, and lichen the rest of the year. Many of them were goats. Especially common were the hadrosaur-like duckbill forms. Their predators included the ubiquitous mice and rats—but there were also carnivorous squirrels and huge birds of prey that seemed to be trying to emulate the pterosaurs of the oxygen-rich Cretaceous skies.

On the northern fringes of the continents a belt of tundra had formed. Here the descendants of pigs and goats cropped the thin foliage of summer, and huddled together to endure the winter. Like the vanished mammoths, some of these creatures had grown huge, the better to retain their warmth, until they were great round boulders of flesh. On the tundra the predatory rats had grown their incisors into huge stabbing instruments, the better to penetrate those thick layers of fur and fat.

They looked something like the saber-toothed cats of earlier times. There were even populations of migrant bats who had learned to subsist on the vast swarms of insects that formed during the brief tundra spring.

None of these new species, of course, would ever bear a human name.

There was one key difference in this latest recovery of life, compared to its last great trauma after Chicxulub. The rodents had not evolved until some ten million years after the comet impact. This time, though, when the days of recovery came, the rodents were everywhere.

Rodents were formidable competitors. They were born with incisors ready to gnaw. These great teeth were deep-rooted in powerful jaws: Once rats had been able to gnaw through concrete. Their teeth enabled them to eat food hard and tough enough to be inaccessible to other mammals. But the rodents' ability to proliferate and adapt was more fundamental. Rodents lived fast and bred young. Even among the giant species like the rat-cheetahs, females had short gestation times and produced large litters. Many of those kits would die, but every one of those dead babies was raw material for the relentless processes of adaptation and selection.

Given empty spaces to fill, the rodents evolved quickly. In the grand recovery after the disappearance of man, the rodents had been the big winners. By now, on land at least, Earth could be described as a kingdom of rats.

All this had left little room for the descendants of humans.

Crowded out by increasingly ferocious and confident rodents, the posthumans had given up the strategy—superior intelligence—that had brought them such success, and disaster. They had retreated, seeking sheltering niches and passive strategies. Some had become small, timid, fast-breeding runners. They were like vermin. Some even burrowed into the ground. Remembrance's folk had returned to the ancestral trees, but now the rats were invading even that ancient shelter.

The elephantine humans had tried another approach: becoming so huge they were protected simply by their immense size. But this had not been entirely successful. You could tell that from the design of their gazellelike back legs. Elephants could not have run very quickly, but they had not needed to; in their day no predator existed that could have taken on a full-grown proboscidean. Facing the power of the rodent predator families, the elephantine posthumans had had to retain the power to flee.

But even this had not been enough.

The mouse-raptors were social creatures. Their sociability was deep rooted, reaching back to the colony structures of the marmots and prairie dogs, which had lived in hierarchical "towns" of millions of animals. They scouted, seeking prey or water. They kept sentry watch for each other.

They hunted cooperatively. They communicated: The adults called to each other continually with cries, squeals, and the drummings of those powerful tails that sent long-range shudderings through the ground.

For the posthumans, the sociability of these raptors made them simply too effective as predators. The numbers of the big herbivores had steadily dwindled.

But that was bad for the raptors too. And so, in time, the elephantines and the mouse-raptors had developed a kind of symbiosis. The mouse-raptors learned to *protect* the herds of slow-witted elephantines. Their presence would deter other predators. By their behavior and signals they could warn the elephantines of other dangers, such as fires. They could even guide them to water and good grazing.

All the raptors asked for in return was to take their share of meat.

The elephantines passively accepted all this. They had no choice. And over enough time, selection had shaped the elephantines to fit the new conditions. If the raptors chased away the other predators for you, why be fast? And if they did your thinking for you, why be smart?

As their bodies had bulked up, the people's minds had shriveled, casting off the burden of thought. They were like domesticated chickens, whose brains had been sacrificed to make longer guts and a more effective digestive system. It wasn't so bad when you got used to it. Under the mouse-raptors' unthinking guidance their numbers had even increased. It wasn't so bad, so long as you turned away when your mother or your sister or your child was taken.

Not such a bad life, to be farmed by rodents.

The light began to leak out of the sky. So Remembrance found another stand of acacias, and crawled gingerly into the branches of the tallest tree. It would have to do. At least she was off the ground.

As the light died, so the stars appeared—but it was a crowded sky.

The sun, in its endless swimming around the Galaxy, was now passing through a wisp of interstellar dust and gas, a wisp mighty enough to span light years. Human astronomers had seen this coming. It was the vanguard of a mighty bubble blown in the gas by an ancient supernova explosion, and at its heart was a region where stars were being built. And so the new sky was spectacular, full of bright, hot new stars.

But there was nobody on Earth who might understand any of this. Remembrance spent a sleepless night listening to the squeals, thrums, and roars of predators, while unnamed constellations drifted over the sky.

III

The first few hundred asteroids the astronomers discovered had orbited in their orderly belt between Mars and Jupiter, comfortably far from Earth. These space rocks had been a curiosity, nothing but a theoretical challenge to students of the origins of the solar system.

It had been quite a shock when Eros was discovered.

Eros was found to sail within Mars' orbit—in fact at its nearest to Earth, it came to within less than a quarter of the closest approach of Mars and Earth. Later, more asteroids were found that actually *crossed* the orbit of Earth, making them candidates for eventual collision with the planet.

Eros, that first rogue, was never forgotten. As long as people cared about such things, the asteroid became a kind of mute hero among its kind, better known than any other.

At the beginning of the twenty-first century Eros was the target of the first space probe to orbit an asteroid. The probe was called NEAR, for Near Earth Asteroid Rendezvous. At the end of the mission the probe was made to land gently on the asteroid's ancient ground. Those first astronomers had given their asteroid the romantic name of the Greek god of love. There was much talk of how the probe NEAR had "kissed" the target rock, and the press had been predictably excited that the contact had occurred only a little before Valentine's Day.

But under the circumstances the asteroid's name could not have been more inappropriate.

It had long been believed that Eros, with its eccentric orbit taking it endlessly across the orbit of Mars, was in no danger of collision with the Earth. In fact, it seemed much more likely to collide with Mars itself.

But Mars was gone.

And, over long enough periods, as it responded to the subtle tweaks of the planets' gravitational pulls, the spinning of the sun, and its own intricate, intrinsic dynamic instabilities, the orbit of the asteroid evolved. One million years after the demise of mankind, Eros had sailed close to Earth—very close, close enough to be visible to a naked eye, had anyone been looking.

Some twenty-nine million years after that, it was coming closer still.

Stuck in her acacia tree, Remembrance itched. She scrabbled at her fur, hunting for the ticks and bugs that loved to feast on your blood, or lay their irritating eggs under your skin. But there were places she couldn't reach, like the small of her back, and naturally the bugs congregated there.

It was a painful reminder of how alone she was. As language had declined, the habit of grooming had returned to serve its old function of social cement. (It had never really gone away anyhow.) But Remembrance had had no grooming since before her last sleep, when she had huddled with her mother in her nest.

Hot, itchy, hungry, thirsty, lonely, Remembrance waited in her acacia stand until the sun had once more climbed high in the sky.

Then, at last, she clambered down.

The elephant people and their rodent keepers had gone. Across the empty, dust-strewn grassland, little stirred. The silence was as heavy as the heat. Through dusty haze, she could see a dark smudge to the east that might have been a herd of elephantine pigs or goats, or even hominids. To the west there was a little pocket of motion, a glimpse of brown fur. Perhaps it was a predatory rat with her kits.

To the north, where the mountains loomed purple, she could see that splash of dull greenery. She still had no other impulse than to make straight for the forest's alluring comfort.

Naked, her hands empty, she set off across the plain, slumping every now and again to let her knuckles carry some of her weight. She was a tiny figure crossing a huge, bare landscape, accompanied by nothing but the shadow under her feet.

She found no water, nothing to eat save handfuls of sparse grass. As she lumbered on, she was increasingly distracted by thirst. The silence settled still more heavily. Soon it was as if there were nothing in her life but this walk, as if her memories of a life of green and family were as meaningless as her dreams of falling.

She found herself walking down a shallow slope into a broad bowl of land kilometers across. Before this great depression she hesitated.

A valley was incised across the heart of the bowl—a valley once cut by a river—but even from here she could see that the valley was dry. The vegetation was different from that in the plain beyond. There were no trees here, few shrubs, and only occasional splashes of grass green. Instead, there was a broad mass of rustling violet leaves.

To distrust anything new was a good rule of thumb. But this great bowl lay right across her path, cutting her off from her forested slope, still far away. She could see there were no animals here, no herbivores, no prowling predators.

So she set off, wary, watchful.

The belt of violet purple turned out to be flowers growing in thick clumps, some tall enough to reach her waist, amid spindly, pale blades of grass. She walked on until she was surrounded by the clamoring purple. But there was still no water.

Once there had been a city here. Even now, so long after the city's fall, the soil was so polluted that only metal-tolerant plants could survive here—such as the violet-petaled copper flowers that waved over the soil.

Eventually the purple flowers grew thinner. At the very heart of this strange place she came to the river's shallow bank. The channel was dry, filled only with drifting dust: Ancient geological shifts had long since diverted away the water that had cut this channel. Remembrance clambered down the eroded banks and tried digging into the dusty substrate, but there was no moisture to be had here either.

As she climbed out of the shallow bowl it wasn't long before Remembrance came to another obstacle.

There were trees here—twisted, stubborn-looking trees—and termite mounds, and broad, low ant colonies, scattered like statues over an otherwise dry and lifeless plain. It was not a forest—it wasn't crowded enough for that—it was more like an orchard, with the individual trees well spaced, surrounded by their little gardens of termite mounds and ant nests. These were borametz trees, the new kind. The orchard stirred deep, instinctive feelings of unease in Remembrance. Something inside her knew that this was not the kind of landscape within which hominids had evolved.

But this stark landscape of trees and termites was another barrier across her path, stretching to left and right as far as she could see. And, as the sun began its swift descent to the horizon, she was growing ever thirstier and hungrier.

Tentatively she walked forward.

Something tickled her foot. She yelped and jumped back.

She had disturbed a double line of ants. They were walking to and from a nest—she could see the holes in the ground—along a trail that led to the broad roots of one of the trees. She crouched down and began to swipe at the ants with her cupped palms. She scooped up more dust than insects, but she managed to cram a few of the ants into her mouth and crunched the gritty goodies. More ants clambered around her feet, intent on their task, oblivious to the sudden fate of their fellows.

The tree that was the destination of these ants was unspectacular: It was low and squat, with a thick, gnarled trunk, branches coated with small round leaves, and broad roots that spread across the ground before plunging into it like digging fingers.

Remembrance walked up and inspected the borametz tree skeptically.

No fruit clung to its low branches. There were what looked like hard-shelled nuts growing in clusters from the base of the trunk, close to the roots of the tree. But there were very few of the nuts, less than a dozen. When she tried to prize them off, she found they were bound too strongly for her fingers, and the shells were too tough for her teeth. She pulled off a few leaves and chewed them experimentally. They were bitter and dry.

She gave up, dropping the last of the leaves, and made her way to a more promising food source. The nearest termite mound was as tall as she was, a great rough cone of hardened mud. She went back to the tree to look for a twig. She'd done a little termite-fishing in the past, though she was not as good as Capo had been. She was not even as expert as chimps had been in the age of man. But she might be able to get enough of the squirming goodies to allay her hunger—

She glimpsed a lunging head, incisors like blades scything through the air. *Rat.* She leapt upward, reaching for the branches of the borametz. The branches were narrow, tangled, and hard to grasp. But she forced her way into them, for they were all the cover she had.

It was a mouse-raptor: one of the colony that had herded the posthuman elephantines to the lake. Squealing its high-pitched rage the raptor reared up on its huge hind legs, slashed at the lower foliage with its blood-stained incisors, and rammed the borametz's trunk with its massive skull.

Young, restless, inquisitive, the raptor had never hunted this kind of animal. Tracking Remembrance this far had been a good game. But now the raptor had played enough, and had become curious about how she would taste.

The borametz's gnarled bark scraped Remembrance's skin painfully. The raptor couldn't reach up into the branches. But under the battering of its huge head the whole tree shook, and Remembrance knew she would soon fall, like a piece of fruit. Growing frantic, she squirmed through the branches, trying to get further away from the raptor.

But the branches of the borametz were fragile and easily snapped. They had evolved that way, to discourage birds, bats, and climbing mammals from trying to make a living here.

The branch under her belly gave way suddenly. She fell through the air and hit the ground, but the dirt collapsed under her in a cloud of dust.

Shocked, she fell through a further body-length, landing hard. Winded, she lay on her back. She looked up at a patch of sky and the head of the raptor, framed by a ragged, broken roof of packed earth.

And then the surface beneath her gave way in turn. She fell again, followed by dust and chunks of earth. She landed hard, once again, deeper still. Rubble fell across her face, clogging her mouth and nose and eyes.

There was a smell like milk: milk laced with urine and feces. Something swarmed over Remembrance's belly—something small, but heavy and hot and hairless. She grabbed blindly. She found herself clutching a torso, naked, slithery, moist. Arms and legs beat at her feebly. It was like holding a hairless baby.

But now one of those little hands reached her chest, and claws sliced into her skin. She yelled and hurled the creature away. She heard it land with a thump, and slither away into the dark.

But *they were all around her*—she heard them in the dark, sliding and rustling, saw them in the indistinct light.

Mole people. That was how they seemed. They had loose, fleshy skin that hung in folds around their necks and bodies. They were hairless: Their heads were bald, their pink scalps wrinkled, and they lacked eyelashes and eyebrows. Their ears were small, vestigial; their noses had pulled forward into snouts. They even had whiskers. And they had no eyes: There were only layers of skin covering the sockets where their eyes had been.

They had the arms and legs and torsos and heads of people. But they were all small, none of them larger than a child among her own kind, and yet many of them were adults. She saw breasts and functional penises on those small bodies.

Blind or not, they were flinching from the light. They swarmed away, disappearing into tunnels cut into the ground. The nails of their hands were shovel-like claws, equipped for digging. One touch of those claws had left deep furrows in Remembrance's shoulder.

She was in a nest, a nest of people who squirmed and burrowed. She screamed, driven by a deep horror of these distorted posthumans, a horror she couldn't understand, and she reached up toward the light.

And found herself staring straight into the eyes of the mouse-raptor. It hissed and braced to leap.

She hurled herself into an empty tunnel.

The walls were packed hard and worn smooth by the passage of many, many squirming bodies, and she was immersed in the characteristic stink of milk and piss. The tunnels had been built by the mole folk to take their own slim, scrabbling little bodies, and they were too small for Remembrance. She had to crawl on her belly, dragging herself along with arms and legs that soon ached painfully. It was a nightmare of enclosure.

But there was light. Narrow chimneys snaked to the surface. Thin, angled, they were intended to allow the passage of air while excluding any predator. But enough light diffused down to give her partial impressions of what she was passing through.

Tunnels, branching everywhere, a whole network of them. She could hear echoing spaces beneath and around her, chambers and tunnels and alcoves branching away forever. She caught occasional glimpses of the mole folk—a scrabbling limb or retreating rump, or smoothed over eye sockets gazing blindly.

Fear and dread filled her mind. But she had no choice but to go on.

Without warning she fell through a thin wall, and tumbled through into a crowded chamber. Babies instantly swarmed over her, biting and scratching.

This large chamber was crowded with children, miniature versions of the adults she had first glimpsed. The place stank overwhelmingly of blood and shit and milk and vomit. Struggling, she pushed the babies away. Almost all of them were female. Their soft, hot little bodies were somehow even more repulsive than the adults'. She turned and tried to clamber back up to the tunnel from which she had fallen.

But now adults came tumbling out of the tunnel. These newcomers did not retreat, as had those she had first encountered. These mole folk were soldiers, come to protect the birthing chamber from the intruder.

The first of the soldiers leapt at her, its digging claws extended. Remembrance raised her arm to protect her throat. Under the mole creature's soft weight she fell back into the wriggling heap of infants.

The soldier was an adult, a female. But her breasts were as tiny as a child's, her pudenda undeveloped. She was sterile. Nevertheless, squirming, biting, and scratching, she fought as ferociously as if her own children were at risk.

Remembrance might have succumbed to the soldier's assault, but she got in a lucky kick. The heel of her foot caught the soldier just below her breastbone. The little creature went flying back, colliding with those who were trying to follow her, so they dissolved into a wriggling mass of limbs and claws.

Dimly making out a tunnel mouth on the far side of the chamber, Remembrance hurled herself that way. She went on all fours, wading through mewling infants.

But still the soldiers pursued her. She struggled on through the tunnels, selecting branches at random. She could not tell if she were climbing upward or deeper into the ground. But for now nothing mattered but to flee.

She broke through another wall, fell, landed on something hard, like a heap of rocks. No, not rocks—they were *nuts,* big heavy nuts, the nuts of the borametz tree. Stumbling further, she found an immense heap of seed and roots. This huge chamber was crammed full of food.

Still the soldiers came, swarming, snuffling.

She leapt to the far side of the chamber and dug herself in against the wall, behind a pile of the heavy seeds. She picked up nuts and hurled them as hard as she could. She could hardly miss, and she was rewarded by the crack of the heavy shells on those eyeless heads. There was whimpering and confusion as the front line of the soldiers pushed back into those who followed, trying to get away from this missile-throwing demon.

But not all the soldiers retreated. Several stayed at the mouth of the tunnel, hissing and spitting at her.

Remembrance, exhausted and battered, really didn't care. She couldn't get out of here, but the soldiers couldn't get to her either. She stopped hurling the nuts.

She smelled dampness. She found a place in the earth wall behind her where a thin tree root pushed through. She had broken the root, and now it was dripping a thin, watery sap. She clamped the root to her mouth and began to suck down the sap. It was sweet, and it trickled over her parched throat. She found some tubers under the nut pile. In the near dark, she bit into sweet flesh, sating her hunger.

She lay down over what was left of her stolen roots, with heavy nuts grasped against her chest. Soon the hissing of the impotent soldiers seemed no more disturbing than the noise of a distant rainstorm. Her energy drained, shocked, bewildered, she actually dozed.

But there was movement in the chamber, scrabbling, slithering. Reluctantly she poked her head above the barrier of nuts. She saw mole folk moving around the chamber, but these were not soldiers. They seemed to have forgotten she was here. They were picking up nuts and passing them out of the chamber, into the tunnel entrance. She had no idea what they were doing. She didn't have the intellectual capacity even to formulate the question. All that mattered was that they were no threat to her.

She slumped back into her improvised nest and, nibbling on a bit of root, fell asleep.

The mole folk's underground way of life had started as a response to the aridity of this place—that and the usual ferocious predation. Even the rats couldn't get you if you burrowed in the ground.

Of course there had been prices to be paid. People had shrunk, generation by generation, the better to fit into the growing complexes of burrows. And over time bodies had been shaped by the restrictions of tunnel life: useless eyes were lost, nails became digging claws, body hair evapo-

rated save for vibrissae, whiskers, which sprouted from lengthening muzzles, the better to help them feel their way in the dark.

The aridity had also promoted cooperation.

The mole folk lived off roots and tubers, riches buried in the ground.
But in the dryness the tubers grew large and widely spaced. It was better
for the plants that way, because big tubers did not desiccate so easily. A
solo mole person, however, burrowing away at random, was likely to
starve long before stumbling across the scattered bounty. But if you were
prepared to share what you found, then having many colony members
digging in all directions brought a more likely chance of success for the
group as a whole.

All posthumans were social, like their ancestors, but they specialized
in the way they had developed that sociality. These mole folk had taken
sociality about as far as you could go. They came to live like social insects,
like ants or bees or termites. Or perhaps they were like naked mole rats,
the peculiar hive-dwelling rodents that had once infested Somalia,
Kenya, and Ethiopia, now long extinct.

This was a hive. There was no conscious mind at work here in the
hive. But then consciousness wasn't necessary. The hive's global organization emerged from the sum of the interactions of its members.

Most of the inhabitants of the colony were female, but only a few of
those females were fertile. These "queens" had produced the infants
Remembrance had stumbled upon in the birthing chamber. The rest of
the females were sterile—indeed they never entered puberty—and their
lives were devoted to the care not of their own children, but of those of
their sisters and cousins.

For the genes it made sense, of course. Otherwise it would not have
happened. The colony was one vast family, bound together by inbreed-
ing. By ensuring the preservation of the colony, you could ensure that
your genetic legacy was transmitted to the future, even if not directly
through your own offspring. In fact, if you were sterile, that was the *only*
way you could pass on your genes.

More sacrifices. As the bodies of these colony people had shriveled, so
had their brains. You didn't *need* a brain. The hive would take care of
you—rather as the mouse-raptors took care of the elephant folk they
farmed. There were better things to be done with your body's energy
than fuel an unnecessary brain.

And, with time, the mole folk were even giving up that most precious
of all mammalian inheritances: hot-bloodedness itself. As they rarely ven-
tured out of their burrows, the mole folk did not need such expensive

metabolic machinery—and a cold-blooded scout cost less food than a hot-blooded one. It was done without sentiment. With time, the colony folk would grow smaller yet, smaller than any hot-blooded mammal's design could maintain. In another few million years these mole folk would swarm like tiny lizards, competing with the reptiles and amphibians who had always inhabited the microecology.

So the mole folk scuttled through their spit-walled corridors, their whiskers twitching, fearful and ignorant. But in their dreams their residual eyes, covered by flesh, would flicker and dart as they dreamed strange dreams of open plains, and running, running.

She lost track of time. Suspended in the suffocating heat of the chamber, she slept, ate roots and tubers, sucked water from the tree roots. The mole folk left her alone. She was in there for days, not thinking, with no impulse to act save to eat, piss, shit, sleep.

At last, though, something disturbed her. She woke, looked up drowsily.

In the dim, diffuse light, she saw that mole folk were clambering into the chamber, and out again through a narrow passageway in the roof. They moved in a jostling column, the flaccid skin on their pale bodies crumpling as they pressed against each other, their whiskers twitching, clawed hands scrabbling.

Though the mouse-raptor and other dangers lingered at the back of her mind, Remembrance found herself longing for openness—for a glimpse of day, for fresh air, for *green*.

She waited until the mole folk had passed. Then she clambered over the low heapings of roots and pushed her way into the narrow breach in the roof.

It was a kind of chimney that led up toward a crack of purple-black sky. The sight of the sky drove her on, and she wedged her body ever more tightly into the narrow, irregular chimney, scrabbling at the dirt with her hands and feet, knees and elbows, forcing her chest and hips through gaps that seemed far too small for them.

At last her head broke above ground level. She took in great gulps of fresh air and immediately felt invigorated. But the air was cold. The twisted forms of the borametz trees occluded a star-laden sky. It was night, the most natural time for the mole folk to venture to the surface. She forced her arms out of the hole, got her hands onto the surface, and with a tree-climber's strength she pushed herself upward, prizing her body out of the chimney like a cork from a bottle.

The mole folk were everywhere, running on hind legs and knuckles, snuffling, shuffling, and squirming. But their movement was orderly. They moved in great columns that wound through the termite heaps and ant nests, to and from the borametz trees. They were picking off the nuts that grew in clusters at the roots of the trees, nuts that were sometimes as large as their heads. But they did not seem to be trying to break them open, to get at their flesh. They weren't even taking them into their underground stores. In fact, she saw now, they were actually bringing nuts *up* from the underground chambers.

They were taking the nuts, one at a time, out to the fringe of the borametz grove. There workers dug into the dirt, scattering the thin grass to make little pits into which the nuts were dropped and buried.

Each borametz was the center of a symbiotic community of insects and animals.

Symbioses between plants and other organisms were very ancient: The flowering plants and the social insects had actually evolved in tandem, one serving the needs of the other. And it was the social insects, the ants and termites, who had been the first to be co-opted by the new tree species' reproductive strategies.

Every symbiosis was a kind of bargain. Attendants, insect or mammal, would remove the borametz trees' seeds from their root bases, but they would not devour them. They would store them. And when conditions were right they would transport them to a place suitable for planting, usually at the fringe of an existing grove, where there would be little competition with established trees or grasses. And so the grove would grow. In return for their labors the attendants were rewarded with water: water brought up even in the most arid areas from deep water tables by the borametz's exceptionally deep-growing roots.

It had not been hard for the mole folk, with their cooperative society and still-agile primate hands and brains, to learn how to emulate the termites and the ants and begin to tend the borametz trees themselves. Indeed with their greater sizes, they were able to move larger weights than the insects, and the development of new borametz species with large seed cases had resulted.

For the borametz it was a question of efficiency. The borametz had to expend much less energy on each successful seedling than its competitors. And so it was a reproductive strategy that enabled the borametz to flourish where other tree species could not. Little by little, as their attendants carried their seeds from their orchards into the meadows, the borametz species were moving out into the grasslands. At last, more than fifty million years after the triumph of the grasses, the trees were finding a way to fight back.

The borametz trees embodied the first great vegetable revolution since the flowering plants that had arisen in the days before Chicxulub. And in the ages to come—like the initial emergence of plants on land that had enabled animals to leave the sea, like the evolution of the flowering plants, like the rise of the grasses—this new vegetable archetype would have a profound impact on all forms of life.

As she sat on the ground, still panting, watching the mole folks' baffling behavior, Remembrance heard a familiar soft footstep, an awful hissing breath. She turned her head, slowly, trying to be invisible.

It was the mouse-raptor—the juvenile, the same one that had strayed from its herd of elephant folk to chase her here. It was standing over a line of mole folk who scurried back and forth from tree to planting ground, oblivious to the threat that loomed over them.

It was as if the raptor were taking a small revenge. Few rodents could get through the mighty shells of the borametz nuts. As the borametz spread, the seed-eating stock from which this raptor had sprung—along with birds and other species—would soon be threatened with dwindling food supplies, dwindling ranges—and, in some cases, extinction.

The raptor made its choice. It bent down, balancing with its long tail, and used its delicate front claws to scoop up a bewildered mole woman. The raptor turned her over and stroked her soft belly, almost tenderly.

The mole woman struggled feebly, cut off from the colony for the first time in her life, divorced from its subtle social pressures. It was as if she had suddenly surfaced from an ocean of blood and milk, and she was truly terrified, for the first and last time. Then the raptor's head descended.

Her companions hurried on past the feet of her killer, their flow barely disturbed.

The mouse-raptor turned, its small ears twitching. And it stared straight at Remembrance.

Without hesitation she plunged straight back into her hole in the ground.

Remembrance stayed in the food chamber for several more days. But she was no longer able to settle back into the exhausted fog that had enveloped her.

In the end it was the madness of the mole folk that drove her out.

Even for this arid area, the season had been dry. The mole folk were having increasing difficulty in finding the roots and tubers on which they relied. The stock in the chamber dwindled steadily, and started to be replaced by other vegetation, like the violet leaves of copper flowers. But this unwelcome diet contained toxic elements. Gradually the poisons built up in the bloodstreams of the mole folk.

At last, everything fell apart.

Again Remembrance was startled awake by a rush of mole folk through the nearly empty food store. But this time they did not move in their orderly columns out through the vents. Instead they swarmed madly, surging up and out of the chamber, shattering its roof in their eagerness to be on the surface.

Remembrance, keeping out of the way of blindly scrabbling claws, followed gingerly. She emerged, this time, into full daylight.

All around her the mole folk swarmed. There were many, many of them, running over the ground, a carpet of squirming bare flesh. The air was full of their milky stink, the scraping of their skins against one another. There were far more than could have come from her own colony: Many hives had emptied as a burst of madness swept through the poisoned, half-intoxicated population.

Already the predators were showing interest. Remembrance saw the stealthy form of a rat-cheetah and a pack of doglike postmice, while overhead birds of prey began their descent. For those who sought flesh this was a miracle, as these little packets of meat just bubbled out of the ground.

It was all a response to the shortage of food. The mole folks' overcrowded burrows had emptied as they swarmed everywhere in a mindless search for provision. But in their intoxicated state they were unable to keep themselves from danger. Many of this horde would die today, most in the mouths of predators. In the long run it did not matter to the hives. Each colony would retain enough breeding stock to survive. And it wasn't necessarily a bad thing for their numbers to be reduced in these times of semidrought. Mole folk reproduced quickly, and as soon as the food supply picked up, the empty burrows and chambers would be full again.

The genes would go on: That was all that mattered. Even this periodic madness was part of the grander design. But many small minds would be extinguished today.

As the predators started to feed—as the air filled with the crunch of bone and gristle, the squeals of the dying, the stink of blood—Remembrance slipped away from this place of madness and death, and resumed her long-broken journey toward the distant purple hills.

IV

Remembrance came at last to a great bay, a place where the ocean pushed into the land.

She clambered down exposed sandstone bluffs. Once this area had been under the sea, and sediment had been laid down over millions of years. Now the land had been uplifted, and rivers and streams had cut great gouges in the exposed seabed, revealing deep, dense strata—in some of which, sandwiched between thick layers of sandstone, were embedded traces of shipwrecks and debris from vanished cities.

At last Remembrance reached the beach itself. She scampered along its upper fringe, sticking to the shade of the rocks and scrub grass. The sand was sharp under her feet and knuckles, and got into her fur. This was a young beach, and the sand was still full of jagged edges, too new to have been eroded smooth.

She came to a freshwater stream that trickled down from the rocks toward the beach. Where the water decanted onto the sand, a small stand of trees clung to life. She ducked down and pushed her mouth into the cool water, sucking up great mouthfuls. Then she clambered into the stream itself and scraped the water through her fur, trying to get rid of the sand and fleas and ticks.

That done, she crawled into the shade of the trees. There was no fruit here, but the leaf-strewn floor, cold and damp, harbored many toiling insects that she popped into her mouth.

Before her the sea lapped softly, the water bright in the high sunlight. The sea meant nothing to her, but its distant glimmer had always attracted her, and it was oddly pleasing for her to be here.

In fact the sea had been the savior of her kind.

Torn by great tectonic forces, Africa's Rift Valley had eventually become a true rift in the fabric of the continent. The sea had invaded, and the whole of eastern Africa had sheared off the mainland and sailed away into what had been the Indian Ocean, there to begin its own destiny. So chthonically slow was this immense process that the mayfly creatures living on this new island had scarcely noticed it happening. And yet, for Remembrance's kind, it had been crucial.

After the fall of mankind, there had been pockets of survivors left all over the planet. Almost everywhere the competition with the rodents had been too fierce. Only here, on this rifted fragment of Africa, had an accident of geology saved the posthumans, giving them time to find ways to survive the rodents' ruthless competitive onslaught.

Once this place, East Africa, had been the cradle that had shaped mankind. Now it was the final refuge of man's last children.

There was something in the water. Cautiously, Remembrance cowered back into the shade.

It was a great black shape, sleek and powerful, swimming purposefully. It seemed to roll, and a fin a little like a bird's wing was raised into the air. Remembrance made out a bulbous head lifting above the water, with a broad sievelike beak. Water showered from two nostrils set in the top of the beak, sparkling in the air, expelled with a sharp whooshing noise. Then the great body flexed and dove back under the surface. She caught a last glimpse of a tail, and then the creature had vanished. Despite its immense bulk, it left scarcely a ripple in the water.

In this giant's wake more slim, powerful bodies leapt from the water, three, four, five of them. They swept through graceful arcs and plunged back into the sea, and then rose to leap again and again. Their bodies were shaped like those of fish, but these dolphinlike creatures were evidently not fish. They were equipped with beaks like birds, stretched into long orange pincers.

Behind the "dolphins," in turn, came more followers, likewise hopping and buzzing over the ocean surface. Much smaller, these were true fish. Their wet scales glistened, and fins like wings fluttered at the sides of their slim, golden bodies as they made their short, jerky flights over the water.

The "whale" was not a true whale, the "dolphins" not dolphins. Those great marine mammals had preceded humanity into extinction. These creatures were descended from birds: In fact, from the cormorants of the Galapagos Islands in the Pacific, which, blown there from mainland South America by contrary winds, had given up flight and taken to exploiting the sea. Their descendants' wings had become fins, their feet flukes, their beaks a variety of specialized instruments—snappers, strainers—for extracting food from the ocean. Some of the species of "dolphin" had even regrown the teeth of their ancient reptilian ancestors: The genetic design for teeth had lain dormant in birds' genomes for two hundred million years, waiting to be re-expressed when required.

Invisibly slow on any human timescale, adaptation and selection were nevertheless capable, given thirty million years, of turning a cormorant into a whale, a dolphin, or a seal.

And, strangely enough, all the swimming birds Remembrance saw were indirect legacies of Joan Useb.

As Remembrance watched, a dolphinlike creature erupted out of the water right in the middle of the cloud of flying fish. The fish scattered, their fin-wings buzzing, but the beak of the "dolphin" snapped closed on one, two, three of them before its sleek body fell back into the water.

The sun was starting its long descent toward the sea. Remembrance stood up, brushed herself free of sand, and resumed her cautious knuckle-walk along the fringe of the beach, but something overhead distracted her. She glanced up at the sky, fearing it was another bird of prey. It was a light like a star, but the sky was still too bright for stars. As she watched, it slid over the roof of the sky.

The light in the sky was Eros.

NEAR, the humble, long-dead probe, had spent thirty million years swimming with its asteroid host through the spaces beyond Mars. Its exposed parts were heavily eroded, metal walls reduced to paper thinness by endless microscopic impacts. At the touch of a gloved astronaut's hand it would have crumbled like a sculpture of dust.

But NEAR had survived this far, among the last of all of mankind's artifacts. If Eros had kept up its eccentric dance around the sun, perhaps NEAR could have survived longer yet. But it was not going to get that chance.

The asteroid's passage through the atmosphere would be mercifully swift. The fragile probe, returning to the planet where it had been made, would flash to vapor only fractions of a second before the great body with which it had long ago rendezvoused was itself destroyed.

Earth's evolutionary laboratories had been stirred many times by monstrous interventions from without. Now, here was another stirring. And over the bright scene on which Remembrance gazed, a curtain would soon be drawn.

Remembrance herself would survive, as would the children she would bear in the future. Once again the great work would begin: Once again the processes of variation and selection would sculpt the descendants of the survivors to fill shattered ecological systems.

But life was not infinitely adaptable.

On Remembrance's Earth, among the new species there were many novelties. And yet they were all variations on ancient themes. All the new animals were built on the ancient tetrapod body plan, inherited from the first wheezing fish to have crawled out of the mud. And as creatures with backbones, they were all part of a single phylum—a great empire of life.

The first great triumph of multicellular life had been the so-called Cambrian explosion, some five hundred million years before the time of mankind. In a burst of genetic innovation, as many as a *hundred* phyla had been created: each phylum a significant group of species represent-ing a major design of body plans. All backboned creatures were part of the phylum of chordates. The arthropods, the most populous of the phyla, included creatures like insects, centipedes, millipedes, spiders, and crabs. And so on. Thirty phyla had survived life's first great shaking down.

Since then species had risen and fallen, and life had suffered major disasters and recoveries over and over again. But not one new phylum had emerged, *not one*, not even after the Pangaean extinction event, the greatest emptying of all. Even by the time of that ancient event, life's capability for innovation was much constrained.

The stuff of life was plastic, the mindless processes of variation and selection inventive. But not infinitely so. And with time, less.

It was a question of the DNA. As time had worn away, the molecular software that controlled the development of creatures had itself evolved, becoming tighter, more robust, more controlled. It was as if each genome had been redrafted over and over, each time junk and defects were combed out, each time the coherence of the whole was improved—but each time the possibility for major change was reduced. Extraordinarily ancient, made conservative by the inward-looking complexity of the genomes themselves, life was no longer capable of a great innovation. Even DNA had grown old.

This epochal failure to innovate was an opportunity lost. And life could not take many more hammer blows.

The light in the sky was strange. But, Remembrance's instinctive calculus quickly computed, it was no threat. In this she was wrong. Purga, who had watched the Devil's Tail similarly slide silently overhead, might have told her that.

Before the sun had touched the horizon she at last reached her forest in the lee of the volcanic hills, her target for many days. Remembrance peered up at the tall trees before her, the canopy that strained up toward the sky. She thought she saw slim shapes climbing there, and perhaps those dull clots of darkness were nests.

They were not her people. But they were people, and perhaps they would be like her.

She pulled herself off the ground and clambered upward into the comforting green of the canopy.

Something fluttered past her head. It was a flying fish, coming from the sea. As she watched, it sailed into the forest canopy, flapping its fin-wings earnestly, and settled clumsily onto a nest, air wheezing into primitive lungs.

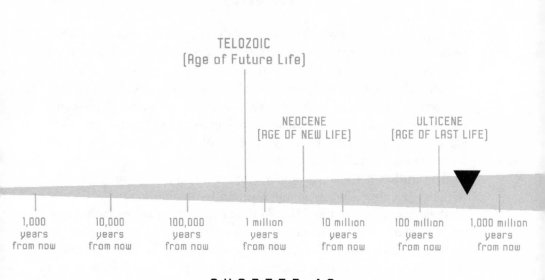

TELOZOIC
[Age of Future Life]

NEOCENE
[AGE OF NEW LIFE]

ULTICENE
[AGE OF LAST LIFE]

▼

1,000 years from now

10,000 years from now

100,000 years from now

1 million years from now

10 million years from now

100 million years from now

1,000 million years from now

CHAPTER 19

a far distant futurity

▼ **Montana, Central New Pangaea. Circa 500 million years after present.**

I

Ultimate dug listlessly in the dirt, hoping to find a scorpion or beetle. She was a mound of orange-colored fur on the rust-tinged ground.

This was a flat, dry plain of crimson red rock and sand. It was as if the land had been scraped bare by some vast blade, and the bedrock wind-burnished to a copper sheen. Once there had been mountains to the west, purple-gray cones bringing relief to eyes wearied by flatness. But long ago the wind had torn all the mountains down, leaving great fans of scattered rocks over the plains, rocks that had themselves eroded to dust, leaving no trace.

Half a billion years after the death of the last true human, a new supercontinent had assembled itself. Dominated by desert, as red as the ancient heart of Australia, it was like a vast shield fixed to the blue face of the Earth. On this New Pangaea, there were no barriers, no lakes or mountain ranges. Nowadays it didn't matter where you went, from pole to equator, from east to west. Everywhere was the same. And there was dust everywhere. Even the air was full of red dust, suspended there by the habitual sandstorms, making the sky a butterscotch-colored dome. It was more like Mars than Earth.

But the sun was a ferocious disk, pumping out heat and light, much brighter than in the past. Any human observer would have cowered from that great fire in the sky.

Under that tremendous glare the heat lay heavy on the land, by day and by night. There was no sound save for the wind and the scratching of the few living things, no sense that things had ever been different on this red planet. The land *felt* empty, a huge place of resonant silence, a stage from which the actors had departed.

As it happened, far beneath the dust where Ultimate dug—buried under half a billion years of deposits, under the salt and the sandstone of New Pangaea—was the place that had been known as Montana. Ultimate was not far above Hell Creek, where the bones of Joan Useb's mother had at last joined those of dinosaurs and archaic mammals in the strata she had searched so assiduously.

Ultimate had no way of knowing her peculiar place in history, still less of understanding. But she was among the last of her kind.

Ultimate went home. Home was a pit carved in the harder rock. It offered some shelter from the wind. This was where Ultimate and her kind eked out their lives.

The pit looked artificial. Its floor was smooth, its terraced walls steep. The pit was in fact a quarry, made half a billion years earlier by human beings, dug deep into the bedrock. Even after all this time, even as mountains had come and gone, the quarry had survived almost intact, a mute memorial to the workings of man.

Trees grew on the floor of the pit, standing stately and alone, like sentinels, with their satellite termite colonies towering all around. They were stubby, ugly trees with perennial needlelike leaves, defiant of time. Little else lived here save the people, and other symbiotes of the trees, and many, many tiny creatures that toiled in the dust.

As Ultimate clambered down the pit's walls, the wind changed and began to blow from the west, from the direction of the inland ocean. Gradually the humidity rose. At last, over the ruined mountains to the west, heavy black clouds began to gather.

Ultimate peered into the western sky. It had never rained here, in Ultimate's lifetime. Most clouds coming from the distant ocean dumped their rainfall long before they reached a place like this, deep in the supercontinent's interior. It took a mighty storm indeed to breach those immense defenses of arid plain, a once-in-a-lifetime monster. But that was what was approaching now. You could feel it in the air, feel that something was wrong.

The people hurried back to their Tree, and clambered into its welcoming branches. Hurried, yes—but still they moved with a languid slowness, as if they were swimming through the air's dense heat.

At ten years old, Ultimate looked something like a small monkey. She was long-limbed, with a narrow torso, narrow shoulders: Even now, in these distant descendants of mankind, the basic body plan of the primates persisted. Her slim body was coated in thick fur, bright red, red as the sand. She had a small head with a large brow and a mobile, expressive face—a very human face, in fact. Small flaps of skin, rather like eyelids, could cover her ears, nose, anus, vagina to trap precious moisture. Her brow was swollen, almost as if her kind had re-evolved the big forebrains of the human age, but behind that brow there was only spongy bone, a great system of sinuses that worked as a refrigeration system to keep her brain cool.

And, though she was fully grown, her body was childlike. Ultimate was functionally female—people still gave birth—but there were no males any more, and gender was meaningless. She had no breasts, not even vestigial nipples. Nowadays there was no need for mother's milk, just as there was no need for the elaborate superstructure of a large brain. The Tree took care of all of that for you.

And she was not bipedal. That was obvious as she made her way back to the Tree: her arms and legs were made for swinging and climbing, her feet for grasping, not walking upright. That particular locomotive experiment had been thoroughly buried long ago. Compared to her ancestors, she was slow-moving, lethargic, like all her kind.

At the Tree, Ultimate looked for her daughter.

The infant's leafy cocoon nestled in the crook of a low branch. Threads of orange hair littered over her swollen brow, the little girl was safely enfolded in soft white down. As the Tree's sap passed along the pale thread of the belly-root that wormed into her stomach, the child stirred and murmured, her tiny thumb clamped firmly in her mouth, dreaming vegetable dreams.

Something was wrong. Ultimate was not capable of much in the way of analysis, but her instinct was unmistakable. She prodded at the tangled red fur on the child's little belly, and smoothed out the fluffy cottonlike lining of the cocoon. The little girl mewled, turning blindly in her sleep. Nothing Ultimate did made that feeling of wrongness go away. Uncertain, she patted the walls of the cocoon back into place.

The wind rose, like a great breath.

Ultimate clambered higher into the Tree's welcoming branches. Hastily she pulled her own cocoon into place around her body, sealing up the leaves. The leaves were thick and tough, like plates of leathery armor. The others were doing the same, people huddling on the branches, so that it looked as if the Tree were suddenly sprouting huge black fruits.

The clouds streamed overhead, blotting out the intense heat of a too hot sun. Ultimate stared. Curiosity wasn't much use now, when there was so little difference in the world across great stretches of time and space. But today *was* different. She had never felt air as moist and heavy and oppressive as this, never seen black clouds that boiled and bubbled like that.

And in the last moment before the storm hit, she glimpsed something new.

Settled on the timeworn plain, it was a sphere. It was twice as tall as she was. It was not blue like the evening sky, nor rust red like the ground, nor the color of sand and dirt like most of the creatures in the world. Instead, it was a shimmering mixture of purple and black, the colors of the night.

On this day of strangeness, here was something extraordinary. She gaped, unable to comprehend. But she sensed that this new thing was not of her world. In that she was right.

But now lightning cracked, and she buried her face in the green, mewling. The leaves closed around her, sealing themselves up seamlessly. In the warm darkness the air grew moist and comforting. But when the belly-root came probing for the valvelike orifice on her stomach, just below her navel, she pushed it away. She was here for shelter; she had nothing to give the Tree today.

And then the storm hit.

Wind and dust came out of the west like a red wall. Dried plants were shattered. Even the scattered, stately Trees were shaken, branches ripped away. People and other symbiotes were wrenched from their cocoons, utterly terrified.

The first few raindrops, landing like bullets, heralded an immense downpour. The rain was so heavy it even began to erode the rock-hard surfaces of the ancient termite mounds. There was nothing to absorb the water, no grass to consolidate the loose soil. Within minutes water was running down every dried-out gully and streambed. A great muddy wave came cascading into the quarry. The water seethed around the roots of the trees, turbulent, tinged red by mud.

But the rain dissipated as quickly as it had begun. The clouds cleared, racing deeper into the heart of the supercontinent. The flood quickly subsided, sinking into the parched sand.

There hadn't been such a storm since Ultimate's mother had first opened her eyes. Nothing in Ultimate's experience had prepared her for such a catastrophic downpour. But the Tree, in its slow vegetable way, understood.

Even as Ultimate cowered, shocked, in her cocoon, she felt the leathery skin pulse around her. She longed to stay here in the moist dark rather than face whatever lay beyond these enclosing walls. But she was made to feel uneasy, restless. The Tree wanted her to leave, to go to work.

She set her back against the cocoon wall and pushed. The leaves came free of one another with a moist, sucking noise. She tumbled out of the Tree, and landed in mud.

All around her people were falling out of the Tree. They took experimental steps and knuckle-walks. The mud felt strange: It was heavy, clinging, crimson stuff that stuck to their legs and feet and hands.

The ferocious sun was shining once more, and the mud was already drying, the water escaping into the air, the ground baking hard. But for these rare minutes the ground was a cacophonous swarm of noise and motion. With visible speed, tendrils, leaves, and even flowers were pushing out of the mud. They had come from seeds that had lain dormant for a century. Soon sacs began to pop. Like tiny artillery pieces, they shot new seeds through the air. Entire reproductive cycles were being completed in minutes.

Insects emerged from their own encysted hiding places to dance and mate over the transient pools. On the ground there were more insects— ants, scorpions, cockroaches, beetles, and their much morphed descendant species. Many of the ants were leaf eaters, and Ultimate could see great chains of them trooping back and forth from the burgeoning plants bearing bits of greenery for their nests.

And there were many, many small lizards. They were hard to see, so well did their reddish skin match the color of the ground. Everywhere they hunted. Some of them had no smarter strategy than to sit with their mouths open by the ant columns, waiting for clumsy insects to stumble in.

One small, sturdy cactuslike plant, a ball of leathery skin and defensive spikes, dragged its upper roots from the soil, abandoning a deep, extensive root system. On roots that quivered like clumsy legs, it tottered toward the still-running water. When it got there, the walking plant subsided into the mud, as if with a sigh. Immediately the inefficient vegetable muscles that had powered its short journey began to dissolve, and new roots began to work their way into the moist ground.

All over the pit people were feeding on the sudden plants, reptiles, amphibians, insects. They were mostly adults: Children were rare in these straitened times; the Tree saw to that.

Ultimate, a rainstorm virgin, stared at all this, gaping.

A froglike creature erupted from the ground. It hopped and stumbled to the nearest of the temporary ponds, where it leapt into the water and began to croak noisily, guiding the emerging females who followed to it. Soon the pond was a splashing frenzy of amphibian mating. Ultimate grabbed one of the frogs. It was like a slimy sac of water. She popped it into her mouth. Briefly she felt its coldness, its heart hammering against her tongue, as if in disappointment that its century-long wait in a cocoon of hardened mud was going to end in such ignominy. Then she bit down, and delicious water and salty blood gushed into her mouth.

But already the pools were drying, the water hissing into the parched earth. The frogs' spawn had hatched, and tadpoles, fast metamorphosing, were feeding on algae, tiny shrimps, and each other. They swarmed out of the water after their parents—and were snapped up by a mass of tiny lizards in a quivering feeding frenzy. But already the young frogs were digging their way into the mud, constructing for themselves mucus-lined chambers in which they would wait out the decades until the next storm, their skins hardened, their shriveled metabolisms slowing into suspended animation.

People were stumbling away from the feeding grounds now. Some were carrying the heavy seeds of the Tree, huge pods as large as their own heads. Like the frogs, this strange day was the Tree's once-a-century opportunity to have the seeds of its next generation buried for it by its armies of symbiotes.

Ultimate saw Cactus chasing a small, scuttling lizard with a plump tail full of stored fat.

Cactus had been born about the same time as Ultimate, and as they had grown up they had learned about the world together, sharing, competing, fighting. Cactus was small and round. This was unusual for her people, who were generally skinny and long limbed, the better to lose their body's heat—and she was prickly tempered, indeed like a cactus. Cactus was a kind of companion, even a sister, but she wasn't Ultimate's friend. You had to be able to see somebody else's point of view to call them a friend, and that ability had long been given up. People didn't have friends these days—no friends apart from the Tree.

Ultimate wanted to follow Cactus, but she was distracted. Suddenly she longed for salt. That was the Tree's message to her, imprinted in the organic chemistry it had fed her while in the cocoon. *The Tree needed salt.* And it was up to her to find it. She remembered where a salt bed was, a few hundred meters away. She was helplessly drawn that way.

But in that direction stood the sphere, that enigmatic ball of black and purple that lowered silently over the teeming landscape.

She hesitated, caught between conflicting impulses. She knew the sphere was *wrong.* The great tide of human intelligence had long withdrawn, but the people had retained a good understanding of the land, its geography, and resources: efficient foraging was an essential skill if you were to find food and water in this desperately arid landscape. So she understood very well that the sphere shouldn't be here. But that was the way to the salt.

Despite her unease, she set off.

The salt lick was almost at the foot of the sphere. She saw how mud had lapped up against its oddly gleaming surface. She tried to ignore the sphere, and began to scrabble in the sticky dirt.

There was no shortage of salt. A hundred million years ago, as the continents had danced toward their spontaneous assembly of this New Pangaea, a great inland sea had formed over much of North America. It had become landlocked, leaving only scattered lakes of brine. But that vanishing sea had left behind a vast bed of salt deposits, a shining plain that had stretched for hundreds of kilometers. The salt bed had been covered by debris washed down from the ruins of the fast-eroding mountains, and now lay buried under meters of rust-red sand, but it was still there.

Before long she had made a hole as deep as her arm could reach, and she was bringing up handfuls of dirt laced with gray-white salt. She chewed on the dirt, letting the salt crystals melt in her mouth, and spitting out the sand. With the salt in her belly, stored for later transmission to the Tree, Ultimate was released from her compulsion.

And again she became aware of the sphere. It had moved from where she had first seen it. And it hovered above the ground; a finger's-width of light could be seen beneath it.

She approached the sphere, walking on her hind feet and her knuckles, a dim curiosity alight in her eyes. Her fear wasn't strong. There were few novelties in her desert world. But likewise there were few threats. In a landscape like a tabletop, predators had a difficult time sneaking up on even the slowest and dullest of victims.

With a tentative fingertip she stroked the sphere's surface. It was neither warm nor cold. It was *smooth*, smoother than anything she had felt before. The hairs on her hand prickled, as if charged. And she could smell something, a smell like the quintessence of the desert itself, an electric smell of scorching, of burning, of dryness.

The burnt-metal smell was in fact the result of exposure to hard vacuum: a legacy of space.

Their foraging done, one by one the people returned to the Tree, climbed into its branches, and folded themselves securely inside its leaves.

Ultimate pulled leathery leaves around her body. The belly-root snaked out quickly, probing for the valve on her stomach, and nestled into her like a reattached umbilical. As her salt-laden fluids began to circulate into the Tree, so Ultimate was rewarded by a soothing sense of security, of peace, of rightness. This mood was induced by chemicals leaked into her body as she exchanged blood for Tree sap, but it was no less comforting for that. This was her immediate reward for feeding the Tree, just as her longer-term reward was life itself. The Tree did not take without giving. Posthuman and Tree were neither of them parasites on the other. This was a true symbiosis.

But there was something wrong. Ultimate felt uneasy, wordlessly disturbed.

Even though the warm sap filled her head with green sleepiness, she kept thinking of how the child had been lying in her cocoon, her thumb in her mouth, the belly-root curled before her. *Something had been wrong.* Every instinct told her so.

The sap pulsed harder into her gut, and soporific chemicals washed through her. This drastic injection meant the Tree wanted her to stay here, where she was, safe in her cocoon. But still that nagging sense of wrongness pulled at her.

She pulled the belly-root out of her stomach, and pushed hard with her shoulder and legs. The cocoon popped open, and she tumbled to the ground.

Briefly she was overwhelmed by light and warmth. Though the day was still bright the sun was low. Inside the cocoon, time swam at a different pace from the world outside—a pace chosen by the Tree. But the ground was hard and dust-strewn. Save for a few raindrop stipples, it was as if the storm had never been.

Nobody was around. All the cocoons were closed—all but one. Cactus was gazing down at her, her small head protruding from her own half-sealed cocoon. With a look of playfulness, Cactus pushed her way out of her enclosing leaves and tumbled easily to the ground beside Ultimate.

Ultimate's sense of anxiety was still growing.

She hurried around the base of the Tree to find her baby's cocoon in the crook of the low branch. But it was sealed tight, and would not yield when she tried to open it. As if this were a game, Cactus joined her. The two of them dug their fingers into the seams between the sealed-up leaves, straining and pushing and grunting.

Once it would have occurred to a person to use a tool to open this pod. Not anymore. Toolmaking was gone, all the artifacts of man had long since rotted away save for a few pithecine nodules buried in lost strata. And Ultimate and Cactus weren't even very good at solving unusual problems, for in their flat world they encountered few novelties.

At last, however, the cocoon opened with a pop.

Here was Ultimate's baby, still swaddled in the white cottonlike material of the cocoon's interior. But, Ultimate saw immediately, the cottony stuff had grown thicker. It had closed around the baby's face, and tendrils of it were pushing into her mouth, nose, eyes, and ears.

Cactus flinched, an expression of revulsion on her face.

Both of them knew what this meant. They had seen it before. The Tree was killing Ultimate's baby.

A new Pangaea.

A hundred million years after Remembrance had gone to her unmarked grave, the Americas had begun to slide east once more. As the Atlantic closed, so Africa drifted north of the equator, in the process pushing Eurasia further north still. Meanwhile Antarctica sailed north to collide with Australia, and that new assemblage began to push into east Eurasia. So a new supercontinent had been born. Africa was the central plain of the new assemblage, with the Americas pressing to the west, Eurasia to the north, Australia and Antarctica to the east and south. In the interior, far from the mediating effect of oceans, severe conditions took hold—ferociously hot and arid summers, killingly cold winters.

All barriers to movement had been eliminated. There was a brutal free-for-all as plants and animals migrated in all directions. It was a chilling parallel to the great global mixing that humans had forced during their few thousand years of dominance of the planet—and, just as it had been before, a world united was a world reduced. There had been a rapid pulse of extinctions.

And as time wore away, things got worse.

The new supercontinent immediately began to age. The great tectonic collisions had thrown up new mountains, and as they eroded, their debris enriched the plains with chemical nutrients like phosphorus. But now there were no new mountain-building events, no new uplift. The last mountains wore away. Rainwater and groundwater, percolating through the soil, leached out the last nutrients—and when they were gone there was nothing to replace them.

New red sandstones were laid down, rust red, red as the lifeless Martian deserts had been—the signature of lifelessness, of erosion and wind, heat and cold. The supercontinent became a great crimson plain spanning thousands of kilometers and marked only by the worn stumps of the last mountains.

Meanwhile the reduction in sea levels exposed shallow continental shelves. As they dried out they quickly began to weather, drawing oxygen out of the air. On land many animals simply suffocated to death. And in the oceans, as the pole-to-equator temperature gradient flattened out, the circulation of the ocean slowed. The waters stagnated.

On land, in the sea, species fell away like leaves from an autumn tree.

In a desiccating world the familiar games of competition, of predator and prey, were not so effective anymore. The world didn't have the energy to sustain great complex food webs and pyramids.

Instead, life had fallen back on much more ancient strategies.

Sharing was as old as life itself. Even the cells of Ultimate's body were the result of mergers of more primitive forms. The most ancient bacteria had been simple creatures, living off the sulfur and heat of hellish early Earth. For them the emergence of cyanobacteria—the first photosynthesizers, which used sunlight to turn carbon dioxide into carbohydrates and oxygen—was a disaster, for reactive oxygen was a lethal poison.

The survivors won by cooperating. A sulfur eater merged with another primitive form, a free-living swimmer. Later an oxygen-breathing bacterium was incorporated into the mix. The three-part entity—swimmer, sulfur-lover, oxygen breather—became capable of reproduction by cell division and could engulf food particles. In a fourth absorption some of the growing complexes engulfed bright green photosynthetic bacteria. The result was swimming green algae, the ancestors of all plant cells. And so on.

Throughout the evolution of life there had been more sharing, even of genetic material. Human beings themselves—and their descendants, including Ultimate—were like colonies of cooperative beings, from the helpful bacteria in their guts which processed foods, to the mitochondria absorbed eons ago that powered their very cells.

So it was now. Joan Useb's intuition, long ago, had been right: One way or another, the future for mankind had been cooperation, with one another and the creatures around them. But she could never have foreseen this, the final expression of that cooperation.

The Tree, a remote descendant of the borametz of Remembrance's time, had taken the principle of cooperation and sharing to its extremes. Now the Tree could not survive without the termites and other insects that brought nutrients to its deep roots, and the furry, bright-eyed mammals who brought it water, food, and salt, and planted its seeds. Even its leaves, strictly speaking, belonged to another plant that lived on its surface and fed on its sap.

But likewise the symbiotes, including the posthumans, could not have survived without the succor of the Tree. Its tough leaves sheltered them from predators, from the harsh heat of the climate, even from the once-in-a-century rainstorms. Sap was delivered through the belly-roots, just as the Tree took back its nutrients by the same conduits: infants were not breast-fed but were swaddled by the Tree, nurtured by these vegetable umbilicals. The sap, drawing on the deepest groundwater, sustained them through the mightiest supercontinental droughts—and, laden with beneficent chemicals, the sap healed their injuries and illnesses.

The Tree was even involved in human reproduction.

There was still sex—but only homosexual sex, for there was only one gender now. Sex served only for social bonding, pleasure, comfort. People didn't need sex for breeding anymore, not even for the mixing of genetic material. The Tree did it all. It took body fluid from one "parent" in its sap and, circulating it through its mighty bulk, mixed it and delivered it to another.

People still gave birth, though. Ultimate herself had given birth to the infant that now lay in its leafy cradle. That heritage, the bond between mother and child, had proved too central to give up. But you no longer fed your child, by breast or otherwise. All you had to give your child was attention, and love. You no longer raised it. The Tree did all that, with the organic mechanisms in its leafy cocoons.

Of course there was still selection, of a sort. Only those individuals who worked well with the Tree and with each other were enfolded and allowed to contribute to the circulating stream of germ material. The ill, the weak, the deformed, were expelled with vegetable pitilessness.

Such a close convergence of the biologies of plant and animal might have seemed unlikely. But given enough time, adaptation and selection could turn a wheezing, four-finned lungfish into a dinosaur, or a human or a horse or an elephant or a bat—and even back into a whale, a fishlike creature, once again. By comparison hooking up people and trees with an umbilical connection was a trivial piece of re-engineering.

In the myths of vanished humanity there had been a kind of foreshadowing of this new arrangement. The Middle Ages' legends of the Lamb of Tartary had spoken of the Borametz, a tree whose fruit was supposed to contain tiny lambs. All of mankind's legends were forgotten now, but the tale of the Borametz, with its twining of animal and plant, found strange echoes in these latter days.

But there were costs, as always. Their complex symbiosis with the Tree had imposed a kind of stasis on the postpeople. Over time the bodies of Ultimate and her kind had specialized for the heat and aridity, and had simplified and become more efficient. Once the crucial linking was made, Tree and people became so well adapted to each other that it was no longer possible for either of them to change quickly.

Since the snaking umbilicals had started to worm their way into posthuman bellies, since people had first huddled in the protective enclosure of borametz leaves, two hundred million years had worn away unmarked.

But even now, even after all this time, the symbiotic ties were weak compared to more ancient forces.

In its slow vegetable way, the Tree had concluded that for now the people could not afford another baby. Ultimate's infant was being reabsorbed, her substance returning to the Tree.

It was an ancient calculation: in hard times it paid to sacrifice the vulnerable young, and to keep alive mature individuals who might breed again in an upturn.

But the infant was almost old enough to feed herself. Just a little longer and she would have survived to independence. And *this was Ultimate's baby*: the first she had had, perhaps the only one she would ever be permitted to have. Ancient drives warred. It was a failure of adaptation, this battling of one instinct against another.

It was a primordial calculus, an ancient story told over and over again, in Purga's time, in Juna's, for uncounted grandmothers lost and unimaginable in the dark. But for Ultimate, here at the end of time, the dilemma hurt as much as if it had just been minted in the fires of hell.

It took heartbeats to resolve. But in the end the tie of mother to child defeated the bonds between symbiotes. She dug her hands into the cottony stuff and dragged her baby from the cocoon. She pulled the belly-root from the infant's gut, and bits of white fiber from her mouth and nose. The child opened her mouth with a popping sound, and turned her head this way and that.

Cactus watched, astonished. Ultimate stood there panting, her mouth open.

Now what? Standing there holding the baby—in defiance of the Tree that had given her life—Ultimate was out on her own, beyond instinct or experience. But the Tree had tried to kill her baby. She had had no choice.

She took a step away from the Tree. Then another step. And another.

Until she was running, running past the place where she had dug the salt—the sphere was gone now, faded from her memory—and she kept running, her baby clutched in her arms, until she came to the walls of the quarry, up which she scrambled in a flash.

She looked back into the great pit, its floor studded with the lowering, silent forms of the borametz trees. And here came Cactus, running after her with a defiant grin.

II

The land was bare. There were a few stubby trees, and shrubs with bark like rock and leaves like needles, and cacti, small and hard as pebbles and equipped with long toxin-laden spines. Protecting their water, these plants were little balls of aggression, and Ultimate and Cactus knew better than to tackle such risky fare until it was essential to do so.

You had to watch where you put your feet and hands.

There were pits in the desert's crimson floor. They were bright red, a little like flowers, barely visible against the red soil, but with knots of darkness at their centers. Foolish lizards and amphibians, and even the occasional mammal, would tumble unwarily into these waiting traps—and they would not emerge, for these pits were mouths.

These deadly maws belonged to creatures that lived in narrow burrows under the ground. Hairless, eyeless, their legs reduced to scrabbling finlike stubs with sand-digging claws, they were rodents, among the last remnants of the great lineages that had once ruled the planet.

This time of openness and lack of cover did not favor large predators, and the survivors had been forced to find new strategies. The frantic activity and sociability of their ancestors long abandoned, these burrowing rat-mouths spent their lives in holes in the ground, waiting for something to fall into their mouths. Shielded from the excesses of the climate, moving from their burrows only when driven to mate, the rat-mouths had slow metabolisms and very small brains. They made few demands of life, and in their way were content.

But for creatures as smart as Ultimate and Cactus, the rat-mouths weren't hard to avoid. Side by side, the companions moved on.

The companions came to a little gully. It was nearly choked: the rain-storm had filled it with pebbles and stones. But there was still a trickle of silty runoff water. Ultimate and Cactus crouched down, Ultimate shielding her baby, and they pushed their faces into the water, sucking at it gratefully.

Ultimate found green here, in the damp. It was a kind of leaf, prostrate, dark, slightly crimped. Its form was very ancient, too primitive even to have the wherewithal to grow up toward the light. It was actually a descendant of a liverwort, all but unchanged by the passage of time, a barely modified copy of one of the first plants ever to colonize land— a land that had not looked so different from this harsh place. The times had come around, and the liverwort found room to live. Curious, Ultimate plucked the leaf from the rock it clung to, chewed it—it was waxy, sticky—and kissed her baby, letting bits of the leaf trickle into her mouth. The baby chomped with a sucking noise, her little eyes rolling.

Close to one of those pebblelike cactuses, Ultimate spotted a beetle, silvery-backed, toiling to push a dried-up pellet of dung along a miniature crevasse. Ultimate briefly considered making a grab for the beetle.

But as the beetle passed the shade of the cactus, a tiny crimson form shot out of the darkness. It was a lizard, smaller than Ultimate's little finger, and its head was a lot smaller than the beetle itself. But nevertheless the lizard clamped its jaws on the toiling beetle's rear end. Ultimate could hear the miniscule crunch: The beetle waved its legs and antennae, but it could not get away. The lizard, its burst of energy expended, spread great sail-like fans from its neck and legs. The cooling fans made the lizard look twice its resting size, though its red color gave it good camouflage against the Pangaean dust. Saved from overheating, it began the slow, luxurious process of sucking out the beetle's salty vitals from within its carapace.

But it wasn't to be given that luxury. From nowhere a small bird came running on to the scene. Black-feathered, its wings vestigial stubs hidden beneath its skin, it was flightless. Without hesitation, and with lethal precision, the bird lunged at the lizard with a yellow beak full of tiny teeth. The lizard released the beetle and tried to squirm away under the cactus, its sail-fans folding. But the bird had hold of one fin and it pulled the lizard back into the light, shaking its tiny body.

The mutilated beetle crawled away—only to be scooped up by Cactus's little paw and delivered to her mouth.

There were plenty of birds around; that great, ancient lineage was much too adaptable not to have found a place even in this harsh, much-changed world. But few birds flew nowadays. Why fly when there was nothing to flee, nowhere to go that wasn't exactly the same as *here*? So the birds had taken to the ground, and in the great shriveling, had adopted many forms.

Meanwhile, disturbed by the bird's attack, more lizards erupted from under the cactus. There were many of them, all of them smaller than the sail-fan caught by the bird, smaller than Ultimate's own fingernail. They were so tiny, Ultimate saw, they had to clamber over pebbles and irregularities in the dirt as if they were hills and valleys. They scurried in all directions, disturbed from their daily slumber, and made for cover in the rocks and pebbles.

Ultimate watched, fascinated.

As new Pangaea's great drying had continued, the larger species had fallen away. In the barren emptiness of the supercontinent there was nowhere for a creature the size of Ultimate to hide, still less a gazelle or a lion. On the largest scales the ancient game of predator and prey had broken down.

But on smaller scales, a new ecology proliferated. Under Ultimate's feet there were holes in the rocks, crevasses in the sand, holes in borametz tree trunks, tangles in root systems. Even in the flattest landscape there was topography where you could hide from predators, or wait to ambush prey, or simply hole up and avoid the rest of the world—if you were small enough.

But if the world of the smallest scales was still rich in opportunity, it was a world largely excluded from the hot-blooded kind.

All hot-bloods had to maintain their high body temperatures. But there was a limit to how much insulating hair and fat you could grow before you became an immobilized little puff-ball, how fast a pulse you could sustain. The last of the shriveling mole folk, their tiny hearts rattling heroically, had been as small as a centimeter. But a centimeter-scale was still huge. There was plenty of room below this, plenty of ways to live.

But all these niches were taken by insects and reptiles and amphibians. Small and skinny, the cold-bloods hid from the heat of the sun and the chill of the night, under rocks and in the shade of trees and cacti. In a handful of dirt it was possible now to find tiny, perfectly formed descendants of frogs and salamanders, snakes—and even the endlessly enduring crocodiles. There were even tiny lungfish, silvery little creatures hastily adapted for the land as the inland waters had dried. This largest of continents was dominated by the smallest of animals.

Without the Tree's support, such large hot-blooded mammals as Ultimate's postpeople could never have survived so long. They were like throwbacks to easier times, out of place in this marginal environment. As the Earth warmed relentlessly, as the great desiccation continued, even the Tree-based communities shrank back and died, one by one. And yet they were here: And yet here was Ultimate, the latest link in a great chain that now passed back through a hundred million grandmothers, morphing and changing, loving and dying, back to Purga herself, and into the formlessness of the still deeper past beyond.

Ultimate and Cactus watched the tiny scramblings in the dirt. Then, hooting, the posthumans fell on the scrambling lizards. Most of them were too small to catch—you would close your hand around them only to see them squirming out the other side—and even when Ultimate managed to cram one into her mouth it was too small a morsel to be satisfying.

But they didn't need to eat the lizards. They were playing. Even now you could have fun. But in the silence of New Pangaea their whoops and hooting cries echoed from the bare rocks, and as far as could be seen they were the only large creatures moving, anywhere.

The sunset came quickly.

The air was scrubbed clean of dust by the rains. As soon as the sun touched the horizon, darkness striped across the flattened land, small ridges, dunes, and pebbles casting shadows tens of meters long. The light in the sky faded from blue to purple, quickly sinking to black at the zenith. It was like a sunset on the airless Moon.

Ultimate and Cactus huddled together, the baby between their bodies. Every night of her life Ultimate had spent in the Tree's enfolding vegetable embrace. Now the shadows were like raptor fingers reaching out for them.

But as the temperature fell, so Ultimate's adaptations to the desert came into operation.

Her skin was actually hot to the touch. During the day her body stored heat, in layers of fat and tissue. In the cooler air of night, her body was able to radiate a lot of the heat back to the environment. If she had not been able to perform this trick of refrigeration she would have had to lose the heat by sweating—and that would have used up water she couldn't afford to waste. And Cactus and Ultimate were breathing, deeply and slowly. That way a maximum amount of oxygen was extracted from each lungful of air, and a minimum amount of water was lost. Meanwhile Ultimate's body was manufacturing water from the carbohydrates in the food she had eaten. She would finish the night with more water in her body's stores than when she had started.

But still, for all this remarkable physiological engineering, the two of them could do little but sit and endure the night, breathing slowly, lapsing into a kind of dull half dream as their bodies' functioning slowed to a crawl.

While above them a bewildering sky unfolded.

Ultimate had a grandstand perspective view of the Galaxy. The huge spiral arms were corridors of brightness that spanned the sky, studded with pinpricks of sapphire-blue young stars and ruby-red nebulae. At the center of the disk was the Galactic core, a bulge of yellow-orange stars like the yolk of a fried egg: the light had taken twenty-five thousand years to travel here to Earth from that crowded core.

In human times the sun had been embedded in the body of the huge flat disk, so that the Galaxy had been seen edge-on, its glory diminished by the obstructing dust clouds that littered the disk. But now the sun, following its slow orbit around the core, had sailed out of the Galaxy's plane. Compared to the random scattering of a few thousand lamps that had marked man's sky, this was like glimpsing the lights of a hidden city.

Ultimate cowered.

A bony hook rose in the sky. It was the Moon, of course, an old Moon, tonight a narrow crescent. The same patient face that had peered down on Earth since long before the birth of man was all but unchanged across half a billion years. And yet this thin crescent Moon shone more brightly over the new supercontinent than it had over the more equable lands in the past. For the Moon shone by reflected sunlight—and the sun had grown brighter.

Had she known where to look Ultimate might have made out a dim smudge in the sky away from the Galaxy's disk, easily visible on the clearest nights. That remote smudge was the great galaxy known as Andromeda, twice the size of its neighbor. It was still a million light-years distant from Earth's Galaxy—but in human times it had been twice as far away as that, and even then it had been visible to the naked eye.

Andromeda and the Galaxy were heading for a collision, still another half-billion years distant. The two great star systems would pass through each other like mingling clouds, with direct collisions between stars rare. But there would be a vast gush of star formation, an explosion of energy that would flood the disks of both galaxies with hard radiation. It would be a remarkable, lethal light show.

But by then there would be little left alive on Earth itself to be troubled by the catastrophe. For the brightening of the sun was life's final emergency.

Morning came with its usual stark suddenness. Scuttling lizards and insects disappeared into the nooks and crannies where they would ride out the day, waiting for the richer opportunities of evening.

The baby mewled. Her fur stuck up in clumps, and the pucker where the belly-root should sit looked inflamed. She kept up her complaints, her bulbous little head turning to and fro, until Ultimate had chewed some more liverwort and dribbled it into her mouth. Cactus, too, was grumbling, picking dirt and bits of dried shit from her fur.

This morning it didn't seem such a good idea to be out here in the middle of nowhere, so far from home. But as she held her baby Ultimate knew she had to stay away from the Tree—stay away, or lose her baby. She clung to that one irreducible fact.

Ultimate and Cactus began to work their random way across the landscape, heading roughly away from the quarry. Just as they had yesterday, they ate where they could—though they found no water—and they avoided the rat-mouths and other hazards.

And, at some point past noon, when the sun had begun its climb down the sky, Ultimate suddenly found herself facing the sphere once again.

She had forgotten it existed. It did not occur to her to wonder how such an immense object might have gotten *here* from *there,* in the quarry.

Cactus showed no interest, once she had figured out that you couldn't eat the sphere. She passed on, grumbling to herself, picking bits of crimson dust out of her fur.

Her baby asleep in her arms, Ultimate walked up to the sphere's purple-black bulk. She sniffed it and, this time, tasted it. Again that unidentifiable electric tang subtly thrilled her. She lingered, somehow drawn. But the sphere offered her nothing.

But suddenly Cactus was howling, thrashing on the ground. Ultimate whirled, crouching. Cactus's left leg was somehow pinned, and blood spurted from her foot—and Ultimate heard the crunch of bone, as if poor Cactus's limb had been taken in some vast mouth.

But there was no mouth to be seen.

No teeth and claws held Cactus. But slashes appeared on her chest and torso, dripping with startlingly bright blood, as if out of nowhere. Still she fought. She swung her fists, kicked, tried to bite even as she screamed. She was landing blows—Ultimate could hear the meaty sound of flesh being struck, and there were peculiar bits of discoloration in the air over Cactus, purple and blue. And the blood itself was starting to outline her assailant in crimson splashes. Ultimate could make out a long cylindrical torso, stubby legs, a wide, snapping mouth.

But Cactus was losing her fight. Her legs and upper body became trapped under the shimmering mass. She turned to Ultimate, and reached out her hand.

Instincts warred in Ultimate. It might have been different if she could have imagined how Cactus was feeling, the mortal fear that flooded through her. But Ultimate could not; empathy had been lost in mankind's great shedding, along with so much else.

She had hesitated too long.

That great blurred mass raised itself up and came crashing down on Cactus. A thicker, richer blood gushed from the helpless posthuman's mouth.

Ultimate's shock evaporated. With a squeal of terror she turned and ran, her squealing baby clutched to her chest, her feet and her free hand clattering over the dusty ground. She kept going until she came to an eroded ridge of crimson rock.

She flung herself to the ground, and looked back. Cactus was still. Ultimate could make out nothing of the vast transparent thing that had destroyed her. But new creatures had emerged, as if from nowhere. They looked like frogs, with sprawling bodies, leathery amphibian skin, splayed, clawed feet, and wide mouths equipped with needle-sharp teeth for rending and gouging. Already the first of them had opened up Cactus's chest and was feasting on the still-warm organs within.

The invisible predator had done its job. It lay exhausted in a pool of Cactus's blood. It was too weary even to feed itself, and it relied on scraps brought to it by its greedy siblings. The meat could be seen being shredded by its grinding teeth and then passing into its gullet and stomach, where digestive processes would begin to absorb and transform it.

As the world had emptied and been eroded flat, the lack of cover was the killer. In a landscape like a pool table, you just couldn't hide a one-ton salamander, even if it was painted as red as the rocks. That was why most of the big animals had quickly disappeared, outcompeted by their smaller cousins.

But these creatures had adopted a novel strategy: the ultimate camouflage. The great redesign had taken many tens of millions of years.

Invisibility—or at least transparency—had been a strategy adopted by some fish in earlier times. There were transparent substitutes for most of the body's biochemicals. A substitute had to be found for hemoglobin, for example, the bright red protein in blood cells that combined with oxygen to transport that vital substance through the body.

Of course no land-going creature could ever be truly invisible. Even in these arid times all animals were essentially bags of water. If you were actually immersed in water—where those long-extinct fish had once swum—something approaching true invisibility could be achieved. But light moved differently through air and water; in the air the final land-going "invisible" actually looked like a big bag of water sitting in the dirt.

Still, it worked pretty well. As long as you kept still you were hard to see—just a mistiness, a slight distortion here and there that might easily be mistaken for a bit of heat shimmer. You could huddle against a rocky outcrop, ensuring that you presented only your least visible angles to any prey. You even had fur, transparent-like fiber-optic cable, which transmitted bits of background color to baffle your prey further.

But even so, few species had adopted the stratagem, for invisibility was a blight.

Every invisible was blind, of course. No transparent retina could trap light. On top of that the creature's biochemistry, limited by the use of transparent substances, was a lot less efficient. And there was no shielding, even for its innermost parts, from the ferocious light, heat, and ultraviolet radiation from the sun, or from the cosmic radiation that had always battered the planet despite its great shield of magnetism. Its organs were transparent, but not transparent enough to let through all the damaging radiation.

Already Cactus's killer was in agony, and soon the cancers developing in its transparent gut would kill it. And it was neotenous. It would die without reaching puberty. None of the invisible kind had ever lived long enough to breed true, nor would their genetic material, damaged by radiation, ever have been able to produce a viable offspring.

Sickly, helpless from birth, these wretched creatures began dying before they emerged from their eggs.

But that didn't matter, not from the point of view of the genes, for the family benefited.

This amphibian species had reached a compromise. Most of its young were born as they always had been. But perhaps one in ten was born invisible. Like the sterile workers in a hive, the invisible lived through its brief, painful life and died young, all for a single purpose: to retrieve food for its siblings. Through them—through their offspring, not its own—the invisible's genetic legacy would live on.

It was an expensive strategy. But it was better to sacrifice one in ten of each generation to a brief life of agony than to succumb to extinction.

The presence of food in its stomach and waste in its lower gut made the invisible easy to spot, of course. So when they were hungry again its siblings would starve it, waiting for all the waste to pass out of its system, rendering it as transparent as possible. And then they would set it to work once more, under the lethal sun, hoping to have it snatch one more meal for them before it died.

The sphere had made its own observations of these events.

The sphere was a living thing, and yet it was not. It was an artifact— and yet it was not that either. The sphere had no name for itself, or for its kind. Yet it was conscious.

It was one of a great horde that now spanned the stars, in a great belt of colonization that swept around the Galaxy's limb. And yet the sphere had come here, to this ruined world, seeking answers.

Memories stretched deep. Among the sphere's kind, identity was a fluid thing, to be split and shared and passed on through components and blueprints. The sphere could think back, deep through thousands of generations, but it was a memory trail that ended in mist. The replicating hordes had forgotten where they came from.

In its way, the sphere longed to know. *How* had this great star-spanning swarm of robots first originated? Had there been some form of spontaneous mechanical emergence, cogs and circuits coming together on some metallic asteroid? Or had there been a Designer, some *other*, who had brought the progenitors of these swarming masses into being?

For a million years the sphere had studied the distribution of the replicators through the Galaxy. It wasn't easy, for the great disk had rotated twice since the origin of its kind, and the stars had swum about, smearing the robot colonists across the sky. Great mathematical models had been built to reverse that great turning, to restore the stars as they once must have been, to map back the replicators' half-forgotten expansion.

And at last the sphere had converged on this system, this world— amid a handful of others—as the putative origin. It had found a world of organic chemistry and creatures interesting in their way. But it was a dying world, overheated by its sun, the life-forms restricted to the fringes of a desert continent. There was no sign of organized intelligence.

And yet, here and there, the ancient rocks of the supercontinent had been marked deliberately, it seemed to the sphere, with cuts and gouges and great pits. Once there had been mind here, perhaps. But if so it was vanished from these wretched, crawling creatures.

The sphere represented a new order of life. And yet it was like a child, wistfully seeking its lost father. The last traces of the Martian robots' original blueprint, assembled by long-dead NASA engineers in computer laboratories in California and New England and much modified since, had been lost. It was somehow appropriate that this greatest, and strangest, of all of mankind's legacies should have been created entirely accidentally—and that those created should have been abandoned to their fate.

There was nothing more to be learned here. With an equivalent of a sigh, the sphere leapt to the stars. The small world dwindled behind it.

Ultimate huddled in the dirt until the scavenging siblings had finished feeding. Then she stumbled away, clutching her baby, not even noticing that the sphere had vanished.

III

Ultimate kept heading west, away from the borametz quarry.

At night she wedged herself with her infant into crevices between rocks, trying to emulate the comforting enclosure of the Tree's cocoon. She ate whatever she could find—half-desiccated toads and frogs buried in the mud, lizards, scorpions, the flesh and roots of cacti. She fed the child a chewed-up pulp of meat and vegetable matter. But the child spat out the coarse stuff. She was still missing her belly-root, and she mewled and complained.

Ultimate walked, and walked and walked.

She had no strategy in mind save to keep moving, to keep her infant out of the chemical clutches of the Tree, and to wait to see what turned up. If her thinking had been sophisticated enough she might have hoped to find more people, somewhere she could stay, maybe even a community that lived independently of the Trees.

It would have been a futile hope, for there were no more such communities anywhere on Earth. She didn't know it, but she had nowhere to go.

The land began to rise slowly. Ultimate found herself walking on coarse sand and gravel fans.

After half a day of this she came to a place of low, smooth-shouldered hills. She could see how these eroded stumps went marching off to the horizon, to north and south, for kilometer after kilometer, all the way to the dust-laden horizon and beyond. She was walking through the remnant of a once-great mountain chain, thrown up by the ancient stitching together of the continents. But the dust-laden winds of New Pangaea had long since worn down the mountains to these meaningless stumps.

When she looked back she could see her own footprints, accompanied by the scraping of knuckles, marked by the messy places where she had stopped to feed or make waste or sleep. They were the only trail through these silent hills.

It took her two days to cross the mountains.

After that the land began to descend again.

On the plain, a little more vegetation grew. There were spiky trees with gnarled branches and clumps of needlelike leaves, like bristlecone pines. Around their roots sheltered a few leaping mice—hardy rodent survivors, ferocious conservers of water—and many, many lizards and insects. She chased tiny things like geckos and iguanas, and munched their flesh. But on this looser ground Ultimate had to be cautious, watching for rat-mouths embedded in the ground, and for the quivering, invisible mass of an ambush hunter.

As the land descended further, the view to the west opened up. She saw a great plain. Beyond a kind of coastal fringe, the land was white, white as bone, a sheet that ran all the way to a knife-sharp, geometrically flat horizon. A thin wind moaned in her face. On its breath, she could already taste the salt. Nothing moved, as far as she could see.

She had come to a fragment of the dying inland ocean. There was still water out there—it took a long, long time to dry out a sea—but it was a narrowing strip of water so saline it was all but lifeless, and it was framed by this great white rim of exposed salt flats, a sheet that extended to her horizon.

Tucking her baby's face into the fur on her breast, Ultimate continued her dogged descent.

She reached the place where the salt began. Great parallel bands showed where water had once lapped. She scooped up a bit of the salty dirt and licked it. She spat out the bitter stuff immediately. There was vegetation here, tolerant of the salty soil. There were small, spiky yellow shrubs that looked like the desert holly and honeysweet and spurge that had once clung to life in the Californian deserts of North America.

Experimentally she broke off a bit of the holly's foliage and tried to chew it, but it was too dry. Frustrated, she hurled the bit of twig away over the salt.

And then she saw the footprints.

Curious, she fit her own feet into the shallow indentations in the ground. Here had been toes, here a scuffing that might have been caused by a resting knuckle. The prints could not have been made recently. The mud was baked hard as rock, and her own weight left no mark.

The prints set out, straight as an arrow, across the salt pan, marching on toward the empty horizon. She followed for a step or two. But the salt was hard and harsh and very hot, and when it got into minor cuts and scrapes on her feet and hands it stung badly.

The footprints did not turn back. Whoever had made them had not returned. Perhaps the walker had been intent on reaching the ocean proper, on walking all the way across North America: After all, there were no barriers now.

She knew she could not follow, not into the belly of this dead sea.

And it would have made no difference even if she had. This was New Pangaea. Wherever she went she would have found the same crimson ground, the same searing heat.

She stayed on the desolate, silent beach for the rest of the day. As it descended the overheating sun grew huge, its circular shape quivering. Its harsh light turned the salt plain a washed-out pink.

This had been the last significant journey ever undertaken by any of her ancient, wandering lineage. But the journey was over. This parched, dead beach had been the farthest point of all. The children of humanity had done with exploring.

As the light failed she turned away and began to walk up the sloping ground. She did not look back.

In the years after Ultimate's death Earth would spin on, ever more slowly, its waltz with its receding Moon gradually running down.

And the sun blazed ever brighter, following its own hydrogen logic.

The sun was a fusion furnace. But the sun's core was becoming clogged with helium ash, and the surrounding layers were falling inwards: The sun was shrinking. Because of this collapse the sun was getting hotter. Not by much—only by around 1 percent every hundred million years—but it was relentless.

For most of Earth's history, life had managed to shield itself from this steady heating-up. The living planet used its "bloodstream"—the rivers and oceans and atmosphere and the cycling rock, and the interactions of trillions of organisms—to remove waste and restore nutrients to where they were needed. Temperature was controlled by carbon dioxide—a vital greenhouse gas, and the raw material for plants' photosynthesis. There was a feedback loop. The hotter it got, the more carbon dioxide was absorbed by the weathering rocks—so the less greenhouse effect there was—and so the temperature was adjusted back down. It was a thermostat that had kept the Earth's temperature stable for eons.

But as the sun got hotter, so more carbon dioxide got trapped in the rocks, and the less there was available for the plants.

Eventually, fifty million years after Ultimate's time, photosynthesis itself began to fail. The plants shriveled: grasses, flowers, trees, ferns, all gone. And the creatures that lived off them died too. Great kingdoms of life imploded. There was a last rodent, and then a last mammal, a last reptile. And after the higher plants had disappeared, so did the fungi and slime mold and ciliates and algae. It was as if evolution had, in these final times, reversed itself, and life's hard-won complexity was shed.

At last, under a blazing sun, only heat-loving bacteria could survive. Many of them had descended with little modification from the earliest life-forms of all, the simple methane eaters who had lived before poisonous oxygen was spread into the atmosphere. For them it was like the good old days before photosynthesis: the arid plains of the last supercontinent were briefly streaked with gaudy, defiant colors, purples and crimsons draped like flags over the eroded rocks.

But the heat climbed, relentlessly. The water evaporated, until whole oceans were suspended in the atmosphere. At last some of the great clouds reached the stratosphere, the atmosphere's upper layer. Here, assailed by the sun's ultraviolet rays, the water molecules broke up into hydrogen and oxygen. The hydrogen was lost to space—and with it the water that might have reformed. It was as if a valve had been opened. Earth's water leaked rapidly out into space.

When the water was gone, it got so hot that the carbon dioxide was baked out of the rocks. Under air as dense as an ocean, the dried seabeds grew hot enough to melt lead. Even the thermophiles wilted. It was the last extinction event of all.

But on rocky ground as hot as the floor of an oven, the bacteria had left behind desiccated spores. In these toughened shells, virtually indestructible, the bacteria, dormant, rode out the years.

There were still convulsions as asteroids and comets sporadically fell onto the parched land, more unremarked Chicxulubs. Now there was nothing left to kill, of course. But as the ground flexed and rebounded, huge quantities of rock were hurled into space.

Some of this material, taken from the edge of each impact zone, was not shocked, and therefore it reached space unsterilized. That was how the bacterial spores left Earth.

They drifted away from Earth and, propelled by the gentle, persistent pressure of sunlight, they created a vast diffuse cloud around the sun. Encysted in their spores, bacteria were all but immortal. And they were hardy interplanetary travelers. The bacteria had coated their DNA strands with small proteins that stiffened the helical shapes and fended off chemical attack. When a spore germinated it could mobilize specialized enzymes to repair any DNA damage. Even some radiation damage could be fixed.

The sun continued its endless circling of the Galaxy's heart, planets and comets and spore cloud and all.

At last the sun drifted into a dense molecular cloud. It was a place where stars were born. The sky was crowded here; dazzling young stars jostled in a great swarm. The fiercely hot sun with its ruined planets was like a bitter old woman intruding in a nursery.

But, just occasionally, one of the sun's spaceborne spores would encounter a grain of interstellar dust, rich with organic molecules and water ice.

Battered by the radiation of nearby supernovae, a fragment of the cloud collapsed. A new sun was born, a new system of planets, gas-stuffed giants and hard, rocky worlds. Comets fell to the surface of the new rocky planets, just as once Earth had been impact-nourished.

And in some of those comets were Earthborn bacteria. Only a few. But it only took a few.

Still the sun aged. It bloated to monstrous proportions, glowing red. Earth skimmed the diffuse edge of the swollen sun, like a fly circling an elephant. The dying giant star burned whatever it could burn. The final paroxysms lit up the great shell of gas and dust that lingered around the sun. The solar system became a planetary nebula, a sphere shimmering with fabulous colors, visible across light-years.

These glorious spasms marked the final death of Earth. But on a new planet of a new star, the nebula was just a light show in the sky. What mattered was the here and now, the oceans and the lands where new ecosystems assembled, where creatures' changing forms tracked changes in their environment, where variation and selection blindly worked, shaping and complexifying.

Life always had been chancy. And now life had found ways of surviving the ultimate extinction event. In new oceans and on strange lands, evolution had begun again.

But it had nothing to do with mankind.

Exhausted, dust-laden, her body covered by a hundred minor scrapes, bruises and prickles, her baby cradled in her arms, Ultimate limped to the center of the ancient quarry.

The land seemed beaten flat, with the sun poised above, a great glowing fist. And at first glance there was no sign that anything still lived on this desert world, none at all.

She approached the Tree itself. She saw the big pendulous folded-over shapes of cocooned people, inert and black. The Tree stood there, silent and still, neither reproving nor forgiving her small betrayal.

She knew what she had to do. She found a folded-up ball of leaves. Carefully she prized the leaves open, shaping them into a makeshift cradle. Then she placed her baby carefully inside.

The baby gurgled and wriggled. She was comfortable, here in the leaves; she was happy to be back with the Tree. But already, Ultimate saw, the belly-rope had snaked into its orifice in the child's stomach. And white tendrils were pushing out of pores in the cradling leaves, reaching out for the baby's mouth and nose, ears and eyes.

There would be no pain. Ultimate had been granted that much knowledge, and comfort. Ultimate stroked the child's furry cheek one last time. Then, without regret, she folded up the leaves and sealed them up.

She clambered off the ground, found her own favorite cocoon, and snuggled inside, neatly closing up the big leathery leaves around her. Here she would stay until a better time: a day miraculously cooler and moister than the rest, a time when it might be possible for the Tree to release Ultimate from this protective embrace, to send her out into the world once more—even to seed her belly with another generation of people.

But there would never be another impregnation, never another birth, never another doomed child.

One by one the cocoons would shrivel as their inhabitants, sealed in green, were absorbed back into the bulk of the borametz—and in the end the borametz itself, of course, would succumb, thousands of years old, tough and defiant to the last. The shining molecular chain that had stretched from Purga through generations of creatures that had climbed and leapt, and learned to walk, trod the dirt of another world, and grown small again, and mindless, and returned to the trees—at last that great chain was broken, as the last of Purga's granddaughters faced an emergency she could not withstand.

Ultimate was the last mother of all. She couldn't even save her own child. But she was at peace.

She stroked the belly-root and helped it worm its way into her gut. The Tree's anesthetic and healing chemicals soothed her aching body, closed her small wounds. And as psychotropic vegetable medications washed away the sharp, jagged memory of her lost baby, she was filled with a green bliss that felt as if it would last forever.

It wasn't such a bad way for the long story to end.

epilogue

There had been a sighting of another band of feral kids, this time on Bartolome Island. So Joan and Lucy had loaded up the nets and tasers and hypo rifles, and here they were limping over the Pacific in their sun-powered launch.

The flat equatorial sunlight reflected off the water onto Joan's pocked skin. She was fifty-two now but looked a good deal older, such was the damage that had been done to her skin, not to mention her hair, by the environment she had endured since Rabaul. But Lucy had met very few truly *old* people in the course of her short life, and she had few points of comparison; to her, Joan was just Joan, her mother, her closest companion.

The day was bright, the few clouds high and streaky. The sun beat hard on the big solar cell sail spread over Lucy's head. Still, they had packed their heavy-duty ponchos, and every few minutes the women glanced at the sky, fearful of rain that might wash down more of the high dust onto them, the toxic, sometimes radioactive grit that had once been fields and cities and people that was now wrapped around the planet like a thin gray blanket.

And, as always, Joan Useb talked, and talked.

"I always had a soft spot for the British, you know, God rest them. In their heyday they didn't always behave well, of course. But the human story of the Galapagos was otherwise pretty unhappy: mad Norwegian farmers, Ecuadorian prison camps, everybody eating the wildlife as fast as they could. Even the Americans used the islands as bombing ranges. But all the Brits did to the Galapagos was send over Darwin for five weeks, and all they took away was the theory of evolution."

Lucy let Joan's chatter wash through her head, these random echoes from a world she had never known.

Frigate birds wheeled overhead, pursuing the launch as they had pursued the fishing vessels and tourist boats that had once plied these waters. They were great gaunt black-feathered birds that always reminded Lucy of nothing so much as the pterosaurs of her mother's books and fading printouts. In the water she thought she saw a sea lion, perhaps attracted by the buzz of the launch's electric motor. But these cute mammals were rare now, poisoned by the toxic garbage that still circulated through the sluggish oceans.

The Galapagos were a bunch of volcanic cones that had been thrust a few million years ago above the surface of the Pacific, here on the equator, a thousand kilometers west of South America. Some of them were little more than a jumble of volcanic boulders, piled up one on top of the other. But others had undergone their own geological evolution. On Bartolome, for instance, the softer outer shells of the older cones had worn away, and the stubborn plugs within had turned crimson red as the iron they contained had rusted. But newer lava had flooded around these older formations, fields of lava bombs, tubes, cones, like a gray-black lunar sea washing around the feet of the stubborn old monuments.

But there was life, here on these new, half-formed islands: Of course there was, a scrap of life that had once been the most famous in the world.

She saw a bird standing gaunt on a small promontory. It was a flightless cormorant: scruffy and black, a thing of stubby useless wings and oily feathers. Standing alone on its bit of volcanic rock, it peered out to sea— patient and still, like so much of the wildlife in this predator-free place, as if waiting for something.

"Ugly, ugly," Joan murmured. "These islands, the birds and animals. Wonderful, of course, but ugly. Islands have always been great laboratories of evolution. The isolation. The emptiness, populated by a handful of species who raft or fly in, and then radiate into all the empty niches. Like that cormorant. That's how far you get in three million years, apparently: halfway between a pelican and a penguin. Give it another few megayears, though, and those useless wings will have become genuine flippers, the feathers properly waterproof, and I wonder what they will become *then*? No wonder Darwin's eyes were opened here. You can *see* selection working."

"Mother—"

"You understand all that, of course." She grimaced, her masklike face twisting. "You know, the fate of the old is to turn into one's own parents; this is just the way my mother used to speak to me. No conversation that didn't turn into a lecture."

They pulled into the shore by a shallow beach. The launch grounded itself, and Lucy hopped out, her sandaled feet crunching on the coarse black sand. She turned back to help her mother, and then the two of them made the launch fast and briskly hauled out their gear.

As Joan began to set up the traps, Lucy took a couple of the hypo rifles and went patrolling along the beach.

The beach itself was an eerie place. The black lava sand was littered by equally black rocks. Even the sea was made to look black, like a sea of oil, by the darkness of its bed. In the distance she could make out mangrove, trees capable of exploiting the salty water, a splash of green against the mineral black and red.

And marine iguanas were lined up here like fat meter-long sculptures, their expressionless faces turned to the sun. They were themselves black, so dark and still it took a second glance to recognize them as living things and not an eerie formation of rope lava. Stranded here on Darwin's laboratory after rafting across with tortoises and turtles, the iguanas' ancestors had been dry-land creatures, tree climbers. They were gradually adapting to living off algae they strained out of seawater. But they would spit out the excess water—the air was filled with their hawking; the little jets spouting from their mouths sparkled in the sunlight—and they had to rely on the heat of the sun to bake the thin repast in their stomachs.

Lucy kept her rifle ready. If feral kids were around, it paid to be wary.

During the scramble for places on the last few boats back to the mainland, kids had been dumped here by desperate parents. The weak ones had quickly died, leaving their bones to litter the beaches and rocky outcrops, like the bones of sea lions and iguanas and albatrosses. But some of the kids had survived. In fact the word "kids" was a misnomer, for they had already been here long enough to spawn a second generation, children who had grown up knowing nothing but these barren bits of rock and the endless oceans, kids even more wordless and without culture than their parents. Feral kids, without tools, with only a rudimentary language—and yet human, capable of being cleaned up and educated.

And also capable of taking a bite out of your leg.

Joan's traps were simple: nothing much more than concealed nets and snares, baited with rich-smelling spicy food. When she had set them up, she and Lucy settled down out of sight in the shade of an outcrop of tuff—crumbling, easily eroded lava—and prepared to wait for the feral children.

Since Rabaul, life had been hard for Joan and her daughter—but then it had been hard for everyone on the planet. Even though her grand empathetic project had been crushed, Joan hadn't stopped working. With wide-eyed little Lucy in tow, she had retreated here, to Galapagos.

Paradoxically these fragile islands had been relatively well preserved through the greater global catastrophe. Once seventeen thousand people had lived here, mostly emigrants from mainland Ecuador. Before Rabaul there had been a constant friction between the needs of this growing, resentful population and the unique wildlife, nominally preserved by Ecuador's national park legislation. But the islands had always been fed by the mainland. When everything had spun apart after Rabaul, when the ships had stopped coming, most of that population had fled back home.

So the islands, largely free of people—and their companions, the rats and the goats, and their waste products, sewage and oil—had, in their modest way, begun to prosper again.

Joan and Lucy—and a handful of others, including Alyce Sigurdardottir until her death—had settled in the ruins of what had once been the Charles Darwin Research Station on Santa Cruz, and, with the locals who remained, had devoted themselves to helping the creatures that had so intrigued Darwin himself through the unfolding extinction.

For a time there had been communications. But then the high-altitude electronics-busting bombs, fired off at the height of the messy multipolar wars, had wrecked the ionosphere. And when the last satellites were shot out of the sky, that had been the end of TV, even speech radio. Joan had long maintained a regime of listening, as long as their sets and power lasted. But it had been years since they had heard anything.

No radio, then. No contrails in the sky, no ships on the horizon. There was no outside world, for all intents and purposes.

They were getting used to the isolation. You always had to remember that when something wore out it was gone forever. But the supplies left behind by those vanished thousands—tools and clothing and batteries and torches and paper and even canned foods—would sustain this little community of fewer than a hundred for their lifetimes and beyond.

The world might be ending—but not here, not *yet*.

Humanity had not vanished; of course not. The great terminal drama that was unfolding around the planet had many years, even decades to run yet. But sometimes, when Joan thought about the very long run, she realized she could see nothing ahead for Lucy, still just eighteen, and her children after her; none at all. So, mostly, she didn't think about it. What else was there to do?

At Lucy's feet, crabs scuttled across the rocks, brilliant red against the black surface, with stalk-mounted sky-blue eyes.

"Mom—"

"Yes, dear?"

"Do you ever wonder if we're doing the right thing for these kids? I mean, what if the grandparents of those marine iguanas had said, 'No, you can't eat that gloopy sea stuff. Get back up the trees where you belong.' "

Joan's eyes were closed. "We should let the kids evolve, like the iguanas?"

"Well, maybe—"

"In order for the descendants of a handful of the kids to adapt, most of those alive now would have to die. I'm afraid we humans don't have the moral capacity to sit back and let that happen. But if the day comes when we can't help them, well, that's when Papa Darwin takes over." Joan shrugged. "Adapt they would, that's for sure. But the result might not be very much like *us*. To survive here, the cormorants have lost flight, perhaps the most beautiful gift of all. I wonder what would be taken from us. Of course that's just my prejudice. Isn't it a wonderful thought to imagine that however cruel the process of evolution might seem to us, something new and in some senses *better than us* might some day come out of it?"

Lucy shuddered, despite the heat. "That's scary."

Joan tapped Lucy's leg. "Scared is good. It shows you are starting to use your imagination. The implications of who we are and how we got here—sometimes it scares *me*, even now."

Lucy clutched her hand. "Mother, I have to say this. Your view of life is so *godless*."

Joan drew back a little. "Ah. I knew this day would come. So you've discovered the great Ju-Ju in the sky."

Lucy felt unreasonably defensive. "You're the one who has always encouraged me to read. I just find it hard to believe God is nothing but an anthropomorphic construct. Or that the world is just a . . . a vast machine, churning through our tiny lives, morphing our children like a handful of algae in a dish."

"Well, maybe there is still room for a God. But what kind of God would *intervene* the whole time? And isn't the story wonderful enough on its own?

"Look at this way. Think about your grandmothers. You have many ancestors in each generation, but only one maternal grandmother. So there is a molecular chain of heredity, leading from each of us into the deepest past, as far as we can see. You have ten million grandmothers, Lucy. Since that comet wiped out the dinosaurs and gave those first little ratty primates a chance, *ten million*. Imagine if they were all lined up, side by side, your grandmother beside her own mother, and then hers in turn.

"Human faces at first, of course." Among those faces would have been the disciples of Mother, ancestors of the African population from whom Joan was descended. And if Lucy could have followed her European father's line back she would have seen, among the morphing faces, Juna of Cata Huuk, and a little deeper Jahna, the girl who had met the last Neandertal, themselves descended from Mother's band. "But then," Joan said, "the subtle changes come, from one generation to the next. Gradually their eyes lose the light of understanding. Implosions: a shrinking forehead, a shriveling body, an apelike face, and at last the great anatomical redesign to restore the wide-eyed creatures that lived in the trees. And back further, shrinking and shriveling, eyes growing wider, minds simpler—" The last common ancestor of humans and another hominid species, the Neandertals, was a quarter of a million years deep. Deeper still the shining line passed through Far and her beautiful, upright folk, and then through the pithecines and back to Capo's forest, and deeper, deeper yet, Purga, who had scurried past slumbering dinosaurs by the light of a comet. "And yet," Joan said, "each one of those ten million, almost all of them uncomprehending animals, lying side by side like frames from a movie, was your ancestor. But you met none of them, Lucy, and you never will. Not even my own mother, your grandmother. Because they are gone: all gone, dead, locked in the ground. *No motion has she now, no force / She neither hears nor sees / Rolled round in Earth's diurnal course / With rocks, and stones, and trees.*"

Lucy said dryly, "Wordsworth, right? Another dead person."

"The world is unfortunately full of dead persons. Anyhow, *that's* our story. And I think, in my glimpses of the great encompassing mechanism that has shaped us all, I've seen a little of the numinous. That's enough of God for me." Joan sighed. "Of course you'll have to figure it all out for yourself, which is most of the fun, of course."

"Mom, have you been happy?"

Joan frowned strangely. "You never asked me that before."

Lucy stayed silent, not letting her off the hook.

Joan thought about it.

Like all her ancestors, Joan had emerged from deep time. But unlike most of them she had been able to peer into the dark abysses that surrounded her life. She had come to know that her ancestors were utterly unlike anything in her world, and that nothing like herself could survive the most remote future. But she knew, too, that life would go on—if not her life, if not *this* life, as long as Earth lasted—and maybe even longer. And that ought to be enough for anyone.

"Yes," she told her daughter, and hugged her. "Yes, love. I have been happy—"

Lucy silenced her with a gesture. Now Joan could hear it too: a rustling, a subdued, wistful crying. They peered around the rock.

A little girl had been caught in the net. No older than five, naked, hair matted, she was crying because she couldn't get to the plate of spicy vegetables Joan had set out.

Joan and Lucy showed themselves. The girl shrank back.

Carefully, their hands open, with measured footsteps and soothing words, they walked up to the feral child. They stayed with her until she calmed. Then, tenderly, they began to pull the net away from her.

There is grandeur in this view of life ... that ... from so simple a beginning endless forms most beautiful and most wonderful have been, and are being, evolved.

—CHARLES DARWIN,

op. cit.

afterword

This is a novel. I have tried to dramatize the grand story of human evolution, not to define it; I hope my story is plausible, but this book should *not* be read as a textbook. Much of it is based on hypothetical reconstructions of the past by experts in the field. In many cases I have chosen what seems to me the most plausible or exciting idea among competing proposals. But some of it is based on my own wild speculation.

I'm very grateful to Eric Brown, who kindly commented on the manuscript. Professors Jack Cohen and Ian Stewart of Warwick University were very generous with their time in providing expert advice to shore up my layman's guesswork. I'm also indebted to Simon Spanton, for support above and beyond the call of editorial duty. Any remaining errors are, of course, solely my responsibility.

—Stephen Baxter
Great Missenden, U.K.
May 2002